Broken Pebbles
& Papillion Wings

Broken Pebbles
& Papillion Wings

PW Stephens

Published by PWS

© Copyright P W Stephens 2020

BROKEN PEBBLES
& PAPILLION WINGS

All rights reserved.

The right of P W Stephens to be identified as the author of this work has been asserted in accordance with Copyright, Designs and Patents Act 1988.

No part of this publication may be reproduced, stored in a retrieval system, or transmitted, in any form or by any means, electronic, mechanical, photocopying, recording or otherwise, nor translated into a machine language, without the written permission of the publisher.

This is a work of fiction. Names and characters are a product of the author's imagination and any resemblance to actual persons, living or dead, events and organisations is purely coincidental.

Conditions of sale.

This book is sold subject to the condition that it shall not, by way of trade or otherwise, be lent, re-sold, hired out or otherwise circulated in any form of binding or cover other than that in which it is published and without similar condition including this condition being imposed on the subsequent purchaser.

ISBN 979-8-566-01745-7

Book formatted by autumnalmusingformating

Part One Contents
The Book of Jacob

- Chapter 01: The Pebble and the Boy
- Chapter 02: Growing Pains
- Chapter 03: The Viking King
- Chapter 04: Birth of a Monster
- Chapter 05: York Avenue
- Chapter 06: Into the Fire
- Chapter 07: Sunshine and Stick Insects
- Chapter 08: Changes
- Chapter 09: Alice and the Looking Glass
- Chapter 10: Father of the Bride
- Chapter 11: Living by the Sword
- Chapter 12: Triggered
- Chapter 13: Changing of the Guard
- Chapter 14: It Follows
- Chapter 15: The Summer Breeze
- Chapter 16: The End
- Chapter 17: Wires
- Chapter 18: News from Home
- Chapter 19: Sepia Tone
- Chapter 20: The Crow and the Girls
- Chapter 21: Fragmenting
- Chapter 22: The Drugs Don't Work
- Chapter 23: The Nightmare Sleeps
- Chapter 24: In Dreams
- Chapter 25: The Curtain Call
- Chapter 26: The Harlequin

Part Two Contents
The Book of Alice

- Chapter 01: The Light and the Lighthouse
- Chapter 02: Scar Tissue
- Chapter 03: Ruby Slippers
- Chapter 04: Between the Infant and the Abyss
- Chapter 05: The Tell-Tale Heart
- Chapter 06: Sliding Doors
- Chapter 07: Johnno was a Local Boy
- Chapter 08: Nurse Bonnie
- Chapter 09: Freudian Slip
- Chapter 10: The Hand that Rocks
- Chapter 11: Brand New Start
- Chapter 12: The Last Day
- Chapter 13: I Do
- Chapter 14: I Move the Stars for No One
- Chapter 15: The Butterfly Collector
- Chapter 16: To Whom It May Concern
- Chapter 17: Glad Rags
- Chapter 18: The Kraken and Her
- Chapter 19: The Light Between Us

Part Three Contents
The Book of John

- Chapter 01: Thirteen Steps
- Chapter 02: Equilibrium
- Chapter 03: Saving Yourself
- Chapter 04: To Dance with my Father
- Chapter 05: The Snorkeler
- Chapter 06: The Red Door
- Chapter 07: The Esmee Nijboer
- Chapter 08: I am Mother
- Chapter 09: Hometown Blues
- Chapter 10: Bronte in Winter
- Chapter 11: Not a Date
- Chapter 12: Rolling in the Deep
- Chapter 13: Girl in the Picture
- Chapter 14: The Oberon Deep
- Chapter 15: Demons and Desires
- Chapter 16: Building Bricks
- Chapter 17: Running
- Chapter 18: Nom de Guerre
- Chapter 19: When One Light Goes Out
- Chapter 20: Double Jeopardy
- Chapter 21: Courtin' Zombies
- Chapter 22: See Me Fall
- Chapter 23: Angela Rowe
- Chapter 24: Relatable
- Chapter 25: My Dorian Gray
- Chapter 26: Alice

Part Four Contents
The Book of Dorothy

- Chapter 01: The Mirrorverse
- Chapter 02: Fighting with my Family
- Chapter 03: I've a Feeling
- Chapter 04: A Mothers Torment
- Chapter 05: Finding Dorothy
- Chapter 06: Pack Mentality
- Chapter 07: Older & Wiser
- Chapter 08: The Gorgon
- Chapter 09: Oyster Shells
- Chapter 10: Finding Voice
- Chapter 11: Requiem
- Epilogue

Authors Note

I always wanted to write fiction. I grew up escaping my school life with James Herbert and Stephen King permanently by my side. My thirties had me trying to escape different things altogether, with Lovecraft and Poe now my travel companions. The thing that had always held me back from pursuing writing as my life's vocation, was a lack of belief in myself. It was that belief that stopped me picking up a pen until I was nearly forty years old. This late start turned into a blessing in disguise, as it seemed that my ability to write an edgy thriller benefitted from life experience, from seeing the world through different lenses and on different levels. It begs the question; can you write true gothic horror if you have lived a young, clean and unblemished life with no voices in your head? I'd like to think not, as it was my journey that shaped the way that I write. Is there really an Evan, Alice or even a Jacob? Not as I know of, but my ability to scribe their stories comes from understanding that the world they inhabit is the very same world I lived in.

Doth the Kraken...

Acknowledgements

Thank you to my family and friends for your unwavering support.

To my daughter, Grace Natasha, whom I love more than life.

To my Sam, who proof read every draft with me, without complaint.

To the crows that call my name as I walk home in the dark.

To the Kraken that haunted the shadows of my youth.

To the boys that bullied Jacob so badly that he had to write a novel about it.

To Poe, Lovecraft and King for inspiring me.

And lastly, to Whitstable, Canterbury and Rye Harbour. You built my dreams with a reality of ocean waves and cobbled stone.

For Sarah

In Ballycastle's embrace, where wild waves roar,
Lady Sarah blooms on the rugged shore.
Celtic blood courses through her veins,
A spirit untamed, where freedom reigns.

Brunette locks dance in the breeze,
A symphony of whispers through ancient trees.
Slim and graceful, she walks the land,
A guardian of nature, with a heart so grand.

Blessed with beauty, she wears it with grace,
Yet, her essence transcends the surface's embrace.
For in her eyes, a wild fire gleams,
A soul ablaze with Celtic dreams.

On the cliffs, where only seagulls cry,
Her spirit soars, where others lie.
Independent and free, like the ocean's song,
In her heart, the ancient rhythms belong.

A white witch, her powers unfold,
Not in darkness, but in kindness told.
She dances with shadows, under moonlit skies,
A silhouette against stars, where magic lies.

Lady Sarah, a beacon on the Irish coast,
Where Celtic blood and spirit boast.
In the arms of Ballycastle, she has grown,
A guardian of love, in a world made her own.

Part One
The Book of Jacob

1

The Pebble and the Boy
Autumn 1994
Tankerton, Kent UK

In late Autumn, one might assume it was too cold to be sitting on the biting wet stones of Tankerton seafront, but Jacob never conformed to normality and it seemed like he wasn't the only one. Who was this girl with hair of October leaves and November embers? She, who has watched him vividly for an hour or so as she sat opposite him on the far side of the heavy wooden groynes that separated the same stretch of beach that they shared. He had been out all morning taking photographs of different coloured stones with an old German Franka 25 that his grandad had given him at the beginning of the year. A gift that sadly came before his passing not a few weeks later. It was certainly a robust piece of kit that had surely seen some amazing stories unfold in its twenty-year life. Jacob loved it though and found its dents and scratches endearing, whilst the grainy washed look 35mm film gave each picture more character than he knew any flashy Nikon would provide.

'You know, if rocks are what you are after, there are plenty more on my side of the fence,' said the flame haired young girl that had somehow used Jacobs daydream to sneak up on him unseen. He couldn't remember ever having met such a beautiful girl, not that he had witnessed many during his short tenure on earth; but those he had met certainly held nothing on her, *so why is she talking to me?* Jacob asked himself within his thoughts.

'You know you don't say much' the girl was clearly mocking him but held a playful giggle in her tone which brought a smile to Jacob's lips non the less.

'Sorry,' he said adjusting himself to a more masculine pose. 'I'm Jacob, Jacob Brooking,' he stuttered his name like he had a stammer, much to the amusement of his new shadow who was trying and failing to catch his gaze, probably due to the fact he couldn't stop looking at his feet.

'I know who you are you big wally, you just joined the Howard George, right? I'm Alice.'

'Alice ...' Jacob repeated her name softly back to her as if letting it sink in. 'That's a beautiful name and one I would surely remember, but I'm not sure I recall seeing you around school because, well ... you know, it's a boy's school,' Jacob knew that what he was saying was factually accurate, Alice though, seemed to giggle at him even more.

'Doesn't mean I 've not noticed you at the fence everyday, I notice lots of things, you don't play well with the other boys, do you?' Jacob finally mustered the strength to look up into her eyes, *my god,* eyes so beautiful and blue that they could easily be cut from the very things that dreams are made of.

'Have you been stalking me?' Jacob asked.

Alice smiled, her perfectly straight bright pearls gleaming back at him, 'let's say admiring instead of stalking shall we?'

She took a seat next to him on the old worn blanket and watched intently as he balanced different shaped pebbles one on top of the other.

'You're an interesting boy aren't you Jacob, and you seem so different to the other idiots on the boy side of that big fence that separates our schools.'

'How do you mean?' Jacob inquired with a quizzical look upon his face.

'Well for a start you are taking pictures of rocks on a wet beach at the weekend, whilst all your class mates are probably playing football.'

Jacob laughed loudly 'I guess that does make me a little different.'

He reached over and picked up an azure coloured rock that had been worn down into a perfect oval by an aggressive and violent ocean.

'They are not rocks though Alice, they are pebbles and do you know what I love about them?' Alice didn't answer but motioned for him to continue.

'I've always loved how there are no two pebbles the same, the same colour, the same shape or weight; each one unique, each one special.'

'That's beautiful,' said Alice 'But what about these two?' She held back a curious grin and held up two clearly matching pebbles.

'See, you think you have caught me out, but you're not looking at the big picture, well, the little picture really,' Jacob smiled as he took both pebbles from her and turned them over and over repeatedly in his hand whilst running his thumbs across them as if he was trying to summon a Genie.

'Look at this one ... its flawless right?' Jacob held out his left hand and Alice ran her index finger over the top of the exposed pebble whilst not fully understanding his point. 'Now this one,' he said opening his right palm, which led Alice to mimic the same procedure of gently following the lines of the pebble under her fingertips' soft caress.

'Ok, so there's a tiny crack in it, I get it, but they are nearly the same and I think you know I'm at least a little bit right,' Alice nudged her shoulder into his with a smile.

'The crack represents a journey, an incident and I guess a history, something has happened to this rock, that didn't happen to the other, and that thought process gets my mind excited.'

'Because its broken?' Alice quipped.

'No Alice, because it's unique,' Jacob smiled.

-

That night, as Jacob reached under his pillow for the battered old Sony Walkman that sung him to sleep each night, his thoughts turned to Alice, he thought of her curly red hair, of her bottomless blue eyes and of her beautiful laugh, the laugh that seemed to pull him ever closer to the frightening Abyss that was undoubtably his Oubliette. Never had a word been more fitting to a soul, she had made his forget, if only for a moment, if only for a heartbeat and for that brief dreamlike passage of time, he had felt real.

I hate you!

Jacob span around quickly, pulling off his headphones as he searched for the source of the voice. His bedroom was a mess, a pig sty his mum would say for sure, but it wasn't a large room in any way shape or form and it took but a moment to confirm his suspicions that no one was there. He slowly replaced his headphones and the sound of Paul Weller filled his ears once more. As he lay back on his pillow and closed his weary eyes to think again on his day with Alice, he couldn't help but wonder, what a girl like her could ever see in him. The perennial loser, whom no family or friend had ever believed in, could never be of interest to a girl like Alice. What had compelled her to talk to him? He would never understand it and right now he just wanted to enjoy the moments as they came, with a date in the park organised for tomorrow and phone numbers swapped, he could certainly feel warmth in his heart as he started to fall into a comfortable slumber. 'No monsters under the bed tonight,' he whispered as the waking world left him for the embrace of sleep.

I HATE YOU! Said the voice once more.

Jacob sat bolt upright as he felt a wet and viscous tentacle wrap around his ankle, teeth and barbs punctured flesh as, despite his futile struggle, he found himself dragged under the bed by the strength of a Kraken, a Kraken born from the mind of a thousand terrified sailors.

Spring 1995
Canterbury, Kent UK

Jacob hobbled down the stairs gingerly as his legs failed to respond to the instructions his young brain was giving them.

'Mum, I can't feel my legs again.'

'Well, rub them, honey. I'm not sure what you do in your sleep, as this is happening every day now.'

Jacob's mum, Marie Brooking, was an amazing mother and a fantastic woman. But she rarely minced her words, and today she seemed genuinely concerned with her eldest son's inability to walk properly. Jacob was ashamed that at 15 years old he still slept with his legs crossed, just to make sure there was no chance of one stray foot falling out from under the duvet, as everyone knew what a dangerous place outside of the quilt was for any leg to be. And it was this and this alone that gave him dead legs in the morning.

He sat at the table and was greeted quickly by a bowl of Coco Pops and a cup of milky tea. His baby brother sat opposite him, trying to get all his Weetabix under the surface of his milk without spilling it from his bowl, so as to avoid the crunchy breakfast that no young boy wanted. He was failing miserably.

'Mum, I don't feel too good,' Jacob said for the third time that week.

She sighed curtly without taking her eyes off the task at hand. 'What's wrong now?'

'It's my stomach again. I feel sick.'

'Well, you can't have any more time off, Jacob. The school are already on my back with concerns about all your time off.'

'BUT MUM!' he protested, in a whine so high pitched that the dog's ears pricked up. 'Oh Christ,' Jacob cried. 'The dog!'

'Muuuuuum, the dog's on fire,' Samuel bellowed.

Jacob's younger brother, five years his junior, always liked to overreact, but this time Jacob had to admit that Samuel was right to raise the alarm so noisily. Peepo always point-blank refused to move from her spot right in front of the fireplace, and today was no different, even though her jet-black fur was starting to smoulder. *It must be nice to be that lazy,* Jacob mused. I bet she has no dramas in her life. Well, apart from her heavy smoking habit, he giggled to himself. Jacob jumped down from the table and patted her down before forcibly sliding the overweight beast a couple of feet across the carpet. She had always been a pot-bellied dog, and moving her was never easy. 'Mum, I really don't feel right,' said Jacob, his words turning into a plea for help.

'He only doesn't want to go to school because they call him Gummy Bear,' Samuel mocked.

'SHUT UP,' was the immediate response to his brother.

'Just say to them that sticks and stones will break my bones, but names will never hurt me,' Mum preached as always.

Little did she know that they did use sticks and stones to beat the life out of his bones most days, and usually they would call him names while they did it.

Gummy Bear.

Gummy Bear.

Gummy Bear.

Jacob heard the voice in his head. But it didn't sound like the kids at school. Its repeatedly aggressive cackle almost overshadowed the words. Jacob hated the voice in his head but had come to accept its presence in his life. He just assumed everyone had one. He hoped other people's inner voices were nicer than his, and he honestly suspected they would have to be. He had once tried to describe it to his dad, but he felt silly talking to him about inner turmoil. Stern-faced in the presence of emotional weakness, his parents would say, 'Just smile and be happy. What is the point in talking negative, son?' So, Jacob had decided this was something that was best dealt with alone. He had always felt ashamed talking of such things with his hard- and endlessly working dad. Paul Brooking worked three jobs, often far from home, just to keep his family fed. He didn't deserve to hear on a daily basis how pathetic his son was.

'I suggest you stop daydreaming and finish your breakfast. And for god's sake sort your tie out,' said his mum, breaking the hazed look on his face.

'Yes, Mum,' he replied with an acceptance that left him feeling hollow.

I hate you, Gummy Bear, the voice said.

I know, he thought clearly and with absolutely no fight. *You tell me every day.*

-

The Howard George School for Boys had never been a nice place to be, and Jacob didn't have one fond memory or many friends to make the experience worthwhile. Well, he had Alice, who was in the neighbouring girls' school and would meet him at the fence every day for lunch, just so they could talk music that she clearly only pretended to like to impress him. He loved that she did that and would show her due respect by always giving her his Marathon bar, which more than likely she would break in half for him to enjoy with her. But to get to her, he would of course have to get through to lunch, and right now he wasn't sure how promising that seemed.

'Your coat looks shit, Gummy Bear,' they laughed.

'Your parents are clearly poor.' Simeon Bennett mocked him while at the same time punching him in the shoulder repeatedly. 'No wonder no one likes you.'

He's got you there.

That was a mistruth, of course, as Jacob was sure lots of people liked him in his small unique circle that he kept. It was just his ability to attract the attention of this wolf pack of baying idiots that meant he was often avoided by everyone, lest they might stray too close and attract the attention of the bullies themselves.

'You're scum,' shouted David Taylor, the brute of the group and the axe handle to Simeon's sharp wit. He looked down at the pinned Jacob and spat on his coat.

Jacob tried to recoil in disgust but was being held in place by a third goon, who was unidentifiable due to his position behind Jacob's back.

Simeon started to do his usual party trick of emptying Jacob's bag all over the classroom floor before spitting inside it. Jacob's dad had once told Jacob to fight back and earn the respect that, in his opinion, was the only thing that would stop kids like this. But the one day Jacob had caught David with a low blow hard enough to do some real damage, it had resulted in a beating far worse than he had ever received previously, and they had dragged him by his throat behind the sports block after classes had ended and punched him repeatedly while screaming, 'DON'T YOU EVER HIT ME BACK EVER AGAIN.' It just wasn't worth it.

Simeon looked down at him, sneering like a demonic version of the Cheshire cat from *Alice in Wonderland*. Slick, jet-black hair and matching thick brows framed his dark, rat-like eyes, which seemed far too small for his elongated face. He was always smiling, yet Jacob doubted he had ever been happy. He had heard rumours that he was the way he was due to a sexually abusive father, but no one was brave enough to bring this up in conversation. He had heard of a boy, David Shelly, from the year above, who'd mentioned it in conversation the previous term and hadn't been seen at school since.

Simeon Bennett had been kicked out of his last school for violence towards a teacher and had joined the Howard George just a year before, instantly using all his wit and guile to get the stronger and more thug-like David Taylor on board. David, whose straw-like mop of hair sat on his thick, square forehead like a bird's nest, always stunk of smoke and was rarely clean to any respectable level, which left Jacob feeling saturated by his bullies' touch. Heavier and thicker set in physical appearance and mentality, David was actually the less imposing of the pair due to the clear absence of a brain, but he was always the one who left Jacob bruised. And today was a bad day for Jacob.

With a sharp yank, his third oppressor pulled him backwards off his chair. Jacob hit the floor with a sickening crack that drew all the air from his ribs in one giant expressive breath.

'See you later, Gummy Bear,' whispered Simeon, as he smiled maliciously like the Grim Reaper, all teeth and no lips and his mouth almost too wide for his face.

As they walked past his winded frame, David gave him a solid boot to the side of the face, drawing a shriek of pain from Jacob. This final act appeared to have been carried out to reiterate that they thought of him as scum.

Jacob sat up. His cheeks were flushed and his face was stained with tears. He hadn't realised he was crying. He started to collect his belongings and put them back into his satchel, using his gym top to wipe the spit off everything first. It was only then that he looked up to see the other members of his class staring at him from the safety of their desks. Unsure whether the looks on their faces were pity or ridicule, he decided he had best get out as quickly as he could. He shoved the rest of his things away before pulling himself up to his feet, his face throbbing and his ribs feeling like a knife was wedged in the cage that held his breathless lungs. He scrambled out of the classroom without even closing the door behind him. The further he got from the door, the louder the whispering from the other students became as they talked once again of how lucky they were not to be him.

-

'Baby, what happened?' asked Alice as she reached through the wire fence to brush his bruised cheek with her fingers.

He recoiled slightly. His face was still sensitive, and the area she caressed was flooded with a burning sensation. 'It's fine, Pebble. It's just boys doing boy stuff, I guess.'

'You don't truly believe that, do you, Jay? That this is normal behaviour for boys? Or even animals, for that matter?'

'It doesn't matter what I believe. I'm sure I deserved it regardless. And no, before you ask – I really don't want to talk about it.'

'OK, grumpy bum,' Alice retorted with an air of mischief. 'Why don't you kiss me instead?' Her head tilted to the ground as she spoke, but she looked up at Jacob through her auburn bangs.

He smiled the kind of smile that came deep from inside, with no falsity to it whatsoever, as he realised he could never resist her when she did that. No matter his mood, she would always bring him round, without even trying too hard. Her hair just failed to hide her piercing blue eyes, and her glossed red lips wore a smile that transformed her from cute to something else entirely as she took her bottom lip between her teeth.

Oh god, he thought as instinct took over. He pressed his face up against the fence as tightly as he could and pursed his lips together as far forward as the wire would allow. And there she was, the warmth of her lips seeming to defrost the pain in his cheek almost immediately. As they reached for each other and linked fingers through the mesh, she started to withdraw, and he gently took her lip between his teeth.

When she was finally released, she looked at him open-mouthed. 'Jacob Brooking, what would my father say?' She giggled. She turned her back to him before starting to walk away with a skip in her step and the slightest of wiggles in her bum. Well aware of what she was doing and fully aware Jacob was watching, she headed back to class.

'I love you, Jay,' she called over her shoulder.

'I love you, Alice Marie Petalow,' he whispered as she disappeared through a door.

All of a sudden, his world felt darker.

Shame you don't deserve her, isn't it, Gummy Bear? said the voice as Jacob drew in a deep breath.

It would be a long walk back to class. Maybe Simeon and his minions would ignore him if he just shut his mouth and sat at the front of each class where the teacher could always reach him. Or maybe the barbs would turn to punches once more and would do him a favour and finally silence the voice in his head. Maybe then he would have peace. Ending it had often seemed like the only option to him, but like the voice said, he was too much of a coward.

Do it, the voice said. *I dare you.*

-

The dark was his protection. He couldn't see a thing, and that meant nothing could see him. But it was also his enemy, for the shadows were where the creature slept, where it plotted and where it watched. Hiding from monsters under his quilt was becoming a far-too-regular occurrence. For a boy of 14 years, Jacob had to admit that he felt a little childish. He had told his mother a few days before, but her attention always seemed elsewhere as she dealt with the demons of her own past.

'Just be brave, Jacob. You're a big boy now. You don't hear Samuel complaining of monsters hiding in the shadows, do you?'

'No, Mum, he doesn't.'

Marie Brooking lit another cigarette and ruffled his hair. She loved him, Jacob knew that, and he certainly had no right to complain about his upbringing, but he had always felt like he was the wrong piece in his mother's picture puzzle. Like she was disappointed he wasn't quite the child she had wanted him to be.

He had told his brother too, but Samuel had started to freak out at the thought of a creature in the room next door, leaving Jacob no choice but to pass the whole thing off as a joke. So, he was here alone, as per usual. His exhalations were trapped inside the confines of his safe house, and his breathing was becoming difficult. The quilt was tucked under his body so tightly that no limbs could reach for a hold on him. Jacob had pictured himself as a caterpillar getting ready for its transformation, a chrysalis of anxiety and panic. It had started when his father had turned the hall light off and closed his own bedroom door with a heavy thud. Jacob felt alone; in fact, today he had felt more alone than ever.

That Morning

Jacob climbed into his dad's car and excitedly turned on the cassette player. His father's taste in music was, at least in Jacob's young eyes, second to none. A lover of soul and country rock, Paul Brooking inspired his son in more ways than he would ever know, but the first way he was to influence Jacob was with music. The Electric Light Orchestra came on, much to the delight of Jacob, who quickly pulled on his seat belt as his father got in the car. The nearly new Peugeot 505 GTI was an amazing car to sit in, and he would admit to anyone who would listen that sitting by his father's side was his favourite place to be. The blue velour seats were warm and welcoming, and the sporty nature of the car seemed to hug him as his father went round corners with youthful abandon. His father had offered to drop him off at his friend's house. It wasn't a long walk there, but the rain that showered down on the cold

December day would certainly have made it an unpleasant one.

'Did you read that article I left you out, son?'

'The West Ham United one? It doesn't make for great reading, but I think Harry is the right guy for us. I know you disagree, though.'

'It's not that I disagree, as I'm not sure there is anyone better out there right now in terms of leading us forward. There's just something about his car-salesman nature that rubs me the wrong way. Still, we should beat Charlton at home this weekend.'

The rest of the journey played out in silence. That wasn't uncommon for time spent with Paul Brooking, a man who didn't believe in conversation for the sake of it. When Paul said something, it always paid to listen.

The grey Peugeot rode the kerb gently as they arrived at Dinger's house. He wasn't a friend that Jacob's father particularly liked. Paul had accused him on more than one occasion of only hanging out at the Brooking house because Jacob had the better computer. No comment had been made today, though, with the play having been organised at Dinger's house for a change.

'Thanks, Pop,' said Jacob as he unbuckled his seat belt and leaned over to kiss his father on the cheek.

Much to his surprise, his dad pulled away and instead just tapped him on the leg with his open hand.

'Getting a little old for a kiss goodbye, son. You just go and have a good day.'

He doesn't love you anymore.

'Oh, OK, Dad, sure, I'll see you at home later,' Jacob said in shock as he climbed out of the car and gently pressed the door closed.

He still kisses Samuel goodbye.

Yeah, but Sam's younger, thought Jacob, trying his best to convince himself that this wasn't a personal thing. But it wasn't something that he was ever going to forget. Jacob had always wanted to be treated like a young man and not a kid. But now that time was here, he was frightened. He just couldn't shake the feeling that it was the first sign of his father giving up on him.

Paul Brooking, though, never gave that moment another thought, for Paul loved his son.

I can see you, said the creature, as Jacob felt the weight of its mass press down on his mattress.

I can smell you, said the creature, as it wrapped its long viscous tentacles around Jacob's cocoon.

I can taste you, said the creature, as it enveloped him in such a grip that Jacob thought he would surely be crushed.

They are right to bully you at school, the creature spat viciously.

They are right to love you less than your brother, you are pathetic and I taste only the weakness that drenches your skin as you cower from me, like a beaten dog, under the very cover of darkness that you know gives me strength.

Jacob wasn't sure if the voice - or the creature that projected it, for that matter - was real, but he knew that the pain was real. He knew that he couldn't breathe and that he was starting to black out. Why it hated him Jacob didn't understand, and his hope that the other kids at school were tormented by monsters of their own had been misplaced - the few students who had been willing to talk to him about it had found no middle ground with him at all. It seemed he was alone in his relationship with the shadow leviathan, and as the weight of its mass started to crush him, and his ribs started to splinter and crack, he realised that actually he had very little in his life other than the creature's hate. His parents seemed to not even recognise his place in the family anymore. His brother had started calling him Gummy Bear, just like the kids at school, and what chance did he possibly have with that beautiful girl from the school next door? The last of his air escaped his lungs and his body started to convulse.

'Son, I'm here, little buddy,' said his dad, pulling the quilt from around Jacob's constricted body and holding him in place as he thrashed around like he was afflicted by some kind of demonic possession.

'Dad!' called Jacob. He reached forward with tear-stained cheeks and rasping lungs.

'I'm here, son, just breathe.' Paul pulled his son into his chest and kissed his brow. 'Where has all this come from? For weeks now I've seen you at war with yourself, and I can't for the life of me understand where all this angst is coming from.'

Jacob couldn't find the words to explain what he was going through. He felt broken, alone and like no one else would understand his pain. What could he say to his father now that would help him rationalise his conflict?

'It was just a bad dream,' said Jacob, trying to regain some composure. 'I couldn't even tell you what it was about.'

'OK, son. Just know that I'm only next door, OK?'

'Yeah, alright, Dad, thanks.'

Jacob's father left the room and left the door ajar, just enough for the hall light to shine on his son's face. Leaving the landing light on may have seemed like a small gesture to others, but to Jacob it meant the world.

2

Growing Pains
Spring 1995
Canterbury, Kent UK

Even though she was a slight girl, Alice was still finding it hard to balance on the toilet seat. She had been hiding in the cubicle for ten minutes, as the three girls who had come into the bathroom shortly after her were not friends of hers, not in any way whatsoever. Graffiti marked the inside of the door: 'Katlyn Baily is a slut'. The girl in question was on the other side.

'I just don't get what Alice likes about that retard Jay Brooking,' Katlyn said while the three of them applied too much make-up to faces that at such a young age needed little.

'She's a whore, Katlyn, you know this,' said Chloe with a cruel bite in her voice. Chloe Durby was the sinister one in the trio of vultures, as Alice called them. While Katlyn was the poor little rich kid who lied and complained about anything and everything despite its irrelevance to her own life, it was Chloe who, Alice imagined, tortured cats in her garden each day.

The last member of the group, Emily, was quieter, and Alice had always thought that she was in the clique because it was safer than being out of it, rather than because she had an innate desire to be mean to others. But she would still agree with everything the girls said in public.

'Well, she's not a whore, is she, girls?' said Katlyn with bold assurance.

'And why's that?' asked the two mocking birds by her side in unison.

'Because she doesn't get paid,' Katlyn laughed. 'I'd fuck Jay for money. But I wouldn't touch him for free.'

'Not that the ginger tramp is anything to look at either, so maybe they're made for each other,' Chloe snorted.

Alice was seething at what she was hearing but knew that getting her head flushed down the toilet by three bigger girls was not going to solve anything at all. Instead, she focused on her footing and controlling her breathing so she would hopefully go unnoticed until they left.

'I have a friend in his class, they say he talks to himself,' Emily joined in. 'They say he refuses to talk to many of his classmates except a very select few and that Alice is his only true friend.'

'Alice Petalow doesn't have any friends,' said Chloe. 'That's why I never understood why she's always so undeservedly fucking happy.'

'It annoys the shit out of me,' said Katlyn, who seemed genuine with every statement.

Alice felt her heart break as she racked her mind to try and figure out what she had done to any of these girls to deserve the words she was hearing. She heard the door to the bathroom open.

Over her shoulder, Chloe shouted, 'See you later, Ginge. Don't stay in there all day.'

The three girls started singing as they skipped down the hall in search of another victim to tear down. And they would find someone, they always did. People like Alice were the carcasses that these vultures would feed off. Alice knew her place in the school social structure. And she felt a wave of pride wash over her for escaping a bathroom beating at the vultures' hands, even though they had known she was in there all along. She climbed down from the porcelain pedestal and opened the cubicle door. The mirror stared back at her. The dirty mirror had a large crack running diagonally through it, which seemed to cut her image in half. Her hair was tied in a tight French plait and her eyes were glazed over as she looked at her reflection and tried to laugh off the girls' comments, but it wasn't coming easily.

The left side of the crack was warped and reminded her of a circus mirror in some house of horrors or freak-show parlour. Her forehead was elongated and her jaw misshapen. Yet to the right of the break was a crystal-clear reflection of a confused 16-year-old girl who couldn't figure out why anyone would be as mean to her as the three vultures had been. Alice knew in her heart she couldn't have lived with herself if she had ever made anyone feel as low as they constantly made her and her friends feel. The warped reflection seemed to be smiling at her as she adjusted the collar of her blouse.

'And what are you smiling at?' Alice quipped.

Failure, the reflection answered.

Before Alice could figure out how to respond to a completely inanimate object talking to her, the door to the bathroom burst open. Chloe led the charge like a raging bull, and Katlyn followed her with an air of graceful authority. Emily was last. She pulled the door closed behind her and guarded it while looking squarely at the floor.

'I've changed my mind,' said Katlyn. 'I'm sick of you, Petalow, and I think you need to learn a lesson for listening in on our conversation.' She drew a pair of scissors from her waistband. 'Chloe, grab a little of that beautiful hair, would you?'

Alice wanted to scream for help, but what would have been the point? She collapsed into the corner of the room, cowering from what was about to happen. The mirror just kept smiling at her as long locks of her beautiful red hair fell to the floor around her.

3

The Viking King
1995
Mile End, London Docklands UK

The *Commodores* rang through the tinny speakers of the paint-splattered radio hanging from a makeshift hook rammed into the back wall of the dockyard fish market in Mile End, east London. Jay had always loved the band and today was a great day to hear them play. It took him back to car journeys with his dad. Riding in the back seat of that old grey Peugeot while his baby brother poked and prodded him to antagonise the life out of him. His dad always had some Motown cassette on, or something full of soul. It had been the catalyst for Paul Brooking's oldest son to become the romantic and unique young man he had become, one who truly believed in the task in front of him today, although it was too many years of listening to Motown that had led him here on this suicide mission, and his belief that love could somehow always find a way would be the reason he died.

Jacob was sitting in what could only have been a 1920s Catholic-school chair, built with the sole purpose of causing pain and discomfort to all that sat in its tight embrace. His adversary in this game of awkwardness was a lot more 'the man' in this power play. Twice the size of Jacob in size and stature. His office in the very rear of the stinking hangar was covered in photographs commemorating his achievements in life. First was a black-and-white sepia piece of this grey-haired behemoth with his brothers in arms, possibly in the Falklands, standing on some ridge in the pouring rain. The war appeared to have taken its toll. From their hollow expressions, it was clear that each man had lost something. He was too well spoken to be a paratrooper, so Jacob suspected he'd been a Royal Marine. Then he was dressed in a shirt and tie at the rugby club, possibly five years later, with his team mates from Canterbury RFU around him, and he was holding no fewer than six trophies at an end-of-season awards presentation of some kind. These were interlaced with a plethora of fishing-trip pictures. In each one, he was holding a hooked fish that was easily as big as Jacob himself. Not a great sign for what was to come, Jacob mused, as he sympathised with one large pike in particular. But one final picture took his eye more than the others. This one didn't hang from the wall. It stood to proud attention on the man's desk. It held within its frame the most beautiful woman Jacob had ever seen. Possibly in her 40s, she had red hair like that of an autumnal dream. Her eyes were a piercing blue, the likes of which he had never seen nor believed could exist. By her side was her daughter – his Alice. A perfect reflection in all but age. Jay had loved Alice since the day he first saw her. More than anyone he had ever seen. And he could make that statement knowing he had seen more of the world than most 16-year-old boys. He doubted another creature could stop his heart and yet keep him alive like she did all at once. Like in the Star Wars film he had loved growing up, he would go to the dark side for her, without hesitation, and no mystical wizard with a laser sword would tell him otherwise. His concentration was halted swiftly as Mr Petalow senior, noticing Jacob's gaze, put the frame down on its front with enough force to make his simple gesture an exclamation point.

'What do you want, Brooking?' he barked.

This wasn't a good start, Jay thought, as his heart rate kicked up a notch.

John Petalow was six foot four with cropped silver hair and a beard to match. He had the same piercing eyes as the two ladies in his life, but his seemed to send a different message. Where theirs were welcoming, warm and mischievous, his were full of calculating intellect. His pupils were a little too dilated, like those of a hungry great white shark. Menace radiated from the very air that was released from his lungs. He sat in a huge leather chair, with oak legs that looked to have been carved from a tree so giant only the man upon this throne could have done it.

'Well, boy? Do I look like I built this business up from nothing by sitting in this office waiting for children to reach puberty?'

'Sir – John. Sir John,' Jacob stuttered in hilarious fashion. In his head he wanted to argue that he had already reached puberty, but he decided it would take him down a discussion he didn't want to start. In fact, the further he stayed away from that subject, the better.

'Mr Petalow will do, boy,' he declared. 'Now, please,' he went on, his tone softening at seeing Jacob's unease. 'What is it you need here?'

'Alice, Mr Petalow – I need Alice. Or, rather, I would at least like Alice to come out with me on Saturday evening. Maybe to the cinema or theatre. Could I at least ...'

Jacob was cut short by John's hand shooting up. Mr Petalow looked like he was stopping traffic, but Jacob knew he could just as easily have been stopping a rampaging herd of buffalo.

'What makes you think Alice's mother or I would allow this during her studies? Tell me, what do you offer her?'

'I'm a good man.'

The voice laughed at the same time as the Viking king. Jacob felt that the voice was laughing at him pretending to be good, while Alice's father was laughing at his belief he was a man.

'And I've loved Alice since the day I met her. I would do her no harm and I would keep her safe.'

'It's my job to keep her safe,' John Petalow boomed, his words now coming from deep inside a hollow void where Jacob was sure his heart should be. 'Tell me, boy, are you even working since you left school? And left school with nothing, I hear, or am I misinformed?'

'No, sir, I am not working as such, but I want to be a chef. It's all I've ever wanted to do. I've applied everywhere but to no avail.' He could feel his palms leaking at such a profound rate that he panicked they would all drown and even the fish on ice would have the means to swim back to the Thames.

HE'S NOT BUYING YOUR LIES, said the voice with a cackle.

Mr Petalow just looked at him. Maybe looking through him would have been a better way to describe it. Jacob had no idea if he should return the gaze or if he should avoid it, like the Medusa from that Harryhausen film he had loved as a child, the hero of which had always been an idol to him. But instead of finding his inner Perseus, he settled for looking into his lap, where his hands were shaking.

'Listen, son. Jacob, isn't it?'

HE KNOWS YOUR NAME.

HE'S TOYING WITH YOU.

Mr Petalow reached into a secure drawer under his desk. Jacob's chest tightened at the thought of what he was hiding in that drawer. Maybe the severed fingers of all the previous prepubescent boys who had dared to date his teenage daughter. Or, worse still, it could be the instrument that removed those fingers.

Mr Petalow pulled out a pen and tore a piece of paper from a notepad on his desk. He scribbled for a second and then with one ridiculously muscular hand pushed the note across the desk.

'You're nothing. I don't believe you will ever be more than nothing, and Alice deserves something. I want her to have something with someone more,' Mr Petalow said with weight.

'Sir,' Jacob blurted.

'DON'T interrupt me, son. If you're talking, you're not listening, and right now I really need you to listen. This is the number of Pierre DuPont, head chef and patron of the Travelling Trout. He needs a junior chef right now, and I hold favour with him. It's a prestigious establishment. You will be bullied and overworked for little pay, but it will give you an opportunity.'

'What for?' Jacob asked meekly.

'To prove me wrong, Jacob. Come back to me in six months, and if you have nailed that position down, you can take my daughter out, as at least then she would have finished her exams.'

Jacob's mouth opened to protest, but he found himself too weak to argue. Six months was a long time. And he had set his heart on taking Alice out this Saturday.

YOU'RE NOT GOOD ENOUGH.

Jacob rose from the confines of his torture chair and offered his hand. 'Thank you, Mr Petalow.'

Jonathon Petalow stood, and it suddenly hit Jacob just how huge his adversary was. It was like he was cut from a single monolith of granite.

He shook Jacob's tiny hand and whispered in his most subtle voice yet. 'This isn't all about Alice. You do know that, right? Don't let yourself down, and don't let me down.'

HAHAHAHAHAHAHAHA

Shut up, Jacob thought.

NO, YOU'RE A FOOL.

SHUT UP, he repeated in his head.

NO!

NO!

NO!

NO!

4

Birth of a Monster
Spring 1996
Canterbury, Kent, UK

Alice had been battered during what had been the most intense 60 minutes of lacrosse she had ever played – a 13-9 loss to a Maidstone side that, on a different day, couldn't have held a candle to the league leaders at Canterbury WLC. Alice was only playing in the colts, as she was still short of 18, but the side she had faced today had been full of adults each a little quicker and more educated on tactics. The freeze pack on her knee was starting to become useless as the afternoon sun, on a particularly warm May afternoon, melted the ice quicker than she could replace it. Another graze on her forearm would need cleaning when she got back to the locker room; Alice had picked most of the gravel out, but she could feel throbbing as though a foreign object was lodged deep inside her skin. Alice was normally the motivational coach for the locker room. She was the club's top scorer, at least in the colts, and found it easy to give the pre-match pep talk, but today she was struggling to find a good reason why she wasted her Saturday afternoons getting beaten up with hard balls and harder sticks.

'You looked good today, Pebble. Just wasn't your day, I guess,' said Jacob as he joined Alice on the side lines and took her hand into his own.

'Our bloody defence let us down again, but can you blame them when the opposition is fielding a team of semi-professional players? Thank you for coming to watch me though, bubba. It means a lot, even if we lost. I know you don't get much time off.'

'Don't be silly. I only took that job to shut your father up, so getting to watch his daughter run around in these little shorts for an hour is kind of bliss, to be honest.' Jacob tugged at the waistband of a figure-hugging pair of white shorts.

'Baby, please come back home and find something in Canterbury,' pleaded Alice as she discarded the ice pack. 'I know you are doing well, but I can't see why you have to be stuck out there on the outskirts of London.'

'I promised your father a year, and I want to prove the old fool wrong. And things are going bloody well. Who would have guessed? Jacob Brooking, young chef of the year.'

'I am proud of you, Jay; I just miss you. It's unfair that I must be alone whilst all those waitresses get to flirt with you every day.'

'Even if that were true, do you honestly think that I could ever have eyes for anyone but you? Never could I find such beauty in another, my love.'

Jacob went down on one knee in a mock proposal, and Alice reacted by pushing him over for trying to be funny.

'You'd better get cleaned up if you want us to spend some time together before the Viking king takes you away from me,' said Jacob from his new position on the Astroturf.

'Yes, boss,' replied Alice, bending over to kiss Jacob firmly on the lips. 'I'll be quick.'

'Great game, losers! Reminded me of when we were kids playing junior league,' taunted a spiteful blonde who could only be a year or two older than Alice. 'Hey, Ginge, good job missing that open goal at the end. Real classy bit of play to spoon it into the crowd.'

'If you call the group of boys getting far too excited about your bust a crowd, then, yeah, I guess you are right, blondie,' retorted Alice with a smile.

'The fuck you say to me? You snotty bitch, I will wipe the smile off your face before I go out there and fuck that cute little thing that was watching you.'

The blonde girl rounded on Alice but got no rise from her, as Alice refused to take her head out of her locker.

Coward, the voice whispered.

'I didn't say anything,' said Alice. 'Anything at all actually. You must have misheard me.'

'That's right, you misheard her, blondie. So why don't you climb back onto your coach and fuck right off,' said Holly, Alice's best friend and the club's vice captain.

'Or what?' snapped the blonde. 'You gonna eat me, tubs?'

Holly stepped forward, towering over her much slighter opponent. 'Oh, you fucking wait and see what I do.'

'Come on, Laurie, let's leave the kids to play with each other, yeah,' said one of the older girls. She pulled the blonde round and shuffled her out the door.

'Take care, ladies,' said the Maidstone captain, who was the last of the opposition to leave the locker room.

'See you later, bitches.' Holly waved as she bounced her curvaceous hip off of Alice, almost knocking her into her locker.

'Yeah, see you in the play-offs, ladies,' said Alice. She pulled off her kit and dumped it in a pile on the floor. 'Why does everyone we ever speak to have to treat us like we're a bunch of weak-willed fairies?'

Holly laughed. 'You speak for yourself, ginge. I don't get much trouble.'

'That's because you look like a hungry, hungry hippo when you're pissed off, Holl.'

'You little ...'

Holly was cut off by sounds of laughter from outside and went to see what the commotion was, while Alice struggled to get a towel around her.

Jacob was sitting next to, and talking to, the blonde. She laughed and touched his arm before bouncing up and heading over to the coach.

Alice tripped over herself as she tried to get her jogging bottoms on. 'What's going on out there, Holl?'

'Nothing. Just Jacob talking to himself and the Maidstone bitches all trying to squeeze those big heads onto the coach.'

'He does that a lot,' said Alice, wondering how much of her boyfriend's craziness she should divulge in public.

'Babe, you knew Jay was crazy when he met you. Don't pretend this is a new thing.'

Alice's inner voice started to laugh with a dry rasping cackle. She looked at herself in the locker-room mirror as she threw some perfume on and tied her hair back. *That will have to do*, she thought.

The mirror's reflection of her was moving a fraction slower than she was – a vision that didn't change as she rubbed her eyes and tried to regain her focus.

He's not the crazy one ... is he?

Autumn 1997
Canterbury, Kent UK

The seaside town of Whitstable was home. It was where they both lived. But they had grown up to be the young adults they were now on very different sides of the county. Alice had been born and raised just ten miles up the road in the historic city of Canterbury. She had enjoyed a much more privileged childhood on the cobbled streets of the heritage site. Culture poured from every narrow alley, each containing a unique shop or store selling handmade crafts or jewellery. Students from schools across Europe visited each day to see the cathedral lit up at night. A magnificent sight at any age. But for a child it was the best place in the world for letting your imagination run wild. And Alice had come back to her city of origin to pick up supplies for a big art project the college had entrusted her to run wild with. The picture she had in mind was beautiful, and this city would be her inspiration, as it had been so many times before.

This particular Saturday wasn't a beautiful day by any stretch of the imagination, though. Rain lashed down on the stone streets and ran in rivers through the cracks, with little estuaries forming into puddles at the soles of Alice's pumps as she pressed her body tight against the wall to avoid the biblical downpour. She had found a haven under a tiny shop awning angled over the doorway to a vintage fudge confectioner. The awning was doing its best to deflect all but the worst of the storm, although Alice had resigned herself to getting soaked to the bone due to the sheer volume of rain coming down. She had run blindly down this alley for shelter, but now that she was trapped here, she saw it was filled with tiny and unique shops selling anything you could desire. It had an almost magical feel to it, and even in this horrid weather she couldn't help but marvel at the unique beauty of the city. Canterbury was old and it showed here, as the cobbles met the uneven brickwork and gave everything an almost drunk appearance. All off-kilter and crooked. And it was that which made it so attractive to Alice. Sweet seventeen and full of confidence, Alice took a hairband from her wrist and tied her hair into a tight bun. Pulling a dark blue woolly bobble hat from her shoulder satchel, she covered as much of her hair as she could and buttoned her coat up as far as it would go, readying herself for the dash to the bus stop, because, she whispered to herself, 'It's just a bit of rain.'

She sprinted out of the alley to her right and into the open high street. The rain still thundered down aggressively and was stinging her head and back, even through her clothing, with its sheer force. Hitting the ground hard and at pace, with every step sending up an explosion of rainwater, she sped towards the cover of the bus shelter, which was just a few hundred feet ahead of her. Being vice captain of the college lacrosse team meant stamina was not an issue, but traction was proving a problem, as her feet kept slipping on the wet cobbles. She rode her luck a few times, until the inevitable happened. As she took a sharp left around the edge of a parked taxi, her right foot went from underneath her, and in one rapid motion she crashed down to the wet stone and found herself on her back, staring up at the sky. In a heartbeat, all the air was forced out of her lungs, and her hot breath bellowed from her like she was a mythical dragon in a legendary tale of valour and heroism. As flashes of light danced around her vision like some pyrotechnic display, she was suddenly hit with a sharp lancing pain through her shoulder blades, which prevented her from moving. Every attempt to raise herself up felt like something was stabbing deeper into her body and was soon to pierce her heart. Alice gasped as her lungs allowed her to breathe again. All of a sudden, a hand reached down and clasped her arm in a muscular grip.

'Alice,' the boy asked, 'are you OK?'

Her answer was a tear-filled croak, but the boy smiled as if he understood.

'I'll take that as a yes, shall I? Here, try and sit up. Did you hit your head?'

'No,' Alice slurred. 'Just my back and my bum.'

Visibly in pain, she was pulled upright by the stranger.

'OH MY GOD - I know you,' Alice said, embarrassed.

'We go to the same college, so I should hope you at least know me a little,' Thomas Levit joked.

Alice breathed deeply as Thomas took her hands and smiled.

'One, two and three,' he said, pulling her to her feet.

Alice stumbled a little at first, and Thomas wrapped an arm around her waist to support her. He was a broad man. Muscular with little body fat and hands like shovels. Pulling Alice to her feet was akin to lifting a child for him.

'So, no Jacob today?' he asked, holding her steady as he guided her to the bus shelter.

'He's working as always. He decided against college. He was never the academic type, I guess. How do you know my Jacob? I wasn't aware you had gone to the Howard George.'

'Nooooooo.' Thomas laughed. 'I'm a King's boy, but we have mutual friends through rugby.'

'That's right – you're first team captain at Canterbury. I'm sure I watched you play in the cup final last year with Dad,' Alice recalled.

'Your dad is a legend at our club. John the Viking Petalow has a photo on every wall of the clubhouse, and in each one he's lifting a trophy.' Thomas seemed starstruck as he spoke.

Alice couldn't believe what she was about to say to possibly the coolest guy in her year, if not on the whole campus. 'Well, if you have a few hours spare you're more than welcome to come and meet him. He's only at home doing chores for Mum. I promise he's not always the superhero you guys make him out to be.'

'I'd love to, but does that sound a little bit like a date?' Thomas sounded hopeful. 'Will Jacob mind?'

'Of course it's not a date.' Alice laughed. 'I couldn't do that to Jay, but I do think Dad would enjoy having a man about for an hour or two. He gets bullied by Mum and me constantly.'

'Well, I would be honoured to be the man who saves him from such turmoil. Shall we go, my lady?' Thomas extended his arm out and Alice looped her own into it, neither of them noticing the rain had stopped.

-

'So, this is the famous Petalow ranch?' said Thomas, closing the wrought-iron gate behind him. 'It's smaller than I thought.'

The sun was out and steam was rising gently from the grass on the front lawn.

'What did you expect? A castle, maybe?' Alice slipped her key out of her back pocket and put it in the door, but to her surprise it opened before she could turn it and her father filled the open frame.

'Bloody hell, Alice, I'm used to you bringing home strays, not the captain of the under-23s.' John kissed his daughter on the head. 'Great game last Saturday, Thomas. You really have those backs working as a unit at last.'

Thomas met the compliment with a strong handshake and a wry smile. 'We have a long way to go, but at least we are reading from the same play book now.'

'Good lad, Tom. I have every faith in you to sort them out. I didn't know you and my Alice were friends?'

'We kinda just happened, Dad,' Alice giggled. 'He rescued me from a fall and drove me home.'

'Well, Tom, I owe you a debt of thanks for that.' John finally let go of his hand and turned to his daughter, scanning her from head to toe. 'Are you hurt?'

'No, Dad, just wet from the landing.'

'Well, I'm glad, and I suggest you go and get the kettle on for this fine young man while I pick your mother up from her mission to bankrupt us.'

As he said his goodbyes and approached his oversized Range Rover, which seemed all too appropriate for the Viking king, he turned and gave Alice one last look, mouthing *I approve* at his bemused daughter, who just shook her head in response.

Thomas closed the door behind him and was instantly aware of the fact that he enjoyed being in this position. John Petalow was a legend at the rugby club, and there was no doubt in his mind that legendary status would be his too if he ended up banging the Viking's daughter.

'I'm just changing out of these wet clothes,' Alice said while bouncing up the stairs, stripping as she went. 'Get the kettle on, Tom.'

'Yes, my queen,' said Thomas, whose search for the kitchen took him down a hallway filled with pictures of

Alice's mum, whom he was amazed to discover was a prettier and bustier version of Alice herself.

'What I wouldn't do to get my hands on that,' he whispered, knowing full well that even the great Thomas Levit would be pushing his luck to try and hit on John Petalow's wife of 30 years.

In the kitchen, he picked up a framed picture that had mother and daughter in red bikinis on some ridiculously clean beach with white sand pooling around their feet. Just as he was about to put the picture back to rest, Alice grabbed him from behind and shrieked, 'Stop eyeing up my mother, she's happily married, don't you know.'

Without conscious thought, Tom grabbed Alice and pulled her into a kiss she didn't see coming.

Alice pulled away from his grip immediately. 'What are you doing!'

'Surely it's clear to you?' Thomas proclaimed calmly. 'Or are the rumours of Jacob neglecting you for work exaggerated?'

Alice didn't know how to attack this situation without upsetting Tom or his ego, as in fairness he had been nothing but a gentleman all day to this point.

Thomas once again placed his right hand on her wrist and leaned in to kiss her. Still in complete shock, Alice didn't pull away but clenched her lips tightly into the kind of face you make when you suck on a post-tequila lemon wedge.

'Thomas, whatever you think is happening today isn't going to happen like this,' Alice affirmed as he pulled back.

Thomas remained calm but increased his grip on her wrist to a point where she was aware of his strength.

'So, what has today been about then, Alice? Come to meet my parents, come in my house – was this all a game to you, or did you just want the lift home?'

'No, of course not, Tom. Don't ever say that. I never even thought you would look at me like that. I mean, look at you, for god's sake!'

'Well, I do look at you like that. And now you know how I feel, surely it changes things between us.' An air of arrogance not noted before had slipped into his voice, and without warning he forced himself forward again, pushing his tongue straight through her lips in a motion that nearly caused Alice to bite it clean off. Instead, her free hand shot up in an aggressive half arc that ended up with her watch catching the side of his ear. Thomas recoiled, bringing his hand up to the wound. A small gash on his inner lobe was bleeding.

'You fucking bitch. Who the hell do you think you are? No wonder Jacob works away. I bet he's fucking every waitress at that crappy restaurant.'

'Get out of my house now, Tom,' Alice shouted. Her eyes were beginning to well up, but anger drove her, not fear.

'Fine. I don't need this shit from the likes of you anyway.'

With that he turned to head towards the front door. But as he reached the hall next to the kitchen entrance, he stopped in his tracks. His broad shoulders filled the frame of the door. 'You know what, Alice? Why should I leave with nothing when I feel you owe me? Or should I have just left you to lie in the pissing rain, looking like trash?'

'Thomas, just go.'

'No. I think I'll stay if it's all the same with you.'

He moved back towards where she stood, looking straight through her.

Alice had backed herself into the corner of the kitchen without realising and was suddenly aware she had no idea how far he was willing to take this.

'Stop it right now, Tom,' she barked sharply. 'You know this isn't going to happen. I'd never cheat on Jacob, so why not just leave?'

Thomas had stopped responding to her directly and instead seemed to be conversing with himself. He took her this time tightly by both arms and squeezed her together like a human accordion.

'Tom, please – you're hurting me.'

'I'm not hurting you. This is what you wanted, remember? To come over, to be with you. Didn't even hesitate when your dad said he was leaving us alone, and then what? You ran upstairs to get changed and came back down in this little summer dress.'

'I was soaking and filthy and it was the first thing I found, so don't you dare try and justify this. GET OFF OF ME!'

Tom came in again and started planting wet kisses and small bites on her exposed neck and shoulders, while Alice tried without success to fight him off. Her anger now turned to fear and she screeched at him again and again, until he pulled his face level with hers to spit more venom. Not yet broken by his animalistic behaviour, she brought her head forward into his with all the might she could muster. Every fibre of her body wanted to be free of his disgusting grasp, but as her brow connected with the forehead of a man used to being hit hard, Alice realised she had made a massive mistake. She collapsed to the floor, and for the second time that day the world around her went dark, with the only light coming in aggressive, flashing white spots. She could still feel herself fighting him, although it felt like one of those dreams where you are trying to run yet feel weighed down by some phantom apparition.

Flashes of Thomas's broken face hit her at intervals every few seconds between lances of pain from behind her eyes.

'See, I knew you wanted it. Why else would you stop fighting me? You're not that hurt if you want me this bad.'

Alice was unsure if her head was completely smashed to pieces, because she felt like she was fighting for her life and screaming at the top of her lungs. Yet some conscious part of her mind was telling her the truth. She was completely and silently still.

'Get off me,' she cried in her head.

Without warning she felt her underwear tear under pressure and almost instantly the warmth of something running down her leg. She screamed again inside her prisoned mind at the thought of wetting herself, but it suddenly occurred to her it might be something else. Something worse. The sharp pain in her head left her for a moment as her insides turned to fire and she was violated beyond her threshold for pain.

'You dirty bitch,' he laughed, 'but I'm still game, as you clearly are.'

Alice was crying inside at the realisation that he genuinely thought she wanted this.

'Get off ... GET OFF!'

As she felt him enter her over and over again, her body started to convulse at the damage being caused inside of her. The screaming in her head wouldn't stop and was now overwhelming her senses like a perverse choir of murdered girls begging for release. But it took over everything. She heard nothing but screams. She felt nothing but pain. And she broke, with everything she held within her turning to blackness.

-

She woke up unsure of how long she had been out for but realised quickly that she was alone. Her head throbbed violently as she tried to stand unaided, but rather predictably she fell against the kitchen worktop. She felt and then saw the trickle of blood and semen running down her thigh to her calf, and she just about made it to the sink, where her stomach emptied itself of everything it held, including its own lining.

They won't believe you.

Alice looked around for the source of the voice, but no one was there.

Why would they? Silly little Alice.

Alice looked over to the kitchen table, where a note stood proudly folded into a tent shape.

She staggered over to it, and her heart sank once more at the words written within.

Alice, I had an amazing time. Dinner? Tom xxx

Finally, her body allowed her to cry, and she sank back down to what had become her most common position today. As she lay in the mess that had been created, she brought her knees up to her chest and sobbed uncontrollably.

'Jacob,' she whispered.

He won't believe you either.

5

York Avenue
Autumn 1997
Canterbury, Kent UK

Alice had been sitting in the cold bath for three hours straight while the tap kept running and what was now freezing-cold water poured into the overflow. She hugged her knees tightly into her chest and kept the last of the heat from leaving her body, although her hands were shaking enough to start a small fire had they been wrapped in kindling. She had stared blankly at the same spot without moving since she had dragged herself upstairs. She was still fully dressed, and the blood had tainted the water, which had become a murky brown. She knew no one would believe her. She felt plagued by the events of the last six hours; she felt like she could never be cleansed of the thoughts that were eating away at her soul. She had scratched away most of the skin from the inside of her legs and crotch, and yet she felt as dirty as she had the second that Thomas had touched her. Tears were still rolling down her cheeks, and her eyes felt too wide to ever truly close again. The hurt in her womb hadn't subsided as such, but the lancing pain that had previously torn her asunder was now a deep and thunderous ache, the likes of which one could only experience after the nightmarish violence of the past 24 hours.

A loud knock at the door shook Alice to her very foundations and caused a wave of water to be thrown across the floor of the bathroom.

'Alice, are you OK, petal? You've been in there for hours. Is everything OK?'

Alice struggled to get her words together in a way that would mask her emotion, but she knew that silence would be worse. 'I'm OK, Mum, just really bad period pains. And I'm missing Jacob, I guess. I'll be out soon, you don't need to worry.'

Alice didn't believe her own lies, so she doubted her mother would either.

'OK, sweetie. We're here if you need us. Your father was going to cook some dinner, but I'll tell him you're a little off colour. I'll bring you up a glass of wine and a water bottle.'

Alice reached forward and turned off the tap while pulling on the plug chain until she felt the little pressured pop of air from beneath. She pulled herself slowly up to a half slump, and, for just a second, she caught herself in the antique mirror hanging on the back of the door. Her heart froze. The reflection looking back at her wasn't hers; rather, it was a version of her reimagined by fear. Her eyes were as black as the depths of the ocean and her bones almost sick with malnutrition, but it was still her, and for that moment the reflection looked back at Alice almost quizzically, weighing her up like a warrior scouting its enemy before a battle.

She stepped out of the bath and placed one foot on the bath mat, expecting resistance to meet her wet flesh, but instead she sank straight into a void where the floor should be. She tumbled into darkness until her world went black, and she fell until she hit the surface of a dark world she never saw coming.

She awoke dazed and confused from the journey, with no idea where she had come from or how long she had been unconscious. She put one hand down to raise herself up from the thin, hard-wearing carpet.

'Where am I?' she murmured to herself as she tried to stand, realising something was really out of place. She was at least three feet shorter than she should have been, and, looking at herself in the reflection of her mirrored wardrobe door, she had a strange sense of coming home. She felt as though she was in the bedroom in which she had grown up, in a small property on York Avenue, just outside the city. She hadn't lived here since she was six years old, and as she looked at herself in the mirror and saw an innocent young Alice, with a tight French plait and white knee-high socks, looking back at her, a sudden and unparalleled sense of dread washed over her. She had very few memories of this house, but there was one thing that she had never forgotten, something that had left her crying in her parents' bed each and every night, and she knew it was coming for her.

Alice had to hide, and, as always, this place had no intention of helping her. The walls had always seemed so tall, the ceiling so high and the windows so large that with bright sunlight washing over the plain white paint, the room felt a thousand times larger than it actually was. And yet, as had always been the case, Alice could see no place to hide, and hiding was imperative, because she knew what was coming. She could hear its footsteps already, close together and moving at pace, while a childish giggle was carried on the air in the distance. Alice dropped to her knees and kitten-crawled under her bed so as to be hidden by the thin, overhanging quilt, which she prayed was enough protection. She wrapped her hands in a seal around her mouth. The giggling increased when it entered the room, and as it paced around, searching for her, its tiny shadow was the only thing

Alice could spy through the small slit that separated the quilt from the floor. Alice knew the drill: it would leave her bedroom and search elsewhere, and she would have to make a run for the staircase; it didn't ever follow her outside, and if she could get to the front door, then she would be safe, although the more she thought about it, the less she seemed convinced that she had ever made it outside, and it became apparent that the safety of the "outside" might just be something she had made up as a child to give her hope.

The giggling continued and followed Alice's stalker down the hall and into her parents' bedroom. This was her opportunity, but she had to move quick, and she could feel the fear pulling her back. For just a second, the tormenter's laughter stopped, and Alice took only a second to turn a belly shuffle into a sprint as she darted for the staircase, which, she realised all too late, seemed a thousand steps deep. Alice must have been halfway down when the giggling started up again. It sounded close, and her heart was racing. She bounded off the bottom step and headed towards the 20-foot-high front door. Chancing a look over her shoulder, she saw *It* standing there, watching her from the top of the stairs, causing her to scream in fear. She turned back to her escape plan and realised with a sinking heart that she couldn't even get close to reaching the knob to what was now a thousand-foot slab of gloss white wood so giant in stature that she was unsure she had seen a mightier door. Alice knew what was next, but as she heard the rapid pitter-patter of feet closing in on her, she also knew that this was playing out exactly as it always did. Running straight into the light of the kitchen, she dived for the safety of the round kitchen table, whose dinner cloth would provide her with some cover, if only for a moment; she knew, as she pressed her hand hard over her mouth to stop her heavy breathing giving her location away, that her relief would only be temporary. It was only ever a matter of time.

The laughter stopped, as did the sound of tiny footsteps, and Alice knew it was time. She leant forward, holding her breath, and went to lift the dinner cloth up from where it touched the floor, but before Alice even touched it she started screaming with the shrill pitch of a girl being murdered, as the nightmare in front of her yanked the sheet up and lurched forward.

Alice woke up crying on her bathroom floor. Her dress was still sodden and her hair was drenched and matted, and a six-year-old demon version of herself was giggling at her from the mirror.

You're it, the creature called as it ran into the shadows, leaving Alice to pull herself over to the toilet, where she threw up until only blood was leaving her body.

6

Into the Fire
Winter 2000
Biggen Hill, London UK

The Travelling Trout was a beautiful gastropub nestled in the Kent countryside. Not far from London, the area was affluent to a high degree, and all the chimney stacks you could see belonged to big detached houses with far too much land to share. The pub itself was an Edwardian property surrounded by the beautiful Biggin Hill woodland, which gave the pub a haunted look. Cast-iron street lamps cast a warm glow over the stone walls and the thatched roof, which housed a family of barn owls that were now protected by the RSPCA and so were unlikely to be evicted anytime soon. Jacob had never understood why anyone would want to evict the little beauties in any case, as they ate all the bugs. A line of expensive cars filled the car park, and another big Audi pulled into the gated entrance and drove up the gravel track. This was an old English pub. But it was really high end.

Matt entered the rear of the building to searing heat and the noise of industrial fans. He passed Jacob some fresh herbs he had taken from the garden. Jacob was barking orders at the waiting team as Sam hurriedly dropped hot pans into his sink of soapy water, creating an aggressive sizzle. The kitchen was roasting hot, even at this time of year, so Matt always tried to hide in the preparation section at the rear of the kitchen, far away from the flames. He started unloading the dehydrator, knowing Chef was about to collar him on it, while Sam the kitchen porter and general dish pig looked on, oblivious to the world around him.

7.10pm

'Where is my carving knife? Sam,' demanded Jacob, 'where is my carving knife?'

'Erm, it's out the back, Chef.' Sam looked at the ground as he spoke.

'Why is it out the back, Sam?'

Jacob stopped what he was doing and looked Sam square in the face, while Matt slid quietly into the background so as not to get caught as collateral damage.

'I was opening a ... well, a jar,' said Sam unapologetically. 'I was opening a jar.'

'With my carving knife?'

'Yes, Chef.'

'My knife?'

'Yes, Chef.'

'Sam. Find my knife. Put it on the pass. Then I suggest you get out of my sight.'

'Yes, Chef.'

'Matt?'

'Yes, Chef.'

'If you see Sam touch my knife again, I give you permission to beat his ass blue.'

'Oui, Chef.'

7.15pm

'SERVICE!' shouted Jacob while patting the little bronze bell incessantly for attention.

The two wild venison fillets that Jacob was presenting under the heat lamps were glistening in their own buttery juices. One at a time, he took them onto his little wooden chopping board, which was weathered with cuts and scars from years of abuse, and sliced them into four disks, fanning the meat out. The perfectly seared exterior was offset by the scarlet centre. They had been rested to perfection, retaining all of their juices.

He took each fan of meat, lay it atop the celeriac and potato boulangère in the centre of the plate, and gave it a gentle squeeze to form a flower-like shape. Turning the plates to make sure everything was symmetrical, he took a tablespoon from a little steel tankard of hot water that he held by the pass and gave his chocolate and juniper jus a stir before drizzling a little over the centre of the meat and spiralling out to dress an inner circle on the plate.

7.16pm

'SERVICE!' he shouted again. 'Matthew, parsnip flutes – where are they?'

'Here, Chef.' The scrawny young chef de partie scurried from the back with a tub of what looked like shards of golden glass.

Jacob placed one atop each plate, cresting the meat like a crown before once again rotating each plate to be sure of continuity.

7.17pm

'BLOODY SERVICE!' Jacob shouted, slamming his hand down on the bell one last time. A young waitress rushed through the double door to the side of the pass and straightened herself out before looking at the check in front of her.

'Table seven, Molly.'

'Yes, Chef.'

'And Molly, they reach the table the same way they leave here, OK?'

'Yes, Chef.'

The petrified young girl scurried away with a plate in each hand.

7.18pm

'Matthew, I need two sea trout on my board and a venison garnish up in three minutes.'

'Yes, skipper,' he responded without hesitation.

Jacob put a stainless-steel pan on the heat and sprinkled it with sea salt and a little lemon-tainted rapeseed oil. The young chef returned to Jacob with two large trout fillets, and as soon as he placed them on his blue chopping board Jacob was seasoning both sides and scoring the skin, which he then pressed down into the hot pan before sliding it into the oven to dress his venison plate as he placed the latest fillet onto his resting rack.

7.19pm

'Do you have a minute, Chef?'

Jacob looked up to see Robert standing there. Well dressed as usual, in a rural fashion. His tweed jacket and flat cap made him look like he had returned from a shoot with only his shotgun and springer spaniel missing. Robert Richardson was the owner of the Travelling Trout. As well as being a very well-respected restaurant owner, he was a fair man, and he had looked after a very inexperienced Jacob five years before.

'Of course, boss. As long as you don't mind talking while I work, I'm all yours.'

Jacob didn't take his eyes off the plates he was preparing, but Robert knew he had his full attention.

'Pierre has officially quit his position as head chef. I know it's been a turbulent few years, but I'm hopeful that he taught you something in that time about running this kitchen.' Robert was looking for a reaction, and he appeared to get one as Jacob paused while taking his trout out of the oven. 'You are one of the best chefs I know, but can you do the orders? The logistics? Manage the team?'

'Rob, Pierre was a great chef – maybe too good. But he won't be missed,' said Jacob, flipping his trout over with a little pallet knife to reveal the crispy, salt-mottled skin he had hoped for, before placing it next to the venison on the rack.

'I'm glad you feel that way, Jacob. You know I don't do formal, so what do you want?'

Jacob stopped, looked up and gazed into his boss's predatory eyes.

'Thirty-six thousand to start. We promote Matty to sous chef and get a new chef de partie. He has buckets of potential and won't cost us much more.'

'Deal.' Robert leaned in and offered his hand through the hot lights on the pass.

Jacob gripped his hand firmly and shook it vigorously.

'Matthew,' he called out.

'Yes, Chef?'

'You're promoted to sous chef.'

'Thank you, Chef,' Matt replied without stopping what he was doing.

'And Matthew.'

'Yes, Chef?'

'Where's my bloody samphire?'

'Coming, Chef.'

'Thank you, Rob.' Jacob smiled and released his boss's hand. 'We won't let you down.'

'Good show, Jacob. Enjoy your service, boys. Oh, and Alice has just arrived with her mum. I've put her on table one.'

'Thank you, boss. I'll be out in five.'

7.22pm

Tossing the fresh samphire into the hot pan the trout had previously occupied, Jacob started to construct the plates.

'Matt, come here, mate.'

'What's wrong, Chef?' said Matt, whose chef whites were splattered with a claret sauce.

Jacob offered his hand and placed the other on his young apprentice's shoulder. 'In the week since Pierre left, you have been a rock for me, and, honestly, I need you more than ever now in the coming months.'

'I'll do my best, Jay.'

'I know you will, and that's all I ask. Now, help me get this last check out so I can go see my beautiful girlfriend.'

7.25pm

'SERVICE!'

The trout sat on its bed of samphire, a smear of hollandaise sitting beside it, dressed in fresh dill leaves. While Matthew applied the finishing touches, Jacob was meticulously inspecting the plates. One more rotation of the dishes and Matt got a pat on the back before Jacob rang the bell a final time.

Molly came through the door, but to Jacob's surprise she was followed by a giggling Alice. She truly was the best thing he had seen all day, and she was dressed so quintessentially Alice that a brief moment of nostalgia and love overwhelmed him. She wore a green floral dress, white neck scarf and bangles galore. Her hair was straightened, and the extra length brought it down to near her breast line.

'Pebble, you look amazing. I was trying to get out to you, but I had this to get out first. Table nine please, Molly.'

'Baby, it's fine.' Alice leaned in and kissed him. 'I know you're busy, but what's this good news Robert just told me you have?'

'Well, it turns out I'm the new head chef.'

Alice screeched. 'That's amazing! So he met all your demands?'

'Without any hesitation.'

'I guess that means congratulations to you too then, Matthew.'

Matt couldn't look at Alice without blushing, so he ran to the back of the kitchen while trying to look busy, murmuring his thanks as he went.

'Let's just hope I'm good enough,' Jacob joked.

Alice pulled Jacob by the arm so he was out of the busiest part of the kitchen and placed her hand on his cheek. 'Baby, I believe one thing more than anything I've ever believed.'

'What's that?' replied a hopeful Jacob.

'That you got this, baby. You got this.'

Spring

It was three years since Jacob had accepted the position of head chef at the Trout. Three years of graft, three years of missed sleep, combined with convincing Alice every six months that she didn't need a holiday just yet.

'But Jay,' she would complain, to no avail.

She understood, but the desire for a little time with her boyfriend was of course something he could understand.

Years of hot pans and stupid waiters and here he was, frozen in anticipation, with the letter from the *Good Food Guide* on his desk in front of him, and he was too scared to open it. He had never felt good enough for anything or anyone, and to avoid the obvious failure that any journey would bring, he had always avoided starting any journey at all. That was until he was challenged to 'be enough for Alice' - he said the words out loud, throwing his thoughts out into the public domain, although no one was there to hear him. No one would disturb him today; no one had even offered him a coffee this morning.

He finally gathered the courage to move to the right side of his desk, and with a deep breath, he allowed himself to collapse into his chair. *You can do this, Brooking*, he told himself, taking the letter into his hand. It felt important. It had weight to it, and as he opened the corners of the envelope, he noticed the off-white quality of the paper, thick and textured like it meant something.

Jacob held the letter out in front of him and started to read.

'To all those concerned at the Travelling Trout ...'

Jacob opened the door to the restaurant, and two things awaited him: complete and utter silence, and his entire team standing and looking at him – even those that weren't on the rota to work today had come in.

At the front of the ensemble was his beloved Alice, who, just like the rest, was trying to gauge his reaction for any subtle giveaways. Jacob walked gingerly into the restaurant and propped himself up against the bar opposite his team, refusing to give anything away just yet. Alice – who was in a very formal-looking black skirt and white blouse, her hair pulled back into a tight ponytail, and with a touch of black eyeshadow, which brought out the exceptional brightness and beauty of her blue eyes – looked like she was ready to explode. Her hands were clenched tightly and she couldn't stop fidgeting. She had been helping Jacob run the floor since finishing her art degree in June and felt truly invested in what was about to happen.

'I didn't know you were eagerly waiting out here, guys. Had I known, I may just have taken another hour to build the suspense a little more.'

Raising no laughter from his terrified crew, he decided to put them out of their misery.

'Firstly, I would like to thank you for all the hard work you've put in this past year. Everything you do gets noticed by myself and Robert, despite his usual absence, so whatever the outcome, I need you all to understand one thing. I value you all as a team and as a family, and if one day I have my own restaurant, I will take every one of you with me.'

'Thank you, Chef,' said everyone in the crowd, until Alice took a step forward.

'Jacob.' Alice motioned with her hands.

'Yes, of course.' Jacob stepped forward, a few feet from where Alice stood, holding the letter out in front of him. 'With everyone here in front of me, I'd like to show you this.'

He held out the letter from the *Good Food Guide* and then lowered it in one motion to reveal a large sapphire and platinum engagement ring, which the restaurant lights made twinkle like a candle. In one continued fluid move, he lowered himself down onto his right knee.

'Alice, without you I wouldn't have even started this journey, and without you I wouldn't have made it this far, and, yes, without you we wouldn't now be a three-rosette restaurant.'

The crowd cheered – all except Alice, who was shaking and looking at her Jacob, tears of joy chasing her mascara down her face.

'It would be an honour to be your everything, if you would do me the honour of being my wife,' said Jacob.

Alice collapsed into his arms, putting her forehead against his. 'Yes, baby,' she whispered. 'A thousand times yes.'

They kissed over and over, with Alice peppering Jacob's face with little pecks as he placed the ring on her finger.

'I'm so proud of you, baby,' Alice said.

'You deserve as much credit as me, Pebble.'

'I'm going to marry you, baby,' she said with tears still flowing down her face.

'Yeah, you are,' Jacob laughed, pulling her up to her feet so that everyone could gather round her to offer congratulations.

'Matthew, get over here,' Jacob demanded.

'Yes, Chef,' said Jacob's most loyal team member. 'Congratulations and all that.'

'Don't congratulate me, son – we did this together. And with that in mind, I'm promoting you to head chef with immediate effect. But keep it on the low low for now.'

'But Chef, I'm confused. You're the head chef.'

'I have different plans, mate, but let's talk later.'

'Thank you, Chef,' said Matthew, offering his hand. But instead, Jacob embraced him in a bear hug and said quietly to his young protégé.

'You got this, son.'

7

Sunshine and Stick Insects
Summer 2002
The South East Coast UK

She could hear the honking outside, but she was sure he could wait a little longer. The dress she had settled on was a perfect vision of summer class. A burnt orange colour, light and floral, low cut and shorter on the thigh than her dad would allow if he was here to see her bound out the door. And bound she did as she shut her bedroom door on a plethora of dresses, all tried on and thrown about her bed with gay abandon. After kissing her mum quickly at the bottom of the stairs and pressing a finger to her lips to hush a dress-related protest that was surely coming, she was free.

The sun was shining down harder than she could imagine was possible in the UK even at this time of year, and not a cloud touched the canvas of blue above her. She ran straight to Jacob's car and jumped in. The air conditioning hit her like an ice-cold slap across her brow, and she licked her lips before leaning in for a kiss. Jacob was there, ready to receive. His lips, far too perfect to be wasted on a man, were warm to her touch, and he pushed her mouth apart to gently probe her with his wanting tongue. He always liked to remind her of the power he had over her. She felt a tremor of excitement run up her thigh. And then, as always, he sharply pulled away and started talking about his day. She listened intently as he enthused about the latest Lenny

Kravitz song he had heard just an hour before. Not understanding a thing he was saying, she still loved hearing him talk so passionately about music. He had always claimed it was a dying industry. That writing music that meant something important just never happened in this day and age. Alice sat and watched him as he negotiated the roads ahead. She loved him. For all that he was and all that he was yet to be.

As they made their way down the Kent coastal trail, it was hard not to fall into a blissful daydream. To the left was a drop of 200 feet; at the bottom, the ocean reared up against the cliff face, like some ancient war was taking place on an elemental level. They drove south towards Dover, before stopping for an iced coffee in the little town of Sandgate, which overlooked the ocean from the top of the cliffs. The warm breeze from the sea washed over them like a light blanket. A few speckled clouds appeared, blocking just enough of the afternoon sun to stop their already tanned skin burning. To the right of them was the most fantastic array of homes - so expensive that they would forever be out of reach to all but the richest folk in town. But it was nice to dream, as Alice always did when they made this journey. Not that they didn't do OK. Alice had been running her father's company for two years - at least, the financial part of it. Her dad called her his PA, but she knew this was a little in jest. He hated the office work, and she had taken that off his hands, to her mum's delight, although the promise of more free time had turned quickly into more time for fishing. Jay had become the Travelling Trout's youngest head chef and been instrumental in winning the restaurant's third rosette just last year. Things were certainly on the rise. Alice knew she would swap it all for a little more time with Jacob, and, deep down, she knew he would swap it all for another rosette. But she loved him all the same. Because how could you not, she thought, as he ran his fingers once more up the inside of her thigh.

'Jacob Brooking, I suggest you behave, unless you are planning on following through with your actions right here in front of Doris and her husband.' Alice motioned to an elderly couple holding hands over a pot of tea by the fence, before looking back into Jacob's gaze and biting her bottom lip with playful intent.

'In that case, my beautiful Alice –' Jacob leaned in to kiss her, but at the last second he changed direction and stood up, offering his hand. '– we had best be off.'

'You bastard,' she laughed. She teased him, telling him that he would pay for that later.

Back on the road, Alice looked down to see a text from her father flash up on her phone.

'I hope your dress is not as short as your mother has described to me, young lady? You're not married yet,' read the message.

She sighed and slipped her phone into her clutch bag. Dad still hadn't accepted the relationship, but after six years of permanent rejection, he at least gave an occasional nod of acknowledgement when he saw Jacob now. Having them in the same room was tough, but it was possible.

The Mercedes purred as they took the winding descent to the coastline. The scorching red leather stuck to her leg and refused to let go as she adjusted her frame slightly. Jay pressed down a little more on the throttle. She loved being driven around by him, and the close line he walked between gentleman and bad boy was never more visible than when he was behind the wheel of his car. She watched him as he focused intently on the road. He wore a tight V-neck T-shirt in the same gunmetal grey as his Mercedes. The T-shirt was cut in half by a low-hanging rope necklace, with just a metal loop attached to the end in a knot. In his beige chino shorts and with bangles everywhere, he was like a walking catalogue model. His mirrored sunglasses hid his constant moody glare. Actually, moody was the wrong word. Maybe troubled was more accurate. She loved how deep he was as a person and as a man. It was certainly a rarity with men her age, but it always seemed like he was at war with himself. Always giving the impression that he was mid-argument with an invisible enemy. But she understood that more than most. At least her demons only spoke back to her in the reflection of the mirror. *I'm sure he's fine*, she continued to muse. The pressure of work was constantly pushing the boundaries of control, and she was forever proud of him for all that he had achieved, especially knowing full well that this journey had started for the sole purpose of winning over her father.

They reached sea level and continued to push further south towards Dungeness. Houses along the route became less clustered as a wilder and more rustic beach line started to dominate the view. He loved it here. This was Jacob's safe place. When things had been hard, before they were allowed to see each other, this had been where he had escaped the world. And now it was a place they both shared. They would follow this road down past Camber Sands and head into Rye for a walk down by the harbour. Down along the estuary past the nature reserve, where the grass was allowed to grow unhindered. Where long-legged birds played in the marshland and spiders made webs in reeds without fear of them being broken by passing traffic. Eventually, it would meet a shoreline of pebbles, all multicoloured and broken, like a shattered stained-glass window. That's where Jay had given her the name Pebble.

'You're unique,' he had said. 'No two pebbles are alike, and that's what you are – unique.'

It had hurt to walk on them without shoes on. But Jay had rightly proclaimed this to be the reason no screaming kids could be seen whenever they came. And he was right. It was their beach. Only the occasional dog walker would pass them as they sat on a blanket, nibbling on an exotic picnic he had prepared. You could almost see France on a clear day. Jacob would sit quietly staring out to sea, almost hypnotised by its beauty. She loved it. Loved that they shared something so very 'Jacob'. He had let her into his world. A world where he let no other. A world he held so precious was now their world. The whole area was just an amplification of Jacob's own character. Untamed and unmanageable to any great degree. To walk here was to walk through Jacob's heart. But, strangely, it seemed to be the only place to calm his soul.

'Baby?' Alice chirped. 'You've missed the turning.'

'Have I indeed?' he scoffed. 'Maybe you're confused as to our destination.' His lips creased into a playful smile.

'I thought we were going to Rye as normal, bear?'

'We are, Pebble, but first we need to make a detour, as there's something I need to show you.'

'OK, bear, but don't forget, the last time we did that in public, the farmer got a fright.'

Alice restrained her laughter until Jacob erupted, and they giggled until he pulled into a restaurant car park just off the main stretch, only a short walk from the beach.

She knew this place despite never having been. In his youth, Jacob had never shut up about it. The Gallantry was a fabulous restaurant with an amazing reputation. Renowned for its local produce, it wasn't as prestigious as where Jay worked, but it was charming and rustic in ways the Travelling Trout could never be, with a loyal following to boot.

Jacob unbuckled himself and gave Alice a quick look. She opened her mouth to ask the obvious questions that were lining up, but he shot forward and planted a long kiss on her lips. He took her bottom lip between his teeth as he pulled away. She found herself speechless as he started to get out the car.

'Come on, Pebble,' he said.

As she opened her mouth to respond, another voice got there first.

'Good afternoon, Mr Brooking, and welcome back,' said the far-too-attractive stick insect in front of them.

'What's going on, baby?' she asked, with a little more demand in her voice this time.

'Well, it was supposed to be a surprise for later in the year, but amazingly the pen-pushers were quicker than we thought. This, my beautiful Alice, is my new place of work.'

'Don't be silly, Jay,' Alice laughed. 'I know you speak highly of this place, but they will never be able to match your wages at the Trout.'

'I know, I know, and I thought you would say that, so I took my plea to the owner.'

'And what exactly was his response? Because I'm fairly sure he didn't offer you the £50K a year you're currently making.'

'You're right,' Jacob grinned. 'He said that if I wanted that kind of money, I'd best buy the place.'

Alice could clearly be seen putting together the jigsaw in her mind.

'Baby ... You haven't bought this place, have you?'

'Would you be mad at me if I had?'

'YES, I BLOODY WOULD BE MAD,' Alice screeched, while somehow retaining an idiotic smile. 'How? Why? When?' she asked.

Jacob walked around the car and gripped her waist. His eyes locked on hers.

'Pebble, it's OK. It's ours. I've done this for us. We can run it together. You always said the next step was to buy a restaurant, and you must have known this place was on the dream list.'

Alice slowed her breathing. A deep sigh came from the back of her throat.

'Jay, it's not that I think it's the wrong decision. God, it's probably the right decision. But it should have been OUR decision.'

'Well, I think it's a fantastic move, Jacob,' the stick insect interjected, laying her hand atop his forearm. 'This can only be positive for us.'

'Us?' Alice snapped.

'Yes, us here at the Gallantry. What else would I mean, Mrs Brooking?'

'It's MISS Petalow,' Alice snapped.

The stick insect smiled. 'Of course it is. My mistake.'

Alice looked down, and in the reflection of the car mirror a familiar face looked back.

SHE WILL TAKE HIM AWAY, YOU'RE PATHETIC, the reflection bleated.

'Baby,' said Jacob, 'I have a little paperwork I need to grab from Evan, and then we can drive down to Rye and talk it all over.' He opened the car door for her to get back in.

Alice looked him straight in the eye and let out a heavy sigh before climbing back into the passenger seat. Jacob closed the door behind her and walked over to whoever this tart Evan was. Alice watched him put an all-too-familiar hand on the small of her back as he guided her into the restaurant. She felt herself falling.

The car journey to Rye had felt strained at best. Jacob started talking work, and she all but phased out most of what was being said, giving stock replies to all his questions. She was happy for him but couldn't help but feel that no consideration had been given to her feelings on this matter. Didn't he trust her or value her opinion? Or was she just less of a part of his big plan than she had believed?

It was a little cooler now that the sun had dipped and the fine hairs across her arm were picking up goosebumps. 'Jay, can we just go home? I'm not feeling great.'

He decelerated sharply and threw the car onto a grass verge.

'You're mad at me, aren't you?' There was an air of superiority in his voice. 'This is the thanks I get for trying to do something for us?'

'But it wasn't for us, was it, Jay? It looks more like it was for you and your new best friend.'

'Evan? She's just the restaurant manager. Why do your insecurities always get in our way?'

'Maybe if I hadn't been made to feel like the third wheel in yours and Evan's decision, I'd have more faith in what was going on here,' Alice barked, with absolute faith that she was right. 'I mean, you are expecting me to run it with you. What happened to me going to do my master's after university? What about my dreams, Jay?'

Jacob knew he didn't win these situations often and started to panic.

'Alice, you're the most beautiful woman I know and have ever met. I tell you every day I love you without fail, and this is all for ...'

'DON'T YOU DARE SAY IT'S ALL FOR US! THAT'S ALL YOU EVER SAY!' Tears started to fall from her face. 'When have I ever asked you for anything other than YOU?'

'You're right,' he said in a resigned tone, 'but you don't know what it's like. I've never felt good enough for you, and certainly not the world you come from. I just wanted to make you proud.'

Alice tried to calm herself, but spoke with enough authority that she hoped her point would still hit home. 'Since we've been together, I've tried not to keep secrets and I've made no secret of the fact I am nothing but proud of you, so I need to know if WE will ever be enough for you? Or will you always be trying to prove something to someone?'

YOU WILL NEVER BE ENOUGH, the voice in his head barked.

'You're all that I want, Alice,' Jacob said through a trembling voice.

Alice noticed his clenched fists shaking against his legs and regretted taking him to this place of self-hatred that she knew she would struggle to pull him out from.

'Baby, it's OK. We have said our piece. Let's just head home.'

But Jacob was gone, and Alice knew he wouldn't be back tonight. It would be a long journey home. And she knew nothing she said now would make a difference.

'I hate myself. HATE HATE HATE,' he shouted, punching himself repeatedly in the thigh with his fist.

WE HATE YOU TOO, the voice gargled like it was laughing. Laughing with water filling its poisonous mouth.

Alice reached over and put her hand over his fist. 'I could never hate you. And I know that means nothing to you when you're upset, but it's true.'

SHE LIES.

SHE ALWAYS LIES.

NOT LIKE EVAN.

8

Changes
Summer 2004
Camber, East Sussex UK

'Let me get this straight,' Evan mused. 'Her father still hates you.'

'Oh yes,' Jacob grinned. 'He hates me alright.'

'Despite the fact you have done all he ever asked of you and more.'

'Yep.'

'You supported his daughter through her degree.'

'I did.'

'And he wouldn't pay for her tuition because he wanted her to go to university further away from you.'

'Yep.'

'So you paid for Alice.'

'I did.'

'And saved for this restaurant at the same time.'

Jacob nodded.

'And when you asked his permission to marry her?'

'He said I needed to prove I was ready.'

'So you proposed anyway, you rebel.' Evan was grinning, marvelling at Jacob's audacity.

'I did.'

'But now he wants to come to the wedding.'

Jacob sighed. 'Of course he does.'

'And Alice of course wants her dad there.'

'Of course,' Jacob said with a distance in his voice.

Evan reached over the bar to put her hand on top of his. Her long, painted nails wrapped around his fingers with a gentle squeeze. 'You're a better person than I am, boss, as honestly I wouldn't deal with that amount of disrespect, especially when you're as successful as you are.'

'Don't call me boss, Evan,' said Jacob, bringing her hand to his lips to thank her for the kindness before releasing her to take a sip of his drink. 'I don't look at you as one of our minions.'

Evan was behind the bar, polishing the wine glasses that she had just removed from the wash, while Jacob was emptying the last of his expensive Japanese whisky into his tumbler. End-of-week paperwork was spread out in front of him as he tried to find out why his turbot had increased in price so dramatically over two invoices.

'You have been a massive help to us during the transitional period,' said Jacob. 'I couldn't have had such a problem-free takeover without your hard work.'

'Don't be silly, Jacob. You and Matt have that kitchen nailed down, running better than ever, and bookings are already up on last year.' Evan placed her hand gently under his chin and raised his eyeline up to hers. 'That's down to you, and there's a buzz around Camber because of what you are doing here.'

'That's down to *us*,' Jacob said while raising his glass, which Evan happily toasted with the expensive French white Jacob had poured her.

Evan came round Jacob's side of the bar and sat beside him. She straightened out his collar as she perched and patted down his crisp white shirt.

'I do love it when you help us out front, Jacob Brooking, but if you could look a little less fabulous, you might find the waitresses get more work done.' She smirked while giving his biceps a gentle squeeze.

'Don't talk to me about distracting the staff while sitting there in that bloody dress.'

Evan jumped to her feet and twirled around. Her black dress rode up as she spun, revealing her toned thighs, while her thinly strapped top fought an epic battle to contain her more than ample cleavage. 'You approve, kind sir?' She giggled.

'I certainly do, my most treasured employee.' He jumped to his feet and took her hands, and they both danced to the New Orleans blues playing over the restaurant speakers. 'But I can't afford for our male staff to keep dropping plates every time you bend down to get a glass.' They both fell into laughter and collapsed into their seats.

'So, tell me – any doubts?' Evan asked. 'About Alice?'

Evan looked at him with complete devotion, hanging on his every word.

'Sometimes the situation with her family gets me down, and between you and me, she's not been the most sexual person the past ten years or so.' Jacob paused for a second after this and almost had to force himself to say a little more. 'But no, of course not. Anyway, what about you and that dumbass bodybuilder? Please tell me you've ditched him.'

'Of course I ditched him. Right after he bought me this marvellous dress, of course.'

Once again they found themselves in a fit of laughter.

'That's my girl. He was never good enough for you, Evan. Punch higher, as few men should be lucky enough to get the opportunity with you.'

She smiled and looked at the ground, blushing. Her long blonde hair fell from behind her ears and covered her face. She pulled it back into a loose ponytail and exposed her neckline to Jacob.

'She didn't think I could do this, you know. Alice, I mean.' Jacob seemed to speak with genuine sadness. 'She looks at me the same way her father does at times, with doubt and very little faith.'

'I see that,' said Evan. 'She hated me from day one, and I think it's because she knew we would make this place work and prove her wrong.'

'You may just be right on the money there,' Jacob agreed. 'And you're right. She does hate you,' Jacob said with good humour.

'She must see the way you look at me,' Evan joked with gusto.

Jacob got up and put his coat on to leave. As he walked past Evan, he leaned in behind her and left a lingering kiss on her cheek. 'Once again, my beautiful Evan, I think you might be right on the money. Let me know you're home safe, angel.'

Jacob pulled a mustard yellow scarf around his neck and slid out the door, singing to the music they had previously danced to.

'I will, Mr Brooking.' Evan smiled while touching her cheek gently where the kiss still tingled. That smile stayed the duration of the night. Evan rarely didn't get what she wanted from life, and Evan, of course, knew exactly what she wanted.

Winter 2003

Evan and Heather 8pm

The Voodoo Lounge in Ashford town centre, was a club that seemed to have been transported from the depths of the Louisiana swamps. Candles flickered with an excited enthusiasm at every table and in every window. Old glass liquor bottles of all shapes and colours were being used to decorate every unusable flat space in the building, giving a cluttered effect that almost made it feel like an organised dumping ground. Voodoo dolls and skeleton masks hung from the walls, with random words scrawled like graffiti in and around each one. *New Orleans*, *Cajun*, *Gumbo* and *Big Easy* were written almost haphazardly, while *Mardi Gras* adorned the top of the bar proudly. The dancefloor was heaving. So many people were crammed into such a small space that it gave the impression that the whole dancefloor was a living, moving and breathing organism, swaying as one to the modern R&B music, which didn't suit the theme at all. Evan Laurie sat opposite her equally blonde doppelgänger in a corner booth lit largely by the four candles surrounding them, with only the empty wine glasses making the scene one of a bar and not some witches' coven.

'What is wrong with you, Ev? I have never seen you turn down attention from a guy that looks that good.' Heather Hollis had been Evan's best friend for longer than either of them cared to admit and she would never hold her tongue on a night out. The Heva and Eva show didn't hit the town as often lately, so it surprised her that her best friend was a little off-colour.

'Well, I've never seen you turn down anything from any man, regardless of how many bags he needs to wear over his head,' replied a tipsy Evan with a little grin. Her face was masked in immaculate make-up, and her swollen lips, which had recently been botoxed, were thick with ruby-red gloss.

'How bloody dare you?' snapped Heather. 'I'll tell you now that I rarely drop below a seven.'

Evan laughed out loud, taking Heather's hand firmly. 'But that's seven out of a hundred, my beautiful friend.'

Heather couldn't help but laugh too. 'You cheeky bitch.'

'BITCH? Do you kiss Mumma Hollis with that mouth?' Evan giggled.

Heather put a finger against her bottom lip. 'Nope, the only one I kiss with this mouth is Daddy Laurie.'

Evan slapped her friend's bare leg, causing a little squeal of excitement as Heather started to see the old Evan reappear.

'So, what's going on Ev? You seem a little quiet for the usual Saturday night at club Heva. It's not a boy, is it?'

As soon as the words left her lips, she noticed the smallest flutter in Evan's long lashes.

'Oh my lord, it's a bloody boy, isn't it? And judging by the fact you haven't told me anything about him, and this is me we are talking about, I'm guessing it's someone you shouldn't be thinking about. Tell me I'm wrong, Evan?'

The smile disappeared from Evan's lips, replaced with the smallest of sighs and a bite of her bottom lip. 'No, Hev, it's not someone I should be thinking about, but I am, quite a lot, really.'

Heather stared like a bird of prey into her squirming eyes, even though she was doing her best to avoid the gaze. 'It's your bloody boss, isn't it? That guy Jay you keep going on about.'

Evan bit her tongue, but the look in her eyes betrayed her.

'I don't suppose I need to warn you of the consequences of pursuing the owner of 55% of the restaurant you work at – the guy who's marrying the girl who owns the other 45%?'

Heather knew that the chances of stopping Evan were slim to none. Once Evan had set her heart on something, she rarely let anything get in her way.

'I think,' said Evan with an air of mischief, 'that we need another round of tequila.'

She bounced out of the booth, with all the eyes in the place drawn to her curves, and danced over to the bar, ignoring the queue as she always did, because Evan Laurie didn't stand in line for anyone.

Alice and Holly 8.30pm

'Holly, that can't be right,' Alice choked.

'Two lines again means pregnant, bubba, and this is the third test in 30 minutes. You're as pregnant as they come, so am I happy for you or disappointed on your behalf?' said Holly with a hint of apprehension.

'Oh shit,' said Alice. She fell against the wall and slid down to the floor. 'Shit! Shit! Shit!'

Holly realised that the time for humour had ended, while also realising that she held something in her grasp that her little cousin had just peed on. She dropped the test into the empty sink and then sat down next to Alice. Her mother was a Petalow, the sister of Alice's father, but although they were related by blood, Holly and Alice had always considered themselves friends first and foremost. With just six months separating them, they had been in the same academic year and had been inseparable since pre-school. Holly was far shapelier than Alice, and her faux red hair was a more aggressive shade than Alice's autumnal tones.

She wrapped an arm around Alice as she saw tears escaping the hands that shielded Alice's face. 'This is a good thing, right? You wanted kids at some point?'

Alice pulled her hands away, exposing a mascara massacre right out of a gothic horror story. 'Of course we wanted kids, but now? With everything that's going on, with the wedding and Jacob? What is he going to say?'

Holly squeezed Alice closer to her. 'What about Jacob?'

Alice was trembling as she struggled to find a reply. 'He's just ploughed everything we have into the restaurant, and he's so stressed, like he never stops.'

Holly guided Alice's face around with a gentle touch. 'When is Jacob not stressed, and when is he not under pressure? Why don't we forget about everything that revolves around money and Jay Brooking and think about the one question that matters right now?'

Alice looked up as Holly asked the one thing she hadn't often had to answer.

'What do you want, Alice?'

Alice and Jacob 9.45pm

Tick tock

Jacob was stuck in the tiny box room that had become his office these past few months. His large mahogany desk – a piece of antique furniture that he had loved at first sight during a rare trip north to the Derbyshire town of Buxton – barely fit in the space. Once, when he'd been filing invoices for his accountant, he'd stretched out to yawn, the type of yawn a bear might make after awakening from its winter hibernation, and in doing so he had realised he was touching three of the four walls: his feet were against the skirting underneath his desk, and his palms were flat against the oppressive walls. It was a prison of isolation and paperwork, and Jacob had been trying to fight the urge to drive to the restaurant to pick up the missing invoices he had left on his work desk. His obsession with getting all his paperwork done on his one night off had become a compulsion that he was finding hard to shift. The paperwork didn't need to be done, it could wait until tomorrow, but it would bother Jacob – that wasn't how he worked at all. He would wait until Alice got home from her night out dancing and then enjoy a late-night coastal drive to grab the paperwork. 'Yep, that's what I'll do,' Jacob whispered to himself. Maybe Alice would come with him. He hadn't spent enough time with her since buying the Gallantry, and he was aware that it was bothering her. Her demeanour had been distant and a little shut off this past week. *Must try harder* was his mantra for dealing with Alice, yet time had constantly seemed to slip away from him lately.

 Tick tock

 He heard the slow rotation of the front door's brass lock and the clicking of pins sliding out of place, before the slight pressure change pulled up the hairs on the back of his neck. The cold sea air, pungent with the scent of the ocean, flooded the corridor. Jacob heard Alice hanging up her coat.

 Tick tock

 'I'm in the office, Pebble,' he called out, while staring blankly at the paperwork in front of him, as he had done for hours. The constant ticking of the wall clock had been mocking him. Its relentless noise was like nails dragging down a blackboard.

Tick tock

Alice wrapped her arms around Jacob's shoulders after she approached him silently from behind. He smiled at her poor attempts at being a second-rate ninja but played along anyway.

'Oh my god, baby, you scared the life out of me, my dear heart is racing,' Jacob said dryly while hiding a playful smile. 'Are you OK, my angel?'

Although she was windswept and full of freckles after a weekend of early summer sunshine, Alice was the absolute picture of grace.

Am I OK? Alice thought about this for a few seconds before dropping herself onto his lap with an exhausted sigh. She leaned into his oncoming kiss and held it for longer than Jacob had accounted for, causing a little gasp as she finally pulled away.

'We need to talk, Jay.'

Tick tock

-

'You're pregnant?' Jacob choked on the words as they left his mouth almost unwillingly.

Alice stood in the middle of the kitchen, her hands linked gently in front of her waist, almost protecting the asset she had known nothing about just a few hours earlier.

'Yes, Jay. I know it's hard to believe with all the romantic and passion-filled time we haven't been spending together,' said Alice. His unwillingness to look at her gave Alice a strength she never had when his emerald eyes were gazing on her. 'Jacob, you need to talk to me, please.'

You can't do this. You are not your father. You are not half the man he was, the cackle was loud in his mind but for once easily ignored.

Jacob spun around and jumped towards Alice, picking her up in an embrace that took her clean off her feet. He spun her around in a circle that caused her red hair to fan out like a phoenix. 'Alice, this is wonderful news. How you could think that I would react differently is beyond me. I love you, Miss Petalow, with a warmth my heart feels with only you by my side. No being or object comes close to the unbridled joy that you, my heart, have brought me with this news.' Jacob spoke poetically as he dropped her back down to the floor. Her feet skidded on the hardwood flooring.

You are not your father, the voice grew in volume but still struggled to break through Jacob's walls.

'I need to go into work for an hour to pick up these bloody invoices, but I promise I'll be back so we can celebrate. This is a celebration, right?'

Jacob held his Alice tightly, while she struggled to find her voice through what had become a beaming smile.

'Yes, of course, my love,' she said. 'Of course it is.'

With that he picked up his car keys and headed for the front door, with only a brief moment of pause as he took Alice by the hand and kissed her gently on her forehead.

'I love you,' they said in unison, before Alice was left alone to ground herself from the whirlwind that her Jacob had just become.

Jacob and Matt 11pm

'I get what you are saying, mate, but brioche burger buns are not getting on that menu just because your latest celebrity chef man crush has convinced all the lonely housewives that it adds a touch of class to a simple dish, and I don't give a flying fuck how good your bastard burger patty is.' Jacob had been talking with his prodigy at the Travelling Trout for the whole journey to the Gallantry, during which time he'd realised that Matt needed the occasional reminder that *Menu by Jacob Brooking* was still emblazoned at the top of the Trout's menu and he was still executive chef there. 'Matt, if you feel the Trout needs a burger to bring a dish to "the people", then you serve it open on some bloody good home-made sourdough or something. Put a bit of theatre, OK, son?' He could hear Matt sigh down the phone, followed by what sounded like an empty mop bucket being kicked.

'Yes, Chef, I hear you.'

Jacob smiled, as he'd been exactly the same when he was Matt's age, but with experience he'd come to see that Matt needed his reins pulling at times. 'I know it's frustrating, but until your name is above the door – and I promise you it will be one day – you have to toe the line a little.' Jacob slumped into the pitted-green leather armchair and took a deep breath. 'Look how far you've come these past few years – youngest head chef of a three-rosette restaurant in the country, when it seems like yesterday your spotty little arse was turning mushrooms for me in the prep room. I will back you all the way if you come to me with your own ideas and not something you have stolen off a TV chef, and you know I'm bloody right.'

Matt finally conceded and let his defences relax. 'Yes, Chef, I know you're right. I get it. How's Alice getting on since the move?'

Jacob couldn't help but smile, thinking of his conversation with Alice just an hour before, but he knew it was too soon to say anything. He swapped the mobile over to his left hand, freeing up his right to pour a little Tennessee bourbon into his favourite tumbler. The cube of ice he had taken from the bar had lost its structural integrity ten minutes before, but it would do for now. 'She's OK, mate. Her father is still a royal pain in my arse, and I'm not sure how long I'm going to put up with her not backing me when it comes to his relentless difference of opinion. I have a list of people I wouldn't mind dragging through the mire and his name is at the top and underlined in bloody red pen.'

Matt boomed with laughter at Jacob not mincing his words. 'You know Alice, Chef – she doesn't stand up to the big man. Does he at least give you cheap fish still?'

Now it was Jacob's turn to laugh. 'Does he fuck, but you know what, none of it will matter when I get that ring on Alice's finger, because I'll be damned if I let him keep treating me with such emotionless disdain.'

'Still carrying that chip on your shoulder, I see, Chef,' Matt said playfully.

'Well, I guess you can kiss my arse too, you little turd. Now get back to masturbating over whatever celebrity chef is currently giving you a semi-on, and I'll see you Monday for the summer menu brief, OK?'

Matt chuckled. 'Yes, skipper, see you Monday.'

John Petalow will always hate you, the voice was calm and collected. *You know this, don't you?*

'I do, and I will always hate him,' Jacob whispered.

Jacob and Evan 11.30pm

Jacob threw his phone onto the table and sank the last of his bourbon before standing and straightening himself out in the mirror. 'You got this, Brooking; you need no justification from that bloated old Viking.' He pulled his jacket over his broad shoulders and went to open his office door, only to find it spring open, with the slender figure of Evan standing there to greet him. She looked ridiculously stunning. Like Monroe only better, her hair half up, with ringlets rolling down her shoulders and over her heaving chest, her make-up pristine, and her eyes focused on Jacob. She was dressed all in black, with a skirt that barely contained her dignity and a top that could barely contain her bust.

'Hi, you,' said Evan quietly, but before Jacob could ask why she was here on her night off and especially this late at night, she hushed him by placing a finger on his lips. She pulled her knees together, dragging one foot to the side as if trying to figure out her next move. She reached out for Jacob's hand as she noticed him taking her in. Evan stood tall in stiletto heels that finished in an ankle boot, her legs toned and muscular for a woman so slim, and infinitely longer than they needed to be for the height of the girl. Her black skirt and thin-strapped summer top could have looked whorish on anyone else, but a short-line leather jacket and a low-slung belt that served no purpose other than an aesthetic one had brought the whole thing together with style.

'Evan,' said Jacob, 'are you a bit drunk or a lot drunk?'

He could not take his eyes off Evan's lips, which looked ready to explode at the mere mention of imminent pressure.

'Just a little bit, boss,' she said. Their hands played delicately with each other. 'But I have to say, I'm drunk enough.' She pulled him into her, sinking her hot wet tongue into his wanting mouth.

Tick tock

'Evan, what are you doing?'

Jacob recoiled in shock, falling into his armchair like a ball into a catcher's mitt, pulling his fingers to his lips as if poisoned by a venomous snake.

'Don't play coy with me, Mr Brooking. That wasn't the kiss of a man that didn't want to be kissed, and I've not missed the signals you've been throwing my way.' Evan followed him to his chair and mounted him, not unlike a lady side-saddling a stallion. 'I know what you want,' she said with both a hiccup and a smile.

Jacob jumped to his feet, spinning her around in the process of trying to maintain her equilibrium. He pinned her by the waist so that she was half sitting on his desk.

'Oh, Jay.' Evan bit her lip before pushing all the paperwork on the desk to the floor. 'Right here, is this where you want me?'

Take her.

'Evan, I have neither the vocabulary nor the time to tell you how very beautiful you are to me, or to tell you how much brighter my days are with you by my side.' Jacob took her opposite hand in his. His worn and calloused fingers interlinked with her slender digits, which were tipped with deep scarlet pointed nails. 'But we can never be more than we are right now.'

Evan looked at him quizzically but with a wanton desire. 'What we are right now? What exactly is that, Jay?' Her free hand rose up to stroke Jacob's stubbled jaw. She leaned in to kiss him, this time with a gentle certainty that told Jacob this wasn't just the drink talking. As Evan's full lips touched his own, he felt no desire, none whatsoever, to pull away.

She's beautiful, the voice soothed.

She's much more... us.

Jacob raised his own free hand and ran it through her golden locks until he was cradling her head in a kiss that grew increasingly into something that might overcome them.

Tick tock

The clock snapped Jacob back to the real world – one where he was staring into the abyss of the situation he was falling into.

'Evan, you need to go.' Jacob spoke softly but with purpose, yet he was still to move his hand from her neck and their foreheads still touched.

'OK, Jay,' Evan said, kissing him a few times more for effect. 'But we do need to talk about this tomorrow, so dinner at mine after work, please. Don't let me down.'

You need to do this.

'OK, Evan, I'll be there.'

She leaned in and kissed his lips one last time, while her hands spun him around so that he was pushed tightly against the desk. Her hands dropped down between his thighs and rose to squeeze the growing bulge that had appeared unknowingly in his jeans.

'Until tomorrow, my love,' she called while power-walking out of the office door.

Tick tock

Jacob slumped back into his armchair to try and figure out where the ticking clock was sounding from, as there was no such device in his work office.

9

Alice and the Looking Glass
Spring 2004
Knightsbridge, London UK

Jacob couldn't take his eyes off her. But he couldn't breathe. Her face had never looked more radiant, and her eyes shone with supernatural power, the blue almost seducing him to drop to his knees. Still he couldn't breathe. Her hair seemed longer and fuller than ever before. Like November fire, it lit up the darkness that surrounded them. Yet he still couldn't breathe. Her voice was gentle and kind, yet she was crying, and as he stood opposite her on that dark plateau outside of Medway Hospital, he couldn't draw breath, as she repeated over and over, 'This is what you wanted, right, baby?' She was holding a stillborn child in her arms, in front of her blood-soaked white gown.

Jacob woke up screaming. Tears flooded his face as he searched for Alice in the dark. His fingers wrapped around her and he pulled her closer than ever before while he tried to control his breathing.

  'Baby, what's wrong?' asked Alice, as she struggled to open her eyes and wipe the dribble from her lips.

  'Nothing's wrong, baby. Nothing at all. Just a dream.'

> *THE WRONG LIFE WAS TAKEN AND YOU KNOW IT. SHE WILL NEVER FORGIVE YOU. MURDERER...*

Dr Vivian Phillips sat next to Alice on a long green chesterfield sofa that wouldn't have looked out of place in the Nome King's palace from her favourite film. Alice had always felt a kinship with Dorothy, and right now she wished a flying monkey would grab her and take her back to Oz and the Emerald Palace. Indeed, Alice looked on in complete awe as the doctor perched on the edge of her sofa, appearing to be the spitting image of Judy Garland herself. The same age as Alice's mother, she carried herself like a movie star from the 1940s. In fact, there was a photograph on her desk that Alice could have sworn was Veronica Lake, but in actuality it was the good doctor on her wedding day many years before. She was the sexiest woman Alice had ever seen, and yet not one inch of flesh was on show. But the respect Alice held for the doctor was not because of her stunning good looks, but due to her absolute command of everything in the room. When Alice had first entered her domain, she had felt trust and respect for everything Doctor Phillips was offering. Her office was filled with books and memorabilia from her travels. There were golden artefacts from Egypt and South America and silks from India and Thailand. Vivian Phillips hadn't graduated and opened a practice here in London. She had lived. And she had knowledge that couldn't be taught, but could only be found through exploration. Alice had been waved over to sit on the green couch while the doctor had finished a phone conversation in what Alice thought was fluent Italian. After hanging up, she had joined Alice holding an expensive leather-bound notepad and fountain pen and had offered her a drink in a soft, well-spoken Hertfordshire accent. Alice doubted Dr Phillips had ever said a single word without intent. Procrastination did not seem her forte.

Alice felt at ease. But she knew in her heart that no lie she told would be bought by her adversary, so she wasn't even going to try. She pulled the cushion from behind her back and held it across her stomach. Failing at first to find the words she needed and had hoped to find the strength for, she looked at Dr Phillips for help.

'Alice, it's OK. Don't feel rushed because I'm here. Let it come naturally. Tell me about the baby.'

'The baby?' Alice had a tremble in her voice. 'Jacob wasn't happy when he found out I was pregnant. In fact, quite the opposite.' She adjusted herself on the chair. 'I was afraid to tell him, especially with the restaurant doing so well and the wedding planning taking so much of our spare time.'

Dr Phillips leaned in towards her. 'How was Jacob's involvement in the wedding?'

'Minimal to say the least. He would always find a reason to work his day off. It feels like he is changing his mind.'

This came out more like a question she was trying to answer rather than the statement she had intended to make.

'I know it's not easy for him,' she continued. 'He gets a hard time from my family, especially my father, who has never welcomed his presence in my life.'

Alice spoke from the heart, and it was plain to see for Dr Phillips that because of the love she held for Jacob, it hurt her to see him struggle so.

'He's never been allowed to feel like he's enough for me,' Alice went on. 'He puts his heart and soul into improving himself and the business so someone will cut him some slack and remove that chip from his shoulder.' Alice exhaled slowly. 'I just wish he could see the truth.'

'What truth is that, Alice?'

'That he was always enough to me. That this idea that he has to lock horns with my father means nothing to me, and actually I think that battle ended without him realising many years ago. He is what he is and my father's the same. There is no judgement there, so, honestly, I think he is fighting himself.'

Alice stood up and walked over to the window, which had a beautiful view over Notting Hill Park.

'He gets so angry when he's challenged,' she said, 'yet I feel the argument he ends up having is completely internal. Like all his thoughts and ideas contradict each other.'

'So, no joy for your big news then.' The doctor's tone was still calm and gentle.

'He was happy for a minute, before he seemed to confuse himself with how this might play out. Then anger kicked in, like I'd ruined a plan I knew nothing about.' Alice paused and looked to the floor. 'Then he asked me to have the abortion.'

'Just like that?' the doctor asked.

'No, not quite. He said we should consider our priorities – that the business needed us and that the wedding needed to come first, before we properly planned our family life together.'

'He said all the right things to convince you?'

'I guess so. But as conflicted as he seemed, I do believe he meant what he was saying.'

'Did he go with you? You were 18 weeks – that's not an easy process.' The doctor patted the couch next to her. 'Was there any support?'

Alice moved and sat back down beside the doctor. 'He dropped me off and picked me up the following day – if you can call that support.'

'Did you tell him that they found the baby still on your arrival?'

'Honestly, I didn't see the point. I guess the outcome was the same regardless, so why complicate things?'

'And how do you feel now, Alice?'

'About Jay?' Alice asked.

'About the baby, Alice.'

'Hollow. I thought I was making the wrong choice but for the right person. And, yes, before you say anything, I know that's wrong and stupid beyond measure, but I guess now I know that whatever choice I had made would have been irrelevant. It's made me question if I even deserve to be a mother.'

'I'm not here to judge your choices, Alice. I'm here to guide you to your own answers. How do you feel about Jacob now?'

'I constantly hear myself in the mirror. It tells me I'm not good enough for him, that I hold him back and that I'm not pretty enough for him and that he deserves more than I offer. And sometimes I think it's right.'

'Yet all the other people in your life say the opposite. Why do you think that is?'

'Because they don't know my Jacob,' Alice snapped back, all of a sudden feeling less like Dorothy and more like Alice tumbling down a rabbit hole.

10

Father of the Bride
Autumn 2005
Camber, East Sussex, UK

There was a thunderous knock at the door.

'Come in,' Jacob shouted with gay abandon. He didn't have much time, and his blasted tie wasn't falling right at all, but he was doing his best to look presentable on his wedding day. Of all days, surely this was the one on which his tie must hang impeccably. Jacob looked over his shoulder to see the hulking figure of Alice's father squeezing into the small room, much like a rhino trying to turn around in an elevator. His father-in-law was an intimidating man to everyone. Even the muscular frame of Jacob seemed quite pathetic compared to the behemoth that was John Petalow, and it wasn't even muscle that made the man so big; he was just huge, his arms like tree trunks and his barrelled body like a samurai's suit of armour. It was Jacob's hotel, but even he would have been hard-pressed to take the much larger bridal suite off his fiancée, so they would have to dance around each other here.

'What can I do for you, John? I must confess, I'm a little pressed for time,' Jacob said as he turned back to the mirror.

Don't turn your back on him, you fool, said the voice in a shrill and almost surprised voice.

In the next few minutes, Jacob would realise two things: firstly, that his years of training at the gym and playing rugby for Canterbury meant absolutely nothing when it came down to life and death; and, secondly, that the monster in his head didn't always lie to get him into trouble.

John Petalow's hands were like shovels, and as he gripped Jacob's neck from behind, much like an adult lion might carry a new-born cub, there was nothing Jacob could do to escape. His face was smashed up against the mirror in front of him, causing a crack that ran from top to bottom. Jacob tried to speak out in protest at the violence being forced on him, but his oppressor's massive hand was restraining his airway to the point that nothing but a whimper was escaping his throat.

'Son, of all the things I am known for, after breaking necks, the thing I am known for most is never forgetting, and I remember saying to you many years ago, when you sat in front of me, begging, like a dog, to take my Alice from me, I said, "If you're talking, then you are not listening, and right now I need you to listen." I remember those words clearly.' John Petalow leaned in close to Jacob's ear and, in a low growl, said, 'Jacob, do you remember those words? Nod once if you do, OK?'

Jacob felt his head nod once as John's hand shook him like a rag doll.

'Good. Now the same rules apply. So when I let go, you are not going to speak, because I need you to listen. Nod again if you comprehend what I'm saying.'

Jacob once again felt the involuntary shake of his neck result in the most basic of nods, and then he felt himself released. He crashed down to one knee and drew breath like never before, although he showed enough resolve to stand and face John, knowing better than to say anything. He gritted his teeth and prepared for the bullshit "if you ever hurt my daughter" speech that he was certain was coming.

He was wrong. And the next few words out of John's mouth knocked the colour out of Jacob's tanned skin and the broadness out of his shoulders.

'I know about you and Evan Laurie. You were seen by my delivery driver, at the crack of dawn the other day. He had ten kilos of Scottish salmon for you that he couldn't get a signature for. Why? Well, I'm glad you asked. It was because when he went to find you, you had that restaurant manager of yours bent over your desk. Tell me, Jacob, am I missing anything so far? Nope? Then I shall carry on.'

As he spoke, John never took his eyes off Jacob's, and Jacob felt smaller with every second that the gaze fell over him.

'You had the fucking cheek to ring me a few hours later, to tell me, ME, just how disappointed you were that my delivery drivers have stopped bothering to ask for a signature when they leave their invoice. "It's just bloody lazy" were your words. The thing is, that delivery driver wouldn't have said a word to me had I not called him into the office to reprimand him on your behalf. Does that taste good, Jacob? Because I hope you choke on that fucking irony.'

John finally turned his back on Jacob.

'This is what we are going to do,' he said, in a quieter tone, knowing that he didn't have to shout anymore to be heard. 'I will not have Alice hurt. As much as I detest your very existence in her life, it would destroy her to know what you are, so you cannot tell her, and no one else can know, so you need to manage that slut you are keeping.'

Jacob raised himself up to his true height. 'She's not a slut, John.'

The Viking king responded in kind and instantly towered over Jacob's false bravado. 'You have some fucking cheek, son, fucking fronting up to me. I will tear your cunting face off. Sit down, SIT FUCKING DOWN.'

Jacob did as he was told in an instant so that his lecture could continue.

'You have 12 months. That's time to build the business and sort out your double life. In 12 months we are going to talk about this, and if your affairs are not in order and Evan is not long gone, then I will take Alice from you, and bury you in a travellers' field.'

He reached down and grabbed Jacob's shoulder with such force that Jacob almost buckled in half like an accordion.

'Jacob, I can't emphasise this enough, do you understand me?'

Jacob nodded.

'Then I will say no more, and I will go and tend to my daughter before her big day begins. I'll see you out there, son. Don't let me down.'

What will you do now?

Jacob took a pocket square to the trickle of blood running down his forehead. *As we are told,* thought Jacob.

We do not answer to him and I fear no physical power that he possesses, said the creature with venom.

Then what do you fear? Creature in my thoughts, voice that watches me trip up at every hurdle while apparently giving me advice to survive. What do you fear? WHAT? Asked Jacob without parting his lips.

WE FEAR EVAN!

And you have no idea what you are doing, do you!

'Did I ever really know what I was doing?' Jacob voiced in reply.

-

YOU LOOK DISGUSTING.

No, I don't. Not today I don't. I'm not listening to you.

Alice in truth looked more divine than ever before. It was a virtually impossible task to dress her up in anything that would increase her desirability as a woman. But today was no ordinary day. Her classic dovetailed ivory wedding dress hugged her delicate size-eight frame, which only a woman as humble as her couldn't have appreciated having. The clean and uncluttered dress fell strapless from her petite bustline, hanging on as though by invisible wizardry all the way down her body until the most delicate curve of her hip broke the angle just a touch, before the dress fell once again into a simple fantail spread out behind her. The thinnest of splits running from the ground to just past her knee revealed the most exquisite of strapped heels, with ribbon running from the shoe and looping three times around her ankle and lower calf. The tall, slender heel would have been a nightmare to walk in for anyone without the lightness of movement this angel had always possessed. Her hair was tied back for the first time in what seemed like forever, not counting the simple plait she threw in each night before bed. A tight bun crowned her head, with diamonds, studs and slivers of silver hairclips catching the light every time she moved. These were matched by a diamond bracelet that her mother had given her that morning as a wedding gift. A necklace she had picked out herself as an engagement present fell between her cleavage, where a slender V cut out of the dress line revealed more of her inner and lower breast than her father would have approved of had he been part of the buying process. The tiny stone that hung from the white gold pendant sitting just below the centre of her breasts highlighted their ample shape all the more. Only the sapphire on her engagement ring broke the colour code. 'You're too unconventional for a diamond engagement ring,' Jacob had said, reminding her that she was unique. 'You shouldn't wear the same ring as all the other brides.' But at least it had matched her eyes.

She looked to die for. And no voice, real or otherwise, would make her believe a different viewpoint. Not today.

They were to be married on the beach just down from their restaurant in Camber. It was a beautiful day with crystal-clear skies and a gentle breeze, which stopped the guests, in shirts and ties and stunning summer frocks with matching hats, from overheating. Alice hadn't seen it herself yet, but her bridesmaid had reported a scene like Ladies' Day at Royal Ascot, as they waited for the most beautiful of them all to arrive.

The Gallantry had made a wonderful effort for its owners. The bridal suite was dressed in white and orange rose petals, and more than a hundred little gift boxes from the staff were arranged in the corner, all wearing burnt-tan ribbons. Alice felt like the princess she hoped she looked like. If only just for a day, she thought.

Alice took one more deep breath and took herself in for the last time top to bottom. The beech mirror stood seven feet from floor to ceiling and for once her reflection was her own. It seemed like the doubting voice in her was silenced completely. The witch that haunted her days was nowhere to be seen, and Alice prayed it would stay that way. A noise startled her from her blind side, and she adjusted her view in the mirror ever so slightly to see her father standing there proudly.

'You look wonderful, monkey,' he said adoringly while placing a reassuring hand on her shoulder.

She knew she would always be monkey to him, just as he would always be Pappa Bear. The only thing she had never doubted was the love she received from her mum and dad.

The only thing you have never doubted?

Really?

WHAT DOES THAT TELL YOU ABOUT YOUR PRECIOUS FIANCÉ?

She shook her head clear and sat on the edge of the mattress, trying her best not to crease the masterpiece she was wrapped in.

Her father joined her on the queen-sized bed and took her tiny hand in his shovel-like palms. 'You look just like your mother on our wedding day, and it never ceases to amaze me just how alike you both are in beauty and in soul.'

'Don't be silly, Dad. Mum is much more beautiful than I am.'

'And she would say the same thing about you, Alice Marie, and that is why you are both so beautiful to me.'

He looked down, as though composing himself.

'Listen,' he said. 'I've never liked Jacob.'

'NOOOOOOOO! Really? I have never picked up on that,' Alice giggled.

'Just listen, you little diva. I'm trying to impart some knowledge here. He works hard, he's ambitious, he provides for you, and I guess some really distant people might squint and find him an attractive man. So have you ever thought to ask me why I don't like him?'

'I just always assumed it was because he was so bloody flaky at times. So inconsistent.'

John Petalow laughed with a deep bellow. 'Yes, inconsistent for sure – and full of himself. But no – it's because he reminds me of me in one very specific way.'

Alice chose not to comment and instead let her father move the story forward at his own pace. It was rare to hear him open up like this, and she felt honoured to be part of the conversation.

'When I met your mum, well, I wasn't a good man. The war had taken its toll on me and I had blood on my hands.'

Alice was surprised to hear him mention the Falklands, as it was a subject everyone avoided with him. 'But I thought you knew Mum from school?'

'I did know her, but she never knew me. I was a big ungainly rugby oaf, and she was the prom queen. She was all class, and I'm not sure she noticed me until the day I returned home. She was working the bar at the welcome home party. It was at the Ship and Winkle Inn, just down from your grandad's house. She grafted all night, while a load of us battered young veterans sat quietly, not talking about what we had seen and done on that shitty little island.

'I got talking to her after more than a few pints of Guinness had restored some of the courage I seemed to be missing.'

Alice was engrossed in this story – a story she had only ever heard in snippets from her mother.

'That night, as we said goodnight, she placed a hand on my cheek and said, "John, I am going to fix you."

'And as I looked into her eyes – the mirror of yours – I knew that as long as she was with me, she would never have to fix me, as it's her very presence that fixes and completes me.

'And that's what scares me.'

Alice was both concerned and confused. 'What, Pappa?'

'I know you look at him the way your mum looks at me. I know he needs you to fix him the way your mum fixes me.

'I know what I did. I know where I have been to be broken, what I have done to others to be broken, and I know what I am always capable of, with only your mum being the difference between the man I am and the wreck that I could have been.

'I look at Jacob though and I honestly don't know what he has done or what he is capable of to be so broken that you look at him the way your very tolerant mother looks at me.

'But I'm being silly.' He smiled. 'You clearly both love each other, and despite what you all think, that has always been enough for me.'

Her father rose to his feet and offered his arm. 'Shall we? It's time, my beautiful girl.'

Alice rose and looped her arm into his. She smiled and kissed her dad gently on the cheek before turning to exit for the short walk down to the beach. Catching herself briefly in the mirror and noticing her skin looked a little grey, she heard her reflection whisper to her.

But you know what he's capable of.

YOU KNOW.

'Yeah, I know,' she whispered, as she held her stomach ever so tenderly.

11

Living by the Sword
Winter 2005
Old Romney, Kent UK

'Look what you made me do,' Evan spat, as Jacob ground his jaw to take the sting out of the slap that had woken his bones from a long day in the kitchen. Evan couldn't really hurt Jacob in a physical way. Despite being a more imposing figure than Alice by virtue of her dancer's body, she still gave up seven stone to his very broad frame, and he sometimes wondered if not really hurting him was the exact reason she hit him; she got to release her frustration on Jacob, who was strong enough to shrug it off and would just stay quiet while taking the occasional blow on the chin. There had been one occasion when she had really wanted to make him feel pain. When he had shrugged off an open hand, with no sign even of a whimper, she had let her frustration get the better of her and scratched his face with her long, sharp, painted nails – a method she employed knowing full well that he would have to explain the injury to Alice somehow. This had left Jacob with a conundrum of sorts: he didn't want to show Evan any kind of weakness, and yet he could certainly do without Alice finding out about the affair he had unknowingly started three months prior. He decided that the easiest thing to do was to wince, clench his jaw and pretend that she had hurt him in more ways than merely stripping away his masculinity every time they got into a fight.

'Evan, you know I have to consider her role in this. She owns half of the company by default – a company you work for. Do you really want that drama?'

Jacob was trying to shrink himself down so that Evan would feel she was fully in control of all aspects of this situation. This wasn't his first dance with her.

She turned her back on Jacob and shook her giant blonde mane like she was trying to regain some form of composure, but Jacob knew this was only the beginning of this evening's games. 'I don't remember you being too worried about Alice and her role in the company when you wanted your dick sucked, Jay, so don't give me that shit. GOD, YOU ARE SO FRUSTRATING.'

Jacob had been trying to work his way out of this relationship since the minute it had started, but when Evan wanted something, she got it, and Jacob had found it easier to nod and agree to everything she wanted rather than start a fight, and that had included sex. He had to admit that the sex was amazing – not that it wasn't with Alice, but it was aggressive and lascivious in an almost primitive and carnal way. It was the only time he felt in charge of the situation with her. So, it happened a lot and often after a blazing row like this.

'I need to head home tonight, Ev. You know this. I can't just not go home.'

He knew instantly he had said something wrong. Evan turned back around to face him, with hate filling her eyes.

'HOME, JAY?' She threw her hands towards the ground in childish frustration, and angry tears glossed her eyes. 'You know, there was a time when you wanted to be "home" with me, Jay. When did that change?'

Jacob was acting slow but thinking fast about how to get out of this situation. 'Baby, you know what I meant. You know how I feel about you, about us.'

Evan stepped dangerously close to Jacob's space and was shaking with an adrenaline-fuelled rage. 'No, Jacob, I don't know how you feel about me, because I'm this big fucking secret, am I not? Do we go out with my friends or my family? No, we don't, because of how you feel for your precious Alice and her love for you.'

Evan swung for Jacob once more and was surprised to see him catch her wrist just before her open hand connected with his cheek. For a second, they paused, looking each other up and down, waiting for an opening to appear.

Hahahahahahaha!

The creature's laugh threw Jacob, giving Evan the avenue of attack that she needed. She brought her left hand up and caught him with a glancing blow to the temple. Jacob snapped and pushed her forcefully away, his muscular frame sending his athletic but slender opponent tumbling onto and across the huge bed behind her, leaving her crumpled on the floor on the other side of it.

Fool! She will definitely tell Alice now, the creature mocked and warned all at the same time.

'Baby, I'm sorry.' Jacob rushed over to Evan's prone body. He helped her sit upright, realising with relief that she wasn't physically hurt. He witnessed the first real tears he had ever seen her cry. He put his hands on her cheeks and kissed her on the lips - a kiss that was unreturned.

'Baby, I'll sort it, I promise,' he said, kissing her once more, getting a little more return than the first time.

'Promise me we can do something with my friends at the weekend, Jay. I don't want to be a secret forever.'

Jacob kissed her again before he whispered exactly what she needed to hear. 'I promise, Ev.'

Liar! the voice shouted.

'I'm sorry I hurt you,' Jacob said, pulling her forehead against his own.

LIAR! the voice screamed.

'I'm sorry, too, baby,' Evan said, pressing her lips passionately against his.

I want Alice to find out, the voice snorted. Because then I can get to her as well. I wonder if her broken-hearted disappointment will taste as good as your constantly sweet fear of conflict. Let's see, shall we?

Jacob could hear every word the voice was saying but chose to push it to the back of his mind. One battle at a time was all he had to win to survive. *Just get through the next few hours*, he kept thinking, over and over. *Just get home to Alice, and tomorrow can take care of itself.*

Coward, screamed the voice, *you're a coward and a fraud.*

I know, Jacob replied in his mind, before pulling Evan up onto the bed. His lips lightly fluttered against her belly as he pulled down her black silk shorts, which were already wet with excitement. *When have I ever denied those monikers, my old friend?*

I'm not your friend, Jacob, the creature snapped.

'Then why the hell do you KEEP TALKING TO ME!!!!!!!!' Screamed Jacob, drawing a confused look from Evan.

12

Triggered
Winter 2006
Camber, Kent UK

Jacob Brooking had been sitting on the tiny gardening stool opposite his father's memorial stone for two hours. A fine rain had turned to mist in the warm air and left him feeling like he had got dressed after a shower without drying himself properly. Yet he had found it impossible to leave his father's side. He felt comfort here and a peace that often eluded him. The day was drawing to a close and the sun was slowly meeting the world's end as the light began to fade. The temperature was going to drop soon enough, and Alice would be upset if she got home to an empty house once again. Jacob knew he should go home, to save his own hide, if nothing else. But something had stopped him leaving. Not something he could understand, not something physical. Just something subtle that he couldn't quite comprehend the origin of. There was a voice, soft but full of malice and sharp intellect. A voice that sounded familiar yet alien and not of this earth. A voice that resonated from his own head and seemed to follow him everywhere, except, for some reason, this particular spot.

-

The creature had no master and yet could not leave this place. It hated the man. The man who had imprisoned it here in this hollow of darkness, surrounded by webs of vanity and self-indulgence. Jacob, it had suspected he was called, although over the years the other man things had called him many different names. But it was irrelevant to the creature, whose hate was real and justified, so the man's moniker mattered little. The creature hated the fact that without the poor excuse for a human, it couldn't exist. It hated that more than anything. That the prison holding it here would let it see the open world through the eyes of the man but would not let it escape. Well, not for long periods of time, at least. The dripping-wet leathery skin of the creature trembled as it began to move. Like a monster straight from the darkness of the Mariana Trench, it writhed on a bed of long tentacles, each covered with an array of suckers and barbs. Its oversized head was too heavy for its body to support easily. It slunk slowly from its exposed space, its long black tentacles pulling it forward one after another, each making a slapping sound as it whipped down on the moist ground. The creature was so black that it seemed light was scared to touch it, although amazingly its eyes still shone like lifeless ebony beacons. As empty as the voids above, the eyes seemed so reflective that a person might see their own soul looking back at them, if they were unlucky enough to be in the presence of such a creature.

The creature pulled itself into a dark corner of the man's mind, its octopus-like body able to fit into places its mass shouldn't have allowed. It wrapped its wet, slime-ridden tentacles around the frame of the nest it had found and backed into it as far as the nest would accommodate, looking somewhat like one of the shiny black spiders that live in tunnelled holes in your garden wall, its dripping maw grinding against itself in constant frustration. It had a three-pronged version of a beak, like that of a bird of prey, in place of a mouth. Its words were not spoken; instead, they resonated within the air. The man didn't deserve the happiness he felt, didn't deserve anything of the sort, and the creature wouldn't let him be happy. Couldn't let him be happy. He would get only the pain the creature would reflect on him from its own tortured existence. But the creature couldn't kill him. It knew this, knew it needed him to survive. But it would make him suffer. It would make him hurt and it would enjoy the feeling.

The creature's massive eyes blinked as it thought of all the times it had ventured outside of the man's mind. It took a tremendous amount of effort to leave the prison, and even then it was only possible when the man was weak and his guard was down. But it was always worth it. To see him scared, to see him hurt and to see him fall. Each time, the creature would push a little further, a little harder and for a little longer. But the creature would always retreat when the man's blood flowed. The creature, with no concept of an afterlife, was unsure what would happen to it if the man never woke. But it was sure their paths were linked in such a way that they could never travel alone. So it would always retreat when the man hurt himself, although it would savour every drop of blood that drained from him. And for a time it would be content.

It closed its soulless eyes one last time to rest. It had toyed with him today, had whispered terrible things in his ear. Just enough to create a little doubt. Just enough to make him hate himself the way the creature hated him. It hadn't even had to be specific. Single words often enough.

Ugly.

Useless.

Pathetic.

He was easy to throw off his confident stride. For all his muscles, he was weak of will. He was still the child that had spawned the creature all those years before, but even toying with the man was exhausting for the beast. It needed to rest, and it would leave him be for a few days while it regained its strength. Its mind slowed as it fell into a grave slumber. But the hatred was still there. It was always there. Its maw still gritted. The prison that the man kept the creature in would be its playground. But it was still a prison regardless. One of flesh and of bone. The creature opened its mouth to yawn one last time before it fell deeply into the abyss, and at that moment Jacob breathed out, and for the first time on that rainy Saturday, he felt a little better as he raised himself up. He folded up his little stool that had been his perch and headed back towards the car.

'Goodbye, Pops,' he whispered, as the creature turned in the sleep of the wicked, thoughtless and content with the work it had done.

-

'To what do I owe the pleasure of your company?' Jacob asked with a tremor in his voice akin to a young boy asking for an answer he didn't want.

He couldn't be doing this, could he? Could he really be hiding under the cover of darkness from a malevolent evil he thought was long gone? He was sandwiched tightly between the wall and the sports mattress he'd had made specially to try and ease the constant ache in his shoulder. The ache had been with him since he had attempted to swan-dive into a crystal-clear lake in Connecticut one summer's evening while on holiday with his parents. The water had been so clear he could see the bottom like it was a high-definition photograph, but he had misjudged the depth on a giant level and had crunched fairly conclusively into a heap in barely six feet of water. Almost unwilling to climb out of the water due to his embarrassment, Jacob eventually broke the surface and did an amazing job of hiding the dislocated limb's searing pain. The pain from that incident had never healed. He had vowed that day that he would never again do anything stupid to impress a girl. He wished that he had kept this promise, as 'You shouldn't have done that' seemed to be the sentence he used most in his life.

He had come into the room to look for an old photo of his dad when the radio, which was playing Absolute Soul throughout the house, had stopped him in his tracks. 'How Can You Mend a Broken Heart' started to play – the classic Al Green version, not the original Bee Gees one or the poorly constructed Pendergrass version. His dad's favourite song. At first it warmed his soul to hear it, especially while he was looking for something related to his old man. But the longer the song played, the wider his eyes dilated, and the faster his heart raced.

WHY DIDN'T YOU MOURN? The voice screeched.

DO YOU THINK I'D FORGOTTEN, CHILD?

And suddenly he was 12 years old again.

1991

The Medway towns were not an amazing place to grow up. This commuter area just outside London was apparently coastal, but Jacob, like everyone else, refused to believe that being attached to the Thames river's filthy largest estuary made it coastal. But it was home. And it was all he had ever known.

It was a Sunday morning in late September, and that same song he could hear playing in the recess of his mind was playing on the old radio that Dad had used whenever a garden choir had beckoned. Mum was in the kitchen, as she always was on a Sunday. One of her fantastic roast dinners was en route – god, he could taste it. It was beef, no doubt about it. Overcooked and dry as a desert summer, but somehow it would still be delicious. Not one for following British protocol, Mrs Brooking would make sure there would be mint sauce and stuffing to go with the

Yorkshire pudding. It may not have been traditional, but it was their tradition. The Brooking way.

Dad was mowing the lawn and Peepo was chasing him round the garden. The young Labrador puppy was as scared of the lawnmower as she was the Hoover, but would always chase and bark rather than flee, a flight animal she was not. Paul Brooking pushed the old green mower around the garden with a strength Jacob knew he would never have. His dad was a great man. A man some would say he idolised too much, making the task of filling his shoes in the future impossible. But it was because of him that Jacob Brooking of London Road in Rainham, Kent, had led a safe and happy childhood. He owed his mother and father an unpayable debt. And it was that debt that would forever overshadow his own achievements.

Suddenly, without noticing the day go, it was dark and no one was with him. He could hear his mother asking him to go to bed, but he couldn't see her. It was school tomorrow, and he struggled to get up in the morning. He looked through the rear patio door to where his dad had been in the garden just seconds before, but no one was there. The light was fading fast and not in a way that looked natural to him. It was more like some giant mythical god had poured a pot of black paint over the end of the garden, and the void-like mass was moving slowly towards the house, trying to envelop his home. He ran upstairs to his bedroom, busting in the door with as much force as a 12-year-old boy could muster, and leapt onto his top bunk. The bottom bed was empty since his baby brother had demanded his own room. Jacob quickly hid his toes from whatever might be lurking outside of the quilt's protection and pulled his Sony Walkman out from under his pillow. Seeking the protection of his music, he checked the tape. *American Anthems*. A collection of songs that a friend had given to his dad, which had now been passed down to Jacob in the hope it might grow his knowledge of great music. Peter Cetera came on and he was safe. All was good again.

Jacob knew this was a dream. He knew full well he wasn't 12 years old anymore. But he was home. So how could he be down? Well, unless this wasn't a dream. Unless it was school tomorrow. Where the bullies were. Where Simeon Bennett would terrorise him. Where he would spend every lesson trying to hide in plain sight so as not to get noticed. Jacob would of course pretend to be sick in the morning, as he did every day. It worked at least once a week. It amazed him that not one person ever commented on this. How had no one noticed? He'd had one day off sick every single week for five years in a row. Maybe they did notice. Maybe no one cared.

With the quilt pulled up to his nose and 'Glory of Love' playing loudly in his ear, he looked into the dark opposite corner of the room. Waiting for it to appear. As it always did. But nothing yet rose from the shadows. Maybe tonight would be different. Maybe it had left him. Maybe ... His Walkman slowed a little, as though the batteries were dying, and then with a sharp whine it stopped. The curtains swayed in the draft from the window that his mum would never close, and the moonlight broke through like a laser just for a moment. And it was there. The light caught it for a second. Pure blackness like obsidian liquid. It writhed and grew quickly. Leaking darkness, it slunk across the ground like one of the jelly octopuses he had thrown against the wall as a child to watch climb down as if alive. It moved unnaturally in a way only a creature with no bones could move. Jacob's breathing was now so intense that he swore his heart would burst as the black kraken reached the foot of his bed. As it did every night, it pulled itself up onto his bunk one wet black limb at a time, reaching under his blanket to wrap itself tightly like a python around his ankle. Jacob felt the powerful pinch of its barbed suckers attach to his flesh. It pulled with the force of a thousand horses, and he disappeared into the darkness he knew and feared so much.

2006

His eyes opened bloodshot and filled with tears. He was back in his marital bedroom. And he was back staring at the writhing black shadow in the corner. He couldn't yet see it – rather, he could see where it wasn't. Once again, the light seemed to avoid its very touch. But like his childhood, this kraken struck fear into him with a different weapon. He wasn't a kid anymore. He was 17 stone of muscle and sinew. He had been afraid of nothing in a physical sense for years. So the beast didn't reach for him. In fact, it backed away. Expanding its shadow against the wall, it increased in size and stature, like a midnight-coloured peacock.

ALICE WON'T TOUCH YOU BECAUSE YOU'RE DISGUSTING. YOUR BODY, YOU CLOTHING AND YOUR WHOLE DEMEANOUR REEKS OF FAILURE.

The sound came from his own mind, despite the creature in front of him clearly being the source.

SHE MOCKS YOU. YOU HEAR HER FAMILY SAY YOU'RE NOT ENOUGH. GIVE UP!

I can't, Jacob whimpered. *I love her. I know I don't deserve her, but I love her.*

NO, YOU DON'T, YOU LOVE YOU.

Why are you back? I haven't seen you in years.

YOU'RE AS DISAPPOINTING AS A HUSBAND AS YOU WERE A SON. HOW WAS YOUR FATHER'S FUNERAL, BY THE WAY? I NOTICED YOU DIDN'T CRY. YOUR MUM MUST HAVE BEEN SICKENED BY YOU.

He had wanted to cry. His heart was broken. He just couldn't. He had felt hollow and couldn't feel the emotions he had wanted to feel on the outside that dark day. But he had felt them a thousand times over every day since.

YOU WERE NOT THE SON HE DESERVED AND YOUR TEARS MEAN NOTHING NOW.

Jacob reached up to his stung eye sockets and noticed he was crying his eyes out. He was also shaking like an untethered washing machine. But worst of all, he felt like he was sinking into the carpet. He was definitely slipping into the floor around him. No, he wasn't sinking; he was shrinking. He was already half the size of his adult self. Now he was smaller and lighter than he ever remembered being, his clothes draped over him like loose robes. His heart raced as he felt powerless once more. Before he could react to what was happening, the shadow tentacle reached forward, sensing his childlike fear, and gripped him tightly around his legs with so much force he felt like his bones were shattering. Then, with a thundercloud-like clap of noise, he was yanked into the shadows and awoke underwater.

The kraken was wrapped around his lower torso now, and he was being dragged deeper with each second. As he thrashed around for air, he could see the moon as a pinprick of light above the surface. He couldn't escape. He could barely move at all. He could feel a beak biting at his ankles, and the water around him warmed as it filled with his own blood, heating him and somehow choking him at the same time. Water was filling his lungs, and the more he tried to scream, the more water got in. Through the sheer panic, he didn't notice what was saving him. The more he bled, the less the kraken gripped him. The blade-like maw of the creature was sharper than a surgeon's scalpel, and he could feel pieces of him being quickly dissected, until, finally, with an almost disappointing groan, it released him.

But it was too late. His body fell into a death roll, like a puppet having its strings cut one at a time, and he started to jerk and spasm in an almost chaotic dance. His eyes filled with blood as the pressure of the deep finally took him into a sleep he craved.

'WHAT ARE YOU DOING?' Alice screamed at him, her face one of pure terror as she saw her husband slumped in the corner, tearing the flesh from his arm with his fingernails.

Jacob looked back at her, taking a second to figure out where he was before erupting into floods of tears.

Alice ran over and wrapped herself around him, pulling him closer than even the kraken had managed and kissing him repeatedly on his forehead. 'Baby, why are you doing this again? Talk to me. I'm here. I'm always here, and I'll always help you if I can, but you have to let me in.'

See, you don't deserve her, it whispered, as if Alice would somehow hear its shallow, shrill voice within his mind. *You never did.*

'I know I don't,' Jacob whispered in reply.

'Don't listen to her,' Alice responded without looking up at the creature.

13

Changing of the Guard
Summer 2006
Knightsbridge, London UK

Jacob had been sitting opposite the doctor for what felt like an hour. She was just looking at him, observing his every move. Testing him somehow. Judging his reactions to every point she had put to him. But it had been so long since she last spoke, he was losing track of the conversation.

'I don't quite understand.' Jacob rose to his feet. 'You're saying I have more than one personality?'

The doctor watched him stand and then gave a gentle sigh as he stomped around like a scolded child.

'Sit down, Mr Brooking, please. You need to listen to what I'm saying in its entirety. Don't just take the negatives from every sentence and disregard the rest. I'm here to help you, so please sit down.'

'You sound like my wife,' quipped Jacob.

'I'll take that as a compliment, having spoken to your beautiful Alice.'

Vivian Phillips was the best psych doctor money could buy and she knew it, so she never pussy-footed around anyone or anything. Alice had put Jacob onto her after going to her to cure that silly body-hatred thing Alice always talked about. He never understood it. She was the most beautiful woman he knew. Surely she saw that same reflection in the mirror.

Dr Phillips moved from the desk where she had been leaning and sat on the green chesterfield next to Jacob. A beautiful woman who must have been in her mid-50s, she carried herself in body and form in a manner that any girl half her age would have been envious of. Jacob struggled to understand his emotions towards her. Was he petrified of her or besotted with her? He wasn't sure. But he was pretty sure it was a decent amount of both. Tall and curvaceous, her body seemed to be on a mission to free itself of the white blouse that was tucked tightly into her high-waisted black trousers. Her dark hair was pulled back into a neat bun, and she wore thick-rimmed black glasses. She waited for him to speak, opening her hands in a gesture of calmness.

'OK, what's the script, Doc? Explain it to me like the idiot I clearly am.'

'You're far from an idiot, Mr Brooking, and I am not your enemy, so please be less curt in your tone, if you don't mind.

'You have a condition where your impulsive behaviour will often dominate your emotional behaviour and certainly your rational behaviour.

'You will often see things differently to everyone else, take conversations completely the wrong way, and you have abandonment issues, which may leave you acting irrationally.'

She paused after each sentence to gauge his reaction and to make sure it was sinking in.

'It can be treated with both psychological and medical treatment,' she continued, 'and, given time, you might live a life with zero side effects.

'But the possibility that you have either bipolar or, more likely, personality disorder isn't what worries me. I'm more concerned that you're showing signs of schizophrenia to a level where your psychosis is blurring your version of reality on a massive level. I'm unsure of your ability to distinguish clearly between what is real and what is fabricated by your sense of escapism.

'Tell me about the squid that haunts your dreams.' Dr Phillips noticed the reaction the word 'squid' had received. 'Does it ever appear in your reality?'

'I'm not a psycho, doctor.'

'No one is calling you anything of the sort, and this is a condition more common than you would believe. Now tell me. Do you ever see this squid in ...?'

'IT'S AN OCTOPUS.'

'Sorry, Jacob – do you ever see the octopus in your waking world?'

'Sometimes, but more often I hear it.' Jacob seemed to sink in stature as he slumped in his seat. The colour drained from his face. 'I hear its voice throughout the day, mostly when I'm under duress. If I'm having a bad day or I've fought with Alice, it tells me things I don't want to hear.'

'Always negative, I assume? Telling you that you're not good enough, that you're unable to perform whatever task has been put before you?'

'The voice isn't my friend, doctor. It hates me.'

'"It", Mr Brooking? "It" is you. You're hearing your own voice throw self-hatred at you, and we have to find a way to silence that mindset. You can't allow it to be given form or voice. Does the creature use your own voice?'

'I guess so. But it always sounds like it has half a mouthful of water. Like it's drowning in its own hatred of me. Doctor, I want to be better, but I'm not crazy, and I can't go on some stupid mind-numbing medication. My working day is non-stop. The restaurant has Michelin inspectors due any day now, and we are a sous chef short for the next few weeks.'

Dr Phillips took a measured and deep breath. 'Mr Brooking, I need you to understand the seriousness of your condition. Alice found you harming yourself while screaming at this black monster to leave you alone. I'm amazed you have got this far into a fully functional life without ending up in hospital or worse.'

Jacob looked down at his left arm, which was heavily bandaged from last Monday's incident. Tears of frustration started to well behind his eyes.

'I'm not crazy,' he whimpered.

'Mr Brooking. Jacob. JACOB BROOKING.'

The doctor's last words found their mark as she raised her authority to a level he wasn't used to people using against him.

'I'm going to advise we have an assessment done at Nightingale's Hospital, Royal London,' she said. 'I'll be with you the whole journey. We will come out of it with a much clearer view of where you are and how we move forward.'

'I don't want anyone to know about this. I want complete confidentiality. Even Alice.'

'You might find her support invaluable during the coming months. I implore you to reconsider not telling your wife, but it has to be your call. Mr Brooking, are you taking this all in? Mr Brooking?'

'OK, OK. I need to go. Just let me know about this hospital thing, and I guess I'll be there.'

Jacob shook the doctor's hand and left the room without another word. He moved swiftly out of the building and halted at the edge of the drive, searching for his car. His heart rate rose as anxiety took over and he started to panic.

This couldn't be real. What would Dad have said? What would his mum say? And where was his car? His eyes darted left and right and he could feel the frustration building in his heart. His lungs started to close up and restrict his breathing.

I just want to go home, he cried to himself as he slumped down on the kerb.

SHE DOESN'T KNOW YOU, UNDERSTAND US OR THE RELATIONSHIP WE HAVE. YOU KNOW YOU CAN'T LIVE WITHOUT ME. YOU HONESTLY THINK YOU COULD HAVE ACHIEVED ALL YOU HAVE IN THIS WORLD WITHOUT ME?

With a sudden, cold realisation, Jacob looked up and saw the Mercedes parked in front of him not five feet away. He pulled himself up to his weary feet, feeling like the weight of the world was trying to drag him back to the ground.

Managing to unlock the door, he fell into the low-profile seats with a thud and pulled the seatbelt over his already restricted chest. It felt like he was being cut in two as it snapped closed around him.

He pressed his thumb down on the bright red starter button and the large AMG-tuned engine purred into life like a mechanical monster emerging from hibernation. Taking hold of the steering wheel to move off, he found himself frozen still, unable to release his hands from the death grip they had on the wheel. Sweat started to pour from him, running off his brow, making his eyes sting with venomous spite. He realised quickly that it was not just his hands that were frozen, but his whole body. He started to wet himself as he lost all measure of self-control. Floods of tears now mixed with the sweat dripping from his chin. His clothes were sodden. His paralysis had held him in a fierce embrace for what felt like hours, but was more likely minutes.

A loud knock on the window woke him from the nightmare dream state that was holding him prisoner. His vice-like grip released instantly as he looked to the right to see a concerned Doctor Phillips.

With all his might, he pulled his hand over to the window control and opened the gateway to the telling off he knew was coming.

'Mr Brooking,' the doctor whispered in the most gentle voice. 'Tell your wife. Tell Alice. And I'm going to be blunt here: tell her tonight.'

'OK. Tell Alice. Right, I can do that.'

He raised the window back up and pulled away with a little squeeze of the accelerator.

Tell Alice, he thought. *I can do that. She thinks I'm crazy anyway.*

SHE THINKS YOU'RE PATHETIC.

NOT LIKE EVAN.

LET'S NOT TELL EVAN.

—

'I think we should go away for a bit,' Jacob suggested. 'I think the break will do us good.'

'No way are you suggesting a holiday!' Alice couldn't believe what she was hearing. 'Not a chance.'

'It's a little more than a holiday, Pebble. I've organised a year-long excursion to the West Coast of the United States.' He took Alice's hand and sat next to her. 'Dockside accommodation in San Diego, and we get a boat.'

'Are you fricking kidding me? A bloody year? How could we ever afford that?'

'We can't, but we will. I'm just waiting for you to give me the go-ahead, and we can leave in two days.'

'But what about the restaurant?'

'I'm going to employ Charlie, the manager at the Mermaid, to work with Evan.'

Alice scrunched her brow. 'But what about the Mermaid?'

'The brewery is pulling the plug soon due to a buyout, so we are effectively doing Charlie a favour. He's well up for it.'

'OK, but what will we do for money?'

'I thought you could sell art from the dock and I could do some consulting while we're there. But relax – we have savings, and we're entitled to take some money out of the business as well. We didn't build this empire for nothing, you know.'

Jacob laughed. 'Oh my god, are you crying?'

'Baby, it's been 12 years since we first kissed, and we haven't been away for more than a day or two at any point during that time. We couldn't even have a honeymoon due to your bloody choice of career, so, yes, I'm fricking crying.'

Jacob pulled her into an embrace and kissed her head. 'I know it's been hard and I know I've not been easy to deal with at times, but I've always tried to be the best man I can for you.'

'I know, baby, I know.' Alice looked up cheekily. 'Is San Diego a hot place to relax?'

'Yes, you can go bikini shopping.'

Jacob looked down and saw his phone flash up with Evan's name on it, like a warning sign. He reached down and flipped it over, knowing it was something he would have to deal with sooner rather than later.

You're in trouble now.

'I'm going away for a bit,' said a very coy Jacob as he hurtled along the coastal roads.

'You need to come see me, Jay. Don't do this over the phone, please. Or should I be having this conversation with Alice instead?'

'Evan, don't be stupid. She's a joint partner of the business that employs you. What would that achieve?'

'I'm telling you now, Jacob, if you don't change your plans, all hell is going to break loose.'

She hates you.

'If you want to remain with us at the Gallantry, I need you to give me this,' Jacob told her.

'Who do you think you are, Jay?'

Who do you think you are?

'You don't tell me how to act,' Evan shouted. 'Fuck you, Jacob!'

She's going to tell Alice everything.

Jacob put the phone down. Within seconds, his phone rang again. He pulled over and blocked Evan's number. His phone rang again, this time with the number withheld. He ignored the call until it rang out.

Within a minute, the glove box to his Mercedes sprang to life as Alice's phone started to vibrate. Jacob had taken it without consent after telling her a bullshit story about needing to change her number for the States; as yet, it hadn't gone through the process, and he hadn't wanted to take the risk of leaving it with her. He had blocked Evan on all her social media until this died down, hoping that she wasn't tech savvy enough to notice. After the news he had got from the consultation, he couldn't stay here right now, as he was unsure which choices over the last few years had been his and which had been his apparent psychosis. All he knew was Alice had always been the right choice and being with her was always the choice he would make. A break and then a new start was all it would take to make this right. His phone rang again. He answered knowing what was coming, but also knowing it was something he had to deal with.

She will end you.

'Don't you ever put the phone down on me again, you piece of shit!' screamed Evan.

'I can't take this, Evan. I need you to stop.'

But she won't stop.

'I'll stop when I'm fucking ready, Jacob.'

'How is this going to make anything better, Evan? It can't!'

'I'll do what I need to do, Jacob, to make sure I'm not made a fool of, do you understand me?'

SHE WILL END YOU.

'What can I do, Evan?' Jacob begged. 'What can I do to stop this?'

The phone went silent. Jacob's hands-free system emitted a burst of static that hurt his inner ear, as though it was trying to convey Evan's hatred.

'£5,000 in my account by 3pm and I won't say another word on the matter.'

'Five grand and I have your word?'

'Don't you dare fucking talk to me like that!' Evan screeched. 'I don't have to give you my word, Jacob, when your "word" means shit to me.'

'OK, I'm sorry. Before 3pm. I'll do it now.'

He put the phone down and immediately pulled away from the side of the road. His body trembled with fear. He tried to find the strength to control his breathing. Anxiety was taking over, but he was free, and his world could start again. He knew that this was a close call, though, and his heart was letting him know how lucky he was.

You can't escape me, though.

AND YOU CAN'T BUY ME OFF, the voice said with pure hatred.

-

Free of doubt and with a clear direction in front of him, Jacob had found the strength to push forward. The bank was an ancient stone building reminiscent of a cathedral wing. In the centre of Canterbury, this was no surprise. It fitted in perfectly with the flow of the medieval city's style.

As he pushed through the heavy security doors, however, he was greeted by an air-conditioned modern room that was a hive of activity. Old gents were out collecting their pensions, just happy to be out of the house, while young families tried to pay bills with screaming kids in tow and well-dressed bank workers fluttered around them like bumble bees trying to pollinate as many flowers as possible.

Jacob walked up to the bank teller and introduced himself. The teller told him that the regional accounts manager would see him in a few minutes. Jacob was led down a long corridor where the murky green carpet was heavily worn down the middle from years of endless trudging by demotivated employees, who must've been dragging their feet as they struggled to deal with handling so much money while having so little themselves.

The bank clerk sat him down in a large office with a very formal feel to it. The furniture was incredibly efficient and cost-effective but was warmed slightly by two small potted cacti and a large coffee mug that had World's Best Dad written across it. Right next to the desk was a picture on the wall of the bank manager in question, sitting with his picture-perfect family on what looked like a Butlins holiday, one girl on his shoulders and a slightly older one holding his hand, while his beautiful, pregnant-looking wife was on the other arm. Jacob couldn't help but feel safe here.

'Mr Bennett will be here in just a second, Mr Brooking,' said his handsome but ever-so-camp new friend. 'Can I just ask, Mr Brooking – are you OK?'

'I think so, thank you.' Jacob smiled as his ego told him that his new friend clearly had a crush on him.

So, Mr Bennett was his man. Jacob sat quite contently back in his cheap plastic and foam chair. But before he got too settled, he had to rise back to his feet as the door behind him opened.

'Hello, sir,' the bank manager said, shaking Jacob's hand enthusiastically. 'I apologise for keeping you.'

He placed his other hand on Jacob's shoulder and guided him back to the chair. The manager seemed to look him in the eye with friendly scrutiny, as if taking him all in for just a moment.

'Before we start, is there anything you need? Coffee? Tea? Or maybe just a glass of water?'

Jacob sat down. 'No, I'm fine, thank you.'

The bank manager was a tall man with tidy black hair that was receding slightly across his angled brow. He was clearly a smart man, whose slim frame boasted a little pot belly that told Jacob that here was a man who enjoyed more than the occasional pizza night with his family.

'So, what can I do for you, sir? And please forgive me – I don't have the paperwork in front of me, so I don't have your name.'

'Brooking,' Jacob replied.

The bank manager smiled. 'Well, what can I do for you, Mr Brooking?'

'I need to transfer £5,000 from my personal account to a partner of mine at work, but it needs to be done within the hour, and as I don't have my bank cards with me, they told me to come and speak to the main man.' He coolly pointed at the bank manager.

'That's not a problem, Mr Brooking. But before we proceed, are you sure you're OK?'

'I'm fine, really,' Jacob said in a paranoid tone, wondering why people kept asking him the same question.

'I only asked, Mr Brooking, because apart from being as pale as the paper I'm about to write on, you are visibly shaking, and you have clearly been crying, sir.'

Jacob looked down and saw that the bank manager was right. His sweaty, nervous hands were moving outside of his control.

'I don't know what to tell you,' he said. 'I thought it was OK. I've been going through some stuff today and these past few days. I've had a few hard choices that needed a few tough resolutions, so I guess I've been struggling more than I thought, obviously.'

'Mr Brooking, it's OK. We've all had weeks where the tough call was the right one.'

'Please, call me Jacob. Mr Brooking is a much wider man than his son, I promise you,' Jacob joked.

'Hang on, Jacob Brooking? From the Howard George School?'

'That's me, unfortunately,' Jacob replied.

'Jacob, we went to school together. Simeon Bennett. Surely you remember, mate?'

Simeon got back to his feet and once again offered his hand.

'Sim?' Jacob stood uneasily, unsure of the reality in front of him.

Simeon rolled his eyes, and then smiled. 'I always hated that you lot called me Sim.'

He thinks you were friends.

'Look at you, though, man. I'm so proud of you, getting out of that godawful school and making a name for yourself.' Simeon seemed a little starstruck. 'In fact, I took my wife to your restaurant for our anniversary, but I wouldn't have put this man in front of me as the name I saw above that restaurant door.'

'What do you mean?' Jacob asked.

'What do I mean? Are you kidding me? I look like a taller and fatter version of the rat-faced kid that used to chase you round school. You, on the other hand, look like a *GQ* magazine just shat you out.'

'You're too kind, Simeon. I must confess, I never thought you liked me at school. You were not the nicest kid to have chase me round the playground.'

'I had a rough childhood, Jay.' Simeon glanced at the picture on the wall. 'If I was ever out of line, it was only down to my own unhappiness, a pain I've promised to never put my own kids through.'

With that said, Jacob took Simeon's hand and shook it well.

'You seem like a great dad, Sim, sorry, Simeon, and I hope one day I can be that man.' Jacob spoke honestly and somehow felt lighter for doing so.

'Right, let's stop reminiscing about the bloody Howard George and sort your money out. Five thousand pounds, you said?'

14

It Follows
Spring 2007
San Diego, California USA

As the day drew to a close on the San Diego coastline, it almost looked like the sun was falling into a warm bathtub. The sky, a fading viridian green, melted slowly into a sea of deep teal, while the sun itself, a pale, burnt-terracotta version of its normal vibrancy, started to rest peacefully on a bed of oceanic mist, which took the edge off its impetuous glare. Flocks of gulls chased a large and battered-looking trawler that was returning to dock. The ship had the words *Sarah Grace* written upon its bow in a deep claret that contrasted beautifully with the fresh white paint job, which did little to hide the age of the vessel. Jacob realised that this ship had been under maintenance at the Marina Cortez, and its belly was clearly empty of anything the gulls might desire for dinner. Yet they chattered loudly among themselves and fought for the right to take the first bite of a meal they were yet to discover was a fabrication of their dreams. They would all be disappointed and hungry tonight.

    Jacob lay at rest on a jade leather chaise longue, his hands on his chest and his fingers interlaced in stoic contemplation. His head was propped gently against the arm of the chair, just enough for him to take in the beautiful sunset, which danced gently like an autumnal kaleidoscope as the light began to fail. He reached over and took his crystal tumbler off the small slate coffee table that Alice had picked up at the goodwill market the weekend before last. They were not a poor couple, by any means – in fact, quite the opposite could be said about the Brooking empire, as he had often called it – but that had never stopped Alice looking for a bargain. She claimed that something used, worn and even damaged would always carry more character than anything new and shiny. *Maybe that's why she loves me so much*, Jacob had thought to himself, giggling, before sighing at the reality of how damaged and worn he was.

   Jacob could have sworn that he could hear some light jazz that was being carried on the wind from a nearby Parisian hipster café, but he had to wonder if it was just his imagination playing tricks on him once more, as it seemed far too perfect a backing track to the scene being played out in front of him. It was almost impossible at times to know what was real and what was his mind's psychosis, as he knew how much the internal voice loved to trick him with alternative versions of his own reality, and yet he had felt far more settled here in the States. The move had been relatively stress free. Alice had taken an instant shine to all the locals, who had already given her a backlog of commissions for paintings and sketches of their coastal homes. She'd found a rhythm here that he had rarely seen from her previously, and seeing her happy had warmed his soul beyond words. As well as his own mental health seeming to settle, he had also noticed that Alice was taking compliments with a more natural vigour. This would often lead to her bouncing over to him for a passionate embrace. Maybe this trip had been good for them both. Jacob sipped his Tennessee bourbon and pondered what he would have to do to make this move permanent. What was really left for them in the UK? Just bad memories and two families who had shown nothing but disappointment in Jacob and all he had ever brought to their lives. He snarled as he thought about his godawful father-in-law, who looked down on Jacob as he held his wife and daughter up on that perfect pedestal, while Jacob's own parents had noticed nothing about his life positive or otherwise, as they had only ever existed within their own bubble of team Samuel, who had carved out quite a successful career as a semi-professional golfer and then a golfing coach. They had been to every championship he had ever competed in, no matter how small. Yet had they ever eaten or even stepped foot in one of his restaurants? He couldn't remember if they had, but it couldn't have been a long visit, that was for certain. Nope. There was nothing for him there, especially since his dad had passed. His mum was now more withdrawn than ever.

You're as selfish as you always were, the voice whispered.

It didn't have the energy to fight with real conviction, which made it all the easier for Jacob to ignore.

He finished his bourbon, the ice now melted in the Californian evening air. *I was never good enough for their perfect little girl, so I'll just take her away*, he thought, as he lay his head back down.

Where was Alice, anyway? She had disappeared over an hour ago with the promise of a cold meat platter once she had Skyped her mother. He loved it when she cooked dinner, even if it was just leftovers of things he had cooked over previous days. Despite his obvious skill in the kitchen, he had always hated his own cooking, and the joy of anyone else bringing him food was unparalleled. Jacob still carried his muscular rugby-playing frame from his youth and had maintained it in the gym most days, but it was this constant need to be fit that caused him to be almost permanently hungry. She would hopefully throw on some of the apricot white Stilton that he'd had sent all the way from the Sussex coast, and at quite the cost. The Yanks were great at many things, but the subtle nuance of fine cheese was not their strong point. Alice had named him the dairy pirate, smuggling culture into the relaxed West Coast vibe for three months straight. Jacob had pointed out that the lack of a parrot meant he couldn't be a pirate of any real worth, so Alice had instead suggested a wooden leg. When he'd looked at her in bemusement, she'd kicked him in the shin hard enough that he'd collapsed. He'd proceeded to chase her round their large yacht, which came as part of the rental agreement on the dock house they rented.

He picked up his empty glass and sat up, stretching his arms out wide and arching his back until it cracked into place. The warm air was dying around him, and the sun was only a sliver on the horizon as it put itself to bed for the night among the flock of miserable seagulls now floating on the water. The chill from the air made his skin feel like a gentle current was running through it and told him it was time to head into a warm embrace and a platter full of food. He rose to his feet, fully taking in the beautiful view one last time before turning to open the porch door.

'Honey, I'm home!'

Jacob closed the door behind him. A crystal tumbler like the one he was carrying smashed in an explosion of noise against the frame of the door. Shards of glass and splinters of wood showered his face, luckily avoiding his eyes, as the thickest part of the tumbler's base fell to the ground. He looked around to see Alice slumped on the floor. Wet from the tears she had been crying, her hair was stuck to her face, and her mascara had run all the way to her neckline. Her bloodshot eyes were a dark royal blue, instead of the electric azure that normally pulled his soul into hers.

'Why, Jacob?' Alice growled quietly.

'Baby, you're scaring me,' Jacob replied. 'Why what?'

'Why did we move here, Jay? Honestly. Tell me honestly.' Her voice was deep and broken. 'Why are we here?'

'Because we deserve the break, baby. You kno ...'

A shoe hit him in the gut, and Jacob winced, feeling the venom with which it had been thrown.

'What on earth have your parents said to you this time, Pebble?'

'DON'T CALL ME THAT! I AM NOT YOUR FUCKING PEBBLE. AND DON'T YOU DARE PIN THIS ON MY PARENTS.'

Alice staggered to her feet. 'Why don't we talk about the email I just received from Evan instead?'

She knows, whispered the voice.

'Well, Jacob? Shall we?' Alice was growing in stature with every step forward. 'Shall we talk openly and honestly as husband and wife about how we swore to always be together in everything we did?'

You deserve this.

'Shall we talk about you fucking Evan Laurie for a month before our wedding and then paying her to keep quiet?'

You can't win this.

'Or how about how you had me murder our baby so that you could get away with it a little longer? No?'

Alice was only a few feet away from Jacob now.

'SAY SOMETHING TO ME YOU FUCKING PIG!'

That seemed to come from Alice and the voice in his head at the same time. Jacob couldn't differentiate between them.

Alice reached forward and gripped him around the throat. Her nails pinched his flesh and broke the skin.

Jacob couldn't respond. He had convinced himself not only that Alice would never find out about the affair but that it hadn't actually happened at all. He honestly believed at times that his psychosis had made it all up. That it had just been a friendship out of hand. That it was nothing.

'You told Evan you loved her.'

'But I didn't,' Jacob muttered.

'I suggest you find somewhere else to sleep right now, Jay, because I can't look at you one second longer, and you clearly have nothing to say and no explanation worth hearing.' Alice grabbed a set of keys from the glass bowl next to the door and shoved them into his chest. 'Why don't you go and sleep on that precious boat, since you love it so very much.' Tears were rolling down her face as she turned away in disgust.

Jacob took the keys and went out onto the front decking. The cold night air caught him off guard. He walked down towards his Audi, which was parked at the bottom of the yard. He took one last look over his shoulder at the devastation he had caused.

Alice was curled up against the door. 'You may as well keep on running, Jacob. It's all you have ever known how to do.'

Jacob heard her words but just looked at the ground instead.

LOOK AT HER, YOU COWARD.

'I did nothing wrong,' Jacob muttered once more.

YOU DID EVERYTHING WRONG.

YOU NEVER DESERVED HER.

15

The Summer Breeze
Spring 2007
Somewhere in the Pacific Ocean

The ship was being thrown aggressively back and forth on the waves of the Pacific Ocean as if it were a paper vessel trying to navigate a hurricane. The witching hour had brought more lashing rain and a thunderous grumble born from a war between the gods – a war that was being waged ever closer, with each angry boom from within the clouds sounding louder and more violent. Jacob's mum had always said that a storm was just furniture being moved in heaven, but he doubted that was the case here. That good Christian belief seemed weak compared to what was clearly a very Greek and very angry Zeus throwing down the law to a very disobedient Poseidon, as each bolt of lightning was matched by another crashing wave of titanic proportions. It would have been nearly impossible for another vessel to make out the ship's lines against the maelstrom. Her form was all but invisible, except for the sheet lightning that illuminated her hull every few minutes. For a second or two, white light reigned, before the waves once again dropped her out of sight underneath the massive swell of an angry sea. One tiny speck of light remained throughout, though, almost like a firefly dancing in a Louisiana swamp. The tiny candlelight came from the ship's living quarters and lit up the small aft window like a beacon of hope in a place of endless sorrow.

It had become the only constant in what was a violent dance that the ship was enduring very much against her will.

Jacob sat in the small cabin on the lower deck of the yacht – a vessel he had got as part of the deal to take on the boathouse for a year – and mulled over his first lines. The diary in front of him was leather-bound and heavy like some book of ancient lore. The weapon in his grasp, a fountain pen of a delicate design, had a craftsmanship that radiated expense. A gift from his father many years before, it was something Jacob held dear. It was more than just a pen to him. He saw the gift as a symbol of his father's final wish: that Jacob would open up at last, with the pen serving as the means to aid that unusual practice of telling the truth – unusual for Jacob Brooking, at least, a man who had got used to telling the truth only when things were good. As of now, things were far from good. As the violent motion of his surroundings did their best to throw his stomach off course, he found comfort as he pressed the nib of the pen down on the first page. In the light of a pair of large candles, Jacob started to talk honestly, for the very first time, to Alice.

To my heart

The apology you are owed cannot be voiced with mere words. In fact, my meagre existence here in this life is really an affront to the true remorse I feel, for I have left my life forfeit with my actions towards you these past few years. I'm sorry, Alice – not for my past catching me up, but for taking far too long to tell you exactly what drives my every action throughout the days when you are not by my side, for it seems that when my hand is entwined with yours, I fear nothing and fall rarely. Your love it seems, is the anchor that holds me through storms and your patience the rudder that guides me, and now you are lost to me, and I have not one person to blame but myself. So, I am sorry – sorry for being too proud to tell you how far I have so often fallen from the pedestal you put me on. I am a man falling from grace, at a rate I cannot control, and a man who knows that redemption is further from reach than it has ever been before.

Day 5

    I have been at sea now for a few days. I had started writing this letter to you in the hope of seeing you that same day I first put pen to paper, yet fear consumes me – fear of confrontation with you. Truth be told, confrontation with anyone scares me more than anything rational should scare a man, yet here I am, still writing instead of turning this ship around. What has become of me? When did I become so weak? The shrink has told me I need to write everything down, because I panic when I get myself into heated procrastination, and who am I to argue with Dr. Phillips? "Write it down, Jacob, then read it back to them later when emotion has left the room." And so I guess that's what I'm doing – writing down what I should have been able to say to your face so many times before, and for that I am once again sorry. Maybe when I dock I'll find you waiting, and I can read this to you in the hope it will adjust your view on the choices I have made, yet I feel my heart will be broken to find you gone, and maybe that is the fear that stops me from turning the wheel right now. I've done all I can to push you away at times, and yet the idea of a life without you scares me more than the nightmare creature that fills my waking dreams. Its hate has haunted me all of my life. The constant fear of the darkness only exists because of the ominous threat It poses my sanity from the shadows, yet the pain and suffering it has brought constantly to my life pales in comparison to the void that your absence has left within my ever-diminishing soul.

Day 10

I'm sorry for Evan, I'm sorry for what I did in its entirety, but I know it hurts you more that it was her. I never loved her, but I enjoyed feeling like I was good enough for someone, like I was enough. I'm a bad man and my heart has always been filled with a darkness born out of hatred, a hatred that in turn was born from the chip on my shoulder. I never felt good enough for you, I never felt good enough for your father, who constantly expected more from me. But with Evan, I felt a kinship with her own self-loathing, and that made me feel enough for her, and just for a moment then I felt enough for someone. But I was wrong, and by the time I'd realised my mistake, it was too late. You know what she can be like, you know the violence of both her words and her actions, and it was the fear of what was surely to come which stopped me from walking away the second it happened, and for that Alice I am so truly sorry. It has only reiterated what I already knew: I have never been the man you needed me to be. But I do see now that you loved me even when I hated myself, and had I realised that at the time, then maybe I would have acted differently.

Day 36

I've shut the engines down for a day while I try to find my bearings. I've realised that the few classes in open-sea navigation that I took after getting this boat have quickly been forgotten. Once again, my ego has blinded my ability to learn lessons that might actually benefit my life. I wonder how many times I have ignored your advice because I thought honestly that the great Jacob "fucking" Brooking knew better. I always said that my only dream in life was to be like my father, to be a good husband and eventually a good dad, but the apple has fallen pretty far from the tree with me. I'm a disgrace to my family and to yours, and I can't help but feel that this is karma rounding up on me for the final kill. The voice in my head has screamed at me from dawn until dusk today. It hates me, tells me I'm stupid for writing this, as you will be long gone by the time I have summoned the courage to return to you. But it's wrong. It must be. Because I love you, and I know you still love me, you must still love me. Even as I write, its shrieking and bitter voice is cutting through my resolve to survive this ordeal. I need you here to guide me. It wants me to hurt myself, wants me to end my apparent sad existence, and there is a part of me that thinks it might be right.

Day 42

   I have no words to explain the loss I feel knowing I will never see your face again. I want to make things right. I want to explain the choices I have made, and maybe, just maybe, you will look upon me as you once did.
   I've held off writing too much lately in the hope I might get to explain my feelings face to face, but it seems that even with all the will in the world, fate is still against me this time. At 2.37pm yesterday I finally ran out of diesel, and no soul seems to be answering any distress call I have sent. I guess I have run for so long, I never considered I might eventually run out of road. With my biggest fear always the idea of being caught by my demons, it's come as quite the

revelation to find the only thing I'm running from is my own heart. Indeed, it's quite the surprise to me that no matter how far or fast I run, I can't escape my own true self. So now I am here, with my only companion the cold presence of death. He hangs over me once more. I feel his skeletal hand clamping metaphorically down on my soul with focused desire. He wants me, and I feel this time he will take me. I will write more soon, my Alice, in the hope that even when I'm gone, you might find this book and know that I am truly sorry.

KNOCK KNOCK KNOCK

Jacob was woken with abject horror by the sound of a visitor's warning. He turned about in earnest to locate the source of his wake-up call but found nothing – nothing but the shadows dancing to the one lamp that still had a candle burning brightly.

KNOCK KNOCK KNOCK

'The window,' Jacob whispered.

Rising with the stiffness of a man who had slept in an armchair at his desk and the apprehension of a man searching for a body where there should of course be none, he moved across the bedroom to peer through the circular window, which was lined and latched with polished brass. He could see nothing except the setting sun and an assault upon the glass, one of salt water from both above and below. The dying light lit up the sky like a rescue flare, with the burning sun sinking into the ocean as if melting into the sea. But he could see no reason for the knocking. Maybe his guest was just a seagull pecking his reflection in an act of territorial masculinity, or maybe Jacob was still dream-

KNOCK KNOCK KNOCK

Jacob spun around in panic as the same noise that had shaken him from his slumber moved from the window to the large wooden door that led to the upper deck. He moved down the hall towards it, readying himself for both the rescue he knew he wanted, and the disappointment he knew he deserved. The dancing candlelight threw shadows against the walls in unnatural shapes that played out a story, and the closer he got to the door, the more real the stories became to him. He saw a ship bobbing on rough seas, and a beast from beneath the waves rising up and pulling it deep below the surface. Jacob's hand gripped the doorknob, and the fear of the moment seized him. His sweat-filled palms made the brass feel wet in his grasp.

'No – this can't be ...'

Jacob realised that it wasn't sweat on his hands, but blood. Darkness all but consumed him as panic sought to control his actions.

KNOCK KNOCK KNOCK

Jacobs attention was brought back into the room, the noise now behind him. He turned, expecting to see a monster or a demon. Instead, he saw Alice. She was laced in the white of her wedding dress. Her womb was dripping with scarlet, and her hands were outstretched.

'GIVE HIM BACK TO ME, JACOB,' she cried in a howl of pain.

Jacob looked down to find himself holding the unborn son he had made her give up. The child's body was drenched in blood. His eyes were shut tightly, as if they had never opened, and his tiny hand was tightly gripped around Jacob's thumb.

-

Jacob woke up at his desk, screaming, his face drenched with sweat and his eyes filled with tears. He swallowed hard as the dream faded and he took in the quiet all around him – no Alice in sight, no voice, no creature, just empty, dead silence. Silence, that is, except for the slow drip, drip, drip of the blood running off his forearm. The nib of his fountain pen poked out of the top of his arm, embedded in the deep wound he had made in his flesh.

-

Jacob hadn't moved in hours. The water was deadly still. Not a ripple crossed the perfectly mirror-like sheen of what was possibly the calmest ocean that could exist on this earth. He had sailed in the Pacific before, but he couldn't recall ever hearing of this place, a shallow where he could just about see the bottom beneath almost waveless tides, although he couldn't recall much of anything lately. No current of real strength was pulling the boat, and there was no tide of relevant power to cause much more than a gentle sway. The place was home to a thousand wrecked pre-combustion-engine ships that had simply stopped without the air to move them forward. And this was where the last of his diesel had burnt up.

    The carcasses of skeletal 16th-century ships were littered around him. No signs of life except for the boys. The boys had been with him since he had pulled to a standstill. The first was a rather large and menacing barracuda, which lived among the wrecks in the shallow waters beneath him. Even within the confines and safety of his ship, Jacob felt sure that this fish had a plan, that this fish of ungodly length had developed a scheme to get him sooner rather than later. The second of his two new friends was of course the large obsidian octopus that dominated a rock formation aggressively breaking the surface of the water. It appeared each dusk to soak in the last of the sun's rays, but it bore such a resemblance to the kraken in his dreams that he was unsure if it was real or just his aching eyes playing tricks like some perverse mirage. It was close to midday, now, so a more pressing issue was at hand. Could and more importantly would a seagull eat a dead body rotting on the deck of a boat? Or, even worse, a dying body not yet devoid of sensory feeling? Jacob had been toying with this riddle for days and had promised himself that whatever happened, he would decide today and accept the verdict regardless. He thought over and over on this as he lay motionless on a worn, thick shag rug. The rug had previously been happily at rest in the living quarters of the *Summer Breeze*, the 40-foot sun chaser that had been his home for two long months; but Jacob, with great effort, had dragged it to the top deck, as he refused to die in what he considered to be a readymade crypt. If he was to go, it would be with the sun or the moon on his back.

    His parched and broken lips, which were cracked from a combination of dehydration, the roasting midday sun and the spiteful evening chill, had sent a shot of pain through his mouth as he swallowed, and it hurt him more than physically, as his demeanour was that of a proud man, and now he couldn't even swallow without wanting to cry. He felt pathetic. Unchanged since the day he had left San Diego, his sullen look now broke into the smallest of smiles as he realised he hadn't even seen a seagull for two weeks, so it was a moot point. Could he really have travelled that far from land? By his watch, it was the 28th of June and he had run out of fuel a month ago. Where the tide had taken him up until the boat had settled on this motionless mirrored plane of glass he couldn't work out, and the more he thought about it, the more it occurred to him that it had said the 28th on his watch for at least two days. The 28th. Alice's birthday was a month away. What were the chances? It had been two months since he had walked out on the argument. Since he had left her sobbing and heartbroken on their patio deck. Again, he was suddenly aware of the pointlessness of all these numbers, as like it or not he was here with no propulsion, no food and no water – which was, of course, an irony not lost on a man surrounded by nothing but water. With the last of his strength slipping away from him, he was fully resigned to what was inevitable. He was going to die.

His wildly cut hair, once a beautiful chestnut brown, was sun-bleached and reminded him of the autumns he used to witness on his breaks to New England during his youth. A time that seemed so simple to him now. And a time that seemed a lot further away than the 25 years it had actually been since his last family holiday to the East Coast with his folks. His bearded face was narrow and gaunt, and his eyes, which were once bright crystals of emerald that were always considered too green to be his natural eye colour, were now glazed with a white sheen, as blinking had apparently become too much and was beyond him. A man so obsessed with his body and so driven by people's opinion of him now lay dying on the top deck of the majestic ship. His muscles were wasting away and his skin was broken and thin. He would die surrounded by regret. And one in particular would follow him to the boatman's call. He wished she was there. If only to hold him as he slipped away.

Out of nowhere, there was a noise, faint and delicate over the deafening silence. It was distant, but it was definitely there. What was it? His thoughts rushed at him all at once. A ship or a plane maybe? Help? Could it be help? He turned his neck up to the sky as much as his broken body would allow and looked through the deep blue of the open air above him. And his brow creased in sadness as he realised that the two large gulls circling above him might just answer his question after all.

-

Two more hours passed as Jay lay dying on the mahogany deck of his yacht. The two seagulls that he had once thought his enemies were now sitting on the plush cushions lining the bench next to where he had made his final home. Jokingly, he had named them Tommy and Gina, because they looked like a very loving couple as they nestled up together. Tommy had a long curved yellow beak and was the larger, while Gina was more speckled in colour, her face more eloquent and her grey beak small and pointed. He smiled at his new friends and realised he hadn't felt any kind of depression in weeks. And somehow, without the constant voices of others to cloud his thoughts, his own voice had finally prevailed. How much of the last year was real? How much of the last ten? Or was it all psychosis? Had he ruined his relationship with Alice over nothing but confusion over what had been his own voice? Certainly, he had done nothing but love her since he had met her, so why would he push her away? He had done nothing but miss her since the day he had walked out on her. A world of regret had heaped itself on him since the day his engine had choked and died. He had spent his twenties overcompensating for the work his bullies had done with him. He had gone on to believe the world owed him everything for what he had been through. That chip had never left his shoulder. And now he would pay.

  His girl was amazing. He had never deserved Alice. At his best he was punching well above his weight. Yet his swollen ego had led him here to die. Well, he was truly humbled now. And he would die here humble and alone, and all because when his doctor had diagnosed his bipolar and all the other self-destructive conditions he had, his ego had made him walk out the room, never to mention it again. Having these mental conditions wouldn't kill him. Denying his conditions, the honest conversation with his wife, would be what did it.

He would die here. And for the first time in his life, Jacob Brooking admitted he probably didn't deserve it.

Summer 2007
San Diego, California USA

'Hi, my name's Jacob and I have bipolar disorder with traits of personality disorder and extreme psychotic delusions,' Jacob said to the group before taking a seat nervously among a mixture of people all either looking through him like he was glass, or looking at the ground around him with an unwillingness to accept his presence. He had heard them whispering in the corridor as he had arrived at the conference centre for the first of his group therapy sessions. 'There's nothing wrong with him,' they had said. 'Look at his expensive watch,' one had murmured with nasty intent. 'I heard he pulled up in an Audi R8, so what could be wrong with him?' Jacob had ignored them and just shuffled into the circle of truth.

He had barely spoken since the Hawaiian naval vessel had come across him stranded at sea. He remembered little from the rescue event other than the giant Marine medics who had carried him off the *Summer Breeze* and below the surface of the *USS Boston*'s main deck. He remembered his sunburn being treated with freezing-cold creams and lotions. He remembered eating for the first time in weeks and then throwing it all up before having to eat once again. And then he remembered the doctor who looked like his father.

'Talk to someone, Jacob, before it's too late,' he had said with concern.

Now, three weeks later, he was here. He assumed someone had told Alice he was alive, and he hoped that this would be the first step to proving he was serious about fighting this demon inside him, but as of yet he hadn't found the strength or the courage to speak to her or even message her.

'Hi Jacob,' said the group in a drone-like unison.

'Hello, Jacob,' said the group leader. Duncan Stewart was a small man with round features and a receding hairline whose thin gold-framed glasses made him look like the brains behind an evil genius in an old Russian spy film. In fact, he was clearly a god-bothering scout-leader type. He was pleasant enough, if a little tactile for Jacob's taste.

'Or do we call you Jay?'

'Either is fine,' said Jacob without looking at him.

'I've read your file, Jacob, and, let's be fair, there's some heavy stuff in there, so only communicate what you feel comfortable with, and maybe let's just spend this week listening to the rest of the group.'

Duncan brought his eye level down to try and catch any sign of agreement from Jacob but caught nothing.

'Who wants to go first?' asked Duncan.

'I'll go first. I want to talk about my useless son.'

Jacob looked up to see his mother sitting there knitting right in front of him.

One year earlier

'What do you mean, you're ill? There's nothing wrong with you.' Marie Brooking didn't even look up from her newspaper.

'Well, I think it's obvious that I've always struggled, Mum. I'm unsure how you and Dad never noticed.'

'Noticed what, Jacob? You've been a popular guy all your life.'

'Mum, even if that was relevant to what I'm saying, which I can assure you it isn't, I'm not sure how you can say that. Name one of my friends without saying Alice.'

'All I'm saying is I've never noticed anything that you might say makes you disabled.' Marie pronounced the word disabled as though there were quotes around it. But still she didn't take her eyes off the paper on the table in front of her. 'Ultimately, Jacob, you just have to be positive, as really what does all this negativity bring you?'

This would be different if it was your brother.

They actually like him.

'Mum, I'm not sure you are getting this at all. I'm struggling with a mental illness. I'm not disabled as such, but it certainly doesn't go away with just positive thought.'

She must be so disappointed in you.

'Are you telling me you never noticed signs?' Jacob was starting to get irate at his mother's inability to see anything wrong with his childhood behaviour. 'What about school?'

'You were fine at school, Jakey.'

'No, Mum – I hated school, every day. I honestly don't remember having one good day at school. How do you of all people not know that?'

She thinks you're lying.

Shut up, Jacob thought.

I think you're lying.

'SHUT UP.'

Just making excuses for years of cowardice.

'SHUT UP SHUT UP SHUT UP.'

'I hope you're not talking to me, Jacob Brooking,' his mum snapped.

'No, Mum, of course not. I'm just talking to myself.'

Marie looked up and tilted her head. 'Is that a sign of your disability?'

'Mum, it really would mean a lot if you could take this seriously. Maybe come to a meeting with me or something.'

'Jacob, you know I love you. Isn't that enough? Have you spoken to your brother lately?'

Oh, here it goes.

'He's working so hard right now,' his mum went on. 'I do worry about him.'

Jacob sighed. 'I know, Mum. I worry too.'

Doesn't worry about you, does she?

Jacob got up to leave, as the situation was quickly getting away from him. He kissed his mum on the head and thanked her for the coffee. 'Thanks for the help, Mum.'

What help?

'Just remember to keep positive, Jacob, my boy.'

She returned to her paper without another thought.

2007

Jacob shook his head clear as the girl in front of him, who was clearly not his 62-year-old mother, finished her story.

'That's great, Annabelle. Thank you for sharing.' Duncan looked around. 'Who's next?'

A man who now looked like Alice's father stood up to speak. Jacob, realising what the monster inside him was doing, quickly intervened.

'I'll go next,' said Jacob, 'because otherwise this will be a long day for me. Let me tell you about the voice in my head.'

16

The End
Summer 2007
San Diego, California USA

Three months had passed since he had left home. No one had heard from him, and now he was back on the lawn of the dock house, trying to find the strength to turn that door handle. But he was scared, he was frozen, and his heart was pounding. The medication has stopped the voice in his head to a certain extent, but he knew Alice would never forgive him regardless, and he didn't need a monster in his head to tell him that. But he was here and that had to be a start.

-

Three months had passed. No one had heard from him, and he had pissed so many people off that very few questions were asked regarding his whereabouts anymore. But she was alright.

'I'm alright,' she whispered while straightening herself in the mirror for the fiftieth time.

Screw him. Screw Jay and his narcissistic face. Despite her best efforts, her long curly auburn hair kept falling over the earrings her mum had sent her all the way from England for her birthday. Uncontrolled mane or otherwise, it was only the second first date she had ever been on, so if he didn't like the way her hair fell, then she could afford to be picky, and she was sure there were men out there who would love how untamed her hair could be at times. How untamed she could be full-stop. Her freckles had come out today with the sun, and her button nose was covered all over. Her piercing blue eyes cut through everything, though. With her whole look screaming subtle class and her demeanour carrying a deserved swagger of classic beauty, it was left to eyes of crystalline aquamarine to stop time where it stood. To be caught in that gaze was to get lost in a place of oceanic wonder.

A strapped summer dress fell over the curves of her slender athletic frame and danced around her knees. Her exposed shoulders revealed more freckles, which went all the way down her arms. Her fingernails were painted in a clear and clean gloss. The dress, a summer-sale buy from a trip into San Diego, was white lace flecked with tiny turquoise flowers that matched her eyes. The only accessory was the necklace. Bright and gleaming in the sunlight, it matched her sparkly azure five-inch heels. It was the necklace that Jacob had bought her for their anniversary. What a disaster that sunny June day had been. An embarrassed flush of colour washed over her once more as she remembered everyone looking at them as Jacob screamed at her less than an hour after giving her the gift. For that reason, she had toyed with selling it, but she loved it like no sane person should love an inanimate object.

What had she seen in him? All he had ever cared for was his job and his money. Ambition to be more and to have more than he had was all he dreamed of. She had never been part of that plan, she saw that now. And he had never been the man she had hoped he would be. The man she deserved. *And look at you now,* she thought. *Look at what you have become.* 'You're everything he wouldn't have allowed you to become,' she proudly voiced.

She grabbed her door keys and smiled one last time in the hall mirror, her pearl-white teeth lighting up her face.

Her reflection looked back at her and snarled.

WHO THE HELL DO YOU THINK YOU ARE?

I HATE YOU.

'I know you do,' said Alice.

HATE, the mirror proclaimed back, with all that I am. I'm disgusted we share the same form. You were never good enough for him. You were never good enough for anyone of any calibre. WHERE IS HE NOW, PIG?

The mirror screamed at Alice, but it wasn't Alice looking back at her. It could have been. The same basic shape was there, the same clothes, the same eyes. But that was where the similarities ended. Her skin appeared bloated and cracked. Her hair was greasy. No, this wasn't Alice at all. But Alice thought it was. She believed it was her true reflection. But she still couldn't figure out why or how it was talking to her. She had always heard the voice berating her in the back of her mind. But this was different. This wasn't a quiet echo within the silence of her thoughts. It was confrontation. She was watching her reflection in a full-blown argument with herself, yet her real lips hadn't moved once. The new two-dimensional version of herself, though, didn't seem to care about the laws of physics.

The only man to ever love you has left you for a common tart. He was pathetic, half a man, and still too good for you. DO YOU MAKE ANYONE HAPPY? the demon reflection screeched.

'No, I don't, I guess I never have.'

Alice wept. Her eyes filled slowly with the kind of salt water that only comes when you're ready to give up. It had been a month since she had cried, and three months since Jay had left her. She thought she was coping. Yet here she was losing an argument with herself. She missed her mum and dad. She missed Canterbury. And she missed her husband.

'I FUCKING HATE YOU,' Alice screamed.

Her hands, previously frozen, snatched at her phone, fumbling in frustration at her inability to turn it on. She found his number. She had to talk to Jay.

Go on, ring him.

I BET HE DOESN'T ANSWER.

She held the phone to her ear and, despite herself, let hope slip into her heart that his familiar east London accent would answer.

Yet nothing but three loud beeps greeted her. Her eyes glazed over with a final realisation that Jacob wasn't coming back. The weight of the situation washed over her like a lead blanket, and she began to crumble from within.

Alice looked up from her phone. As she stared at the nightmare creature, leering back at her from the mirror, she noticed the reflection wasn't crying at all. She reached up to her face and caressed the wet trail driving a path down her face. Why was she crying when the creature wasn't? That's what broke her finally.

Alice snapped from the very deepest part of her soul. Her entire mind turned into anger, and she launched her phone at the mirror with a force she didn't know she had. Like a supernova, the mirror exploded into a million shards, each shining like a swarm of fireflies as the hall light caught them in its warm embrace.

She slumped to her knees with the pieces settled around her. The last of her strength faded away as she realised her hope of silencing the demon voice was gone, because the one creature was now replaced by a thousand laughing Alice demons. Each shard had an image of Alice within it, and each one mocked her. All laughing at her, mocking her and grinning. Each one more grotesque than the last. But all with an unnaturally large smile filled with broken and filthy teeth.

Hours passed. The laughing continued. The mocking, like a murder of crows fighting over roadkill, just didn't stop. Alice sat there, broken into as many pieces as the mirror. She had only ever loved one man since her father, and she had pushed Jacob away because she knew she wasn't enough. How could she be?

And yet just as she believed the last of her strength had left her, she summoned something from inside her very core. A resilience not to let the demon Alice win. She reached down and picked up the largest shard of glass she could find and brought it to her throat.

'DO IT,' Alice said.

This time it wasn't the reflection talking. Those words came from her own lips as the demon looked on in horror and fear.

Don't do it! We need you.

Blood started to trickle down the shard of mirror.

Jacob stood in the doorway, looking down at the kraken-like creature climbing out of the remains of a shattered mirror frame, its barbed tentacles pulling at Alice's wrists, trying to stop her cutting her own throat.

'Get away from her. GET AWAY FROM HER.'

17

Wires
Summer 2007
Psychiatric Hospital of San Diego CA

Alice had been lying deadly still on the hospital bed for what seemed like days. The room was clinical and open, with nothing inside it that didn't have a purpose. She lay on her side, crunched into a foetal position, with just one white pillow folded beneath her plaited auburn hair. Her gown was a horrible green hue that left her lower back exposed for no reason that she could understand, especially as the only reason she was here was the damage done underneath the white compress bandage around her throat, yet she didn't have the strength to question the doctors. And what would have been the point? The antipsychotic drugs they had filled her with had left her almost paralysed with exhaustion. The sun radiated through the open blinds, highlighting the fact that everything in the room was bright, sterile white. The hairs on her skin were raised slightly and surrounded by her summer freckles as she lay motionless, staring at the card on the bedside table next to her.

   It contained a simple message of get well soon and had a rather sad-looking picture of a navy-blue heart emblazoned on the front, an irony not lost on her own very lonesome real heart.

   Just past the card was the glass door to the en suite, and within its reflection was the main reason Alice had been lying there mesmerised for hours. She had never believed in antidepressants, or in medication in any form, really. But for so long she had been unable to see anything in the mirror that wasn't tainted by the nightmare creature that was her demonic reflective image. If she just glanced at herself quickly, she would see a perfect reflection. But if a choice had to be made - hair up or hair down? A dress or something more comfortable? - the creature would take over, always announcing its presence first. Its gargling voice was like a tremor through her head, telling her nothing but spiteful and hate-filled mistruths. Then, as her reflection would fade to grey, her skin would peel and crack and her teeth, rotting and broken, would start to fall out. She would see only the creature's image. Only that version of herself would remain. And the broken Alice would take over.

But not now. Now her reflection was real. What she saw was still far from perfect. The image seemed blurred a little. Fuzzy where it came to the finer details. Like it was still not her, just a lot more her than normal. And she could still hear the creature trying to scream at her. Yet somehow it seemed further away and trapped in such a way that Alice struggled to make out what it was saying. For the first time in a long time, her exhaustion overcame her fear and all she had the strength to do was look at this imperfect reflection of herself while she waited for tomorrow to come and Jacob to pick her up.

'Jacob,' she whispered to herself.

Alice hadn't seen him in months, except when he had walked in and saved her from taking her own life during what had been the worst psychosis she had ever had. Actually, the more she thought about it, that was the first psychotic episode she could remember since she had thrown him out. She mused for just a moment that maybe the siren creature she saw was connected to Jacob in some obscure way, but she quickly discounted the notion. She was just broken, numb and unable to move in any substantial way. She was still feeling too much right now. The stitches in her neck were small, but they felt like an alien body nesting in her skin, and a gentle throbbing pain reminded her of what she had done to her body that dark and painful day. Her mouth was dry, so she tried to move to reach the plastic safety cup beside her, but her strength had left her as the medication did its best to calm her, to stop her doing anything other than just breathe. Instead, she just lay there, on her side and on her own. Looking straight at her reflection in the glass door. Awaiting the return of the siren, which, somewhere in the distance, she could hear calling her name.

The door to her room opened slowly and with care, and a doctor walked in carrying a small leather-bound file filled to bursting point with paper, all bearing Alice's name. Doctor Luke Fisher was a handsome man, who looked far too young to be in the lofty position of psychiatric consultant, but he had been polite to Alice every time he had stopped in over the past few days, so she gave him a pass each time. His thick-rimmed spectacles made him appear very geek chic, and his naturally curly and messy hair was unashamedly unkempt. Alice thought he would look more at home busking on the high street back home in Canterbury. More Ed Sheeran than Doogie Howser MD.

'Good morning, Alice,' he said with a warm West Coast accent. 'How are you feeling today?'

Alice opened her pastel-pink lips to reply, but no real sound came out.

'Well, that's better than the last time I asked,' the doctor said kindly. 'But at some point, you need to take a step forward with us in beating this.'

Alice averted her gaze in an act of defiance.

'OK, Alice, I'm not here to stress you out, and for that matter neither are any of my staff, but I do need to discuss a few things with you regarding the scars on your thighs and the reason you tried to take your own life.'

Realising this conversation was going to happen at some point whether she liked it or not, Alice took the offer of the doctor's hand and tried to sit upright. He passed her some water and took a seat beside her.

'The scars on my leg are old and from an angst-filled version of myself that I don't really recognise anymore, doctor,' she said while patting her leg almost sarcastically. Her throat hurt at the first full sentence she had uttered since the surgery. 'I don't think that's the problem here.'

'With all due respect, Miss Petalow, I have spoken to your doctor in the UK, and I have your case history here.' He patted the leather binder. 'These scars on your right thigh are completely fresh.'

Alice laughed like it was a lie. 'How fresh?'

'Miss Petalow, you didn't have them when you came here four days ago.'

Alice took her gaze away from the doctor and looked down to where she had just patted her thigh to see small patches of claret forming on the crisp white sheet that covered her lower half. Confused and scared tears started to form and roll down her cheeks.

The doctor relocated to the far side of the room and beckoned over the two nurses who had entered the room behind him. 'How did she hurt herself in a bloody safe room?' he asked them angrily, before realising that Alice could hear him. At that point, the trio lowered their voices so that they were almost inaudible.

They are talking about you, said the distant voice.

They think you're crazy.

'Jacob,' Alice whispered in hope.

Have you learnt nothing, the voice intoned quietly in response.

Autumn 2007
San Diego, California USA

'Well the term "Shared psychosis" is the common definition of what is actually a very rare occurrence, and one of you is going to find this really hard to deal with, I'm afraid,' said Vivian Phillips. 'You need to understand the journey that each of you is about to go through, and preferably without turning on one another. Normally, I'd suggest you go your separate ways whilst you undertake the various therapies we have on offer, but that's not an option, is it, Mr and Mrs Brooking?'

Jacob and Alice looked at one another.

'No,' said Alice. 'Whatever it is, we face it together.'

'Why will this be harder for one of us?' asked Jacob.

'The honest answer will not be easy to hear, Mr Brooking,' said Vivian, 'but I think one of you is to blame, as a shared psychosis usually forms in one and then transmits to the other. If you take away the primary, the secondary will eventually get better, if that makes sense.'

Alice leaned forward with nervous anticipation. 'So, I could be making Jacob ill with my body dysmorphia?'

'Actually, Mrs Brooking, I think it's Jacob who is unknowingly projecting the effects of his personality disorder onto you as his closest companion. Your condition has come much later on in life, whereas Mr Brooking has been affected by his psychosis since his teens.' There was a sadness in Vivian's voice as she shared the one thing she'd been reluctant to say since she'd landed at San Diego International. 'I think you will both struggle to get better while you are together.'

Alice immediately started to well up.

'Doctor,' said Jacob, 'I went through hell and back trying to get myself right for Alice. I nearly died on the godforsaken boat trying to figure myself out. Surely that's a good thing?'

You went to three group therapy classes. Is that really trying?

The creature was subdued, but its voice still rang through Jacob like a church bell, causing him to grip Alice's hand all the harder, a motion that she noticed and reciprocated, whispering, 'It's OK, baby.'

'A few group sessions doesn't fix what you're going through,' said Vivian. 'You are suffering, Jacob. This will be a long, slow process. Are you really willing to risk Alice for that period of time?'

'That's my choice to make, not yours,' snapped Alice in defiance, as she raised her husband's hand, their fingers tightly entwined.

'Mrs Brooking, I couldn't make you leave your husband even if I had the power to do it, and neither would I want to, but you have to understand that folie à deux can be temporary, and you could live a life free of its effects, given time. But Jacob's condition is forever. Things may get better and easier to manage, but he will always be a risk to himself and others with this level of psychosis.' Vivian leaned towards them. 'I just have to advise you to talk about this and communicate about the options in front of you.'

Alice was about to rebuff Doctor Phillips, but before she could do so, Jacob stood up and offered his hand.

'Thank you, Doctor,' he said. 'As always, I'm not hearing what I want from you, but certainly I'm glad I know where I stand moving forward.'

So, you're leaving her, you pathetic excuse for a man.

Jacob reached down and took Alice by the hand. Still weak from the surgery to her neck and the medication flowing through her veins, she struggled to get up without assistance, and despite her fiery demeanour, she was truly struggling right now.

You think leaving her will help? it laughed.

I OWN BOTH OF YOUR SOULS.

18

News From Home
Winter 2009
San Diego, California USA

The San Diego sun was sinking into its final throes as a low-lying sea mist fought to conceal its light early. This was Jacob's favourite part of the day. He'd done two consultancies for the little dockside restaurants just down the strip, and he was about to meet his beautiful Alice for a late lunch that she wholeheartedly deserved after a morning of selling her pictures to a local art gallery. The Alice Petalow range was actually outselling some much more prestigious names in both the shops she sold from, and Jacob was more than a little proud of what she was achieving. Things had been better for them recently, but winter had crept up on them, and Jacob hoped that the magic of the West Coast wouldn't be lost with the change of season. It rarely snowed this far south, but there was certainly much more bite in the air, and when the sun dropped below sea level, it paid to be dressed a little warmer. Jacob sat once again on the decking in front of the boathouse. Marshmallows for his s'mores caramelised on long steel skewers over a roaring firepit, next to a carafe of mulled wine that Alice had lovingly made. Jacob had to be honest, she had done a beautiful job, and he doubted any of his chefs back home could do any better.

Back home - Jacob laughed. Had it ever felt like home? Thinking about the UK, now, reminded him of being kicked from pillar to post by every bully at the Howard George. It reminded him of his family, who never seemed proud of anything he did, and his in-laws, who constantly looked down their noses at him. It reminded him of Evan, who scared him more than any man ever had, and of a litany of mistakes he had made. Alice was his home, and he hoped beyond hope she decided to make the move here permanent. After all, things had been better, for a little while at least. They attended therapy together every Monday and Friday and never left each other's side during the day unless work called.

Jacob's train of thought was pulled quickly from the moment as the breeze picked up a little, causing the firepit to spit aggressively at him while he cautiously rotated his marshmallows in a tight formation.

'Alice, it's nearly ready,' Jacob called. 'It's just a few minutes away, so get your sexy little butt out here.'

Jacob was full of spirit, with Christmas joy abundant in his voice. No reply greeted him, so he gave her another minute before he called once more. Again, his words went unanswered. He started stacking his chocolate and marshmallow sandwiches in soft sugar crackers he had made earlier in the day. It wasn't at all sophisticated, but it was decadent in all the right ways and had become his favourite indulgence that he'd picked up from the natives.

Pulling his tired body up off the bench, he went in search of his wife and found her slumped in the kitchen doorway, tears streaming down her face, a smashed telephone in her grasp.

WHAT have you done?

Ignoring the voice, Jacob ran towards her. 'Baby, what's wrong?'

'It's Mum. Mum's died.' Alice wept into her hands. 'What will I do without my mum?'

Jacob collapsed next to her on the floor and embraced her, wrapping his arms around her as if protecting her from the cold outside. 'I'm here, Pebble, I'm here.'

For a moment, Jacob was all there and nowhere else. She lay cradled in his arms, sobbing as he stroked her back and gently kissed her forehead. He knew nothing he said would help her, so he did all he could to show her that he loved her, to show her that he had her safe in his embrace.

'I've got you,' he whispered. And he meant it.

-

I have always hated flying. It's not who I am; it's not who I will ever be. And I know that's why you are here, why you are watching me. I can feel you here. Your presence is cold on my skin, and your glare constantly tells me that you know I'm afraid. You always appear when I fly. But I must confess, I've not seen you in so long that your presence surprises me. Even after all these years, you still feel new to me. I know you can't hurt me, that your words are just empty threats. That, actually, you are just a process of my mind playing the hate game once again. It's a song I've heard a thousand times. And, yet, as I look at you now, down the aisle of this bloated jet, lying in the open doorway of the cockpit like a coiled spider, too much mass squashed into too small a space, I am once again afraid. Yet I know it's unreasonable, because you are not real. You are not the monster I see in front of me, all teeth and tentacles. You are me. And I will not let this fear choke me. Not now, not when Alice needs me. We don't need you.

BUT YOU DO NEED US, JACOB.

AND WE THINK YOU KNOW THIS.

4pm UK time Wednesday

Alice had said very little during the flight. She had very little to say anyway, but she'd appreciated Jacob holding her hand throughout the journey, even if she knew it was more of a comfort to him than to her. He'd always hated flying but had never let it stop him, and she couldn't help but admire him for that. He'd gripped both her hand and the armrest tightly all the way from Washington, only letting go as the wheels touched down at Gatwick.

As they rode in the taxi on the two-hour drive back to Whitstable, he tried to reassure her a few times, but he knew her heart was broken, and he wasn't going to gloss over her pain with positive reinforcement. Still, she was glad he was there. She didn't want to sleep alone right now, not that she had slept since getting the news three days ago.

6pm Wednesday

Alice opened her arms into a wide embrace and bounded into her father, who gripped her like she was a child once again.

'It's a shame it took something like this to get you back home, monkey.'

Alice knew he had a point, so she gripped him tighter to avoid the combative response she would normally give him.

'Jacob, how are you?' asked the Viking king, not caring what the answer was.

'I'm fine, John. If there's anything I can do, then please don't hesitate to ask.'

John Petalow looked through Jacob with his piercing blue eyes, almost cutting him in two. 'There's nothing you can do, Jacob. There's nothing either of you can do.'

9pm Wednesday

'All these years together, and this is the first time I've been in your bedroom,' said Jacob, trying to lift the gloom a little as they got ready for bed.

Alice slipped a navy silk nightie over her head. It got caught on her ponytail, and she spun around, like a dog chasing its tail, as she tried to twist out of the tangle.

Jacob reached over and unravelled his half-naked wife, pausing to kiss her gently on her forehead.

Alice looked up into Jacob's deep emerald eyes. 'Thank you, baby, for everything.'

'I haven't done anything,' Jacob replied softly.

'You have, baby. You really have. Do you think I don't know you after all these years? The last few months have been wonderful, and I've really seen you try to be the Jacob I know you can be.' Alice paused for a second, before adding a touch of weight to her next sentence. 'I know how much you hated the thought of coming back to Kent. I know this isn't home to you.'

Jacob sat on the edge of the bed and took Alice by the hand. 'My beautiful Pebble, I've never felt at home. I feel constantly lost, like a ship at sea being thrown about by storms and ungodly forces, yet by your side I find comfort, I find warmth and I find nutrition of my body and soul.' Jacob pulled her face round to his own. 'So you never have to thank me for anything that requires me to stand by your side.'

11am Thursday

Alice stood cold and alone, looking down at her mother's recently filled grave. Earlier, the coffin had been lightly covered with a few handfuls of soft dirt that were thrown down onto it by the people who had been close enough to Angela Petalow to be allowed the honour. Alice had been standing there for an hour, while Jacob sat guarding her from a distance of a few hundred feet. He knew not to bother her. This was her time to grieve. He would pick her up if she fell, but for now he waited quietly and patiently. Alice looked up as it started to rain, the cold wind biting and snapping at her exposed neck. A rumble of distant thunder rolled overhead. As she brought her eyes back down to sea level, Alice was surprised to find another woman standing opposite her. The newcomer looked directly into the tear-filled eyes of a heartbroken daughter.

Alice looked at the woman and knew straightaway she wasn't real. She had black eyes and rotting skin and wore a black dress that draped around her, pooling five feet in every direction, like Batman's cape, giving the impression of shadow falling all around her.

I can't remember the last time I saw you without a frame around you. Alice looked at the apparition of the witch in front of her and showed no change of emotion, completely unfazed by the fact that her antagonist had chosen to appear on this sacred day. *Do you really think you can scare me today of all days? I've lost and buried my best friend. So, say what you want, bitch, as it really changes nothing in my empty and desolate heart.*

The creature looked at Alice silently and with utter contempt, tilting its head to the side, almost confused by the audacity of her words.

What makes you think I'm here for you?

The creature's mouth didn't move, and yet Alice heard every word. The rain lashed down harder. Alice dropped to her knees. Her frozen limbs left her watching what unfolded in front of her with little choice. The creature's arms extended down into the grave. Limbs stretched to unnatural lengths as bones broke and skin tore and, finally, the monster tore her mother's body straight through the lid of the coffin.

DO YOU THINK EVERYTHING IS ABOUT YOU?

OH ALICE DEAR, NO!

It was the monster's voice, but the creature spoke through her mother's pale and broken corpse, the lips moving like that of a ventriloquist's puppet. The creature held Angela's body out to Alice almost as an offering, before it rammed its clawed hand straight through Angela's back, tearing the very heart out of her and holding it out for Alice to see, black blood oozing through its fingers. Alice couldn't speak. The creature's jaw cracked open like a boa constrictor, far wider than was physically possible, with the snapping of bones becoming the only sound Alice could hear. Angela looked helplessly at her daughter as the monster put the heart straight into its gaping mouth and, like a seagull trying to eat an overly large fish, swallowed it down whole. The monster clamped its razor-sharp teeth closed with a wicked smile, before its long forked tongue started licking the rotten black blood from its jaws. Alice finally screamed, her throat almost torn open by the magnitude of her release, and in a heartbeat the rain stopped, as if her very voice had commanded it. The creature was gone too, taking Angela's corpse with it and leaving the stench of death lingering in the air.

'Baby, it's time to leave,' said Jacob. 'Your father will be waiting.' He placed his jacket over Alice's freezing shoulders. 'And I'm not sure a scream, no matter how loud, will wake the dead in the way that you want.'

Alice turned around and put her head against Jacob's firm chest.

'I saw it,' she sobbed. 'The creature from the mirror.'

'And did you stand up to it, like the therapist told you to do?'

'I did, baby. I mean, I tried. I really tried.'

Stand up to me?

Is that what was happening as I took your mother's soul to hell? Your mother's heart tasted only of disappointment.

'All you can do is try, Pebble. Your mum would be proud of you. I'm proud of you.' Jacob pulled her in close and kissed the top of her head. 'Never stop being you because of that thing I've inadvertently created.'

'This isn't your fault, Jay.' Alice looked up at him and put a hand on his cheek. 'We both have our demons.'

With no more to say, they started walking back to the car, not letting go of each other for the whole journey back across the sodden grass. If they had nothing else, they at least had each other.

19

Sepia Tone
Winter 2009
Canterbury, Kent UK

John Petalow sat stoically in his favourite chair, a beaten old throne of cracked leather and worn brass. It was an impressive size, and it had to be for the measure of the man. The deep burgundy of the chair fought to dominate a white living room that had only last year been given a fresh and modern look at the behest of his beautiful wife. But John would not consign his chair to a slow death in a second-hand shop. It was his thinking chair, his planning chair and apparently now his melancholy chair, where he would think of Angela and the day she had saved him. He had been fixed from that first kiss 42 years ago. So, what was he now? The old John was seeping back in every day, as proven by the argument he'd had that morning with a fish supplier. A fight that could easily have been avoided for the sake of a lost order of sardines, but he had almost relished the opportunity to put someone in their place and would have throttled the guy on the phone had he been within striking distance. Angela would have told him off, told him to apologise to the poor man, and he would have done it too. He would never let his queen down. But she was dead. And he had no one to answer to anymore – well, except Alice. His angelic daughter had fallen asleep in her mother's jumper while they looked at old photographs of Angela, in which she'd never looked more lovely. He'd covered Alice up with an old throw to keep her warm and pulled her hair from her dribbling lips. She was the very picture of her mother in her thirties and had the pure-of-heart attitude to match that same fire-filled spirit. By all accounts, she hadn't slept since the day her mum had passed, so he sat quite happily, listening to her snore like an overtired puppy; occasionally, she would kick her leg and let out a murmur of discontent at whatever she was chasing in her dream. It was probably a husband that didn't abandon her at the first sign of trouble. Jacob was upstairs, already packing their bags for a flight tomorrow that John knew his daughter didn't want to take. It was too soon. She needed to be home, and this had always been her home – not halfway across the globe, playing fairy tales with that idiot. He could hear Jacob clattering around up there. Maybe he would cave Jacob's skull in and then dump the body in the river that ran behind the house before Alice awoke. Or maybe go and drop him off the coast somewhere in his fishing boat, let a few hungry sea bass nibble at him. John found himself smiling a little too honestly at that thought process and decided a murdered husband probably wasn't what his daughter needed right now. She needed her mum, just like he needed his wife, but right now all she had was him and Jacob.

1984

John waded through a rock pool, trying to find the little fishing net Alice had dropped while trying to catch a small crab running through a shallow.

'You know,' said Angela, 'we really did create something beautiful, didn't we?'

Alice was sitting in her swimming costume, trying to grab the ocean every time the tide washed up to her feet, a tiny giggle bursting from her when the water reached her toes.

'We did, lover, we really did,' said John, bending down to pick up the rescued net from under his foot.

Long before Alice had been born, they had come to Broadstairs beach every August as a summer date. This was the first time they'd brought their little monkey, and it warmed their souls to hear her laugh so freely, her curly red hair thrusting out from under the little white sun hat that Alice would take off as soon as they turned their back. Not that John ever turned his back for long – he was overly protective of them both. He walked over and sat next to his wife, who offered him an overdue kiss. Her bathing suit made her look almost Audrey Hepburn-like, with oversized sunglasses to match. As he pulled his lips away from her, he had to gaze in wonder at just how lucky he was.

'What are you looking at me like that for, baby?' Angela asked playfully.

'Just telling myself not to wake up, because you make me think I'm dreaming at times.'

Angela took her glasses off.

'My darling,' she replied, with nothing but regret in her voice as she brought her other hand up to his cheek. 'You are dreaming.'

-

John awoke in his armchair with a shudder as the painful realisation of the dream seized him. That would be the only way he would see her now, in dreams and in photographs. And it broke his heart.

'Dad.' Alice was awake and upright, the throw wrapped around her like a cowl.

'What is it, poppet?' he replied, rubbing his eyes.

'I want to stay, Dad. I want to come home.'

SHE DOESN'T WANT YOU.

SHE NEVER WANTED YOU.

'But I love you, Alice,' Jacob pleaded.

Alice took his hands in hers and softened her expression to an understanding smile. 'Baby, your love for me has never been in doubt, even in your most despicable moments, and I promise that I love you more than you will ever know. But I need to come home, and I want you to come with me.'

Jacob released her grip with a broken-hearted sigh that resonated from deep inside his blackened soul. 'I can't stay here, Pebble. I hate it more than you know. I've found peace away from this place that I've not found anywhere else.'

Alice took a deep breath before saying the thing she had dreaded more than anything. 'And that's why I have to let you go, baby.'

THIS WAS HER FATHER'S IDEA.

Jacob's demeanour changed in an instant. 'Was this your dad's idea?'

'No, Jay, it wasn't anyone's idea, but thank you for once again blaming every choice you don't agree with on my father. You are aware I have a mind of my own, right?'

SHE'S WALKING AWAY.

'Don't walk away from what we have, Pebble, please.'

Alice looked her husband in the eye one last time before she turned for the door. 'I'm not walking away from anything, Jay. Don't you see? I'm tired of running from things, so it's time to come home. Where you see your place in all that is completely up to you.'

2010

Alice pulled the protective wrap off the brand-new sign above her new studio. Papillon Noir. Written in a gloss ebony on a white backdrop, the sign was exactly what she had wanted, and the local company she had used had captured her vision with gusto. She had found the store by accident while shopping for her father's birthday present one sunny afternoon. She had tripped almost acrobatically over the front step while dancing down the little cobbled street with her headphones playing far too loud and had ended up almost falling through the 'For sale' sign. It was an old building with stone walls and exposed brickwork. She had fallen in love instantly and had pressed her face tightly against the glass door as she tried to figure out how best to turn this beautiful room into a business. And now, just three months later, it was nearly ready. She had used up most of her inheritance in advance to make it happen, but she knew that this was her true calling in life. She pulled back the smaller sign underneath like it was the unveiling of her life plan.

'Papillon Noir by Alice Petalow,' she read out loud with glee, completely content with her choice of font and colour. Her name was written in a rich jade green, giving it an air of class that prompted her to whisper to herself, 'That'll do nicely, Pebble.'

Alice hung the last of her watercolours up on the brick wall behind the small seating area she had designed for her more prestigious customers and took a step back to check it was level with the others. The shop was now filled with her own work, a lot of which Jacob had sent over to her from the US, and it left a feeling of pride resonating within her. Photos she had taken at various beaches across the world were available to buy for a small fee, with the larger paintings fetching upwards of £1,000 each. Whitstable was an affluent town, and she could really make this work if she played up to the right people, so she kept a couple of overpriced French wines in the back for those who needed a little help loosening up. In fact, a glass of Château Cheval was exactly what she needed now to celebrate. She poured herself a glass and slumped onto the forest-green chesterfield to admire her handiwork.

'I wish you were here to see this, Mum,' she said to herself.

Not for the first time, she felt a surge of loneliness wash over her as she realised the creature's voice was not the only one that had left her recently; she could no longer hear her mum's reassurance, and it scared her that she was doing this alone. But she was going to make this work. She had to make this work. This was her opportunity to shine.

20

The Crow and the Girls
Summer 2011
San Diego California USA

The girl was a perfect representation of a teenage boy's dream. With the curves of her body making her look like a Coke bottle, she could have been a centrefold. Curls of brown hair rolled in cascades down the length of her spine, pooling into the small of her back with an almost chaotic beauty. She was angelic – or at least she would have been had she not been passed out and drenched in sweat. Jacob watched her lying face down on the Egyptian cotton sheets that he had purchased the day before at an obscene cost and nearly spat his wine out in disgust at what he had just done to a girl half his age upon them. He would cut her loose in a few days, of that he had no doubt, and yet an hour ago he could have told her he loved her. In truth, he couldn't love anyone but Alice. He would give the girl some excuse about work or maybe going back to the UK. But she wouldn't be the last to fall for his charms. In fact, she probably wouldn't be the last this week, and it sickened him that he didn't need a creature in his head to tell him how sad and pathetic he had become. But whether he needed that negative voice or not wasn't relevant, as it hadn't said anything lately that had caused him too much bother. On his bad days, he heard whispers and hisses of spite, but even these were few and far between, with the meditation and group therapy pulling him through what the doctor's elixirs could not. The creature that had spoken to Jacob all his adult life had retreated into the recesses of his mind, causing a calm to wash over him that he had never felt before. He felt that he could describe his bipolar best through colours, and that there was very little middle ground. If he was manic, he was red; low would be blue; and the rigmarole of day-to-day life left him vanilla, with no shades in between. And yet since he had started his treatment, he had only felt grey. Somehow, the monster, although retreated, seemed more dangerous than ever as it whispered rather than screamed its intentions to him.

The bedroom at the boathouse had full-length windows running along the west wall, and the setting sun was reflecting off the latest conquest's skin in a kind of holy radiance. Jacob poured himself another glass of Harlan Estate Cabernet Sauvignon and continued to hate on himself for the man he had become and the situation he once again found himself in. He wanted her gone but couldn't quite figure out how to remove her without having to talk to her first, and talking to her was not something he wanted to do.

    As he took another sip of his wine, his eyes were drawn quickly to the large carrion crow watching him from the patio railings on the other side of the open French doors. The bird was easily the size of a seagull, and Jacob could hear its beak clashing against the railing as it tried desperately to rid itself of an itch. Jacob admired the beauty of the beast for a moment more before turning his attention back to the wine glass in his hand. 'How have you ended up here again?' Jacob whispered to himself, wondering how much Californian poison was left in his cellar. The crow answered his question with a loud *kraa*, which echoed through the bedroom, and opened its wings into a flutter that gave the impression that it was flexing its dominance over the scene. This impression hardened as the flutter turned to flight and the giant creature glided through the open door and perched on the thigh of the unconscious wench. Jacob didn't even react; he had seen too much these past ten years to be scared by such things, and he knew full well this could easily and most likely be part of an oncoming psychosis.

You know you can't stop, said the voice calmly and quietly.

And do you even want to stop without Alice here to pull you up on your behaviour?

Its voice, now almost constantly persuasive rather than the spiteful aggression Jacob had known for so many years, seemed to be coming from the direction of the crow rather than the space at the back of his mind where only the dark things were kept.

The bird started to walk up and down the bare skin of the girl. Its long, sharp talons, as ebony as anything Jacob had ever seen, were piercing her soft flesh with each little hop the bird took, leaving a trail of thin blood lines running the length of her leg. The natural reaction to this would have been to help the poor girl, who didn't even stir at the pain. But Jacob couldn't find the compassion to help a person he held absolutely no feeling for.

You really are broken, the creature called out as the crow tilted its head at Jacob with a knowing glare.

Jacob grinned, hearing the voice whisper in his mind. The creature's barbs had very little power over him since his doctor had found a balance of antipsychotics that worked; the medication helped Jacob safely across most hurdles and gave him the strength to argue back. Jacob could even find the creature's comments amusing at times.

'You know I don't have to listen to your shit anymore. I can shut you out at any time,' Jacob scoffed arrogantly.

Then why don't you, Jacob? the creature cackled. *Why don't you just wish me away? And maybe, while you're doing that, you can click the heels of your ruby slippers and take yourself home too? Oh, but you can't, can you? Because there is no one there for you anymore. Tell me, Jacob, do you keep me here sedated in the back of your mind just because you are lonely?*

Jacob let out a deep sigh as he listened to the voice echo simultaneously from behind his eyes and from the beak of the bird. He knew the creature was right, but he had to admit that he took just a little pleasure taunting It all the same. It was what It had done to him for 30-odd years.

The crow turned its attention back to the girl and started to take little bites out of her skin. Strips of fair flesh were consumed with each dip of the crow's fat neck, and yet Jacob still couldn't intervene.

Downing the rest of the glass, he pulled himself up while letting his bath towel fall to the floor around his feet. He felt no shame in front of the large bay window and didn't even blink at the baying murder of crows watching him from the patio. He counted six at first, with two more joining the flock a minute or so later. With both caws and kraas as his orchestra, he presented himself brazenly in front of his audience while he emptied the last of his wine bottle into his glass – a glass that was swiftly downed, before a loud snore brought his attention back to where it needed to be. He glanced over his shoulder to find the lead crow staring through his very soul.

Your humanity has left you, Jacob. You think you have me controlled, but look at what you have become.

The crow snapped its beak at him before driving it deep into the meat of the girl's leg.

'SHUT UP,' Jacob shouted with authority but absolutely no anger as he threw the empty bottle, which smashed into the bedside unit, destroying a lamp and a picture frame in the process.

The drunk waitress from the dockside bar down at the beach sat bolt upright, her complexion whitewashed with fear, panic and intoxication. 'Oh my god, what just happened?'

The bird disappeared, as Jacob had imagined it would. There was no sign of the horror it had inflicted on her leg. He turned back to his view and watched the seemingly real crows leave one by one.

'Sorry, love, did I wake you?' Jacob smirked without even turning to face her.

'God, my head's killing me.' The girl struggled to wake herself and rubbed her eyes frantically. 'Honey, can you take me out for something to soak some of this wine up?' She stretched her arms wide above her head.

'Sorry, Clare, I have work to do. In fact, I'm going to be a little snowed under for a few weeks now.'

'It's Clara! And you didn't seem that busy with work when you were trying to get my clothes off in the bar last night?'

She's called you out quicker than most, maybe we have misjudged her.

'You need to go, love,' said Jacob. 'I can't help being busy. I'll call you in a day or two.'

'You know what, jerk, don't bother.'

Clara started grabbing pieces of clothing from around the room and virtually fell out of the front door, still putting her boots on. Her mood mattered little to Jacob, who doubted he would ever see her again. And, honestly, he didn't care.

What have you become? the creature laughed.

I don't know, Jacob thought. *But I know it's better than hurting Alice.*

Spring 2012
Canterbury, Kent UK

The chime of the little copper bell rang once more as a man opened the door for his partner. Taking her hand, he helped her up the front step before guiding her through the open door into Papillon Noir and its bustling interior. Alice greeted them with a wave and a nod but was mid conversation with another couple, who were about to blow a filthy amount of money on two of her oil paintings of the Reculver coastline, just a few miles down the road. For now, the newcomers would have to wait, and in fairness they seemed content to browse the work on the wall.

Business was good and the money was growing daily; Alice was already starting work on a second studio just a few miles outside of Canterbury city centre.

'OK, you have a deal,' said the stern-faced old husband, who had clearly been dragged here kicking and screaming by his much younger and more attractive trophy wife.

Alice was fairly sure this woman wasn't spending her own money, and thinking of what such a pretty young lady would have to do in order to get what she wanted from this fat old aristocrat made her skin crawl, although in fairness they probably both got what they wanted from the relationship.

'Thank you, Mr Whittingham,' said Alice. 'I'll organise our courier to deliver both pictures framed to your door on Friday, if that works for you both?'

Alice offered her hand to close the deal and the old pervert kissed it like she was one of his handmaidens. She shared a short look with his wife and realised quickly that the woman didn't give a damn. *You would be doing me a favour* was the message that the woman seemed to be conveying to Alice, who felt her skin crawl again. Still, five grand for three pictures was a good deal, and it made her realise that maybe she was a better artist than she gave herself credit for.

As soon as the transaction was concluded, Alice bounded over to the new couple. 'I am ever so sorry about the wait. Is there anything I can get you to drink while you have a look at what we have to offer?'

'No, my dear. We know what we are here for.'

The man pointed to a large oil painting above the entrance. The painting was of the Camber beachfront in East Sussex: golden sand and a deep blue ocean contrasted by a morning sunrise that almost looked like a photograph.

'The Camber piece. Well, I have a funny story about that if you would care to listen?' Alice offered the seating to the couple with a wave of her hand.

The couple sat down, and Alice continued with a sparkle in her eye but an almost regretful tone in her voice.

'Me and my husband - well, ex-husband - own a restaurant in Camber, and for the time that I lived there, I would walk down to the beach each morning and try to draw the ocean. Nothing would ever look right. It was as if the paper was rejecting the magic I saw in front of me.'

The wife, who was gripping her husband's hand, motioned to Alice to continue.

'And then, years later, I was sitting at home one night and I saw it, and even though I was thousands of miles away, I finished it in one sitting.'

The husband stood up and took Alice's hand. 'We'll take it. We loved it anyway. The story just adds another layer to it.'

'Great. Would you like it gift-wrapped or delivered?' Alice asked, before being interrupted by a man at the door.

'Or I could help you take it to the car,' said Jacob, taking off his sunglasses and looking his wife directly in the eye.

Alice closed the door behind the couple before wrapping her arms around Jacob. 'What are you doing here? I haven't heard from you in months.'

She went to release him, but he held on tight and kissed the top of her head continuously.

'I've just missed you,' he said, 'and missing you has slowly turned to needing you.'

Jacob finally let her go and placed a hand on her cheek.

Alice pulled away from him slowly. 'I get that, baby. But why now?'

'I've finished my therapy. I'm happy with my medication. I guess I finally felt ready to come home.' Jacob pulled up her chin with his index finger. 'Baby, I've moved home.'

Jacob finished the sentence by kissing her powerfully on the lips.

In reply, Alice slapped him hard across the face. 'How dare you think you can just waltz back into my world, into my gallery, and after nearly two years just slide back into my life?'

Jacob brought his hand up to his stinging face. He didn't dare reply until Alice had finished speaking.

'I've not heard a voice in my head for nearly 12 months, baby. I wanted to be right before I spoke to you. I couldn't risk making you ill.' Jacob placed his hands gently around hers. 'I love you, Alice.'

'Don't,' Alice snapped.

This prompted Jacob to bring himself down to Alice's eye level and interlock his fingers through hers.

'I LOVE YOU!' he said, one last time, before Alice jumped forward and pushed her tongue straight into his mouth.

Dumbstruck by the sudden move, Jacob staggered back a little, but failed to shake Alice's grip. Like a strong tide throwing a child to shore, she pulled him and guided them both into the back room. Jacob first took in the smell of paint and new canvas, noticing how messy the studio was in contrast to the pristine gallery. Before he had time to dwell on it, Alice pushed him up against a workbench and started to unbutton his jeans, her tongue not leaving his mouth. She made light work of his belt and dropped to her knees. Jacob, still not knowing what had hit him, let out a deep moan as she pulled his growing cock from the confines of the tight hipsters he always wore.

'Baby, I ...'

Jacob's words were cut off as Alice took him deep into her wanting mouth. Gladly accepting his fate, he ran his fingers through her hair and fell into a world of bliss that lasted only as long as Alice allowed, because as soon as he was hard enough, she pushed him aside with commanding authority and pulled herself up onto the workbench. Alice hoisted her light blue summer dress up around her thighs, and in one fluid and almost perfectly practised motion, she lost her underwear, gripped a fistful of Jacob's hair and forced his head between her thighs. She knew what she wanted, and she was getting it from the only man she had ever wanted it from. She bit down on her lip so hard that the metallic taste of her own blood filled her mouth.

'Baby, I want you,' Alice begged.

He rose up to kiss her lips, pulling her legs around him. He easily entered her wanting body and drove himself into her until they were a writhing body of orgasmic pleasure. They didn't stop to take breath, as is the way with two people in love when they have been kept apart for so long. Jacob's strokes were slow and measured but deep and powerful nevertheless.

'Come for me, baby. I want to feel you inside of me, I've missed you so much.'

Jacob didn't need telling twice, and as his hips ground against hers, faster and deeper than ever before, he kissed her and filled her with everything he had to give.

'Pebble, I love you,' he said in a gentle voice, broken only by his need for oxygen. They soon lay in an embrace, trying to regain their breath, with Jacob stroking Alice's back gently. She clung to him like a koala, and no words were needed to explain the feelings of fear and excitement they both felt.

Alice waited to hear the voice reappear, but she heard nothing. She hoped that Jacob had the same luck, but the creature had other ideas as to what he deserved.

21

Fragmenting
Summer 2013
Whitstable Bay, Kent UK

A year had passed and finally Whitstable felt like home once more. The sound of the ocean lashing against the coastline felt like an old friend, while the smell of fresh fish coming off the harbour took him back to his youth every time he opened the car window.

Jacob was waiting in his Mercedes outside of Papillon Noir for Alice to finish getting ready. Why she hadn't chosen to get changed at home he couldn't figure out, but he admired her drive in pushing the business forward, as she had no doubt worked right up until the very second he had pulled up outside and beeped his horn. He had found a different Alice on his return to England. She was strong and independent. She was still 'his Alice', of course, but she was also something more now, and he couldn't stop telling her how very proud of her he was.

His daydream shattered as the car door popped open and his flame-haired soulmate looked back at him from the passenger door.

'Hey, handsome.'

She giggled like a schoolgirl, like she always did when she saw him, and he wouldn't have changed it for the world.

Jacob patted the passenger seat. 'Baby, we'll miss our table if you don't get that cute little ass in this car.'

Alice, who was wearing a beautiful summer dress in a dandelion-yellow shade, slid in next to him. Light caught the glitter on her pristine white heels, which matched a bangle on her left wrist. Her style was always simple, yet she accessorised with such elegance that she never had to wear designer clothes. Jacob was fairly sure that since the day he had met her gaze across the playground all those years before, she had never once looked bad. In fact, it was a constant sense of wonder to him how he had ever got such a beautiful creature to look at him in the same way he looked at her.

They pulled into the car park of the beautiful seaside pub. The Sportsman at Seasalter was the best restaurant in the area, and they had made it with ten minutes to spare. Jacob jumped out of his Mercedes and rushed over to the passenger side to open the door for his beautiful wife. He was ever the gentleman; it was a character trait he had got from his father and one that Alice had always found highly attractive in her man.

The sunlight was starting to fade as they were shown to their table. Jacob was pleased to see his favourite dish on the specials board as they passed it.

'You see that, Pebble?' Jacob nudged Alice as he pulled the chair out from under the table for her.

'Your slip-sole special? I did, my love. I might have it too today to see what all the fuss is about.'

An attractive young waitress was immediately on hand with a wine menu, but Jacob interjected quickly with a smile.

'I can't drink tonight,' he said, 'so just a mineral water for me, but my beautiful wife will have the most ridiculously priced glass of champagne you have to offer.'

The waitress smiled at Alice and tilted her head, pulling the wine menu to her heart. 'A special occasion, Mrs Brooking?'

'I don't think so,' said Alice. 'Oh, Jesus – it's our anniversary.'

She mouthed an apology to her smiling husband as he reached for her hand across the table.

'Pebble, you are working so hard that I didn't want you stressing over tonight. I love you.'

Two courses in, the conversation was flowing as easily as ever, with Alice giggling herself into tears on more than one occasion. Things had really seemed different these past few months, and Jacob's return had never felt like a mistake. But as she topped up her glass with the last of the wine, she realised her anniversary was about to fall apart. Alice went pale with shock at the sight of the man being seated behind Jacob.

'Pebble, are you OK?' Jacob asked, concerned for his wife, who looked like she'd seen a ghost.

Her silence did nothing to put his concerns to rest, so he turned to see what had paralysed his wife with fear.

'Is that Tom from the rugby club?' he said. 'I've not seen him in years, the pretentious prick. I never liked him. Looks like he's put on some timber, though.'

Jacob smiled to himself as he turned back to his meal, content that nothing serious had startled Alice. But as he looked at her again, he realised something was still wrong. 'Baby, what is it?'

Jacob took her hand, and Alice jumped as if she had left the room for a second and not realised she had returned to the table.

'Baby,' said Jacob, 'what on earth has got into you?'

Alice shook her head clear and tried her hardest to remain calm. 'I'll tell you on the way home, baby. Let's not ruin our dinner.'

WHAT THE FUCK WAS THAT?

SHE'S HIDING SOMETHING!

-

Jacob stood behind Alice as he wrapped her large Moroccan silk scarf over her shoulders, kissing the back of her neck as he did so. He was unsure what had been wrong for the last hour, but it hadn't taken away from how much he wanted to ravish her. Nothing would stop that happening tonight. Noticing Thomas looking at her, Alice dropped her gaze and turned to leave. Jacob got the door for her as they said their goodbyes to the waiting team, before making their way over to the car.

'So, tell me, what's been up?' Jacob asked politely, but making it known that his curiosity as to what had nearly ruined their night had been piqued.

'Can we talk about it when we get home, baby?'

Alice didn't want to say any more than she had, which only drove Jacob harder.

He pulled her round by her arm. 'Pebble, what the hell happened?'

Alice knew by his tone that she couldn't escape this situation any longer, and she let out a sigh of immense proportions. 'OK, but I need you to stay calm.'

But she knew that wouldn't happen.

-

Alice had been sitting alone in the car for 20 minutes. Jacob hadn't said a word during the whole conversation they'd had; however, his facial expression had said enough to put the fear of god into Alice. To his credit, he had held her hand tight while she explained her history with that pig Thomas, and he had brought her hand to his lips gently before he got out the car, whispering that he loved her as he walked back to the restaurant front door without breaking stride. She hoped he was OK, but more than that, she hoped he didn't kill Thomas. She wanted Thomas dead of course, and she had done for years, but she wasn't prepared to lose Jacob for 15 years in the process.

The car door opened, and Jacob jumped in without a mention of what had happened.

'Shall we go, my beautiful Alice?'

He pressed the ignition and pulled away before he had even put his seatbelt on. His knuckles were red and bruised and there were flecks of blood on the sleeve of his shirt. It was clear what had happened, but Alice didn't care; she just needed to know he was OK.

She placed her hand on his thigh. 'I love you, baby.' A stream of tears trickled down her cheek.

WHORE, the reflection in the window whispered to Alice.

Ten minutes before

Thomas lay bleeding on the floor of the restaurant bathroom. His mouth and nose were busted open in a mess of claret and broken bone, while one of his eyes had swollen so badly it would be a month before he saw clearly out of it again, and yet as he tried to draw breath into his cracked ribcage, he knew he couldn't go to the police. He knew he had more to lose than Jacob did. Jacob's blood-stained Timberland boot crunched down on Thomas's hand, and through the ringing in his ears, Thomas heard the last warning he would ever get in relation to Alice Petalow.

'If you EVER so much as look at her again, I'll kill you. If we walk into a restaurant, you walk out, do you understand?'

Thomas nodded as best he could. He started to black out as he watched his attacker walk away. His last sensation before his body shut down was a complex mix of guilt and hatred, but underneath it all was a question. *Who had Jacob Brooking been talking to while he was hitting me?*

Monday

Why was Thomas in her house, anyway?

Can you answer that?

'She's allowed friends,' Jacob bit back.

Sounds like they were more than friends, don't you think?

'I know what you're doing.' Jacob clenched his fist at the unseen adversary. 'It won't work, I'm telling you straight.'

What I'm doing? all I'm doing, is telling the truth.

'I won't let you get to me.'

A resilience in Jacob's voice made the creature grin within his mind.

Do you think I'm stupid, Jacob?

'Sick, evil and twisted, maybe, but no, I don't think you're stupid, although maybe I am for having this conversation with myself.'

Then ask yourself where I'm getting my thought process from. For if I am you and you are me, then surely you know the truth, the same as I do?

'What truth?' Jacob snapped.

She wanted it while you were winning her father's favour, laughed the creature.

'Shut up.'

Tuesday

You must have noticed.

'I noticed nothing, and I had an amazing time,' Jacob said while making the bed that he had just shared with his wife.

Well, sure you did, but did she? the creature mocked.

'Of course she did. She always does.'

She felt distant to me, like she was somewhere else or with someone else.

'Don't be stupid.' Jacob laughed. 'It's hardly an area I struggle with, is it?'

Your ego means nothing here. She wanted you to take her from behind an awful lot last night. Strange, no?

'Not really, why would it be?'

She normally likes to kiss you while you make love, doesn't she? Seems strange that has changed since you sorted Thomas out. The creature gurgled its deep and broken laugh as it spoke.

'I know what you're doing.'

I'm just letting you know what I saw last night, and you had better believe that I see everything.

'Just shut up.'

But ...

'NO! SHUT UP!'

Wednesday

You never were a good chef.

'Because she didn't finish her lunch? Give me a break. She wasn't hungry.'

Jacob wasn't about to be pulled up on his cooking; it was the one thing he was sure he was good at.

She didn't look interested, in lunch or in you.

Jacob had no time for the creature's games today. 'SHUT UP!'

What exactly are you going to do if I don't, you disgusting and pathetic excuse for a man? YOU HAVE NOTHING THAT SCARES ME.

'I preferred you when I was haunted by you at the bottom of my bed. This medication just makes you talk more.'

Jacob's voice trembled, but he believed in every word that he threw at the creature. Lately, the creature had just spoken to him. It never appeared to him physically, like it used to. The antipsychotics he was taking day and night seemed to keep the worst of its voice at bay, but he still heard it speaking to him, and it had been worse since Sunday's incident. Jacob looked down at his still-swollen knuckles. Why had Thomas even been at her father's house, a place that Jacob had rarely been welcome? It was a question he didn't need the creature to ask; he had asked it a thousand times himself. Why had he been working 16-hour days just to show John Fucking Petalow he was worthy of being on Alice's arm, while she was making friends with the captain of the rugby team? Jacob waited for the voice, but nothing came, and he had a sickening feeling that wasn't a good sign.

Thursday

Jacob had been looking in the shed for at least a quarter of an hour, and yet the gloss paint that Alice swore was buried in here was still missing. He was getting frustrated and didn't want to be in this nightmare haven for arachnids, some of which were bigger than the desert recluse he would sometimes see run across the deck in San Diego. Jacob pulled out a drawer from under his workbench and saw the missing paint hiding under the old picnic blanket they used to take to Camber with them each summer, but as he pulled the blanket away, he disturbed the queen of all spiders, which had apparently made its home, with its sac of a thousand children, underneath. It ran at him as if startled by the light, and Jacob, in a hurry to avoid the raging beast, fell backwards, smashing his head against the lawnmower, which was hanging against the wall.

'I fucking give up today,' he swore, as he brought his hand to the back of his scalp to find the extent of the damage.

The spider, startled by the sudden noise and movement, darted under Jacob's old toolbox for safety.

'Yeah, you'd better hide, you little bastard.'

Jacob brushed himself down as he stood up. Through the shed's cheap plastic window and the patio doors to the cottage, he could see that Alice was on the phone to someone. The conversation looked heated. Was that why she'd sent him out to look for something she knew was hidden away? Was it another man?

YOU KNOW WHO IT IS!

The screaming went through Jacob, and he looked for the source of the voice, as for once he didn't feel it originate from within his own head. The origin was somewhere within the confines of the shed. As the noise spun him around, he felt drawn to the rear. The back of the shed was pitch black and looked longer than Jacob remembered it. He took a few tentative steps forward, noticing that the more he tried to look into the dark corners, the narrower and more nightmarish they became. Eventually, something took his eye, something glistening white and grid-like just in front of him. Carefully, he reached forward to take it, his eyes drawn to it because it was the only thing in the recess of the shed that wasn't ebony black. Before Jacob realised his mistake, the white grid opened into what was actually a mouth containing a thousand tiny white fangs. The giant spider, which was easily eight feet in height, lurched forward as its shiny jet-black body was caught by the light pouring in through the window. It clamped its massive jaws onto Jacob's upper arm and shrieked with joy as it tasted the man's blood exploding in its mouth. Jacob cried out in pain, but he fell silent again as the spider's arms wrapped around him. Its eight limbs were all chitinous, like those of a crab, but with coarse black hairs protruding from every crack in its armour. Still trapped in its bloodied jaws, Jacob found himself face to face with the creature. Its many eyes, all like obsidian stone, were polished to such a degree that he could see his image in every one, yet in every eye the reflection was different. All were versions of Jacob, some laughing hysterically, others crying and heartbroken, all of them alone, but one of the faux Jacobs lay on the ground, his arm torn open and bloodied. The creature bit down again, and

Jacob felt his arm bone shatter into pieces as the spider tore it clean off, as easily as pulling chicken from the bone. Jacob pulled away and thrashed around the shed while the missing limb was replaced by a pressured fountain of crimson. Unable to take the pain, Jacob blacked out, leaving the giant creature smiling, with blood rolling off its hard carapacelike rain off a windshield.

Friday

'So, you woke up in the shed with your arm torn to shreds by the gardening shears and no giant spider in sight?'

'No spider and no sign there ever was one.' Jacob spoke quietly; he was completely defeated.

Dr Phillips looked over her glasses at Jacob. 'How long has it been since you last self-harmed, Mr Brooking?'

'Two years, give or take,' Jacob replied, with a little pride still intact.

'And you feel the medication is working?'

Jacob sat upright before he answered, looking Vivian Phillips square in the eye. 'I think I could certainly up my dose.'

NO! NO! NO!

22

The Drugs Don't Work
Summer 2014
Whitstable Bay, Kent UK

Alice stomped her feet theatrically in a show of frustration. 'I wanna go out, Jay!'

'Then go out, baby,' Jacob responded calmly, without looking up from his book. 'I'm not stopping you.'

'I want to go out *with you*, douchebag,' said Alice, in full tantrum mode, almost jumping up and down while she protested.

'Why do we need to go out today? It's Sunday. That's my day of rest.'

Jacob gave a little grin at his joke, but he knew it was about to backfire.

'Well, I'm sorry, my lord, but the flaw in your statement is that we don't do anything any day anymore!' Alice took a seat next to him. 'I'm sorry, baby. I know the medication is hitting you hard, but the sun's shining and our cameras have sat idle for months now. Just come for a walk with me, maybe?'

Jacob looked up from his book and got trapped in her eyes like a deer caught in headlights. 'Of course, let me get dressed.' His response was half-hearted, like everything he did lately.

She's bored of you.

'I know,' Jacob whispered to himself as he put on a clean shirt.

Better off without you.

'She would be, I have no doubt.'

-

It was hot down on the seafront, the kind of hot he imagined would set vampires on fire even if they were in the shade. Jacob had stripped down to the skin, with only his jean shorts and olive-green Adidas on, to try to cool off a little. His skin was burning under the intense heat of the sun's rays, and he felt good for absorbing some of the sun's power; he felt almost fixed and recharged by its light. He had hoped to get some nice pictures of Alice, but it had become impossible to keep up with her as she bounced excitedly from rare flower to exotic butterfly. She was a feather from the wing of an angel, and she was forever caught in the gust of a whirlwind. She was infectious with her positivity, though, and after being shut in the house for two weeks trying to deal with the effects of his change in medication, it was a blessing for Jacob to be soaking in more than the effects of the sun. Alice darted over to the fence of the nature reserve, which ran parallel to the harbour bay, and stood watching the herons fish for dinner, their long legs wading in and out of the marshland as smaller birds played around them. Jacob pulled his camera up to his eye and adjusted his lens to bring Alice into focus. She looked radiant as always, and her hair seemed all the more electric in the light of the summer sun. Jacob was hesitating to take the shot due to a figure lurking in the background who was clearly intent on draining the colour from his picture, as she wore nothing but grey and black while doing a fantastic impression of the word dishevelled. Her hair was as long as Alice's but almost black with filth. She hovered behind Alice as if she was about to pick her pocket, and it gave Jacob a sense of unease that felt strangely familiar. He pulled the camera away and rubbed his eyes before bringing the camera back up to refocus. His dark guest had left the shot. Actually, she had more than left the shot; she was gone. Jacob couldn't see her anywhere. He quickly snapped three shots while Alice pretended not to pose, and he smiled at his luck as she turned to face him, bit her lip and then ran off giggling. He walked slowly behind his excited girl as she flitted from side to side, skipping to a beat she could clearly only hear in her own thoughts. He knew he didn't deserve her. He knew she deserved more than he offered her. He hadn't wanted to come today; he wished he was home now. He had promised everyone that he would stick to his medication, and no matter the cost, he wouldn't break that vow. But it had hit him hard. He hadn't adapted well to the lithium. He was sleeping most of the day, while Alice ran two studios, and he was hardly being proactive when he was awake. He was getting to the gym at least, but even then he was a hood-up, music-on kind of guy. No one dared talk to him, and he was glad of that. He hadn't shaved in weeks, and he had never had a full-enough beard to pull off the fuzz that adorned his face. The constant tiredness wasn't just physical, though, as he actually felt numb inside too and imagined that he was coming across completely uninterested in everything Alice was bringing to the table each night. That was of course far from the truth, and he had never loved her more. But Jacob was finding it hard to get excited about anything of late, and Alice was noticing more each day.

'Come on, misery guts,' she called over her shoulder.

'I'm here, baby,' Jacob called out, not wanting to spoil her day.

He caught up with her staring out to sea, her beautiful red hair fluttering in the breeze, and was instantly in love with her all over again.

'Baby, you still love me, right?' said Alice.

'What? Of course I bloody love you. Where has this come from?'

Alice slipped her fingers through his and returned her eyes to the ocean. 'You never want to do anything with me anymore, baby. I feel like getting you to spend time with me is an effort you would never consider unless I was nagging you to do it.'

Jacob knew she was right, but it wasn't because he didn't love her. If he knew anything in this life, he knew that. 'I'll try harder. I promise I will.'

Jacob could hear a voice in his head saying something, but it was too distant to understand, and so, assuming the medication was doing its job, he allowed himself to be a little more positive for a second.

'How about a paddle?' he suggested.

'Mr Brooking, you do know the way to my heart after all.' Alice giggled as she skipped and stumbled down the pebble bank into the sea.

'I love you,' Jacob whispered to himself. 'I'd do anything for you.'

Winter 2014

Whitstable Bay, Kent UK

In the floor-length mirror was something Alice had only seen once before: fear and panic in the black soulless eyes of the creature. Its hands, withered and claw-like, were pressed against the glass portal, and it was pleading for help.

It was still Alice in demon form, and yet the creature seemed to be making more of an effort to look like its counterpart as it tried to find a middle ground to meet Alice on.

SAVE HIM, it begged, for it knew without him there was no existence.

WE LOVE HIM.

The creature dropped to its knees as it gazed at the real world from its prison and saw the only thing that could possibly scare it. Jacob was lying in Alice's lap. He gripped her hand tightly with one of his own, while his left arm fell limp to the side, cut from elbow to hand. The creature watched tears roll down Alice's face as she grieved for the man she loved. And then, in Jacob's last heartbeat, it ceased to exist. And it was free of its prison. Dissipating into the nothingness of the void, it failed to hold its form, and then there was silence.

One hour before

You won't do it.

Jacob sat in the freezing bath, horrified at the task in front of him. He was sure of what he had to do, but that made it no less painful. He was tired of his existence and his sad little life. He had been unhappy for so long that he couldn't remember a time when he had felt consistently content in his world. And yet his own misery wasn't the reason he was here in the endgame; it was the misery he had put onto Alice and the realisation it wasn't getting any better after 20 long years together. For a long time, he had infected her with a negative mindset that was down to him not accepting the chip on his shoulder, which had developed solely from years of being bullied. When he'd refused to believe that someone as fantastic as Jacob Brooking could have any kind of mental illness, he'd started to transfer his condition onto her. And now, heavily medicated and too tired to respond to the voices in his head, he realised she was bored of him. She hadn't said as much, but he knew she deserved more. He didn't want to go out anymore; his drive was gone, his passion was waning and his ability to surprise her had been lost so that he could safely live a mundane life. And his beautiful Alice – so creative, so full of life – well, she deserved more. He could just leave, of course, but he knew he would always be drawn back to her. Jacob had watched her flourish when he was in San Diego. Watched her start her own company and watched that company grow. Her painting had improved beyond recognition, and her work now fetched obscene amounts of money on a regular basis. His Alice deserved someone of equal stature, someone who would help her smile and could excite her with every touch. She deserved to be free, and as he picked up the short-bladed lock knife that he had taken rock climbing with him years before, when he had a life outside of his cage of misery, he knew that she would be.

DON'T DO IT.

The pain was overwhelming and frightened him into believing he had made a grave mistake. He clambered out of the bath and stumbled at every hurdle, smashing his body against every piece of furniture en-route to his phone, which was downstairs on the kitchen table. He realised he wouldn't make it that far when he fell down the last six steps and collapsed in the hall. The bathroom towel wrapped round his forearm was soaked red and dripping with blood. He was starting to feel the life slip away from him, when the front door opened and his wife, in shock, froze in the entrance.

Save him, the voice said to Alice, sounding as scared as she looked.

'JAY, WHAT HAVE YOU DONE?'

She rushed over to pick him up, but Jacob was too heavy for her to lift. He collapsed down again, falling into her lap; his wound bled freely onto her white dress and a puddle started to form around where they lay. Alice fumbled for her mobile phone, but before she could enter any numbers, Jacob used the last of his strength to push it out of her hand; the phone clattered to the floor, swimming in the red fluid that was pooling around them both.

'Baby, what have you done?' Alice repeated. 'I need to call the ambulance.'

Jacob looked up at her and used his right hand to hold her tightly. 'You deserve to be free, baby. I can't do this anymore.'

Alice felt her heart implode. Erupting in rage at what was happening in front of her, she screamed at Jacob, for she knew that she couldn't lose him. 'FUCK YOU, Jacob. You're a coward. Don't you dare do this to me.'

She looked at the cut flesh under the drenched towel and felt her stomach rise to the back of her throat.

'Don't let it win.'

Alice kept whispering that same sentence over and over.

She looked up and saw her demon self in the full-length mirror, begging for help.

YOU HAVE TO SAVE HIM.

WE NEED HIM.

'Don't let her win,' she said.

Her head dropped as she cradled Jacob in her arms.

'Baby, don't do this to me,' she begged.

'I love you, Pebble.'

Jacob closed his eyes and rolled into her lap as if preparing to fall asleep. His arm dropped limp to the side as the last of his blood pumped onto the floor. Tears overwhelmed her, and she let out a guttural pain-filled scream.

SAVE HIM, it begged. WE LOVE HIM.

Alice looked up at the mirror and realised that the creature was gone, replaced by a more horrific picture – that of her dead husband cradled in her lap as she wept uncontrollably.

23

The Nightmare Sleeps
Winter 2014
Rainham, Kent UK

'I can't believe no one showed up, Sam,' said Alice softly. She was sitting with her brother-in-law in the front row of Rainham Church – the same church Jacob's and Sam's parents had been married in.

'Jacob made his own choices a long time ago, Alice, and you know that making and keeping friends was never his forte.' Sam took her by the hand. 'This isn't on you, sis. You do know that, don't you?'

Sam spoke with kindness in his heart. He wasn't muscular like Jacob had been, but he was taller and just as broad – a real man's man, who had never seen a hair product in his life. For him to talk so tenderly was a surprise, but one Alice was truly grateful for.

'He loved you, Alice, and if I'm completely honest, I've been unsure at times that Jacob could love anything in his life other than you.' Samuel put his hand on her shoulder. 'Jacob hated himself, even at his most arrogant. But you, Alice – you were the only thing he never doubted and the only thing he ever let in that later on in life he didn't regret. I hope as time passes you see that, and it helps you through the tough nights ahead.'

2004

Alice stood at the front of the church as Jacob, Sam and two of their uncles carried Paul Brooking to the front of the ceremony. A deep mahogany and trimmed with brass handles, the coffin was simple but clearly heavy and sturdy, exactly as her father-in-law-to-be would have wanted. They walked him down the aisle while an old ELO song played over the old church speakers. All of them were at least six feet tall, and yet the burden upon them took its toll. Paul had been a much-loved man within the Brooking family, and his loss would be felt in many circles. Jacob turned and walked towards Alice as his younger brother, who had always seemed like the older of the two, wrapped an arm around him. Jacob hadn't said anything all day. He was yet to show any emotion at all, and Alice worried that he had fallen in on himself, as she had seen him do so many times before. She had watched as his beloved grandparents had died, and as his Labrador had been taken to the vets to be put down, and she had witnessed not one tear being shed. Just silence, before months of emptiness and self-harm, both mental and physical. He took every loss as something personal to him, as if he was feeling guilt for any hurt he might have caused. He couldn't mourn his loss because of the anger he felt at himself for letting that person down. Jacob sat with her and she placed her hand on his, his stoic glare not showing a trace of emotion. She could see it happening once more. Maybe he would be OK. But she knew that was unlikely. Alice would be by his side, as it was all she could do, and she would love him as she always had, but she knew that the next few months would be hard, and she just hoped that he came out the other side.

Present day

Alice walked out to Jacob's freshly filled grave without realising that she had even left the church. A light rain fell around her; the cold bite of winter was starting to creep into every day.

'I love you,' Alice whispered to her lost love, before the last of her tears dried up on her flushed cheeks.

I love you too.

Alice shot around, not knowing where the words had come from, but certain it had been Jacob's voice that spoke them. She had to be dreaming; there was no other way to explain it. She couldn't calm her heart rate as she spun around in circles, looking for the source of the voice.

Find me, Pebble. Jacob's words were more powerful than before. *I'm here, find me.*

There was nothing around Alice other than gravestones, a few trees and an old path flanked by tall, expensive mausoleums, which she imagined rich families buried their loved ones in. She ran as quickly as her short heels would allow across the wet grass and skidded to a halt as she hit the gravel path.

I'm here, Jacob whispered.

Out of the corner of her eye, she saw a shadow of her love move between the stone buildings. She chased him to that spot, but as she turned the corner, she was met with a dead end.

Don't give up, I'm here.

This time, the voice came from behind her. She turned around so quickly her footing nearly went as her world spun in circles. Once again, Jacob flashed quickly between two buildings, almost mocking her as he called out.

I love you, Alice, he said one last time, as she rounded the corner behind him and found him there waiting.

An ancient stone water fountain built into the wall of the mausoleum towered over her. Rainwater poured through the open mouth of a gargoyle in a waterfall of crystal light and was pooling in the stone basin beneath. Within the water, she could see her Jacob.

'Baby, what's going on?' said Alice.

Apprehensively, she reached forward and broke the fall of the water with her outstretched hand. She watched, bemused, as Jacob's image danced and shimmered with the movement of the water.

I'm here, I'll always be here, and whenever you can see yourself, know that it will be me looking back at you.

Jacob reached forward and looked like he was going to take her hand but stopped just short of the water's end.

'I can't believe you're gone, baby. Oh god, I feel sick at the thought of living life without you.'

Alice wept once more, as Jacob smiled back at her through the streaming oasis.

'What do I do without you?' Alice begged, pressing her hand into the waterfall.

Pebble, you've got this, you always had this, so just carry on being you.

As he spoke these words, she swore she felt his touch.

'But I don't even know who I am without you by my side,' Alice said, with utter defeat in her voice.

Jacob smiled and whispered as he began to dissipate into nothingness. *You will always be you to me, whomever you now choose to be.*

Alice woke from her daydream with a jolt as the vicar rested his hand on her shoulder.

'It's not often I find people out here on dark, wet days, Mrs Brooking. Shall we get you home before you catch a cold? I'm sure your day has been long enough.'

Alice responded with a nod and let the vicar guide her back towards the car park, where she was saddened once again by the fact that the only car there was hers.

24

In Dreams

Summer 2015

Whitstable Bay, Kent UK

The sun was pouring through the window like a flood and filled the bedroom with the colours of heaven. Alice didn't have to stir, because as had been routine since Jacob had passed, she had woken up long before the sun had even thought to rise. She lay on her side of the bed, looking at the empty space, as she did every morning. The smell of his aftershave still lingered on his pillow, no doubt down to the bottle of 212 she kept in his bedside table. It had become a habit to spray his pillow once a week, and it genuinely helped her sleep, but she knew it wasn't good for her in the long run; she knew it would have to stop.

The radio came to life as her alarm went off; Aretha Franklin was the order of the day.

Who's zoomin' who indeed, Alice thought, as she sat upright with a stretch that caused several of her bones to pop. She jumped out of bed with the verve and inner gusto of someone half her age and looked out the window at the glorious sunshine, leaning on the windowsill for just a second to soak in the rich nutrients from her favourite star while taking in the glorious blue sky that surrounded it. She gathered her thoughts into something productive and decided to get dressed, with a rush of excitement filling her at the prospect.

'Morning, baby,' Alice said to her bathroom mirror while popping her toothbrush into her mouth. 'I have an entire diary of appointments to keep today, and honestly I'm not sure how I'm going to do it all without dying in that ridiculously hot studio of mine.'

Alice's words were mumbled at best, as she spoke while brushing her teeth. But since the recipient was her bathroom mirror, she doubted the clarity of her words made much of a difference. A mouthful of Colgate shut her up for a minute while she tied her hair back into the kind of loose ponytail that most models would spend hours perfecting.

'So, how do I look, my love?'

You look like my Alice, like the most beautiful woman I've ever met.

Jacob looked back at her from behind the mirror and smiled. Alice knew it wasn't real; Jacob hated his smile, and the reflection only smiled at her because she loved it. But real or not, these reflections were all she had, and she couldn't give them up.

Alice kissed the mirror, leaving her print on Jacob's reflection.

'Have a good day, baby.'

Well, I'm not going anywhere, am I? Jacob replied.

Alice placed her hand on the mirror, suddenly a little heartbroken. 'You have made that promise to me before. Please try and keep it this time.'

-

The day did not go to plan. Four meetings and only a few small sales of photographs. It was ridiculously hot in the shop, and Alice was impatiently waiting for her last client so she could run across the road and get herself an ice cream from Sundae Sundae. 'Pistachio and mint,' she whispered to herself, gazing longingly at the store through the window. Sweat dripped down her neck as her little air-conditioning unit struggled with its heavy workload. She would not be denied that ice cream. 'I have worked hard for that bloody ice cream,' she said to herself.

All of a sudden, the doorbell rang and snapped her attention back to the room.

'You must be Mr Jones. Welcome to Noir Papillon – to – to Papillon Noir,' stuttered the off-guard Alice to possibly the most beautiful man she had ever seen.

'Please, call me William,' he said, offering his hand.

Alice gladly accepted, noticing that both his arms were covered in tattoos from wrist to shoulder. His right arm had a nautical theme, full of anchors and old ships, whereas his left was more mythical, with a strong emphasis on what looked like Japanese cultural history. Alice, still a little out of sorts, looked up into his eyes, which were even more blue than her father's. William had white hair with a short but full beard of matching colour. His ears were pierced with two small black rings, and he had a delicate handlebar moustache that was curled to precision, which left Alice thinking he looked more like one of those new-age hipster barbers than a man who might spend thousands of pounds on her work.

'Miss Petalow, you seem a little lost in something. I can come back if you prefer?'

'No, I'm being rude, Mr Jones. Please, come and take a seat while I fetch you a coffee.'

Alice dropped down next to William on the leather seat as if her legs had forgotten how to keep her standing. 'So, what you are saying is you want to buy everything I have in the studio? I don't want to scare you off, but what on earth would you want with so many paintings?'

'My parents are hosting their annual ball in a few months, and all of the parasites of the Kent Art Society will be there. Unbelievably, I've managed to convince them to let me hold an auction there, with the profits going to my foundation.' William did not break eye contact as he took Alice by the hand. 'We could really use your help on this. In return, I'll make you the star of the event. You have a wonderful reputation within this community, and this could increase your exposure tenfold.'

William, realising how passionate he got at times, let go of Alice's hand and apologised.

'No, it's fine,' she responded. 'I'm truly flattered, and of course I would love to help. What is it your foundation does?'

'We are a conservation group for animal and wildlife habitats. My parents, of course, hate me for it. They always assumed I'd use their millions to grow the family empire, and I'm not sure they know what to do with an eco-warrior son.' William looked at the floor. 'My parents are good people but more selfish than I am when it comes to the world we live in. But enough about me. Do we have a deal?'

'We most certainly do, Mr Jones. I will just have to work out the value, which may take a few hours. If you're in a rush, I can call you with a figure later?'

Alice stood ready to shake on the deal of a lifetime, but William instead rose to give her the hug he had been eager to give from the second he had entered her world.

'I'm in no rush, my Papillon. Why don't I go and grab us an ice cream while you get started?'

Alice giggled for the first time in a long time, and then blushed. 'An ice cream sounds wonderful.'

Autumn 2015
Whitstable Bay, Kent UK

The night was wonderful. Alice's pictures were auctioned for three times the amount she had sold them to William for. It boosted her confidence immensely to see her work so sought after, and it made her feel truly special to speak with so many important people within the art community, people whom she had never been lucky enough to mix with before. It filled her mind with ideas for future projects, and a few high-end commissions were booked off the back of the evening.

But when the rush of the night died down, she was in a position that left her conflicted in so many ways. She was walking home along the seafront, a journey she had made a thousand times before, a journey she had loved making with Jacob, and yet as she made it tonight, she was struggling with the fact that it wasn't Jacob holding her hand; it was William. Of course, she fancied him. How could she not? William Jones was in all probability the product of a Norse god who had mated with a playwright equal to Shakespeare in talent. But he wasn't Jacob. How could he be? Then again, she kept asking herself, was that a bad thing? Jacob, in all fairness, had been a very inconsistent part of her life. And yet when things had been good, they had been amazing, and Alice felt like she was betraying that memory even by contemplating the fact that she most desperately wanted to kiss her new partner in crime. Jacob had died less than two years ago. Surely it was too soon. What would everyone say, and more importantly what would Jacob say?

   'I can't do this,' Alice said, pulling her hand from his.

   'I'm sorry. I never meant to break any kind of boundary with us.' William seemed distraught that he might have compromised his blossoming friendship with Alice. 'Please don't think ill of me for overstepping myself.'

'No, William, I'm being silly. It's just ... I don't know, I'm a little lost, and I ...'

William placed a warm hand on her chill-bitten cheek. 'Alice, I ask nothing from you but your company and your beautiful smile.' His demeanour was open and kind. 'And if anything I have done or will do should jeopardise that, then I fall at my own mercy for ruining such a beautiful thing that I have found.'

Alice looked into his crystal eyes and swore even in the darkness of the witching hour on a cold November night that she could see her reflection in his soul.

'It would be a crime I could not forgive myself for,' he said.

He turned and carried on walking along the seafront, this time with his hands secured in the pockets of his tweed trousers. But, to his surprise, Alice caught up with him, looped her arm through his and pulled herself closer to him. They continued in matching stride, both content with what had been said.

Alice turned to face her protector as they reached the door to the ocean-view cottage that Alice had called home for the past year. Bought with the money from the sale of her and Jacob's shares of the Gallantry, the cottage was a fresh start for Alice, and she'd made it her own in every respect. It was as Alice as any building or inanimate object could be.

'Would you come in for a tea before you head home, Mr Jones?' she asked nervously, looking at his chest so that she avoided the bewitching effects that his eyes seemed to have.

'I think you deserve the rest your mind surely craves after such a wonderfully successful night. You should be proud of what you have done today. I know I am proud of you.' William took both of her hands into his own and kissed her gently on the cheek. 'Rest well, my Papillon.'

His words fell away as he turned and walked into the night, leaving Alice clutching her heart for a moment.

'Goodnight, Mr Jones,' she whispered to herself as she closed her front door, resting her head against it as she bolted the lock into place, a sigh escaping her in sadness at once again being at home alone.

She hadn't seen Jacob's reflection much of late. He seemed distant and fleeting at every visit. Did he know how conflicted she was? She walked to the end of the dark hall, where a large, ornate mirror leaned casually against the wall, and placed her hand against it.

'Help me, baby,' she said in a choked voice. The guilt she was experiencing as a result of having feelings for William outweighed her pride in the night's work and the money that had been raised for his charity. 'Where are you, Jacob?' she pleaded.

I'm here, I'm always here, he whispered back.

Alice fell to a slump next to the mirror. 'Baby, I'm sorry. I'm so sorry. I've been weak.'

Don't be sorry. You have done nothing but be the woman I fell in love with, my beautiful little Pebble. Or was it Papillon?

25

The Curtain Call
Winter 2016
Whitstable Bay, Kent UK

'I can't let you go,' said Alice as she fell to her knees in front of the small bookcase that carried the last memories of her marriage.

A black-and-white portrait shot of Jacob stood proudly in a silver skeleton-edged frame next to their wedding rings on the top shelf. Below that was a montage of Polaroids taken with a vintage camera her father had bought her 20 years before. The pictures were of moments they'd shared over the years and were all very natural, full of smiles and laughter. Underneath that was her first Canon SLR: a dusty old bit of kit that was considered cutting edge when Jacob had bought it for her. It still contained a full reel of unprocessed pictures of wild flowers and rare birds at Rye Harbour. Undoubtedly, it would have a few shots of Jacob she had squeezed in stealthily while he wasn't paying attention – although she had a feeling he always knew what she was up to, since he always looked like he was flexing in every single picture, a fact he denied with vigour. Every time, Jacob would smile and say, 'I'm not flexing.' She could hear him now, and, honestly, right now she needed to hear him.

Alice grabbed both wedding rings off the shelf, putting hers on its rightful finger and Jacob's on her thumb, and walked over to his old chair in front of the fire, collecting a heavy wool blanket from the back of the sofa as she walked past. She wrapped herself up in the blanket like a silkworm ready to transform and sat watching the open flames dance and spit in a display of exotic colours, doing their utmost to light and warm the cold, stone-clad room. As if Alice had found her final resting place, she drifted off into a comfortable sleep, in which she almost instantly felt Jacob take her hand.

'This is a dream, isn't it?' asked Alice, already knowing the answer, as she and Jacob walked hand in hand along the beachfront.

'Your whole life is a dream, my beautiful Pebble. Tell me, have you ever stopped dancing through life?' Jacob said playfully, which caused Alice to grip his hand all the tighter, as she knew this was a moment worth savouring.

'What do I do, baby?' said Alice with a heavy heart. 'It's getting harder each and every day to sit alone looking at your picture. I need you. I need you to help me.'

'Pebble, I couldn't tell you what to do when I was alive. What on earth makes you think I have that kind of power now?'

Jacob leaned in and kissed her, his lips warm to the touch and softer than velvet. Alice closed her eyes as Jacob's hand released hers, only to fall around her waist and pull her closer. His free hand began exploring her hair as he gently probed her mouth with the tip of his tongue. As she felt him pull away, she opened her eyes and, with a sickening blow, realised he was gone. Not even a goodbye this time. She pulled her dress from under her and sat down on the beach, looking out to sea.

'What do I do, baby?' she asked Jacob, knowing no answer would come.

She slipped off her sandals and spread her toes out in the soft sand. The warm air from the sun washed over her as she remembered why she had loved coming here so much. Closing her eyes, she thought of William and of his determination to win her heart. She smiled at his overly polite nature and his willingness to help everyone he met. Could she ever really love another man? Could anyone ever really love her, once they knew where she had been? He seemed to, despite her unwillingness to let him in. And Dad seemed to like him. That was certainly new. Maybe he was going soft in his old age. Or maybe he had fed off her pain all these years, the way she had fed off Jacob's.

'I hope you have found peace, my forever,' Alice said painfully as she sat up and looked out over the calm blue ocean. She pulled herself up and, carrying her sandals in her right hand, started walking towards the sunset. In her left hand, she played with her wedding ring. Slipping it off and holding it in the palm of her hand, she decided that when she woke up, she would come up with a plan for the two rings, as, surely, holding onto something that meant so much was never going to help her move forward.

Wake up.

Alice opened her eyes in a panic and checked her surroundings. She was still wrapped up in the armchair. The fire kicked up amber fireflies into the dark room.

Find me.

Recognising Jacob's voice, Alice stood up, confused and scared. The cold stone floor bit her toes.

Find me, Pebble. I'm here.

Alice moved through the living room to the door where the voice had originated.

I love you.

'Baby, where are you?'

I'm here, Jacob whispered.

Alice walked past the kitchen to the base of the stairs.

I'll always be here in your heart.

Alice rushed up the stairs two at a time and dashed into her bedroom, her heart pounding. And there he was. Jacob stood where her reflection should have been, in the full-length mirror leaning against the wall. There in his prime. His hair was that slightly longer length, which she loved more than she would admit. A clean and crisp white T-shirt hugged his muscular frame, and jeans and sand-coloured Timberland boots finished his look. His wrist, however, which would normally be covered by bangles, had a scar that ran from there to his elbow, and it was a sight that caused her heart to sink.

Alice moved towards Jacob's reflection. 'Baby, what's going on?'

You know what's going on, Pebble. He put his palm up to the mirror. *It's time to go.*

Alice burst into tears. A mixture of joy and heartbreak overwhelmed her as she brought her hand up to touch his. For just a second, she swore she could feel their fingers entwine. For just a second, she felt him.

'What will I do without you?'

Alice sobbed, looking at the floor as if hoping that the world would open up and swallow her where she stood.

I love you, Pebble.

'I love you, baby,' she cried, as she looked up and realised Jacob, her Jacob, was truly gone. And she realised the reflection in front of her was a very rare sight indeed. It was her own.

And then, out of nowhere, his voice echoed once more in her mind for what she knew would be the last time.

You've got this.

For the first time in 20 years, she felt truly alone.

Spring 2017

She knew she could do it, she had complete faith in herself, and yet this last step was feeling more improbable with every passing second. It was the simplest of tasks, too, with not a thing stopping her, and yet she failed at every opportunity to take what could be the most important step of her recent existence.

'You can do this, Petalow,' she said, with more fire in her belly than the previous two or three times she had said it, although her words, which were meant for self-motivation, served only to delay what needed to be done.

In a daffodil 1950s Lindy Bop dress tied high on her waist, with a white belt, designed to look like an oversized bow, sitting just above the curve of her hip line, she certainly looked the part. Her fiery red hair curled into ringlets as it flowed from underneath a white headband and spilled over her right shoulder, giving her the look of a young Maureen O'Hara. She felt as good as she looked, and there was no doubt in her mind that she was more than capable of doing this. So, with a final push, she took the last step forward and went to knock on William's door. Hesitation held her back for one last second before her knuckles made contact with the gloss navy-blue door.

To her surprise, it opened instantly and as if by some magical force.

A smiling William Jones stood proudly in the doorway.

'I did wonder how long it would take you to knock on,' he jested loudly, but his demeanour was that of a man who was ecstatic to see the girl of his dreams.

Alice stepped straight inside his personal space and placed a finger over his mouth.

'Oh, do shut up, William,' she said. She leaned in and, this time without hesitation, pressed her ruby red lips hard against his.

Somewhere deep inside of her, the creature stirred, disgusted by the unbridled joy the woman was feeling. It grunted and spat as it turned in on itself. They had always called it the Voice, but for now there was only silence. For now, it would rest; and, for now, it would wait. The creature was human in frame yet moved unnaturally, like a marionette with its strings tied wrong. It had a feminine kind of appearance, but with its grey broken skin and jet-black eyes, it lacked any softness. The Alice creature had called Alice a witch, but it knew she couldn't fathom its true form or existence in any rational sense. For now, it was irrelevant. It was weak and it had no voice. Backed into a corner of Alice's mind, the creature closed its eyes and began to dream of the things that only the wicked might dream about, until, once again, it was given the power it needed, to feed.

26

The Harlequin
Somewhere in the Void

'If you continue to wear so many masks, my son, you will one day forget which one your true face is.'

Jacob read the quote out loud from the crumpled note it was written on as he sat on the beach in the thundering rain. He had given up caring about the downpour when he realised there was nowhere for him to shelter for at least a mile in any direction; instead of sprinting for cover, he had sat slumped against the sea wall, accepting he was going to get wet. As always, he was overdressed for his location, in a classic white linen shirt with the cuffs rolled back to his elbows, matched with a tweed waistcoat and a cross-hatch flat cap that made him look like a farm owner about to have his cow named "best breed" at the Kent County Show. All he had in his possession were his book, an old first edition of *The Rats* by James Herbert that he held tightly in his embrace, and a few quid to buy himself a coffee on the way home. He had left his phone at home, so as not to be distracted by the online world while he tried to clear his thoughts out here in the real world, but finding the note had preoccupied him more than any social media app could have done. It was a note from his father, hidden inside Jacob's favourite book maybe 25 years ago, just before he had gone off to start his apprenticeship in London. Paul Brooking had always had a way with words, either written or spoken, although admittedly he shared very few of either. A quiet man from a working-class family, he had loved both his sons more than anything and had prided himself on being a family man. This little nugget of advice would have been placed there with wholehearted purpose. As a boy, Jacob had always put on a front, completely dissatisfied with the young man he was, and he had often changed his friends and surroundings to avoid anyone finding out what a loser he felt like most of the time.

He had stolen and broken both hearts and material possessions to try and prove to the world that he was the man that he claimed to be. He had thrown away everything that had ever mattered to him to prove that he didn't need anyone or anything. And his father had seen through it all and never intervened, never pulled him up; instead, he'd tried to guide him with music. Jacob remembered every song his dad had ever asked him to play. There was a day, many years ago, long before Alice had lost her dear mum and long before Jacob had lost his best friend and father, when Jacob's father had given him the album *Stanley Road* by Paul Weller on cassette, passing it to him with the words, 'If you listen to every song on this album properly, I'll never have to teach you a life lesson ever again.'

Jacob would of course not be so lucky, he could have used his fathers wisdom throughout the entirety of his life, but he understood the sentiment well enough. His father was a man of few words, but everything he said had weight and purpose. Jacob had idolised his father, and it was failing to emulate his achievements as both a husband and a son that had caused Jacob so much pain these past 20 years. 'I've only ever let you down,' he would whisper every time he thought of his relationship with the greatest man he had ever known. The voice of the creature, now muted in the back of his mind, would agree with Jacob in a heartbeat, but really there was no need. Jacob had made peace with the man he had become. He had made peace with his failings as a son, as a brother and as a husband. He was wounded and hardened with a body made up of scar tissue. And he had started to realise each day just how tired he had become. Yet today he felt lighter, almost free of the burdens that had tied him down for so long. In fact, he felt a little dreamy, as if everything was a little more beautiful. As the rain had started to fall upon his aching skin, he had felt warmed by its gentle wash. He could nearly smell the rain today, and each breath Jacob took seemed to take him to a new high. Jacob wondered if this was something he had always been able to do and this was merely the first time he had noticed.

As the rain subsided and a break in the clouds brought a ray of light more bright and vibrant than any he had ever seen, Jacob realised he wasn't sure how he had got here. He couldn't remember leaving the house.

'Hang on,' Jacob said out loud.

He bounced up to his feet with a mixture of shock, confusion and surprisingly renewed mobility, the arthritis in his left knee, a product of lower-league rugby throughout his youth, having completely cleared up for the first time in years. He spun around, realising that he had no idea what beach this was, causing the sensation of not knowing how he had got here to become panic at the thought that he didn't even know where "here" was. As if sensing his fear, the sky cleared completely, and the warmth of the sun washed over him like a comfort blanket, bringing with it an immense calm. He couldn't remember ever feeling safe in any capacity unless ...

'Alice.'

The whisper escaped his lips like he was talking in his sleep. He had only felt safe with Alice by his side. But where was she now? His thoughts on this morning were still whitewashed, like looking too closely at the sun. The last thing he remembered clearly was waiting for her to come home from work. He had missed her terribly, and yet he'd had a feeling of fearful trepidation due to her imminent arrival. Why? Why would he fear his beloved coming home? What was he afraid of? The monster! Jacob remembered fighting with it throughout the best part of the day. It had been trying to stop him from doing something, but Jacob was unsure what, or why that would have caused him to be afraid of Alice coming home, which was always the best part of his day.

'It's going to be OK,' said a familiar voice – a voice both soft and full of the kind of wisdom one can only gather over many lifetimes.

Jacob knew it had come from behind him, and yet his body wasn't ready to turn around. He knew the voice like he knew his own – better, even – and yet it couldn't be. How could he be here?

'You're safe here, you never have to be scared again.' The man's voice moved closer as footsteps displaced the pebbles beneath.

'You left me when I needed you most.' Jacob's words were joined by the sound of his tears dropping onto the book, which was firmly clenched in his hand. 'I couldn't find you.'

'I never left you. I've watched you every day since you were born. I've been with you through it all, Jacob, and do you know what I've learnt over that time?' He placed his hand firmly on Jacob's shoulder. 'It wasn't your fault, son.'

Hearing his father's last words, Jacob spun around and wrapped his arms around his father's core. Although he was sure he and his father were the same height, he felt small in his dad's tight embrace.

'I love you, Dad,' Jacob whispered, refusing to relinquish an embrace he never thought he would get again.

'Welcome home, son,' Paul Brooking whispered while kissing his son's head repeatedly. 'I love you too.'

-

And then, Alice awoke... Alice had been lying deadly still on the hospital bed for what seemed like years. The room was clinical and open, with nothing inside it that didn't have a purpose. She lay on her side, crunched into a foetal position, with just one white pillow folded beneath her plaited auburn hair.

Part Two
The Book of Alice

1

The Light and the Lighthouse Somewhere in the Void

Jacob couldn't decide on a way forward. This was a pivotal decision, one that had to be made with a clear mind and a calm heart. If he hung out the washing on the east-wing line, it would surely dry better away from the sea mist; but those bloody crows – damn those bloody crows – they always left mess all over that side of the grounds, and they cared little for the brilliant white of his T-shirts. The west wing was getting increasingly hit by ever-more-aggressive waves smashing against the coast. The ocean spray lashed hard against the white stone walls of the lighthouse, like a giant primordial lash, bringing a thunderous clap like shingle thrown onto a tin roof with each giant splash. Jacob was unsure how long he had been living on this gargantuan rock surrounded by a violent sea and a murder of monstrous crows, but he knew he was happy and that this place almost defined him, with its melting pot of beauty and uncontrolled environmental destruction. It was as if someone who knew Jacob intimately had created this place for him. 'The east wing,' he murmured to himself, knowing he was taking a chance. He carried the wicker laundry basket across the lush green of the lighthouse's back yard and over to the wood house, where the washing line sat loosely on the ground.

'KRAAAAAA,' the closest crow called from the large birch tree that the other end of the line would attach to.

'Kraa yourself, you big bag of feathers!' Jacob responded.

As Jacob pegged his clothes on the line, his attention was pulled back to the lighthouse. He swore he could hear his father calling from the kitchen. *Maybe lunch is ready*, he mused while he hurried his pace, eager to see what his dad had created for a well-earned break in play. They had a good system here. Paul Brooking would wash the clothes, while Jacob hung them out; his dad would cook lunch, while Jacob always made dinner; and Paul loved to tend the garden, while his son looked after the welfare of the lighthouse itself – not that they had ever seen a ship to warn. Jacob hadn't yet figured out how this place worked or even if it had a name. But they had made it a home, and they were happy. The larder was somehow always full, and although the weather threatened, it had always been kind.

'I'm coming, Pops,' called Jacob as he pegged up the last shirt. He looked up briefly to warn the crows that any attempt to ruin his work would involve grave consequences, but to his amazement, not a feather could be seen. In fact, he couldn't see a bird in the sky. 'Not even a gull to ruin my washing. Maybe my luck's in.' Jacob smiled, picked up the empty wicker basket and began his stroll back to the lighthouse so as to enjoy another five-star lunch with his best friend.

'Son, I've been calling you,' said Jacob's dad as he put a platter of cured meats and smoked cheeses down on a giant oak chopping board at the centre of a circular table.

'Dad, this looks beautiful,' said Jacob, taking his place in a chair next to a sleeping Peepo. The black Lab had been waiting for them at the window the day they'd arrived, and Jacob had to admit that his heart had lifted immeasurably to see her beautiful shiny wet nose at the window as his father had led them along the beach to what would become their new home.

'Hold on, son, the best is yet to come.' Paul Brooking pulled a loaf of rosemary bread from the Aga. Steam and herb-filled aromas filled the kitchen, and an almost incandescent glow radiated off the bread. Paul laid it down next to a dish of sea-salted butter and smiled.

'Dad, you never cease to amaze me. This all looks bloody lovely, and Mum would be proud if she were here.'

Jacob pulled a slice of ham from the table and slipped it to Peepo, who instantly pricked up her ears as Jacob whispered encouragement to the forever-starving beast.

'You can wash your hands again if you insist on feeding that bloody dog,' said Paul without even turning around.

Jacob laughed. 'What exactly am I going to catch from not washing my hands in this place?'

'What exactly do you think this place is, my boy?'

'Oh, sweet Jesus, Dad, you know I can't answer that. The words always seem to escape me even as I try to speak them, and honestly, Pop, haven't we been through this little dance enough times?' Jacob, although defiant in his reasons, was still a son who did as his father asked, and so he jumped to his feet, sinking his hands into the soapy water Paul had got ready for the plates in advance. 'You know, Dad, I've never cared where this place is, or even what our purpose here may be, but I'm truly glad I'm here with you and Peepo.'

As he went to sit back down, he noticed that Peepo had vanished. Where she had gone in a closed room of this size was a mystery, but Jacob gave it little thought, as, honestly, where could she go?

Jacob and his father ate everything at the table except for a few crusts, which were for the nest of swallows above the barn gate, and a few scraps of meat for Peepo, if and when she ever returned from her mysterious hiding place.

'Let me help you with that,' said Jacob as his dad tirelessly cleared all the plates. He reached across the table to grab the empty glasses, when something happened that shocked him frozen. 'Dad! What's happening?'

Paul looked around to see his son's left hand slowly disintegrate into an ashen vapour trail that left a mist of fireflies dancing out of existence.

The glass remained unmoved by Jacob's efforts to take it, and the fear was spreading through him like the flame that tore away at his arm.

'DAD, I'M SCARED! WHAT IS HAPPENING?'

Jacob was in full panic mode as the fire spread up his arm and into his shoulder. Each limb disappeared as the flames consumed him, as though he were a sheet of paper. Jacob looked up at his father to see him all but disappear himself.

'Don't be scared, son, you must have known this was coming.'

'What was coming? Dad, what was coming?'

Paul Brooking smiled at his son as he finally vanished. 'I love you, son, but you didn't really think this was real, did you?'

Jacob looked down as the last of his visual self finally vanished into nothing, and a veil of darkness washed over him.

He felt no pain. And he felt no peace. Jacob Brooking, by all accounts, felt nothing.

Summer 2009

St Martin's Hospital, Canterbury

'William,' Alice croaked as she woke with the throat of a woman who hadn't uttered a word in two years.

The man in question stood with his back to Alice on the far side of the room, mid-conversation with one of the nurses, and he didn't even flinch at the frail voice that had escaped her. Alice pulled herself up with great unease, and the nurse drew William's attention to the patient.

'Alice, you're awake,' the doctor said as he hurried eagerly to her bedside.

'William, what's going on? Where am I, and what on earth are you wearing?' asked Alice, gently pulling his stethoscope.

The doctor smiled a toothy grin through his grey beard and shone a pen light into Alice's deep blue eyes. 'So many questions, Miss Petalow, and we can answer them all, but for now please just breathe and let me take a look at you. Two years is a very long time to be in and out of a catatonic state.'

Alice's heart rate increased and her breathing followed suit as the confusion started to overwhelm her. 'WILLIAM, WHAT'S GOING ON?'

The doctor leaned in once more. 'Alice, who exactly do you think I am? You keep calling me William. Is that someone you want me to contact?'

The nurse came to take Alice's pulse. Alice sat shaking as she tried to piece her world back together.

'You're William, my boyfriend,' she said. 'You just told me you loved me whilst on our first weekend away.'

The doctor raised his hand. 'Alice, I'm not William, I'm Dr Williams, and I've been overseeing your stay here at the hospital for the past 23 months.' The doctor pulled up his security pass from the lanyard round his neck and presented it to Alice.

'Consultant J. Williams ... No, NO, I don't understand.' Alice's voice started to fail as her throat fell into an uncontrollable tremble. 'WHAT IS HAPPENING TO ME?'

He's not listening to you, the voice came from nowhere, and Alice barely registered it anyway.

'Alice, we need you to breathe,' said the doctor, while the nurse called for support.

He's forgotten you, he's going to leave you, just like Jacob did, called the voice.

'Jacob,' Alice murmured on hearing the name voiced in her head. She rocked back and forth, struggling to control her breathing like the doctor had asked.

'Do you need Jacob?' the doctor answered. 'We will call him as soon as you settle, he was just here yesterday.'

'WHAT?' Alice stopped hyperventilating. 'But Jacob's dead.'

She hadn't used her legs in two years, and her attempt at making it to the toilet was futile to say the least. Dr Williams tried to catch her, but Alice still took a rather nasty hit to her knee as her legs immediately buckled, like those of a newborn giraffe trying to find its footing, and she hit the ground.

Alice opened her mouth to breathe for what felt like the first time since the doctor had told her the news. But she struggled to draw in anything of sustenance and started to suffocate, despite there being no restriction on her airway.

'Breathe, Alice, you need to calm down.'

'MY DEAD HUSBAND IS APPARENTLY NOW ALIVE AND MY NEW BOYFRIEND, WHO APPARENTLY IS NOT MY BOYFRIEND AT ALL, IS THE DOCTOR TELLING ME ALL THIS,' Alice screeched while gulping huge breaths in between each and every word. She bellowed once more, 'And YOU – YOU, who looks identical to the man who just today, as sunrise touched my eyes and awoke me from dreams, told me he loved me, as he kissed me gently good morning – YOU, of all people, want me, ME, to calm down?'

Alice was overwhelmed and emptied her stomach of whatever protein-rich fluid had been pumped into her these past two years with the sole purpose of keeping her alive. Her world went to darkness once again, and the last of her strength slipped away into nothing. The only remnants of consciousness in her weary and broken form came from a tiny twitch she made every time she heard the voice in her head call out to her.

Alice, come back to us!

2

Scar Tissue
Summer 2009
St Martin's Hospital, Canterbury, Kent

Alice hadn't spoken in minutes, but Dr Vivian Phillips didn't have any desire to rush her through this; after all, she wasn't on the clock today. She had been brought in especially. Alice's parents had paid a handsome sum to make sure Alice got all the help she needed from a doctor who knew her personally and had experience with her broken past.

'So, I've been in an induced coma since I cut my throat?' Alice asked.

'Not quite. We pulled you out of it as soon as your stitches healed fully. You were induced because you wouldn't stop trying to tear them out. You nearly bled out on us twice, Alice.' The doctor held back a genuine sadness at the fall of her favourite client and pushed some photos across the desk.

The images showed Alice on the same hospital bed she had woken up on not a day before.

'But these photos show I'm wide awake,' said Alice as she flipped through the pictures, which were dated by month starting a year earlier.

'When you were taken out of the coma, you remained in an unresponsive catatonic state for a further 12 months. We could get nothing from you other than one thing.' The doctor slid one last photograph across the table and placed a painted and finely manicured nail on the image. 'He came to see you every day for the first four months, and then every few weeks after that. He even brought you flowers on your birthday just the other day.'

'Jacob's alive,' Alice whispered.

'Yes, quite alive, although at times over these past few years, I believe he's struggled to believe that's a good thing.'

'Have you kept seeing him - you know, in a professional sense? Is he OK?'

'I believe he's on his way here now. But, Alice, it's been two years. You have to be prepared for a different Jacob to walk through that door. His therapy has been intense, but you would be so very proud of him.'

Alice found a smile for the first time since she had woken.

'But I saw him die - I held him in my arms as he bled out. What do you think that could have meant?'

The doctor smiled. 'Do you think maybe that was your way of forgiving him and letting him go?'

They sat in silence for a moment while Alice soaked in what she was hearing.

'Alice, there is one more thing we need to discuss, if you are up for it? Before we induced you, before the doctors could stop you tearing your stitches out, well, you kept screaming out a name.'

'Thomas,' Alice interrupted, with fear edging into her voice.

'Let's talk about Thomas for a little bit – that's if you're strong enough?'

'Yeah, erm ... I mean, of course.' Alice sighed and looked at the floor. 'To be honest, I'm so very tired of keeping secrets designed to protect other people.' She reached up and scratched at the long-since-healed scar on her neck. Then she raised herself up and gingerly moved over to the en suite, stopping at the mirror to take a look at the horror looking back from beyond the reflection. 'But before we start, can we find a way to shut this bitch up who won't stop screaming in my head?'

Alice's reflection laughed at the audacity of such a pathetic specimen calling her a bitch and smiled a fang-toothed grin as a way of acknowledgement to Alice's true self.

You fucking piece of shit.

Jacob stood tall as his reflection voiced its unwanted opinion from the protection of a broken old mirror crudely stuck onto the men's-room door. A bigger and better mirror surely wouldn't have stretched the budget of the best private hospital in Kent.

Don't ignore me.

'I'm not ignoring you, Ahab,' Jacob replied. 'I thought we were going to try getting along. Remember what Dr Phillips told us to do.'

You cannot reason with me.

'Well, clearly not today, as you are being an intolerable fool, so, yes, maybe I will ignore you.'

She's better off without you.

Jacob straightened his collar. 'Well, on that, old friend, we can at least agree.'

7 April, one year before

'Let me get this straight – you want me to give that bastard a name?' Jacob seemed more interested than normal, and the light in his eyes shone for the first time in months.

'What, pray tell, would giving the bloody thing a name do to help me?'

'Giving it a name, Mr Brooking, will grant you two things – firstly, the ability to differentiate its voice from your own internal thoughts, and, secondly, a better degree of power, if and when you fight back.'

Jacob laughed. 'Fight back? I'm not sure I've ever won a fight against that thing, certainly not one of any consequence.'

Dr Phillips raised a perfectly kept eyebrow at Jacob and peered over her black-rimmed glasses. 'If you have never won a fight with the voice inside your head, then surely you will need all the help you can get.'

She was right, he needed help, as he had hit a bit of a rut of late. The kraken within his mind was nowhere near the threat that it had been in the years before, but it was still there each and every day. He had learned to ignore all but its most abusive barbs, yet at least once a day it would find its mark. That was fine when it was just him he had to worry about, but now there was someone else to consider.

The present

Jacob took a deep breath and placed a firm hand on the bathroom door, both fear and excitement causing his heart rate to dance like the jungle drums in a 1940s King Kong film. Jacob feared he was not the titular ape in this analogy, but rather the petrified young British explorer, out for glory but with no idea what peril lay ahead. 'You've got this, Jay.' Jacob pushed through the door and fell straight into a confident stride as he took the corridor that led to Alice's ward. He had tried to make an effort, with a crisp white shirt paired with a navy tie and matching trousers. He had brought it down a notch, into a more casual look, with an informal sleeve roll that exposed the shipwreck tattoo on the underside of his forearm, a reminder of his time lost at sea aboard the *Summer Breeze* – a reminder of a time lost to himself. He rattled as he walked the halls, with more bangles and beads than a Thai monk. He wanted to impress her, needed to impress her, not because he wanted to win her back, but because deep down he knew that this was all his fault.

-

'You look like the woman you should be, Miss Alice,' said the ward sister, who had been kind enough to help Alice put some make-up on.

'I look rough and you very well know it, Miss Bonnie, but thank you for trying.'

Alice walked gingerly back to her bed and, with a little help from the ward sister, managed to get herself upright against a couple of large pillows that had lost their volume after one too many Sister Bonnie pat-downs. Bonnie Belmonte was a strong woman of Antiguan descent, and her thick Caribbean accent hadn't left her over a 30-year tenure in the UK.

'You are,' she said, 'what my grandma used to say, a duppy conqueror.'

Alice giggled at the strange phrase. 'And what exactly is a duppy?'

'A duppy, my sweet girl, is a ghost, and you are a ghost conqueror.' Sister Bonnie smiled as she took Alice's hand, her beautiful white teeth separated by a gap in the centre of the top row. 'You have got this, child – on that I promise.'

Alice gave her hand a delicate squeeze. 'Can you tell me about these scars?' She pointed at the tiny marks that ran over her arms and legs.

'Those are from you rolling about the floor like a loon, in a thousand shards of broken mirror. Apparently, when Jacob carried you screaming into the San Diego ER, you were bleeding from so many small cuts that they were lost as to where the actual injury was at first.'

'And what of this big one on my belly? How did that get there? I noticed it when you helped me bathe earlier, but I was unsure if it was just my mind playing tricks on me.'

The sister took a hold of Alice's hand once more and leaned in close. 'My dear child, you really don't remember a thing, do you?'

Alice shook her head as the sister pondered how to answer.

'I think the story of that particular scar is one best told by Mr Brooking,' said Bonnie, 'for I feel I won't do the story any real justice.'

Alice let the sister's hand go and smiled softly. 'I'm sure it can't be any worse than the story that brought me here.' She ran her fingers over the hairline scar on her neck. 'Thank you, Sister.'

'You're very welcome, Miss Alice. Now be strong, for I hear footsteps on my ward floor.'

As Sister Bonnie left Alice to finish the last part of her journey alone, she passed a very nervous-looking Jacob in the doorway and took a moment to place a hand on his forearm, her midnight ebony skin contrasting with his pale colour; he clearly hadn't seen too much sun in the last two years. 'You be kind to her, child. You may have been coming in for one-way conversation these past two years, but today I reckon she might have a little in return.'

Jacob hoped that were true. He nodded and rounded the doorway, apprehension as to what might be said ruining the excitement that had been building every day for the last two years.

And then ... There she was ...

Alice sat on the hospital bed in a white summer frock that fell around her ankles. Her hair was tied back to reveal a slim neckline. She was almost gaunt from a two-year liquid diet that had given her exactly the nourishment she needed to stay healthy and alive but little sustenance. She had certainly lost a dress size or two. But where her body was frail, her sapphire-blue eyes still shone bright with bewitching power, and just like the last time Jacob had seen her sitting upright, they were filled with tears once more. She didn't speak just yet, she couldn't. Instead, she held out her arms and Jacob rushed to fill them with the kind of embrace one can only experience when your love returns from the dead. Both of them held on tightly to what was once lost and refused to let go in fear of reality kicking in, a reality where they were once again apart, and once again alone.

'I thought you were dead,' Alice cried while she peppered his brow and cheeks with kisses.

Jacob brought his hands up to cradle his wife's cheeks and kissed her lips firmly. 'I am not so easily lost to this world, my beautiful Pebble, but I must confess, I am eager to hear about this journey you have endured in its entirety, as it sounds quite the caper indeed.'

'Baby, the nurses said you visited every day. I know it seems crazy, but whenever you were telling me about your day, it seemed to be shaping my dreams. The story in my head was almost mimicking the stories – at least, that's what my nurse has been telling me.'

Jacob smiled and sat next to his wife, taking her hand in his own. 'Had I known that, I might have tried to brainwash you.'

Jacob laughed and Alice punched him in the arm, causing him to hold it in mock pain.

'I'm serious, Jay. The nurses told me your stories. When you started to benefit from your therapy, I saw it happen. When the medication took its toll on you, I saw it happen. And when my mother ...' Alice paused and closed her eyes for a heartbeat to try and find the strength to finish her statement.

'She had a stroke about 12 months ago,' Jacob explained. 'Strangely, it tied in almost to the day with you waking up from the induced coma and falling into that unresponsive state. We nearly lost her, and quite honestly we are lucky to have you both here with us today.'

Alice looked up and took in what Jacob was saying. Every word, no matter the grim nature of the subject, was a pleasure to hear. His absence had been hard, and his presence by her side was a joy she had felt she would never feel again.

'I wonder why I took the news of her falling so ill as a death in my world. What do you think my mind was trying to tell me?'

Jacob took a deep breath before he answered, struggling to find the words. 'I think your mind was confused, for the same month that your mum fell ill, I lost Grandma.'

Alice took her husband in her arms and pulled him close. 'Jay, I'm so sorry, I wasn't there, I didn't even ... What happened?' She shuffled closer and held Jacob's arm tightly.

'She had struggled since losing both my gramps and then my dad. I think she just stopped taking care of herself, and in the end that took its toll. It wasn't your fault, baby, far from it, but maybe the guilt of not being there for me manifested itself through your dreams.' Jacob sighed but looked into Alice's eyes with relief. 'I'm just glad you are back with us, Pebble; we have a lot to talk about.'

'That sounds ominous,' said Alice, yawning. The two years of sleep had taken their toll.

'I'll say no more until John and Angela get here.'

'John and Angela? I'm not sure I've ever heard you call them by name before. It's usually "your mum" and "your dad", and with no small amount of disdain, either.'

Alice was only half joking, although Jacob would have struggled to disagree. He had never bonded with them as Alice would have wanted – not until recently, anyway.

'Pebble, things have changed these past 18 months, and a lot of it has been for the better, but I must confess I have mixed feelings about how this might play out. So, can you do me a favour? I need you to know how much we all love you and how very proud you should be of us all.'

Alice almost couldn't believe what she was hearing. 'Us all? I have to say it's a pleasant surprise to hear you talk about my family like this. I guess I can take solace in the fact that some good has come from all this.'

NO.

NO GOOD COMES FROM THIS.

IT'S NOT REAL.

8 May, one year before

'Ahab? A strange choice even for the most dedicated Herman Melville fan,' said Dr Phillips. 'Tell me, why name it after the captain and not the whale? After all, the whale would be apt, in terms of both scale and design.'

'Because the whale was just trying to go about its business,' said Jacob, 'trying to live its best life. Captain Ahab was the true monster. He was dedicating his whole existence to killing that whale, to sinking that whale and taking its life into the bleak void of the cold ocean floor. This thing inside of me is much more like that. It's the evil trying to harm the innocent.'

'Do you believe yourself an innocent party, Jacob?'

'I don't believe I'm guilty of the kind of crime that deserves the punishment I so often receive,' said Jacob defiantly.

'Then I'm glad to say, Mr Brooking, that we are getting somewhere.'

3

Ruby Slippers
Summer 2009
St Martin's Hospital, Canterbury, Kent

'Are you ready to talk about her?' said Dr Phillips with an air of caution in her voice.

'Evan? I hope that bitch rots in hell.'

Dr Phillips seemed hurt by Alice's words, a reaction not missed by Alice.

'No, Alice, not Evan, but at least we've established that you're not ready to talk about that part of your life yet. I meant your mother. It must be an amazing feeling to know your mother is alive. How does that feel?'

'Oh ... Honestly, it doesn't feel real that either of them is still here. Jacob or my mum. It's a dream to me, and my mind won't allow it to take root – not until I can see, touch or hear them, I guess.'

'Well, they shall be here soon enough. I hear Jacob was already on his way to see you when he got the call, and your parents are close behind.'

'Jacob and my dad in the same room, and I'm too weak to run away – please, Doc, put me back to sleep.'

Doctor and patient shared an awkward laugh that turned into an even more awkward silence – one that was broken in the most unexpected way.

'You might find this hard to believe, but your father has a new-found respect for Jacob,' said the doctor.

'I'll believe that when I see it,' said Alice.

'Remember these words,' said Dr Phillips, 'if you remember nothing else that I tell you. It's OK that things have changed in your absence. You might even be pleasantly surprised.'

Two hours later

Angela Petalow wrapped her arms tightly around a daughter whom she had thought was lost to another world. Tears of joy and disbelief ran down her cheeks as an overwhelmed Alice held her with equal vigour and love. They refused to break the embrace, and they couldn't find the words to form coherent sentences. 'I love you' was all that could be heard escaping from both sets of lips in between the crying and smattering of long-missed kisses. But the joy and relief they felt was radiating off of them in such abundance that Jacob felt warmth just to be in the presence of such love.

'I never thought I would see you again,' said Alice, kissing her mother squarely on the lips.

'All that matters is that you are here with us now, because we have so longed for this day.' Angela turned and placed a cupped hand on Jacob's face. 'Isn't that right, my favourite son?'

Alice was so overwhelmed with joy that she didn't allow the shock of such an unusually sweet moment between her mother and husband to break into her thought process.

'That's right, Mum, this day has been long overdue,' said Jacob, caressing his mother-in-law's hand in return.

'Oh my god, what has been going on between you lot while I've been away?' said Alice. 'I feel like I've woken up in the twilight zone.'

Angela took her daughter's hands and sat next to her on the edge of the bed, feeling an instant contentment, one that she never thought she would feel again. 'In times of hardship, sometimes the smallest things can bring us all together.'

Alice furrowed her brow. 'What on earth are you talking about? I'm not sure me being asleep for two years would qualify as a "small thing". Actually, speaking of things that are far from small, where's Dad?'

'Well, I guess I would be here.' The deep and brooding voice of her father split a path between Angela and Jacob like he was parting the Red Sea. His huge frame filled the doorway with its unnatural width and height, and his demeanour was stern and unmoving, as always. John Petalow was a man mountain and a colossus, one who had always hated her husband for never being "quite enough" for his Alice, and yet she could see something different in him, something kind and protective. Where once he had been a bull, now he carried the air of a giant stag – majestic and family orientated, despite its strength and indifference towards others outside of the herd. 'I was parking the car, love. I dropped your mother off at the entrance because she couldn't wait to see you.' He took a few strides into the room with his arms still folded and kissed Alice square on the forehead. 'Welcome home, monkey.'

It was unusual to hear so many words from her father, even under such a unique situation, but Alice knew that he was happy to see her back on her feet – well, at least sitting upright.

'And this, my son, I believe to be yours.' John Petalow unravelled what Alice had assumed was a defensive crossed-arm gesture and passed the most beautiful auburn-haired child to Jacob.

This isn't real.

'Jacob, what's going on?' said Alice as her heart rate grew in both speed and aggression.

The silent child smiled at Jacob while holding onto his tie as if for dear life.

'Alice Marie Brooking, I present to you your daughter, Dorothy Gale Brooking.'

LIES LIES LIES LIES

As Jacob turned her in Alice's direction, Dorothy pushed away from the mother she had only ever experienced as asleep or in a trance-like state. The flame-haired princess had never known her mum, and all the knowledge she had of her was from the stories her dad would tell her each night. Alice was struggling to figure out what was happening – what had happened – and her confusion threatened to send her back into the false reality she had just come from. Alice reached out tenderly to hold the shrinking child's hand but fell short as a young Dorothy cowered from a touch she had never known, leaving Alice to fall forward and into an abyss she, once again, couldn't have seen coming.

-

Alice had fallen like this before, after the assault by Thomas many years before, but where on that occasion she had blacked out and woken up on the carpet of her childhood home, this time she hit the ground hard, and the jolt through her body shook her to her bones as she rapidly decelerated to a standstill. A foot of water had broken her fall, enough to stop serious injury, but the air was knocked from her in one huge and forced exhale that left her gasping.

'Alice!'

She could hear William's voice calling her, and yet as she rose to her feet to check her surroundings, only two things embraced her – darkness, and the murky ocean that rose up to her knee.

'Alice! Come back to me.'

William's voice was coming at her from every angle and she felt her equilibrium tested as she took to her feet in the abyss of pure midnight. Alice spun around on a floor so black it possibly didn't exist and looked for the source of the call, but to no avail. Her movements caused ripples in the water, which looked more like oil, and this brought movement to her attention. Things were swimming about her ankles within the dark liquid. Obsidian tentacles whipped about in a frenzy, making it look like the ground beneath her was actually alive. This couldn't be real ... *Could it?* Remembering back to a session with Dr Phillips, Alice clenched her fists tightly and closed her eyes. She focused only on her physical self and released the tension slowly from her fists, before opening her eyes once more.

There sat in front of her was the image from the hospital ward. She was lying on the bed, catatonic and oblivious to her apparent daughter pointing at her motionless body. Alice was watching it play out as if on a screen. She could see her mum rushing around, screaming for nurses to come and help, while her father just placed a reassuring hand on her shoulder. Jacob, with Dorothy held tight in his arms, looked like the father she knew he would be. His eyes were locked on hers, and she could see him mouthing the words, 'You've got this, Pebble, we believe in you.'

'Alice!'

Alice shot round and looked behind, to see herself seemingly unconscious once more, this time on the soft tartan rug of the picnic that William had set up. His hands pressed tightly on her motionless heart, as he knelt by her side. But this was different, because William was looking straight at her, not at the image of her motionless corpse in front of her.

'It's not real, Alice, come back to me.'

'William, I can't move,' said Alice as she met him in conversation for the first time in the surrealness of the abyss.

'Baby, you have to try. It's not real, any of it,' William shouted, trying to stay strong, just in case Alice needed to use his voice as an anchor.

'What's not real, William?'

Then, as though afraid of something he could see behind Alice, he scrambled to his feet, falling backwards as he hurried.

'NO!' he screamed. 'It can't be.'

Alice turned to find the vision of her family replaced by her mirrored demon self.

Hello Alice.

It wore the same white frock as Alice and yet the frock was stained and filthy. This creature of broken skin and missing teeth was grinning, its over-sized fangs the only thing on the apparition that were not rotten with decay. Once again, Alice was frozen still. The creature, with limbs of unnatural length, stepped forward to grip Alice by her arms. The creature's bony fingers, each ended with black, razor-sharp talons, pierced her flesh as it spoke in its wicked and broken tongue.

IT'S NOT REAL, CHILD.

Alice fell into panic. The stench of the creature's breath was almost overwhelming. Alice clenched her fists and closed her eyes once more. Ignoring the pain in her arm and the hot acrid breath of the oppressor, a feat that wasn't easy as she felt her blood trickle down her wrists, she slowly unclenched her hands and opened her eyes with a bellowing shriek to find her hand holding a tiny ruby shoe, and as she looked up, once more in the real world of the hospital ward, she was faced with a confused Dorothy, a young lady almost amused at the audacity of this new woman in her life, who had stolen her shoe.

'Dorothy,' Alice whispered.

'Dorothy,' Jacob replied reassuringly.

Dorothy said nothing, while pointing at her father with a smile.

Alice watched Dorothy giggle as she reached up to Jacob's face, letting the bristles of his short, well-kept beard tickle her hand. Alice herself tried to hold it together, knowing, without any doubt, where that scar on her belly had come from.

4

Between the Infant and the Abyss
Summer 2009
Faversham, Kent, UK

It had been a week since Alice had woken from her nightmare, and yet she felt more out of place in the waking world than she ever had before. She was sure that this was real, but that didn't mean she had wanted it to be so. She sat in the passenger seat of Jacob's Mercedes and watched the beautiful green countryside of Kent zip past at speed. She was unsure how to feel just yet. Everyone kept telling her how happy she should be for having finally woken up, which would have been fine had she had any recollection of being asleep, yet what had actually happened was that the snow globe of her life had been shaken with such vigour that nothing really made sense anymore. She had an 18-month-old child whom she had no recollection of even carrying. She had a husband and a mother back from beyond the grave and a boyfriend who in reality was not her boyfriend and had no idea what the daft young coma victim was talking about. None of it made sense. She had tried to write it all down with Doctor Phillips, and, on paper at least, it all tied in. William, her boyfriend in the dream world, looked like Dr Williams in the real world. She had imagined her mothers death when Jacob had sat by her side one night and spoken of Angela having a minor stroke. It all added up – even the day that Dorothy would have been conceived fell into place. Alice couldn't fathom how she had never noticed a bump of any kind, although she did remember the struggle of getting into her dress on that awful day of mirror shards and Jacob's return. One thing still didn't click, though: why she would imagine Jacob's death and his eventual release from her life.

'Jay, tell me again about the news you gave me this year – you know, when you used to sit by my bedside.'

Jacob took a while to answer. 'Well, I told you about your mum, and about the shop that I saw for sale – the one I thought would make a great studio for you.' Jacob fidgeted with obvious unease as he continued to reel off things that were not of any help to Alice. 'And then I told you that, erm, that I'd met someone.'

Alice felt weak. She was confused and heartbroken at the news that she could never have seen coming, even though there was no reason for it not to have been a possibility.

'Then why are you here, Jacob, if you have met someone else? Or am I missing something? Why don't you help me to connect these dots?' Alice was glad that her supposed daughter was in her father's Range Rover just ahead.

'Because you are my wife, Alice, and despite the fact we broke up – and you cannot deny that we did – it doesn't mean I stopped loving you or even wanting you back.' Jacob sighed deeply and took a moment to find the right line of defence. 'I came back to you that day in San Diego because I wanted to make things right with you. I'd had extensive therapy and had come a million miles from the person who had left you those three months before, but I never planned to find you cutting your own throat open, I never planned for you to go to sleep for two years, and I certainly never planned to meet anyone, even though I had no idea if you would ever wake up.' Jacob tried to take

Alice's hand but was quickly rejected. 'Alice, I never thought you were going to wake up, and yet I still came and sat with you each day in the blind hope that you would.'

The Mercedes pulled into the Petalows' driveway. John was carrying a fast-asleep Dorothy into the house.

'I'll get the bags out,' said Jacob. 'Do you need a hand getting to your room, love?'

Alice scowled and reached for the door, but Jacob stopped her with a firm grip on her arm.

'Alice, I've done nothing wrong here.'

Alice sat back once again. 'Then you won't mind telling me everything, will you?'

Everything? Well, this is going to be fun, said Ahab.

Yes, old friend, you might want to stay out of this one, thought Jacob.

Autumn 2008

Faversham, Kent, UK

'Double espresso, Mr Brooking?' said the barista at Barton Millie's Coffee Cup, one of those modern types of coffee house where the staff all had tattoos and suede aprons.

'Yes please, Jessica, and would you be so kind as to run it over to my table with a smoked cheese croissant?'

Jacob handed over a crisp ten-pound note from his money clip and refused the change with a wave of his hand. His morning had been productive. He had worn his best navy suit and tie to try to show the other shareholders at the Gallantry that he was still in charge of the operation despite having to sell 30% of the restaurant to cover Alice's medical bills. He needn't have bothered, as he had methodically picked the shareholders – Canterbury's best offerings of poor little rich kids who just wanted to own a share in a fancy restaurant – so as to ensure they would always feel subservient to him.

He sat at the small table that he frequented most days and laid out his newspaper, pondering for a moment just when exactly he had become so calculated. Still, it seemed to be working for him, as business was on the up: his take from the business seemed to have enjoyed a slight growth, despite his drop in shares and a reduction of time spent in the kitchen. He still wrote the menus and tasted the dishes, and a random fiery tirade at a slack member of staff always kept the crew on their toes, but mostly his days were filled with Dorothy giggling to herself and him marvelling at how such a broken man could create such a happy and perfect thing. Dotty wasn't here today, as he had work to do; she would be sitting in the garden with her gramps. John Petalow had softened since her entry into the world eight months earlier, and the giant of a man would sit and play with her for hours, while Angela would tend to the various wild flowers that filled the Petalows' five-acre garden.

With work out of the way, it was Jacob's time to breathe. Being a single father had come to Jacob with ease; it was the only thing he had found easy in all his years alive. Keeping her happy and safe had given him a focus he had never experienced before. It was all about her, no one else. Dorothy Gale Brooking and her beautiful smile had killed his selfishness in just a few months, and the bond they shared had proved to him that it was possible to love someone so much that it fixes you on every level.

Jacob Brooking had never felt so normal, and it was a good place to be. He would still hear the monster in his thoughts, from time to time – that was normal. As Jessica brought him his coffee and croissant, he noticed her blush, and yet the voice mocked him, tried to bring him low once more.

She thinks you're a loner.

Well, she wouldn't be wrong. Jacob smiled, fully aware that friends were not really his forte.

And old, the voice cackled.

Well, that's just rude. Let's not forget that you are the same age as me, you old bastard.

Jacob had developed a better way of dealing with his inner voice of late. Dr Phillips had told him that if he couldn't win the fight with his inner demon, he should stop fighting it.

'Thank you, Jessica. How's that boyfriend of yours? Still keeping you happy, love?'

'You know how it is, Mr Brooking. Until he pulls his finger out, I'll always be on the lookout for something better.' Jessica turned to hide her blush and gave an obvious wiggle to draw his attention down.

'Really, Jay, you will flirt with anyone, but do you have to tease "the help" with your endless charms?'

Jacob looked up and nearly choked on the first bite of his pastry.

'Oh my god – Evan. I don't know what to say. I ...'

Well, you're fucked.

'Don't panic, Jay, just bloody give me a hug so we can kill this awkwardness.'

Evan opened her arms up to Jacob, which did nothing to ease his fear, but he surprised himself and stood to embrace her all the same.

'Of course. I'm sorry, Evan. How are you?'

'I'm really well, thanks. May I join you?'

Evan motioned at the seat opposite and then pulled herself into the spot. Skinny jeans so tight they were almost painted onto her perfectly curved rear drew Jacob's attention with little effort, despite the crippling fear in his heart.

Evan sighed. 'I must confess, I had kind of hoped you would look worse than you do, Jay.'

Jacob tried to force his grin to look natural, but failed. 'From you I take that as a compliment. Evan, listen, I need to say ...'

Evan cut him off quickly. 'I'm sorry too, but I don't think us bringing up the past is how we enjoy this impromptu coffee, do you?'

Jacob relaxed slightly and drew in his puffed-out chest. 'I am sorry, though, I need you to know that. I'm not that guy anymore.'

Evan reached over the table and placed a reassuring hand on his. 'Jacob Brooking, I'm not made of glass, OK? And if the rumours are to be believed, I hear you have had a harder few years than I.'

She knows.

'I didn't know my news had spread so quickly and was so important to the community in general?'

Evan smiled softly and seemed genuine as she squeezed his hand ever so slightly before releasing it. 'Jay, your wife tried to kill herself and then gave birth to your child whilst in a coma – a coma it seems she might be in for the rest of her life. Do you think that's not gossip-worthy, especially when we share a lot of the same friends still?'

Jacob laughed.

'OK, they may be employees to you,' said Evan, 'but they are friends to me, you big meanie managing director you.'

Evan parted her plump lips to reveal her perfect white teeth and a smile that had always had a power over him, much like her long blonde hair, which today was straightened and fell over her shoulders and past her breasts, almost to her lap.

'You look good, Evan. You always did. Can I get you a coffee whilst we catch up?' Jacob rose, knowing the answer already.

'A flat white please, Jay, and then you can tell me all about it.'

Jacob looked confused. 'All about what?'

Evan leaned forward, rested her elbow on the coffee table and gently cradled her jaw while twirling her hair between her fingers. 'About San Diego, Jacob. About what happened when you left me.'

Summer 2009

Canterbury, Kent, UK

'Jacob, how could you?' Alice felt an overwhelming desire to scream, but the medication was doing its job of keeping her calm, at least on the surface.

'We broke up,' said Jacob. 'I went away for three months, and we haven't spoken a single word to each other in two years. I never thought you would wake up. I thought my life was just me and Dotty, and I bumped into her randomly. Would it make a difference if it was anyone else?'

For once, Jacob didn't sound like he was making excuses. His life hadn't stopped for two years, and he wasn't going to apologise for any choices he had made while struggling on his own.

'Well, I wonder if my parents would love you so much if they knew?' said Alice, sounding a little spoiled and hurt.

'They already know. I asked your mother's advice before I moved forward. How could I not? They have helped me raise our child, I had to show them that respect.'

Alice turned her gaze from him. 'Respect, Jay? What about respect for me? How about anyone in the world except for her?'

Dorothy let out a cry that immediately brought Jacob over to the mock playpen he had built for her out of cushions stolen from the couch.

'What's up, little boo?' said Jacob as he picked up his terrified daughter from the floor. 'Tell me.'

Dorothy clung to Jacob like he was about to vanish. Jacob went and sat next to Alice and tried to offer Dorothy over, but she wrapped her arms around her dad's body all the tighter.

'She hates me, Jay. That's why she doesn't want anything to do with me.'

'She will come around. This is all new to her. She hadn't heard you talk until last week, and now she's listening to you shout at me.' Jacob knew he had made a mistake with that last comment and so quickly tried to deflate the situation by waving Dorothy's hand at her angry mother.

'Don't you dare use this little club you two have going on to deflect what you have done, Jay. Not her – not Evan.'

Alice's voice was in check, knowing that scaring Dorothy was probably not the best way into her heart, but

Jacob knew that he didn't have much choice other than to agree with Alice on this.

'You're right,' he said. 'I should have been more thoughtful. Together or apart, I owed you that, Alice. I was lonely, and knowing you had started dating so quickly after I had left on that godforsaken voyage ... Well, I didn't think.'

Alice looked up at Jacob, confused. 'How do you know I was dating, when you were apparently lost at sea?'

'Because when I held you in my arms, blood pouring from the gaps in the compress I was forcing onto your neck wound, your date turned up to ask why you hadn't showed up to meet him at the Harbour Café. He walked in and attacked me, thinking it was me who had hurt you, but I wouldn't put you down. He eventually guided the paramedics into you from the road.' Jacob's voice trembled as he thought back to that day once more. 'Pebble, you can believe what you want, but I have not sat idle since that day, none of us have, and I'm sorry but I was struggling at the end to do it alone.'

Ten months earlier

'Jacob, hi, it's Evan. I know you have a lot going on, what with the baby and looking after Alice and all. I just wondered if I could lighten the load a little and make you dinner this week. Let you be you for a night. It doesn't have to mean anything.'

Do it, we like Evan.

'Evan, I don't know what to say. That's so kind of you to offer, and certainly it's unexpected. Let me see if I can find a sitter for the night. I'll get back to you soon as.'

You're not even going to try, are you? Coward!

'Great,' said Evan. 'I'm excited for you to see the new place, and I expect you to bring the wine – your taste is too expensive for my purse.'

You won't go.

I'm not sure you deserve a girl that attractive.

'Too expensive for your purse? Evan, your purse is a £1,500 Prada job. I know that because I bought the bastard thing.'

You don't have the backbone to follow through with this.

'Yeah, but you didn't fill it with money, my darling Jacob. Right, I'll let you get back to whatever you were doing – or whomever, should I say.'

That was an attack, you know it was.

Jacob held up the full diaper that he had been trying to change while speaking to Evan with the phone pressed between his shoulder and ear. 'Trust me when I say this, I would swap whatever it is you are doing with the task I'm handling right now.'

'All the more reason to get back to me with a positive answer, then. Goodbye, Mr Brooking, text me when you get the chance.'

'I'm on it. Give me an hour or two.'

Jacob put the phone down. He could barely hear his own thoughts due to Dorothy screaming at his poor attempt to replace her nappy, and all the chatter the voice in his head was throwing his way.

I'm going to bloody go, he thought, *I need a break.*

What you need and what you deserve are two different things. She will probably slit her throat when you walk through the door, just like Alice di..

JUST LIKE ALICE DID? Is that what you were going to say? Because I'm tired of that broken record. I'm going because I want to go, and nothing you say will stop me. Jacob could hear himself shouting, even though the conversation was in his thoughts.

With that, the creature went silent, and then it smiled a smile that exposed every fanged tooth in its kraken-like beak.

Yes, Jacob, you are going to do exactly what you want to do. All this is on you, it always was.

This time, the creature whispered, and its smile remained long after the sun had set.

Summer 2009

'So, this is it, then?' said Alice, defeated not only by the news, but by Jacob's honest account of it. 'We are not going to work this through and sort our marriage out?'

'I'm not saying anything other than this. You have come back into a world that has kept turning in your absence. We need to get you fit and healthy, Dorothy needs you to adapt into the mother that I know you are going to be, and you need to find yourself once more. I'll speak with Evan, but you must know that this, all of this, is all about you getting well, not us getting back together.'

Jacob stood up and held Dorothy out so her mother could kiss her brow.

'Goodnight, my angel,' Alice whispered.

Dorothy once again shied away into Jacob's arms.

'Goodbye, Pebble. Call me if you need me for anything.'

Before he could reach the door, Alice said his name.

'Thank you for being honest with me,' she said. 'I don't like what you have told me, in actual fact I hate it, but you never would have been this honest before, so I guess you have changed.'

Jacob smiled, gave a slight nod and pulled the door behind him.

-

Hours passed and Alice didn't move. *Why her?* was all she could keep asking herself. *Why Evan fucking Laurie?*

BECAUSE IT'S NOT REAL. COME BACK TO US, ALICE. IT'S NEVER BEEN REAL.

The voice took Alice by surprise, for she had made a point of asking her father to remove all the mirrors from the house, and it was so very rare to hear it speak without a reflection. In fact, the only time she had ever heard the voice speak that clearly without a reflection had been at her mother's funeral, in the world that apparently wasn't real ...

Alice snapped, and the tears of confusion that she had shed so many times these past few days returned with a vengeance. 'Where am I?' she sobbed, digging her nails once more into the soft flesh of her thigh.

5

The Tell-Tale Heart
Autumn 2008
Faversham, Kent, UK

As I take a seat upon this magnificent leather sofa, a sofa of deep stitches and brass finishing, the one that I have admired for so many years, it saddens my heart once more that I didn't have the courage to talk to you about this before, without, that is, having to pay for an hour of your time.

True! I'm negligent, very, very dreadfully negligent. I had been and am always such; I make as little time for you as you do for me, but why will you say that I am in love? The adoration I may have for this man has sharpened my senses, not taken them on flights of fantasy, not dulled them with words that you and I both know have little meaning in this real world, this painfully dreadful world. I know my senses are acute. I know my own mind. I have seen all things in the heaven and in the earth. I heard many things in hell and have come close to living them at times. I KNOW THIS WORLD! How, then, could I be in love? For to be in love, one must not be of this realm.

Take my candour, please, and observe how healthily and how calmly I can tell you the whole story.

-

It is impossible to say how first the idea entered my brain; but once conceived, it haunted me day and night. I lusted for the man whose affections I had previously won. He had never wanted me the same. But he had never given me insult; even in the days before he left, he had begged forgiveness. For his gold I had no desire, although it certainly had its charms, and he had given it freely. Yet the idea came to me that he was more than just a flight of fancy out of nowhere. I think, in the end, it was his eyes! Yes, it was this! He had the eyes of an avenging angel, a viridian green, with a crystal pupil that refracted light as if not meant to give true reflection of such a wondrous creature. Whenever it fell upon me, my blood ran hot and my pulse rose in both tempo and depth; and so by degrees – very gradually – I made up my mind to take the heart of the man once more, and thus rid myself of the powerless longing forever. Not because I loved him ... Because I didn't want to be so powerless to a man I was getting no return from.

  Now this is the point. You fancy me in love. You, a woman of culture and class. A woman of higher education than most can dream of. Women in love know nothing. But you should have seen me. You should have seen how wisely I proceeded – with what caution, with what foresight, with what dissimulation I went to work! Does that sound like the madness of love? He never knew that my new place of work – another restaurant – was opposite his regular coffee shop, a chance that fate had thrown at us both. Fate ... another made-up word for an irrational concept. I was never more taken by the man than during the whole week before I came to you today. And every morning, about midday, I pulled the silk rope of our blinds and opened them – oh so gently! The restaurant was so dark that no light shone out, yet enough was let in for me to see him each day. Oh, you would have laughed to see how unknowingly I had let him into my life! I undid the blind just so much that a single thin ray fell upon my vulture's eye. And this I did for seven long days, every morning at midday, but I found my eye impossible to close; and so it was impossible to do the work; for it was not the man who vexed me, but his power that held me so, unbeknownst to him. And every morning, when the day broke, I went boldly into the window bay and spoke courageously to him, calling him by name in a hearty tone, and inquiring how he had passed the night. Yet I would have to stop when the others came near, lest they think me mad. So, you see he would have been a very profound man, indeed, to suspect that every day, just at twelve, I looked in upon him while he sat by the window and drank his elixir of caffeine and dark magic.

 Upon the eighth day, just yesterday in fact, I was less than my usually cautious self, a whimsy caused by lack of sleep from an unrelated matter of mind, and in letting in the light, a rare mistake was made. A watch's minute hand moves more quickly than did mine and I lost a quarter of an hour to his gaze. Never before that day had I felt my powers so greatly diminished. I could scarcely contain my feelings of loneliness since the last sight I had of the man, whom you laughably say I must love. To think that there I was, opening the blinds once more, little by little, and he not even to dream of my secret deeds or thoughts. I fairly restrained a chuckle at the idea; and perhaps he saw me, knew I was there; for he moved once more to the table I forever saw him at, as if he knew no other table would provide me with ample view. *He knows*, I told myself, for why else would he always sit there? Now you may think that I drew back, but no. My room was as dark as the cobbled streets were light, and with the veil of darkness, the veil that protected me each and every day, doing the job that I had called on it to do, I watched once more, and so I knew that he could not see the opening of the blinds. I kept quite still and said nothing. For a whole minute that felt akin to an hour I did not move a muscle, and he could not see me. I did not catch acknowledgement in his eyes of green, jade and emerald – yes, emerald. He was still listening to music, an earphone in one ear and one hanging loosely about his neck, just in case a pretty little waitress chose to talk to him. But they could only dream of such a man; just as I have done, night after night, thinking of the man and his lips upon my flesh. And yet you say I am in love. Does my clarity of thought stand for nothing? I care little for your fantasy and the use of words better left in the poetry books of forgotten scholars.

When I had waited a long time – minutes? Hours? Days perhaps? – but very patiently, without seeing him change position, I resolved to open a very, very little crevice in the window itself. So as to maybe breathe a little of the same air that he himself had taken into the very lungs I so desired would breathe their warmth over my shoulder once more. So, I opened it, you cannot imagine how stealthily, until, at length, a bright sunray, like the thread of a spider, shot from out the crevice and fell full upon my vulture's eye. The window was open, it was open wide, and I grew scared as I saw him look in my direction. But I could see nothing to tell me of the crime being caught. The man's face or demeanour remained unbothered, a stroke of luck, as I had directed the ray, as if by instinct, precisely upon the damned spot where I stood watching. He sipped at his elixir and mouthed the words of such a song that I could not imagine. I was fully aware of my actions and of his, and have I not told you that what you mistake for love is but over-acuteness of the senses?

Now, I say, there came to my ears a low, dull, quick sound, such as a watch makes when enveloped in cotton. I knew that sound well, too. It was the beating of my heart. It increased my longing, as the beating of a drum stimulates the soldier into courage.

So I was exposed to him, but even then I kept still. I scarcely breathed. I held the blind motionless. I tried to see how steadily I could maintain the ray upon the form. I understood I was exposed and yet felt thrilled within my own form. Meantime the hellish tattoo of my heart increased. It grew quicker and quicker, and louder and louder, every instant. Mark me well, for I have told you that I am nervous: so, I am. And so I was at the hour of twelve, before our patrons joined us for lunches, drinks, the clamour of false lives and wishes unfulfilled. But amid the dreadful silence of that empty restaurant, so strange a noise as my own heartbeat excited me to near uncontrollable terror. Yet, for some minutes longer I refrained and stood still. The beating grew louder, louder! I thought my heart must burst, and now a new anxiety seized me – the sound would be heard by a customer or member of my crew. The hour had come for me to focus my attention elsewhere! And with a loud yell of frustration, I threw open the front doors and leapt into the cobbled streets, quickly pulling down the awnings to protect our al fresco diners from the very rays that had exposed my eye. Moving quickly and in open secrecy as I kept my back to the man, through fear that he might recognise me once more, in an instant I dragged my menu board to its home upon the floor and pulled the heavy wooden slats into position. I then smiled gaily, to find the deed so far done. But, for many minutes, as I retreated back within the sanctuary of the dark, the heart beat on with a muffled sound. This, however, did not vex me; it would not be heard through my blouse, not by kin nor patron alike. At length it ceased. The feeling dead until tomorrow. I placed my hand upon my heart and held it there many minutes. There was no pulsation that felt abnormal. The rush that the man had pulled upon me had subsided, as it did each day. His emerald eyes would trouble me no more.

If still you think me in love, you will think so no longer when I describe the wise precautions I took for the concealment of my emotions. As the bell sounded upon the hour, there came a holler at the street door. I went down to greet it with a light heart, for what had I now to fear? There entered three handsome men, who introduced themselves, with perfect suavity, as men of the local law firm. They were led to a table with a view of the beautiful town that surrounded them. Their drinks order was taken with jollity and efficiency, for what had I to fear? I bade the gentlemen a good lunch and a good stay.

The men were satisfied. My manner had convinced them. I was singularly at ease. They sat, and they ate in silence before they drank and enjoyed a little hubris, whilst the talk of success and women's hearts won dominated the air about them, and whilst I answered cheerily to any question thrown my way. I was pleasant and open as I always am and have been, for they chatted of familiar things. But, ere long, I felt myself getting pale and wished them gone. My head ached and my heart more so, and I fancied a ringing in my ears; but still they sat and still chatted. The ringing became more distinct. It continued and became more acute. I talked more freely to get rid of the feeling, forgetting my place as host; but it continued and gained definiteness, until, with certainty, I found that I had to make my excuses and return to the safety of the cellar.

My heart once more pounded within my chest and I found myself short of breath. A young server joined me, of young years and fair face, no knowledge of the world yet imparted on her soul. Although not seeking safety like I, she proudly proclaimed, 'Miss Evan, the table by the window, the table of money and of arrogance, they ask for you, Miss Evan, they clamour for your time once more.'

I waved the young cherub away with a gesture of indifference. Why would they not be gone? I paced the floor with heavy strides, as if frustrated by the desires of the men, when it was the desires of one man I wanted and nothing more. Oh God! What could I do? I rallied my thoughts and I took to my task.

'Gentlemen, what shall it be?' I asked with the mime of someone who might actually enjoy that damned profession. But I heard nothing over my own racing heart, as I looked up through the window to see him leave, the man who took my breath from me with nothing but his presence. My heart now throbbed, and I feared all would hear it. It grew louder, louder and louder still! And yet the men chatted pleasantly and smiled as if ignorant to my plight. Was it possible they heard not? Almighty God! No, no! They heard! They knew! They were making a mockery of my torment! This I thought, and this I think. But anything was better than this agony! Anything was more tolerable than this derision! I could bear those hypocritical smiles no longer! I felt that I must scream or die! And now, again! It grows louder, louder, louder, louder!

'Gentlemen, but a moment, please.'

I opened the front door to find the sun, the air and the cobbles of the street, but he was gone, and with that, also the beating of my heart. Only emptiness remained, and the hollow shell of the cold woman you raised took herself aside to devalue the incident as nothing more than tiredness.

So, you may say I am in love, but really, do I sound of such a fantastical mindset? When I remember everything so calculatedly and without whimsical nostalgia, does that really tell you of love, mother?

6

Sliding Doors
Spring 2010
Faversham, Kent, UK

Look at you. Look at your skin as it catches the few rays of morning light trying to squeeze their way through the curtain break. You are beautiful, in a different way to Alice entirely, but no less so. I can't help but be mesmerised by the ringlets of blonde hair that fall so naturally, and how, even as you sleep in front of me, well, you look like you are posing for a shot. I'm waiting for you to open your eyes, so that I can kiss you without fear of waking you, because every girl who puts up with me must surely deserve more rest than others.

Jacob leaned over despite himself and gently laid his lips on her brow. He whispered I love you and slipped out of the bedroom. How had this happened to him? He had been through so much drama in his life – most of it caused by his own poor mindset, of course – that he didn't understand what he had done to deserve two beautiful women in his life, but he did have them, and he was happy.

He entered his kitchen in only his olive-coloured hipster briefs and danced a little as the stone tiles caught his bare feet off guard. He had always regretted not getting the underfloor heating here, as this kitchen floor was so beautiful he doubted it would ever be brought up for another. He methodically poured filtered water into his minimalist glass coffee jar and watched the drops of dark roast slowly fill the pot drip by drip. Jacob had always preferred the pour-over method of coffee-making. Yes, it took three minutes to get a cup, but the depths of flavour were the wake-up that his senses needed to take on the day. He hadn't heard Ahab in his mind for a few days, although he still jumped a little when the toaster broke the quiet perfection of the drip, drip, drip and spat out a slice of his home-baked loaf. He lavished its surface with salted butter and gripped it between his teeth while picking up both drinks.

The sensation of swapping from cold stone to warm carpet sent a tingle up his calves. He nudged the bedroom door open with his bottom as he entered the room backwards, and there he was, only his underwear to cover his shame as he stood, his large thighs constrained by the elastic and his flat stomach rippling with muscles that had only appeared since his dramatic boat diet two years before. With a milky tea in one hand and his drip-poured coffee in his right, he stood, toast in mouth, and marvelled at what lay before him. For as she lay, uncovered by sheet or clothing, a painted nail gently bitten in her mouth and her other hand squeezing the most perfect breasts Jacob had ever seen in life or for that matter on screen or in a magazine, she took Jacob's lust as she had taken his heart.

He placed the hot drinks and the toast on the bedside table, a piece of furniture he had taken from the boat he had been stranded upon. Then he leaned in and placed his lips on hers as he took his place above her, his hands exploring her body from her hips all the way up, until he pinned her arms above her head and entwined their fingers.

Her big eyes sparkled in the morning light as his tongue left her mouth with a gentle pull on her bottom lip.

'I can't believe the first time you say those words, it's when you think I'm asleep, Jay. Really, what is a girl to think?' Evan smiled innocently, which for her was never an easy feat, before leaning in for another kiss. Just before their lips touched, she whispered seductively, 'I love you too, Jay. I think I always have done.'

-

Look at you. Look at your skin as it catches the few rays of morning light trying to squeeze their way through the curtain break. You are beautiful, in a different way to anything I have ever deemed to fit that word. I can't help but be mesmerised by the colour of your hair, which is both the dark brown of your brooding father's and the autumnal fire of my own, and how even as you sleep in front of me, well, you look like you are a gift from heaven. I'm waiting for you to open your eyes, so that I can hold your little hand without fear of waking you, because every girl who puts up with me and your father surely deserves more rest than others.

Alice leaned over despite herself and gently covered Dorothy with the soft blanket she had kicked off during the night, before slipping out of the bedroom. How had this happened to her? She had been through so much drama in her life - most of it caused by her own poor mindset, of course - that she didn't seem to understand what she had done to deserve to have such a beautiful little woman in her life, but she did have her, and she was happy, she was sure she was, although still confused as to moving forward. Dorothy clung to her dad and could not speak a word to Alice, and, in turn, Alice had found it very hard to bond with her, although she knew it was early days.

Alice entered her parents' kitchen in her university hoodie and a pair of Jacob's old joggers. Her bare feet tingled and warmed as the stone tiles caught them off guard with the under-floor heating her father had fitted a few years back, apparently to help with his gout. He never complained about physical stuff much, so Alice couldn't argue with her father's expensive answer to his pain; it was his money, after all. She poured herself a green tea and threw some Cheerios into a bowl for Dorothy. She hadn't heard her stir just yet but knew it was coming. She may have struggled to bond with Dorothy – she still felt like she was looking after Jacob's child two days a week – but she had the heart of a mother, and taking care of Dorothy certainly wasn't a chore. Lost in her thoughts, she jumped a little when the toaster broke the silence and spat out a slice of Jacob's home-baked loaf. She lavished its surface with margarine and her mother's strawberry jam and gripped it between her teeth while taking her tea and Dorothy's breakfast back to bed.

The sensation of swapping from hard stone to the softness of the carpet in the hall sent a tingle up her calves. She nudged the bedroom door open with her bottom as she entered the room backwards, and ... There he was, with only his underwear to cover his shame as he lay on his side upon Alice's bed, his chiselled body a patchwork of tattoos and his smile half hidden by his grey beard.

Alice dropped her tea, which smashed to the ground, quickly followed by the jam-covered toast.

William sprung to his feet. 'Are you OK? Let me help you.'

Alice looked around the room, noticing it to be the bedroom of the cottage in her dream.

'Dorothy!' she called as she ran out of the room, leaving William picking up the broken mug. Alice panicked. This was home, her make-believe home but her home, so there was no bedroom in which she would find her daughter. She darted from door to door, just to check her sanity wasn't as fractured as she feared, and found nothing. She ran back into the bedroom, where William was soaking up the green tea with a towel. She shrieked at what stood behind him, reflecting in the very mirror in which she had parted ways with Jacob's memory all those years ago. Her hair the red of grease and just as unclean, her flesh broken and unclean, her teeth rotten and broken apart from the pair of long pristine fangs either side of her forked tongue, which were highlighted all the more by the unnaturally large smile that this demonic version of Alice was always wearing.

'Alice, what's wrong?' asked William as she slumped to the floor in front of him, unable to breathe and unable to cry.

Welcome home, child, voiced the demon Alice with the wicked smile of the unclean.

7

Johnno was a Local Boy
End of summer 2007
Psychiatric Hospital of San Diego, USA

'What do you mean, she's pregnant?' asked Jacob.

'What I mean, Mr Brooking, is that we have had to put her into an induced coma due to her insistence on taking her own life, and this is more complicated due to the fact she is at least 16 weeks pregnant. You didn't notice your wife's small bump? Have there been any other signs, Mr Brooking?'

The woman tasked with minimising the damage Alice had done to herself just 12 hours before was Doctor Creed, the head of surgery. She was a woman of pure business – make-up free, hair impeccably scraped back. Everything seemed to be measured to perfection. Even the cactus on her desk sat upright at a perfect angle, and this was something that filled Jacob with the confidence he needed to get through the situation.

'No. I mean, I don't know. I've not been around so much the last three months. In fact, as I walked in on her cutting her throat, it was the first time I had seen her in 14 weeks.' Jacob fell into the seat opposite the doctor, completely bemused by the situation. 'Will the baby be OK?'

'The baby seems fine, and her heart rate doesn't appear to be affected at all by her mother's condition. If worst comes to worst and we can't get Alice right, then we can safely deliver like this, but let's hope we don't have to.'

Jacob wasn't listening. '*Her* heart? She's a girl?'

The doctor smiled. 'Yes, Mr Brooking. You are having a daughter.'

Jacob looked up, concerned. 'You seem to suggest she might not wake up. How much of a possibility is that? Please be honest.'

'I don't know any other way to be, Mr Brooking. But right now, nothing is certain. We don't expect anything to happen quickly. She needs to heal, both outside and in. Whatever demon she is trying to fight, we need to help her as best we can, and right now that means leaving her to rest.'

Over the Atlantic

'This is his fault, love, I'm telling you. It's that bastard Jacob, he's caused this.' John was livid. To hear that his Alice was in a critical condition had broken his heart, and John Petalow dealt with heartbreak the only way he knew how – with anger directed at the person he felt was responsible.

'You don't know that it's anything to do with Jacob. The last few times I spoke with Alice she seemed genuinely happy with everything, and I think Jay had a lot to do with that.'

Angela had always been John's voice of reason, but right now that wasn't going well with him.

'He is a drain on that poor girl's happiness, and you know it.' John spoke with the kind of tone that he usually reserved for the people who worked for him; it was rare for his wife to catch this end of the deal. 'Do you remember her as a teen? Always singing, always dancing. Everything she did had an aura of love and happiness. Where has that Alice been the last 15 years?'

'I know you don't like Jacob, I know you're worried about Alice. Do you not think I'm holding back the tears right now? Believe me, I am! But you are not helping, so shut up, remember you are a bloody Petalow, and get some rest.'

John knew better than to reply to this tirade from his wife. Instead, he tried to get comfortable so that he could sleep. The first-class seat was still too small for him; flying any other class wasn't even an option for him, as these were the only seats that fit him, bar the cargo hold. He downed the cheap bourbon that the flight attendant was claiming to be single malt whiskey and closed his eyes. *Bastard Jacob Brooking, ignoring my warning. I'll tear his arms off.* John drifted off with a wry smile, as he knew that was wholly possible for him to achieve. Unfortunately, he slipped into a dream that wasn't such a satisfying image.

He saw friends being killed in front of him. He saw the inside of **HMS** *Oberon*, the submarine that had been his prison for all those months. He and his very advanced Special Boat Service team had been on that sub in the Falklands during the summer of 1979, long before the war had started, and yet he still saw death.

Jacob Brooking stood there with him. The dead body of his daughter and the rest of C Squadron lay littered around them, mixed with the dead bodies of a dozen other submariners, butchered beyond all reason, with their throats cut or their hearts punctured. Jacob, wearing an Argentine uniform that seemed to fit him as if he'd been born into it, smiled with malicious intent. His hands were covered with blood, and at his feet was Alice, whose neck was broken and bloodied by a clearly one-sided struggle. John's heart started to race. He screamed his daughter's name and lunged at Jacob, but he was easily overpowered by a simple sweep of Jacob's arm, which brought him crashing to his knees.

'She's been mine for long enough now, Viking king. I will do with her as I please.'

In one motion, Jacob brought his hand down on John's exposed neck, meeting no resistance and taking his head clean off. John's decapitated head rolled like a hellish marble drawn from the nightmares of the damned until it came to rest next to the motionless body of his daughter, dead eyes looking back at his own, no speech able to escape his guillotined vocal cords.

-

As Jacob sat in the first-class waiting lounge, ready for the abuse he was sure to receive, he couldn't help but wonder what would have happened had he not returned to Alice. Was it his proximity to her that had made her do it? Could she sense him returning?

That's madness. I'm thinking like a madman. How could she have known I was coming? I saved her.

Jacob had been trying to convince himself of this for the whole journey to San Diego International, and he was no closer to succeeding after an hour of sitting at the bar, nursing a bourbon.

You're going to be a single father with a brain-dead wife. Good luck explaining that to the Viking, laughed the monstrous voice with a wicked cackle.

This wasn't my fault and you know it; Alice has always had her demons, just like I do.

Her demons didn't exist until she found out about Evan, or before you dragged her away from her family. Or shall we go further back, to when you bought a restaurant behind her back before convincing her to murder her unborn child? Was that not your fault either, Jacob? JACOB???

'WHAT?' shouted Jacob, much to the surprise of the barman, who had been minding his own business.

You know this is all on you.

'But what the hell can I do about it now? I'm here, aren't I? Trying to make things right. What more can I do?' Jacob whispered to himself.

'You can start by bringing the car around to the front,' said a tired voice from behind.

Jacob turned to see Alice's mum standing there with her arms open.

'Hello Angela,' he said, jumping down from the bar stool to accept the hug he didn't realise he had needed. 'Where's John?'

'Getting the luggage sorted. He's ... eager to see you. I guess that would be the way to put it.'

Angela found a false smile to go with this statement, but it did nothing to hide the reality of the situation. John Petalow wanted answers, and he would wring them from Jacob's neck if he had to.

-

John Petalow gripped Jacob by the throat and pinned him against the wall of the hospital waiting room with such brute force that a calendar on the opposing wall fluttered to the ground.

'She's pregnant?' shouted John, blinded by rage. 'You bully my only child into trying to take her own life and you knock her up for good measure. Why? So she can't escape your narcissism. I should fucking kill you, Brooking.'

The Viking king might have been a huge man, but like most apex predators, knowing that he had no equal often meant he would forget to guard himself, and this was one of those times. Jacob wasn't the beast that his father-in-law was, but he was still a fairly fit young man who had been in enough scrapes in his life to know how to protect himself. You couldn't defend against a man like John Petalow for long, so instead Jacob drove a balled fist upwards, catching John on his chin with a thunderous uppercut that rocked him back a few feet. The Viking king wasn't a man who could be dropped by normal means, and even a punch of real quality wouldn't have come close to hurting him. In the aftermath of the incident, Jacob mused that his knuckles had taken more damage than John's face. However, something changed in John's eyes. A modicum of respect washed over him for just a moment, and he brought his hand up to his jaw and rotated it in a circular motion to check it wasn't damaged. Then he crossed his arms and uttered a single word: 'SPEAK!'

'I didn't bully her into anything. There is more to this than either of us understand, of that I am sure.' Jacob pulled himself straight. 'And, yes, I got my wife pregnant. That is something that can happen between two consenting adults, especially when they are husband and wife.'

'I warned you,' John growled. 'I told you to sort your life out.'

'And I have,' responded Jacob sharply. 'So stop jumping on my back. You may be Alice's father, but you damn sure are not mine.'

'So what do you intend to do here? Are you going to run away, like normal? Bury your head in the sand again?'

'I'll tell you what I'm going to do. When this child comes – which I have been assured can happen safely, whether Alice is awake or not – I will be as good a father as my own, and not a bully and a judgemental arsehole.'

John smiled at hearing Jacob fight back for a change. 'Careful there. Those are some big words you're throwing about, and I'd hate for you to break your other hand on my face.'

'I'm going to do right by her.'

'Her,' muttered the Viking king.

'It seems you are having a granddaughter – or should I say princess to your throne, my liege.' Jacob bowed theatrically as he spoke.

'Enough of that shit. I will only let so much go. Sit down.' John eased his giant frame into a plastic hospital chair and pointed to the one opposite. 'Listen, son, if you do what you say, I will give you my full support, as will my Angela. But I want something in return, and I promise you won't like it.' John leaned forward. 'We want you to leave Alice, and we want her home.' He raised his hand instantly to block the reply he knew was coming. 'Hear me out. She's not happy, we both know that. But when was the last time you were happy? The last time you were not on the run? Alice is not the answer to your problems.'

Jacob sighed. 'I don't think that matters anyway. She found out about Evan and left me about three months ago. I say left me – kicked me out would be more precise. And, as you say, I did all I know how to do. I ran.'

'I guess that explains my friend's missing boat.'

Jacob nodded. 'Some weeks stuck afloat, then some spent getting my head right. I'm not the man you knew before. I'm not even the man Alice knew. But you're right. There is no happy ever after with us.'

'So we have a deal, son.' John offered his hand.

'Yeah, we have a deal. And any help moving forward would be greatly appreciated.'

'I'll talk to Angela as soon as we get back to the hotel.'

'What's wrong?' said Jacob, noticing how defeated John looked. 'Isn't this what you wanted?'

'My daughter in a coma, pregnant, divorcing her cheating husband ... I'm not the monster you think I am. Let me tell you a secret.' He paused for a second. 'I mean what I've said, and I will honour our agreement to help you, but if you tell anyone what I'm about to tell you, I will gut you like a seabass. Not even Alice. OK?'

Jacob nodded, taken aback that his father-in-law, of all people, might tell him something that he wouldn't tell his own daughter.

'I have another child. Before Alice, I had a one-night stand with someone I'd met through ... well, it doesn't matter how we met. We never saw one another again – at least, she never saw me. I'd been with Angela for a few months when I saw the lady in question pushing a new-born baby. I knew it was mine. Don't ask me how I knew – just trust me. It was her baby, and it was mine.

'I was a coward. Instead of talking to her, I slipped away into the shadows in the hope that I never saw her again – a wish that came true. A wish that I have always regretted.'

Jacob couldn't find the words to convey his surprise. This story told of a man that he didn't know. Jacob realised that John hadn't always been so fearless.

'That's why I respect you in this,' said John, 'and that is why I am the father I am. I failed that child. I won't fail them both.'

'I get that. And thank you. I won't let any of you down in this, I promise.'

John rose quickly and placed a giant hand on Jacob's shoulder. 'I know you won't.'

As John walked away to give the news to his beloved wife, Jacob called out to him.

'John ... I'm sorry that I punched you.'

John Petalow smiled but gave no reply. He didn't need to. He had made ground today with a young man he never thought he could respect for anything, and that was enough.

8

Nurse Bonnie
Spring 2010
Canterbury, Kent, UK

Bonnie Belmonte had known the Petalows had money, but never had she expected such a beautiful home in such a rural location. Alice had been inviting her over for brunch every day since her release. They had grown quite close during her stay at the hospital, and there were only so many times Bonnie felt she could delay before Alice took umbrage at the excuses, so here she was. Bonnie knew it wasn't the most professional thing to visit a patient's home, but she had been eager to catch up with the gossip, and Alice had promised cake – and Bonnie Belmonte loved cake.

    She pushed open the wrought-iron gate and marvelled at the beautiful garden, which was kept by a particularly green-fingered Angela Petalow. The pinks of lupins and the blues of delphiniums took her eye first, before the vivid red dahlias, which were arranged either side of the large oak door, actually gave her pause for thought and honest appreciation, especially as it was barely into March, a time when most other people's gardens were only just starting to bloom. Bonnie imagined that Angela's garden was like this all year round. *That's some voodoo gardening, I tell you, girl,* Bonnie thought as she knocked on the front door with a double crack of the brass door knocker.

There was no reply, other than the faint sound of Dorothy crying in the distance. Bonnie assumed that Alice was tending to her daughter and would be down in a moment. She rapped against the wood a second time, continuing to look around the wondrous garden. When her third knock went unanswered, curiosity got the better of her, and she started to stroll around the back of Manor Petalow.

'Alice, sweet child, are you to keep me waiting all day?'

At the rear of the house, large French doors overlooked an enormous back garden. Bonnie was about to call one last time, when Dorothy screamed from the window above her. She tried the handle of the back door and let out a sigh of relief when the door sprung open.

'Alice, are you OK, child?' called Bonnie, as she walked through the kitchen and made her way towards the large staircase and the source of the crying. All the doors on the upper floor were closed. She pushed open Dorothy's bedroom door. The child's face was flushed and full of the tears of a young girl too small to escape her bedroom yet old enough to know she had been left alone for longer than was normal.

'Hey, my littlest Brooking, what's wrong, my child?' said Bonnie as she reached down to pick Dorothy up from the ground.

Dorothy's little arms reached up to greet her saviour, her beautiful red hair unbrushed and matted with tears.

'Where's Mumma, my sweetness? Shall we go find her?'

Cradling her tightly, Bonnie took Dorothy out onto the landing. She noticed that one of the doors was in fact ajar, and that what was keeping it ajar was someone's foot.

Without hesitation she rushed Dorothy back to her bedroom and sat her down on the bed.

'Dotty, my child, will you sit and play for just a few more minutes whilst I go get Mummy? I promise I'll be right back, and I'll leave the door open, OK?'

Dorothy nodded and crawled over her bed to hide under a mound of fluffy teddies, grabbing a regal-looking hare that sported a waistcoat en route.

Bonnie went back across the landing and entered the room where Alice was lying flat on her back. She knelt beside Alice and checked her pulse. She had seen her like this a thousand times, her eyes wide open and glossy but unresponsive and wider than looked naturally possible. Bonnie rolled her into the recovery position and placed a pillow from the bed under her neck.

'Alice, I know you can hear me, so do yourself a favour, poppet. Wake up before you fall too deeply. Do you really wanna lose another two years? No? I didn't think so. So, wake up.'

Bonnie was instantly back in work mode and her tone was strict and unwavering. She took out her phone, dialled 999 and asked for an ambulance.

'This is Sister Bonnie Belmonte of St Martin's Hospital. I'm with a patient of mine, Alice Petalow. We are just off Perry Lane at Preston Hill, the Petalow Manor, just by the large oak tree. It's set quite far back from the road, but you should find it at, erm, hang on ...' She scrambled through her pockets to find the scrap of paper that she'd written Alice's address on. 'Right, at CT3 1ER. Alice is a mental health patient. She appears to have slipped into a catatonic state. She is breathing with a pulse of 65. I've tried to see if she is responsive to pain, but nothing so far. She doesn't appear to have self-harmed, so I've put her in recovery to continue my assessment.'

'Bonnie,' Alice croaked. She was struggling to pull herself up against the frame of the door. 'Bonnie, I - I slipped back into ... I don't know how long I've been out. Where's Dorothy? Oh fuck, WHERE'S DOROTHY?'

Alice fell back down to her knees as Bonnie reached out to catch her.

'Take it easy, child, Bon Bon has got you.'

Bonnie led Alice to the bed and sat her upright, taking time to check her eyes and her breathing once more. 'Little Dotty is just fine, but I must confess, you have given me a scare. What was the last thing you remember?'

'I remember my alarm going off and I remember making breakfast, then ... then nothing.' Alice looked lost. 'I feel like I've been out for minutes, but you're here and my alarm went off at 7 a.m.'

'Then you have been out for about five hours, and that's OK because no harm was done. Paramedics are on their way - more than likely they will just want to check you over. Let me sort your little monkey out and I'll let them in when they arrive. Where are Dotty's bits?'

Alice looked guilt-ridden as she thought about the neglect of her daughter. 'Everything you need is in the storage cupboard outside her room. What do I tell Jacob when he arrives to get her later?'

Bonnie picked up Alice's chin with her index finger and whispered kindly, 'I'll worry about Mr Brooking, just like I have done for the past two years. Let's worry about you first, though, my sweetness.'

Winter 2009
Knightsbridge, London, UK

'What's the last thing you can remember clearly from San Diego that you know with absolute certainty was a memory of reality and not the false perception that you then started to build for yourself?' asked Dr Phillips without once taking her eyes off Alice, who was stretched out, eyes closed, on the long leather sofa.

'You are asking what you think is a simple question, but in all honesty it may be the hardest thing I've ever had to answer, for what is real in my head has often been what has led me astray. You have to understand that if I didn't see Jacob standing in front of me, breathing in front of me, then I can tell you now as a matter of fact that I saw him die and it was real.' Alice took a deep breath before she continued. 'My memories do not come at me like I was in a dream, for I do not see blurred lines, faint sounds and vacant tastes. I must confess that as crazy as it seems, I see only reality in what I saw, like looking at a photo album – I see every colour clearly, see every face and hear every seagull that would mercilessly fight for the leftover croissant that I swear I can still taste the remnants of.'

'The problem you have is your own imagination. I have sat here with stupid people, people with far too much money who think they have the same problem you have, but they don't have the mind to create the world that your fabulous mind has created. Your world-building is second to none, and that's why you struggle. So instead of looking at what looked like or had the smell of a reality that your mind could easily build, I want you to look at something else.'

'Which is?'

'It's fairly textbook that the things that happened in your false reality were created to solve the issues in your heart. Your mum died because you felt you had let her down. She had been married for decades, put up with all your father's tantrums and mood swings. Didn't you mention he had PTSD from his time in the navy?'

'I did, yes.'

'You felt like you had let her down by not surviving the marriage like she had. Jacob's death was no different. Yes, you were mad at him for what he did to you, but ultimately you just wanted him to be at peace, and you didn't know how to solve his issues without laying him to rest. The art studio had always been a dream of yours. You told me that in session one. So, is it any surprise that you ended up there?'

'And William?'

'The looks of a Greek god, tattoos and a six-pack. He's educated, a millionaire, and he works with endangered animals for a living.'

Alice sat up and opened her eyes. 'It's too perfect.'

'Of course it is. William wouldn't exist in any reality except a false one, or I wouldn't be gay, Alice.'

Alice paused for a moment, slightly taken aback by this revelation. 'So, what do I need to look for?'

'You are looking for what didn't look real. You need to reverse that. Start looking for things that were not part of your script, little moments that surprised you because they were never part of your plan. What do you remember of Jacob that you saw in San Diego, that you never could have seen coming?'

Winter 2006
San Diego, California, USA

Alice had been holding tightly onto Jacob's arm for the duration of the long walk home from the French restaurant in town. The air was warm even in December, but struggling to get out of the British mentality of what winter was all about, she had worn a pink glittery bobble hat and equally vibrant scarf to accessorise her white cashmere sweater and matching jeans. Jacob had taken them out to celebrate her first commission coming in. The fact that she was painting again had given Alice an almost childlike happiness. She would bounce around the house, constantly sketching and screaming out ideas. This was the Alice he had fallen in love with all those years ago, the Alice that he had treated right and the Alice he wanted to spend his life with. They danced through the night to imaginary tunes they were playing through their minds, and the clicks of their heels fell in time with every step. They loved each other. Although those feelings were also false due to the nature of what was to be revealed some months later, the situation was real, and what Jacob was to say next would change Alice's opinion of her husband forever.

'Baby, baby, stop.' He ground to a halt, pulling Alice round to face him.

She smiled. 'Hey you.'

'Baby ...' Jacob hesitated, his words choking him up from inside.

'Jay, what is it? Talk to me.'

'Alice, I'm really sorry ... I've been thinking about everything, everything that brought us here, to this place.'

'San Diego? It was a plane, my love,' said Alice playfully, before noticing tears rolling down his cheeks. 'Jay, you're scaring me. What's wrong?'

'I'm sorry that I made you give up our child. I've regretted it every day since, and I see you walking into that hospital every time I close my eyes.' Jacob trembled, as if voicing his true self made him vulnerable. 'It haunts me in my day and more so in my dreams.'

'You didn't MAKE me do anything. Where has all this come from?'

'We are both aware that had my outlook been different, then we would be pushing a pram right now. It was my broken mind that talked us out of that choice, and I can't take it back, I can't ...'

Jacob was quickly becoming inconsolable. He fell to the floor and wrapped himself around Alice, who crouched down to join him.

'Oh sweetheart,' she said, 'we can't know what would have happened. Whatever has led us here has worked out for a reason. We could have had that child and broken up a month later. Who knows if I can even carry successfully after ...' Alice realised her thoughts had drifted away from her. 'You just don't know. But, baby, I do know this ...'

Jacob responded by gripping Alice a little tighter.

'I know that I love you,' she went on, 'I know that I'm happy, and I know that "where we are" is a beautiful place.'

'You mean San Diego?' asked Jacob with a whimper.

'No, you bellend, I mean us, where WE are, is beautiful!'

Jacob lay there, safe within Alice's warm embrace, while the ocean lapped the shore to their right. Neither of them said a word. Alice occasionally kissed Jacob's brow, and they didn't let go. It felt like home.

Knightsbridge, London, UK

'I hated seeing him upset, but at the same time I don't think I've ever loved him more, or even known him more. That Jacob there was the Jacob I never expected to see.'

'You had seen him cry before, though, held him as his heart broke?'

'But this was the first time I'd ever heard him tell me honestly why he was hurting. That I think is the most real memory I have from San Diego. I got to see the man I love for the first time, and I got an apology I both didn't expect and didn't know I needed.'

'What are you feeling now, Alice?'

'Like I want to remember more!' said Alice with a renewed fire in her eyes.

9

Freudian Slip
Spring 2010
Knightsbridge, London, UK

'Say it,' Dr Phillips demanded with force.

'I don't need to say it,' cried Alice. 'We both know what happened.'

'You need to say it, Alice. You give it power by protecting it.'

'I'm not protecting it. I'm not protecting him.'

'Say it, Alice.'

'I can't.'

'Say it!'

Alice was beside herself. 'I ... I can't.'

One hour before

Alice loved her meetings with Dr Vivian Phillips, for she had known her so long that she was almost like family – she certainly felt closer to her than to any of her aunts and uncles. Alice wasn't stupid. She knew that she was paying – or, rather, her father was paying – for the privilege of being listened to. That being said, Alice felt she had a deeper connection than Dr Phillips' other patients would have with the esteemed psychologist. *After all,* Alice thought, *she knows my deepest, darkest secrets.* Her father had spent a fortune on her therapy and had never even met Dr Phillips, so Alice had to make this work.

'Why won't you talk about Thomas?' Dr Phillips asked astutely.

For a slight-framed, middle-aged woman, the good doctor was still the most frighteningly intimidating woman that you could hope to meet. Her £2,000 suit was not only immaculately fitted but pressed and ironed in a way that told Alice that it was done by a man who did it for a living. A lady of class like Vivian Phillips did not iron, press or even hang her own clothes; if Alice was sure of anything in this reality, it was that. But Alice wasn't intimidated by her, even if she knew just by looking at her that Vivian couldn't and wouldn't ever be messed with. The power radiated from her. But Alice knew there was a kind heart behind the professionally curled hair and Parisian styling, and she also knew that the reason Vivian always sat next to her, rather than across the breadth of the giant oak desk, was so that Alice felt like she was having a human conversation.

'Why don't we talk about the mirror once more? I feel like the depth of your issues are coming from there, and while your ability to change the subject is second to none, I think, deep down at your core, you know that this is where our focus should lie. So tell me, why do you think the mirrored reflection takes "your" form?'

Alice sighed. 'As I've mentioned before, it is, at least in my opinion, the reflection of the true character I am.'

'But Alice, you know that you have a kind heart, an intelligent and creative mind, and, let's be fair, most women would die for your figure and that gorgeous mane of auburn hair. So why would a diminished and almost demonic reflection be a personification of your true self?'

'People don't really look at me like that though, do they? I mean, after everything I've done.'

'What exactly do you think that you have done in this world to even make that statement, Alice? List off a few things.'

'Well, I mean Jacob wouldn't have strayed if I'd have been perfect, would he? And I was pretty easily convinced to give up my child.'

'We have been seeing each other long enough now that you know I'm not buying into any of this. Jacob's misgivings are not your fault. Jacob's decision to push for an abortion based on his own very poor choices was *not* your fault.'

'So, what do you think I see in the mirror? Because we have spoken before on this and normally you do more listening. Today I feel you are pushing me to say something.'

'Is there something you need to say? When you came out of that deep and dreadful sleep, you told me you were tired of protecting people. You know who you were talking about, don't you?'

'Thomas. I was talking ... about Thomas.'

'Are you strong enough to hear my perspective on this? It will be something you don't want to hear.'

Alice nodded. Her hands became agitated, gripping her thighs through the denim of her jeans in the way a passenger might put their foot on an imaginary brake during a reckless driver's journey.

'I think you see yourself in the reflection because you find it easier to blame yourself than to blame Thomas for what he did. I believe the rotting flesh and broken teeth are a sign that you are trying to see through that image of yourself, that you want to blame his behaviour and free your conscience of the self-imposed guilt you currently feel. You know when you look at that monstrous reflection that it may look like you, but it's not you, it's Thomas, haunting you, mocking you. You have to free yourself of that blame.'

Alice looked up to see the doctor looking straight into her eyes as if her whole life was on display. 'But what if I was to blame? I mean ...'

'Alice, you were not to blame. No woman deserves what you went through. Stop protecting him.'

'But I invited him round, when Jacob was working so hard and ...'

'What happened, Alice? Say it,' Dr Phillips demanded with force.

'I don't need to say it,' cried Alice. 'We both know what happened.'

'You need to say it, Alice. You give it power by protecting it.'

'I'm not protecting it. I'm not protecting him.'

'Say it, Alice.'

'I can't.'

'Say it!'

Alice was beside herself. 'I ... I can't.'

'SAY IT!'

'Thomas ...'

'Thomas what?'

'Thomas ...'

What did Thomas do, slut? I don't remember a thing

'What did Thomas do?' whispered Dr Phillips.

'Thomas Levit raped me,' Alice said, not realising that she had stopped crying.

-

Alice wandered about the large office, picking up various trinkets and ornaments from Dr Phillips' many trips around the globe. 'So, you want me to try and picture him, in the mirror, when I feel attacked.'

She was agitated, bordering on angry, and this was exactly what the doctor needed from her.

'In the long run,' said Dr Phillips, 'we need you to stop seeing anything in the mirror except your true reflection. Right now, I want you to start fighting the right battle, and it's not your own reflection you should be fighting, so push for him, when your demon self appears. Call him out, and I believe he will come.'

'Then that's what I will do,' said Alice gratefully. 'Thank you again.' She was standing on Dr Phillips' side of the desk. She picked up a picture in an ornate gold frame. It had a much younger Vivian Phillips atop a camel with another woman sitting behind her, embracing her waist like a koala scared to fall from a tree. 'Where was this taken?'

'Oh my, that would be 1978 I believe, in Cairo. A few years before you were born, Mrs Brooking.'

'It's Ms Petalow again, I'm afraid.' As she replaced the picture and picked up the next, a photo in a much less elaborate frame, Alice caught her breath. 'But before we get on to Jacob, can you answer me this – why do you have a picture of this slut on your desk?'

Alice almost shattered the glass as she pointed at a very young, very innocent Evan Laurie.

'That "slut", Alice, is my daughter. Is this the Evan you have spoken about?'

Alice looked apologetic at the name-calling but stayed resilient in her tone. 'How would you not have picked up on that? It's hardly a common name.'

Vivian took a seat behind her desk and gestured for Alice to move to the sofa. 'I didn't realise because her name is not, and for that matter never has been, Evan. My daughter is Evangeline Phillips. If she has taken to being called Evan, it is clearly to try and upset me. We don't really talk anymore. I saw her once last year, in this very office, and that was it.'

'That would explain why she doesn't share your surname, either.' Alice was angry, but also frustrated that she had no place to direct the anger, with it clearly not being the fault of the doctor that her daughter was the woman she was.

'Tell me, what does she go by now? My daughter of a million masks.'

'Evan Laurie. And, yes, she is the one who stole my husband from me.'

'Evangeline Laurie Phillips - it's her middle name. The name I gave her to remember a love lost many years before. We ... We are not as close as I would like. In fact, quite the opposite.'

'Is she close to her father?'

'Evangeline has never known her father, and maybe my dedication to forging this career is what pushed her away. You might hate her, Alice, but my daughter has been moved from nanny to nanny, from boarding school to boarding school. She is truly loved, but she doesn't know love, not like you do. I won't ever excuse her actions. For many years we fought like cat and mouse as I tried to curb her affections for always getting her own way. But I will say this. When I saw her last year - when she sat in the very chair you are sitting in now - she spoke as a woman who was genuinely in love. It was a side of her I've never seen, and it made me happy.'

Doctor Phillips stood proudly and came around to offer her hand to Alice. 'Unfortunately, I feel this situation now compromises our relationship and concludes our business here. If you need further help, then I have a list of people you can speak to, but honestly ... I think you've got this.'

10

The Hand that Rocks
Spring 2010
Faversham, Kent, UK

Jacob was called into work unexpectedly, and the moment he left, Dorothy started screaming. In the supermarket, she had a full-blown tantrum. Alice tried to control the situation by picking her up, but a distraught Dorothy kicked out aggressively, hurting Alice's chest. When they returned to Jacob's, Alice put her to bed in the hope that she would wear herself out, but young Dorothy showed unflagging commitment to the cause. The headboard cracked against the wall as Dorothy took her frustration out again and again on the frame of her bed. She lay on her back, kicking as if her life depended on it, while her tiny vocal cords provided the shrill noise of an ancient sea monster. How a child who had refused to speak to her since the day they had first met had the audacity to cry and scream at Alice was beyond her comprehension.

'This isn't real,' cried Alice. She gave up trying to calm her down and instead collapsed into the corner of Jacob's bedroom so as to completely shut herself down. She texted him to come home; he read but didn't reply to the message. She was on her own here, and she wasn't coping. All she could hear was the crash of the pine frame and the constant screaming, which was uncomfortably offset by one of Dorothy's toys playing 'Twinkle, Twinkle, Little Star' over and over on repeat.

'Alice, come home to us!'

The voice shouted passionately from everywhere and nowhere all at once. But it wasn't Alice's nightmare self.

'William, William, I can't cope, I don't know what to do.'

Alice cursed herself as she spoke, for she knew that William wasn't real, knew it was her own schizophrenia trying to find an angle into her fragile mind, but now, right now, she needed something; she needed him.

'Alice, I'm here, just follow my voice home.'

'William, I don't know what to do. She won't stop crying.'

'She's not real, none of this is. You have to find a way to see through this illusion of lies and mistruths.'

'I'm trying, baby, but I don't know how to do what you're asking of me. And I'm scared I'm going to do something that I will never be able to undo.'

'My beautiful and sweet Papillon. Remember what Doctor Phillips taught you. Think back to your safety training.'

Alice let out a whimper as she tried to gather the strength to follow through on William's plan. She took to her feet, clenched and balled her fists, drew a deep breath, and closed her eyes.

'That's it ... Follow my voice. And don't open your eyes ... not until you feel me take your hand. Hold your grip tightly, and don't let go ... Now tell me, Papillon ... Can you hear the child crying now?'

'No, William, I don't think I can. Just that infernal nursery rhyme. It seems louder than ever.'

Alice, her eyes still shut and her hands still clenched, felt a calm wash over her.

'Then you are free, my sweet girl ...'

'Open your eyes ...'

-

'ALICE! WHAT HAVE YOU DONE?'

Jacob's shout came out of nowhere as Alice realised that she had moved, unbeknown to her, straight to Dorothy's bedside.

Before she could see what she had done – she was gripping a pillow so tightly in her hands that blood, caused by her nails digging into her palms, was soaking through the material – Jacob thrust her aside, forcing her to crash heavily against the chest of drawers next to Dorothy's bed.

Dorothy wasn't moving. Jacob picked her up with one hand and ran from the room, dialling on his phone as he moved.

'Ambulance. Take my address first, 175 Hereford Close. It's my daughter, she's not breathing, I've just found her unresponsive.'

Alice slumped to the ground and started to shriek. She screamed and cried until her throat tore and the blood gargled in her mouth, and then she screamed again. She continued until the paramedic found her lying next to the foot of the bed. She didn't respond to the emergency doctor; why would she, when she hadn't even noticed Jacob rip the bloodied pillow from her hands moments before?

'Alice ... I'm going to need you to calm down, or we might have to sedate you. Dorothy, your daughter, she's OK and she's breathing again.' The nurse took Alice by the shoulders and shook her upright. 'Alice, listen to me. She's going to be OK, so you need to calm down.'

'She's going to be OK,' Alice repeated.

'It looks to me like she smothered herself with one of the hundreds of soft toys in her bed. This isn't unheard of, Alice. It's not your fault.'

'She's going to be OK,' Alice repeated.

'Jacob has got into the ambulance with Dorothy and my partner to make sure that everything is tickety-boo. It seems like the little mite is enjoying all the fuss and attention.' The paramedic sat down beside Alice and nudged her gently with her shoulder. 'I'm not going anywhere, Alice, not until I know you're OK. As soon as you're ready, we can make our way to A&E.'

'Thank you,' croaked Alice.

The paramedic, a stern-faced brunette who had clearly hardened over years of service, flashed a small smile at her distraught patient. 'You and your partner did the right thing and called us right away. You saved your little girl by checking on her when you did.'

Guess you know now, spoke her nightmare self.

'It's all real,' cried Alice.

Now I wonder where you are, said Thomas in the dark of her mind.

11

Brand New Start
Spring 2010
Canterbury, Kent, UK

I'm going away. I know what you're thinking. You think I'm abandoning my responsibilities, you think I'm running away from my problems, but you are wrong, you are all wrong. I have been asleep for two long years, and by all accounts I've been mentally ill for a lot longer than that. But while your worlds kept on moving, mine did not. My real world froze, while I started my own business, met the man of my dreams and lost my two best friends in a fantasy my over-creative mind had drawn up from my deepest fears and highest aspirations. And now ... I'm a mum to a beautiful daughter whom I don't remember carrying. I have no business, and yet I remember building it from scratch ...

> Let's not forget Jacob.

And my husband, my soulmate, the man I saw die in my arms, is now in a happy relationship with the woman he cheated on me with, and I cannot process that. I can't fathom why you would do that to me, Jay, I just can't. And yet you seem happier than I've ever seen you before. You, Jacob, Mr Never-happy-with-anything-he-has. Always chasing more, always wanting more. And now ...

> Now he's happier without you.

Now you are content for the first time in your life, and with the only woman I've ever hated. Jacob, I need to do this, and you know I'm right. I've found a little retreat on the beach, a place I can paint and read whilst my memories come back, where I can find myself once more. I need this, and I think you know that Dorothy needs that from me too.

Dorothy will grow to resent you, as will your mother.

Mum, don't be upset. We can write every week. And I want to keep you and Dad apprised on my progress. I want to be able to communicate more about some of the things I've been through, and that will only happen if we are all willing to work together.

They will forget you. Remember when you were in a coma? They pretty much adopted Jacob and Evan.

Dad, after all these years I still can't tell if your silence means you are angry or proud of me, so I'm just going to presume that at least you understand.

All he understands is that his happy family was more complete while you were asleep.

And my beautiful little girl ... I can't convey my feelings for you because I don't understand them, but as I look at your auburn ringlets falling around your neck and I look into your eyes, a deeper blue than mine have ever been and circled by a band of emerald that reminds me of your father every time I look at you, I do know that I want to do everything I can to make you happy, make you safe and make you loved.

Her step mum will love her more than you ever could.

Alice took a deep breath, the last comment taking its toll on her heart with the bitter truth than ran through it. She took the door handle in her hand and tried one last time to regain her composure. 'You've got this,' she whispered to herself before she entered the room full of false confidence. Her parents were there, laughing with Jacob as Dorothy waddled between them all, trying to catch a balloon that bounced above her head, her laughter infectious and impossible to ignore.

'Hey, you guys, thank you for coming,' said Alice, drawing everyone but Dorothy's attention. 'We need to talk. No, that's not right, not at all. What I mean is ... I need to tell you something.'

-

Old Salty Cottage

Melville Drive Sandown

I.O.W. PO22 8SW

14th October

Dearest Dotty

Your father has promised me that he's reading you these, so with that in mind I want him to give you a big fat kiss when you get to the bottom. I want you to know that I miss you terribly and that I'm safe and enjoying the sand between my toes. It is my hope that one day I can bring you back here, so that you can see where I found my way once more. I hope Nanna and Poppa Bear are OK, and that you are looking after your dad. He struggles to even make his bed without a strong woman by his side, so keep on top of him for me, will you? I look outside and I see the leaves are falling and changing into the colours that match both your hair and your fiery temperament, and it reminds me what a beautiful and amazing thing that I have created in you. I have sent you some shells I collected from the beach. Ask your dad to put them on your bedroom window for me, so that when you look outside you know that I am thinking of you.

I miss you,
Mum (Ask Dad to kiss you)

Summer 2010

The coastal roads of east Kent, UK

Jacob knew it was there and yet couldn't quite focus on the bastard creature that had followed him all these years. The shadow it cast was unnatural in so many ways, like spilt ink over a photograph of the room, and it had always been the same. As Jacob approached his 30th birthday, he had noticed the creature's physical presence less each day, maybe due to his ever-increasing tolerance of its presence. He still hated the creature and was always wary of its place in the day, for it never appeared without reason or purpose, and neither of those things were ever really a positive.

'It's not like you to hide, Ahab. What's so wrong that you have taken to skulking around the shadows looking for carrion to pick at? I thought you were a predator. No? My mistake.'

Jacob mocked the creature slightly but still had an air of caution in his voice. He had played this game for long enough now to know it could change in an instant. Content that the kraken, Ahab, would stay hidden under his bed, he carried on getting dressed, finishing his tie with a half-Windsor knot.

'I'll catch you later, old man,' Jacob whispered, patting the bed on his way out of the bedroom. 'Was a pleasure talking to you.'

He heard only a barely audible grumble in reply.

'Are you ready, ladies?' called Jacob excitedly as he bounced down the stairs.

At the bottom, he was confronted by a vision that just a few years ago he could never have imagined he would see, and it warmed his soul that he knew with complete certainty that this was a reality he had built and not destroyed.

'How do we look, Dad?' said Evan.

She twirled round in a circle, holding in her arms a giggling Dorothy. They were dressed in identical summer dresses of yellow and gold, with their hair tied up and bound by gold ribbon.

'You look ... Well, you look perfect to me. I truly am a lucky man to have you both with me.'

Jacob had organised a day of taking photos at a little spot called Samphire Hoe on the Dover and Folkestone borders. A man-made beach that had been developed using the soil dug out when the Channel Tunnel was built back in the mid-1980s, since 1997 it had been a fantastic tourist spot, especially for those with a keen eye and a good lens.

On the drive down, Dorothy and Evan sang nursery rhymes until the journey got too much for the littlest Brooking, and she fell asleep with her fingers in her mouth and dribble on her chin. Evan then pulled herself a little closer to Jacob, while he navigated the coastal roads with more care than he would have done in his old Benz. He had decided to get something family sized when he had become a father, and the big BMW X5 didn't cling to the road as much as his old coupé when driven at speed, although Evan had commented that since becoming a father, he had slowed down naturally anyway, and she had assured him that was for the better, as it was his whole lifestyle that had slowed down.

'I fucking love you, Jay,' said Evan under her breath, knowing Dorothy could be listening. 'This has felt so different, these last few years ... This "us". You know?' Jacob gave her thigh a little squeeze. 'I know exactly what you mean, love. Who would have thought openness and honesty would have made me a more lovable man, right?'

Although Jacob was smiling, he knew there was a modicum of truth behind his statement, and clearly Evan knew it too, as she squeezed his hand in return.

'You didn't know you were poorly, babe,' she said, 'although why you kept it from me I'll never understand. But let's be fair, I was no saint either, and I didn't make it easy on you.'

Jacob was waiting for the creature to cut in at any point, but every pause in the conversation brought only silence. 'Easy on me? Honey, I was petrified of you!'

Evan looked at Jacob in disbelief. 'Petrified? But you are so much bigger than me. What could you have feared?'

'Back then I couldn't deal with confrontation as most people do, you know this, but maybe subconsciously I was also scared I was losing you.' Jacob seemed like he was struggling to admit his past feelings, but spoke without prompt. 'Ev, I convinced myself that what we had was nothing so that it was justified in my head, that the affair was acceptable. But I see now that, actually, I was much more myself by your side than I'd ever been with anyone else.'

Evan smiled and pushed her head into Jacob's shoulder. 'Well, if it led us here, to where we are now, then I wouldn't change a thing.'

'Nearly dying on that bloody boat wasn't much fun, but, yeah, I agree.'

The car went into the steep drop of the tunnel that led down to the beachfront, causing everyone's stomachs to flip for a moment. Dorothy's eyes shot open in a wide stare, shocked at the sudden lurching feeling.

'It's OK, poppet,' said Evan, turning to face her at the sound of a whimper, but she had already drifted back off into whatever fairy-tale dream could occupy the mind of a two-and-a-half-year-old girl.

With Dorothy asleep in the car, Evan and Jacob started to unload the picnic basket and camera from the boot of the car, sharing a kiss in between every little task they performed. As Jacob pulled the boot closed, he leaned into Evan and kissed her with such force that she fell against the car, his hands pinning her in place.

'Wow, where did that come from?' said a startled Evan in between more kisses peppered upon her lips by an almost rampant Jacob.

'I just wanted to show you what I thought of you before I showed you this.'

Jacob pulled away, one hand still on Evan's hip. He reached into his back pocket and pulled out a sealed letter with Alice's name on it.

'Baby, I don't understand,' said Evan, recoiling slightly at the sight of Alice's name. 'What's that got to do with me?'

'This is a signed copy of my divorce papers, and if you help me with a task over the coming months, I'd like to post them through Alice's door, because when I propose to you, I'd like to do it as a free man.'

'PROPOSE?' said Evan. 'When you propose?'

Her mouth was agape. She jumped up into his arms, wrapping her legs around him as he spun about, kissing her pink glossy lips.

'Jay, you have completed me. I'll do anything to spend my life with you both.'

As Evan's feet slowly came back down to earth, and Jacob's kisses became deeper and more passionate, he waited for the voice of Ahab to offer its opinion. He waited, and yet ... It never came.

12

The Last Day
Spring 2011
Sandown, Isle of Wight, UK

'Good morning, Mrs Frodsham,' called Alice as she skipped along the road past the old cottage. 'How are the flowers today?'

Mrs Edna Frodsham had been Alice's neighbour since she had moved here and had never been anything less than hospitable. It was no rare occurrence to see her appear at the back window with a freshly made gypsy tart or Bakewell slice. 'Another week or two before we hit any kind of real bloom, my dear. You make sure you keep warm, pet. It's blowing hard down on the front.'

'I will, Mrs Frodsham, I promise.'

Alice carried on down the road. Her purple bobble hat wasn't really needed, especially as she didn't feel cold today, but it matched her scarf, and she hadn't been able to do much with her hair to stop the wind whipping it up like candyfloss on blustery days like this. She took the cobbled steps down to the seafront, where she had made her home the past five months. Both her fitness and her equilibrium had returned fully after "the long sleep", as she had described it to her local doctor, and with little effort she bounced from stone to stone without catching the crooked and broken edges that had caught her out so many times when she had first arrived. Her Converse trainers sunk into the sand as soon as she reached the bottom, and she instantly regretted not wearing her boots on a day that, although not cold, was far too brisk to go barefoot.

She turned to her right and followed the chalky rock face for 30 minutes before finding the spot she needed, a place where no one else could see her. Her own spot – not one borrowed from Jacob or imagined in her fantasy, just hers. She had come here every day the weather had allowed since her arrival, but today was different, today was special, and she intended to mark the occasion. She took the last few steps towards the final part of her journey. Two large slabs of rock that had fallen from the cliff face many hundreds of years before were her destination. One was curved in the middle and had the look of a fancy chair designed for the aristocracy; the other was more jagged and held anything that Alice wanted to sketch while sitting in her royal chair.

She sat down and took out her sketchbook. She flicked through the pages, seeing numerous drawings she had made of shells and driftwood over the months. Even a crab claw, mottled and dyed by the sun's rays, had found a place in Alice's work. She found the last page completely empty and pulled out a black ballpoint to rectify that.

Dearest Alice

In finishing this book, you have completed the first step of your recovery. You remember once again all that is real and all that is not.

You remember you. Now finish this.

Alice M Petalow

29/4/11

As soon as the date was written, Alice closed the book and took the deepest breath she had ever taken. *This is it, girl. Remember what everyone kept saying. You've got this.* Reaching into her satchel, she took out an aggressive-looking camping knife and removed the safety cover. *You've got this.* She furrowed out a space under the second slab of rock with the blunt edge of the blade, deep enough to fit her leather-bound sketchbook. She forced the sketchbook underneath the large monolith before covering the entrance with loose sand until no trace of it could be seen. *You can do this, Alice,* she reassured herself over and over. She sat back in her cold, hard seat of queens and leaned forward with the knife in her hand. *Last step ... You've got this ...* With a final push, she took the sharp edge of the curved blade and very slowly started to carve her initials into the rock that protected her work. 'Time to go home, Alice,' she said confidently to herself.

Canterbury, one week later

Alice stood with her key in the door. She hesitated, for she knew what was waiting on the other side of it. *You've got this,* she thought to herself as the lock turned with a triple click.

'I'm home, guys. There had better be either a kettle on or a glass of wine poured ready for me.'

There was no response.

'Helloooooo ... Anyone home?'

She was met with the same lack of response as before.

'Welcome home, Alice,' she said to herself sarcastically, while picking up the post from the floor. Three letters for Dad; one for Dotty, which was clearly a delayed letter that Alice had sent a week before; and one for Mrs

Alice Brooking. It had been some time since Alice had referred to herself by her married name, so it made her anxious to consider the contents.

It looks official. It could be anything, Alice mused. *It could be a doctor's appointment. Yes, that must be what it is.*

Alice took a seat on the third step of the stairs – a step that in her youth she had considered her thinking step – and tore open the letter. She read the lines, 'In the family court at Canterbury City, between Alice Marie Brooking and Jacob Paul Brooking ...'

Spring 2012

Faversham, Kent, UK

A year had passed since she had posted back the signed divorce papers, since she'd had anything substantial to do with Jacob, save for Dorothy's birthday party and her infant-school induction. Alice really had no reason to do anything except exchange pleasantries at the midweek handover. She had been polite, more than polite; after all, she got a four-figure cheque through the post each month for her share of the Gallantry. But a kiss on her cheek would be standard, before he would take her hand and tell her she was doing 'really well' – patronising bastard. She wasn't doing well at all, and what right did he have to tell her what he perceived? He certainly had no right to touch her with those dirty and sullied hands, surely thick with the stench of that harlot.

Today it changed. Today she would be honest with him, hear his voice tremble as she released years of built-up angst against his and Evan's false relationship. It had been building.

Her monster still spoke to her every day. Knowing her monster was a representation of Thomas had given it a name, but it hadn't stopped the noise. And she was tired of carrying around her demons. She was tired full stop. Today was the first day of clearing out her closet.

    Knock, knock, knock.

    He's probably fucking Evan.

    KNOCK, KNOCK, KNOCK.

    Yeah, knock louder, cause that will stop him.

    KNOCK, KNOCK …

    'Alice, what the actual fuck? Use the bloody doorbell, that's what it's for. What on earth is wrong?'

    Alice glanced to her right and saw the brass button, but it only took a second to remember why she was banging in the first place, and she quickly turned her attention back to Jacob.

    'You're engaged?' said Alice with disgust.

    'Erm … I guess I am. I was going to tell you when I dropped Dotty off tomorrow.'

    'Well, you don't have to worry now, do you? I ran into Matt yesterday, and he seemed oblivious as to who he was talking to as he detailed how he had never seen "chef" happier than he had recently.'

    'Alice, I'm not sure what you're so unhappy about? We've been separated years.'

    And whose choice was that?

    'And whose choice was that, Jay? Because it wasn't mine.'

    'Alice, stop! I'm not that guy anymore, and do you know what? You are not this girl anymore. So stop and come with me.'

Jacob grabbed his car keys and a second set that she didn't recognise and closed the door behind him.

'I'm not going anywhere with you,' she said.

Jacob opened the passenger door and offered his hand to Alice. 'Just get in the bloody car, love.'

Alice ignored his help and climbed into the car with a slam of the door and a grunt of derision. Jacob looked at the sky and pleaded for a little mercy on his day off, but he knew it wouldn't come.

'Where are we going?' asked Alice. 'Because I can't see what on earth you might think I would care about now.'

Jacob summoned a false smile and took a breath. 'You sound more like your father every day. Just have a bit of faith, will you?'

Alice looked out of the window as the car pulled away, hoping that a tornado would appear, as though they were in an L. Frank Baum novel, and suck them off this plane of existence. This world was just a little too painful for Alice right now, and she felt exposed by its reality.

'I don't get it,' she said. 'I don't get Evan and all her little quirks that seem to make everyone hate her but you. I've never seen you so happy and so bloody composed. You have even left your demons behind, and that's something I just can't explain.'

'Me either, and neither should I have to. I know it makes no sense to you, but honestly I just feel more myself with her, and I can be more myself around her. And you know what? I am happy. Is that so wrong? I mean, I want no different for you, after all.'

Alice scowled but didn't take her eyes off the sky. 'How very magnanimous of you.'

'All that matters now is we try to do what's right by Dorothy, and that's what this is all about.'

Jacob pulled into the tiny parking space behind the row of vintage shops on Whitstable high street and jumped out onto the cobbled streets. 'Well, are you coming?'

'Do I have a choice?' answered Alice.

Good job putting him back in his place, bitch.

'Jacob, what have you done?'

Alice looked up as he pulled away the plastic protection of the brand-new shop sign: 'Le Petit Papillon'.

It wasn't identical to the font in her false reality, but it was close.

'We have built your shop into the old sewing-machine building. It's near identical to the one you built in your dreams.'

'But how did you know?'

'We've been making notes. Me, your mum and dad – actually, everyone you have spoken to about your dream world. I guess we've just figured it out between us.'

'My parents knew about this?'

'Yes. It was my idea. But it was your father who told me I had to do something for you in return ...'

'In return for what?'

'For your share of the restaurant. We valued it at £180,000. This shop has cost slightly more, but this has given you licence to be free once more.'

'The little butterfly,' whispered Alice.

'That's Dorothy, right?'

'Yes ... Of course that's Dorothy. How many other little butterflies do you know? Shall we take a look inside?'

-

Alice was almost speechless when she saw the interior of the shop. 'Jacob, I don't know what to say.'

'Well, thank your dad more than me. He did more of the painting and woodwork. We were going to do a grand unveiling tomorrow, but since you came knocking at my door ... I didn't really have much of a choice.'

'I am still mad at you,' Alice said without looking him in the eye. 'You can't keep buying your way out of everything.'

'I am not buying anything. This has been bought by your shares in the company,' Jacob said with authority.

'And what if I choose not to take this on? After all, you can't make me give up my shares!'

'No, Alice. No one can make you do anything. Have we ever been able to make you do anything against your will? Christ almighty, Pebble, we couldn't even make you wake up before you were ready!'

'Don't call me that, Jacob. My name is Alice. Now answer the question – what will you do if I don't take it on?'

He sighed. 'Then me and your father will have to share a tear-filled hug and I will have to put the bloody building back on the market.'

Alice's eyes glazed over. She picked up a photo from the counter. The photo was of a black-and-red butterfly on a piece of driftwood – a photo she had taken many years before down at Rye Harbour.

'I love it,' she said. 'I hate you for taking the fire out of my voice today. I hate you for asking that tart to marry you. I hate you for being happier with her than you were with me. But I love this.'

'So we have a deal? If so, the building is yours. I've paid the rates and council tax for a year. All it needs is your touch of magic and those bloody amazing pictures hung on the walls.'

'Thank you, Jay. I do really appreciate what you and my parents have done here.'

'It's my pleasure. Just make sure you invite me to the opening.'

'Of course.' Alice laughed. 'Just don't bring that –'

Jacob cut her off quickly. 'Before you say anything more, I want to say one thing. Her life, although strange and vulgar to you, has not been easy. I love her, and she is wonderful with Dorothy.' He handed the keys of the property over to Alice. 'You might find that you have more in common than you think.'

13

I Do
Autumn 2012
Tunbridge Wells, Kent, UK

Evan looked in the mirror and saw every negative that had been pointed out by men over the years. Her bust was escaping her dress and her hair was struggling to stay up in the fashion in which she had intended, her blonde locks being of such length that even when they were curled, their weight was constantly trying to bring them down. Her bright red lips were matched by her six-inch heels, while the rest of her look was that of traditional ivory.

'You can do this, Evangeline. He loves you exactly how you are, remember? He knows your past, and you know his.'

'Evan, you look amazing, you old tart,' said Heather as she fell into the room, with a half-empty bottle of prosecco gripped tightly in her hand.

'Hev, if you are pissed on my bloody wedding day, I will never forgive you!'

'I'm not pissed. I just can't walk in these bloody heels you bought me.'

If one was to describe Evan as a flamingo, then Heather was certainly an ostrich. She was larger than Evan in both physical appearance and personality.

'Heather, you look beautiful,' said Evan. 'Now pour me a glass of that, will you? I am shitting myself here.'

Heather poured a tall glass of prosecco and dropped in a fat strawberry from the breakfast basket for good measure. 'There we go, chuck, but I don't; you do. You look amazing. And you know what?'

'What's that, babe?' said Evan while downing the glass of prosecco.

'He fucking loves you, girl. I didn't think so before, but watching him interacting with you these last few years – well, he never takes his eyes off you. Or his hands, for that matter!'

'I know he loves me. I just hope it continues as Dorothy grows older.'

'Aww, it's amazing what being a stepmother has done to you, babe. I never saw it coming.'

'I never saw it coming myself, but she has levelled Jacob out, and she makes me laugh so much. Who would have thought such joy could come from such a tiny package?'

'Have you bloody heard yourself?' Heather beamed.

'I know, I think this is as happy as I have ever been!'

-

The wedding venue, in the High Rocks forest in Tunbridge Wells, was beautiful in a way that was almost dreamlike. With the evening sun dipping beneath the treeline, a firefly-like swarm of stars had appeared overhead. Jacob stood to attention underneath the arch of wild flowers and looked out at the gathering of friends and family that had come to see them on their special day. He was wearing trousers and a waistcoat in a traditional navy tweed, and a crisp white shirt. A Paul Smith pocket square poked out of his pocket, and his Omega watch was the only other addition to what he hoped was a classic and a lost vintage look. His brother stood with him, wearing identical clothes but hung in a different way. Samuel had always been told, by Jacob no less, that he was the less attractive brother. His style was that of a man who didn't care much for what anyone thought about him. So his shirt was a little less tucked in, and his hair a little less styled. At six feet one inch, Samuel was a touch taller, but they were obviously brothers, and side by side they looked the part.

'Shame Dad didn't get to see you marry the right girl at last,' said Sam, nodding towards their mum, who sat with Dorothy bouncing on her knee.

'Alice was never the wrong girl, mate. I was the wrong guy, though, for sure.'

Samuel put his hand on his brother's back. The violinist started to play, and Samuel leaned in and whispered, 'Damn, son, well done my boy.'

'*It's not so easy loving me,*' sang the female vocalist, who was standing next to the violinist and a man playing an acoustic guitar, whose hair was tied up in a loose bun like a samurai warrior. '*It gets so complicated, all the things you've got to be ...*'

As Evan started to walk down the aisle, all eyes were on her elegant and desirable form, perfectly wrapped in a dress that was short at the front but then trailed off to a small train at the rear.

'*Everything's changing but you're the truth, I'm amazed by all your patience, everything I put you through.*'

Jacob's heart froze. He had been so nervous waiting for Alice, as if he knew deep down they weren't right for each other, yet now he felt completely at ease. Just being himself was enough for Evan and Dorothy. He never had to pretend to be anything more.

'When I'm about to fall, somehow you're always waiting, with your open arms to catch me ...'

Evan stood opposite Jacob. He lifted her veil, to reveal her glossed red lips.

'Ladies and gentlemen, friends and family. We are gathered here today to witness the union of love between Jacob and Evangeline. I believe you have prepared your own vows?' said the minister. 'Evangeline, would you like to go first?'

Evan was shaking but was quickly eased by Jacob, who took her hands within his own.

'There was a time, Jacob Brooking, when I knew I loved you, but I never loved us. All that has changed these past few years. That may be down to a certain young lady.' Evan gave a little wink to Dorothy - a wink that was returned by Dorothy blinking both eyes together tightly. 'Or maybe we just grew into one another. But what I am sure of is you are my best friend, and I have never loved two people more than I love both of you.'

Evan looked once more at Dorothy, but she had disappeared from her grandmother's knee and instead was trying to chase a butterfly down the centre of the aisle, drawing a chorus of delight from the crowd. As she returned her gaze to Jacob, Evan saw the face of a man caught off guard by her honest and, for her at least, articulate declaration of love for Dorothy, on top of her love for him.

With tears starting to well in his eyes, Jacob opened his mouth to speak but felt overwhelmed to do so.

'Baby,' said Evan, giving his hands a gentle shake. 'Just remember the hard part's already done.'

'Evan,' Jacob stuttered. 'I thought I wasn't good enough. Not good enough for my family, for my job, and certainly for anybody that dared to love me. I looked at others to complete me. I looked to run away in hope I might find a piece of me I might like. Then Dotty came along and we found our way and I realised something. I was always enough, and I am a good dad, and I work hard. Let me be a good husband to you, the most beautiful and amazing woman I know, and I promise I won't let you down. You have saved me! I love you with all my heart. You have ...'

Jacob paused for a moment, as if waiting for a disapproving voice, as if waiting for the doubt to kick in. It never came, and he finally felt free to say everything that he had always wanted to say.

'You have saved me from myself, and I will show you from today just how much I love you for that.'

14

I Move the Stars for No One
Autumn 2012
Whitstable Bay, Kent, UK

'Stop it, Dorothy. Can you not see that Mummy is busy?'

Dorothy didn't care that her mum was busy. She was bored and, like most children of that age and of above-average intelligence, needed to be amused by something that would stop her entertaining herself with something inappropriate every time her mum's back was turned. This particular time, she was playing with her mother's paintbrushes. With Alice being the artist she was, they were not cheap, and so Dorothy's misbehaviour was driving her to distraction.

'Baby, those are Mummy's. You have your own, remember? Over here with your books and toys.'

Alice gestured to the little playpen she had set up in the corner of the studio, an art deco version of an Indian tepee. Dorothy still struggled to communicate with her mum the way she communicated with Jacob. She gave Alice a quick look of derision and threw her mother's brushes on the wooden floor before throwing herself into her corner on her belly. Alice let out a frustrated and muffled scream and pulled Dorothy up by her wrists and onto her bottom. 'Baby, please, just help me out and play here whilst I get some work done.'

She instantly regretted snapping at her daughter, but she was so tired. This wasn't a life she had asked for at all.

The little bell above the door chimed like birdsong, announcing the arrival of customers.

'Please, just do this for me,' Alice pleaded with Dorothy before going to greet her new customers. 'Welcome to Le Petit Papillon,' she said proudly, before realising that she knew her customers. 'Mr and Mrs Fitzherbert – I'm sorry, I didn't recognise you for a moment. Not that I could ever forget you in that wonderful coat, Julianne. I wasn't expecting to see you again so soon.'

Mr Pip Fitzherbert, by far the more pretentious and ruder of the two of them, pushed past Alice and pointed at the Viking Bay piece that Alice had painted as an art student at Canterbury University. 'My wife, in all her wisdom, has convinced me to drive all the way back here – despite nearly being on my own driveway an hour ago – so that we can buy this little oil painting of yours. Why she didn't buy it when we were here I just don't know, but here we are.'

'It's a watercolour, Mr Fitzherbert, but of course, I will wrap it for you now. Julianne, have you decided where you might hang –'

Alice was cut off by the catastrophic crash of what she knew to be her current project falling off its easel and smashing on the hard floor, followed closely by the pitter-patter of Dorothy's tiny feet.

'If you could give me a moment,' said Alice, smiling falsely while backing out of the room. This was how Alice's day had begun, and it was how it was to continue.

-

Alice wasn't a stroppy person. In fact, her very nature emanated a constant state of happiness, as Alice was the very picture of a woman who danced in the rain and sang loudly, not caring who could witness such an event. But as she tucked Dorothy into bed that night, she felt frustrated by the day gone by. A day wasted. The one sale to the Fitzherberts had been the only highlight; her brush had laid not one stroke on her three current projects. Dorothy was already fast asleep, the journey home having knocked her out so much that her grandfather had carried her straight to bed from the car. Alice was glad to have dinner with her folks, especially with the business just taking off and Jacob on his honeymoon with his new practically perfect wife, as Alice had taken to sarcastically calling her. It wasn't always easy for Alice to find time to food-shop, let alone cook a healthy dinner for the both of them, and her mother's attention to Dorothy gave her time to breathe.

Alice looked at her daughter, exhausted from her day of destruction, and wondered how she could sleep so soundly after spending her entire day being so very pestiferous. 'Where did you come from, baby? You are the only thing I don't remember – carrying, birthing or holding you. I remember nothing and I doubt sometimes you are real. Is that why you hate me? I don't know what you want from me, for you still refuse to talk to me, like I am nothing but a nuisance to you, getting in the way of you and your father's fun.' Alice turned on the night light as she backed slowly out of the room, trying not to wake her daughter from her slumber. She closed the door slowly and rested her head on it. 'I mean, how could I possibly compete with your perfect little family over at the Brooking family home?'

She cursed quietly to herself, before a soothing voice intervened.

'You are a great mum,' said Angela Petalow as she handed her daughter a mug of lemon-and-ginger tea. 'Never forget that.'

'Thanks, Mum, but I'm still fairly sure she hates me. I never asked for this, and it scares me the way she looks at me at times.'

Alice walked into her room and sat on her bed, while her mum loitered in the doorway.

'She doesn't hate you, Alice. She is still getting used to you having her more often, that's all.'

Alice looked up into her mum's eyes and spoke honestly. 'All I remember is hating Evan, and then Dorothy was here.'

'My beautiful Alice, look how far you have come since you left hospital. It's hard to hear, I know, but Jacob is a great dad too, and having seen Evan with him and then also with our Dotty, well ... I can't argue with the fact that they seem a good fit. Does that take anything away from you, as a woman, as a mother? No! Of course it doesn't. You will find your way in life. You are the most creative and beautiful of all God's creatures, and you will attract those around you that benefit you on a deeper level. That was never our Jacob. Just be you. Dorothy will come around, believe me, my love.' Angela lowered her shoulders and sighed on behalf of her daughter. 'That little poppet is blessed with love in abundance, just like you are. Your father and I are so extremely proud of you.' Angela walked over and kissed her daughter on her brow. 'Get some rest, my love.'

Alice sipped the last of her tea before sliding down under her fleece-lined quilt and curling into a foetal position, one goose-downed pillow held in her tight embrace. Her heart felt heavy, and the drama had taken its toll on her brain's ability to function properly, so she closed her eyes and tried her best to shut off the noise of the day and the bickering mind voices that followed. Then, as everything slowed to a halt, and her mind gave up the fight, nothing came forward, nothing except the silence of the night.

It couldn't have been ten minutes before a crash woke Alice in a startled panic, causing her to almost fall out of bed in a rush to reach her daughter. Dorothy stood next to the spot where her bookcase used to stand and looked first at her mother and then at the smashed lamp on the floor. The glow from Dorothy's comfort lamp picked out the broken porcelain and glass, like a star system scattered across the carpet. Dorothy jumped back onto her bed and defiantly pointed at Mr Blackberry, her regal hare toy, a favourite gift from her father, which lay next to the shattered lamp.

'What have you done, Dorothy? For God's sake, girl, you need to give me a goddamned break.'

Dorothy didn't cry as a result of her mother's outburst. Instead, she lay on her bed and faced the wall.

'You can turn your back to me all you want, Miss Brooking, but I tell you now that you are going to change your attitude or you can go and live with your bloody father from the minute he returns, and you can stay there until you realise just how easy you had it here.'

Alice picked up every shard of anything that had the potential to hurt her daughter's delicate feet and stood the bookcase up with a rage-fuelled burst of strength. She replaced the books one by one before throwing Mr Blackberry on the bed next to a sulking Dorothy. 'Can I go to sleep now, Your Majesty? Is that OK?'

Dorothy didn't respond and cared little for her mother's sarcasm, leaving Alice to close the door behind her and rest her brow once more on its painted wood.

'I didn't ask for this. Why can't you just leave me alone!' Alice cried with a flushed red face.

As you wish, said the creature in the hallway mirror, which looked like Alice, but sounded like Thomas Levit.

Rain lashed hard against the windowpane, waking Alice up from a dream of beautiful calm. She had been walking through a field of sunflowers, with the sun itself baking down on the ground, as she playfully chased a butterfly while skipping to the song of chirping birds and busy crickets.

WHAT'S WRONG, ALICE? called the creature from the reflection in the window. Its form was barely visible, but somehow the water pounding against it was creating a silhouette. It had been years since Alice had kept a mirror in her bedroom, but somehow her demon self always found a way to show its face and communicate its venom, be it a rainy window or a make-up mirror.

Dorothy, check Dorothy. Alice looked at her phone to assess the time. One o'clock was a good time – if all was well and the creature left her alone, then another six hours' sleep wasn't beyond the realms of possibility. She slid out of bed and onto the cold and uninviting floor while blindly fumbling for her slippers. The rain's beat became more aggressive and overpowered all of Alice's other senses as she staggered blindly in the dark, yawning and stretching all the way to Dorothy's room. She went to open Dorothy's door, but the darkness betrayed her, as it was already wide open. Alice rushed over to Dorothy's bed to make sure all was well. She had felt guilty all night for the falling-out during the day. Whatever was wrong with their relationship, Alice was fairly sure it wasn't the fault of her nearly five-year-old daughter. She pulled the quilt back from the heap of pillows and was hit instantly with the dread she had feared the most.

As you wished, my child.

Alice staggered back. *Dad, she will be with Dad.* Seeking sanctuary with the big bear was something Alice herself had done throughout her childhood, especially during violent storms. She turned to go and check but was stopped abruptly by a lancing pain deep within her foot. The pain was so intense that it brought her tumbling to her knees. Alice muffled her scream between pursed lips. She realised she couldn't take her slipper off to look at the source of the pain, as a shard of glass from the shattered lamp had pierced the bottom of her heel, pinning her plush shoe to her flesh. 'Fuck, fuck, fuck,' Alice cursed quietly while biting down on her lip to avoid waking the whole house up. 'Jesus, Alice, you can do this,' she said. She gripped the glass dagger between her two fingers.

Does it hurt?

Alice looked to her right and saw her demon self in Dorothy's mirrored wardrobe. For once, it wasn't wearing identical clothes. Instead, it wore a white communion dress that looked far too small for someone or something of Alice's size. It was just like ... No, it *was* Dorothy's communion dress.

Does it hurt? the creature repeated. It licked its lips and pressed its filthy blood-stained hands against the mirror's glass front, as if trapped in a transparent cell.

Alice ignored the creature and wrenched the shard out with a suppressed yelp. 'I'm not letting you toy with me, creature.' She pulled herself up and hobbled to the door, leaving a bloody footprint behind her with every step of her right foot.

'Mum, Dad, are you awake?'

Alice didn't wait for a reply. She turned the handle to her parents' bedroom door. On the other side, she found everything she had ever feared. No roof sheltered the decaying corpses of her parents, only a hellish, blood-red sky; no carpet lay beneath her feet, only hard stone and hot volcanic ash. Her parents, flayed and desiccated, were lying on their bed, side by side and hand in hand. Yet as Alice battled herself, convincing herself with every look that none of this could be real, a worse sight caught her eye. The sky filled with rapacious black-winged creatures, too large to be birds. Each one shrieked and clawed for aerial dominance over the blood heaven, a dance that saw blood shed by razor-sharp talons and jagged-edged beaks. When Alice screamed at the horror unfolding in front of her, the harpies' focus turned to her, and in that moment Alice realised that behind the sharp beaks of the nightmare creatures were deformed and black-eyed versions of every girl who had ever bullied her at school. With renewed hunger and wanton desire, the beasts swooped down one by one to devour Alice as they had done her parents.

Alice turned to leave the room, but the door she had entered was gone. In its place was the same barren stone landscape that surrounded her. Black stone and a blood-red sky were her everything now. As she started to run, a quick glance over her shoulder told her that her parents' corpses had disappeared. She ran. She ran until she could feel the bile rising in her throat. Her slippers were torn off by the jagged rock. She kept going, kept on running, until the skin on her feet was shredded. The demonic harpies, easily the size of a Rottweiler and with the harrowed and tortured faces of all of her oppressors, ripped her nightdress from her body and took turns in attempting to tear the flesh from her shoulders and back. As Alice rounded a larger slab of obsidian slate that ran down a slope dangerously steep to a woman running so fast, she ran shoulder-first into the front door of a large detached house that had seemingly come out of nowhere. Alice burst through the red oak door, slamming it behind her and pulling across an archaic iron bolt as a means of defence. She didn't know if these creatures knew how to open a door, but as she slid to the floor to tend her bloodied and blackened feet, she realised she didn't care, because this couldn't be real. It couldn't be ... *Could it?*

Three of the closest harpies slammed into the door with sickening thuds as Alice pushed up onto her haunches and added her weight to it to keep it secure. The creatures shrieked and snapped with fang-filled beaks.

'Where am I?' said Alice as she got herself up to her feet.

You are where you wanted to be, Alice, said her demon self as it entered the room from an arched entrance that led to a kitchen that looked more like a torture chamber.

'You're not real, bitch,' said Alice confidently. 'I'm scared, I'm hurt, but I'm not stupid. You have brought me to your false reality far too many times.'

Do I look like a reflection in your mirror to you this time? I have told you where you are — exactly where you wanted to be. Away from your bastard child ... She will be happier with her "better" parents anyway.

'THAT'S NOT WHAT I WANTED, AND YOU KNOW IT ... WHERE IS SHE?'

Alice took a step towards her dark reflection. Her demon self moved with unnatural form and almost supernatural speed, pinning Alice by the throat as its clawed hand clasped her neck, forcing air and blood to spurt out of her mouth.

I move the stars for no one, Alice, and yet here you are, demanding from me, screaming at me, wanting FROM ME...

The creature's clawed digits punctured her throat, drawing yet more blood as it brought its face to hers. Its rotten teeth were black and yellow, with pieces of rotting flesh in every crevice. The creature's torn skin was almost translucent, and Alice could have sworn that there were insects writhing underneath the thin layer of flesh used to bind this form together.

What right do you have to ask anything of me? You wanted peace from the child that you deem not your own. I have brought it, and now you see fit to complain about that, as if I should somehow care what you want.

The creature's grip increased, and Alice pulled on its wrists to prevent her imminent choking, but as her attempts only seemed to pull away rotting flesh from its arms, she soon gave up and let the darkness take over.

Not yet, said the creature.

With a snap of its wrist and a turn of its deformed body, it threw Alice across the room, towards the archway, where she smashed hard against the wall. She fought to stay conscious, air flooding her empty lungs.

You will never escape me; you are just a vessel of my omnipotent form.

Alice scrambled into the kitchen on all fours, bloodying her knees as she went. She pulled herself up eventually and glanced through the rear window to see the harpies picking at a corpse at the rear of the house. A creature with the face of Chloe Durby - one of her tormentors from her school days - plucked an eye from the corpse with its jagged beak, swallowing it down as it craned its neck to the sky. Petrified, Alice spun around to face her demon self as it followed her into the kitchen, almost climbing the unit behind her to escape its gaze.

You ungrateful whore.

'You're not real,' screamed Alice. She fumbled for and then gripped a large, rusty, curved knife, which resembled a garden sickle rather than any kitchen blade.

Brandishing it above her head like a scorpion, she said once more, 'You're not real.'

Bless you, you pathetic piece of shit. You actually think you can hurt me. I told you before, I will eat your soul and then your precious daughter's after that.

'NO!' screamed Alice, as she brought the blade down towards an on-rushing blur of hatred in physical form, one whose mouth had opened unnaturally wide to expose the venom-toothed fangs among the rotten remains of its normal teeth. Alice brought the blade down in an arc that cleaved the creature's face in two. Its eyes fell apart by a few inches, as if the creature was losing its mask. Even its tongue was split like that of a serpent, yet the creature still smiled as its two tongues whipped about independently.

You can't hurt me, child, but I will embrace your fight, for I relish the pain and the flood of human sensations that come with it.

Its claws sunk into Alice's flesh again. It gripped her tightly by the arms to stop her from launching another attack, and then opened its mouth wide like a boa constrictor, burying its teeth into Alice's shoulder and neck.

Yet Alice didn't move, didn't flinch and didn't make a sound.

Have you given up? See, I knew you wanted it. Why else would you stop fighting me?

Alice smiled, and that smile increased despite the dozen puncture marks across her shoulder and neckline that oozed blood and venom.

'Thomas,' said Alice. 'I can see your face beneath my own.'

The creature withdrew and held its hands up to its falling mask. Thomas Levit was staring back at Alice. His face beneath the monster's was perfect, clean and unbroken.

'You have no power over me, Thomas, and if you ever did – well, not anymore!'

The creature screamed and lunged at her, sinking its teeth into her battered body, but again Alice didn't react.

'You have no power over me,' Alice said proudly, as she closed her eyes and clenched her fists. 'YOU HAVE NO POWER OVER ME!!!'

Alice opened her eyes to find herself sitting upright in her bed. She was drenched in sweat and was fairly sure she had wet herself, but she was safe, and this was real, she could feel it.

'Mummy.' Dorothy was at the door.

'What's wrong, poppet?' said Alice, smiling at her beautiful daughter, the mirror of her younger self.

'Mummy, I had a bad dream,' said a tear-filled Dorothy, holding tightly onto Mr Blackberry.

'Go and get into bed, baby, whilst I quickly go and wash. And then how about I come and snuggle in your bed?'

'OK, Mum.'

With a pitter-patter of her tiny feet, Dorothy ran back to her room.

Alice took a deep breath and stepped into her en suite shower. As the hot water ran over her body, her reflection in the bathroom mirror continued to flicker between her own and that of the man who had raped her. But she couldn't care less, and as she wrapped herself in a towel, she ran her hand over the moisture-covered mirror. Only her face remained.

'I've got you now, you bastard,' she said confidently. 'You have no power over me.'

15

The Butterfly Collector
Winter 2012
St Martin's Hospital, Kent, UK

'I can't let you stay in there for long,' said Sister Bonnie with absolute authority.

'I know, Bon,' answered Alice with false confidence. 'It's just something I have to do.'

'I get that, my treasure, I really do. Just get from this what you need and then leave it all behind in that room with him. Do you hear me, Miss Alice?'

Alice nodded slowly but in full agreement. She placed her hand on the door and slowly pushed through with a resolute strength she was eager to show through the entirety of the coming conflict, but as she stepped into the room, the wind was taken from her sails almost immediately. Thomas Levit had been a hard man to find. She had visited all his old teammates back at Canterbury RFC – the ones that her father still had connections with, at any rate – but no one had seen him in years. She had hit social media hard in the hope that his name would pop up in certain circles, and yet again, nothing had cropped up. His whereabouts had come, eventually, from a peculiar avenue. She'd gone to see Bonnie, and they'd gone for an overpriced hospital-grade sandwich in the cafeteria. Alice overheard a group of bitching nurses, who were sitting at the next table, talking about him.

She didn't find out why Thomas was at St Martin's until she stood at the end of his bed.

Thomas Nathaniel Levit, diagnosis: Glioblastoma Multiforme Grade IV astrocytoma. Alice didn't understand what this meant. Treatment: best supportive care. Ward Notes: TLC Two Hourly Turns. No OBS necessary. Nurse to change syringe driver 10/12/12. One of the nurses told her it was as severe a brain tumour as they had ever seen at Canterbury Oncology.

'No less than you deserve, Thomas.' Alice spoke gently, looking at his frail body and replacing the clipboard. Tubes and wires were coming out of every orifice on his body, some natural, others man-made. A machine designed with the sole purpose of keeping him breathing was sat next to him, permanently humming and clicking, and two drips seemed to be doing their very best to keep the reaper at bay.

Thomas looked up. Alice wasn't sure if he recognised her or not. The hums, whirs and clicks kept the room from being silent, if not awkward, and Alice knew that if death did exist as an entity, then he was most definitely sitting at the head of Thomas Levit's bed.

Alice took her time to soak up the reality of the situation that faced her. She had played this confrontation out in her head so many times with every possible scenario, yet this she had not considered. Thomas was gaunt, far too weak to even raise a murmur to communicate with Alice, and that suited her just fine, or so she thought at first. His sunken eyes looked full of fear – maybe the fear of a man who envisaged his victim getting revenge. Alice wasn't here to kill him, though; she was here to win back her life. She walked around the bed and perched on the edge of his mattress, taking his wrist in her hands to prove, both to Thomas and herself, that she was in control of the situation.

Noticing that she could close a very loose loop about his wrist with little effort, she dropped the limp appendage back to the bed with a smile.

'It's been a while,' said Alice. She looked straight into his black-ringed eyes – something she had promised herself she would do. 'I won't beat around the bush. I had to tell you in no uncertain terms that I hate you. I hate you for what you did to me. For not even realising the magnitude of what you did to me, and for the endless suffering you have put me through since that day, just because you needed to give your ego a boost. And then for letting that damage affect my relationship with my daughter.' Alice was unrelenting and focused in her verbal tirade. 'I hate you because as you lie there dying in front of me, you probably see yourself as the victim here.' Alice rose defiantly to her feet and drew herself closer to his almost skeletal face. 'But what I hate the most, Thomas "fucking captain of the rugby team" Levit, is that you are so pathetic right now, so weak, that you cannot even find the strength to come up with some bullshit excuse for your crimes.'

Alice turned her back to him, and her navy-blue dress swung behind her like a cape. The hum and whir of the machines was matched by the click of her heels as she strode away from him. She stopped briefly in the door, without turning about, as she didn't need to face him anymore. 'One last thing before I go. The nurses have told me you have barely any time left and that I am your first visitor in months. So, I hope you enjoy the irony that I might well be the last person you see from outside the hospital walls.' Alice paused to catch both the moment and her breath. 'Goodbye, Thomas. You won't see me again. And believe me when I say that I won't be seeing you either.'

-

Thomas Levit died 48 hours later, alone in his hospital bed, with only the hums, clicks and whirs of the machines for company. He hadn't recognised the girl that had visited him days before, for she was just one of many people he had surely hurt over the years. She'd had her life turned upside down by this monster of a man, who looked at Alice as just another face. The visit, though, had reminded him of the direction that the reaper would lead him, and Thomas Levit, with little show of the violence he had become renowned for, cried in fear until his heart stopped, the beeps turned to a flat-lined pitch, and the shadow of death took him away.

16

To Whom It May Concern
Spring 2013
Whitstable, Kent, UK

The task was simple: clear the air and make things right. With the shop thriving in a way her false reality had seemed to predict all too accurately and Dorothy finding a place by her mother's side at last, it had become more apparent that her life was back on track and that actually having her best friend back on board would benefit both her own life and Dorothy's.

    He seemed happy now, and it pleased Alice to see him so settled, as it was something she had never seen before. He was great with Dorothy too. In fact, he doted on her so much that Alice couldn't believe his devotion at times. Yes, they could be friends; she was sure of it. In fact, despite his good looks seeming to only get better with age, Alice had found herself not looking at him that way anymore. She pondered for a moment if that was down to Evan's touch. Maybe that was why she could look at his handsome face and appreciate it the way she would a friend's. Jacob just didn't tick those boxes for her anymore. He and Evan looked more suited, anyway. She had seen them out shopping one day at the Ashford outlet in the summer and had resisted announcing her presence, choosing instead to awkwardly stalk them for ten minutes to get the measure of their relationship. They had looked like one of those magazine couples that you love to hate for being a little too perfect. From the safety of a Starbucks window seat, she had watched Jacob roll with laughter as Evan tried to play-fight with him. She had never seen him laugh so loud, never seen him so carefree. In Evan she had noticed a change, too. Since they had worked together at the restaurant, Evan had gone for a more natural look, and it surprised Alice just how stunning she was naturally, and more secure within herself. With true love apparently in her heart, that false confidence had fallen away. Alice doubted she could ever be friends with Evan or even come close to forgiving her, but it was a good thing they were happy, as it made Dotty happy. Dotty adored Evan and her dad, which drove Alice mad with jealousy, even if she was truly grateful for it.

Alice dropped the letter into the postbox and instantly felt a little lighter on her feet. *Maybe this was overdue*, she thought as she climbed onto her vintage push bike, the wicker basket on the front filled with flowers to decorate Le Petit Papillon.

Onwards and upwards, Alice Marie Petalow, onwards and upwards.

-

Dearest Jacob

Where do I begin to tell my first true love that I am happy for him, and that I want to be free of the restraints that have kept him from being my best friend these past few years, years that to be fair have not been kind to me? I guess I'll start by saying that you can read this freely knowing that this is not an attack. After all, I know how your mind works. I wanted to thank you and Evan (yes, you read that right, feel free to photograph that and send it to my father) for everything you do for our Dorothy. You are a better dad than I ever could have wished for you to be, and our daughter worships the pair of you. Thank you for finding a focus with her that I never knew you possessed.

   Which brings me to this... I don't hate you, Jay. In fact, I don't even hate Evan. Let's be clear on one thing, I am not absolving either of you of the choices you made when we were together. But I do realise now that you had no idea what was going on in my head during the early years of our relationship, and maybe one day when we are old and you are grey, and we are down at Tankerton seafront chatting away like two old hands, sat on a bench because the walk is too much for us, and Evan is long gone from a Botox overdose (joke), well, maybe then I'll tell you what I was going through. But for now, just know that although you were a giant dick, my suicide attempt was nothing to do with you. That being said, you shouldn't have kept your condition from me for so long. It was that lack of communication that ultimately ruined us – that and the simple fact that you shouldn't have married me if you had feelings for anyone else. Let alone the daughter of our therapist (I know, right – you should have seen my face).

   I don't want to dig up the past, though, and so I'll say no more and we can move forward. I just felt with the conclusion of my therapy last week – a journey that has taken me over ten years, if you can believe it – maybe it was time we drew a line under our past. I know you struggle to always get to Dotty on time in the week, so I thought we could move things about a little, as I'm now settled in the apartment above the studio. So if you wanted to pick Dotty up direct from me rather than driving into Canterbury, you will save yourself 40 minutes in traffic, and although my coffee isn't as good as my mum's, it will be good to catch up once or twice a week.

  We will never be best friends, you and I, and Evan will never share a bottle of wine with me on a summer's night, but I do think we are due some peace in our lives, and honestly I see this as the way forward, and I am incredibly proud of who you have become, Jay. Your father would be too.

  Pebble xxx

To my Dearest ~~Alice~~ ~~Pebble~~ Alice

      Words cannot explain the gratitude I feel for your kindness, a trait in you that I have never deserved to see. You are right in what you say, communication was never our forte and has never been my strong point at all. When I needed to talk to you I couldn't, and when you needed me to listen, I wasn't there. It was a problem throughout our relationship that I forever felt incapable of being the man that you deserved, and in reading your letter that has once again been proved true, I am reminded once more just how lucky I am to have you in my life in any capacity whatsoever. I am touched by your words and your endless empathy for those who wrong you. And you were right, if I had spoken to you of my demons, of my insecurities, then things would have been different, I am sure. I certainly believe that had I spent more time listening to your pain rather than battling that constant chip on my shoulder, well, maybe I could have lightened your load a little. It took me some time to realise that my biggest failing to you was not as a husband, but as your friend, a friend born all those years ~~before~~ ~~on those~~ Tankerton slopes you speak about so fondly. So, with that said, I am truly sorry, Alice, for not being the friend I should have been.

You are a great mum, a fantastic daughter, and seeing you flourish as a businesswoman is such a wonderful thing that I am filled with pride.

I've spoken to Evan and she's moved by your words. She understands that you will never be friends, but she wants you to know she doesn't see you as an enemy, in fact she never has been.

Thank you for showing me a respect I'm sure I don't deserve.

Thank you for being the influence our daughter needs.

Thank you for being the most colourful pebble on my Platonian shore.

All my love, Jacob x

Jacob patted the letter, as if to wish it a safe journey, and dropped it into the post box. *Long overdue*, he thought. He had believed Alice to be the answer to all his problems, yet he saw now that he had always been enough on his own. That's how he knew that his love for Evan was real, because he had never needed her; he just felt happier when she was by his side. Alice had enabled his bad behaviour for far too long, and he had repaid her with nothing but misery. He didn't deserve her friendship, but he was extremely glad that he had it.

17

Glad Rags
Summer 2013
Ramsgate, Kent, UK

Alice wasn't blown away by the idea of tonight. Speed dating had been her best friend Holly's idea; it certainly wasn't something she would have forced on herself. 'We can do it together,' Holly had said. 'We don't do anything anymore. You might as well still be in that bloody coma.'

Alice pulled up at the venue and slipped on her scarlet-red stiletto heels – to drive in them would surely have been a death sentence. She stepped out of the car and onto the cobbles, reset the fall of her strappy white top as it dropped over her curves, and pulled her phone out of her suede clutch bag.

There was a text from Holly:

Alice, I'm not coming. This was all a ruse to get you dating again. So get your ass in there, as I've paid your fee already and I'm tired of you being a loser on your own every night. You're a MILF now, don't forget. Go work that little ass of yours.

The text was frustrating, but not out of the blue. Alice had suspected foul play when her illustrious and bubbly friend had refused the opportunity to get ready together with a few bottles of wine and a shared taxi. *Right, Pebble, you've got this.* She stepped through the hotel doors. With her hair up in a tight auburn bun, she looked the part of the alpha female, even if she didn't feel anywhere near as confident as the image she was projecting.

BZZZZZZZZZ

The buzzer sounded and the first potential knight in shining armour sat down in front of Alice. Already bored by the dull surroundings, she wished she was outside, sketching the seafront.

'I'm Robert, but you can call me "the boy", 'cause my friends think I'm the man. I know, silly right? Although I do have quite a solid investment portfolio – I imagine that's why they gave me the moniker. So, it's OK here ... The Stella seems cheap enough and the fanny is packed in tightly. You know what, though, I think you and me are a notch above the rest. How about we just head off, leave these suckers behind, am I right? No? OK. So what is it you do for a living, Alice, other than day trips to wonderland – you know, because of your name. I reckon you're a secretary, you look like a secretary. I have my own PA. It's like having a wife at work. She makes me coffee and empties my trash bin. Only difference is I don't have to bang her fat ass.'

The fat, balding ginger man in front of Alice didn't stop for breath from the second he sat down, and the sound of the buzzer was a sweet release.

'Hi, Alice. My name's Evan.'

Alice laughed out loud and refused to talk for the duration of the three minutes of allotted time, other than to clarify that she couldn't date a man with the same name as the woman who stole her husband.

'Hello, red,' said the next man, clearly a vegan, his hemp shoes giving it away far too easily. Keith was a miserable man of short stature and clearly stoned. Kieran didn't seem to have a brain cell in his head and fidgeted to such a degree that Alice presumed he had either ADHD or a crack addiction. Gregory wore a pair of old school shoes, along with trousers, a shirt, a tie and a baseball cap, and he smelled of wet dog and cheap lager. The quality didn't pick up for the remainder of the hour, and Alice ticked no boxes to meet any of them again. *You are so much more than this,* Alice told herself as she prepared to leave.

Suddenly, a gentle hand took the loop of her arm and guided her to the door.

'Just keep walking.' The petite girl who had been sitting next to Alice had a thick Tennessee accent. 'The crack addict was ready to make another pass at you.'

They fell into the street giggling, full of the joy that freedom had given them from the dour confines of such a grotty hotel.

'I'm Poppy, and I think you and I deserve a proper drink. That sound good, sugar?'

She looked like a curvy Winona Ryder; Alice was a little jealous of her shape. 'A drink sounds great, but let's move quick before the horde follows us out.'

They joined arms once more and skipped down the back streets until they found a wine bar more suited to the women they were.

-

'So, you're from Tennessee, but live in Kansas,' said Alice, already on her second glass of wine. Getting a hotel looked ever more likely.

Poppy smiled, running her fingers through her dark, pixie-cut hair. The colour was almost replicated in her hazel eyes, which had a haunting depth.

'That is correct, sugar,' she said, sipping on a botanical gin cocktail that Alice had recommended. 'I still can't believe this isn't a thing in the States.'

'What is it you do for a living?'

'I am, for my sins, an art buyer for a gallery back home. I get to travel all over the world and look at the most beautiful paintings. I majored in fine art at the University of San Francisco and never looked back.' Poppy put her hand on Alice's thigh. 'And you are an artist yourself.'

'What makes you say that?' gasped Alice.

'Because I just spent an hour listening to the most interesting person in the room tell men what she does for a living and then reject the hell out of all their dumb asses, and I can't blame you at all.' Poppy's southern drawl was becoming heavier with each passing drink. 'I mean, I'm gay, and even I could see there were slim pickings on that BBQ.'

'OK, I'm open-minded, I probably could have guessed gay if I hadn't seen you in there with me. So what was that about? Or do you just go to pick up demoralised chicks?' Alice giggled and gave her a nudge of the shoulder.

'Oh, you think that's what I was doing? Because, girl, you looked empowered, not demoralised. I like to people-watch and hear bullshit stories. I won't lie, I'm a bit of a social butterfly, and that seemed the only place to be in this smelly harbour town.'

There was something so refreshing about Poppy's company, and Alice was revelling in it.

'Do you know what we should do now, honey pie?' said Alice in a mock accent that failed to mimic her counterpart with any authenticity.

'Hit me, sugar plum,' Poppy responded in a much more successful cockney accent. 'And don't give me no twaddle.'

Alice downed her wine and offered her hand as she slid out of the booth. 'Let's go dancing.'

'Dancing?'

'Dancing,' reiterated an energetic Alice.

Poppy smiled and took her hand, and they ran through the streets of the small fishing town until they found a place to call their own.

-

Alice woke up at about 2 a.m. to her phone vibrating across the glass bedside unit. Its sound was like a jackhammer to her head, and it woke her with a fright as she tried to get her bearings in a room she didn't recognise. She fumbled for her phone. Poppy was passed out cold, still fully dressed and holding onto a bottle of water as if it was the only thing that could save her from the upcoming hangover. *Mum? What does she want at this time?* thought Alice while trying to find her equilibrium.

'Mum ... What's wrong?'

18

The Kraken and Her
Summer 2013
Queen Elizabeth Hospital, Margate, Kent

Evan watched a focused John Petalow stalk the halls of Queen Elizabeth Hospital like a lion caged in a space only twice its size. He was calm enough, yet, like a dormant volcano, it paid to give him some space. She had never been formally introduced to John when she had managed the restaurant floor at the Gallantry. As the owner of the Mile End fish market, John had been sighted often enough, as he ran through fish prices with Matt or Jay over coffee, but Evan had only ever exchanged greetings with him.

    Angela had been very welcoming; it had taken Evan completely off guard when Alice's mum had wrapped her arms around her before placing a hand gently on her shoulder and proclaiming that she could see what all the fuss was about. Evan couldn't believe how much Dorothy and Alice looked like her.

    Jacob hadn't said much since the news had come in of Dorothy's ruptured appendix. Full dad mode had kicked in and he'd been unnervingly proactive in packing some clothes and toys for her and putting them in the car. But the journey to the hospital had been deathly quiet. Jacob had a need for control that often left him anxious about being a passenger in any capacity; whether in a car or a conversation, he had to be in the driving seat. But he had accepted her offer to drive without a fight and had spent the journey looking up at the stars through the panoramic glass roof of the car.

She drew his hand up to her lips and gave it the slightest squeeze before gently pressing her lips against the back of it.

'I love you,' said Jacob without looking at his attentive wife. 'She's going to be OK, right?'

Evan pulled his gaze around to hers with the deft touch of her painted nails. 'This is a procedure the surgeons have done a thousand times before, and you know what a fighter our little lady is.'

Jacob took heart in Evan's words, before rising to his feet to greet a frantic Alice, who burst through the door like a tempest.

'Jay, what's going on?'

'Appendix is being taken out as we speak. It hasn't burst, but it was beginning to rupture, and this was the only action to prevent a serious problem. The surgeon is the best in Kent by all accounts, and Bonnie has already been on the phone to make sure they are doing everything to the letter.'

Jacob's words were strong and honest, and Alice relaxed enough to start saying hello to everyone, wrapping her arms first around her mum and then her lumbering beast of a father. Evan got a nod of recognition that she returned with a raised hand. Evan had never really liked Alice, but the poor girl hadn't had it easy, and even she had to admit that Alice probably had more reason to dislike her than the other way around.

'I've got to go and stretch my legs, baby.' Jacob bent down and kissed Evan on the top of her head. 'Can you keep an eye on things here?'

'Are you sure you don't need the company?' Evan was a little anxious at the prospect of being left alone with the Petalows.

'No, I'll be OK,' said Jacob, missing the reasoning for Evan asking in the first place. 'I won't be long, I promise.'

He slipped out of the door at the back of the room, opposite the entrance Alice had entered, and fell against the wall on the other side. *What the hell is going on?* he thought as the whole hospital moved as if he was on a ship sailing rough seas.

Jacob pulled himself up the staircase, feeling as though he had been heavily sedated. The hall was spinning. As he pulled himself in front of the top-floor fire escape, it became apparent that his delusion of sea sickness was misinformed. This was no delusion. Jacob pushed through into the open air and was hit by a wave of gigantic proportions. Salt, sand and seaweed hit him like a boxing glove as he was thrown to the deck. *The deck? Where am I? No ... It can't be ...*

Moonlight alone illuminated the deck of the *Summer Breeze*, which was being thrown violently around by a storm all too familiar to him. He knew this place well. The smell of the varnished maple deck and the icy-cold seawater that lashed it with every throw of oceanic anger could not hide the sense of anguish that Jacob felt at being back here. He had nearly died here, painfully and slowly, and the motion of the ship rocking violently sent his trauma-filled heart into relapse.

Jacob stepped back towards the fire escape but paused as he heard a familiar sound approaching from behind. The creature was huge and easily filled the corridor with its mass of wet, leathery tentacles, which, one by one, slapped the floor aggressively as it pulled itself towards Jacob at a speed that belied its size and girth. A giant maw sat at its centre, and it had two obsidian eyes that were the very colour of emptiness.

Did you think that you had escaped me?

The creature's voice was clear in Jacob's head, and yet when the kraken opened its beak to voice the words that Jacob could hear transmitted to him, a high-pitched scream, like nails on a blackboard, cut through his soul.

'YOU ARE NOT REAL; YOU NEVER HAVE BEEN,' Jacob screamed above the noise of the screeching creature, howling wind and thunderous waves.

Then why, pray tell, are you backing away from me as though scared? If I am not a real entity, then surely you could let me close my jaws around you, as I have done so many times before.

'I'm a fool, Ahab, my old friend, but I am no idiot. Do you hear me?' Jacob backed into the brass railing that surrounded the deck. 'What you do to me I know is far from real; it is no more real than any dream within a dream. But I know that what I dream with you tends to have rather bloody and violent repercussions for me on the floor of the hospital hallway or wherever I actually am.' Jacob climbed over the railing and felt the cold, hard lash of the furious ocean on his back.

You won't jump, Jacob! You have never had the heart to escape me. After all, who are you without me? You with your happy little family, with your girls. You will get bored, you always do, and then you will be all alone without me by your side.

Jacob smiled, knowing that he had the strength inside to beat the creature once and for all. No fear shackled him, no power bound him. He was, as he had always been, free to make his own choices.

He let go of the railing just as a barbed tentacle wrapped itself around his forearm. Three loops of viscous black mass looped around his limb like a boa constrictor taking the life of a young deer, and as Jacob resisted the creature's pull, its beak snapping viciously at him, he took a moment to stare into the eyes of his tormentor one last time, so he could truly see his nemesis in this game of real life and false death.

-

Alice watched Evan get up to follow her beloved husband not two minutes after he had left, bitter that Evan had been sitting here playing happy families with her parents while she was stuck in traffic. *Who does she think she is?* was voiced over and again within the depths of Alice's overthinking mind.

Before she had the calmness and soundness of mind to convince herself to do otherwise, she was on her feet and chasing Evan up the staircase in angry pursuit. *She has no right to be here, none at all. She's not my family or Dorothy's, and we don't need her here.* Alice's lungs burned as she raced to find her. Turning into the hall, she saw Evan go through the fire escape at the end of the ward. A crowd of onlookers were frantically gesturing between them. *First Thomas, then you. You need to be dealt with. You need to hear my voice, all my voices, as I reprimand you for stepping into mine and Jacob's world.* Alice let the air return to her lungs as she recovered her composure. *I'll show you that I am neither meek nor the quiet little butterfly that you believe me to be.* Alice pushed aside the few people blocking the fire escape with a forceful, no-nonsense apology.

Evan had a tight hold of Jacob, who was standing on the wrong side of the security fence that lined the roof of the five-storey hospital. His eyes were vacant, in a place that Alice had seen him visit many times before.

You know this, Alice, he doesn't come back from this for hours, his psychosis is too deep. It always was...

'Evan, baby, where am I?' said Jacob, grabbing the railing with his free hand.

'I've got you, my love. Don't rush. Just slowly step over onto this side.'

Evan stroked his face and never broke eye contact. He trusted her with his life, and she knew what to do in situations like this, for she knew her Jacob. As he stepped over the low fence and fell into her arms, she instantly sunk down to the ground with him and cradled his head against her breast.

'I don't know what happened,' said Jacob as floods of tears erupted from his red eyes.

'Yes, you do.' Evan caressed and kissed his head. 'You were scared for our Dorothy, and you let your demon back in for a moment. And that's OK.'

Evan kissed his brow and then took his hands to help him up.

'It's always OK to be scared, but I've got you, and we have got this. Together,' said Evan, pulling Jacob to his feet with a groan.

'Thank you, my love.' Jacob, with inconsolable tears still running down his face, wrapped his arms around her tightly. 'Together.'

Alice watched them link their fingers into a tight embrace as they headed off the roof.

'Evan, I ... I hope you are both OK,' said Alice, marvelling at the unison between them.

'Thank you, Alice,' said Evan with the smallest of smiles. 'Shall we go get some coffee?'

'Coffee sounds ... Frankly, it sounds great.' Alice let them past and followed closely behind.

You never pulled him round that quickly. I guess it must be love, she thought gladly, but as she witnessed the bond between Jacob and Evan grow, it was only understanding that she gained. She couldn't forgive them. Deep down inside her, in the place where the demon Alice slept, she thought only of hurting them both like she had been hurt.

19

The Light Between Us
Spring 2014
Reculver, Kent, UK

'You've sold the restaurant?' said Evan as she turned onto the coastal road that led down to the Reculver seafront. 'YOU? You who loves his restaurant?'

Jacob smiled in a way that would have told anyone who looked at him that he was really pleased with himself. 'Sold it.'

'What is going on here, and why the hell am I driving? You never let me drive, and now you're acting more suspicious than a puppy sitting next to a carpet turd.' Despite wanting to know what was going on, Evan was in good cheer. She liked seeing Jacob enjoy his day, even if it was a mischievous game of his, which kept drawing little smiles from his lips.

It felt like the first day of summer. The top was down on Evan's Mazda, and they could feel their skin starting to burn in the heat.

'You are driving because I, good lady, am drunk,' Jacob joked theatrically. 'Well, maybe not drunk, but I've had a few with Matt to say goodbye and all that jazz. And nothing's going on. You really have to stop being so paranoid.' Jacob was giggling to himself like a prepubescent schoolboy now, which only encouraged Evan to press harder.

'OK, smart arse. If you are going to play this game, I guess I'll start playing you at it. So ... how much have you sold the restaurant for?'

Jacob replied as if he was informally reading the price of West Ham United's latest signing in the Saturday paper. 'Two point six million.'

Evan nearly ran into a hedge as the seafront came into view. 'Two point six million *pounds*?'

'I think it's pounds. I mean, I just presumed it would be,' joked Jacob with a pretend hiccup to boot, which drew a slap across his thigh – an action he used as a means to interlock their fingers. 'I love you so much,' he said, kissing the back of her hand. 'I tell you what, park over by this lighthouse and tell me what happened with your visit to your mum's this morning, and then maybe, just maybe, I'll tell you what's going on.'

That morning

Rat-a-tat-tat.

Evan knocked hard on her mother's door. It came across as angry, which wasn't her intention at all. In fact, the opposite might have been closer to the truth. Evan was here to make things right, to make things like they had been before. Well, not as before, she thought, because before was rubbish too.

Evan's mother was a curious woman, a woman of pure focus and unbridled drive, ever the psychologist, unable to switch off and just be a mother.

While she wanted to come across as strong and confident, Evan didn't dare use her own key to let herself in. After all these years, there was no guarantee it would work anyway. In actual fact, had her mother's Jaguar not been parked in the driveway, she doubted she would have known if she even still lived here, such was the deterioration of their relationship. The sad irony was that they didn't even live that far apart. Her mother's coastal home in the village of Seasalter was just a quarter of an hour's drive from her and Jacob's house in Faversham. Yet no chance meeting had occurred.

Evan had booked an hour with her mother as a patient at her practice a few years back so that she could try and explain about Jacob, but Vivian had refused to break professional character, and after an hour of listening to her daughter, she had offered professional advice and seen her on her way at the chime of the clock. Getting paid advice was never Evan's intention, and the point of the visit had been lost on her mother. One hour in six years wasn't enough for any child and parent.

The door opened slowly, as Vivian Phillips struggled with the security bolt while holding her phone to her ear. As soon as she saw who had knocked so firmly at her door, she found a way, in a language Evan guessed was German, to end the call.

'Evangeline!' said Vivian in a state of shock. 'I wasn't expecting ...'

'Oh, just shut up, Mother,' said Evan, before wrapping her arms around her tightly. 'I know you don't do affection, but you are going to take this, and then you are going to get the kettle on. OK, Mum?' Evan went to let go but felt resistance.

'Are you sure you wouldn't prefer a glass of Pinot? I've just opened a little French number.'

Evan smiled at the unexpected warm reception and finally looked into her mum's eyes as she was released. 'Not today, Mum. Just a green tea will be fine, or one of those camomile ones that you used to hide at the back of the cupboard. Here, I'll make it.' She followed her mum into the kitchen, hoping that she would remember where everything was.

'No wine and you are offering to make the tea. Do I assume I need to muster some sort of ransom for the safe release of my actual daughter – you know, the one who usually has a more orange complexion and false lashes.'

'It's good to see that time hasn't taken your sense of sarcasm and wit away,' joked Evan as she finished filling the kettle. 'Listen, Mum, we need to clear the air. Will you sit and talk with me?'

'Of course, Evangeline. I would love to.'

'Don't call me that. No one has called me that for well over a decade. Christ, my husband nearly choked when he heard it on our wedding day. He thought we were at the wrong wedding.'

'Your husband?'

Evan proudly lifted her wedding finger. 'Jacob and I were married nearly two years ago in a small ceremony in Tunbridge Wells. Don't tell me you have become so estranged and disconnected from my world that you didn't hear anything? I'm really sorry that you are only now just finding out, but I guess this is why we need to talk.'

'No, Evange ... Evan. It's me who needs to apologise. I gave up hope of you ever forgiving my behaviour as an absentee mother and just accepted our paths to be different. Do I assume this to be the notorious Jacob Brooking?'

'I am officially Evan Laurie Brooking Phillips, and I can't hide the fact that I am both happier and more balanced than I have ever been because of him.'

'I can imagine he will say the same about you. How is he? How is his ...' Vivian hesitated long enough for her daughter to interject.

'His mental health? Don't worry. He tells me everything. You should have seen his face though when he found out who you were in relation to me. I'm not sure any monster that has chased him through his dreams has ever scared him so much, and that's saying something, as I'm sure you know.'

'He's well, then?'

'He's really well. His bipolar really doesn't affect him too much since getting his medication right – well, unless he's stressed, but even that seems rare nowadays.'

'And his psychosis from the BPD?' asked Vivian, straying a little too close to full psychologist mode for Evan's liking.

'He hasn't heard a voice outside of his own in over a year, bar one incident when little Dorothy was poorly, but that was the exception that proves his recovery. It has taken some understanding on my part, but I went to a few classes on dealing with a mental health partner, and actually I find the whole thing quite interesting now. I start at the Open University next year, to do a degree in mental health nursing.'

'I'm not surprised that you have gone down that route at all. You were always so very gifted; I just felt you lacked direction. I'm so happy you have found something you can embrace. So, my beautiful daughter is a step mum. How is little Dorothy?'

'You won't believe this, but she's my best friend. I take her to dance class once a week and we fall asleep in front of a film nearly every Friday night. She is just amazing.'

'I don't know what to say. You turn up here, hardly any make-up on but looking more beautiful than ever before, you are married, a step mum – and by all accounts an amazing one at that ...'

'Is all this a bad thing?'

'Not at all. I just feel like you have done it all without me. It shows what an amazing woman you are, and honestly I take no credit for it.'

Evan took her mum's hand as a show of support. Vivian didn't cry, for it was not becoming of a woman of her stature, but Evan could see she was struggling.

'I didn't ever hate you because you were a bad mother. I hated you because I missed you, you were never there. But that doesn't mean you didn't teach me anything, and I loved you then just like I love you now.' Evan brushed the hair out of her mum's face and looked her square in the eyes. 'I won't forgive you because honestly that would mean looking backwards, and I only want to look forwards. That is something we do together or not at all.'

'Christ almighty, Evan. Now I know you are taking the piss, as that's one of my lines.'

'I did used to listen to you. I missed you so much that I used to break into your office as a kid and listen to your patient tapes, just so I could hear your voice.'

'Oh god, Evangeline Phillips, they were confidential,' said Vivian, laughing. 'So why now? Why do I deserve your presence in my life when I haven't earned it for many a year, if I ever earned it at all?'

'Because I need your help. I'm scared and I need my hand held through a few things.' She took her mum's hand and placed it on her belly. 'I'm pregnant, and as overjoyed as we both are, there are certain things men are useless at. An overexcited Jacob is a wonderful sight to behold, it wouldn't surprise me if he tried to deliver the little mite all on his own, but I need some female calm and composure in planning all this, if you know what I mean?'

'I'm going to be a grandmother,' said Vivian, with tears welling up in her eyes.

'Yes, Mum, you are.' Evan wrapped her arms around Vivian once more. 'We are going to be a family again.'

The lighthouse

'Wow, Ev, that is amazing,' said Jacob, gripping her hand tightly. 'I am so very proud of you. It is an enlightening thing to be able to move into our bright new world with that all left behind. You must be so happy to have your mum back in any capacity.'

'It will take time for us to find our way, of that I have no doubt. At our core, Mother and I are very different people in every respect, and it's been so long that we almost have to rebuild our friendship from scratch.' There was a melancholy in Evan's voice, but Jacob knew that his wife was feeling better for putting that particular demon to rest. 'Now, my deceptive little harlequin, what the hell is going on here? You wanted the rundown of my day in return for this devious plan you are clearly bursting to tell me, and you got it. So pull your fist out of your mouth and bloody tell me the script.'

'I guess now is as good a time as ever.' Jacob smiled. 'So, the lighthouse in front of you – well, I've bought it. It's ours. It belongs to us. It's –'

Evan jumped across the car and mounted Jacob in the passenger seat. 'Are you shitting me, Brooking, are you actually shitting me?'

'It's ours, and we can raise our little family right here. The lighthouse, the attached cottage, the holiday let at the rear and the annex, which I thought you could turn into an office for your studies and then eventually use as a clinic, if things go that way.'

Evan wasn't listening anymore. She was kissing Jacob between every word and, driven by pure passion, unbuttoning his trousers at the same time.

Jacob smiled at the elderly couple walking past. 'Let's get you inside for a look around, shall we, before we alienate the locals on the first day?'

-

The creature still existed, but somehow the girl Alice had taken its mask away. It had no form to physically manifest into now, but it still existed as an entity, still watched her and wished for nothing but tragedy to befall her miserable fake life. The creature knew it had to wait, though, knew it didn't have the power to raise its voice right now, so it didn't have a chance of getting her attention, let alone of hurting her. Something would happen to give the creature strength, it always did, as was the very essence of life. For now, the mirrored demon self of Alice Petalow would be patient, a trait that it didn't normally possess.

It climbed into a selection of bad memories - one of Thomas, one of a murdered child and one of a cheating husband - and it closed its eyes to accept the sleep of the wicked, the sleep that it needed, and it wondered if it would dream like the girl Alice would dream.

The creature closed its metaphorical mind's eye and hoped that it would dream. But as it drifted off, onto a plane of existence outside of hate and jealousy, there was nothing.

Part Three
The Book of John

1

Thirteen Steps
Chatham Maritime Dockyards
Summer 1967

The Naval base upon the River Medway, not far from the Thames estuary on the north coast of Kent, was old by any standards. John had been told by his father that the main structure of the dockland had been standing since the 16th century, and he had wondered on many occasion if it was just the layers of relayed concrete and years of lead paint that was keeping the place standing, against its will, from finally crumbling to its death. His father, an engineer for the British Navy for some 15 years, was finishing up his term with the building of Oberon class submarines, and the one that sat in front of him, which was to become the HMS Ocelot, was really a thing to behold. John took time away from his studies every weekend to work alongside his fellow sea cadets, assisting the engineers with menial duties such as sweeping and mopping the hardwood floors of the dry docks. This was always met with favour from the dockhands who had spent every Friday night since the end of the war sailing three sheets to the wind, every day spent hung over, at least until the drinks started flowing again. They had to go out in uniform, of course, so they would be so easily spotted if an affray were to happen, a thing not uncommon as civilian men watched drunken sailors coerce their women away. The problem was, a 21.30 curfew often left the dockers drinking hard and drinking fast. What was once a well-disciplined part of Her Majesty's Navy, was now a very different place. John in particular, despite his young years, felt that the last few seasons had seen a much more relaxed attitude to work at Chatters. They were certainly not lazy, and it would take a braver man than the young sea cadet to accuse the old sea dogs of anything of the sort, but something had slipped in the men, as they toiled with finding their place back home, with no war to fight. They had to earn their coin of course, avoiding the wrath of the Commodore and his small army of power hungry Petty Officers was a must; lest you be scrubbing the shitters for the next month. There was one man, though, who hadn't slipped since the bloodshed of Korea well over a decade ago, his drunkenness never impacting the job that he rose for each and every morning. A man whose outspoken nature had ended the chance of any promotion of merit, time and time again, but nonetheless a man who loved the job he did and the country he fought for. Leading Hand Marc Petalow was, by all accounts, an average man; a man of medium build and height, who could disappear into any crowd through the nature of how beige he was. If one looked harder though, through the pristine uniform and boot-neck haircut of sunset blonde, through the quiet demeanour and silent debate, well, you would see a different man entirely. Marc Petalow was a man angry at the world, angry at others for not working quite as hard as he worked, for not caring quite as much as he cared and for getting the recognition that he alone deserved. Born and raised in Arbroath, Scotland, before war and love pulled him to warmer climates, Marc was a stubborn, quiet and stoic man who would never voice his unhappiness, bar the occasional grumble from under his breath. That was, of course, until he got home to a family who in his opinion didn't appreciate him any more than the young lieutenants who snorted at him with contempt and derision. At home, that was when he made his voice heard.

'JOHNATHON!' Marc called his son as he watched him and another cadet share a joke, all whilst they made a pigs ear of polishing the brass on the tops of the bollard posts. It had not been the first time that Marc had picked up on their sloppy work, and it most certainly would not be the last. 'Get over here boy, and I mean sharp.' His voice wasn't raised to a shout but almost growled with deep authority that John knew better than to ignore.

'Yes, Dad?' he asked as he moved double time to his father's location, instantly regretting his choice of words as a sharp glare from his father told him there was going to be hell to pay later.

'What the hell have I told you about calling me "that" at the base? I am Killick, or Killick Petalow if you feel the need to be formal. You refer to me softly again and I will tan your arse boy, understand?'

'Yes, Killick, I understand'

'Now stop fucking about with your boyfriend and get your jobs done, we are not her for fun. You want fun then you can join the cubs, you hear me?'

'Yes, Killick.'

'Now get about your business, before you embarrass me further.'

'Yes, Killick. Sorry, Killick.'

With that, Sea Cadet Petalow went back to putting brass polish on the tops of the bollard posts. He wouldn't dare speak to the other cadets now, at least not when his father was watching. Instead, he peered out into the water and longed for a day where he was afraid of an enemy that didn't share his blood line, an enemy who he could take combat to. An enemy who was not his father.

-

'WHERE IS HE?' shouted Marc as he burst through the door with all the strength and lack of grace that only a drunken sailor might carry.

'He's not here, Marc, and you just let him be OK? You let him be and don't you go hurting our boy again.' said Betsie Petalow as she rose from her armchair to greet her once-again half-cut husband.

'DON'T BULLSHIT ME, BET! WHERE IS HE?' Marc said as he made his way into the front room, pretending to not use the door frame as leverage. The ale and rum mixing aggressively with the fresh air that the walk home had brought.

'He left earlier to stay at camp with a few friends, they have that excursion tomorrow afternoon and, looking at the state of you I can hardly blame him for wanting to stay clear. What's he done today to rile you...swept the floor the wrong way? Too many sugars in your tea? Help me understand Marc, because I'm sick of it.'

'He called me Dad again, in front of the other dockers, and he knows just how I feel about that,' replied Marc as he shot a warning glare at his wife. He did not tolerate much in the way of back-chat.

'Oh sweet Lord, I didn't know it was such a severe crime. By all means, you should arrange a flogging.' Betsie laughed sarcastically. 'I wonder if you go into the armoury and ask nicely, they might lend you that old cat-o'nine-tails that hangs over the door-'

Her words were abruptly silenced by a thunderous open hand across the ear that threw her down across the arm of her chair. A trickle of blood ran down her neck as one of her earrings was torn violently from its place.

'Don't you dare test me, woman. You know better than that by now, surely.' Marc spat venomously, as he hung ominously over her prone form to see if she had the force of will to muster a brave comeback. 'Nothing to say? You seemed so fucking chatty just a second ago.'

'No Marc, I'm sorry. Why don't you get yourself to bed and I'll bring you up your tea.'

Marc Petalow leaned in and kissed his wife firmly on the lips, his breath reeking of booze and whore dock women, and turned abruptly to go upstairs. 'There's a good lass, keep this up and I might let you suck my dick.' His smirk was mirrored by Betsie's fake smile, the same one that she forced herself to wear each and every day.

-

The next week was no different, with John managing to upset his father by being less than competent at the Navy Colts rugger game. 'WHERE IS THAT PIECE OF SHIT?' John heard his dad shout menacingly as he burst through the front door. He had explained to his mother in advance that he might be in trouble, and that was confirmed when his father didn't return home at the normal time. "Normal time", indeed, John had laughed as he even thought it. Normal for Marc was usually three hours past clocking-off and steaming, but even now it was past the time he normally arrived back for dinner each night. The fact that he still had still not returned home past sunset in the middle of summer, could only mean that he was undoubtably more drunk than usual. John was just lucky enough to see his father angrily staggering down the street, so he thankfully had plenty of time to do as his mother recommended.

The crawl space in the wall was a by-product of his father's rage, from an incident that neither John nor his father could recall. He did remember, though, the weekend his parents had moved the heavy oak wardrobe to cover the giant hole in the plaster. He hated climbing through his clothes, knowing that his destination was a night of dust, cobwebs and the bastard spiders that spun them. Over the years, John had kitted out the tiny space, not much more than a few metres square which fortunately turned out into an arch over the garage, with an old pillow and a child's quilt, a quilt that would not keep him warm but might just stop him from getting hypothermia as he spent the night outside the insulated part of the house. It saddened him that he not only needed this small piece of sanctuary, but that it was as much home to him as any other part of the house.

'WHERE IS HE?' He heard his father bellow again. John wasn't a kid anymore, over six foot tall already and only a year off being able to join the Navy proper. Yet, as his father took out his abhorrent rage upon his mother, he could feel his cowering frame shrink into the tiny space it was to inhabit for the night. He heard his mother crash down to the ground as his father's frustrations grew to find a point of release once more. John wanted to intervene, to jump in front of his mother and give her the protection she deserved, but each time he had tried it had only led to deeper bruises for the pair of them. It had never been worth it, and he knew that his mother felt the same way.

'No, Marc, I'm sorry...' He heard his mother whimper, completely defeated, before she went quiet, and John awaited the perilous thumps of his father's drunken footsteps on the old wooden floor. He didn't have to wait long, and he counted the steps down one by one in frightened apprehension. This was the moment where it could all go wrong. If he didn't time it right, there was always a chance that he might be heard, the repercussions of which didn't bear thinking about. So, as the thirteenth step creaked ominously, John took a deep breath and closed his eyes.

Marc stood in his son's doorway. His breathing laboured from rage, and his gait unsteady from alcohol, he stared into the spartan room looking for something to destroy.

'Come to bed, love, it's late.' said Betsie as she carried her husband's tea up the stairs behind him. 'He's not here, Marc, you can speak to him tomorrow about his behaviour I'm sure.'

Marc Petalow flashed a broken, crooked smile at his wife before taking the mug from her hand and thrashing it violently against the wall, an act that showered them both in tea and ceramic splinters. Whilst Betsie cowered, Marc stood defiant.

'MARC! What are you...?' Betsie found herself cut-off as her husband gripped her by the hair and forced her, face first, against the wardrobe door before quickly unbuttoning his trousers and tearing at his wife's dress.

'Not here, Marc, let's go to bed love.' she whispered whilst trying to turn about on him. As always, her pleas went unheard.

But her drunken husband only forced her back in to place in response, as he started to urinate up the back of her leg. He then forced her to open her legs. A short but aggressive tug on her long grey hair quickly curbed any complaint before it could even begin, and Marc grunted like a pot-bellied pig as he quickly, yet no less violently, emptied himself into her.

'Suggest you clean that shit up.' Marc snarled, as he started to stagger towards their bedroom, not even bothering to rebutton his trousers.

Betsie picked up the largest pieces of the smashed mug and went to fill a bucket with soapy water so as to scrub the floor, pausing for just a second in the doorway. 'I'm sorry, Son,' she whispered with a voice laden with guilt, while tears full of mascara streamed down her face.

'I'm sorry too, Mum.' whispered John as the blood ran out between the fingers of his anger clenched fist.

2

Equilibrium

Reculver, Kent, UK

Summer 2014

Evan had finally done it. It had taken a month, and an inner fortitude that she never realised that she possessed, but she had done it. The house, the gardens, and even the lighthouse office which was to become Jacob's place of work, were all perfect. Once a vintage 1920's building almost untouched by modernisation, was now perfectly dressed, perfectly balanced. Every box was unpacked, with everything that had a place being put in its place, and everything with no place having been sold on eBay. The cottage still retained its vintage charm, but it was well-kept and well-maintained. Jacob had repainted the fading outside walls with a coat of brilliant white, whilst the roof had been re-slated by a friend of John Petalow's for a discount price. It was everything she had ever dreamed of; the cottage, the lighthouse, the sound of the ocean hitting the rocks, the beach just a one minute walk from their front door. Their bedroom overlooked the ocean, as did Dorothy's, per her request. Lachlan would have the smallest room upon his arrival, while it didn't have the luxury of a sea view, it overlooked the rose garden, and had the most beautiful sky light that would safely let fresh air flood his little lungs. Evan reached down and ran her hand over the huge bump that had appeared almost overnight. She was only thirty weeks into the pregnancy, but her slim frame could hide no secrets, and her joy at becoming a mother was equally clear to see. She had been lucky so far, no sickness or flux in hormones, and she great. Jacob, though, had been better than great. Every morning since she had started to show, Jacob would wake her up with breakfast and the kind of kiss that had got them into trouble from the first day they met. He would leave her each morning with a decaf coffee and a kiss to her bump. He was working in London today, and she was excited to see his reaction to the house upon his return later. Maybe she would make him a little summer salad that they could eat on the decking, *a little wine for him and some ginger ale for me,* smiled Evan as she opened the bi-folding patio doors that led out from the living room onto the back garden.

Jacob had taken a job as a food critic since his sale of the restaurant, a job that he had instantly mastered. The major broadsheets had eagerly fought over the popular, Michelin-starred, chef-turned-reporter, with the Times being the clear winner for Jacob. Did he miss the bustle of the kitchen? He would say yes, but Evan had never seen him smile the way he now did on a daily basis. His phone went on the bookshelf from the very second he walked in. Music would go on and they would sit talking to each other about their time apart. He would cook lavish dinners while dancing around the kitchen in only shorts and an old denim apron. He was forever sticking spoons of rich sauce in her mouth and Evan, who had been a size eight since she was a teenager, had to keep reminding herself that it was an infant in her bump, and not a food baby that ironically would still be Jacob's doing. Evan was happy and she knew that Jacob was too. She realised now just how much emphasis she had previously put upon getting other peoples' attention. Long gone were the days of her spending all her money on expensive makeup and designer clothes, despite the fact that she could probably afford it more now than ever. She looked at herself differently now. Now, she was enough, just as she was. She was a great wife, and an amazing stepmother, and she hoped with all that she was that she could also be the mother her son would deserve.

'Mumma Evan?' called Dorothy, playfully, as she skipped onto the decking alongside her.

'Yes, Little Poppet, what can I do for you?' Evan replied as she picked up her stepdaughter with a groan, 'God, you are getting to heavy to pick up easily, my lovely.'

'Well I am six, I'm nearly as old as you now,' said Dorothy as she reached down and rubbed, what she called, Evan's magic bump, 'How is Lak…Losh…Larchlan, today?'

Evan gave a little smile at Dorothy's continued struggle to pronounce her unborn brother's name. 'Lachlan is more than fine today, thank you for asking, are you excited to meet him?'

'Yup, yup, yup,' Dorothy replied gleefully as she hopped down and ran to the fence to look out to sea. 'Evan, will my brother be a baby calf?' 'Because my Mummy said that you used to be a cow, but that you are OK now. Isn't calf, what they call a baby cow?'

Evan laughed hard as she looked down at the confused little girl who had surely just meant every word she had said with absolutely no malice. 'No, Poppet, I promise that your brother will be a little boy. I think, or at least I hope, your mum was joking.'

'Phew, because I'm not sure I'd know how to play with a little cow,' smiled Dorothy as she skipped away.

Evan followed her into the house as she heard her phone ring and looked down to see who it was. 'Angela, hi, are you and John OK?' asked Evan, not expecting to see her husband's ex-mother-in-law to call her without reason.

'Hello Evan, yes of course we are, nothing much changes here. I'm in the garden and John's complaining about governmental changes to small business, usual poppycock. Tell me, are you free this Saturday for some alfresco dining? We fancied a BBQ. We know it's Jacob's weekend for having Dotty, so we wondered if you all wanted to come, rather than her not be there, if you know what I mean?'

'Oh, Angela, that would be lovely, thank you so much for thinking of us. But have you asked Alice about this? I mean she seems OK and all, but I don't want to make anyone feel uncomfortable.'

'Of course, and I understand that, so I spoke to Alice first and she said, and I quote, as long as Blondie doesn't make too much small talk with me.' Angela said it all with enough humour that Evan didn't rile at all from the 'Blondie' comment. In actual fact she saw it as a step up from "cow".

'Well then yes of course we would love to, I'll run it past Jay when he gets in but I don't foresee any reason that he would say no. Guess we will see you around...?'

'Say two...ish, that sound OK? And can you get Jacob to make that tiramisu that he does so well?' said Angela hopefully.

'Sounds good to me, lean on me and I'll make it happen. Do you want to speak to the monkey while I have you on the phone?'

'Well, how can I resist? Thank you Evan, and I'll see you at the weekend.'

Evan passed the phone to Dorothy, who ran off into her room so she could explain to her grandmother how much she loved her new cabin bed, as Evan before stepped back out onto the decking to sit down with her book and crème soda. Evan Brooking was happy. So happy, in fact, that it almost didn't seem real.

Alice looked at herself in the mirror and saw, as was to be expected in most people's worlds, her own face looking back at her. There had occasionally been a flicker of something else, almost like her reflection was a badly tuned television set, but today, it was still just her. She had been trying to find something to get excited about today, but nothing had really stuck, and the idea of Dorothy having fun with everyone she loved was the only reason that she was putting herself through this at all. She hadn't seen Evan since the pregnancy was announced, although that was just due to Jay doing most of the taxi work for Dorothy, and she wasn't entirely sure how she was going to handle it all. Especially since Evan was a big part of the reason that she hadn't kept her own first child. It ate away at her that Jacob seemed so thrilled by this pregnancy, when her own pregnancy had just pushed him away. *No, don't do this...everything is different now,* thought Alice, as she re-applied her makeup for the third time. Jacob was different now, he seemed so very settled, and Evan along with him. They were one of those couples it was very easy to hate; Instagram perfect without need for a filter. *You don't care, Alice. So stop beating yourself up. I mean, if you had to choose between Jacob and Poppy...*Alice looked at herself again and frowned. *What am I saying? I'm not gay and even if I was, I doubt I'll see her again anyway.* Alice wrestled with her thoughts as she continued to reapply her mascara. Did the fact that she was trying to convince herself about her own sexuality, in fact, answer the question? Maybe she would speak to Poppy about it one day, but Alice imagined that the kind of strength that that conversation would require was not the strength that she possessed, certainly not right now.

'Man up, Petalow,' Alice said proudly into her reflection as she heard a knock at the door downstairs.

'Hello, Loves,' said Angela as she opened the door to Jacob and Evan.

'Hey, Nanny!' shouted Dorothy as she ran between them all, in search of her grandad. 'Pops...where are you?'

'He's in the garden, I think he's got a present for his little Dotty,' called Angela as she turned to watch Dorothy disappear through the house and straight through the kitchen door. 'Come on in, you two. Evan, how is that little bump of yours?'

'Heavy, you can tell it's a boy for sure, he won't stop moving.' said Evan as they followed Angela into the kitchen. She had never been inside the Petalow house before, yet it felt like home, warm and full of memories, pictures lining each and every wall.

Angela opened the large American-style fridge and pulled out two bottles of beer for Jacob. ' Go give one to Pops would you Jay, oh is that your tiramisu? Bloody lovely,' she said as they swapped hands and thank you's.

'Of course, Mum, I'm on it. Are you gonna be OK, baby?' he asked, looking at Evan, fully aware that he had promised to stand by her side throughout the course of the afternoon.

'Course I'll be OK, go have fun and we will be right behind you,' said a combination of both Evan and Angela in unison.

Jacob strolled over to the BBQ, where John was picking Dorothy up into the sky and peppering her with kisses. 'Here we go, Pops.' he said kindly, while placing the beer on the little table next to them.

'Thank you, Son,' said John as he released Dorothy from the relentless affection and shook Jacob's hand. 'How are you all? Baby OK?'

'We are all good, sir, thank you for asking. Dotty is especially excited to get a little brother, she's been helping to decorate his room by filling it with her childhood toys.'

'Seems so long ago that she was thrust upon us, right?' said John, placing one hand on Jacob's shoulder as they toasted with a clink of bottles.

'Wouldn't change a thing now, but damn that was a scary time. I was petrified of you, and telling you was every worst nightmare combined.' Jacob smiled as he spoke.

'Well that's disappointing,' grinned John. 'That you're not scared of me anymore, I mean.'

They both laughed as John started rolling sausages over, The bitter taste of charcoal filling the air as the roasting summer sun beat down. 'John, I may not fear you like I used to, but I love and respect you now, you and Nanny. You have to know how grateful I am for all the help you have given us.'

'Alright, don't go soft on me you big fanny,' John laughed but was clearly touched by Jacob's words. 'So tell me about this new job?'

Evan watched Angela chase Dorothy out of the flower beds whilst Jacob and John seemed to bond over the quality of the meat. It was a little hot for her with the baby in tow, so she sat under the giant parasol and sipped on her ginger beer, quite content with how the afternoon was panning out. She had never liked ginger beer before she fell pregnant, but found it the only thing that stopped her almost constant indigestion.

'Hey, can I join you?' asked Alice politely as she motioned to sit down.

'Oh my God, of course Alice, it's your home, you don't need my permission. How are you?' stuttered Evan. She was clearly thrown by Alice wanting to join her. After all, it was her request to not make small talk with "Blondie".

'You're looking huge,' smiled Alice before realising she had probably come across as catty. 'Sorry, I didn't mean...'

Evan laughed and nodded. 'Girl, I am huge, you don't need to apologise! I'm sorry though, this must be awkward as fuck with us being here.'

No

'No, it's been long enough and I need to make mine and Dorothy's life a priority. I have to stop thinking about the past.' said Alice, completely ignoring the voice in her mind that was trying to contradict her.

'Well, I hear that you have painted something incredible, Jacob said you should auction it at Blackberries. I believe his words were, and I quote, "it's the most hauntingly beautiful thing I've ever seen, and she should be bloody proud of herself," and you know Jacob, if he thinks something is haunting then it must be dark.'

'Thank you, both of you. I don't think I'm ready to part with it yet, but I'm sure that day will come, just not yet. It's hidden away in the attic right now, I kept hearing... you know what, it doesn't matter. Tell me, how is he doing?'

'Jacob? Yeah he's OK, he seems settled within himself now more than ever, I think giving up the executive chef role has benefited him,' said Evan with a smile and a sip of her ginger beer.

'But he always loved the heat of a kitchen, he said that the violence of a busy service was his biggest release, or was he just trying to get away from me?' Alice gave an awkward laugh to end the question.

'No, don't be daft. Do you know what I think it was? Your dad started a process, one that had begun initially with the kids at school picking on him. Jay Brooking wanted to prove himself to everyone, to the kids at school, then your father who challenged him, and then to all the people who whispered in his ear that he didn't deserve you as his wife,' said Evan kindly. 'He didn't want to be away from you, he wanted to prove as best he could that he was worthy of your love.'

'He really did tell you everything, didn't he?' said Alice, a little hurt that he could so easily be open with Evan, when he had been so closed off with her.

'I'll tell you what he told me; he told me that he didn't want his unhappiness to poison you any longer, an unhappiness that had been there since you met each other, but NOT because you met each other. The kitchen environment was a constant means for him to show everyone that he had made something of himself, to show people that he was enough,' Evan saddened as she spoke of her love in such a dark place. 'But I think that being a dad has shown him that he is man enough anyway, that he always was.'

'He is a great dad, it surprised me how easily he picked it up,' said Alice.

'It surprised everyone, I think,' replied Evan with a chuckle. ' Can I tell you a secret, Alice?' said Evan as she turned to face her old adversary.

Alice took a large gulp of her wine and brought herself face to face with Evan, 'Shoot, I'm all ears.'

'I was always, and I mean always, so very jealous of you.' Evan said honestly.

'Well, you got him in the end, so I wouldn't dwell on that too much.' Alice giggled, a combination of wine and sun making her relax more than she would have normally wanted to with Evan.

'No, you misunderstand, not because of Jacob, but because of all this,' Evan gestured with open arms. 'Believe it or not, I came from a nice home in a lovely area, the same as you did, but my mother never wanted to be at home. Work was all she cared about, and my father...well I've never met him, I couldn't even tell you what he looked like,' Evan put her hand onto her bump and smiled. 'You had everything I wanted, but it wasn't what you thought.'

NO

'Evan, I...I never realised,' said Alice with a genuine sadness in her voice. 'I'm sorry, I always thought Vivian would be an amazing mum, but I never knew about your father. You always came across as the girl who had it all and wanted more, I never stopped to think there might be pain behind your beauty.'

'She is an amazing mum, in her own way. I never went without, it was just a shame that a perverted old boarding school teacher became my only strong male influence. My grandparents disowned mum when she came out, so it was only ever me and her, and she seemed vacant, even when she was sat by my side.'

IT'S A TRICK

'Hello, you,' said John as he bent down and kissed Evan on the cheek before falling in behind Alice, both hands on her shoulders. 'Are you ready for food?'

'Of course we are, Dad,' said Alice as her and Evan stood together. 'Thank you, Dad,' said Alice finally.

'What for, Monkey? It's only a couple of sausages and some pork steaks.' John replied as both girls looped their arms through his massive arms. Even in his sixties, John cast both of them in shadow.

'For everything, Dad, for everything.'

-

'I hope you two are having fun over here?' said Evan as she joined Angela in pushing Dorothy on a swing that had been hand-crafted by John using trees cut from the surrounding woods. Lunch had gone down well, and both Evan and Alice had admitted that they best not sit down through fear of falling asleep.

'We are having so much fun, aren't we, Dotty boo boo?' said Angela with another big push.

'Yep, yep, yep,' replied Dorothy as she swung her legs into the air with unbridled glee.

'Angela, I have to tell you, this garden is divine, how much time do you have to spend out here to keep it looking this good?'

Angela beamed with pride and gave a humble nod of thanks. 'I'm retired now, my lovely. So really it's all I have to keep me sharp and focused day-to-day. I try and spend a few hours a day out here, but it's winding down for the autumn now, another month or so and this whole garden will be golden.'

'It's already golden to me Angela, its truly a beautiful thing, well except...no, I'm being rude.' said Evan, backtracking.

'Except for the ugly bench at the back, the one surrounded by dandelions?' laughed Angela. 'You don't need to worry, Evan, if I could change that wrought iron monstrosity, I absolutely would.'

'Why can't you?' asked Evan, curiosity mixed with an unwillingness to come across as nosey.

'It's John's fathers spot. He's been dead years, since before I even met him. They never had more than a tenuous relationship at best.' Angela's eyes told a sad story that her cheery voice was trying to hide.

'If they didn't have a great relationship, why do you think he keeps it?' asked Evan, as she picked Dorothy up from a swing fail that caused neither harm or upset.

'I think it's always reminded him of what Alice doesn't need in a father and, honestly, of what I have don't need in a husband. Sounds silly, but I think that the bench grounds him. I often find John out there sitting upon it, and in fairness, it's been here longer than I have. There are some days where he might be fighting over a decision, and an hour on the bench will give him an answer.' Angela took Evan by the hand and leaned in closely, aware that innocent ears were listening in. 'I know he can be a big scary man, but that doesn't mean he's stupid. All he cares about is his girls, and he sees what you do for Dorothy. You are an amazing influence on her.'

'Thank you Angela, that means so much coming from you, it's been a concern, one that I have returned to with every decision I've had to make as the potential Evil Stepmother. I feared that I had become the ugly bench in your beautiful Petalow garden.'

'Don't be daft, you and Jacob are a part of Dorothy's life and therefore you are part of ours.' Angela meant every word that she spoke, and Evan felt all the better for hearing it, although the more she saw of the Petalow's, the more she felt the old scars of a vacuum in her chest, the one her own heritage had created.

3

Saving Yourself

Gillingham Kent

Summer 1969

Betsie Anne Petalow had been born in a time where it was understood that you would do as you were asked, especially within the context of a marriage. She was also born into an upbringing of respect for "your" man, regardless of how he behaved throughout the day. As long as he kept a roof over the family's head, and he did just as he had always done, then she would be expected to be the doting housewife. Dinner would always be prompt and served fresh with a grateful smile, baths would be drawn and conversation kept to a minimum unless started by her husband, for why would he want to speak if not to air his own mind? His day was hard enough without listening to his wife's complaints of supermarket sell-outs. Betsie Anne would stand by her husband's side, not out of loyalty or respect, but because she knew that to run would mean to die. She had been sitting in front of her vanity mirror for an hour trying, and failing, for the most part, to cover up last night's argument. Maybe when John was free of all this, maybe when he had the ocean beneath him and a home away from home that the forces would provide, maybe then she would think about her own future, but right now, she had to suck it up. She was older than Marc, not by much, but he had been only a teenager when they had married and had John. Had she met him later in life, she may have been smart enough to turn him down.

'You look OK, Bee, you look OK.' She had used more makeup than usual to cover her bruised cheek, a little foundation seemed to have done the trick of hiding the bruise, whilst a rose blusher had brought some normal colour back to her face. Her John hadn't been so lucky, going to school with a black eye was a normal occurrence for the young lad, but last night she had heard his forearm snap under the pressure of Marc's vicious grip. She had taken him to the emergency room soon as her delinquent husband had passed out at the kitchen table. He wouldn't wake up until the morning, that was for sure. Marc Petalow may have been a violent and spiteful man but at least he was consistent; once out, he was out!

'Where's Johnathon?' demanded Marc, as he walked into the bedroom to find his wife dressing her eyes with liner.

'He has his written assessment today Marc, you know this. I think he's eager to get started.' Betsie replied to her husband whilst looking at him in the reflection of her vanity mirror.

'He may be eager, but he has a long way to go if he thinks he will make it as Docker. Was that a cast on his arm I saw this morning?'

'Yes Marc, he's fractured his bloody arm, do you not remember?' Betsie turned to look at her husband, bewildered at his complete lack of empathy or regret.

'How the fuck has the lanky twat done that?' laughed Marc as he buttoned his blue shirt, ready to return to base. 'No doubt he was fucking around with those nonce mates of his. I honestly don't know where he gets it from at times. He's a liability to our family name Betsie, you need to be tougher on him, don't leave it all to me.'

'How did he do it? Are you kidding me?' asked Betsie in disbelief at her husband's ignorance. 'Well I guess it was just boys being boys, or was it rugby? Actually no...I think perhaps he fell in the shower.' She wanted to strangle him as she spoke, wanted him to know that there were repercussions to his actions, but she doubted he would even recognise the sarcasm in her voice.

'Well, he needs to stop fucking about. He's a man in a few weeks and it's time to pull his shit together. The Navy is no joke.' snarled Marc with belligerence.

Betsie Anne Petalow stood with all the grace of a woman in control and looked her husband in the eye. 'Have a good day, Marc.' she said before kissing him on the cheek and leaving the room. As she took the stairs towards the front door, she felt a tug on the hair that was hard enough to bring her crashing down to the floor. The last ten steps disappeared quickly beneath her, leaving her struggling to draw breath as the air was knocked out of her the very second she hit the ground.

'Just one thing before you go, love, if you ever think I'm too stupid, too slow or too dim witted to understand your sarcastic and venomous tongue, then you are sorely mistaken. Do I make myself clear?' Marc spat from the top few steps of the staircase.

Betsie could only look up at him from the ground that had painfully broken her fall, and nod as tears of pain and of frustration filled her eyes, for it had been a long time since Betsie Anne Petalow had cried tears of sadness over the man that lauded over her from height.

-

John hadn't minded the cast so much. In fact, he believed that walking in to the armed forces recruitment centre with an injury somehow made him fit in a little more. Damn thing was itchy though, itchy like an angry red ant was doing the rounds down there. His father had not had a good night. It was no secret that John despised Leading Hand Marc Petalow, in fact John would see him dead and not miss a night's sleep at his loss to the world, but last night...last night was different. John had seen a man so destroyed by war that his empathy was no longer with him. War had left him devoid of human feeling, an angry bitter husk of a man. Marc would say nothing for days and then explode to life, once drink tipped the balance between a lack of empathy and a lack of regret, and last night, as John sat on the ground holding his as-yet undiagnosed broken arm in tears, whilst watching his mum take the beating that she had "apparently" deserved, he saw something he had never seen before. His father had crashed to the ground and sobbed. Tears flooded his face like a burst dam as the man physically fell apart in front of him. John had seen the pain in soldiers and sailors alike, his time as a cadet taking him to bases all over the south coast, but he had never seen a man so destroyed by combat that he didn't know right from wrong any longer.

'Why do you make me do this to you?' he had bellowed through his hands as he fell into a foetal position on the ground. 'Do you not know just how much I love you both, do you not see that I keep you both in line so that people don't die, so that you don't die?' His voice swapping from a shriek to a whisper and back again with absurd frequency. 'I can't see anyone else die on my watch, I can't deal with the taste anymore. The metallic taste burns my mouth, I feel myself choking on it.' Marc looked like he was having some kind of seizure while he spoke, his body shaking with muscle spasms that made him look like he was trying to slither out the room like a snake. 'I love you both.' Marc repeated softly, over and over. 'I love you both...I love...'

John had watched his father pass out on the linoleum lined kitchen floor and saw him for what he was; not an evil man, not a hateful man, but a broken man. Marc Petalow, a veteran of countless battles in service to the Queen's Navy, a man that had fought for his country in Korea and seen his brothers torn to pieces in the punchbowl that was to be known as the Battle of Bloody Ridge. Marc Petalow, a man who violently beat his wife and son constantly to keep them in line was simply broken beyond repair. Battle-scarred to a point where he clearly couldn't define where the war had ended and down-time had begun. This didn't make John hate his father any less, rather it helped him understand that he was watching a man still fighting. Marc didn't hate his wife and child. He hated the world, he hated that he couldn't save his friends long gone, and he truly believed that the beatings so frequently dished out would be the difference between his family living or dying. John felt sorry for his father.

'Cadet Petalow, you're next.' said the pristinely dressed Naval Lieutenant with the dour tone of a man who had seen too many bright eyed hopefuls line up outside his office.

'Yes, Sir.' said John in an instant as he snapped to attention and marched into the office behind him. Taking the seat offered by the officer as he passed it to step behind the large oak desk.

'John, you are a pain in my arse,' Lieutenant Marvell spoke candidly as always as he threw John's results across the desk and took his seat opposite. 'You got 96%, highest score in the classroom this year.'

'Sir, although I wouldn't disagree that I probably am a pain in your arse, I have to admit that I'm not sure why my high test score makes that more of a valid point today?' John replied, trying to remain professional whilst hiding his pride from nailing the written test.

'John, you are the best cadet we have, clearly the smartest, so why the marines?' Lt. Marvell leaned across the desk, his eyes boring into John's as if he could read his very thoughts.

'I guess I just always wanted to be part of a unit, part of a team.'

'You would still get that with what I have to offer you, son.' The Lieutenant pushed another piece of paper across the desk and tapped upon its surface with authority.

'Engineer,' John read out loud. 'You want me to be a submarine engineer, like my father?'

'Your father is a well-respected part of the fleet and you should be honoured to follow in his footsteps, Johnathon. My boy, you are too smart to be a booty and it was your father that put in the call for this.'

'With all due respect Sir, I'm not my father... and to be frank, if I may be in your company, the fact that he made that call is exactly why I cannot even consider it.'

'So that's it then? I stamp this piece of paper and you are off to Lympstone in four to six months.' Lt. Marvell said with acceptance of the inevitable. 'You will be speed marching across Dartmoor in the pissing rain for the best part of the first year.'

'And I welcome it, Sir.' replied John with undeserved swagger in his tone, standing up as if to emphasise the point.

'Well then, Cadet Petalow...' the Lieutenant said, as he brought down the bright red stamp upon Johns application. 'I wish you the very best of luck.' He stood and shook the good hand of the excited young man. 'Any idea where you want to go, if indeed you are lucky enough to get your green beret?'

'Four-Five, Sir.' Said John without missing a beat. 'As far from Chatham Naval base as I can get.'

'Arbroath...Bloody cold up there, son, brass monkeys, one might say. With that being said, they will be lucky to have you. You have been a fine cadet and will become a fine marine, of that I have no doubt.'

'Thank you sir.' said John who turned to leave as the Lieutenant waved him away.

'John, one last thing...good luck telling your dad.'

John didn't turn about but briefly stopped in his tracks. 'Thank you sir, I think I will need it.'

-

John hadn't been seeing Jane for very long, maybe six months, he guessed, and it had never really had legs in it. They were different people entirely and everyone had always weighed in with that same opinion. John was a man who was proud of where he had grown up. Proud of the streets and the people that surrounded him. Jane, though, was the opposite, she never stopped trying to be above her surroundings and the people that filled them. Borne from the largest council housing estate in the county of Kent, you would have imagined her to be a down-to-earth and charming young lady. Yet scornful looks and disparaging remarks muttered quietly under her breath were hidden by the facade of innocence, as if butter would not melt in the mouth of the queen of council housing. It was for this reason that John, upon his acceptance into Royal Marine training in Devon, had decided that he would have to end things, a choice he hadn't lost any sleep over in the build-up to the impending showdown. John had decided to walk from his home in Rainham some two miles away. He was yet to pass or even apply for his driving licence, what was the point in paying for it, he had thought, when the Navy would do it all for him? The shining sun was beating down though, and the air was filled with the scent of freshly cut grass and summer flowers. If he was to walk, then today was a good day for it, despite the miserable task ahead of him. He doubted she would be too bothered by the news, in fairness he was surprised that she hadn't ended it herself as the weeks leading up to this had certainly had their fair share of cold shoulders, hard stares and unreturned calls. John wished that she had put him out of his misery, despite the fact she had been a firecracker in the bedroom, he had really become quite bored of her bitching and whining. He walked up the street towards her house, the last in the cul-de-sac, and tried to focus on all the negatives they had shared. It was never nice to break up with anyone, and looking back at what they had shared with rose-tinted glasses was not going to help anyone today. John walked down the pathway and rapped his knuckles upon the door. For the area, he had to admit that it was a lovely property. The last house in the street, at the top of a steep hill surrounded by trees, it was almost the castle that looked over the minions. At least from a housing estate perspective. It certainly was a lot bigger than his father's Naval-owned home.

Knock, Knock...John's bunched knuckles hit thin air on the third strike as the door swung open to reveal a pair of laughing faces about to leave the house.

'John! Oh my, what are you doing here?' said Jane as she quickly let go of Roger Benjamin's hand.

'Benji? Well, this is a surprise mate, shall I assume that as my best friend of some ten years, that you are here to offer me emotional support? No? Just coincidence then!' said John as he flexed his hand back into a fist.

'Johnno, it's not what you think.' stuttered Roger quickly, as if caught in the sights of a large calibre hunting rifle.

John pulled his old friend outside by the scruff of his shirt and pushed him into the street. Roger, who was neither as big or broad as the giant youth that was John Petalow, was still a good few years older and more experienced. John would need to be careful how he played this. They had been friends since they were kids, related somewhere down the line by married cousins, they were mates...or so John had thought.

'What the actual fuck, Benji?' shouted John, whilst Jane slunk into the back ground like a venomous shadow.

'Johnno come on, you were going to break up with her anyway.'

'So you thought you had better get in there first?' snapped John as he pushed him once more.

'OK, mate, enough of the argy-bargy, I'll only take so much from you kid...' Roger found his protest cut short as John tackled him to the ground and found the speed to hit his opponent four times across the jaw before he had even been able to register what was going on, both left and right hooks connecting with focused intent.

'I trusted you, you piece of shit I fucking loved you like a brother!' said John as he leapt up to his feet before his opponent could reorganise his thoughts.

Roger Benjamin rolled over onto his knees and spat out both blood and spittle before checking his jaw with a squeeze of his hand. 'She's just a girl, John. You are bang out of line.'

'I'm bang out of line? I think you got this backwards my old sunbeam. You're right though, she is just a girl, and honestly I couldn't give a fuck about that slag,' said John as he straightened himself up. 'But you know better than most that there are not many people in my life that I let in, what a fool I've been.'

'Well the sooner you're gone then, I guess the happier we will all be eh, old friend?' quipped Roger as he rose to his feet with the balance of a man who had just been hit by a car.

'I think you're right, the pair of you are perfect together.' spat John as he turned his back on the carnage. Reaching the end of the street he turned to notice that Jane had returned to her new man's side as she guided him unsteadily back inside.

Fuck this place, thought John with disbelief over what had just happened. Fuck Roger, fuck that trollop and fuck my dad. I'll show the lot of them. 'Just remember what he said, sweetheart, you're just a girl to him, and you are damn sure that's all you were to me.' It was time for John to get out of this place, as soon as he got home he would start packing up his life. Why wait? This was the only way forward.

-

John had been packing his life into boxes for hours on end and it seemed like he had barely touched the surface. He didn't have much in the way of possessions but he had a terrible habit of stopping to reminisce over every old toy or book that he came across. He wasn't taking it all with him to Lympstone, in fact he was taking very little. His father, though, had insisted that he box and store all of his "crap" in the loft before he went, an insistence that John had taken as a compliment, as it surely meant that he didn't expect his son to return any time soon. Thinking that he would pass basic training was of course as close to a compliment as John could expect from Marc Petalow, and John willingly accepted it. His old school report had given him a giggle. *Johnathon Petalow believes himself too smart to be taught by the teachers on site, yet despite what he thinks, the only thing he truly excels at is long distance running and captaining the Rugby team. If he could look past this bizarre fascination with joining the British forces then we might have a good student on our hands.* John, of course, didn't think that he was smarter than anyone, let alone the teachers who bullied and belittled him as much as his drunken father, but he never heard them preach anything that took his interest, with one exception of course. Mr Hawkins had been the only teacher at school that had ever gripped John's imagination with any kind of favour. He was the one that had them all sitting out on the grass during the warmer months, the Americans of Lovecraft and Poe were read, rather than the curriculum of Shakespeare and Dickens. Mr Hawkins was as rebellious as a teacher could get in the 60's, and John had been truly sad when he had heard of his retirement last summer due to Parkinson's. Generations of kids had been touched by his ability to inspire, and the thought of him bowing out like this didn't sit well with John at all.

The Snorkeler, by Johnathon Petalow, he read out in his head as he pulled an old essay out of his English literature book. I remember you, old friend, he flicked straight to the back of the essay to read Mr Hawkins very distinct handwriting, and was not disappointed.

John laid the short story upon his bedside table and continued to pack his young life into cardboard boxes. It would be strange to leave. This bedroom was all he had ever known, apart from the occasional night at his Grandma's, where family get-togethers would often result with six or seven cousins laying head to toe like sardines, blankets pulled so tight that the very effort required to breathe was exhausting beyond reason. He wouldn't miss it, far from it, but it was home, and John Petalow came from a time where "home" still meant something. He took a few deep breaths and finished packing up the remnants of his life, knowing full well that once he left, he would only ever be back to visit his mother. A fact that filled him with joy, sadness, and guilt for abandoning her. He knew he couldn't protect her, and it wasn't a son's place to do so, but leaving her here with that drunken docker seemed like a death sentence that he was unwilling to administer.

4

To Dance with my Father
Reculver, Kent, UK
Summer 2014

The sun was starting to set on the back end of the laziest Sunday afternoon that Jacob could remember, and he had loved it. He and Evan lay out upon the decking, the couple's sun lounger, that Jacob had built for them, held them in a tight embrace as they watched the sun drop into the ocean. Two glasses of alcohol-free cider clinking together as Evan popped a strawberry into Jacobs mouth with a smile. They were happy, and with Dorothy at Alice's all weekend, Evan was hoping to tear Jacobs clothes off the second they decided to head into the house. Sex was a little more awkward as Evan's bump came between them, but was no less enjoyable, in fact quite the opposite was true as she found herself growing ever more sensitive to touch. Jacob ran a strawberry up her thigh, its cold touch causing goosebumps to break out all over her body, the strawberry made its way over her baby bump before tracing a path through her breasts as she bit her lip awaiting its sweetness. He was going to get himself into trouble, although how much more trouble he could get himself into she was unsure, as she shifted her weight uncomfortably in the sun lounger. She was still beautiful, Jacob would say the most beautiful woman he had ever met, and she had put on no extra weight outside of the baby, not that Jacob would care if she had. Her fears that the physical side to their relationship would die out with the pregnancy had found no footing, he still lusted for her every day, and she for him. He was as attentive a husband as he was a loving father, and she was excited to grow their family. They both lay back in the comfort that the lounger provided, and sipped upon their drinks as they enjoyed the peace and quiet of such a beautiful summer evening. Evan had been mad at Jacob for buying this property without consulting her, but that annoyance had only lasted until she saw it. Their home was perfect, perfect to enjoy their life together and perfect to raise their little family. It certainly matched Jacob's character, old-fashioned walls made up of huge stones, all quarried from the very ground they walked upon, had built the beautiful white building to withstand the lashings of wind and rain over the centuries that it had stood here. It was a solid home, that would still be the family home long after both she and Jacob had left this world. Jacob had always wanted to leave something behind, something that told a legacy of more than the troubled youth that nearly died at sea, and Evan knew that this was it. Their family legacy would not be one of pain and suffering, of divorce and mental illness. Their story would be one of love, one of family and friendship. Jacob was her best friend and of that she had no doubt, it had taken time to break down those walls of his, but she knew that she could tell him anything, and she believed with all her heart, that if he needed to open his heart to her, he would.

'Baby? Tell me about your dad, you so rarely talk about him, what was he like?' asked Evan, careful not to upset the moment.

'Mr Paul Brooking? Well, what can I say? The man was a legend to me,' said Jacob with a beaming smile. 'He was a devoted father, I mean truly devoted, who worked jobs that we knew he hated, so that we could survive as a family.'

'I thought he worked at the hospital?' asked Evan as she cuddled up to her best friend, a chill biting her skin as the sun finally took its day rest.

'He did, as a medical gas engineer, right up until we lost him. Things were not always easy though, and when things were tough he also worked an evening job at the local pub serving pints to old drunks, and cleaning up their mess after doors, a job that took up his evenings and most of his weekends too. We barely saw him, but we knew why and we respected him for it.'

'My god, you must have seen less of him than I did my mother.' said Evan, completely understanding his pain.

'I saw him enough to know that he loved me, enough to know I was safe, and enough to know that my mum had the best husband,' Jacob took a deep breath as he relived his childhood. 'I miss him, baby, so much.'

'I know you do my love, oh, if I could bring him back I would move mountains for you, but you know that right?' Evan linked their fingers as they spoke. 'Actually that's why I brought all this up.'

Jacob nearly choked as he took a sip of his cider. 'Because you want to bring my father back from the dead?'

Evan poked him in the ribs with her free hand, once again causing him choke on his drink. 'No you dumbass, I've been thinking of my father... I mean, finding my father.'

'Oh, wow... I mean I can't blame you, but I have to ask where on Earth this has so suddenly come from?' Jacob said, turning to face his wife, a look of intrigue crossing his face.

Evan pulled herself up and swivelled round. 'It's us, our family I mean. I just can't imagine Dotty or Lachlan growing up without you here, with me. I thought I'd found everything here by your side, but truth be told I'm really missing something right now.'

'Any idea what that might be? Or if I can help you?' asked Jacob sitting up to meet his equal.

'OK, don't laugh, I want what Alice has...' said Evan almost wincing at her own statement.

'Well, not to brag, love, but you have already taken the most important thing she had, what more do you want to strip the poor girl of?' Jacob pulled his collar up on his linen shirt in an almost mock imitation of Danny from the film Grease.

Evan once again lashed her husband with a playful slap. 'I swear if I wasn't carrying around your giant child, I would beat you to within an inch of your life.'

Jacob braced himself as he was mounted by his wife. 'OK, so what is it? Hit me up, Mamma Bear.'

'I spent two hours looking at bloody photo albums with Alice and her mother, I saw four or five generations of Petalow, from John's miserable looking father to Angela's Nazi-hunting grandmother, all laid out before me, and all I could think was, I have no pictures of my parents or grandparents, just an absentee mother, who is only just starting to show an interest, that's it.'

'And that's what you want?' asked Jacob kindly. 'An extended family to share social events with and special occasions?'

Evan sighed as a little sadness crept into her words. 'I want parents who are proud of me, of us, of our kids. I watched John and Angela playing with Dorothy at the BBQ and it killed me that I never had that. I won't ever let our two go without, but at the same time I realised what I was missing in my life.'

'You have me, never forget that, and our two monkeys.' said Jacob as he put his hand on his wife's bump and gave a comical flutter of his eyelashes, a move that instantly brought a smile to Evan's face.

'I know, baby, and I am so grateful for that. I guess it would just be nice to know where I came from, that's all,' Evan said as she held on tightly to Jacob's hand.

'I get that, and I want to help, so what can I do?' asked Jacob, as he pulled the hair out of Evan's face.

'I'm not sure yet, I need to talk to my mother first, she has always claimed ignorance on the subject, but something tells me that she does nothing in her life with ignorance in the equation, so that means she's hiding something,' Evan reached down and planted a kiss on Jacob's lips, the kind of kiss that halts you at the gates of heaven. 'But, Mr Brooking, I do have a job for you right now if you're up to it?'

'Oh girl, you don't even know,' Jacob growled as he stood, sweeping Evan up into his embrace as he went. 'I think, since we have been talking family all night, it's time I let you into an old Brooking family secret...' Jacob leaned in and kissed Evan deeply, pulling on her lip as he pulled away. 'We really love a hot blonde.'

'Well lucky for you...well... lucky...' Evan stuttered whilst she lost all the colour in her face, 'I think I'm going to throw up.'

5

The Snorkeler
Summer 1969

He was finally finished. Two bags of essentials to take to Lympstone with him, two boxes for the tip in the morning and three to go in the loft before he left. His room was bare and he was excited for both sleep, and to wake up tomorrow. He wasn't stupid, he knew he had months of vomit-inducing physical hardship ahead of him. John also knew that he would rather be throwing up on a muddy hill than watch his mother get another beating. John climbed into bed and turned on his bedside light to illuminate the old manuscript that sat next to him. The cheap paper had turned yellow in the few years it had been stuffed into the top of his wardrobe, and it carried the musty smell of a childhood only recently forgotten. John smiled as he fingered through the pages of his short story. There had been a time when he had fancied himself a potential author, a time when his father had been away on the Ton-Class countermeasure operations as they picked up the last of the loose mines from the war. On his father's return, that idea had soon been quashed in favour of, as his father had put it, a real man's job. *Your job, Son, is to provide for whatever girl is stupid enough to let you start a family with her. So pick a career where your hands get dirty enough to deserve that privilege.* John repeated his father's words in his mind. He wasn't good enough anyway, his spelling and grammar were sub-par at best, with his skill only coming in the form of a vivid imagination. An imagination born from years of wishing he was anywhere but stuck in this hell-hole.

'The Snorkeler' read John as he turned back to page one. *'By Johnathon Petalow'*

The canal that ran through this pitiful place was as dank and dreary as the rest of the village that had always been home to Madison Brown. Today was to be no exception as the rain tore down in sheets, forcing Madison to quickly find shelter under a cobbled foot bridge that arched over the sleepy canal. She laughed at the pointless exercise, as the rain was so heavy that her brief exposure had drenched her to the very bones, and she doubted she would have got much wetter had she just carried on walking home at a leisurely pace. She pulled her toggle coat in tight around her and suppressed another shudder as the bitterly cold October night closed in. Her mother hated her walking home from work this way, the well-lit roads might take her another fifteen minutes, but at least they were safe. Madison had defended herself with the premise that 'nothing ever happened in this sleepy little place anyway.' I mean, who am I likely to run into on a day like this? she thought with a grimace. Although, there was that time, a time before Madison was even born...She edged forward off of the cobbled stone surround of the path and stepped a little closer to the water's edge. There was a story whispered in the back of the classroom, prepubescent young boys trying to scare each other with moronic ghost stories and haunting tales of village history. The water, dark and void-like, was thick with oil and grease, creating a rainbow of blacks; an unfortunate side effect from busy boat traffic that passed constantly on this route. Madison doubted that much could live in that water, yet she had often seen ducks skipping over the surface baying for food from every passer-by, and they had to be eating something other than the scraps of stale bread thrown in by the locals. Madison took another step forward and looked into the darkness of the water. The story told of a man returned from war, Sam Whitney, a Navy diver of kind heart and no kin. He had found a family in the Forces, brothers and sisters alike. Yet his heart was longing for a conclusion to the endless battle. Years of watching his friends die in horrific ways, had emptied his heart, his conscience unable to deal with the broken morality that was forced upon them all. He had taken the lives of as many Germans who were forced to fight as Nazis, as he had Germans who wanted to be Nazis. Young men oppressed into a life they had no desire to live. He was a good man, just like a lot of the men who he faced in combat. He was also a man who had been betrayed on his journey from Nazi-occupied France, all the way back to his home county of Cheshire. Betrayed, simply because he had fallen in love. The nature of love itself was not the crime, the object of his affection had been though.

His heart, which was his to give to whomever he chose, was given to a German field nurse, captured one night in the raid of a busy dockyard. He had taken a rifle bullet through the thigh during the firefight and Marianne Kruspe, a Red Cross nurse of only teenage years herself, had tended his wounds, then held him with warmth and kindness until the rest of his squadron had arrived, only for them to arrest her on the spot. Her brunette hair tied back into a tight bun only exposed more of her delicate features, a face that, despite the chaos around them, seemed to radiate only light, whilst her almost golden eyes looked kindly into Sam's soul. Locked up for the remainder of the war in the makeshift brig, built into the abandoned U-Boat that had become their temporary base of operations as it found its final resting place, beached and torn open by the rocks of an unwelcoming coastline. He had visited her every day, and every day he had fallen a little more deeply into the chasm of her soul. Sam would bring her books to read and fruit stolen from the nearby French town. They would talk late into the night, until the guard would grow tired of his presence with the enemy and throw a glare so sharp down the corridor that Sam knew not to argue. Other times they wouldn't talk at all and silence was all they needed as their fingers linked through the bars of the makeshift prison. This lasted for as long as such things can last, before envious eyes find a way to tear open what had become whole. Unrest had been growing within the younger members of the squadron, the idea of Sam keeping the Kraut prisoner alive whilst their friends were still dying on the front line, had left a bitter and vicious taste in their angry, vengeful mouths, a taste that he expected to lead to trouble, but not this. Marianne was missing from her cell, he had known something was wrong when the guard had looked down towards the ground upon his entrance, the thick stare of contempt, so often his physical moniker, had left him. What Sam had found instead was the bloodied remains of her uniformed dress, underwear and a cell that had seen a struggle for life. Sam looked back to the guard post and saw it empty. Rage filled his bod as fear and adrenaline mixed into his blood stream. Marine Sam Whitney, would find out what had happened here, and if his fears were correct, he would bring those responsible to justice. A quick search of the boat had brought nothing, but as he stepped outside and into the night, the rain lashing down against his shorn skull, he heard laughter. Not the laughter of one, but the laughter of many. He ran through the rivers of mud that surrounded the dock and came to a halt as he bolted around the corner of the makeshift latrine, his boots almost losing traction under the loose footing. The crowd of hyena-like soldiers and sailors were still howling to themselves as he came to bear on them. Upon recognising his face the crowd started to disperse, slowly at first, but with more purpose once he started to push his way through the numbers. In a matter of seconds he was left completely alone, alone with his beloved Marianne. Her legs the only thing not submerged by the tide as she lay face down, broken and beaten in the thick black mud of the coastline. A coastline dyed red already by the blood of his own brothers, and now hers. It had been said that the death scream he let out at that moment had been the reason that the Nazis had surrendered not a day later. That his pain and anguish had travelled through the ether like oil into clean water, and attacked the very spirits of all those involved in this awful war. Upon his return to Blighty and to his Cheshire home, he had found emptiness. She had given meaning to a war he couldn't find reason within. She had given him hope. More than that, she had made him feel like he deserved a positive resolution after all the soldiers had fallen that he deserved to live. Sam had lost that belief upon her passing, and knew with absolute certainty that he needed to be with his Marianne, whatever it took, no matter the cost. As he stepped into the canal on that cold October night, his bergen full of rocks and masonry bricks, he felt warmth from the void below, felt the familiar touch of his love, the love that had left him on the eve of September not a month before. No…not left him, took from him, taken from him in hate and prejudice. He felt that hatred rise through him as the murky water flooded his lungs. He felt his blood boil as he choked on the dirt-filled liquid that the boats constantly churned out. His body spasmed until his muscles started to clench tightly into a death stance. Sam Whitney died on the First of October 1945. He died looking up at the surface from the depths of the canal, died waiting for his love to look down from the light above him and pull him to safety like she had done once before, and when she came, he would never let her go.

Detective Inspector Emmet Gill had worked this case before, same canal, same circumstance, just a different name. He had to ask himself why parents allowed their children to walk here alone, he wouldn't have ever let his two boys down here on a wet autumn night, well, that's if his cruel faced ex-wife would ever let him see them. Maybe I should drag her arse down here, he mused with an honest grunt as he ducked under the old stone bridge where his junior Detective was measuring the clawed scratch marks that led from the gritted pathway to the murky waters edge. He knew they wouldn't find Madison Brown, they certainly hadn't found the Smith child from last year, or the Hodge girl from the year before that. So what realistic chance they would find Audrey Browns teenage daughter?

'Nothing here Inspector, same as last year,' said the young detective as he stood up to greet his Senior with the bad news.

'Ok lad, let's close off this stretch of the canal whilst we get the brains from central to go through it all with a fine toothed comb, they won't find anything, but we have to go by the book.'

'Yes Inspector, of course.' said the detective as he hurried to work, eager to impress.

Emmet Gill looked past the claw marks and into the dark water. They would dredge the canal, and once again find nothing, just as they had done so before and undoubtably as they would do so again.

'Where do you take them?' he asked, with an empty and faithless heart, as cold eyes looked back at him silently from beneath the surface.

6

The Red Door
Whitstable, Kent, UK
Autumn 2014

Alice climbed into bed after washing the orange stain from her hands and quickly tidying up the innards of the pumpkin she had just gutted. Alice had always had ability when it came to being an artist, her skills with a paintbrush had made her a living more comfortable than most, and her photography was selling equally well. Alice could think of none though, not a Matisse, a Turner or a Banksy, who could carve a pumpkin quite like her. The creation looking back at her from the creating table which sat in the corner of her bedroom, was truly masterful, its teeth razor sharp and eyes full of menace. Jacob had always been the pumpkin king, his armoury of chef's tools had made the perfect carving kit and his skills with a knife were unparalleled, but this...this was as if born from the nightmares of a goblin king. Alice had been fighting the urge to keep slicing into it, not knowing when to stop was a far too frequent a problem for the youngest Petalow, but she had decided that it was finally ready to go on the counter down in the gallery. She had spent more time than was necessary mulling over the sex of her pumpkin, settling on it being a male only because it reminded her of a the scarecrow that her mother kept in the garden during her youth. Mr Peepatch, as he had affectionately been called, had given a younger and more naïve Alice more than a few sleepless nights. It wasn't unusual for her to sit upon her window ledge, almost certain that she had watched it move, controlled by some dark power that was from a place beyond her knowledge. A theory that certainly held more weight after the negative energy of the last few years. Alice knew that monsters didn't exist, she knew that all her recent problems were a product of her poor mental health. But she also knew that there was no chance that the monster under her bed could get her as long as she kept her feet under the quilt at night; everyone knew the stray legs were the quick snacks that kept the shadows full. The almost supernatural paranoia she had been feeling more recently though was, as ashamed as she was to admit it, keeping her up at night, and her new therapist was quite clear that this was completely normal. How could she expect to suddenly be OK just because she had identified the root of her problem? Thomas had made her feel powerless, made her feel weak, but she knew that wasn't true anymore...she was strong and more powerful than most people realised. Yet the voices were still there, and she couldn't quieten them fully. She had good days, days where all she heard was the playlist on her radio and the chatter of customers, but her choir of discontent still found its mark on sleepy days. Mostly inaudible since she had confronted Thomas on his deathbed, but still there, like a hundred voices whispering at once. She was unsure what they were trying to tell her, and the focusing techniques that her doctor had taught her seemed not to help at all, each voice overpowered by the next, with very few sentences breaking through coherently. Strangely though, the few voices that had broken through were almost positive, telling her that she deserved more, that she was above others and she should take what she was owed. She wanted it to stop but, at least, it wasn't the demon creature from the mirror talking to her, which had made a refreshing change. One thing did weigh on her mind though, the idea that she knew where the voice was originating from. It was a nonsense belief really, much like the monster waiting under the bed. She knew it couldn't be real, just a figment of her imagination that had been created from unresolved fear, built from all that had happened the last fifteen years. Alice Petalow got it, she understood, and yet she couldn't shake the feeling that the whispering was coming from her painting. It had been likened to her very own Dorian Gray. A girl so haunted she held the look of an angel that had lost her wings due to falling from grace. Heartbroken at failing her father, and petrified of the solitary road to damnation that lay ahead of her, yet she smiled. The smile held no joy of course, rather it was the smile of sad realisation and acceptance of her fate. The painting had been shut away, already wrapped in its pallet at the back of the galleries loft space, ready and awaiting sale at auction. It was the door to that loft space that had been the fulcrum for the whispers. In the day, with the bustle of the shop and customers, she would hear nothing. But in her quiet hours, when she settled down to read or prepare herself for bed, that's when the voices were most clear, that was when it bothered her most. In the early hours especially, when Alice was half asleep, she could hear it quietly calling her from behind that varnished red door. Her therapist had told her that is was an ongoing process, told her to write down everything that she could decipher so that they could work through it together. That was fine, she thought, and she understood the concept completely. Yet tonight, as she lay on her bed, looking at the red door in front of her that lead to the loft, she had to wonder what on Earth was turning the key from the other side of the locked door.

'I'm not scared of you anymore, try as you might. I have walked paths of fire where my parents were flayed in front of me, and my demon rapist tried to murder me,' Alice said defiantly with a heart full of resolve that she never knew she had. She was strong, and she knew that she could survive herself, but surviving wasn't the issue here as she turned her back resolutely to the red door to find a perfect mirror of herself lying next to her. The doppelgänger looked back at her inquisitively with crystal blue eyes. This wasn't her demon self. Her skin was as flawless as Alice's bone china complexion, her hair the same mane of phoenix flame that adorned her own head. The doppelgänger smiled and words filled Alice's mind without touching her ears.

Get back what was yours, Alice. Retrieve the life that was taken from you! You deserve more.

-

'Doctor, the voices are getting worse, and as scared as I am to admit this, I'm starting to see things once more,' said Alice to her therapist, her hand shaking as she held the phone to her ear.

'Then it's time for us to execute are plan, when can you come into see me?' answered the doctor, hoping that Alice had the strength to pull off what needed to be done.

7

The Esmee Nijboer
Gulf of Guinea
Autumn 1971

John hadn't held his green beret for more than a few months before his first real mission came forward. A spate of pirate attacks from a group of Somali fighters had led the British government to send out a small contingent from Four-Five commando, who had been on a diving exercise off the coast of Guinea for three weeks. He had enjoyed the first few days, after all, the water was far warmer here than both Lympstone and Arbroath where he had previously been shipped from. That was before he realised that the warmer waters attracted more than just diving instructors on deep ocean training. Sharks twice the length of his massive frame would circle him like vultures whilst he tried to perfect underwater demolitions. His training partner, Adley Long, had laughed at John's trepidation regarding the massive fish. The Aussie born rugby player had been with John through all of his basic training and had, without doubt, been the reason that John had found the internal fortitude to last the distance. Adley had quickly been renamed Shrimpy, as despite having lived in sunny Essex for most of his adult life, he still carried the thick Queensland accent, and despite initial protests it would be a handle that he grew to love. Once again they were side by side, but this time the pressure was real. They both hung, half submerged, from access ladders on the 80,000 ton cargo ship, The Esmee Nijboer.

They each had another fire team member placed directly above them, enough rungs between them to make a harder "one shot" target if they were spotted, yet they were close enough to hopefully prevent that discovery from happening. The four man brick had been stalking the ship all night, launching silently as the witching hour had approached. Each man had taken up point on the starboard side of the hull to shy away from the moonlight, no pollution here in the African night sky to mask their entrance, the moon acted almost like a flood light in the clear air. They were ready to move in an instant and, on the command of Sergeant Harris, they would scale the ship to take control of the deck. The short swim from the R.I.B. had freaked John out more than he would care to admit. Not being able to see the sharks had made them all the more menacing within his mind, and he clung to the iron ladder as if waiting to be pulled under at any moment. Most people would look at a man like John Petalow and assume that he wouldn't be afraid of anything, and for the most part they were right. Yet as he looked into the abyss beneath him, he felt like he was being watched, and not out of curiosity. More so, whatever was watching him was weighing up its attack trajectory. He wasn't wrong, either, as merciless minds tried to figure out if the two half submerged men were friend or food.

'Johnno, it's just a big fish mate. She's probably more scared of your fat arse than you are scared of her.' whispered Adley, without looking. He knew his friend was scared, but this was to be his first enemy contact too and he needed to be focused.

'How do you know it's a "she"? Have you seen one, is it down there now?' said John, clearly panicked.

'The girls are always bigger when it comes to sharks mate, and she's a whopper,' whispered Adley with a smile as he focused on looking up the ladder. 'But what is it, John?'

'Just a big fish, yeah I get it, but why do they have to be so fucking big?' John whispered to himself in return.

'Shut up you two, Harris will have you both if you don't get it together. We move in thirty seconds. Be ready ladies.' snarled Boomer. Corporal Desmond Middleton was, for all intents and purposes, the scariest man that John had ever met. The most senior of the group and a championship-level Naval boxer, he looked truly battle worn. His ebony skin was pitted with scars and crow's feet to such an extent that the only parts of his face untouched were eyes so dark that he could compete with the black tips swimming about their feet, and a pristine moustache that fell all the way down to his chin strap.

'Thirty seconds, yes Skipper, have that.' said Stuart Dunn as he brought a knee up and placed his boot on the rung above ready to push off. Flecks of rust from the ladder fell down onto Adley as he prepped to follow closely.

John awaited the signal and tensed his muscles ready to move. He felt tight, apprehensive,...but ready. *Just remember what your father always taught you. Slow is smooth, and smooth is fast.* 'Don't rush this, John,' he whispered as he heard two clear clicks in his ear. Instantly both lead men pushed off the standing rungs.

Fire Team Alpha took starboard, as John and Adley headed towards the portside. She was a huge vessel but Intel had briefed only four night guards, one on each corner of the ship. Supposedly they were watching the hostages as they tried to sleep on the corrugated iron deck, but John thought it a safe bet that they were either asleep themselves or at best day dreaming of a better life, a life away from the situation they had got themselves into. The rest of the x-rays were below deck, probably drunk with one or two of the prettier hostages unwillingly in tow. That was a problem they would potentially have to handle once the deck was dealt with, and that needed to be done without causing the hostages to panic.

Another click sounded in John's ear and was followed almost immediately by two more; the signal that Fire Team Alpha was in position. Adley branched right towards his target while John pressed himself tightly against the wall panelling. As he saw his target looking out to sea, rifle leaning casually against the railing, and completely oblivious as to what was about to happen to him and his comrades, John heard three more clicks from Adley. John paused not ten feet from his target and clicked four times on his radio. Being the last into position, his final click would be the signal to move in five seconds. John's heart had raced up until that point but, as his training kicked up a notch, he nearly flat lined as the seconds counted down. 5...4...3...2...

John launched forward at a speed unnatural to his giant size. His right arm wrapped around the neck of his much smaller target and formed into a triangle choke hold, the strength of which was magnified intensely by John arching his back, lifting his little opponent clean off the floor.

'Ontspan,' whispered John with absolute authority into the ear of the petrified man. 'ONTSPAN,' he growled once more. 'Relax', it was the only word he remembered from the linguistics brief they had on the eve of this mission. John wasn't sure if his sweet talking had worked or if his target had simply passed out, but a few seconds later it became irrelevant as the body in his grasp went limp, and John lay him gently on the deck. Drilled to perfection, he zip tied the x-ray's hands and bound them to the railing. A strip of tape covered his mouth, and John depressed his comms. 'Four, clear,' said John clearly as he dropped the enemy weapon over the side of the ship.

As the other three cleared their targets, the second unit, led by Sgt. Harris entered the fray. Instantly moving in between the hostages, checking each one for sleeper guards and silencing the frightened captives, John and Adley formed up on Alpha team at the door to the lower decks. Shrimpy took the door, with Boomer and Dunny arms ready. John took up the rear, and mouthed the silent count before the door opened and Fire Team Alpha moved in with clinical precision. Shrimpy followed closely behind, then John at speed. The corridor split in two, and Boomer instinctively led team one left whilst Adley led right.

Four loud cracks came from Alpha Team, but before questions could be asked, the radio cracked to life. 'Three x-rays down. Two hostages secure.' The Intel had claimed nine bad guys, so all being accurate, that left two. Adley led to the first door and moved in, with John taking lead in the corridor. 'Clear,' shouted Adley as he came straight out behind John who instinctively started to move to the next room.

John pulled the trigger to his rifle seconds after entering the large mess hall, as the enemy brought his gun to bear. The 7.62 round from the L1 hit the target square in the chest. The round killed the young assailant instantly as it punctured his heart with a small entrance wound, but left his back with a much larger exit. A second round punched a few inches higher before his brain had even registered the first bullet exiting his body. John instantly trained his rifle on the second target who stood with his trousers around his ankles, a crying young girl at his feet. His target looked for his weapon, and panicked as he saw it to be further away than the oncoming Royal Marine. 'GET DOWN!' John shouted with extreme authority before smashing the stock of his rifle into his opponent's face, shattering both bone and teeth in one strike. In seconds, he had kicked the screaming man onto his belly and put his twenty-stone weight through his knee and onto the back of his x-ray's neck. 'Two x-rays down. One hostage secure.' called John as Adley picked up the hostage to lead her to the safety of the deck.

'Well done, Johnno, I told you, the sharks are more scared of you...' Adley laughed as he went to exit the mess hall with the hostage hanging tightly off his arm.

John looked up as the first crack sounded and the shock of what he saw caused his focus to slip. The man beneath him went silent as his neck broke under John's weighted and powerful knee. Adley fell back into the room holding his chest. His body armour had slowed the bullet, but it had entered his lung and was soon followed by three more shots. The young girl screamed and fell, kicking and screaming to the floor. As Adley dropped to his knees, his rifle falling beside him, John saw target ten for the first time. Intel had been wrong. The man, nearly as tall as John but much slighter in frame, brought his pistol up whilst angrily shouting words that John didn't want to try to understand. John Petalow would be dead before he could even aim his rifle, and he felt his heart pound at the sight of his closest friend dying before him. He thought of his mother, so very far away. He thought of his father and cursed the notion that he probably wouldn't outlive him. Then he closed his eyes and...

Crack.

'X-ray down!' shouted Sgt. Harris as he stormed the room, kicking aside the dead hostile as he passed. 'You alive, John?' he asked as he knelt beside Adley.

'Yes, Sergeant,' John barked as he checked the non-existent pulse of his half-naked opponent. 'Adley?'

'I'm sorry, John,' said Sgt. Harris as he called for back-up. 'Are you able?' he asked sternly as he rose to look at John.

'Of course, Sergeant,' John growled. 'Part of the job, right?'

-

The tears that John cried that night told a very different tale from the resolute Marine who carried his friend's body to the top deck that very morning. After the mission debrief and a much needed shower, shit and a shave, John had started boxing up Adley's kit for the return back to Scotland. Spare fatigues, boots, and other necessities for their time here, nothing personal, nothing real. That's when it hit John, he had sweat, cried and bled with this man for over a year, and yet had never asked him what to do if ever he died. John once again felt alone, and he was starting to think that was a good thing, moving forward.

8

I Am Mother
Canterbury, Kent, UK
Summer 1995

Evan sat in her window, watching intently as the gardener drank the iced water that she had left out for him. Bryn Thomas was a new, and welcome, addition to her mother's home. The young Welshman had been brought in to maintain the cars and keep the land as best he could, and Evan enjoyed watching him do it. Just turned seventeen, she was home for the summer after finishing her final year of boarding school. Choosing a university was her mother's order of the day, yet following in her footsteps was no desire of Evan's; she had other plans. Bryn took off his chequered red shirt to reveal a tightly muscled body, like a knotted rope, no fat hid the abs on his stomach as they glistened in the summer sun, sweat pouring off him. Evan couldn't help but touch herself as she watched him run his hands through his curly red mop of hair. Her mum had done something good for once, thought Evan, although she doubted that the "Lady" Vivian Phillips looked at Bryn quite the same way she did. He poured the last of the water over his face to cool himself down and Evan nearly fell from the window ledge as she buried her hand deeply between her thighs and clenched every muscle she had. She wished to see more of Bryn and his tightly wound body, but as she jumped down from the ledge she knew that today would probably be the last day she was to lay eyes on him. Evan was leaving, with no intention of coming back. Her absentee mother would be angry, but that was neither her concern or consideration. University had never been her plan,, and Evan felt that life was too short for following another heart's idea of what was right.

Autumn 2014

She looked like Monroe as she sat looking out of the window at the passing world, she had had a little off her hair yesterday, the length had been making it difficult to maintain as she woke up each and every morning a little larger than before. Sleeping in rollers last night had given Jacob a shock when he woke up, but it had made Evan feel beautiful as her hair cascaded in ringlets about her shoulders.

It made a change from feeling bloated and swollen. Even her mother had commented on how well she looked, and that was certainly a rarity. It had been nice for Evan to start rebuilding her relationship with her. It had been something she had longed for since childhood. Evan had forever looked up to Vivian, it was hard not too, she was as successful and independent as they come. She had wanted to hate her mother for a long time, for the neglect, for putting her career first. There was something stopping her though, a barrier to the hate. A little part of Evan thought that maybe, just maybe, the reason that her mother hadn't wanted to be around was because she resented Evan for her father's absence.

'We have only just started talking to each other again, I have to be sure this is a conversation you want,' said Vivian as she sat down opposite Evan, placing a cappuccino in front of her. 'This isn't the simple chat you think it might be, I can't just tell you about some heroic figure that you might want to include in your life. Damn, I'm not even sure how much I remember.'

The café they had found to sit at in Canterbury High Street was bustling with people, both inside and out, but they had gotten the comfy seats near the window and there was no way Evan was letting her mother escape today without gleaning some information from her.

'Mum, this isn't an interrogation, and I absolutely don't want to cause friction between us, it's your help I want, nothing more, can you give me that?' Evan removed her scarf and adjusted her dungarees so she could attempt to cross her legs, but this was apparently something she could no longer do, and she let out a sigh as she instead leaned back into her chair, cradling her bump.

Vivian felt a rare maternal warmth as she watched her daughter rub her baby bump so tenderly; Evan would be a better mother than she had been. Vivian had never intended on being a parent, and her absence during Evangeline's early years had proven that. She had not intended to be a bad parent, and she felt it a blight upon her character that her beautiful daughter had become all that she was – strong, independent, smart and hard working - whilst she, the absentee mother, had been busy filling their bank accounts by virtue of her professional success. Vivian had provided everything that she deemed relevant for her child's safe upbringing, but completely neglected the one thing Evangeline had desired... a mother.

'Of course I want to help, I do! And I will give you all the time that you want to figure this out, but I will confess early on, I don't know where your father is,' Vivian wasn't lying, Evan could tell that from the off. 'How about I tell you everything I can, we may not be able to do it all in one day, but I'll leave out no detail, and with that you can deduce what you need to moving forward.'

'Mum that's all I want, plus the opportunity to learn more about a youth that you, honestly, never really disclosed. It could only bring us closer, surely?' Evan reached across the table and took her mother's hand into her own. 'We are on a beautiful path, I want you to know that and, whatever happens regarding my father, we will stay on it.'

'How did this happen?' smiled Vivian as she exhaled with pride. 'I have three degrees in psychology and yet my daughter who left school at eighteen to run off with a bartender is actually far smarter than I ever was.'

'Don't talk crazy, Mum,' laughed Evan. 'I wouldn't say I'm "far" smarter.' Vivian gave a rare chuckle whilst giving Evan's hand a gentle squeeze.

'OK, just know this... I'm not sure how easy this story will be to tell...,' said Vivian as she let go of her daughter's grip and took a sip of her latte.

'Because of what you don't remember?' asked Evan as she took her own drink in hand, barely managing to get it to her lips without spilling any of the oversized glass mug.

'No, my love. Because of how much it hurts to think back to Laurie Rosenberg.'

Cambridge University
Autumn 1977

Vivian Phillips had never considered herself gay. She had pursued boys in the past with nonchalant abandon, and she had no doubt that she would again. Yet, as she sat in her Social Anthropology lecture upon her the eve of her twenty-first birthday, there was only one person that held her heart. Professor Rosenberg was more than just her lecturer, she was her friend, and the past few months had been almost magical. Each night they took walks through the university grounds before drinking wine, or taking a punt down the river together. Vivian would talk of the boys in the dormitory and Laurie would complain about her arse of a boyfriend. He didn't deserve her, he never had done. How could he, he was a just an old car engineer and at least twenty years older that Laurie. He claimed to be younger, but Vivian was not buying it one bit. She was only in the first year of her Masters, but she had passed her Psychology degree at Greenwich with aplomb. Her dissertation on soldiers affected by the trauma of blood and shellshock had been published, and received as revolutionary. She was young, that much was true, but she knew the eyes of a man who had seen war and shed blood. Of course, she had only met him the once, an impromptu meeting on the green outside Midsummer House. He had been gripping Laurie's hand so tightly that Vivian could swear he was walking with a scalded child rather than his beautiful young girlfriend. One meeting was enough for Vivian, forever the student, to quick to break down the morals of the man. Laurie had claimed that he was different at the beginning, that he had given her sanctuary when she had come out of her destructive marriage with Peter what's-his-face. He had been no better a partner for her, and each story that she told would break Vivian's heart a little more. Laurie Rosenberg was the best person she knew, and no man could be worthy of her. Especially this Alastair Hart.

'Are you with us Miss Phillips?' said the professor as she watched her favourite student slip into a daydream once more.

'Yes of course, Professor Rosenberg, I'm just struggling a little with the theory behind this, can I have a little of your time after class to make sure I'm on point?' Vivian wasn't struggling with anything, of course, except perhaps why the only birthday present she desired at midnight was the kiss of the only woman she had ever loved.

9

Hometown Blues
Rainham, Kent UK
Winter 1971

The street seemed so much smaller to him now. It hadn't been that long since he was last here, possibly a year, more than likely two. He seemed to have grown so much in that time away though, both mentally and physically. Still, the idea of knocking on his father's door left him with mixed emotions. Not that he was scared, far from it in fact, more apprehensive. Whenever he spoke to his mother, which in itself was a rarity, she still sounded a beaten woman, and that had broken John's heart. He wondered if the hole in his bedroom wall had been fixed yet, although he doubted his ability to fit into the crawl space now. He gave himself a wry smile as he realised that he would never have to climb into that space again. After all, John Petalow had long since given up on the childish notion of fear. His booted footsteps on the London Road sounded like his father's, like the countdown to something negative. With each footfall, he felt a little smaller. The doubt finally creeping in as he paused outside the family home and caught his own reflection in the bay window, only to see the teenage boy that had been so frightened to come home each night. *Don't be stupid John,* he thought, while he felt the gravel of the front path under his feet, *you're not that kid anymore.* The knock on the door went unanswered for longer than felt comfortable, and when it opened...John understood why.

'Where is he, Mum?' demanded John as he dropped his bag in the doorway and took her hand in his.

Betsie Petalow looked at her son from behind the swelling of two black eyes that almost pleaded with him not to react, without using her voice.

'Mum, where is my father?' John said unrelenting, towering over his mother's quivering frame.

'He's at the Cricketers,' she relented. 'But John, he's with the lads, don't go causing trouble, just come in and talk to me, I haven't seen you in so long...'

John was already walking down the road. He was dressed in his civvies; denim jeans that struggled to contain his massive thighs and a black polo shirt that really needed to be a size larger, if only they had made one. Only his desert-issue combat boots gave away any relation to his position within the Forces. He was enraged, he had expected drama this weekend, and it was exactly why he didn't come home anymore. John hadn't expected to see his mother once again battered, before he had even entered the house. The biggest problem now was that the local pub wasn't far enough away for John to calm down.

-

John nearly took the hinges off the twin doors as he burst into The Cricketers with a heavy push from both hands, immediately spotting his father, sitting in a booth with three of his docker mates. Seeing how pathetically lean his haggard old man looked didn't detract from his course whatsoever.

'Well shit me. You have grown, kid,' said Reggie, the landlord, who had served John his very first pint all those years ago. John didn't reply, and Marc Petalow, after a tertiary glance at his bulldozing son, went straight back to his ale.

John's giant hand wrapped around his father's throat and in one rapid motion, tore him upwards from the booth and smashed him down onto the adjacent pool table, never once releasing his choke hold. The two lads who were in the middle of a game quickly stepped back, not wanting any part of what was happening. John didn't need to hit him, he would just hold him here on the felt of the table until his little limbs stopped moving.

'You listen here, you miserable old bastard. If you ever, and I mean EVER, even dream of laying a hand on that poor woman again, I will punish you in ways you didn't know existed. Do you understand?' John said releasing enough pressure so his father could choke out a reply.

'Fuck you,' Marc croaked almost inaudibly, as he gripped John's wrist with both hands.

One of the ex-servicemen, an old Matelot called Burl, who his father had known for thirty-odd years, tried valiantly to save his friend by crashing a pint glass over John's head. He realised instantly that this was a mistake and, without letting go of his father, Marc kicked the knee out from under Burl's overweight body. His face smashed hard into the edge of the pool table, instantly knocking him out cold and leaving two front teeth lodged in the green top.

'FUCK ME? YOU SURE THAT'S YOUR ANSWER?' With a jerk of extreme power, John lifted his father by the neck and slammed him back down into the felt. The room was silent as he went to work. 'I'll ask you again, DO YOU UNDERSTAND?'

Marc was beating madly at his oppressor's arms to try and get free, but it was like a lion cub trying to fight off its father in a lesson of hunter and prey. Marc knew his place in this, and as the world started to turn black he choked out a response, blood and spittle escaping the edges of his mouth.

John released his father's neck, his fingers leaving their mark with bruising so dark that you could almost believe Marc to have been wearing a purple scarf. Before John turned to leave, he nudged the unconscious body by his feet to make sure he hadn't killed him. A small groan confirmed life at some level. *Well at least I'm not going away for murder,* John thought as he walked out of the pub, brushing a small glass shard from his shaven scalp as the doors closed behind him. *Now, what's for tea?*

-

John and Betsie Petalow sat opposite each other, quietly eating the dinner she had prepared earlier for the family's long-awaited reunion. Neither of them said much, just pleasantries about how nothing had changed in the neighbourhood, and how sad it was that John hadn't been able to make his grandfather's funeral. A large brisket of beef sat in the centre of the table, surrounded by a small army of goose fat potatoes and honey-glazed vegetables. They would never get through it alone, even with John's almost bear like appetite. That almost stopped being a problem when they heard the front door open.

'Dinner's on the table if you're hungry, Marc,' said Betsie with a quiver of uncertainty her voice. Her question went unanswered, and the sound of thirteen steps going up the stairs soon followed.

'Don't worry, Mum. I'm here,' said John without looking up from a gravy-smothered forkful of brisket. 'I doubt he will have much to say tonight.'

'Don't talk with your mouth full, Johnathon,' Betsie said as she stood from her chair, 'I need a cigarette.'

'Why don't you sit back down, love.' said Marc as he entered the room and took the seat next to his wife. His loaded service revolver placed on the table in front of him.

Marc sat with the Browning gripped tightly in his hand, his thumb flicking the safety on and off continuously, as if two sides of his personality were trying to work out his next move. John didn't look up from his brisket and continued in his quest to eat a three-man dinner all to himself. Betsie found herself lost for words as she sat next to her husband, unsure of his next move. Marc Petalow was only ever two things, angry at the world, or dismissive of it. This calculating side of him, she had seen enough to know that trouble was coming to bare. She fidgeted heavily in her seat while trying to keep calm. Marc hadn't taken his eyes off the giant frame of his son from the instant he had joined the table, as if given courage by the weapon he carried. A weapon that, frustratingly, wasn't having the effect on John that he wanted.

'So, the youngest Corporal in your regiment's history. And you are already pushing for Special Forces? You must be proud of yourself, Son?' Marc almost spat the words whilst rubbing his neck with his free hand. 'Good to see that I rubbed off on you a little.'

John looked up at the audacity of his father's claim and raised his brow almost comically, before quickly dismissing the attempt to goad him by eating another gravy-soaked roast potato.

'Fair enough, John, you've done it all on your own. You're the big guy now, what you weigh? Twenty stone? Maybe you should pay the bills now you are "the man" and all?'

John refused to bite. He placed his fork gently at the side of his plate and grabbed the buttered bread that his mum always left for the men of the house to mop up with. He wiped it casually around the plate as it soaked in the loose brisket and gravy juices, before pushing it into his mouth in one.

'You really don't get it do you, John? You can't just walk into my pub, with my friends around me and embarrass me like you did. There have to be repercussions. Consequences that you have to pay.'

'Marc, for God's sake, he's our son,' pleaded Betsie as she struggled to remain non-combative to her husband.

'It's OK mum, please...let him finish,' John silenced his mother with a raised hand and a kind look.

'Burl will need surgery on his front teeth. I have to say, the rest of the boys were impressed with your takedown techniques. No wonder the frogmen are pushing you to apply,' Marc sounded almost proud for a second, a second that soon passed as he switched the safety off of the pistol once more. 'You lack respect, John. You hurt my pride today and I can't let that slide. If you want to be the man of the house, then you are going to have to take that position from me.'

'MARC, I WILL NOT LET YOU HURT OUR BO...' Betsie was cut short as Marc pulled the gun level with her face and pushed it into her forehead.

'You, sit down...SIT DOWN AND SHUT UP!' shouted Marc with an authority not befitting a man as slight and wiry.

'That's enough, Dad,' said John as he rose from behind the table and confidently strode over to his father. 'Why don't you point that old gun at me? Mum, just sit down please, trust me.'

Betsie fell into her chair, her body almost convulsing with fear as she prepared for the worst. Marc though, seemed much more focused as he turned to point the gun at his only son.

John only smiled as he reached his father. The barrel of the pistol pressing against his chest. 'You can tell you work in engineering, Dad. If you shoot me there, a guy my size...well sure, I'd die, but not before I rip your head clean off.' John quickly grabbed the barrel of the gun and pulled it up to his brow, pressing it firmly between his eyes. 'If you are going to shoot me old man, I suggest here. I'll drop quick and you should be in the pub by seven to tell all your mates how you put me in my place.'

Marc seemed thrown by his son's confidence. His finger twitched against the trigger of a gun he had never fired.

'Come on, why are you dragging this out Killick, you're not scared are you? Oh my...you are, you're petrified,' John laughed as he leaned into the pistol barrel. 'Do you know, Killick? For so many years, I wanted to be just like you, because you were all I knew. You were my strongest male influence...' John was getting angrier as he spoke down to his wilting father. 'Then I saw the other kids playing with their own fathers, saw them laughing and joking. And do you know what I did? I made excuses for you,' John was bearing down on his father now, his voice a bellow. "My father's been through more." I would say. "My father is protecting us the same way he protected this country, he's defending us." I defended you like no son should ever have to.'

CLICK.

Marc pulled the trigger, to no avail.

'I was wrong to defend you, because you are pathetic. Less than a man. I deserved a better father, and you are damn sure my mother deserved a better husband.'

CLICK.

Marc was shaking as he tried to fire the gun again, the barrel waving around freely in front of John's face.

CLICK.

CLICK.

CLICK.

'Killick, I took the ammo out of that old pistol the second I walked through the door. Don't disgrace me by assuming that I am so naive not to know what a coward like you would do, now that your opponent is bigger than you. I know, Mum knows, we ALL KNOW.'

CLICK.

In one smooth movement, John had brought his hand up, snapping Marc's wrist with a simple twist that dropped the gun to the floor and shattered his fingers. John's free hand then drove up into his father's elbow, forcing him face first into the dining table. Before Marc had even realised what was going on, John had pulled the carving knife out of the remaining brisket joint and plunged it through Marc's hand, pinning him to the table with a scream that told of a coward caught out.

'I'm taking Mum for a walk. I will be one hour precisely and then I will be home,' John kept pressing his father into the table with all his weight born onto, what felt like, a dislocated shoulder. 'When I return, you will be gone. Not for the night, but forever, do you understand?' John brought his lips down to his father's ear. 'If I see you again, even in passing, I will kill you, I...WILL...KILL...YOU!' John growled as he yanked the knife free, causing blood to pour from the wound. 'Mum, get your shoes on and grab your smokes,' John said gently, as he threw the knife down and picked up the empty gun. 'Hope you don't see me again, or God help you, I will make you regret it.'

John let his mother past him as she spat on her husbands disgraced and broken body, before he followed her out the front door. Betsie Petalow was already smoking by the time she reached the end of the path. John quickly put his arm round her so that she knew, as long as he stood by her side, no one would ever hurt her again. They started walking, each taking a long look at the house as they went.

'Maybe it's time I moved house, John,' Betsie said with a tremor in her voice.

'Yeah, you might be right, Mum. Too many bad memories, time for a new start.'

10

Brontë in Winter

Cambridge, Cambridgeshire, UK

Winter 1977

It looked almost daylight as the moon reflected brightly off the shroud of snow that had quietly been settling all evening. Cambridge was a beautiful city on any day, but the winter quilt made it almost Victorian. An effect only exacerbated by the look that the ladies bore, as they fell into the street giggling. Laurie had treated Vivian to a Brontë-themed dinner for her birthday, and they had both worn classic, ivory silk dresses elaborated by gigot sleeves and collars to protect the modesty of such finely-figured women. Vivian still had her bonnet on as she skipped out into the snow, her evening had been joyous and she had no intention of hiding it as she spun about a cast iron street light. Laurie bounded behind her, but tried to restrain herself from the same behaviour her date was showing. Laurie was happy, she wondered in fact if she had ever been so happy. But she was twelve years Vivian's senior, and she knew all too well that she would be frowned upon if this was seen as anything other than a chance meeting. The other professors were known to be quite stuffy and overtly opulent. Hanging out with one of the students, even an adult one, was not the done thing in any capacity. How could she resist being here though, when the only other option was to be at home? Of course she would pay later, when Alastair returned home to realise that dinner wasn't made. But why should she be the one to make it, she thought, when she earnt more than three times his salary? At least this one didn't beat her. Her ex-husband had left her for dead one night after a drunken rampage; Alastair was a jerk at times, but he had never yet hit her. It saddened her that her new benchmark for acceptable relationships was based on the likelihood to avoid physical assault. There was something in his mannerisms, though, something that told of a man who longed to task a crime, a crime that he had previously been caught committing. Vivian looped her arm through Laurie's and they walked towards the green with the whimsy of mischief, their steps leaving prints, a sharp crunch with every footfall. She could quite happily never return home. A tenured position at such a prestigious university was the only reason that she hadn't already left with her new best friend. They had discussed the idea of exploring the world once all this was over; India, Africa and the States were all on their list, and that excited Laurie much more than the idea of staying in Cambridgeshire.

'Thank you, for everything you have done tonight,' said Vivian as she pulled Laurie in close. 'You really have made my day.'

'Oh stop it, it was just dinner and a little Wuthering Heights, you deserved it. As silly as our friendship may seem to others, I've found your companionship to be my saving grace of late.' Laurie said as she halted the walk home and turned to face her date.

'I have to be honest, and please don't think me crazy,' Vivian said taking hold of both of Laurie's gloved hands. 'I have found myself questioning my motives for spending so much time with you, Yes, of course, I see our friendship as pivotal to my happiness since moving from Greenwich. To be blunt, I'm not sure I could do without you, and your bonnet, now...'

'But...' Laurie asked, looking into Vivian's gaze.

'But, I think...I think I really need to kiss you now, I need to kiss you, and it scares me so very...her words were cut short as Laurie brought her finger up to Vivian's lips.

'I can't, I just...I can't...' Laurie pulled her finger away and kissed Vivian on the cheek. 'I am so ready for you, and I say that having never felt this way about a woman before...but I know for a fact that I am not ready for "us" and the drama that would bring.'

The snow started to fall a little harder and Laurie reached up to touch Vivian's cheek, a move that fell short as her mirror stepped back.

'I'm sorry, I shouldn't have...' Vivian said, as she turned and fled into the snow. Laurie knew better than to follow her.

-

Laurie Rosenberg reached her front door and realised that her night, as dramatic as it had so far been, was only just beginning. The door was bolted and an unused dinner plate was on the front step, an inch of snow mounted high upon it. She dare not ring the bell, it just wasn't worth the grief that would surely follow, so, it was to be a night spent freezing in the back of her Ford Cortina. For which, a part of her believed to be better than the alternative.

Autumn 2014

'Mum, that is heart breaking, I'm so sorry you had to go through that. You never really talk about being...you know, about being...'

'Gay? Oh come on, Evan. We are both old enough not to be coy on such things. Besides, you never ask.' Vivian smiled as she stood up to leave. 'Can we finish this in the week, my beautiful, inquisitive daughter? If you want this story told properly, then it cannot be squeezed into a one-day rush job.'

'Of course Mum, I know this is just as hard for you to tell as it is for me to hear. I'm just happy we are communicating.' said Evan rising to leave with her mother.

'Hard for me to tell? If I'm straight with you, Evan, I'm petrified to finish this conversation.'

11

Not a Date
Cambridge, Cambridgeshire UK
Winter 1977

'Fine...if you won't kiss me then I have no doubt someone will...' thought Vivian as stared at Laurie from across the café floor. She knew that the object of her affection was avoiding eye contact with her, as she mingled awkwardly with the other professors. It was frowned upon to be seen out of grounds being overly friendly to a student. Vivian would never have fully fit in to that stuffy old crowd anyway and, truth be told, she had never wanted to. Vivian would be heading home to Kent over Christmas, so this was the last opportunity to make an impression that Laurie Rosenberg would not soon forget. Her brunette locks were tied up, for a change, exposing her slim neckline and accentuating her slender frame all the more. Laurie, though, had her hair rolling around her shoulders in infinite curls. She was not wearing enough layers for the time of year and, with her coat and scarf hanging by the door, her shoulders were exposed to the winter chill. It seemed no warmer inside the café than outside, and Vivian was taking in every inch of her. She was fairly sure that Laurie knew what she was doing, for every touch of her face and every forced laugh at some pompous professor's awful joke all seemed orchestrated towards making Vivian thirst. In response, she had brought a companion on the endeavour to try and make Laurie notice her. Fredrick Grant was a senior, in the final year of his doctorate; a handsome man, humble and with good humour, he had fancied himself a suiter for Vivian's favour on more than one occasion. But for all his wit and "captain-of-the-rowing-club" good looks, he wasn't man or woman enough for Vivian. He was certainly no Laurie Rosenberg.

'You look amazing, my love,' said Freddie in an accent so well-bred that he was obviously a local. 'I mean...that dress, considering the time of year and all...'

'OK handsome, let's cool it just a second. As much as I appreciate the compliments, and I really do, this is not a date. That being said, I really am grateful that you have come out today, especially at such short notice. I hope I didn't put you out?' said Vivian, well aware that she was probably about to hurt his pride.

'Date?' spluttered Freddie as he almost choked on his coffee. 'Who said anything about a date? Not me, not Fredrick Grant. Just coffee between friends,' he smiled, clearly saving face. 'Except we aren't friends really, so I have to ask, what's the script here?'

'I'm sorry, you're right. I'm evil, and there is certainly a script. I just thought that if I was honest with you from the start it might make me seem a little less creepy,' said Vivian as she took his hand, an act that took him by surprise given her previous statement. 'I'm here to make someone else jealous. Do your job right, and I'll tell every girl in my year what an amazing lover you were and just how "much" you brought to the evening.'

Fredrick's first move was to look about the café to find his opponent, but Vivian quickly pulled his chin back around with a delicate touch of her finger. 'OK,' said Freddie, 'I get it. No losing face, as long as you get this guy's attention right? Something like that?'

'By Jove, I think he's got it,' replied Vivian with a smile.

'Well, what does this stud bring to the table then? Clearly, it's something that I'm lacking,' said Fredrick as he tried to sound less disgruntled than he was.

'Firstly...you can cut that out. You are skipper of the Cambridge rowing team, attending arguably the best university in the world, whilst being only six months from potentially being a doctor of law. You do not need to boost your ego with me, half the university will want to kill me just for sharing a coffee with you,' smiled Vivian with kindness.

'OK, stop blowing smoke up my arse, and tell me what he's like?' answered Fredrick, with renewed interest in the operation.

'Well, this "stud" as you put it, is very smart. Not just book smart; smart-smart, and not intense with it. That's not to say that this "stud" isn't intense. They have a look in their eyes that just makes my heart stop, and honestly, I think I'm in love.'

'Well, he sounds perfect, but he also sounds like he's not interested, if you indeed need to sit here holding my hand in a childish ruse to try and get his attention.'

Vivian looked past his shoulder and caught Laurie's eye for just enough time to feel her heart skip a beat.

'You OK there, Viv? Think I lost you for a second. Not winning you over, am I?' Fredrick said in half jest.

'Sorry, I know I've been terrible by dragging you into this, you must think I'm an awful swine,' said Vivian as she watched Laurie put her coat on and get ready to leave. The only sign of a goodbye was a flick of her blonde locks that told of a woman unimpressed by Vivian's juvenile antics.

'Vivian, if you need a friend to make some hunk jealous, I'm always here for you, if indeed I am available, I'm yours, just try being honest about it next time, you daft cow.'

'OK, it's a deal, now piss off before I ruin your reputation.' laughed Vivian as she leant over the table and kissed him squarely on the lips.

'OK, I'm gone. I'll catch you in the new year, Miss Phillips.' Fredrick got up and walked casually out into the winter cold, tightening his scarf as he passed by Professor Rosenberg on the street.

-

Laurie was doing her best to be OK in the face of her heart breaking. People were passing her in the street with little or no regard as the snow started to flutter down around her. She looked as though she were fighting an asthma attack, but the truth was very different. She was fighting her sinking soul, and she didn't know how to make it stop. Vivian wasn't supposed to love anyone else, that wasn't how this worked. She was supposed to be an escape from Alastair. She was supposed to be her muse, her confidante. But then, Laurie Rosenberg was not supposed to fall in love with her.

12

Rolling in the Deep
The North Sea
Autumn 1975

John looked down at the two unopened letters in front of him. The heavy rain had been smashing into his window for what felt like an eternity and it had since turned into a form of white noise that had lulled him in to an almost hypnotised state. You might say it was almost romantic, but that wasn't really who John was. He wouldn't miss the North Sea and its aggressive nature, the rain hit so hard here that it always felt like hailstones assaulting your body. He had been sitting in his bunk for an hour, trying to figure out where the feeling in his gut was coming from. He was far from a superstitious man, so the notion of having a "bad feeling" about receiving any news from home was, frankly, ridiculous to him...and yet here he was. He opened one; good news from the months of arduous selection training that he had just had to endure. He was in, and would be rendezvousing with the SBS within the month down at Hamworthy Barracks in Poole. That positive news had only served to make him more nervous about the second letter. Especially since he recognised his mother's handwriting, combined with the strong aroma of cigarette smoke and furniture polish that instantly transported him home. It could only be about his father and, good or ill, he wasn't sure that he wanted to know the details of any stories revolving around Marc Petalow. In the time since the Christmas incident over a year ago, he hadn't heard a thing from him. That in itself wasn't unusual, as John had never heard directly from his father. But even his mother hadn't mentioned him. They had returned home that fateful night to an empty house, gutted of his clothes and the television that has still been on lease from Radio Rentals. A few whispering neighbours tried to deduce what had happened, but they didn't dare ask John outright. His display of violence in The Cricketers had quickly done the local gossip rounds, and then...nothing. No-one in the street would miss Marc, such was the legacy he had left behind at London Road. John had only ventured home a few times since that day, and each time he had done something to erase further any evidence of his father's existence from the house. He had fixed the wall in his old room first, then sanded the dinner table to remove the notch that the carving knife had left from crucifying his father. His mother had put the house up for sale a few months back, but few views had led to fewer offers, and those offers had been for far less than the value of a home that was within the London commuter belt. It was easy to understand, with the recession hitting home for a lot of families, and John wanted the house gone even if it meant taking a loss. *Maybe this is good news about the sale,* he mused while finally picking up the envelope, *there is no reason it shouldn't be, it's about the house, and it's news not past time.* He picked up his combat knife from its resting place and quickly sliced open the envelope, an act that released more scents from home, and caused a shudder down his spine.

My dearest Johnathon,

Hello my little sailor. I hope this letter finds you well and the weather up in bonnie Scotland is being kind to you? I must confess that the news I bring to you is both good and bad, although which way round you deem that information is dependent on your feelings upon the subject matters.

This Monday just passed, I received a visit from the police, to inform me that your father has been declared dead. He was found missing from his bedsit on Old Chatham Road for over two months. A blood soaked jumper and a suicide note were the only evidence found when the landlord tried to chase him for his unpaid rent. I'm sorry John, not for your loss as such, I know you had no love for the man, more because I imagine you are confused. Confused as to what exactly you should be feeling right now, and believe me, I get it. I'm not sure if I should laugh or cry.

All he left in that place were empty bottles and a note filled with drunken ramblings about how he should have been made a Lieutenant before he retired. He made no mention of either of us. But his Will, it seems, has put the estate to me, although he has drained the savings account, and his service medals to you. I don't suppose you will want to be involved, and I cannot blame you for feeling that way, but just so you have the information the funeral will be held with an empty casket at St Margaret's on the 18th. I will attend only as I feel it is my place under God to see him out of this world. Because I do of course still ask myself, could I have done more to change him?

On brighter news, the house has been sold for just under the asking price and I've been viewing properties over in Canterbury. I'm too old to be surrounded by such haunting memories, and I long for those weights to be lifted from my mind. I don't want to be poor old Betsie at number 175. I want to enjoy the freedom of anonymity whilst I'm still able, and maybe you will come home more often when I'm away from that torturous place.

I'm struggling to picture the range of faces you must be pulling with all this information hitting you at once, so I will say no more. Just know that there are two things I am certain are true.

One, you make me proud every single day, and two, none of this, not the drinking, the violence or even what happened last Christmas, was your fault. Your father was lost a long time before you arrived, my son.

    Stay safe,

    I love you.

    Mum x

The South Atlantic, 12 Months Later

John looked up as Adley fell back into the room holding his chest, his face a picture of abject horror. His body armour hadn't slowed the bullet, and it had exited his lung almost as soon as it hit, tearing through him as though he was made of paper. Ten more shots followed, each spinning Adley about like a marionette whose puppeteer was possessed by the Devil himself. The young hostage girl smiled and fell, clapping and laughing to the floor. As Adley dropped to his knees, his rifle falling beside him and shattering as if made of glass, John saw target ten for the first time. Intel had been wrong. The man, twice as tall as John but much larger in frame, brought his pistol up whilst angrily shouting words from a dead language that John, somehow, understood. Johnathon Petalow was convinced that he would be dead before he could even aim his rifle, and he felt his heart pound at the sight of his friend dying so horrifically before him. The girl rolled in Adley's blood like a pig in muck, still laughing, wearing a smile, far too big for her face, that was filled with razor sharp teeth. He thought of his mother, so very far away. He thought of his father and cursed the notion that he probably wouldn't outlive him. Then...he opened his eyes.

It was freezing cold at RAF Mount Pleasant, despite the morning sun that shone through his bunk window. They had been greeted on arrival, 48 hours before, by snow. Snow that had, thankfully, cleared during the night. John rubbed his eyes as he looked in the mirror, toothbrush sticking out of his mouth like a mock pipe. His dreams since Adley's death came and went, yet something seemed different this time. In the years since the event, John's dreams had changed it into something even more sanguine, more evil...more powerful. John ran a hand through his short blonde hair and looked himself square in the eye one last time. Mission brief was in thirty, and he needed to get his shit together. This was as big as a training mission got, and he had to be on form. *Two hours of broken sleep and nightmares will not be my ally today*, he thought as he spat out his toothbrush and ran it under the tap. *Come on John, pull yourself together.*

-

'Johnno...You awake, sunbeam?' shouted Rupert over the loud hum of the Sea King's twin engines.

'I'm up.' replied John, without opening his eyes. He had been on enough missions to fall asleep on the route to anywhere. The back seats of Jeeps and troop carriers were often full of dozing troops, and helicopters were no exception to John. He wasn't some newly passed Marine, he was in Special Boat Squadron now. The eagerness for battle had subdued, as the short-lived adrenalin rushes were now replaced by a constant need to be prepared. That meant getting as much food and kip in as often as you could, because you never knew when the next opportunity to do so might arise.

'Here you go, Corporal,' Rupert passed him a lid full of weak-as-piss looking tea from his flask. John downed the liquid and passed it straight back, as he looked around at the rest of the team. Wilbur and Barry had their eyes closed, but were clearly awake as they sung some old rugby song over the racket of the rotary blades constant whirring. The Viking King was certainly awake, and meticulously flicking through his mission notes.

'You OK, Skipper?' John shouted over his headset. Tuomo Hakanen was a man held in high regard by all those that served under him. As frightening as he was kind, his men trusted him completely. An English national, born to Danish parents, he fit the Scandinavian mould perfectly. Piercing blue eyes and hair so blonde it was almost white. He was easily the same build as John, but always seemed quicker and more calculated with his movements. He was the adjustable wrench to John's sledge hammer.

'All good here. Are you boys ready for this? We drop in fifteen, and I don't want any fuck ups here. We are being watched after all,' answered the Sergeant without even looking up from the pages.

He was answered by a crescendo of positivity as the boys started to come liven up. 'Yes Skipper, we're as ready as ever.' said John as he rubbed his short beard to try and rustle some life into his face. A bonus of not being a regular any more was that he didn't have to look like all the other boot-necks. Occasionally a beard would help him to blend in; counterterrorism was a big part of the role they had to play within UK Special Forces. Although that was more often than not left to their more famous, Ray-Ban wearing, S.A.S. brothers.

'Why are they watching us, Skip?' voiced Wilbur, as he started to re-check all of his equipment.

'OK, listen in gentlemen,' sighed Sgt. Hakanen as he finally put his notes to bed. 'The Prime Minister, in his infinite wisdom, seems to think that in the next ten years there may be an attack on the Falkland Islands. He wants to make sure we are ready for such a situation to occur, and over the next twelve months we will be conducting test scenarios that will affect the outcome of how well budgeted the UK Special Forces are moving forward, for off-shore defence. This recession is hitting all the branches of our tree, my sons.'

'Do you really think the Argies are that brave, Sarge? They surely don't have the military to support such a coup?' said Barry, his eyes still closed.

'Do you think it matters what I think, boys? It doesn't. Nor does it matter what you think. So let's do our job the only way we know how, and hope the scran on our pick-up is better than the breakfast your wife gave me when I rolled off her yesterday morning, Mr Burgess.' The sergeant didn't break a smile at his own joke, but everyone else let out a hearty laugh, even Barry - until he realised they were laughing at him.

  They were due to drop at twenty feet into the freezing ocean beneath. Full diving gear weighed them down, and meant that they sank beneath the surface almost instantly. They were to swim out to an old wreck not far off Port Stanley. There, they would lay a string of charges in mock warfare conditions before being picked up by HMS Oberon, only a short swim from the target. John hated submarines. He was too broad for them, too tall and, the rest of the boys would say, too grumpy; especially when it meant being stuck in such a small space with a bunch of sun-dodgers. But still, his place was not to question. He was only a tool.

  John fidgeted as he prepared for the jump; he needed a slash, but it made more sense to just go in the ocean, rather than fuck about up here. Trying to get his wetsuit down so he could piss in a bottle would only be a ball-ache. He remembered Adley telling him once that the ammonia-like stench from his piss was what kept the sharks at a distance. From that day, it had become common practice for John to just let rip in his wetsuit as soon as his feet hit the water. He missed his old bunk mate more than he cared to admit, and it paid that he was in a unit of men who had all felt loss. No-one wanted to get too close to anyone else for fear of effect. Caring too much changed how you looked at a combat scenario. They were operators, and they had a job to do, unrestrained by emotion. Still...it would have been nice to have someone reassure him about the lack of sharks.

'Too cold for sharks down here, mate,' Adley would have said jovially, probably before slipping in that it was Orcas that he had to worry about in these parts.

'Johnno, the light's on red mate. Sort your shit out,' said Rupert as he roused John from a rare lapse in concentration. 'You good? You got this?'

'Oh, I'm good my brother. Let's go fishing.' replied John as he stood tall and slapped his dive mate on the shoulder. Rupert May was a good foot shorter than John, but when it came to the more Naval aspects of the regiment, that wasn't necessarily a bad thing at all.

One by one, they lined up ready to make the drop. Tuomo was on door release, and the only one not to stagger as the helicopter rose its nose to kill its forward momentum. 'Just remember boys, your mothers never really loved you, and I'm the only one you need to make proud.'

13

Girl in the Picture

Whitstable, Kent

Autumn 2014

The darkness in the attic was the kind of darkness that could hide any malevolence, no matter it's size or stature. That had always been what had scared Alice the most; not the fact that she heard echoing voices up here, but that the origin of them could be right beside her, and she wouldn't even know. Fumbling for the hanging light-switch, she spun about in the darkness until she felt the chain brushing up against her hand before finally taking it in her grasp. The bulb flickered for a moment before it came to life with a "ping". The attic was no less terrifying under the yellow glow of the single light source, but at least she could find her way now. She had her camera in hand, as she had been tasked by Poppy to take some photos of her "Dorian Gray" piece. It was a shrewd move; Poppy had many contacts across the pond and she could double the audience of potential clients, if it was done right. Alice spied the painting leaning against the bare stone bricks of the back wall, and took a few tentative steps towards it. The blanket that covered it was fluttering from an unidentified draft that almost gave the impression that the painting was shivering. It was as if it was scared to see her, or excited. Alice mused that neither emotion was healthy for an inanimate object to feel, and she pressed forward. She needed to find some strength from somewhere. The journey had been getting increasingly more difficult every time she had come up into the old building's rafters, and she knew that she was far too old to be worrying about supernatural paintings coming to life. Her fears were eased as she pulled the dusty blanket off the frame and saw the beautiful painting that lay beneath. It really did make her proud to see what she was capable of when she stepped beyond painting landscapes. The girl in the painting was beautiful and she looked almost real, from whatever angle you viewed her. Sure, she was haunting; a sadness sat in her eyes that could not be ignored, but she was also, equally, beautiful. She sat upon a stool, dressed in an ivory gown that fell in folds upon a polished wooden floor, looking at the viewer past the edge of the ornate brass-rimmed frame. Alice had painted the piece as modern-gothic, but with no clues within the painting itself to suggest the period it resided within, it felt almost Victorian in its projection. Alice pulled her camera up and took a knee in front of her work. It was too dark up here, and even with the buzzing bulb above her head, the flash would dilute the colour too much. Still it would be sufficient for the purposes of what Poppy had in mind. As Alice's camera flashed continuously, the mechanism clicking over and over in her hands, the fear started to leave her. She had nothing to be scared of; she should be proud of what she had done, it was clearly her best work. She threw the dust blanket back over the frame and shuffled back towards the staircase, snapping the light off as she went. The dark surrounded her again in an instant and with it, a cold chill that brought pin-pricks to her skin. Alice moved quickly, almost bounding down the steps to her bedroom, shutting the red door to the attic with some authority.

'Job done.' exhaled Alice, as she walked over to her bed. She was annoyed at herself, she had no reason to put herself through all this again. Hadn't she been through enough of this subconscious-voice bullshit that had plagued her since her youth? Even so, at least this time they were actually being supportive of her. They were certainly not trying to hurt her, so why should she be scared? Alice sat on the bottom of her bed and quickly cycled through the photos she had taken, the little LCD screen lighting up her face with a blue glow. 'No, this isn't right...for FUCK'S SAKE!' Alice snapped as she went through the seven shots one after another, each shot was as demonic as the last. *It must be the flash, it has to be. What else could it be?* she thought with a snarl, angry that she was going to have to go back upstairs. The girl in the painting was missing from every shot, and Alice was disregarding how the flash had somehow managed to ignore all of the tertiary items in the shot, for to do so would be to admit madness. Instead she came up with a plan to move herself forward, and resolutely jumped up off the bed. 'Guess you will have to come down here then,' she said bitterly, trying not to let darkness consume her mindset. Throwing her camera upon the quilt, she opened the red door and stepped in to go retrieve the picture. The only displeasure she would admit to was the effort she knew it would take to lift it down the stairs. That was, until she took her first step inside, as the door slammed behind her, the darkness closed in, and the key slowly turned from the other side of the lock.

'I'm not scared of you.' said Alice who, contrary to her words, was absolutely petrified.

Alice you have to listen to us. We are trying to help you.

'I know you are,' agreed Alice, as she remembered her plan, a plan forged by her therapist to combat the voices. 'So, tell me what I need to do.' It was pitch black now that the door was closed, and Alice point-blank refused to go up the stairs to turn on the light.

What you need to do, child, is take from them what was taken from you.

'I don't know how to do that, and I'm not sure I would if I could,' answered Alice, with a little more confidence. The doctor had instructed her to try a new approach to combat her inner voice. Reasoning and apathy were to be her way forward, and at this point she was willing to try anything. Alice finally moved quickly up the steps to turn on the light. She walked across to the painting, taking the heavy frame in her hands, and started to work her way back to the stairs. The door was already opening as she approached it. Her breathing heavy, she lay the painting against her bedroom wall and slammed the door closed before she collapsed against it to try and gather herself.

Alice... called out the voice from behind the door.

Alice became angry through the fear, and leaned towards the painting to remove the cloth. 'Wait, how could this be...?' As she looked at the picture in front of her, it was clear that the girl was still missing.

Alice...Don't leave me in here, it's dark. I hate the dark. Please, Alice...

She quickly scrambled away from the door and stood to face it. Without thinking, she had turned the handle and taken a step back. Nothing but an abyss stared back. As the painting collapsed onto its front, the noise of which caused Alice to scream in terror, she knew that something had passed through her. She slammed the door once more, this time locking and removing the key, before looking at the picture frame which was now face down upon her bedroom floor. And that was where it would remain until the morning. Alice couldn't stay there tonight. How could she?

'Hey, Mum...Yeah, I know its late to call, but can I stay with you tonight?'

It had been a week since the incident in the loft, and it had not been a week of easy sleep for Alice. Her mother had returned back with her, at first, to help her sort out the upstairs space. Alice had failed to mention to her mother the details of exactly what had happened and, in fairness, she had become all too convinced that the situation was no more than a fabrication of an over medicated mind. They had found nothing but an empty apartment, and the silence that naturally went with such a place. Really, what else should Alice have expected to find? Her fantasies had gotten the best of her before, and there was no doubt in her mind that it would happen again. The trick was to know when it was happening, so that she could deal with the problem, or just move on from the incident and trust that eventually her anti-psychotics would take care of it. Today, though, was a better day; she was dressed in clothes that could have been taken straight from 'A Christmas Carol', as she walked down Whitstable High Street. A combination of snow and sand blowing in from the seafront whipped about her feet, whilst the cold wind bit at her nose and ears. It had been snowing for hours. The flurries were light, not enough to settle, but instead creating a beautiful, almost traditional, Victorian scene as everyone danced from shop to shop amid the Christmas decorations. Alice had her hair tied up into a bun and wore a winter hat to keep it all in place amid the winter wind's turmoil. A long blue coat, kept together by little wooden toggles much like she used to wear as a child, kept the worst of the wind away and a white woollen turtleneck, that her mum had knitted for her, kept her toasty warm. She had been shopping for seafaring antiques, a commodity that the little port-town had in abundance. She had picked up a little nautical compass; an all-brass skeleton with pearl backing, for a tidy little price. But she wanted a few more bits before she went to meet Dorothy from school. She danced through a crowd of lunchtime drinkers who awaited the doors of their watering hole to welcome them in, as the clock struck noon, receiving a few whistles and cat-calls from them as she went. Alice smiled at the thought that she might ever be attracted to that kind of behaviour. That wasn't Alice Petalow, far from it. She had cancelled on a date only the night before, a date that had been weeks in the making, as her suiter owned a shop just down the road. What had started as a few glances here and there had turned into pleasantries before, out of nowhere, he had come in to the shop last week especially to deliver a hot chocolate for Alice. He was a nice guy; well-spoken, polite and certainly a gentleman, but, Anthony Lawrence of Whitstable Haberdashery had one glaring problem, it all seemed very real. William, the William that she had created in her mind during her illness, still played on her mind constantly. Alice had created him to be the perfect man, the hyper-realism of her psychosis had made him so much more than a fictional being to her. Jacob, not the one who existed now who was living his settled life with Blondie and his perfect little family, but her Jacob, the one who was wild and unpredictable, passionate and full of fire...he may not have been the finished product; a man who had transitioned to truly find himself, but he had certainly set the standard high. Alice felt that she was in need of that craving appetite for life. She halted her walk as she caught herself in the reflection of a shop window. Neither version of Jacob was to be the one who would walk by her side now though and, looking at her reflection, she could only imagined one person to stand in the space next to her. Poppy had called her from Kansas on what should have been Alice's date night with Anthony. They had laughed so hard that Alice had found herself snorting like a pig, something that she hadn't done since her teenage years. That phone call had been the catalyst for her no-show with Anthony, and she hadn't dwelled on it for long. Maybe he had been too attainable, but Alice felt a deeper reasoning behind her decision. She needed romance, real romance and, as everybody knew, to have a true love story you needed a little drama and tragedy. Could she be with Poppy in that way? She was still unsure, but what Alice did know was that she was looking forward to another trans-Atlantic phone call more than she was a date with any man. Alice continued her walk down the cobbled streets and headed towards the harbour market, a spring in her step since she had thought of Poppy. Their call hadn't been all pleasure, of course, as Alice had previously sent Poppy the photographs of the gothic piece that still slept in the attic, and Poppy had tried to work out a minimum price to sell it for at auction. Poppy's reaction had been mixed. She agreed, along with everyone else who had seen it, that it was the most beautiful painting that she had ever seen, and the Kansas gallery that employed her was not short of talent upon its walls. There was more to it than beauty though, as Alice explained in depth why she had needed to keep it locked away. Poppy had listened intently, not wanting to seem blasé to Alice opening her heart and lowing her walls. Once she had finished, it had become apparent that Poppy, the same as Alice, had struggled to look at the girl's painted apparition for too long. Voices echoed in the background of any mind that wandered too deeply into the world that the haunted maiden lived in.

'Daydreaming again?' said Jacob as Alice nearly walked into him.

Alice cursed herself, knowing full well that she could have avoided this meeting, if only she had been more self-aware. 'Well this is a nice surprise, are you OK?' asked Alice politely as she allowed Jacob to kiss her on the cheek.

'I'm well, just doing a little shopping for the baby...you know what? I'm sure you don't want to hear about all that...How are you?' replied Jacob as he realised that he needed more tact in his conversations with Alice.

'Oh Jacob, you know I don't care about all that. It's in the past now, we move forward,'

You do care! Don't fight it. You deserve more.

'...but yes, I'm really well, thank you,' said Alice completely ignoring both the voice in her mind and the calling within her heart to smash him over the head with her bag full of shopping.

Take what is yours. Take what you are owed.

Jacob smiled. 'I'm glad you're OK. Tell me...'

Alice held her hand up, 'I'll tell you anything you need to know, but I'm in a bit of a rush so can we catch up later?' Alice didn't feel comfortable, and the need to escape was starting to overwhelm her.

'Oh, yes of course. Listen, tell Dorothy that I love her and I'll pick her up on Sunday,' Jacob knew when to step back, and he gave Alice a wink as he strode away with a new mobile bassinette in hand.

He won't think of you until he sees you next. No-one thinks of you until you are standing broken in front of them. You deserve more. You deserve what was taken from you.

Alice had lost the desire for public appearance and darted back to her apartment. Her breathing was erratic and her head was throbbing. She could hear her sales assistant pottering about in the studio below her as she ran up the stairs, discarding all her winter clothing as she went. She was tired and only had a few hours before she had to get Dorothy. Alice threw her shopping down and fell face first onto her bed before screaming into her pillow with frustration. Why did it always feel like everyone was either laughing at her failings or ignoring her plight?

Because they are. You know this. Show them the error of their ways. Show them who you are, or WE will.

Alice looked up in shock. She was used to the voice in her head, and the last few days it had certainly found its clarity. But this voice hadn't come from her mind. Her eyes were drawn instantly to the attic door as it swung slowly open. An event that was impossible, as Alice knew that she had locked it tightly before she left. As she reached into her dress pocket and pulled out the large iron skeleton key that was the only means to unlock it, she realised that maybe this voice had more to say than she could bear to hear. 'I listened to what you said the other day, and I agreed with you, I do deserve more,' said Alice as she cautiously stood up and approached the door. 'So I'm not sure what you want me to do...or what I can do?' Alice placed one hand in the door frame and peered into the darkness, and only darkness looked back. There was something there though, the smell of its acrid breath filled the attic entrance. Rotting meat and endless decay filled her nostrils and choked her throat with a taste she had not felt since she had cut her own throat.

We talked about what was taken from you. Yes...yes we did. Did we discuss what might happen if you didn't take back what was yours? NO, NO, NO, NO, NO!

The second that the mirror-demon's voice had stopped echoing in the air, the red door, the colour of blood and nightmares, slammed closed on Alice's hand causing both bone and wood to shatter upon impact.

Spring 2015

Alice had been ignoring the knocking at the door for five minutes, she refused to even acknowledge it and it had become little more than an annoyance as she tried to work. Every time she heard a noise, a tap at the window or a creak in the floorboards, she would jump to attention, only to realise soon after that it was only her troubled mind just craving attention. Her psychosis was now a full time occurrence, the only thing that had kept her from being committed to a high-risk hospital was the fact that her mindset didn't seem to be out to hurt her in any way. The banging at the front door eventually stopped, as it always did, with Alice returning to the most mundane of tasks and continuing her stock-take. A few hours passed before she was ready for a trip to the wholesalers, a sad fact that it was becoming the highlight of her week. A few oils and a stack full of blank canvases was all she needed; she had never liked holding too much stock, it was dead money and despite the high profit margins at the Petit Papillion, it never hurt to be thrifty. A warm spring breeze had started to creep through the open windows of the apartment as she got ready, it was certainly time to break out the first dress of the year. A terracotta number that hung just above the knee, winning the pick. She topped it off with a black summer hat and matching lace scarf, her spring outfit looking more like the offspring of an illicit affair between Easter and Halloween. Purse, keys, sunglasses, all checked off as she bounced down her steps towards her front door.

'Oh sweet Jesus,' said Poppy with a strong southern drawl as she fell backwards into the apartment, only catching herself on the door frame at the last second.

'POPPY? Oh my god, what are you doing here?' said Alice as she instantly started to cry with joy. She jumped on Poppy's back and showered her with the love of a returning best friend.

'Well, I was waiting for your sweet-vanilla ass to come home, but I guess you were just ignoring me, my Sugar.' Poppy smiled brightly as she returned the affection to sender.

'I've never been happier to see someone! Why are you here? Do you have bags?' asked Alice with a smile, tears streaming over her rose-tinted cheeks.

'I'm here to see you, silly, and the only bags I have are these two little ones, and the ones under my eyes' Poppy laughed as she pulled herself up to meet Alice face to face.

'Great, that's so great. Drop them in here and lets go grab a coffee, because I have stuff to tell you that might make you jump straight back on that plane.'

-

'So what you're telling me, in the most inarticulate of terms, is that you, sugar, are crazy?' said Poppy, as she took Alice by the hand to reassure her that her humour was well directed.

'Oh God, I'm scaring you off aren't I?' said Alice as she nervously sipped on her coffee.

'Oh sweetie, no. I knew you were crazy when I met you. Bat-shit crazy to be frank, it's part of your character,' laughed Poppy, her hazel eyes almost oversized in the dark setting of the coffee lounge.

Alice couldn't help but smile as Poppy kissed her hand lovingly. 'When did this happen?' Alice asked, 'We never even went on a proper date, and yet this, whatever it may be, seems to blossom more each time I look at your face.'

'Well, I don't know about you, my beautiful butterfly, but I'm not sure that I've been sober for the last few years, so I'm pretty sure that lack of inhibition is the answer on my part.'

'You are literally the only reason I haven't fallen apart these past twelve months, so drunk or not, thank you...for everything.' Alice was speaking honestly as she saw another girl take a seat behind Poppy. The girl's clothes were the same as her own; but torn and filthy. Her hair was greasy and matted; yet clearly the same burning red that crowned Alice's own head. It was obvious to Alice who it was, long before she saw the flicker of the demon-self flash across the girl's face like a television with a bad reception. The fear of Poppy seeing her in the middle of a psychotic episode held her back from reacting to the monster that sat just behind her Southern Belle.

'So tell me, what is it that you are not letting go of? After all, it doesn't take a doctorate to realise that the girl in your painting is clearly your past self. And it's your complete inability to ignore her as anything less than "just a painting" which proves that you are not ready to let her go. So what is it?' asked Poppy, never once breaking eye contact with her.

Alice stared back, only occasionally letting her eyes drift to her demon-self who sat patiently behind. No words would come to the fore each time she opened her mouth to speak, instead her silence spoke volumes.

'Is it Jacob? Your love was pretty epic.'

'No, God no. I'm past that, we're both past that.'

'Evan being pregnant then? The baby?'

'No, I'm happy for them...really.'

'Because, Sugar, I get it. You gave up your child for them to carry on behind your back.'

'My child was still before I made that choice.'

'Then what do you think it is, Angel? Tell me.'

Alice watched her demon-self lick its lips with a black, forked tongue. It's eyes were not malicious or filled with hate like once before, now they were only hollow, devoid of any compassion. 'I don't know what it is, I just know that I've not slept in three months unless I'm slumming it at my parents.'

'Well, of all the things you know about me, what would you say is my most defining feature?' asked Poppy, as she remained positive enough for the both of them.

'You mean apart from those hazel eyes and that killer bust?' motioned Alice by cupping her much less shapely figure.

'Well, apart from the obviously unending beauty...' smiled Poppy innocently smiling as she rested her chin upon her hands.

'If I had to guess, based on talking to you most nights since that night of drunken splendour all those years ago, I would say it's your joy of boundless adventure.' said Alice.

'OK, I like that, and I can work with it. What, then, makes my adventures "boundless"?' asked Poppy with a smile.

'I'm not sure. You are certainly the most fearless person I've ever met.' said Alice

'What makes everything I do so limitless is that I am completely unrestricted by my past, or my present, if I'm honest. Do you think I'm this happy, care-free girl because I've had an easy life? Because I promise you now that both you and I, Sugar, have far more in common than you know,' said Poppy with sadness. '...the difference is, I don't carry anything around with me.'

'But it's hard to do that when I have to live here. I have responsibilities now, I'm far from unbound.' the sad realisation washed over Alice, as she watched her demon-self smile an unnatural, tooth-filled grin.

'I know, Sugar, I do. But you have to do what you can to move forward,' Poppy said, with absolutely no doubt in her voice. 'So let's go get you a bloody haircut, because you are not the helpless maiden your plaited red hair portrays. Then let's get that painting delivered to Blackberries so that you can spend the next two weeks with me, redeveloping that loft space into something positive'

'Two weeks? I have you for two weeks?' Alice screeched.

'Sugar, you have me as long as long as you need me.'

-

Two empty wine glasses sat on the slate fireplace's ornate surround. They hadn't even made it to the bedroom as the passion that had been manifesting for two years prior had overflowed with uncontrollable desire. To Alice, this was all new, and right now new was good. She reached up and ran her hands through Poppy's brunette pixie cut as Poppy tasted her for the very first time. Alice writhed on the deep shag of her Persian rug as Poppy's head buried itself between her thighs. It had never felt so good. Her orgasm was so unforced and so natural. As her body spasmed, she felt as though she had been electrocuted and all at once she felt loved, wanted and safe.

14

The Oberon Deep

The South Atlantic

Autumn 1976

The water was gut-wrenchingly cold, even through their drysuit's heavy insulation. Upon impact, each frogman dropped twenty feet under the surface from weight alone. No-one in their team was particularly small, and each one carried over a hundred pounds of kit once you added the compressed tanks and explosive charges. So they sank, quickly and efficiently, before Wilfred took point and dropped them further down to a depth of eighty feet below. Then, with his four frogs in tow, he took them due west at pace. John took up the rear, swimming ten feet behind Rupert, whose body was barely visible bar the Lumen sticks that gave his body an eerie green hue. John was, of course, no stranger to cold water dives. He was the only Marine here to have come out of Four-Five, the only one who had regularly trained in the North Sea. Rupert May and Barry Burgess had both come in from the Deal Cavalry Depot in Kent. The pair of donkey-wallopers had gone through selection together, whilst Wilbur Lawson and the Sergeant had trained down in Plymouth with Four-Two. They were both miserable places for sure, but swimming in the Atlantic Channel wasn't quite the same as swimming in the North Sea. It was an experience that John didn't miss one bit, but one that he was hugely grateful for nevertheless, as today it was paying dividends as he powered through the water. The target was an old fishing boat, no bigger than a flat-bed van. How it had been sunk, no-one knew; it wasn't relevant to the task at hand. It was a steel-bottomed ship which was in the right place at the right depth – the perfect tool for the job, it was great practice for charge-laying. As the ship came into view through John's re-breather lens, he saw Fire Team Alpha arch off towards the prow of the ship, while Sgt Hakanen lead the less experienced Beta team towards the stern. The closer they got to the ocean floor the more life they saw, as fish darted in and about the rocks, keen to avoid the heavily-toothed predators that constantly patrolled the area. As anticipated, he heard the clicks from within his comms come to life as each man reached their target point. John realised that the ship, in fact, sat precariously on a shelf that overhung a cavernous drop of at least a few hundred feet. John looked into the depths of the chasm and could barely see the sea bed beneath him. He wondered if this was another reason that this target was chosen, after all it was never supposed to be easy. Conditions in war would rarely be perfect, that was the reality of the job they had signed up for. John knew this, and fully accepted it, as he reached the damaged hull. *The Ariadna Solano* was scrawled across the starboard of the ship, the name of the vessel crowning a huge tear in the hull that answered the question of what had sunk this boat; a collision with another ship seemed the obvious answer. Although, it could just as easily have sunk through neglect, and breached its frame as it found its resting place. The shelf that had caught its decent was not made of sand, rather sharp rock and angular crag. John took position within reach of the hull breach and awaited the signal to progress from Sgt. Hakanen. There was no hesitation from the team. As the order was given, both Wilbur and John proceeded to drill a succession of small circular holes along the length of the hull. Barry and Rupert followed in formation, pushing the shaped charges into the holes created. This was to be a rapid job, met with smooth precision, and it was only two minutes before detonating wires were connecting each charge. That was the moment when the ocean shook and the demo charge, in the care of Lance Corporal Barry Burgess, blew his own arm clean off, turning the ocean into a shockwave of pressure and scarlet. John was the first to find focus following the shockwave blast. The small boat was rolling towards them and would soon fall from its ledge. It would kill them all, and this was no place to die. There was no honour in dying from a training error. John turned and pushed his back into the ship's momentum. Even for a vessel this size, the weight was immense and it pushed John forward through the gravel-strewn floor, until he found purchase against a slab of rock that angled towards the surface. His thighs screamed as they took the weight and his lungs burned as he was squeezed like an accordion. He looked right and made eye contact with Tuomo, who instantly saw what he was doing and recognised that he had been given the opportunity to save his team in the seconds that John was buying them. Barry was unconscious and bleeding out; Tuomo pulled a flare from his belt and swam over to him, pulling him out from under the ship with the strength that had earned him the his reputation. As soon as he was free, he lit the flare and used it to cauterize the wound, a move that would have caused Barry to black out, had he not already been unconscious. John felt his quadriceps tearing as the boat groaned desperately to continue its downward journey. He watched Tuomo swim past, dragging Barry with him by the harness of his air tank. To his left he saw Wilbur trying, and failing, to pull Rupert from under the ship. He looked up and motioned something that John couldn't make out, his lens had cracked from the blast and saltwater assaulted one of his eyes, making it all the more impossible to see in already difficult circumstances. Wilbur braced his legs against the ship as he pushed and pulled at the same time, as John saw the opportunity fading quickly in front of him. He pressed his screaming thighs forward while his barren lungs almost burst from his exhaling roar. His body struggled to keep him from blacking out as the boat moved a quarter of an inch back from whence it came. Rupert popped out from under the weight like a champagne cork, and Wilbur kicked away, pulling him by his harness. Tuomo looked back and reached out an arm to John, who was braced tightly between the rocks and the steel frame that was now starting to bend around his breaking back. Before John could contemplate releasing one of his own hands, the ship's complaints stopped, and it rolled right over John with complete disregard for his life, taking him on its final journey down to the chasm beneath. Then the world went black, and John finally pissed himself.

-

John awoke to the sound of bending steel and the aching frame of a mechanical monstrosity. It wasn't the painful cries of the submarine that scared him, in fact, that was a sound that bade him welcome reminder that he was still alive. It was two questions that scared him. 'How did I get here, and where the fuck is everyone?' he voiced, to an almost deafening silence that sent chills through his very soul. Those two questions were all he could think as he rose up from the infirmary bed with the kind of nausea that could only be down to decompression sickness. It was too quiet. Submarines were notorious for being constantly busy, almost like an ant colony. Hundreds of corridors laced the ship, each as narrow as the next, and there was only so much room for the crew that manned the HMS Oberon. *Was this the Oberon? It surely has to be,* John thought. It wasn't an anomaly to have groups of people trying to pass you on the same corridor junction, all in a rush to complete some important task. John was the size of three men alone and he found himself crouching to get around in some parts of the ship. Even his small unit of frogmen, a team of five seasoned warriors, usually left alone by your run-of-the-mill naval personnel and submariners, were absent as he searched around the infirmary. 'Where is everyone?' he asked again, this time louder and with increasing desire for a response. 'Hello?' he called down the corridor that attached to the main infirmary door. No reply was forthcoming. Worse than that, he could hear nothing at all. Not even a whisper. Just the constant groan of the ship as it toiled in abject pain. The corridors often acted as an instrument of sorts, carrying sound from one end of the boat to the other, but now they brought only the aching sound of the hull as is screeched under the pressure of an ocean that desperately wanted to enter the space that John was inhabiting. Realising that he was still in an open-backed gown, John made his way out of the medical bay, heading through the lower section of the boat towards the bunks that C-squadron had made their home. It was not a short journey, and he was wary of the fact that he would probably run into someone with his arse hanging out, for which the boys would have a good laugh at his expense for sure. They always did, regardless of whether they had any excuse or not; after all he was the youngest of C-squadron's elite. In fact, he was the youngest swimmer canoeist to pass the UKSF selection process. Moving down to Devon with the SBS had been a fantastic career move, plus, it had meant his winters were not so mind-numbingly cold. Cold was certainly something that his rear end was feeling right now, as he moved quickly across the steel grated floor barefoot and bare backed. At first, he had moved with absolute stealth so as to avoid being caught half-naked, but his desire to kitten crawl through the whole ship had begun to wane as he realised that his feeling of solitude wasn't unfounded. He was completely alone. Could everyone be on top deck maybe? Had they docked at Port Stanley, perhaps? John didn't know. 'Where the fuck is everyone?' He repeated over and over as he entered into the shared bunk and grabbed a navy blue T-shirt from his trunk, quickly pulling it over his muscular frame and dropping his gown to the floor in the process. John continued to curse the absence of the rest of his team, as he struggled to get the marine issue combat trousers over his monstrous thighs. He may have been the youngest, but he was easily the brute force of the group. While the rest of the team were lithe and streamlined for swimming and long distance tabbing, John was built like a shire horse; heavy, tall and filled with rippling muscle. He holstered his pistol to his leg and ran a hand through his auburn hair. 'Right, Petalow, let's see what's going on here.' he said, entering the corridor from his box room, only to find the darkness of a void and the overwhelming feeling that he was walking into his own worst nightmare.

The lights had failed, they were little more than an occasional flicker now. The only consistent light was now coming from an emergency bulb that threw nothing more than a red shade over the crimson desolation that littered the floor. Every flash of light highlighted a reality that John could not begin to comprehend. The floor, which just minutes ago was as empty as the infirmary he had awoken within, was now littered with dead submariners. Each of them devoid of blood, with sunken eyes that stared at the ceiling as if pleading with God for help. John knelt down next to the closest body, an able seaman by the name of Julian Carrol. Memories of the poor chap laid out in front of him were sparse, but John had remembered how very in awe the lad had been of his team. He had looked at them as though they were real life superheroes. 'What's happened to you, little buddy?' asked John as he redundantly checked the pulse of Julian's cold-skinned corpse. Corporal John Petalow had seen dead bodies before. He had, in actual fact, made dead bodies himself - many of them. Death was neither something he feared nor cared for. But John had never seen this before, never seen a dozen dead bodies just appear outside his door as if from nowhere. He felt instinct kick in as his heart rate picked up a notch and his right hand started to hover over his holster.

'Pick up the pace, Johnny boy. Or do you want to sleep in the shed again, you little bastard?'

John's hand instinctively found his pistol and, within the blink of an eye, he had it half-drawn and the safety removed. 'Who's there?' shouted John with a practised authority.

'You always were the slow one.' said the voice once more, as the plethora of dead bodies all turned their heads to face him with their empty, lifeless eyes.

John felt sick, as his finger fell into easy companionship with the trigger of his sidearm, but a lifetime of training could not have prepared him for what he was seeing now, or the voice that he was hearing. 'Father?'

'You have no right to call me that name, especially since you claim that everything you've learned to become a man you learnt all on your own.'

John shook his head aggressively whilst pinching his eyes together with his free hand. He didn't believe in ghosts, he certainly didn't believe in heaven or hell, so whatever was going on here he just couldn't fathom.

'You are more like me than you know, Johnny-boy.'

'I'm nothing like you, Dad!' John scoffed, almost tickled by the notion.

'No, Son? Remember that choke you put on me at the pub? I seem to remember choking your mother like that once because she pissed me off, too.'

'That's different, and you know it.' said John as he brought about his pistol, scouting the corridors for the source of the voice. The dead bodies about his feet were reaching for him now, and he was forced to put a round straight into the skull of one that took a hold of his boot. The crack of the shot echoed around the ship like a stone falling down a well.

'What about how calculated you were at dinner that day? Tell me you didn't enjoy putting that knife through the very flesh that created you? I saw the look in your eyes that day, and I saw my own face.'

'I AM NOTHING LIKE YOU!' screamed John as he put two more rounds into a dead sun-dodger who had found the audacity to rise against the natural order and lurch awkwardly towards him.

'You are me, John. You have always been me, and that, my son, is why you were always afraid.'

'No,' said John defiantly. 'I will never treat my family with the contempt and hatred that you constantly showed us.' John spat as he spun around each corner, his rounds finding fresh targets at each junction.

Submariners had many nicknames, "sun-dodgers" and "the great unclean" were the most commonly used. The latter seemed to fit alarmingly well as each body rose up possessed in front of John's very eyes.

'You know, Adley would still be here if you had done your job properly. Did you check your corners? Did you check your-'

'Don't you dare!!!' boomed John. 'I am twice the operator you ever were. I checked every corner, every room, he came out of nowhere.'

'Did he, John? Did he come out of nowhere?' asked the voice of Adley Long, as John rounded another corner to find his long-deceased best friend on his knees with Marc Petalow stood behind him, pistol pressed tightly to the back of his skull.

John knew that what he was seeing wasn't real, he knew that it was either a dream or some nightmarish afterlife where his demons were here just to forever taunt him. Yet he instinctively brought the pistol up to his father's grinning face. 'LET HIM GO, KILLICK.'

'No. Why should I? I found him first, you killed him before. Can I not have this one?'

John looked at his father's smirking face and felt nothing but hatred, whilst his friend looked up with pleading eyes.

'Why didn't you check the corners, John? I thought you were my frie-'

John watched Adley's face explode outwards, Marc's gun easily finding its target from point blank range. 'NOOOOOOO!' John screamed, as he unloaded his remaining ammunition into his father's chest, an action that had little effect as Marc's smile only grew larger, his laugh louder and his teeth sharper.

'You are me, John. What I have done to Adley here is no different to what you did to him all those years before. Don't think that you not pulling the trigger excuses you in the slightest.'

John launched himself forward and wrapped his hands around his father's throat, spearing him to the floor with weighted momentum. 'I WILL NEVER BE YOU!' John spat, only inches from his face, as he felt his trachea splinter under the assault.

Out of nowhere, John felt himself catapulted back across the infirmary as he was restrained by Tuomo and Wilbur against the cold floor, again in his backless gown and again unsure of how he got here. He looked across to see a young medic choking upon the floor, black bruises quickly forming around his throat. 'JOHN, CALM DOWN, SON. YOU ARE SAFE.' Tuomo said with authority as he cradled John closely, still keeping him securely pinned.

'We got you mate, we got you.' said Wilbur as he slowly released John and went to check on the medic.

'What happened?' asked John, as searing pain wracked his thighs.

'You saved us, son, that's what happened,' said Tuomo as he started to release his hold. 'But whatever you do, don't try to stand.'

-

John sat outside the medical bay at Hamworthy Barracks, like a naughty child sat outside a teachers office, ready to take the licks for whatever misdemeanour he was deemed to have committed. Apparently he was a hero, he had saved the lives of every man on his squad that day in the south Atlantic, but he didn't feel like a hero. He reached down to rub the giant scars that had taken over his thighs. He had torn every muscle in both legs to a level where surgery had become the only option. He still felt the tears on cold nights and little muscle spasms were not uncommon on a day to day basis, but he had started walking again after three months on crutches, even if he did look a little unstable at times. Barry "The Mouth" Burgess had had the rest of his arm removed and cleaned up, his new name of "Stumps" was not landing with quite the right humour yet, but in truth, he had dealt with everything well. A career of paperwork and logistics with the Navy awaited, and John saw an emptiness start to form behind his friend's eyes whenever it was discussed. A faulty charging wire had caused the accident, with no blame forthcoming to him or indeed the rest of C-squadron. Sergeant Hakanen was the only reason that John had survived that day, and he was the first person he had seen upon waking up. Refusing to give up on John, the great Dane, upon HMS Oberon answering the distress call to receive Barry and Rupert, had taken a Navy dive team against the Captain's orders, and dropped straight back in to save his young operator. John had been found only loosely pinned down by the ship's hull, he no doubt would have been able to free himself, had the death roll into a two hundred foot chasm not taken his consciousness like a hypnotist clicking his fingers. By the time he was found, he had nothing but vapour left in his air tank, and three small nurse sharks were pulling at his wetsuit to try and reach a wound on his shoulder. John had been grateful of the fact that he had been passed out for that, no matter the short size of the bloody things. Things though, had become very real upon his recovery, his dreams of Adley and his part in his death had become a recurring event. Every night John would wake, his body drenched in sweat, his father's neck missing from his tightly gripped hands. He knew he had done everything right in Africa, he knew that Adley getting shot was just part of the job and that there was nothing he could have done to stop what had happened. Yet, with his father's death bringing him closure, he had found other wounds beginning to open. It seemed his bastard father had been the emotional plug that had repressed any notion of morality. Now Marc was gone, John had to stop blaming him for everything in his life that had previously gone wrong. He had to start taking ownership for his negatives, not just his positives. At least that's what the shrink had been saying. The shrink...he had been a challenge. Special Forces had to have a degree of secrecy, so his doctor was just "The Doctor", much like that Tom Baker crap that was always on the television, and he would probe John twice a week, despite his constant protests. "Soldier Twenty-Two," as he would be known to him, had been given six months of rehab before he was to resume active duty. Time to get his legs back and deal with a few things that he honestly hadn't wanted to face. This was to be his last session before he was allowed some much needed time back home, he was eager to see his mother and visit the new house. He just needed to be John for a little bit, and according to the doctor, feeling that way was a good sign.

'Good morning Twenty-Two, how are you today? Please...take a seat,' said the doctor as he stood, remaining behind his desk.

The doctor was non-descript, slightly balding with tiny, round-lensed glasses that made him look like a member of the Gestapo. He did his job just fine, not that any of John's team enjoyed opening up to anyone. What would always pique their interest though, was the young, beautiful, and ferocious looking woman that sat just back from the doctor with her notepad tightly gripped. Each of them had tried their luck to find out her name. Any attempts at seduction had at best been less than successful, and at worst completely embarrassing. John could clearly see that she was related to the doctor, he imagined perhaps a daughter or niece. They shared the same inquisitive look, like that of a barn owl ready to swoop upon a rodent. John had leaned on his friend Ivy Reid for information; Ivy was secretary to the Commodore, and they often chatted the breeze whilst the nights were winding down. The young lady was by all accounts, only here for a few months. Her destination, Cambridge University; she was only here finishing her current dissertation. That was her excuse for always avoiding people in the mess hall, although John knew the truth - that this young, wannabe psychiatric doctor was simply thoroughly unimpressed with the boot-necks that ran around muddy fields with big guns and bad attitudes.

'I'm OK, Doc, as always, same shit different day,' answered John as he sat opposite the doctor, wincing as he stretched out his thighs. The tightness would remain for months to come, and was a constant reminder of what he had been through.

'Tell me about the dreams, any change?' the doctor asked whilst leaning into the desk.

'The dreams, well...less frequent, more aggressive. I'm waking up with cramp most days, like I've been tensing in my sleep,' John said, almost ashamed of himself. 'I'm scared, doctor. I woke up a few nights ago, drenched in sweat and yet freezing cold, like I was back underwater. I had...'

The doctor waited for him to finish, but intervened when it seemed he needed a gentle push. 'What happened, Twenty-Two? This is a safe place, never forget that.'

John looked up only to meet an inquisitive stare and felt himself shrink. He hadn't felt this small for a decade, not since the days of hiding in his "Narnia" hole at the back of his old wardrobe. 'Doctor, I had somehow managed to tear out a chunk of my hair, it was gripped tightly in my hand, my grasp so intense that I could feel blood seeping through my fingers.' John refused to look over at the doctor's assistant, ashamed of his revelation, and still holding back the fact that on the same night he had woke drenched in his own urine.

'The dreams...,' the doctor replied, without any reaction to John's admission, 'are they still about Adley?'

'Yeah. I mean, mostly. In my heart, I know I did everything right, all by the book, but I don't know...' John looked down at his hands, Adley's blood still etched into every groove.

'Twenty-Two, you can't save everyone, that's neither your job, nor your role in life. I've read the report. Adley's death was not on you. Neither was it your responsibility to protect your mother, you were just a boy.'

John sat back as the connection between his father and his own need to protect those he loved began to unfold in his mind. 'My father...he was not a good man.'

'No. No, he was not, but what has that created in you?' The doctor came around the desk and sat alongside John, his posture open, and a rare smile encroached upon his face. 'You are a better operator for what you have been through, you are a better friend, and a better son. You have been through hardship, that's good, because UKSF do not need operators that are soft, and nothing you have been through has left you soft.'

'Thank you, Doc,' replied John with a half-smile.

'That being said, I want you to take some leave, are you on logistics whilst your legs heal up?'

'Yes, for a few months yet, but I have leave to use up,' said John as he struggled to rise from his seat.

'Well I suggest you go home for a bit, spend some time with family, and then I'd like to reassess before you return to active duty, if that's OK with you?'

'Of course, Doctor, thank you...for everything.'

'No "thank you" necessary, Twenty-Two, just remember, there is no shame in being human. You cannot save the world alone.' The doctor shook John by the hand and saw him to the door before returning to his desk, his pretty little assistant finally downing her note pad in the background.

Six months off active service would be enough, thought the doctor. Twenty-Two was clearly a great soldier and by all accounts a good man, it seemed, but he saw something in the soldier that might hold him back. This soldier cared too much, and that wasn't always a good thing for a trained killer.

15

Demons and Desires
Cambridge University, UK
Spring 1978

She held the cold compress against Laurie's swollen cheek once more and watched her stir. Vivian had wanted for her to be here for so long, but not like this, not hurt, not broken. Laurie had dropped off into a light sleep after an hour or so of sobbing into Vivian's arms, and since then she had just lay with her, nursing her love back to health. She pulled a long strand of golden hair from her face, and tucked it neatly behind her ear. She was so very beautiful to Vivian, and she couldn't understand how anyone that was lucky enough to have her would ever want to hurt her. Vivian had watched Laurie break down from the moment she had opened the door to her, tears pulling her mascara south while she shook almost uncontrollably. She wasn't upset because Alastair had hit her; she had never loved him as one heart should love another. She was upset that, once again, she had let an abusive man into her life. A man who didn't deserve her, who brought nothing to her ability to function successfully. Laurie had always looked to surround herself with people who carried a certain amount of verisimilitude. Yet the romantic relationships in her life had always felt false. Maybe she was gay after all, maybe she just picked testosterone-fuelled men as a method of relationship self-destruction. She knew it wouldn't work, because ultimately she had never wanted it to. As she lay upon Vivian's chest, their hands clasped tightly together and their legs entwined like mating serpents, Laurie opened her heart. Vivian had listened to her talk for hours, occasionally kissing her brow when a narrative had taken an emotional path, and only getting up to remoisten the flannel that was being used to try and reduce the bruising that was now dominating the right side of Laurie's face. All her life, she had chosen men that she felt her stuck-up parents might protest against, without pushing them so far that she might possibly be disowned. Here she was now though, in her mid-thirties, fully aware that she had wasted most of her life trying to annoy parents who likely wouldn't care now.

'I think we should go away. Now that we are finished for the summer, let's just go.' said Laurie as she shot up.

Vivian almost jumped out of her skin, she hadn't realised that she had fallen asleep alongside Laurie, the clock on the wall ticking a few minutes past two in the morning. 'Hang on, what?'

'I think,' Laurie repeated, 'that we should go away. Now that we are finished for the summer.'

'Can we do that? Just go, I mean? Don't get me wrong, I would follow you anywhere, but you are always so worried about what people might say.' replied Vivian as she stretched her arms out, her back cracking as she did so.
'Well, maybe...maybe we don't come back,' said Laurie as she turned to face her shocked partner. 'Isn't that what you always wanted?'

'OK, let's slow this down just a touch. I have two years left of a Master's degree, that *you* are my professor for! Now I am not pooh-poohing anything here, but what plan, exactly, are you trying to get me on board with here?' said Vivian humorously.

'Alright, so the plan needs work, but that doesn't mean it's not a plan. Let's fly tomorrow, anywhere, Istanbul or Barcelona?, My treat.' screeched Laurie, uncharacteristically.

'Well, we have six weeks off, if you want us to go to Catalonia and start hopping from one country to another until we figure this out, then I'm in, I'm absolutely in.' said Vivian, tears of joy starting to form in her eyes. 'Just to confirm though, you are paying right?'

Both girls fell into each other laughing, unbridled glee dictating their actions as they came face to face. The hesitation lasted for only a second as Laurie pushed forward and pressed her lips onto Vivian's, their lips parting just enough to show that this kiss, this one amazing kiss, was no kiss shared by just friends. 'I love you,' they said in perfect unison, before holding each other in an embrace that didn't end until the next morning.

24 Hours Later

As the battered old taxi carried them through the mountain roads leading into north-eastern Spain, the radio playing an almost inaudible version of some Latino version of the Bee Gees, Vivian was in a dreamland. Apart from an ill-advised drunken weekend in Paris last summer, this was only the second time she had been abroad. The air was suffocating in the back of a car, a car that was possibly as old as Vivian herself, but she didn't care, she just rolled the windows down and took in every scent on the breeze. She had not let go of Laurie's hand since the plane had touched down, and she didn't intend to break that bond anytime soon. Laurie had loved seeing the excitement radiate off Vivian, it made her own heart happy, and it had taken away all the fear of what was happening back in the real world. She had left Alastair at a day's notice, packing her bags as he was out working on a private job. She could not bear to think of the destruction he would bring to that poor house as he returned to the note that she had nonchalantly left upon the fridge, ironically under a fridge magnet that she had picked up in Valencia last summer. Vivian had been her escape, not just from him, but from a life that had been slowly strangling her. She would never be able to repay her love for the strength that she could have never have found alone.

16

Building Bricks

Canterbury, Kent UK

Spring 1977

John returned home to Kent on the same day that his mother died. It was chance, poor luck one might say, but the facts didn't change. John was home, and his mother was dead. He had knocked on the door of the new family home in Canterbury, which was answered by a McMillian nurse, tears still in her eyes and the phone still warm from calling the ambulance. This house was, of course, new to John - but it seemed that his mother had made it her own. Betsie Petalow had apparently been silently fighting lung cancer for years, not wanting to bother John with yet another family problem after his father's death. Distraught as he was though, John was pleased that she had died here and not back in Medway. He felt the warmth of this home the very instant he crossed the threshold. This isolated old cottage in Preston, the posh part of Canterbury's bordering towns, was a safe place. There was never a good time to die, a phrase Adley Long had often coined, but knowing that his mother had died feeling at peace gave John a certain brevity that he shouldn't have carried today. He had taken himself on a tour of the house, and found himself resting upon the end of what he at least believed to be his own bed. Betsie had made efforts to make John's room nothing like his old one.

Pictures of her son passing out and receiving his green beret were adjoined by photos of him lifting the Colt's Rugby league title and cup in the same year, back in sixty-six. This felt more like home than "home" ever had, and as he reached over to the bedside table, he picked up something that reminded him of just how wonderful his mother truly was. He held in his hand a typed, fully formatted version of his short story, *The Snorkeler*. Betsie had been a secretary in her youth, a job that she had truly excelled at, and one that she had only stopped doing at his father's behest. Saltwater began to sting his eyes as it dawned on him that she was gone. This woman of strength and loyalty to a fault, of kindness and family morality. She had kept his story and made it something more than special. He would keep it forever and miss her for even longer. More importantly now, he would live his life as she had wanted him to.

    Betsie Anne Petalow had been buried, as per her request, back in her home town of Gillingham. John had mingled as best he could with aunts and uncles that had shown no interest in either his or his mother's life for the past thirty years. This was mostly down to his father's influence he had to admit, but there was still a level of contempt for them that he could not hide. Cousins who he had nothing in common with had tried their best to pretend they were not intimidated by him. They were good people, in their own way, but he could not consider them family. After all, where had they been when his mother was getting a thrashing? That night, he found himself drawn back to The Cricketers pub. In his youth, it was the pub his friends would frequent, all angst-filled teenagers, while John was running up hills every day in preparation for a life in the Navy. It was a working man's pub, full of the factory workers from the old Jubilee Clips factory and old war veterans.

People who just wanted a drink and to be left alone with it, and that was what John so desperately needed right now.

'That's twenty pence to you, John. I'm sorry to hear about your mum, honey,' said the barkeep as she passed over his Guinness.

'You knew my Mum?' asked John as he nodded his thanks into his pint.

'Knew her? Not so much, but we went to school together. It used to break my heart watching her come in here, all beat up. We all hated what your dad was doing to you both.'

'Didn't anyone think to step in though? I mean, when you were all so worried?' John had wanted to sound sarcastic in his delivery, but instead he just came across as hurt. 'Well, anyway, let's hope she's in a better place now. I imagine she went in the opposite direction to my father.' John toasted her once more then retired to a little table in the corner, away from the growing crowd. *Maybe this was a mistake,* thought John as he realised that Gillingham F.C. must have been playing at home this afternoon.

'John, is that you? Bugger me, it is...bloody John Petalow, how are you mate?' asked the rambling drunk as he fell into the seat next to him.

'Benji...how are you, son?' answered John, completely ignoring the question aimed at him.

'Yeah I'm OK, we were just at the game. Kev and Clive are at the bar if you want to join us?' asked Roger Benjamin, an offer ignored by John for the most part. 'What brings you home anyway, soldier? Thought you would be off saving the world or something?'

Look at you! You haven't seen outside of this poxy place since I left, have you? thought John, as he supped on his pint. 'It was Mum's funeral today. I'm surprised you didn't hear something about it, what with this being a one horse town and all?'

'John, I'm so sorry. No, I didn't know. Since your father "passed away" and your mum moved to Canterbury, well...I guess she fell out of the loop. Listen, John, if there's anything I can do-'

'Hold on, what do you mean "passed away"? Why the air quotes?' asked John, getting agitated.

'Nothing, John. Just rumours on the grapevine you know, someone thought they saw him is Essex a few months back, but...'

'My father is dead, just like my mother. It is what it is. There was nothing anyone could do before she died, so I imagine there is even less you can do now,' said John as he slammed down his empty pint glass. 'Anyway, how's the wife?' he asked, knowing full well that Roger had married his ex-girlfriend.

'Jane? Yeah, she's grand fella, she's not changed at all since you last saw her,' laughed Roger uncomfortably. 'Can't believe that was when I saw you last. Looks like the new John ate the John I knew from back then.'

'She's not changed? You mean she's still fucking all your mates?' laughed John, not caring about the reaction it would raise.

Roger ignored the barbed comment, more through fear than respect, and carried on his awkward questioning. 'So, when are you heading back? Must be some muddy gate that needs guarding in a boggy part of Dartmoor?'

Johns crystal-blue eyes seemed to turn darker as his stare intensified. 'Listen, pie boy, I don't like you. And not because of what happened years ago, but because whilst I've been apparently "guarding gates", friends of mine, real friends, have died in my arms whilst trying to defend things more important than you would ever fathom. They were people who knew that the world was bigger than the fucking Medway towns. So don't sit here with me and try to devalue what I have been doing these past six years, because quite frankly, Roger fucking Benjamin, you could not comprehend the things that I have seen.'

'John mate, I'm sorry, I meant no offense,' Roger stuttered in panic, as he looked about the crowded bar for support. Although, looking at John, he was unsure if his two mates would make any difference.

'What you meant is truly irrelevant to me, as I absolutely meant every single word I just said. So take your pint, and find another table. Because if you don't, this is what's going to happen,' John brought his whole body around to face his old friend. 'First I'm going rip your face off, then after I've pissed in your mouth, I'm going to wear your face like a mask, so that I can go fuck your dumb cunt wife. I mean, she's not smart enough to notice the difference right?'

Roger stood up, raising his hands in defeat. 'Alright John, I'm gone. Say no more,' he turned to leave, speaking only once more, as he drifted toward the crowd. 'I'd heard that you had changed, John, but I never thought it would be to this extent.'

'And I'd heard that you hadn't changed at all. Bit pathetic don't you think, especially considering we were sixteen the last time we spoke?'

'This one's on the house, John. I won't get in the way, but please, take it outside if you do kick off,' said the barmaid as she placed another pint of Guinness in front of him.

There won't be any trouble, love. There's not a man in here that wants any from me, anyway,' said John as he looked around the room, all eyes he met falling to the floor. 'Thank you sweetheart, but don't bring me a third, I've got jobs to do.'

After unloading all of the flowers, John spent a little time exploring his new home. His mother had done well; it may have only been a three-bed cottage, but it was huge in stature and surrounded by land. The walls looked like they could survive a medieval siege, a ring of apple trees circled the property like a multicoloured sea-wall. John was a man-mountain. Had he been any more masculine, then he might as well have been born a grizzly bear. Yet here, sat in the garden surrounded by the pink and blue blossoms of the floral wall, he cried. It had always bothered him that his mother had spent her life in servitude to a bully. He had always known that he would escape one day; the ocean had called out to him for as long as he could remember, and the very day he could leave, that's what he did. But John had never dealt with the guilt of leaving her behind, and although she died free, in her own home, she died alone. He decided there and then, as he sat in what was now his garden, that he would see out his last few years with the regiment and then he would settle down here. John Petalow would never be the man his father was, on that he swore to his mother.

17

Running

Cairo, Egypt

Summer 1978

Laurie Rosenberg could not believe her luck as she watched Vivian, her Vivian, go through the bazaar meticulously, smelling and tasting all the different spices available. Yesterday it was silks and fine cotton; today cured meats and ground herbs. Laurie could watch her all day long. Vivian had always seemed so curious of everything, her eyes wide and her thirst for boundless adventure forever unsatisfied. They were dressed in colourful kaftan-style robes of varying colours. Laurie's an emerald green, and her Vivian dressed in the finest golds of Egypt. Bracelets and bangles adorned her wrists and gave her an almost Hindu-like vibe that wouldn't have put her out of place in the George Harrison song, "My Sweet Lord." Her style made her stand out in the crowd, but it was her inquisitive mind that kept Laurie coming back for more, each and every time her heart was captivated by her very personality. Vivian Phillips, her brightest student and now her soulmate. Laurie was unsure quite how this had happened, but she was nonetheless happy it had. There would be hell to pay upon their return to Blighty. 'Professor' Laurie Rosenberg was no more. She had already been assured that her job was to be stripped from her the very second she stepped foot on campus, but in all honesty that was the least of her fears upon returning to the UK. The fallout from her family would be horrific. They were a bunch of snotty braggards and would do their very best to ruin her reputation for sure.

'We will deal with it together. Who cares what they say, or even think, for that matter?' Vivian had said, as she fought to reassure her. She was right of course, but it wasn't every day that she left an abusive boyfriend to run across the world with one of her students that she had fallen madly in love with. Laurie wasn't paying attention, as Vivian reappeared out of nowhere and forced a chilli infused tiger prawn into her mouth. 'I know, right? How amazing is that prawn, isn't it just so...so...recherche?' said Vivian, bouncing up and down with excitement.

Laurie had to finish chewing before she could answer, and she could not deny its elegance as the heat danced off her tongue. 'I wish I'd never taught you that word.' groaned Laurie with a smile. 'But yes, it is incredibly "recherche."

Vivian leaned in to kiss her, and Laurie felt the heat from the chilli once more, as it danced from one set of lips to the next. 'Darling, I've been thinking...'

'Oh shit, that's not good. Do I need to sit down?' joked Laurie with a lick of her lips before Vivian took her by the hand and looked deeply into her eyes.

'I know what you have been thinking, and I think it's time...time to go home.' said Vivian openly.

'How did you know? I mean I know that you are my mirror, we have always known the route of each other's mindset, but still...have I been that obvious in my desires?'

'You talk about home in your sleep, every night. I hear the murmurs, you miss England, I get it. Also, I'm a trained psychologist too, or had you forgotten, my love?' Vivian brought Laurie's hand up to her mouth and kissed it with a delicate purse of her lips.

'I do want to go home, my love, I'm just not sure where to find the courage to do it.' said Laurie with a quiver of fear.

'Well, I'm sure we can do it. However it goes, we will always be by one another's side, we owe each other that much. And we don't necessarily have to go back to Cambridge. "To this affair's conclusion", that's what we promised each other, or had you forgotten?' said Vivian with defiance.

'How could I forget, my love?' said Laurie with a final kiss before Vivian jumped back into her excited child-like persona, diving again from one market stall to the next. Laurie was scared, but she was content, for she knew that as long as they had each other, then nothing else mattered. Except…

'Baby, I have to tell you something. Please don't freak out,' said Laurie, her tone fearful.

'Any conversation that starts with, "Baby please don't freak out" is cause for concern, what have you done?' asked Vivian, herself a little panicked.

Hesitation started to suffocate Laurie's words before they came out, the fear of what she was about to say washing over her like a flood. 'I think, and I say "think" because nothing is confirmed…that I might be pregnant.'

'Pregnant!' gasped Vivian. 'How is that even possible? Oh…I see-'

'Baby don't freak out, nothing is confirmed yet, and I'm scared…' Laurie looked petrified as she spoke, but there seemed to be a certainty to her words.

'I thought you had a tenuous relationship with him, one where you slept in separate beds and fought every day? Not this, I never thought this-' Vivian started to cry as she sat down on the stone wall next to Laurie.

'How dare you!' snapped Laurie defensively, her angst quickly dispersing. 'Do you think that anything I did with him was done willingly? Well, do you? He was a bully, and if you think I asked for this then you are very much mistaken, Miss Phillips.'

'Laurie, I never meant it like that, I...well I'm not sure how I meant it. But I didn't mean it like that,' Vivian tried to take Laurie by the hand, but saw her effort thwarted. Walls that had taken so long to tear down were quickly being raised again. 'Look, whatever happens, we deal with it together. You can't scare me off.'

'Well I'm scared enough for the both of us, honestly I am, so I really hope that you mean that.' Laurie said mournfully, her gaze falling to the floor.

'I do, I mean every word, and I understand why you are frightened. But I will never let any harm come to you.' Vivian jumped from the wall and rounded on Laurie, grabbing both of her hands tightly as she did so.

Laurie looked up through her blonde fringe and smiled at the notion of her junior being the vigilant protector. She knew that Vivian would protect her against most things, but him? She wasn't so sure. 'Thank you, my love. Yes, I feel safer already.' Laurie Evalyn Rosenberg would lie to the love of her life only once in all the time they were together. And that was the one day that she did.

Autumn 2014

'I never knew that was why you were in Egypt. It's beautiful how adamant you both were to stick together. I mean, I'd always known about you naming me after her, but hearing you talk so fondly about another person is a side of you I've never seen. Do you miss her?' asked Evan as she sat at her mother's coffee table with a ginger tea. Her baby-induced indigestion was driving her to madness.

'Of course I do,' sighed Vivian as she joined her daughter to sit. 'Every day, and then twice on a Sunday. I've never loved anyone since.'

'Not even my Dad?' asked Evan, eager to get to the crux of their three-day conversation.

'No, darling. Especially not your father.'

18

Nom de Guerre

Canterbury, Kent UK

Summer 1978

John heard the plastic of the phone beginning to crack in his grip as he processed the conversation. He was not prepared to hear the story being told to him, not prepared for the truth of it. He had been slowly renovating the old bathroom at Petalow 'manor', his hands thick with dust and splinters, his body drenched in sweat. The white T-shirt that he had originally been wearing, long since removed to mop up his giant frame, was now sticking out of the back of his jeans to be used as a hand towel. He carried on listening quietly, responding only with grunts, until the conversation was over. He had always preferred to save questions until the end. *If you're talking, then you're not listening,* he thought. Was that one of his father's sayings? He hoped not, as it had always stuck well with him.

'I'm sorry, John. I don't really know what else to say other than it was him. My Dad worked at the Chatters with him for years, Christ, they even passed out of the academy together.'

'If you are telling me that he's alive, and you saw him with your own eyes, you are asking me to believe something that I really don't want to believe. That being said, we've been friends for years, Justin, and you have never given me reason to think you any less than an honest man.' said John as he took a seat, feeling his body weakened by the news.

'It wasn't just my eyes, John mate. In fact, I may not have recognised him at all on my own. I was with my Dad, visiting family, and as we got off the train at Cambridge he was there. Screaming at some poor university lad that he was looking for some girl.' Justin said, with a little sympathy.

'Did you approach him at all?' asked John, already knowing the answer.

'Different platform, fella, but Dad did call his name out, to no avail. Honestly I thought my old man was just going a little senile at first, but the more I looked, the more convinced I became that he was right.'

'So he didn't even flinch at his name being called? Didn't make a movement to respond?' said John.

'John mate, it was like we were shouting the wrong name at him. Anyway, I can't offer you any more than I've given you. I really am sorry, my man.'

'Hey, this news has thrown me, but it was news I needed to hear for sure, so thank you. I imagine this hasn't been an easy conversation for you.' John knew it hadn't been easy to hear.

'Well, look, whatever you choose to do with this is up to you. I know you didn't have the best of relationships but I guess it's better to know that he's out there right?'

'Right, absolutely. Listen Justin, you take care, and give my love to your mum and dad, OK?' John was already putting the phone down, cutting off his old schoolfriend's reply. John didn't keep many people around in his life, so the ones he stayed in touch with, he ensured were certainly trustworthy. After all, why would Justin lie?

John immediately picked up his old leather phonebook and flicked through the dusty old pages. 'Leanne, Leanne, Leanne...got you.'

'Hello?' answered a girl with a Cornish accent so thick that John always struggled to fully comprehend what she was saying.

'Leanne? Hi, it's John Petalow, I know I haven't called in a year or so, but I need a massive favour.'

'Straight to the point as always, John. Yes, me and hubby are OK, thank you for not asking. What can I do for you?'

'Sorry, my heads up my arse right now. Are you all OK? How's the little man? said John as he backtracked, remembering that he needed this woman's help.

'Oh, so you remember that you have a godson? Yes, he's fine, I'm fine, we are all fine. So..?'

'So....?' Asked John.

'So what do you want, Johnathon?' asked Leanne impatiently.

'Shit, sorry, yes. Do you still work for Cambridgeshire Police? If so, I need your help.'

-

Hart had been Marc's father in-law's name, hardly original, but at least he had taken the name of a great man. John's grandfather had fought and died in service to the country, so had never had the displeasure of meeting his son in-law. John often wondered if he would have approved of his daughter's choice; he very much doubted it. It hadn't taken him long to track Marc down. John was Special Forces, he had friends in all branches of British Intelligence. He may only have been an operator himself, a hammer in a box of surgical tools one might say, but he had worked with people in counter-terrorism for a few years now. His father was a snake, but not a quiet one. He could change his name a thousand times, but he would still be the guy who got drunk each and every night, complaining to anyone who would listen about his family back in Kent, about a wife and son who had betrayed him. In the end, it was his drinking that had caught him out. A drunken brawl one night with a bunch of toffs had left him overnight in a holding cell where he had been bullied by the desk sergeant to give his real name. Turned out he had been living with a woman, a professor at the university, who by all accounts was much younger and prettier than he deserved. John had tried to reach Professor Rosenberg, but with no success. He imagined any woman that was smart enough to teach at Cambridge would not wish to be associated with a man who had faked his own death. John also didn't want anyone else to suffer the destructive influence that his father always brought with him. Apparently, she was on extended leave until early September, so he had sent her a letter and decided to put the situation to bed. What would be the point in giving it too much credence? His father being alive under an alias in a different part of the country was no different to him being dead back home. Marc's tyranny over him had ended long ago, by John's own hand. He had nothing more to fear from the old bastard.

Professor Rosenberg,

    I'm afraid this is a letter that brings you bad news, and I am sad that maybe it comes too late. Your colleagues buckled fairly easily when I asked where I should send this letter. They explained that you had left your partner for a better life, so it was best to write to you here at the university. I trust that if you are reading this, you have arrived home safe from your travels and are eager to get your life back in order. This, unfortunately, is where I come in.

Alastair Hart is not who he seems. His real name is Marc and he is a fraud. He faked his own death a few years ago, although that may be overselling it. What he actually did was disappear from his miserable life leaving only a suicide note. He is a rapist, a drunk, a terrible father to his son, and a violent husband to a woman, that I'm sure he hasn't told you, he was still legally married to until her recent passing. I rescued my own mother from his rage. I cannot do the same for you, it is neither my place, nor is it my burden to carry. He is as dead to me now as he was the day I found out that his black heart still beat.

If I can suggest anything, it is this, you need to get out whilst you have the freedom to do so. If you have left him already, like your friends say you have, then don't let him back into your world. Your colleagues seemed only to want to help me to help you, so know that you have more support than my mother ever did.

I'm sorry. Sorry that you are on a journey that I have long since finished walking.

Johnathon.

19

When One Light Goes Out
Seasalter, Kent UK
Winter Early 1979

Waking up to a hangover was one thing, but as the street light outside slipped through the blinds like an assassins knife, junior surgeon Eden Rhodes realised that this hangover had come on a workday. The young surgical resident squinted at the glowing digital clock as she rolled over to assault it, punching its snooze button right before it had the audacity to attack her with its incessant beeping. It was going to be a long day, and her bones ached as she pulled her unwilling body to the bathroom. It had been a great night, and a worthwhile venture in team building. Most of the ward had come out for Christmas shenanigans, and most of them had left earlier than she had, but it had been fun. Today was a good opportunity to showcase her skills to the new head of surgery, Dr Baldwin Lynch, who had never given her more than a passing glance since she had chosen surgery as her respective path. She had aced medical school and done her time carrying out the menial tasks without ever causing a stir. Yet getting noticed for the bigger operations seemed to more difficult than she previously thought, with the louder and more charismatic male surgeons always getting the nod ahead of her. Today would be different, though. She was shadowing Dr Lynch for the whole day, and the man had his hand in all the best operations. She took a long look at herself in the mirror before she attempted to abolish the demons of last night's misdemeanours. She didn't look half as bad as she felt, and that was a start. She made her way down to the kitchen, hearing her roommates groaning and snoring as she passed each bedroom door, envious at the fact that she was the only one working today, and popped some bread into the toaster. *Coffee, toast, bus and everything's going to be OK,* she thought as she grabbed the marmalade from the fridge and gave herself a shake. *You got this.*

—

Eden had always enjoyed catching the early bus, at six-thirty in the morning when there was barely anyone awake, she never had to worry about sharing her seat. She was not enjoying last night's wine still sloshing about in her stomach, though, the three rounds of toast doing little to subdue the motion sickness that she felt was almost beating her to death with every bump in the road. Flashbacks of singing karaoke with one of the district nurses kept flashing into her mind, a Chaka Khan hit from the summer had clearly been the anthem for the night, as she slowly recalled singing it three or four times. Each time the crowd booed for a change of song. Had someone thrown something on stage for her? She quickly patted down her leather jacket and tried to recall the incident, pulling a pair of off-white briefs out of the side pocket with disgust. She felt the acidic burn of her stomach trying to leave her throat as she quickly threw them across to the opposite side of the bus, a little scream of disgust leaving her lips as she realised what she had been holding. Whose briefs they were she did not care to find out, so discarding the evidence seemed like the logical thing to do.

She jumped off the bus as they pulled up at the hospital with ten minutes to spare. She bid a courteous farewell to the driver, in an attempt to conceal the guilt that she felt, knowing that he would find a pair of used pants on his bus a little later. She walked into the hospital with a smile and a skip in her step, already feeling a little better about the day in front of her. That was until she made it to the bathroom, just in time to throw up, and the process of making herself presentable to Dr Lynch started all over again.

'You're late,' said Dr Lynch looking up from his notes. 'And drunk.'

'I'm not drunk doctor, but I am late. It won't happen again,' replied Eden as she composed herself under the meticulous glare of the head of surgery.

'I do not suffer fools, Miss Rhodes, so make sure it doesn't. Would be a shame to throw your career down the pan so early in its journey.'

'Yes doctor, of course,' said Eden as she fell into step alongside him. His march down the ward was almost military and she struggled to keep pace with him without looking like she was jogging beside his wide gait.

'First things first, we have someone in maternity at the moment. Damn child's not budging so I need you scrubbed in for a caesarean in the next ten minutes. Have you done one before?' asked Dr Lynch, without breaking stride.

'I've closed on one, but not performed the procedure start to finish.' replied Eden, almost out of breath.

'Good. You don't need to worry about the rest, I'll perform the operation with Dr Mason, but I want you in there observing the process before I let you stitch her back up. Any questions?'

'No doctor, no questions,' said Eden as she felt the bile rising in her throat once more.

'That's it, I can't move another bloody box while I'm carrying this little cow, I'm spent,' said Laurie with utter defiance.

'I said that we should pay a company to do it, just saying...' said Vivian with a grin that hid the fact that she was just as exhausted.

"I said we should pay a company to do it," repeated Laurie in a mocking voice that sounded like a teenage girl. "My name's Vivian, I'm so perfect, I'm so wonderful."

'Oh it's like that is it?' giggled Vivian as she cleared her throat to start her own little skit. "My name's Laurie, I'm so old that when I give birth it will probably be to a grown-ass woman."

'You little shit, did your mother never teach you to respect your elders?' laughed Laurie, slapping Vivian on the behind as she climbed up into the van once more.

'She did, but she was senile by the time she was your age, so I just presumed it was the confused ramblings of a mad woman.' Vivian smiled from inside the van, knowing that her heavily pregnant partner could not enter to retaliate.

'When you get out of that bloody van, I swear to God, I'm going to kick your...'

'Alright Grandma, calm down. You know I love you just as you are.' said Vivian as she blew a kiss straight at Laurie.

Laurie caught the kiss and threw it on the ground with a little stomp of her feet to follow. 'You are not winning me over that easily, Miss Phillips.'

'Oh God, I love when you call me that. I'm sorry Miss, I've been bad. Maybe you should spank me?' smiled

Vivian as she looked innocently at the ground and clasped her hands together.

'I hope this isn't a sign for the future, you bullying me every day, I mean,' said Laurie with a smirk, as she took a seat on their new garden wall.

'Well, I can't promise that our house will be jibe-free, but I can promise you that I'll always make it up to you, or at least try to,' replied Vivian as she slid the last box to the edge of the van's open door. 'How are you feeling about all this? I think we picked the right location, don't you?'

'Honestly, I feel safe. Am I glad that we have the ocean almost touching our street? Yes, of course, but mostly I just feel like we can just start our lives all over again now. I feel reborn.'

That night, in the chaos of a half-unpacked home, surrounded by empty boxes and the remnants of a takeaway dinner, they slept happy. They were deeply in love, of that they had known for a long time, and now they had the grounds to start building a future together, a family; their family.

-

This couldn't be real, this couldn't have happened. Vivian was going to wake up any second now and see her unique, beautiful and very real Laurie lying next to her. Amniotic fluid embolism. That's what they had said as they walked out of surgery, right before Vivian fought her way past a number of nurses, and one very determined security guard. He hadn't known what to do with her, as she screamed and writhed like an eel. In the end though, as she stood in front of the surgical table, she wished that the poor lad had managed to stop her. This wasn't her Love. This wasn't the woman she had entered this hospital with. A junior doctor, who had been appointed the grim task of stitching up Laurie's wounds after the failed attempt to save her life, rushed over to try and catch Vivian's fall, as she felt the very life-blood drained out of her.

'Get me some help in here!' shouted Eden as she tried to calm Vivian down. She was acutely aware that she was coated in the blood of the poor girl's partner, comforting her like this seemed so wrong. 'WE NEED HELP IN HERE!'

'The baby, what's happened to the baby?' screamed Vivian through the tears of her shattered heart. 'Where is our child?'

'She's OK, just breathe. We have moved her to the ICU for the time being, but she doing just fine.' said Eden as she tore off her surgical gloves to hold Vivian's hand.

'She? We...we have a girl?'

'A beautiful girl, with more blonde hair than most have at birth. She was over eight pounds, it's no wonder Miss Rosenberg was struggling to move her.'

'Is that...is that why she died?' asked Vivian, as she looked upon the pale face of Laurie's corpse on the surgical table. Her tears were filled with anger and the pain of imminent solitude.

'No, it was just one of those freak occurrences that rarely happen. Our head of surgery said it's the first time he's seen it in twenty years at the table,' replied Eden, softly. It's just chance. That's all these things ever are, and I am so very sorry that it's your family that has had to suffer.'

The nurses that Vivian had previously fought past quickly gathered around and got her to her feet. She couldn't fight them off. She didn't want to, she had nothing left to fight for.

Seasalter, Autumn 2014

Evan knew what was coming, she had seen it a mile off, the way her mother had stumbled through the last part of the story had only confirmed the inevitable. "Mother." That word seemed so false to her now.

'I was there with you the day you were born. I fought for a year to be given full custody of you,' said Vivian pleadingly, a tremor in her hands causing to fidget uncomfortably in her seat.

'You named me too, I guess? Or is that just a massive coincidence?' asked Evan, with a fire in her voice that hadn't been heard in years. Remnants of the person she once was fighting and clawing to the surface.

'Of course I did,' said Vivian defiantly. 'I have been your mother since you first opened your eyes, I didn't pick you up at the shelter six months down the line.'

'It's just all a little late for truth time, don't you think? I mean, I have to ask...would you even have told me, had I not been pressing you for information?'

'Do you know what? No...probably not. But I'll tell you why - because I've not thought about you being anything less than my biological daughter since the day you were born!' Vivian brought herself face to face with her daughter, forcing the tremor to stop through sheer force of will, for she was not used to being the one on the back foot. 'More than that, you have no one else, there isn't some other family out there, ready and willing to pick up the reins. There never was. I haven't seen or heard from that bastard man since the day he punched poor Laurie in the face. Alastair, or Marc, call him what you want. He was a rapist and a drunk, and all he wanted was to ruin other people's lives. He never wanted, or tried, to contact me regarding you.'

'Mum?-'

'I have only ever loved you, and I'm sorry that at times you have not deemed that enough,' interrupted Vivian as she pulled a photograph out of her tote bag. 'I looked through every resource I had, but without knowing his real, full, name I couldn't find him. I couldn't even tell you if he was alive.' she said as she put the photograph down on the table. 'That's all I have, what you do with that picture is up to you.'

'MUM!'

'What is it, Evan? I'm doing my best to have a moment here. You are the one who is always accusing me of being an emotionless shrew. Well, I'm struggling here OK?'

'Mum...my water's broke.'

-

Jacob had not left her side for close to a day and a night, almost throwing Vivian out of the room the second he arrived with her emergency bag in tow.

'He's beautiful, and I'm so proud of both of you. How we have created something so pure, with our two blackened souls, I don't think I will ever understand.' said Jacob as he held his son for the first time.

Evan watched them both with doe eyes. 'Do you know what? I was thinking the exact same thing. Lachlan Paul Brooking, welcome to our little world.'

Jacob watched as his new heir gripped his little finger with his tiny hands. 'Your sister is so very eager to meet you, my son.'

'I hope Dorothy knows that I love her just as much. Just because she's not mine does not mean that I don't see her as my family,' Evan said as she painfully thought of her mother's revelation.

'She knows, my love. She talks about you no differently than she talks about me, or her mother. Do I assume from you making that point, that we need to talk about what your mother has told you?'

'Not today, my love. I'm not ruining this day for anything.' said Evan, as Jacob lay her new born son back in her arms.

20

Double Jeopardy

Canterbury, Kent UK

Autumn 1978

The banging on the door had awoken John from a night's sleep that had kicked his arse. Bad dreams had thrown him from one side of the bed to another. His T-shirt had become so twisted that at one point it had begun to choke his massive frame. On compassionate leave since his mother had passed, John had been slowly finishing the renovations to the house. Betsie had been a tidy woman and a real mother's mother, but she had really struggled with her illness closer to the end, and John understood that he probably should have been home more to help. It had been quite cathartic, for him anyway, to tear down and rebuild walls. The place needed an overhaul and brick-by-brick he was doing it.

The banging repeated upon the heavy oak door, more aggressive and seemingly more impatient than before. Three more loud knocks shook his head, as he brought a giant hand up to rub his eyes of sleep. His head swam as if waking from a drug-induced night, and his mouth felt like a rat had died in its moist embrace. Whomever was banging on his door had better know that were always consequences to waking a bear early from hibernation. John complained audibly as his heavy feet caused the un-carpeted staircase to groan under the his massive weight. As he reached the front door, he had to take a few deep breaths to convince himself that he was not angry, just tired. He had been up plastering the hallway until nearly two in the morning and it was only six now. He was mithered and grumpy, and another barrage of furious knocking caused John's temper to snap.

'What the fuck do you want?' said John as he threw open the door, ready for conflict, as he always was.

'Hello, Son,' said Marc Petalow, as he pressed the snub-nosed barrel of his revolver against John's forehead.

John didn't blink, he didn't even react. If anything he began to press his head forward, the gun's barrel meeting him with equal pressure. 'I wondered how long it would be until your cowardly arse turned up on my door step,' John growled with hatred. 'I'm putting the kettle on. You can stay out here or come inside, but don't for one second think that I'm intimidated by you and that little toy gun.'

Marc followed John into the kitchen, not lowering his aim from his son's head the whole time. 'So, from your reaction, can I assume that you knew I was still alive, Son?'

'You can assume whatever you like, Marc, as quite honestly I don't give a fuck.' John said as he made himself, and only himself, a steaming black coffee, before taking a seat.

'There's no need to be like that, John. I'm only here to talk.' Marc took the seat opposite John as he spoke, resting his aiming arm upon the table, the gun now squared at John's heart.

'The idea of you being here to "only" talk, seems a little frivolous when you walk in pointing a gun at my skull.' As John spoke, he was taking in the room. Ever the operator, he had to judge his every situation. In full combat mode, his mind analysed different scenarios and worked out the odds of survival. A sledgehammer rested against the oven door just a few feet away, and a rack of large kitchen knives sat just behind them, more out of reach but certainly easier and quicker to wield. Both would be useless in a gun fight though, but if Marc didn't have the gun, well... John would not need a weapon.

'I want half the money from this house. You give it to me without quarry and I give my word you will never hear from me again.' said Marc, using a kinder tone.

'Do you believe that your word means anything to me now, if in fact it ever did?' said John as he felt his pulse lower to almost a dead line. Like a tiger ready to pounce, he could not be anxious now. He had to be coiled like a viper, ready to strike with precision instead of panic. Panic got people killed, and John was not going to die today, not by Marc's hand.

Marc thought carefully as he planned his next approach. The tick-tock of the wall clock became the dominant sound in the room as each of them planned attack and defence. 'I took nothing before, Son. I'm entitled to this. Your mother even got my pension because you wanted me gone.'

'Don't you dare put this on me! Whatever you lost to my mother, it was no less than she deserved for the abhorrent life that you made her live.' John spoke with certainty and clarity. There was no mistaking his words; Marc was to get nothing today.

'You forced me out. I left my life behind for you and your mother to live the fairy-tale life, and where did that get you both?' Marc grinned, crow's-feet tightening across his leathery skin. 'You have, by all accounts, become a trained killer, and Betsie Anne is dead.'

Hearing his mother's name was all John had been waiting for. In one fluid motion he threw his boiling coffee into Marc's face and lurched forward, instantly knocking the gun's aim towards the ceiling, gripping the piece in such a way that his giant index finger blocked the hammer from being able to drop, despite his father's attempts to pull the trigger. He screamed as the liquid seared his eyes and skin, his free arm trying to rid his body of the cause of the pain, as he buried his face into his elbow, rubbing back and forward as steam rose up from his head. Marc would not let go of the revolver, his tenacity for hate seemed to equal John's huge strength advantage. John reached to his right and felt his hand clench around the neck of the same sledge hammer he had been using to rebuild the house. Brick by brick, he was going to cleanse this house, and that notion stuck in his mind as he swung the hammer in an arc that brought its head into Marc's forearm with more force that most men could muster. A sickening snap was quickly followed by a spray of blood, bone had torn through skin as Marc finally relinquished his grip on the gun. John didn't hesitate as he opened the barrel and held the gun skywards, as the brass casings fell to the floor like weighted confetti. John threw the empty weapon in the sink as if it were a child's toy. The sledgehammer still clenched in his right hand, he returned his attention to his father.

  Marc looked up at him through bloodshot eyes, his skin blistered, and his broken arm pulled tightly across his chest.

  John pulled his seat back into position and sat opposite his father, no remorse for his attack and no sorrow for the pain that was now tearing his father apart. Through Marc's heavy breathing, the sound of the ticktock clock became dominant once again, as John weighed up his options, his gaze never leaving his broken and bloody opponent. 'Help me out here, Killick. What exactly am I supposed to do now? Let you go? So that you can go back to ruining other people's lives as Alastair Hart? Or worse still, so that you can rock up here once more, on a day when I am not so ready to receive you? WHAT?'

Marc laughed through the pain, his broken form shaking uncontrollably as he became increasingly desperate for alcohol. 'Well, I'm not sure that you're going to kill me, my boy, so let's just chalk this one down to a loss and I'll be on my way. I best stop underestimating you before it's too late.'

'You almost sound remorseful...but I'm not letting you leave. I won't let you ruin that poor child's life like you ruined mine,' John said as he stood back up, throwing his hammer against the floor. He reached over to the kitchen knives and took the largest, its ten-inch blade refracting the light around it. 'You get one opportunity to end this now. Your own life, or mine. I won't kill an unarmed man.' John slammed the knife down on the kitchen counter and turned his back. 'I can't go to jail for killing you, Killick. You're already dead, remember? So know that if you choose to attack me here, I won't hold back again.'

Marc picked up the kitchen knife with his working hand and twisted it about in his grip, rage filling him once more. Rage at everything he had been forsaken by; the Navy, Betsie, Laurie, and once again, his own son. Marc rose unsteadily and arced the knife down towards John's neckline. The move was telegraphed with anger, and John saw it coming even though it was on his blindside. Marc, however, did not see what happened as his twenty-stone son twisted and ducked all at once at a speed that defied logic. John took Marc's weaponised arm and reversed it, ramming the knife back awkwardly. He drove it through his father's chest and followed through until he collapsed backward, John slamming on top of him like a closing coffin lid. 'I never loved you, Dad. I only ever feared you, but not anymore. Take that with you wherever you go.'

Marcus Alastair Petalow died by his own son's hand that day, and, as he slipped into darkness, all that he could think of was just how unfair life had been to him. John shed no tears as he buried the body at the back of the garden. The tick-tock of the kitchen clock still echoed in his mind, as it mimicked each spadeful of dirt thrown upon the sack that was to be Marc's final resting place. John had never wanted this; he had wanted a real father, just like his mother had wanted a real husband. Someone strong yet kind, intelligent but not calculated, someone he could have looked up. So he made a vow as he dragged his mother's old cast-iron bench across the newly covered grave, that was the only thing that she had brought from the old house. Ironically, it was the bench where she had used to sit and smoke while Marc would beat her son so very violently. John finally dropped, exhausted, onto it as it settled into its new home, and he ran his fingers over the black iron that had turned an almost green hue as it aged.

'I will never put my family through any of this, Dad. You let me down and I won't make the same mistake.' said John as he finally stood up, realising with a sigh that he now had to scrub the kitchen clean of any evidence of struggle and, with that, any evidence that Marc Alastair Petalow had ever existed in his damned life.

21

Courtin' Zombies
Chatham Maritime Dockyards
Early Winter 1979

John stood to attention in front of his C.O. He had been on a ten-mile slog through the moors to try and clear his mind ready for this meeting. He had given in his papers; one more job and he was free to leave, a hero of the regiment. Of course Captain Gerhardt was disappointed, he had believed to his very core that John Petalow was a career frogman, but he couldn't blame him after the double thigh rupture. John had never shown signs of being in pain; he never backed out of PT and was probably the fittest guy in the regiment, but the ice baths would only take him so far, and he walked like he had the British flag stuck up his arse. The head doctor was telling a different story though. John never slept more than an hour or two at a time, his restless legs shaking throughout the night, dreams of his fallen comrades keeping him from allowing anyone else to take the high-stake risks in any particular mission. The captain knew, with the certainty of a man who had seen this many times before, that John Petalow would leave the forces, or die within its embrace. He brought the acceptance stamp down upon the papers and watched as John gave a little smile from the corners of his mouth. Twelve months in which not to die? The captain didn't fancy his chances.

Londonderry, Northern Ireland

'You are a saint' said John as he gratefully accepted a mug of steaming coffee. Bronagh Morrow, a curvaceous brunette from Derry, had become more than just a host since putting John and Tuomo in digs six months ago. Her laugh was infectious, and her dinners reminded John of home every time he took that first bite. Of course, she had no idea that she was housing a pair of trained killers, All she knew was that John and Tommy Sutton were brothers on a building contract, far from home, and eager to get fed and settled each night.

'You're always welcome my love. How did my boys get on today? I see Tommy is already out cold.' said Bronagh, full of life and good cheer.

John had to admit he quite fancied her, in an older woman kind of way, but he knew he had to stay focused at all times. Tuomo may have done this before, but John was a newbie to deep cover. Without his rifle and comms, he felt almost defenceless.

'Tommy's OK, he just works too hard. He's a bit of a martyr.' Tuomo had given himself a more British-sounding name, lest it raise more questions than necessary.

'Well, both of you work so hard. Always exhausted - get yourself some rest my beautiful John, then I will wake you both up with a fry up in the morning.'

'Bron, you really are too kind to us, and if I thought for two seconds that you would move to England with me when this bastard contract was up, well I'd marry the sweet Irish arse off you.'

Bronagh looked at John with careful consideration. 'Do you mean that, John? Because I look at you the same way. It will be a tragedy the day that you leave here. I know this isn't the best place to be right now, but there is a place for you, always. I hope you know that.'

John leaned forward and placed a kiss upon her forehead. His newly-grown beard tickling her brow. 'I think, my most beautiful Bronagh, that you will always be just a little bit out of my reach. And that, my love, is the biggest tragedy of all.'

-

The light of the full moon shone through the open window. John had fallen asleep with the curtains undrawn, but now he was wide awake, and he could not find the motivation to get himself up to pull them closed. So instead, he just lay there, looking up at the sun's little gothic sister and he thought of home. He had given notice that this tour would be his last. His mind was becoming as tired as his scarred physique.

'Hey, you' whispered Bronagh as she crept in to the room.

John rolled over to find her standing over him, her curves falling out of every part of the silk nightie that she had adorned for the night.

'Bron, I don't...'

'Shhhhh,' said Bronagh, as she placed a finger over his lips. 'Let's not talk about being out of reach. Not tonight.'

John reached over for her as she pulled back the quilt, running her long nails over his naked stomach before taking his cock in her hand. He pulled the strap off of her nightie and watched as her heavy breasts fell out, instantly taking her nipple in between his teeth as she rubbed his length with passionate vigour. She groaned as he felt the climax rising in his loins.

'Don't, I'm going to come, this feels amazing...' sighed John as he started to buck underneath his experienced host.

'Good, I want you to come...and then I want to spend the next thirty minutes prepping you for round two." replied Bronagh as she sped up her stokes and quickly felt him explode all over her hand and wrist. One by one, she licked her fingers clean before running her lips up John's body to his mouth. He could taste himself as she pushed her tongue into him, but as she ran her nails over his swollen testicles, he didn't care. She caressed him with hand and mouth until he was once again ready for the heat of her body, and as she climbed on top of him, his huge throbbing member filling her like no man before ever had, she knew that she didn't want this night to end.

-

'HOW COULD YOU? I trusted you! Do you know what you have done, I can't lie to him, I can't...'

'Bron, what on Earth is going on?' said John as he awoke, far too quickly, from the hour's sleep he had barely managed. He rubbed his eyes as he sat upright, only to find Bron pointing his beretta at his face.

'I can't believe I bought your bullshit! Builders? Brothers? Is it all lies? You're army, and you have either no idea who my family is or you are as stupid as you are audacious.'

'Bron, whatever you think this is, it's not you we're here for, I promise you. This is just bad luck.'

'Bad luck? You have no idea who I am do you, or who my brother is? How could I have been so stupid?' sobbed Bronagh, as a door was smashed in further down the corridor.

'Bron, what is going on?' asked John as he got up, the cold steel of his own pistol pressing against his chest before he had chance to do any more than stand.

'I'm sorry, John. I didn't expect to find a gun under your pillow when I came in last night...'

The door burst open and four men, each with assault rifles, barrelled into John pinning him down. Each of their faces disguised by balaclavas, they stared blankly back at him before the butt of one of the rifles hit his temple so hard that he instantly blacked out. He would soon make up on the sleep that he had missed.

-

How long had he been sitting tied to this chair? John's wrists were bound tightly by coarse rope, and his early attempts to escape had done little except cause a trickle of blood to evade from his tearing skin. Without degloving he would not be escaping by force, that much was obvious. He had been able to count the hours, roughly, by the position of the sun breaking through the cracks in the barn door, but even that luxury had been taken from him when the sack cloth had been pulled over his head. Tuomo was here with him, or at least he had been at some point. Since the blinding by hessian sack, it was hard to tell what was going on around him. The grunts of a bored guard and the scent of cheap tobacco were the only sensory clues that he was still alive. That wasn't necessarily a good thing, as John knew what was to come. The Provisional IRA were notorious for their ruthless forms of torture. In fact, they had done a pretty decent job of busting him open just dragging him here. One of the thugs had made sure that John would not be at full capacity whilst being kept captive.

'You still with me, Johnno?' asked Tuomo with a purposefully beaten and dejected voice. Special Forces were renown for being chipper in the face of grave adversity, but they were not playing the role of soldiers right now, and it paid to be more dejected and down-trodden. The angry Brit-hating muscle that had been left to watch them was hardly going to put up with ego-fuelled banter from his custodes.

'I'm OK mate, still here. Be strong fella, all be over soon.' John replied under his breath.

'Well, you're not wrong there. It will be over soon enough for you, you feckin' eejits.' said the guard with an accent so thick they could barely understand him.

'Tosser.' murmured Tuomo, unable to fully commit to holding back.

'Tosser, eh? That's not okay boy, I am not okay with that at all.' said the man assigned to guarding them, as he put out his cigarette and pushed his stool out from under him.

John held back his scream to all but a growl, as he felt cold steel puncture his thigh, just above the knee. He couldn't tell exactly where in his thigh the blade was, he just knew it hurt like hell as he felt one of his back teeth crack under the pressure of his clenched jaw.

'Johnno, what's happened?' called Tuomo, as he tried to shake the sack off his own head.

'I'll tell you what's happened big guy, I've just skewered your mate here with a Phillips-head. It's a simple tactic really, and I swear to God I've got pretty fucking good at it over the years. If you give me shit, I'll hurt your mate, and vice versa. And in case you were wondering, the more that shit stinks, the higher the hurt.'

'You motherfucker-'

'Tommy, it's OK, just leave it. They're in charge here.' said John, unwilling to get stabbed again on account of his commanding officer having a short temper.

'Yeah "Tommy", do what Johnno says. He's clearly the smart one here' said the guard as he picked his stool back up. 'You see, you hardcore Army-boys, fearless and all that, you always look out for your mates. You think that fighting for a cause is the same as being willing to die for a cause? You fecks know nothing about loyalty to a bigger cause.'

John could feel the metal lodged in him, the scarring from the Oberon operation torn open once more, blood soaking his lower leg and slowly filling his shoe.

'I'm going for a slash boys. Don't go anywhere, will you?' scoffed the Irishman, thinking he was funnier than he was, to a crowd that did not appreciate his efforts.

'John, you alright buddy?' asked Tuomo as quietly as he could while still being heard.

'I'm OK, Skipper. I can barely feel the fucker anymore.' John winced as he spoke.

'Shit man, it's still in there? We have to get you out of here. We need comms with intel, and we need to get help. If we get out, could you walk?'

'I've walked with worse, Skipper, I promise you that,' said John, '-but it's irrelevant if we can't come up with a plan to escape. You got any ideas?'

John didn't receive an answer; instead he heard three sets of footsteps and the weighted crack of a crowbar striking flesh and bone before it clattered to the floor.

'Let me introduce myself, Johnathon. My name is Keelan Morrow, and I am the Vice Chief of Staff in Northern Command. May I ask who I am talking to?'

'Johnathon, you already said.'

'Don't be smart with me, son' said Keelan in his thick Belfast accent. 'I promise you, I'll make you regret it.'

'I'm a Corporal in the British Navy. Petalow, 363887.'

'Navy? How did you crash an SAS party? Not seen a frogman in these parts for years.' Keelan pulled a chair in front of John, and took hold of the screwdriver.

'Petalow. Corporal 363887!' replied John.

Keelan twisted the screwdriver in response, motioning for one of his minions to remove the sack from John's head. 'Listen. Name, rank and number is all well and good, but I'm going to be honest with you, you're going to die with us here.' John bit down as the pain nearly overwhelmed him, before spitting his newly broken tooth into Keelan's face.

'Petalow...'

Keelan was not a big man, he looked more like a politician than a terrorist, which John instantly mused was ironically the same thing in a lot of ways. His shorn hair was ginger at the sides and vacant on top, liver spots covering his brow.

'Johnathan, this is what's going to happen. People above me need to know what your operation had uncovered, and they cannot rest until they know everything. So here are your two options,' Keelan said as he wrenched the screwdriver out of John's leg. 'One, you tell us everything, and I mean everything, that you and your friends have uncovered here these past six months, and I will personally see to it that you get one round in the temple and your body sent home. Or, option two, we torture you endlessly until you break, which you will, and then when you tell us everything, I will personally dismember you and have your body thrown at an army checkpoint. I hope you understand that the torture will last for days, regardless of how quickly you tell us anything.'

'Johnathon Petalow. Corporal 363887' replied John, defiantly.

'OK.' said Keelan, as he motioned for the muscle next to him to act. The man pulled out an old beretta pistol and put seven rounds into Tuomo who was still bleeding on the floor from his earlier wound, his body convulsing now as each shot hit home.

'Jonathon, I have some business to attend to, so why don't you think about it for a day or two?' said Keelan as he lightly slapped Johnathon's cheek. 'Someone dump his mates body at his feet, maybe it will give him some perspective.'

John watched him exit with his entourage as soon as they had dumped Tuomo's corpse with him. He had seen many die by his side but, for the first time, no emotion now came to him except rage. The pain had stopped, in his leg, in his heart and his mind. He listened to the remaining guard chatting with Keelan outside and planned his escape.

-

A few days passed before they moved Tuomo's body, the stench was making his captors sick, and even the torturer was struggling to focus. John's T-shirt was soaked with blood and three more of his back teeth sat in line upon the dentist's table next to him. No man should have to suffer like John had in the last 48 hours. There were a litany of holes in his body made by lance or blade, and a pair of shears had removed one of his nipples. John though, hadn't talked. Name, rank, and number were all he was going to give them, for he had nothing now but country to fight for. With no siblings, no parents, and no children to mourn him, honour and pride were all he had to take with him. He didn't even have any hobbies, except fishing and rugby. Being an operator was all he knew, and he would die doing his job right.

'It seems he either knows nothing, or he's willing to die hiding it.' said the wiry man who had been his inquisitor the past few days.

'Maybe you haven't stepped it up enough?' said Keelan.

'I couldn't lie to you, even if I wanted to. If I stepped it up any more, he would die on this chair.' said the inquisitor as he wiped some more blood from his fingers.

'Then wrap this up, remove his limbs and dump him at that checkpoint Boughton Street.' Keelan said as he walked over to John once again, pulling his head back by the scruff of his hair.

John tried to hide a smile as he watched Keelan leave again with his full entourage, including the muscled guard that had so far kept them him in check. Just the scrawny interrogator left, readying his bone-saw. John was broken; he was drowning in his own blood and close to death, but he was not ready to let go just yet. The would-be surgeon leaned in towards John's neckline. He was preparing to cut his throat before he dissected him, for who would want to hear those screams, and pressed the blade against his throat. With all the strength of a man fighting for his life, John pushed his bound body forward, the chair following him, and his twenty-stone frame crashed down on top of the stick-thin Ulsterman. John felt the man's ribcage shatter beneath him, but knew the battle was only just beginning, as the screams of his oppressor echoed around the barn. John had to end this quickly, on the off-chance that another lackey had been left outside. He opened his mouth as wide as he could and sank his remaining teeth in to the man's throat. Arterial blood covered them both in an instant, as John felt his windpipe snap in two, and his bite closed completely. The man, who was about to die still believing in his cause, finally stopped struggling as the world around him turned to red. With the conclusion of the fight, John did the only thing he could, and passed out.

-

Corporal John Petalow woke up only a few hours later, his head swimming and his body broken. He had to move. He forced himself up on to his feet, the chair still strapped to his back making it difficult to move easily. With a deep breath he launched himself backwards, crashing onto his spine as the chair shattered beneath him. He felt a large piece of wood puncture his skin, but the relief he felt as his arms moved, unbound for the first time in days, flooded John with endorphins. John stumbled over to the dead surgeon and took the car keys from his pocket. John was free, and he refused to ever be caught like this again. He was out - all he had to do was find his way back to Checkpoint A.

22

See Me Fall

Seasalter, Kent UK

Early Winter 1979

The tears didn't stop. Nor did the screaming, and Vivian's soul continued to slowly empty. What did she want? She couldn't be hungry, as she had eaten more than the doctor had recommended. In fact, Evangeline had eaten more than Vivian had of late. She doubted that anything was wrong with her digestion, after all, she was shitting like a Great Dane. Maybe she was tired. But if she was tired - if that was indeed the reason for her distress - then why didn't she just sleep? After all, she had been in her cot for hours. She looked just like her mother; Evangeline Laurie Phillips was as blonde as the sun, and clearly born with the same fiery spirit. Vivian rubbed a little whiskey on her gums, just in case the poor mite was teething, but nothing felt like it was coming through yet. She wanted to pick her up, but the thought of teaching her daughter such needless dependency frustrated her. Vivian's own parents had disowned her for deciding to raise a bastard child from a lesbian relationship, but they had at least brought her up correctly before then. The best nannies, the best boarding schools...she had never gone without. She had been deemed a disgrace to the family name for falling in love with a woman, and yet she could not complain about their methods of parenting prior to that. They had been tough, for sure, but she had turned out alright, Vivian thought. She had never felt unloved, not really. She had been doing her best to finish her masters at Canterbury but, even part-time, it was proving more difficult than she could ever have imagined, especially with a child in tow. The crying continued in to the night, as Vivian tried to finish her paper on Frederick Nietzsche's influence on Western philosophy. She wasn't sure how much more she could stand. Evangeline wasn't even officially hers yet; another hearing at Maidstone court was booked for next month and there was no certainty she would prevail. Vivian struggled to understand the problem; No, she was not a blood relative, and no, she wasn't legally connected to Laurie before her death either, but it was not like there was a queue of people awaiting to look after her. Evan's father was AWOL and, anyway, he hadn't even been put on the birth certificate. Both sets of grandparents had abandoned their responsibilities the second they discovered the details of their daughters' allegedly sordid relationship. So, who better than Vivian?

'Please, tell me, what do you need? I can't give you any more!' pleaded Vivian as she finally relented and picked up Evangeline, who, to her amazement, stopped crying the very next second.

Winter 2015

Lachlan looked up at his mother, as she bounced him gently between her thighs, with a smile that had rarely left his face since birth. His emerald eyes shone with mischievous desire, almost enough to rival his father's.

'He's getting heavier every day now. I don't think he's lost any weight since the day he joined us!' said Evan, as she made faces at her giggling son.

'Well he won't lose any now, baby. Especially the way he eats...' Jacob laughed.

'Mum said that I used to eat as though each meal was my last, we never could figure out why I was so skinny,' chuckled Evan as she blew a raspberry on Lachlan's belly.

'Dorothy is the same, although I feel she's got my frame.' Jacob said as he grabbed Lachlan's toes.

'Well that's no bad thing, my love, she definitely has more of you than Alice in her features, but that hair will always be the crown of a Petalow, for sure.' said Evan without malice. Her respect for everything that Alice had been through now far outweighed their history together. 'Pass me my bag will you baby? I think he needs some more cream on that dry elbow.'

Jacob reached in to the baby bag and pulled out the Sudocrem from in-between the mountains of wipes and nappies. 'Here we go, stinky bum,' Jacob said as he then proceeded to drop the remaining contents of the bag on to the floor. 'Well done, dumbass,' said Evan with a smile. 'It's lucky you're so pretty.'

'Hey, I never pretended to be anything other than a trophy husband. You know what you were getting into when you put a ring on it,' said Jacob smugly as he repacked the bag, noticing something under the armchair as he picked up a loose nappy. 'What's this, baby?' he asked as he looked at the photograph in his hand, it's quality was poor and it's colour faded.

'I wondered where that had gone, I assumed I'd lost it,' said Evan as she looked at Jacob, still holding the picture. 'It's my father apparently. I've not even had the courage to look at it since Mum dropped that particular bombshell on me.'

Jacob turned the picture over in his hand, as if trying to figure it out from another angle. 'Baby, I've seen this picture before, but I swear for the life of me, I just can't think of where...'

'That's impossible-' said Evan, as she wiped a little cream into Lachlan's elbow crease.

'I'm telling you now...wait...Yes. I know where I've seen this...You want me to show you?' asked Jacob knowing this wasn't going to be at all easy for his wife to deal with.

'If I look at that photo, it's only to shut you up,' said Evan, as she lifted Lachlan in to his crib. 'Come on then, let's do this...'

'Hey, I thought this was important to you? I don't want you to feel pressured by me, I just want you to be happy," said Jacob, concerned with his wife's change of heart.

'It was, I mean it is. I think...I just realised that, in the grand scheme of things, managing my own family was more important than wasting time thinking about a family dynamic that never even existed.' Evan took the photo from Jacob and kissed him square on the lips as she sat next to him.

'I'm telling you though, baby, I know where I've seen this picture-' reiterated Jacob, with absolute certainty.

'You have seen it...' said Evan, in shock, '...and, unfortunately, so have I.' Evan couldn't believe what she was seeing. This was the only photo that her mother had of her birth father. It also happened to be the only photo that Angela Petalow had of John's father, Marc.

'No, this can't be. I know you said that your birth mother was older than Viv, but that would make you and John...brother and sister. Christ, that would make you Alice's auntie-' said Jaco, stunned.

'I know-' said Evan as she stared blankly now at the old photograph.

'You need to speak to your mum. Tell her what you know, and see if it ties up.' said Jacob as he put his hand on his wife's knee to reassure her.

'Yes. Yes you're right, I'm just a little caught off-guard. When I started this journey, I was looking for something positive. I never thought for one moment that the father figure I was looking for would be such a bad man, that his own son would disown him before he died.'

'Evan, my beautiful wife, I am not a bright man...'

'Well that's a lie.' interrupted Evan as she looked up from the photograph.

'Let me finish,' said Jacob with the faintest of smiles, 'I am not a bright man when it comes to always knowing what the right path is. For years I was trying to match up to my own, very perfect, father. Then, after years of failing to be that man, I turned my hand to being John Petalow.'

'How did that work out for you?' asked Evan.

'Not well,' laughed Jacob. 'I was a worse John that I was a Paul. Had one of my idols been a Ringo, I might have pulled it off.'

'So, what's the lesson here?'

'The lesson here my love, is that I had no idea what family even meant until Dorothy turned up, then you, and Lachlan of course. Then everything finally made sense. It's not about who is here or who is not. It's not about who you want to be, or the dreams you leave behind. It's just about those ten little fingers and ten little toes, and keeping them safe. You are a great mother, and a great stepmother. And you will continue to be so, regardless of genetics, or family history.'

Evan felt the emotion of the situation finally overwhelm her. The walls that she had kept so high for so long now tumbled as if made of sand, as she sobbed in to her husband's arms, unashamed at what her younger self would have perceived as weakness.

23

Angela Rowe

Whitstable, Kent UK

Spring 1980

John had been nursing his pint for over an hour. He felt numb to the world and being back home now felt almost unreal to him. He should have been happy; barring an impending war, he was now on permanent leave until his contract ran down. The idea of doing a job that no longer required his blood to be shed sounded like heaven to John, although he felt he did not deserve any respite. He had applied to join Canterbury Rugby Club the day he returned home. They had virtually bitten his hand off when they realised that he was the captain of the Navy team that had a seven-year winning streak over the Army. John knew it would be a few months before he could train, though. He still felt the occasional phantom sensation of metal through his thigh. Both body and mind still needed time to heal. Time was something that he had in abundance now yet, as he struggled to find any joy in himself, the time felt almost as painful as the torture. The pint of Guinness staring back at him was his only friend - maybe that was why he was so stubbornly refusing to drink it, he mused.

'John?' asked the barmaid, as she put a hand on his shoulder. Her approach from behind had caused John to nearly snap her wrist, as years of muscle memory alerted him to a threat. 'John Petalow?'

'Yes, that would be me...how are you, Angela?' replied John as he turned and smiled.

'You remember me? I must say I'm surprised. Can I join you for a minute, just to catch up?'

'You're kidding, right? Angela Rowe, the school darling? Every girl wanted to be you, and every boy wanted to be with you. How on Earth could I ever forget?'

'You exaggerate, you didn't want me,' said Angela teased as she took the seat alongside him.

'Angela, I spent my entire tenure at that bloody school wishing I could be with a girl like you, all my friends felt the same. Honestly, I never believed that you knew I existed.'

'Oh, I knew you existed, you prat. You were captain of the rugby team, plus you were dating scummy Jane."

'Scummy Jane, who could forget?!' said John.

'You did know she was cheating on you, right? With-'

'Roger? Yeah, I caught them at it,' laughed John.

'Wow, I did not know that! How did that go down?'

'Not well for him, I have to admit. But it was all such a long time ago. It never would have worked with you and me anyway...' said John as he finally sipped at his pint.

'Really? How come you think that?' asked Angela, as she leaned over the table, her beautiful red curls spilling over her shoulders.

God, you have not aged a day. More womanly, yes, more feminine, certainly, but skin still like pristine bone china and locks of her hair like liquid fire, thought John as he looked deeply into her eyes for the first time in over ten years. 'Well, all I ever wanted was to join the Navy.'

'I remember - Marines, right?'

'That's right, all my young life, the only plan was to escape Kent.'

'I understand that. But I never would have interrupted your dreams, John, even if we had been together.'

'No, I don't suppose you would have. But then, you may very well have given me good reason to stay, and that was exactly what I was trying to avoid.' John said as he placed his hand on hers.

Angela motioned to reply but ended up just smiling at him, a little dumbstruck and clearly lost for words.

'So, what happened to you after school? I'm assuming this isn't your career plan?' said John as he motioned at the typically old, and typically British, pub.

'Nooo...I went to art college in Canterbury, but being absolutely bang-average at anything creative meant I had to work here whilst doing a second degree in bloody accountancy.'

'That sounds thoroughly like your parents' choice?' said John.

'Thoroughly boring, don't you mean? Anyway, what about you? I'm assuming you got in to the Navy?'

'Got in, got far, and got out. Nothing more to it,' replied John as he looked back into his pint.

'There has to be more to it than that - did you travel? Did you see the world, in all it's glory?'

'I saw too much. I saw things that I will never forget, and things I cannot talk to a lady about.'

'A lady? You really are the gentleman that I remember from school. The same one that picked me up when that black ice took my legs from under me.'

'You remember that?' smiled John, as he thought back to the last winter he had spent at school.

'Of course I remember, John. You were over six foot tall at thirteen years old, you always stood out more than you know,' said Angela as she played with the curls of her hair.

'Well, listen...'

'Hold that thought hon, I had better do some more work before Tits McGee fires my arse,' interrupted Angela as she stood.

'That old Scot still running this place? I thought he'd be dead,' laughed John.

'It won't be for much longer, I'm sure. Meet me after work and walk me home?' asked Angela, without waiting for the answer.

-

Angela watched John whilst she worked the end of her shift. His smile had disappeared the moment she left the table, and from then on he had just sat looking into his pint glass with mournful sorrow. He looked hurt, but not physically. He looked tired, but not tired in the way that might be fixed by an early night. "Big John" Petalow looked like the shadow of that same young man she had known at school. That was, until she had sat with him, and the veil seemed to lift, albeit it only for a moment.

'You ready to walk me home, good sir?' asked Angela with a smile.

'Yes, of course, my lady. Do you still live on London Road?' replied Johnathon as he stood.

'I do, still bound to my parents tyrannical reign.' Angela laughed, as she latched on to John's arm.

'Well then, my beautiful Angela, we had better take the long road home.'

24

Relatable
Whitstable, Kent UK
Winter 2015

Evan had been watching Jacob sit on the tiny gardening stool opposite his father's memorial stone for two hours. The sun was setting, and it was turning cold. Still, he found it impossible to leave his father's side. He seemed so comfortable there, as though he was sat with an old friend, and Evan had not wanted to disturb him. Lachlan was fast asleep, there was no rush, and she had been making notes to prepare for her impending meeting with Alice in the morning. Evan could not begin to imagine what Alice's reaction might be, she certainly knew how much she had struggled to process the realisation herself. How could it be that two women's lives could be so entwined? Evan admired Alice, for she was the girl who was stronger than she'd ever been. How she had coped with losing a child, Evan could not comprehend, especially now that she had Lachlan. It would be difficult, she knew that much, but Evan needed to close the book on her past and this was the only way to do it.

'I'm sorry, Dad. I'm sorry I couldn't mourn you when I should have, and I'm sorry I couldn't tell you this before.' Tears rolled down Jacob's cheeks. 'I have missed you so much since you left, and I cannot tell you how I have struggled to live up to the high standards you set for me as a father, a son, and a man. I have made so many mistakes in your absence, and with each one it has become more apparent that I've let you down...'

Jacob put his hand on his father's memorial stone and closed his eyes for a moment, as if to try and communicate his words through a more physical medium.

'I promise you, I won't let them down like I have done you. I'm going to be better, and I will make you so proud.' He opened his eyes and sat back down. 'You would be so proud of Sam, too. He has two boys that look the spit of you. Whilst Dotty looks like her mum, thank the lord, but she certainly has your spirit, which is enough for me. She would have loved you, Dad, we all still do.'

Jacob exhaled. He took to his feet, folding up the little stool that had been his perch, and headed back towards the car. He felt better. A little sad still, perhaps, but he was so much less in turmoil as a result of his one-sided conversation.

'Are you OK, baby?' said Evan as Jacob came towards her.

'I'm good. More than that, actually – I'm happy, truly.'

Evan reached for him to kiss him deeply on his freezing cold lips. 'I'm so very proud of you.' His newfound ability to mourn had really helped him grow as a man.

Jacob smiled. 'Proud of me? I'm proud of us, love. Look at how far we have come.' He looked over Evan's shoulder and into the back seat of his BMW. 'How is our little man?'

'Fast asleep at last. If I wake him for a feed when we get home, we might get him to sleep through.'

'I love you, Evan Brooking-Phillips. Never change – just as you are is all I have ever wanted.'

'Aww, baby...do we need to look at moving your medication review? I know you have many, but I am not sure I've met this particular personality,' Evan joked, grabbing him tightly, and kissing him passionately, before he could form a smart reply.

They put their heads together one last time before a parting kiss saw Jacob head to the driver's seat.

'Let's get home,' said Evan as she slid into the passenger seat next to him. 'I still need to figure out what I'm going to say to Alice tomorrow.'

'Goodbye, Dad, I'll see you soon,' said Jacob. He started the engine. 'He would have loved you, Evan.'

Evan placed her hand on his. 'He would have loved us.'

-

'Are you sure you want to do this, baby?' asked Jacob, squeezing Evan's hand.

'I have too. She deserves to know, we both deserved to know,' Evan replied, her hand shaking in her husband's grip. 'I love you, so much. Never stop being this version of you.'

'What version is that, my love?' Jacob said as he brought her hand up to his lips.

'The version of you that supports everything that we do as a family. The version of you that constantly has my back.' Evan returned his kiss with another, and got out of the car. The door to Alice's flat lay just a few feet away.

25

My Dorian Gray
Autumn 2015
London, Kent, UK

The oil painting was hanging on the main wall of Blackberries auction house. Alice hadn't moved in over an hour, and the longer she looked at the painting, the more it seemed to look back at her. Alice thought of the philosopher Friedrich Nietzsche, who made the point that you couldn't stare into the abyss without the abyss staring back at you. The strokes of oil, both of light and of dark, certainly held that power over her right now. An almost hypnotic restraint kept her sitting painfully still as the girl within the strokes looked straight into her soul.

'It's an amazing piece,' said the tall man who had appeared out of nowhere and placed a hand on Alice's shoulder. 'But, sweet Jesus, it scares the life out of me.'

Aiden Hewett was the head auctioneer at Blackberries and commanded a great deal of respect within the professional circles that Alice kept.

'How are you, old friend?' asked Alice politely, raising her hand up to touch his.

'I am well, although I would be better if my friends would keep from referring to me as old.' Aiden, who was in his late fifties, had the angled look of an owl, with the slender frame of a marathon runner. His black turtleneck jumper only elongated his look further. 'I didn't know you were here in person; I know you had two pieces on sale today, but –'

'Three. I had three pieces on today. One was under the pseudonym of Angela Marie.'

'This is one of yours? Well, I must say, this is a departure from your usual style, and it has clearly worked for you. Why the change, may I ask?'

'It was my Dorian Gray, and it's a side of me that I didn't want to associate with my other work. My clientele back in Kent are a little on the pompous side.'

'That makes sense from a brand perspective, I guess,' said Aiden, taking a seat next to Alice, 'and explains you using ... your mother's name?'

Alice nodded. 'She doesn't know, but I'm hoping she will take it as a compliment. You said my change in style had clearly worked for me, but I thought you weren't a fan of this particular piece?'

'I most certainly am not, but did you not watch your own auction today? Have you really just sat here, transfixed by the eyes of what looks like a lost version of yourself reflected within a mirror?'

'I'm sorry. You know how I hate watching my own work sell in front of a baying crowd. Did they all sell?'

Aiden reached into the leather satchel by his side and pulled out a piece of yellow paper, passing it to her with a smile. 'Your two normal pieces of work went for a little over your asking price of £2,000. And this monstrosity – well, what does your receipt say?'

'This can't be real?' Alice stared at the receipt, dumbstruck. 'I mean, I think this is my magnum opus, I truly believe that, but still - who would pay £250,000?'

'I believe the buyer was a Miss Palette. Part of an American gallery based out of Topeka in Kansas.'

'You are shitting me?' choked Alice with a chuckle.

'Miss Petalow - we don't use that language here. But, no, I am not "shitting" you.'

The girl in the painting watched them talk for a further half hour before two burly men covered her with a green felt blanket, took her from the wall and placed her securely into a crate. The painting, one made of tears, sweat and toil as well as canvas and oil, was a picture of a girl not unlike Alice. A girl haunted by her reflection, a girl frightened by something that would not leave her shadow, and a girl saddened by a world built on lies and the monster who sold them to her.

-

Alice had missed two calls whilst getting out of the bath, she knew it couldn't be too important, so she had got herself comfortable before ringing back. With spending so much time covered in paint and varnish, it had really become a chore to keep herself looking well kept, so clean and tidy had become the order of the day as she took last week's polish off of her nails. With Dorothy at her grandparents for the weekend, she had decided that the second the studio had closed, this was to be a self-care night. Her long auburn hair was tied into a tight Dutch plait, and she had smears of moisturising night cream under her eyes. Her "independent woman" playlist was playing over her little stereo, and the remnants of a delicious homemade linguine carbonara sat in the sink downstairs. Alice had felt a lot worse than she did right now, even the voices had stopped pushing her so hard for vengeance upon all those had wronged her over the years. Poppy had helped. Without her, Alice was unsure that she would even be here now. They were deeply in love, of that there was no doubt, but making that relationship work was another thing entirely. Would Poppy relocate for her? Who could say? But it certainly wasn't a conversation she had dared approach with her yet. All she knew was, with a mixture of joy and melancholy, was that she was bound to living in Kent because of her Dorothy. So whatever was to happen, was to happen here, and really that was no bad thing. She had learned, with Poppy's help, to love her home once more. Her condition was the problem, not Whitstable, not Canterbury, and not Jacob and Blondie. With her painting finally gone, and her past along with it, she could start to move forward with her life.

'Hey Mumma Bear!' shouted Dorothy down the phone.

'Hey you, why are you not in bed yet, young lady?' asked Alice with a smile, not minding that her daughter had a late night with Nanny and Pops, who were no doubt lavishing her with attention.

'I just wanted to ask about our holiday, Mum, where are we gonna go? Pops is asking, he needs to know if he has to book some free time to help run the shop with Nanny while we are away,' said Dorothy.

'Dorothy, it's your holiday,' said Alice, who was doing a fine job of filing her nails in the comfort of her armchair while balancing the phone awkwardly on her shoulder. 'So you get to decide where we go next summer.'

'I know, Mum, but you deserve a holiday, too. It's not exactly been a quiet year for you, has it?'

'I love that you are thinking of me, but you are making this choice. You've got a few weeks yet, but it will obviously be cheaper the earlier we book it.'

'Okay, okay, keep your knickers on,' said Dorothy. 'I'm on it.'

'Cheeky. Say hello to your grandparents for me, would you? And Dorothy...'

'Yes, Mumma Bear?'

'I love you, Poppet.'

'I love you too, Mum. Sleep tight and don't let the bed bugs bite.'

'I will. And you my love,' said Alice with a smile. Dorothy was right, they would need to book the flights soon if they were not to pay through the nose.

Alice put the phone down and finished her nail maintenance before she got ready for bed. The apartment above her studio wasn't the biggest, but it had an almost regal feel to it. Original oak beams separated each room and Edwardian window frames gave a stunning view of the ocean. Alice loved the ocean dearly, for she slept so much better with its tide gently lapping against the empty oyster shells that littered the bay. Alice felt content within her home, within her life, and within her world. It had been a long time coming, and with business getting ever busier, she knew it was only a matter of time before everything else clicked into place. She washed her teeth in her en-suite, examining her reflection. She saw a few more wrinkles than normal as she massaged the cream into her skin, a grey hair or two hiding among her red locks but, overall, she looked good. She looked more like her mother as she approached her forties, but then that was hardly a bad thing, as her mum was the most beautiful woman she knew. She rinsed her mouth out and gave herself a smile in her bathroom mirror before heading to bed. Her phone lit the room up with a jet of synthetic light and a small beep just as she entered the room. Alice climbed into bed and reached across to where the phone lay.

How about Kansas? read the text from Dorothy. *I hear the locals are friendly, hint hint :)*

Alice smiled at the thought of seeing Poppy once more. They spoke daily, but she hadn't had the pleasure of her company since the after-party of her auction in London eight weeks before. The night had ended with a parting kiss that, even on her best day, Alice could not have explained. *A trip to the States would be great, Alice replied. I'll look into it tomorrow.*

A loud knock at the front door woke Alice sharply. *Who the hell is that?* she thought. It was just after 7.30 A.M., although she felt like she had only just gone to bed. She held her throbbing head. The room was spinning. She rubbed her eyes and searched for her sense of reality. She had barely opened them when she realised something wasn't right. Her apartment was fully carpeted, and yet, as Alice slid out of bed she felt only cold, hard, wood underneath her feet – the same floor that she had had in 'her' cottage all those years ago, in her false reality.

I'm not buying into this. I've been doing this far too long, thought Alice with an inner chuckle. She was far too used to being exposed to the false realities that her broken brain would invent.

'Are you OK, Papillon?'

Alice turned in shock – shock but not fear, as she knew that in this place there was nothing substantial to fear, to see William looking back at her. He rubbed his neck with both hands before pulling his chiselled body upright.

'I know you can't be real, but, damn, what a pleasant surprise.' Alice said with thirsty excitement, before she leaned in and kissed him passionately. She knew that he wasn't anything other than a fiction created by her cruel brain, but she had missed seeing his face.

William pulled away after two more deep kisses ended with Alice mounting him and pulling at his boxers.

'What on Earth has got into you?' said William, both confused and aroused in equal measure. 'This isn't the wake-up call I was expecting.'

'God, you even smell the same. I will say this, my mind really has an eye for detail when it comes to fucking me over, doesn't it?' Alice went back in to finish the job she had started on William before the loud knock at the door hit once again. 'Hold on, baby. They are clearly not going to let us alone. I'll just play the game, I guess. After all, I'm usually brought here for a reason. But you'd better still be here when I return, my handsome-but-imaginary man.'

Alice rolled off of William's flustered body and, remembering her way through her old imaginary home, made her way to the top of the stairs.

'Oh my,' said Alice. 'This is new.'

She was at least seven months pregnant.

'Wow, I could get used to this,' Alice cooed, rubbing her baby bump. 'It's not real, Pebble. Just enjoy the moment, you daft cow.'

There was another knock on the door.

'Hold your horses. I'm bloody coming. Don't you know I'm carrying a child here?'

Alice struggled to the bottom of the stairs and opened the door.

'Alice – sorry, I know it's early, but I need –'

'It had to be you. My bloody mind couldn't leave me upstairs with William, could it? Please continue, Evan.

Honestly, no dream is fit for purpose without you trying to screw me over.'

'I just need to talk to you about something. Can I come in?'

'Please, Your Majesty, come through to the kitchen.' Alice made a regal gesture of welcome. 'Tell me, will Our Royal Highness be joining us, or have you left Jacob alone in bed at home?'

Evan walked through to the kitchen and placed her hands on the sink, almost bracing herself for the conversation ahead. 'I don't even know how to start this without sounding crazy, but I hope you at least understand my intention for coming here and that you see it's not to hurt you.'

Alice had moved to within inches of her without making a sound, and Evan looked down to see a large kitchen knife buried in her abdomen, pushed up to the handle. The blood being released was minimal, but as Evan's body went into survival shock, she knew that pulling the knife out would drastically change that.

'Alice, what have you...?'

Alice drew closer and strengthened her grip on the knife. 'Don't you "Alice" me. You know you had this coming, and if this false reality is the only place that I'm free to do it, then so be it.'

That felt good. You know it's not real, so do it again.

'I've needed this psychosis of mine to work for me for a change,' said Alice, twisting the knife, 'and I have to be honest, it feels so good that I'm tempted to do it in the real world.'

Now get back up to William, before you wake up.

Alice pushed Evan to the ground and turned about with a swagger, only to find Jacob standing there, pale with horror. He rushed over to Evan and pulled a pile of kitchen towels from the counter.

'WHAT HAVE YOU DONE, ALICE?' he screamed. He drew the knife out of Evan's belly, using the towels to stem the blood loss.

Why do they all rush to her side all the time?

'Come on, Jay, William's upstairs, so let's not waste what little time we have together. She doesn't even exist, a bit like you, really, but if I have to be stuck here, I would rather be upstairs with you.'

'Alice, she is going to die here in my arms if you don't call an ambulance, so CALL A FUCKING AMBULANCE!'

Might as well give up on this. Once again it's turned to shit. My mind clearly hates me, thought Alice as she closed her eyes and clenched her fists as the doctor had shown her.

'Alice,' cried Evan in absolute agony.

Alice opened her eyes and realised she was still in the cottage kitchen. *Focus, Pebble, you've got this.* Again, she closed her eyes and clenched her fists tightly.

'Alice, you're...'

—

Alice didn't move, time flew by her as she repeatedly clenched her hands over and over again, but her stance was solid. She watched the chaos unfold in front of her while tears rolled down her face, a face that was turning ghostly pale as she realised the world in front of her was being slowly destroyed. Still she didn't move, that was, until the police officer slammed her into the kitchen table. To the officer, it would have felt like she was resisting, but in truth Alice was rigid with fear. He wrestled her clenched fist behind her back as the paramedics saw to Evan and another officer tried to calm down Jacob, who was trying to help the paramedics fix his dying wife.

'What have you done, Alice?' cried Jacob as he watched the officers escort his ex-wife outside. 'ALICE, WHAT HAVE YOU DONE?'

-

It had not stopped raining. Jacob refused to leave Evan's bedside, as she continued to bleed from a wound which was proving near-impossible to halt. Every time the surgeons suppressed it, another leak had sprung up and each time it only became more difficult to source the new bleed's location. Before the night was over, Jacob held his wife as she slipped away. No words found their way out of Evan's oxygen mask, but she hadn't taken her eyes off him as her grip on his hand slowly relaxed. Jacob's heart was broken, and the tears flowed continuously until support had arrived. He sat in the arms of his brother, Sam, as he tried to find some of the strength that he was going to need in order to move forward without Evan, his love, by his side.

-

The rain thundered down, ricocheting off the ground all around Jacob's umbrella. He wore all black on this day; a day that he had hoped would never come. Evangeline Laurie Brooking; Loving mother, wife and daughter, read her memorial stone. It sat in the centre of more flowers than he had believed one person's death could muster. He was tired; tired of all these people being here, tired of the loneliness in his heart. There were parts of him, deep parts of his personality, that had only existed with Evan by his side, and they had all disappeared with her passing. The funeral had been warm and full of love albeit a little perfunctory. Evan had always been popular, and it made his heart ache all the more when he saw how many people had been touched by her presence. Her best friend from boarding school, Heather, had done a beautiful reading of a poem that they written together. It was the only time in all the years that he had known her that she had not cracked a joke, and Jacob's heart broke all the more for her, too. Everyone had dispersed now, leaving Jacob standing over his wife's final resting place. He was alone now; his joy gone, his soul empty. John had declined to attend, instead sending flowers and love from both himself and Angela. He was still totally unaware that it was his own half-sister that they were burying. John had thought it might be considered disrespectful to stand with Evan's friends and family, when it was his own daughter that had killed her. Jacob would tell him the truth - but not yet; it wasn't the right time, and Jacob had a family of his own to console. Alice was still in custody, but word from Vivian had told of a woman completely out of touch with reality. By all accounts she would not serve any prison time, but the hospital that she would no doubt end up in was not the kind of place that you were allowed to leave by choice. The look in Alice's eyes on that day was totally devoid of any clarity, her pupils had been so dilated that her eyes looked almost black. Alice hadn't meant to kill Evan, Jacob knew that for sure, but Evan was still dead, and Alice had to answer for that. Jacob had carefully tried to explain everything to Dorothy, without discrediting her mother in anyway. He only told her that mummy was poorly, and that she needed to go to a special hospital where she would receive the best care. As for Evan, he hadn't quite found the strength to dive too deeply into it. Dorothy was still so young, she wouldn't understand, especially when Evan was such a big part of her life. For now he had told her a simple truth, that Mumma Evan had gone away, and that she would miss her little Dotty every day. The whole truth of the situation was to be a story for another day. For now, she had a baby brother to help take care of.

You must have known that your mistakes would come back to haunt you, said the voice from Jacob's peripheral.

'No. No, I am not letting you back in,' growled Jacob as he gritted his teeth. 'She wasn't the only reason that I had you beat.'

Of course she was. You never had me beat before, why was that child?

Jacob refused to turn around to face the beast, which he knew had taken physical form behind him. He knew it wasn't real and yet, he could feel it's hot breath upon his skin, the small hairs on his neck picked up as he saw the shadow casting over him. 'You have no power over me, creature, so leave me to mourn my love. I have neither the strength nor tolerance to allow fear into my heart right now.'

What you desire is neither my concern nor my problem, you disgusting excuse for a man, it never has been. But I will give you today... and only today, said the creature as it laid a shadow-veiled tentacle across Jacob's shoulder. Its viscous texture reeked of death and decay. Jacob cared nothing for its presence and was unphased by its contact at first, until the chattering of its razor sharp beak began in his ear.

I'll be seeing you soon, child...

26

Alice
Canterbury, Kent UK
Autumn 1981

It had been seven months of bliss. Of course, he had struggled re-adapting to civilian life, but as John looked across the bed at Angela, he knew that these had been the best seven months of his life. Angela had stayed by his side as he began to leave footprints on the world that weren't bathed in the blood of his enemies. On the side-line of every rugby game that he played, waiting in the reception of every psychiatric evaluation, she was there. Johnathon Petalow did not know much, but he knew how very lucky he was each and every time he woke up next to her. She slept like an angel, with hair of autumnal fire rolling like waves over her naked chest. She looked as though she were a mermaid, who might perch atop a giant plinth amidst a raging sea. She was tranquillity within his chaos. So tranquil was she, that John had to check upon her frequently for fear that her breathing had stopped. She was his anchor and his rudder, she would hold him safe whilst steering his path through storms of conflict. It wasn't unusual for him to wake before her. The military routine had not totally left him, and 5A.M. was his natural waking time. He had vowed to try and change, yet, at the same time John did not see a problem with spending the first hour of his day watching her sleep. He would get up and make her breakfast soon, she deserved no less as Queen of the Petalow manor. He had proposed to her just four weeks ago, and to his joy, she had accepted his declaration of love. They were to be married in the September of next year, something small and personal. Neither of them were introverts, but they kept few friends between them and John had no family that he wished to share his day with. Angela's parents had been encouraging of their relationship from the start. Her own father was a Navy man, who had fought at Dunkirk, and he appreciated the values that John was bringing to the table and so had instantly helped fund both the wedding and John's new venture. John had been working as a dockhand down at Whitstable harbour since his return to civilian life. It was a job that he was certainly over-qualified for, but at least this particular role was less complicated than any of his previous positions. Now, though, things were set to change. Two ships to call his own, neither of them large vessels, but still worthy of respect within the bay community. Dogfish and pollock would break-up the standard catch of mackerel throughout the summer months, and Dover sole was the winter catch that sat in front of him now. John had hired two captains, more than competent enough to man his boats and each coming on board with their own ship-hands. They were good men, who had shown him nothing but respect from the day he opened the doors to J Petalow's fish market. His harbour cold-store was small compared to others but, because of this, it at least always looked full. His small office at the back of the building showed him a view of a permanently bustling front counter that had built an early reputation for itself as the best fishmonger in town. John was grateful for all the help that he had received in setting up his new life, and he wanted to repay Angela and her family by giving them all the love and respect that they deserved. John slid quietly out of the bed and slipped on his dressing gown. His body ached still, from the yesterday's game, and his bones cracked as he stretched out his limbs to welcome the morning. The stairs creaked under his weight as he tried desperately to make it downstairs without waking his fiancée. He had put on a little timber since leaving the Forces but, if anything, it had only made him all the more imposing. The cold stone flagging of the kitchen floor had him dancing for a second as filled the kettle. John loved a Sunday morning; no work, no rugby, just him and his lady at home with the radio playing. He popped some bread in to the toaster and grabbed some of the Rowe's homemade family jam from the refrigerator he had just fitted. As he closed the door, he dropped the jar in shock. Glass shattered, and sent shard-filled strawberry preserve in all directions, as John quickly assessed the threat in front of him.

'Who the fuck are you?' demanded John of the shadowed figure in front of him.

The figure did not move. His hooded face somehow concealed all features with an impossible shadow.

'I asked you a question, boy, I won't ask again,' growled John as he stepped forward to within striking range.

The figure only stared back at John through an emotionless veil.

John's movements were swift and, as always, belied his size as he slammed both hands in to his opponent's chest, causing him to crash hard against the bare brick wall of the kitchen. The force of John's attack shaking the very foundations.

The mysterious visitor bounced off the wall with a sickening thud that brought him to his knees yet, unfazed, he brought his hooded gaze back upon John's towering frame.

'STAY DOWN!' growled John as he reached over for the phone, the click and whir as he dialled 999 failing to distract him from the intruder, who now stood up to full height once more. John watched him rise as only static greeted his ears from the phone line.

'STAY DOWN!'

The figure took a step towards John, raising his hands towards him in a gesture which John could not conceive as either aggressive or passive.

John responded by smashing the telephone handset around his uninvited guest's head. Repeated blows finally butted him to the ground, where John instantly bought his weight to bear.

'J-J-John...' stuttered the prone figure, as his opponent wrapped his hands around his throat. Except, as John tightened his grip, a veil seemed to lift, and John realised that it was not a "he" at all.

'Angela! No...what have I done?1 John reached down to cradle his fiancée as she choked up blood. 'Darling, I thought you were someone else. I...I never meant to hurt you...' cried John, as he held her tightly in his giant embrace.

Angela squeezed his arm in response. It wasn't the first time this had happened. Her eyes glossed over with tears as she struggled to swallow. She knew that John needed more help than he was getting.

'I'll speak to my psychiatrist tomorrow. I'll tell her that I need to up my sessions. This needs to stop, I would rather pack your bags than hurt you again, Angela.' John said as he sobbed into her shoulder.

'It does need to stop John, but moving me out isn't an option either. We have to do this together.' Angela said, as she brought her hand up to her head. A lump had already appeared where the phone had struck.

'I would rather lose you than hurt you Angela, of that there is no doubt. You deserve so much more-' John said, softly.

'John, I'm pregnant. So whatever you believe I deserve is going to have to take a back seat to what *we* both need right now' said Angela as she looked up at John's face.

'You're pregnant?' John asked, smiling.

'I'm pregnant!' exclaimed Angela, although clearly still in pain at the assault. 'We are going to have a baby.'

Winter 2015

Alice held her father's hand from across the small metal table. This wasn't a prison, although in everything but name it might as well have been. It was a hospital; one which and Alice was not allowed to leave, of course. It would be a long time before that could even be considered, but at least she wasn't confined only to her room. Although the first meeting with her parents felt formal, they could easily take a walk through the hospital grounds. This was the best place for Alice, she knew it, and all who loved her knew it.

'You have nothing to be ashamed of you, you needed this help for a long time and I was negligent in not getting it for you earlier.' said John as he looked in to his daughter's eyes; eyes that looked vacant where once they were the colour of life itself.

'It's not your fault either, John' said Angela as she put her hand atop them both.

'As long as you need to be here, we will support you as best we can. Poppy has moved over to run the shop for you, and we have Dorothy covered between us and Jacob'

'Jacob...Is he...OK?' asked Alice as her attention snapped back in to the room.

'Don't think too much on Jay, he has his own battles ahead of him, too' said Angela as she squeezed her daughters hand.

'He hates me, doesn't he?' asked Alice, already knowing the answer. She couldn't blame him, psychosis or not, she had killed his wife, the mother of his son.

'He doesn't hate you, he misses her. He's lost, but we will help him find his way,' said John 'Dorothy is with us whilst he gets Lachlan sorted.'

Did you get what you deserved, Alice?

Alice ignored the voice that whispered in her mind. It was nearly time for her medication, and each day that she was here was another day that the voice lost more of its power. She would beat this thing, no matter how long it took.

Part Four
The Book of Dorothy

Six years later

1

The Mirrorverse
Somewhere in the Void

The Mirrorverse; that was the name that had been given to this place. Given by great men, revered men, who knew that its true name would drive the sanity from any person the very instant that the first syllable was uttered. "The Mirrorverse." It sounded a poor epithet for a place of such magnitude, such grandeur, such scope. It was as big as the galaxy and not a day younger, and shadows hid within its depths concealing monsters the size of planets. Revered men had spoken of The Mirrorverse's existence for thousands of years; the Egyptians knew, as did the Mayans, and yet the closer each civilisation got to unlocking its mystery, the quicker their end was reached. There were places, on Old Earth, where texts that had been poorly translated into the modern tongue spoke of a darkness within the light. The Necronomicon, written in old Arabic with each word etched in the blood of its own believers, sat upon the shelves of the Miskatonic University in Arkham, Massachusetts. There were only a handful of people who could read the dead text, and it could tell them nothing now that they did not already know. The Hoomans had always believed in Heaven and Hell; one praised, the other abhorred. They had never considered, for all their brilliance, that both Above and Below might just be the same place, only from a different perspective.

-

He had lived here all his life, a life that could be compared to only a candle's flicker in the void's omnipresence. Delta roamed the stone plains with his many sisters and a father who said nothing, other than what needed to be said. They had a role to play here, a small role in the grand scheme of things, but a role nonetheless. Their task was to keep the demon in the dark, for she would not dare leave the woods whilst they patrolled the outskirts. He was unsure why this menial task was the role of his pack but, as his father had commanded it, he had to follow through. Alpha's word was absolute. The demon was powerful against smaller foe, but she was no physical threat to their pack. The child of something much more powerful - a deity that had been asleep for longer than this galaxy had existed, she spoke pure darkness through a forked tongue and razor sharp teeth. The pack kept her in check, listening for the whispering of the leaves that spoke of her movements, as if eager to betray her. There were still things here that threatened them, though. The giant bear would revel in its call to arms, and rain glorious death upon them with one blow of its giant paw. The Great Bear though, would need reason to fight, and his place at the grand gate would never be abandoned for any less than a direct threat to the Mirrorverse itself. The mother of the Mirrorverse was different, though; The Great Devourer; the Gorgon. She had so many names. Regardless of what you called her, the very air around her flexed with unseen power. Her darkness had claimed the lives of hundreds of Delta's kin throughout decades of war. She was afraid of nothing, for she had no reason to be fearful; her life was immortal. She had been one of the first - she had seen the Mirrorverse created and then watched galaxies burn under her blood lust. Here though, she was just a vessel, her true omnipotence much larger than could fit on to the surface of even the largest planet, but her power was not lessened by her smaller stature. The Mirrorverse worked by reflecting the Hooman universe to its extremes; the demons might not always inhabit the same flesh and bone but always took what was best and worst from the Hooman's perception, and magnifying it. Delta was terrified of the Great Devourer, and he dreamed often of her catching him and tearing his life from his very flesh, as she had done to so many of his kin. Her beauty was enough to hold your heart still as her shadow surrounded you. Your body could be drunk empty of all that made you real as eyes of blood red stared deep into your soul. Creatures on this side of the mirror were not supposed to feel fear, yet Delta was more afraid of her than anything, but he would be sure not to let any of his pack see him show it. He could never disrespect the pack in such a way, fear was for the weak, and if he was caught showing such a Hooman emotion then, at best, the Beta's would swiftly kill him. Better that, than his father reminding him of what true fear was.

Reculver, Kent, UK

Dorothy had found her mother's diary just a few months before Alice was due for release. Her hospital stay had been intense, and to have her home would be an overdue blessing. Dorothy had helped Auntie Poppy with tidying the apartment in preparation for her return, and that was when she had found the journal; a thick, leather-bound book tied with red ribbon, the gold leaf emblem of a butterfly embezzled on the front. Alice and Poppy had sold the books as novelty photo albums in the gallery, but none other held the secrets that this journal held, none held the darkness. It had weighed heavy on Dorothy as she turned each page and she began to understand her mother's past, especially in relation to her father. She understood now, where once she hadn't been able to comprehend, her father's affair, Alice giving up and losing a child, her psychosis, and the mirror demon's endless taunts that stemmed from an incident that Dorothy hoped never to have to deal with.

She closed the journal on the last page, which had detailed Alice's continued psychosis relating to a painting that Dorothy hoped never to see. It had told Alice that reality was a blur, that she should take Evan's life to find clarity, to take what she was owed. Dorothy had resented her mother for a long time. She had grown up with Evan and her father, whilst her mother seemingly flitted in and out of her life in a haze. Things had changed now, and Dorothy was unsure how to feel. Her father had been the biggest constant in her life; he had been a model parent and her best friend. Yet he was complicit in her mother's downfall. His relationship with Evan had broken his wife's heart and, in knowing this, Dorothy felt as lost as her mother had been, and she was unsure how to pull herself back around from this feeling. That night, she found herself dreaming of dark things; shadows and feelings of loneliness were met with increasing apprehension. When she awoke, Dorothy found herself jumping at things that did not exist. The mirror demon had not spoken to her, and it had not approached her, but still it had been there. In flashes. In the distance. She knew that this was not a road that she wanted to start upon for, it seemed from her mother's diary, it was not a road that was easy to leave. She toyed with the idea talking to Poppy. After all she was the neutral patsy here, and had been almost like a big sister to Dorothy since Evan had passed. Poppy's love for Alice, in spite of everything, was the most real thing that Dorothy had ever witnessed. Dorothy trusted Poppy, and after finishing her mother's journal, she now felt that she couldn't trust anyone. The next night, Dorothy lay out on the patio as the sun slowly dropped in to the sea and a cool breeze whipped around the lighthouse. Her father was putting Lachlan to bed, and Dorothy had finally decided that she wanted to talk with him about a few things once he was done. She also felt sure that he was not going to enjoy the conversation.

'Hey, Monkey. You okay?' said Jacob as he came and sat on the sun-lounger next to Dorothy.

'Hey, Dad. I'm OK, just doing a little reading…' replied Dorothy as she sat up to greet her father. 'Listen, can I ask you something?'

'Of course, hon, what can I help you with?' replied Jacob as he realised, all too late, that the book that Dorothy was holding was Alice's treasured diary.

'Can you tell me how you met Evan, I mean, how you really met Evan?' asked Dorothy as she turned to face her father.

'Listen, I've been playing the honest game a long time now. I see what you're doing, and I don't appreciate you trying to catch me out, so if you have a proper question, baby, just ask.' Jacob said gently, but in such a way that let his daughter know he was no fool.

'OK then. Did you cheat on Mum?' said Dorothy rising to the challenge.

'I did worse than that…I broke her heart and betrayed her trust but, before you attack, can I ask where is all this coming from?'

'So you and Evan played a part in where my Mum is now? All these years I've blamed my "mental mother," when it was you who pushed her over the edge!'

'Alright. Firstly, watch your tone, young lady. I'll only so much sass from you,' said Jacob with a little more bite in his voice 'Secondly, you have no idea about my role in your mother's downfall.'

'Then tell me, Dad. Fill in the gaps that you clearly think I have in my story.'

'What you have missed in reading your mother's story, is my story. I was so sick back then, I had my own demons. I was undiagnosed from both of my conditions, and I had voices in my head telling me that my actions were justified.'

'Is that because of your bipolar? Is that why you go to group once a month?' the bitterness from Dorothy's voice slowly being replaced by curiosity.

'More my borderline personality disorder. You don't see it, because you have only known this version of me, but back then I was in a bad place. Now, none of this is an excuse. I held my hands up to your mother, and to the world, but then you came along and I've tried to be the best version of me ever since.'

'Thank you Dad,' Dorothy said, after a moment, 'I know it's not easy for you to talk about the past.' who was now acutely aware of how much he missed his wife. 'Did Pops ever find out?'

'I told your Grandad, and he beat me to within an inch of my life. But he saw the effect you had on me and we have been fairly solid ever since. He even loved Evan, by the end.'

'I'm sorry I accused you of anything, Dad. You have always been there for me, and I had no right-'

'Baby, if you have read that book, and I mean really read that book, you will know that your mother had problems that didn't relate to me, or Evan. The bigger question, though, is how did you even get hold of that thing?' asked Jacob with an ice-breaking smile.

'Not going to lie, Dad - I stole it, like a common thief.' Dorothy said, as she held it tightly to her chest. 'I'm seeing Poppy for lunch tomorrow, I'll slip it back I promise.'

'I don't think Poppy would care, but your mum will, and she's back with us next month.' said Jacob with an air of apprehension.

'She didn't mean to take Evan from us, Dad, I didn't need to read the diary to know that.'

'I know baby, I do. But take her she did...and I miss her so very much.' Jacob stood and kissed Dorothy on the head. 'Now enough sadness, this beautiful sunset doesn't deserve it.'

'OK, Dad. I'm sorry. I just have a mind that needs to work things through.'

'Your room is filled with fantasy books - you have Lovecraftian horror, in between your Dr Seuss. So, I understand that it must be scary to find a little bit of reality in all that fiction,' said Jacob as he put his hand on her shoulder. 'Never think you can't ask me anything. If I know the answer, I promise you I'll give it to you.'

-

Whitstable Bay was the only place where oysters and chips was considered a normal thing, and it had become Dorothy's favourite summer pastime to catch up with Poppy once a week on the seafront to enjoy the local delicacy. She had put on one of her mother's sunflower-yellow dresses, and tied her hair back with a piece of loose ribbon. If you had known Alice Petalow in her teens, you might have believed her to be sitting right there in front of you. The August sun baked down as hordes of sightseers bustled about with ice cream cones and little buckets full of colourful pebbles and crabs, torn from the safety of the many rock pools.

'Here we go, Sugar, get your chow on,' smiled Poppy as she dropped down on to the pebbles with the two paper plates of food.

'So, what's going at home? Your dad still pissed at you?'

'Nah, he's alright. Although I should have maybe been a bit more tactful about accusing him of destroying Mum's life...I heard him crying on his and Evan's anniversary the other day. I'm not sure he will ever move on.'

'He loved her, even your mom knew that,' said Poppy as she looked at the oyster in her fingers 'Damn girl, I sure am a long way from Kansas!'

'Yeah, he really did. He still makes her side of the bed as if she's coming home.' replied Dorothy, with sadness.

'You think that he's not going to be okay with your mom coming home full-time? Because honestly, honey, I could shit with excitement!' Poppy's Southern drawl had lessened over the years, but soon returned when she was excited, or drunk. It was after twelve, so it could well have been both.

'He hasn't mentioned it much, although he did say that you had something to tell me?' said Dorothy as she gave Poppy an anxious look.

'MOTHERFUCKER!' said Poppy as she realised Jacob had thrown her under the bus.

'Oh God. It's bad, isn't it? What's happening, Poppy-dawg?' asked Dorothy in a panic.

'Listen, honey. It's not bad. In fact, you might be the only one who might see it that way...I've spoken to your mom, and we have agreed between us that a soft return to Whitstable is the safest option.'

'A soft return? What...? Poppy, it's not like you to beat around the bush...'

'Well, actually...' Poppy laughed.

'STOP IT! You know that's not what I meant!' laughed Dorothy, a little uncomfortably.

'It means, you won't be here when your mom gets out. I'm sending you all to my ranch for the summer.'

'Your ranch? but...Oh my God, that's in bloody Kansas! Why...? Mum will want us to be here!' said Dorothy defensively.

'Your mother needs to take one day at a time. Let her get back, let her sleep in her own bed, let me take her to see John and Angela. If she comes home to see the man whose wife she killed, and the daughter she feels like she failed, then she could slip straight back into shit-town, Sugar!'

'I get it, OK? God knows, I bloody get it. But you have to understand that I have never really known her outside of that hospital cafeteria, so I've been looking forward to building a relationship with outside of those boundaries.'

'Dorothy, my beautiful girl, if stealing and reading your mother's diary has taught you anything, it should be that our Alice, for all her strength and resilience, is one fragile cookie.' Poppy reached over and plucked an auburn hair from Dorothy's mouth before giving her a toothy grin. 'Do you want her back to quickly bend? Or do you want her back for good?'

'OK, you win. I'll shut up. Just one last question,' said Dorothy as she smiled and looked up through her fringe. 'Does your place in Kansas have a pool?'

–

The journey to Kansas was as long as it was uneventful, and the rain that lashed upon the windows served as the soundtrack for the entirety of the flight. Dorothy hadn't said much. In fact, for the fifteen hours that she had been seated, only a fraction of that had been spent with earphones out. Her love of music came from her father and, like him, she had an eidetic memory. If she liked a song, Dorothy Brooking would know it inside out; artist, title, year...She had been listening intently to everything that eighties synth had to offer, as she watched her father play with Lachlan. The bond between father and son was obvious to see, and Dorothy felt distanced from them both. She had done since she had been forced to incite her mother's past. As much as she loved them both, they were both cause and effect of her downfall. Jacob's explanation had not given her any closure, although it had demonstrated to her how much he had changed; that bad people can change. Did that excuse his behaviour beforehand, or Evan's for that matter? Evan. The name stirred so many emotions within her. On one hand, she was undeniably the villain in her mother's story, yet Dorothy had only fond memories of her step-mother. She remembered the love, friendship and comfort of the woman who had saved her father from self-destruction. Dorothy was conflicted, and she knew that she was going to have to find her own way through the emotional maze that now encompassed her past.

'It's hot. Too hot,' said Dorothy as she breathed in the dusty air outside Kansas International. 'No-one told me it would be this hot.'

'It's mid-western States in August, baby, what did you expect, honestly?' replied Jacob as he tried to control Lachlan whilst also managing the majority of the luggage. 'Isn't hot a good thing?'

'Well yeah, but there's hot and then there's hot. And this is definitely the latter.' huffed Dorothy.

'Look,' said Jacob as he tried hard to understand his teenage daughter, 'I know you didn't want to come. I know you want to see your mum. I know that you did your best to ignore me for the entirety of the flight, and yes, I know that it's too hot-'

'But...' said Dorothy, without looking up.

'But, young lady, we are here regardless. So can we at least try to enjoy our holiday, try to enjoy the sunshine, and the break away from school, and work?'

'OK, boomer. Calm down, Jeez!' chuckled Dorothy.

'Boomer?! I think you need to wind your neck in, before I drop you back at the zoo where I found you!' smiled Jacob as he restrained a laugh, a laugh that felt genuine. Maybe he had needed this break away more than he could have cared to admit.

2

Fighting With My family
Kansas, Missouri, USA

Len Prince was not a man to be rushed. It was 2pm, and that meant tea time, and tea time was no time to be hare footed. He had watched the brunette pull up just short of an hour ago, parking right outside his gate with complete disregard for his procedures. He granted her a pass; it was hardly a busy hospital and the occasional new in-patient or release of someone that had served their term was all that passed by him each week. Wednesdays were different, of course, with laundry and food deliveries throughout the day. But today wasn't Wednesday, it was Monday, and on Mondays, Len had his tea at 2pm. So Len allowed her, in all his magnanimity, to sit outside his gate until he had finished his brew, it was the least he could do. He leaned back in his old leather chair, black duct tape holding the decrepit thing together as it creaked under his weight, and took another sip of his tea. Six security monitors stared back at him, nothing moving in any of them other than a line of static that continually chased the top of the units dusty frame. Nothing much happened here that required security of any kind, but Len had worked here close to fifty years, and it was a source of pride that he had manned the gates with little to no incident. He had seen young men and women dragged screaming from the safety of their parents' cars, as the iron gates opened like the mouth of a giant leviathan, and he had seen those heartbroken parents leave with the weight of the world hanging heavy on their weary shoulders. It hadn't been all bad, Len had met his wife here some forty years before; his beautiful Ivy. No other woman had touched his soul in the same way as his departed wife. Ivy had blessed him with three wonderful children who, in turn, had given him a litter of grandchildren. Len was full of gratitude for all that she had given him, and it was that sense of appreciation that stopped him from ever rushing anything; life was to be savoured, much like his tea. There had been whispers from some of the carers, who were far too polite to speak out loud on the matter, that Len Prince was past due his retirement. He could hardly disagree. There was a part of him, deep down in the recesses of his mind, that knew that the day he stopped getting up for work would be the day he died. His beautiful Ivy had died of cancer, but Len believed it was no coincidence that it happened only a few months after she retired herself. As much as he missed his wife, he wasn't quite ready to join her yet. After all, who would man the gate?

-

Poppy was nervous, and Poppy even on her worst day was never nervous, she didn't really have the mentality for it. Right now, though, her piss was running cold over the prospect of picking Alice up. The six years that Alice had spent in recovery hadn't stopped the two of them building an amazing relationship; one of complete trust, tenderness and understanding. Things were changing though, Alice was going to be home full time, not just for a long weekend or a day visit. They had enjoyed a number of mini breaks together the past four years, once her two-year mandatory sentence had ended, but this was the real world, a world that Alice had resolutely refused to re-join. Poppy had been running the gallery as best she could in order to finance Alice's continued stay at such a prestigious hospital, but the fees had hindered any growth the business might have had the potential for. She would say that she wasn't totally ready, which Poppy understood, but the money had started to run out and now, for the first time in a long time, Poppy was panicking about the one thing she had been longing for. It wasn't unusual to spend a perfect few days with Alice in high spirits, only to find her cowering under the bed in the midst of the witching hours. Escaping her demons had been a treacherous path at best, and it filled Poppy with such pride that Alice had found the strength to finally accept that she needed to re-establish herself in the world proper. Poppy only hoped that she had the tenacity to push through if she relapsed. Work, bills and parenthood to a hormonal teenager were a far cry from the world she had become accustomed to. This was a big step for both of them, and it was with no small amount of trepidation that Poppy sat waiting at the hospital gate.

'Hello...Miss,' said the security guard as he tapped on the car window with the knuckle of his index finger, a move that nearly scared Poppy to death. 'Sorry, you can't park here I'm afraid. Pick-ups only, and even then you would have to pull into one of the allotted bays.'

Poppy regained a measure of composure before slowly rolling down the window of her old Mustang. It was more a polite gesture than a necessity with the roof folded away behind her, yet it seemed rude to talk through the glass. 'I'm sorry, sir, but I am picking someone up at...Well, it was supposed to be half an hour ago now, but she's yet to emerge...' said Poppy as she smiled at the sweet old man, in admiration of the fact he had yet to retire from the rigmarole of his working days.

'No, you can't be picking up today, young miss. All our out-goings have gone for the day. No more pick-up's now until Friday I'm afraid,' said the security guard with absolute certainty. 'I don't know much my dear, but I know my pick-up and release schedules, as if my own hand had scribed the dates and times. Which of course is true, because they did.' he said with a playful smile.

'That doesn't make any sense...Alice said to get her today, I'm certain of it -' said Poppy in a confused panic.

'Alice, Alice...' said the security guard rubbing his chin with a wrinkled hand. 'Red hair?'

'Yes, bright red,' smiled Poppy, hopefully.

'Blue eyes? Tall and slender?' He nodded as he wagged his finger at her.

'Yes, bright blue, and a waist half the size of mine. Give or take a few stone that is,' joked Poppy with a smile.

'Oh yes, but she's long gone. Left after breakfast this morning, was in a focused hurry. I can't blame her after six years, do you know she was our longest...'

Poppy quickly cut him off uncourteously. 'What do you mean she's gone? What direction did you see her head? Why would she be allowed to leave on her own?' Poppy was flustered at the revelation and found her tongue running faster than her brain's ability to form coherency.

'Miss, I don't mean to sound bold, and please forgive me if I come across that way, but the lady you describe completed her compulsory stay here almost four years ago. We could not have stopped her leaving if we had indeed tried,' said the security guard with complete honesty 'Now, I should tell you, that it is not my place to inform you where our patients are heading. But since you seem unlikely to accept that answer, I will instead recommend that you heads towards the train station.'

-

'Where are you?' Poppy said angrily, phone pressed between shoulder and ear. The countryside passed by her at speed, as her concern for Alice dictated her pace. 'I thought I was picking you up?'

'Baby, please don't panic. I'm at the library, six years without a proper occult section hasn't made research any easier,' replied Alice, seemingly unaware of the panic she had caused.

'The library? So you're in Canterbury?' probed Poppy, relieved that her love was safe. 'What do you mean research, Alice? What's going on?'

'No of course not. Canterbury won't have what I'm looking for. I'm at Treadwell's in London, why? Where are you?' said Alice, still oblivious to the worry she had caused Poppy.

'Where am I? I'm looking for my bloody girlfriend, who told me to pick her up from the hospital, the same girlfriend who is off playing Harry-fucking-Potter somewhere in London!' snapped Poppy as her ability to rationalise her partner's actions began to wane.

'OK, I've fucked up, I get it. I just…need to do this, and quite honestly it's not worth me explaining because you wouldn't understand,' said Alice with a newfound conviction to her voice.

'Right… fine. I guess I'll see you when I see you then. You can let me know when you will be home, or not. I wouldn't want to interfere where clearly I'm not needed, or wanted!' said Poppy as she ended the call to only silent protests from Alice.

Alice did not want to upset anyone, least of all Poppy, but she had been driven these past few years by a desire to look deeper into her psychosis. It had not been a fruitless endeavour. 'Sorry, Miss? Can you help me?' Alice said to the lady who was slowly brushing books down with a vintage feather duster.

'I will certainly try my dear, what is it you need?' The woman looked as if she had spent her whole long life dusting books within the confines of this shop, and she had a kind face. Alice felt no fear in asking her the uncomfortable question.

'I'm looking for a book...it's old. Too old for me to afford I'm sure, but I wondered if I could just take a look?'

'Well, what is it called my lovely? I can't help you much without the title.' smiled the assistant as she put down her duster to concentrate on the new task at hand.

'Okay, this might sound strange, but I'm looking for the Necronomicon. It's the book -'

'The book of the dead...' replied the assistant, whose skin almost started to look thinner at the very mention of it.

'Yes, that's it. I'm surprised you have heard of it, if I'm honest,' said Alice, a little hope creeping into her voice.

'I know of it only because of my husband, Graham. He's obsessed with the occult. He has been to see it on display over in the States. Massachusetts or thereabouts. Tell me, please, just out of curiosity, what would a beautiful woman like yourself need with the book of the dead? It may be fiction, but it apparently it has a darkness within its pages that makes the night look like daylight.'

Alice noticed a change in tact from the assistant, as an almost defensive tone slipped into her voice. 'Honestly?' replied Alice, 'I'm just trying to make sense of a journey I have travelled, and the research has lead me here. Tell me, is your husband free?'

'He's pottering around in the back. I'm not sure how much he can help you, but he's there, same as always. Buried in the darkness of books that don't belong on the shelves of any normal bookshop,' replied the woman, as she raised a pale hand and pointed towards the back of the store. 'Just remember one thing...'

Alice listened intently, as she placed a hand on her arm.

'Whatever he tells you, if indeed he can tell you anything; it doesn't change the journey you have been on, or the lessons you took from it.' With that, she smiled a crooked grin that revealed tea-stained teeth, and returned to her feather duster. Alice smiled in reply and headed towards the back of the shop, unsure if she was doing the right thing, but too far into the process to stop.

-

For a shop no wider than your average London terrace, Alice felt as though she had been walking into its depths for longer than was physically possible. The size and shape of the walls seemed to become more erratic the further she went. It was one of the city's oldest shops, which was exactly why she had come; no Waterstones could have offered her the information that she so desperately desired. She ducked under a low beam, as she the ceiling came in low and the walls hugged her tightly, before it opened up in to a room with a sunken floor. The room held no windows, only tall bookshelves which seemed to lean in towards her. Each one was filled with giant tomes, that had clearly never felt the touch of the feather duster.

'Hello? Are you Graham?' asked Alice, as she took a seat next to an elderly man who was so deep in thought that he hadn't even registered her entry into the room. The man looked weathered from a life of obvious toil yet, as he looked up towards his young patron, it was clear that there was a sharp intellect still running the machine.

'You can't have it. Even if it was mine to give, which it is not.' said Graham as he put down a leather-bound book, etched with intricate silver.

'The Lesser Key of Solomon,' read Alice as she tilted her head to read upside-down. 'I'm sorry, sir, but you needn't worry. That's not the book I'm after.'

'I know it's not! What do you take me for? Do I look a fool to you?' snorted the man as he leaned forward to fully absorb his counterpart's features.

'No...no of course not. I'm here for...'

'The Necronomicon? Yes I know. And like I say, you cannot have it, even if it was mine to give.' said the old man abruptly.

Alice sat back in the old chair, the worn suede felt as though she was the latest of millions before her to sit upon it. 'How did you know it was that which I seek?' she asked, quizzically.

'You think to be the first who has been sent here by my wife? You think maybe that you are unique? I'm afraid you are not, and whilst I wish that I could give you hope, hope that whatever it is you have been through has a meaning or purpose, I can only offer you one thing,' said the man sadly.

'Please, anything you have will be more than I currently possess.' said Alice pleadingly.

'I can offer you only the chance to leave here with more questions than you entered here with,' said Graham as he reached for a small copper bell which he rung with well-practised gusto. 'And for that, we will need tea.'

-

'Does it exist? The book I mean?' asked Alice with curiosity.

'Two books exist. One a work of fiction written by the late HP Lovecraft, and the other that it is based upon, which is buried deep in the vaults of the Miskatonic University over the Atlantic. One is a dark yarn of demons and cosmic horror, the other is a gateway to places that regular folk cannot comprehend.' The old man had no doubt. He wasn't recalling old memories. He knew what he was saying, and he said it with the fear of a man who may very well have opened those pages.

'Your wife, sorry - I don't know her name...she said that you had been to see it, did you get to read any of it?'

'Tabitha? She has suffered by my side for close to sixty years now. Yet, she still seems to not know how to keep her mouth shut when it comes to my personal work,' Graham smiled, as if acknowledging that he wouldn't have her any other way. 'You cannot read the book my dear, although many have tried. Parts of it read like ancient Greek, certain words and sentences stand out more than others, old Gods and dead kings for example, but the rest is almost unintelligible.'

'Because of the condition of the book?' asked Alice eagerly.

'No, not at all. In fact, the book is somehow as if brand new. Bound in human flesh from centuries past and written in blood, yet it looks like it was written yesterday, the pages still warm from the violent etchings of madmen.'

'So what's stopping some fancy scholar translating it word for word? Surely there are people out there that can do that?' said Alice, fearing that she was only getting what the man had promised, more questions and fewer answers.

Graham smiled as his wife appeared and lay an ornate silver tray upon his desk. 'Thank you dear, would you like some tea? Alice, wasn't it?'

'Please.' replied Alice as she smiled at Tabitha, who quickly retreated to the front of the shop.

'The reason it cannot be translated is quite simple. Very few people can understand the ancient Sumerian that the rest of the book is written in, and the two that tried... well, they are both dead.' sighed Graham, as he passed over a bone china tea cup that was filled dangerously close to the top.

'How did they die?' asked Alice as she took a sip of the piping hot brew.

'Sumerian is a dead language. Who knows what they read? But it sent them mad. For ten years they scribbled notes on a thousand bits of paper, and not one of them made sense. Eventually they head to the coast down at Rhode Island and, without a word, they just walked into the sea. No bodies were ever found.'

'Oh my, that's awful. Have you managed to read their notes at all?' asked Alice, not expecting a positive answer.

'Tell me, Miss Alice, before we waste the day, what word is it that you are searching for me to say? For it would be much easier if we spoke freely here, within this speakeasy.'

'The Mirrorverse,' answered Alice, as she put down her tea and tried to put on her "business face".

Graham's eyes told of a sad story, as he thought of all the people before her who had asked the same questions. His chair groaned as he got up from his resting place. His body wanted to make the same noises, and his back cracked as he reached up onto the top shelf of the bookcase behind Alice. 'Entry into the Mirrorverse is something I would not wish upon anyone, and, if you have escaped the place, I would let it go. But if you cannot, then read this. You can't take it with you, but you can take your time reading it here,' he said, as he placed a hand on her shoulder before passing her a book of mossy green hue.

'It's real, isn't it?' said Alice as she clutched the book tightly.

'If you are asking me if have I seen it, I would have to say no. I can neither confirm or deny its existence within our world. What I have seen though, is a hundred women like you, looking for the same answers.' Graham said, as he took his seat beside her once more.

Alice looked at the book in her hand, *The Realm of the Dark Queen*, she read aloud in her head, as she looked at Graham. 'What do you know about it? Is there anything that has been shared by these women before me?'

'I only know that it is a place, much like our own, where mirrored versions of our flesh and bone are inhabited by older, darker beings. Beings who do not die, just transfer to another body with each vessel's decay. I know that they are malicious, and wicked with a passion for slipping into our own world via the minds of the broken and beaten.' Graham took a long sip of his tea before he looked back up at Alice. 'But what I also know is this; they are all just words on a page, the ramblings of mentally- ill or abused women who are sensitive to the things that I don't quite understand. Like a medium who talks to the dead, I don't understand it, but it doesn't mean it's not real.'

'Thank you. Both of you. Are you sure you don't mind me reading a little?' said Alice as she clutched the book to her chest.

'Of course. Take your time, just be careful. Understanding your demon is one thing, but you can too easily give something access to your mind by leaving a door open, and that is something I do not want for you.'

Alice watched Graham open his own book, before she opened hers and silently began to read. *In the beginning there were four. One who would create, one who would destroy, while the others, they would laugh.*

-

The Palette ranch was a truly beautiful thing to behold. Untold acres of land stretched out into the Kansas flats, with only the haze from the rising sun that baked the dirt beneath stopping you from being able to see the curvature of the earth. The beauty was equally matched by its grandeur. Dorothy had settled quickly into her place by the pool, and it was unlikely she would be moving too far from her sun spot any time soon. Next to her lay an open copy of the Grimm Fairy Tales, its pages rustling playfully in the faint breeze whilst condensation pooled at the base of her iced tea. Her auburn hair was tied into a loose plait that trailed the length of her back and contrasted with the white of her summer dress. She sat upright with her hands upon her knees as if meditating upon some great mystery, her eyes pressed firmly closed. On first viewing it would be safe to assume that she was in a place of calm, but Dorothy's mind didn't work that way, it never had. She was uptight and frustrated by her inability to understand why they were here, now...of all times. Six years she had waited to spend quality time with her mum, six years of having nothing except a relationship built on letters and phone calls. Yet, instead of fronting the welcoming committee, she was here; slowly burning in the mid-morning sun. So, she sat and bit her tongue and wished that she was back home. Poppy had given them a list of places to visit whilst they were there, but she saw no real reason to leave the poolside. After all, she was already angry at the world, at least here she was isolated. She tried to control her breathing as she battled within herself. It wasn't as if this was a horrible place to be. In fact, at any other time she may well have been infatuated with the rustic charm of the place, but this was not any other time, this was here and now. Dorothy opened her eyes to the shriek of a hawk that swooped down majestically right in front of her. Its talons opened wide as it fell quickly from the sky in a failed attempt to catch a small lizard, who had been minding its own business upon the stone wall surrounding the pool area. She watched in wonder as the hawk beat its wings frustratingly in an effort to gain altitude once more, angry at its wasted attempt. She imagined that things like that happened every day in a place like this, but to Dorothy it was all very new and exciting. Her heart was happy for the little spiny lizard, but her mind told her that maybe the hawk had a nest of chicks to feed. That was Dorothy's problem; she never stopped thinking. Her teacher and her family had often watched her drift into fantasy when she was supposed to be focused on some important task. She decided to leave some food out for the hawk a little later, for if Dorothy understood anything, even at her young age, she understood life and death. Her mother's diary still burned into her mind, the collection of books had opened her eyes unto the ruthless nature of the world. Feeding the hawk would not change much in the scheme of things, but it would make her feel a little better, and that was enough for now.

'You know you can't sit out here forever, Dotty. You got to start socialising sometime,' said Jacob as he joined his daughter by the pool. 'I mean, if you're gonna sit here all summer then I might as well have sent you to a spa back in Blighty.'

'I wish you had, Dad, and stop calling me that. I'm not a child anymore, contrary to popular belief.' Dorothy was done playing the child in this family, she didn't need wrapping in cotton wool, and she wasn't afraid to let everyone know.

'OK, I get it. No, you're not a kid, and you don't need your old man telling you how to live your life anymore. Is that right?' said Jacob as his heart broke a little more.

'Yeah that's right, so I'm going to see out this week and then I'll get a flight back home to see my mum, if that's OK with you!' Dorothy's question was of course rhetorical, and her sarcastic tone only hurt Jacob more.

He thought about cracking down on her, as he knew his own father would have done many years before, but he knew that wasn't the way to break through to Dorothy. She was far too stubborn, a trait she had inherited from her Grandpa John. How he could use his father's guidance right now. Jacob had been missing him more with each passing year and with Dorothy rebelling, it was becoming harder to manage his own mental health once again. 'Do you know what I miss most?'

'Surprise me,' said Dorothy, who had returned to her state of meditation.

'I miss my best friend. The one you used to be before this defensive teenager appeared a few years ago, wanting to fight everything that I put before her. I miss you, my Dotty, who didn't hate me for wanting to protect her.'

'Protect me? Is that what this is? Who, and what exactly, are you protecting me from, DAD?' spat Dorothy with anger, as she uncrossed her legs and spun round to face her father.

'Of course it's you I'm protecting! You think I've brought you out here for your mother's sake? What if she's cold towards you, or overwhelmed? I don't want that affecting you. She needs to be given time to adjust so that your reunion is as harmonic as possible, and I don't need to worry about you being hurt, this has never been about anything else to me, and if you believe differently then you are a fool,' said Jacob.

'So I'm a fool am I? That's what you're saying?' Dorothy stood up to her father and gritted her teeth with frustration.

'Don't you dare, young lady, sit your arse back down before I start treating you like the child you proclaim not to be.' Jacob could not believe his daughter's audacity, and tried to retain composure throughout the conversation.

'Oh, go to hell. I don't need this crap,' said Dorothy as she shook off the hand of her father, as he grabbed at her walking past.

'Dorothy, get back here. We need to talk about this...' said Jacob, aware that she had already gone. He slumped down upon the sun lounger and listened to Dorothy destroy her bedroom before hearing the door slam behind her. She couldn't go far, the land around them was all owned by the ranch. He would let her cool off and then, hopefully, find a way to reconnect with her. *What's the worst than can happen?* thought Jacob, as a familiar voice echoed around the back of his mind.

3

I've A Feeling
The Mirrorverse

Dorothy would not be dictated to, or told how to act. Yes, she might have been a Brooking, but the blood that ran through her veins was pure Petalow. Like her Grandad, John, she knew her own mind. The wind kicked up around her ankles; grit and sand stung her bare legs as if it was angry at her. She felt a little like a witch, as if her foul mood was dictating the weather's aggressive nature, especially since it had been glorious sunshine only a few minutes ago. Surely a man as smart as her father understood the need she had to be with her mother at such a time. After all, he was a resolutely family-orientated man himself, and had never shied from that fact. The storm kicked up a notch as she growled with discontent at her situation, Jacob would never let her leave early and very well she knew it. A gust of wind nearly exposed parts of her that a young lady ought never to have on display, causing her to continue her journey at more of a waddle, compared to the power-walk that she had been maintaining. A second gust nearly took her footing as she felt herself lift away from the ground ever so slightly. The wind back home never felt like this, even on the coast. Sure, there were days when it was pointless to go out with your hair down, but never days where she felt the traction torn away from her feet. Dorothy felt the pressure change dramatically, both her ears popping in unison as the howling wind turned into a sudden and violent roar. She stopped in her tracks as it became apparent that, in her haste to escape her father's bullshit excuses, she had lost her bearings and was now in a place where there was little protection from the elements. She scouted the area from whence she came; the ranch and the group of buildings, that had been of no insignificant size, had all disappeared from view. In fact, it was quite evident that almost everything was now out of sight, as Dorothy realised all too late that this might well be the beginning of a tornado. Sand was thrown into violent funnels that surrounded her, as if she were a spider flushed down a bath plug, leaving her all but blind to everything but the most immediate of structures. To her right she could see the beginnings of a tree line, but whether she could make it there without being picked up from the safety of the ground beneath her, well...that was a question she had neither the time nor the courage to answer in that moment. She sprinted as though the Devil himself chased her, and she made it to within a few feet of a bank of huge oak trees before the wind picked her up again. This time, it was as if she were a snowflake in a hurricane. Inches quickly became feet, and without any power to fight such a force, she was quickly turned upside-down and thrown back down to the ground, where the only thing that welcomed her was the warm blanket of unconsciousness.

-

It was the screeching that woke her. Like an old steam train slamming on its emergency brakes, the noise almost ruptured her eardrums as it sounded out at indiscriminate intervals. Dorothy rubbed her eyes clear as she tried to sit upright, and her head felt as if it was spinning on all points of the compass at once. How long she had been unconscious for was a mystery. She didn't remember blacking out, only the storm throwing her to the ground as it continued to thunder around her.

You don't get wind like that in Canterbury. Dorothy thought to herself, as she looked around to find her bearings. The ground beneath her was rough stone, and dust whipped about her violently, obscuring her vision. The screeching came once again, and she looked to the skies to see three giant bird-like creatures, circling about her like vultures. *They can't possibly be the source of that noise.* She covered her ears and watched their giant shadows grow ever larger upon the floor. Then, the screeching stopped, as did the dust-storm, and Dorothy was able to take stock of her new surroundings. Stained glass littered the ground around her, pale light refracting off the dagger-like shards of red and yellow. Her best guess was that this was some sort of church. The roof had long since disappeared. Perhaps the storm that had brought her here had also torn the lid off of this old building. Truth be told though, Dorothy had no idea how she had got here, or even any idea where "here" was. This certainly did not look like Kansas anymore. Dorothy staggered backwards, as the screeching resumed, much closer and more aggressive than before. She turned to face the source of the noise, and her eyes struggled to make sense of the sight in front of her. 'What...what are you?' she asked, not expecting any answer.

The creature perched atop a broken pew, much less a vulture than a beaked gargoyle. It pondered upon Dorothy with childish curiosity. It ruffled its obsidian feathers, as its curiosity turned to hungry desire. 'Wat is you?' It snapped, through a razor sharp beak. Cold beady eyes looked straight at her.

'You looks like no Monkay I know before.'

Dorothy struggled to find any words with which to answer the giant bird-creature. The thing reminded her of a pelican...that is, if pelicans were the size of pterodactyls. 'You can t-t-talk?' stuttered Dorothy as she tried desperately not to show any fear, in a situation where screaming felt like the only appropriate reaction.

'Is you food? Is funny Monkay food? For us?' squawked the creature, sounding not unlike a parrot repeating its most heard phrases, as it was joined by its two brethren.

'No! I am not bloody food!' shouted Dorothy. 'Why on Earth would I be food, you big bag of feathers?'

'Bag of feathers?' replied the first vulture.

'If Monkay no food, what is Monkay?' croaked the second, with a raucous cackle.

'Monkay look like food to me...' said the third, smaller, fatter creature as it picked something red out of its beak with a talon the size of Dorothy's forearm.

'I. AM. NOT. FOOD!' repeated Dorothy, as emotion started to get the better of her. 'I need to go, I need to find...'

'What Monkay then?' said One.

'What Monkay need?' crowed Two.

'Marinade!' cackled Three.

Dorothy instantly turned to storm away. 'I need to find my dad, and you three idiots are not helping me in any way.'

'What help Monkay need?' Two said, as it hopped from one pew to another, trying to catch up with Dorothy as she reached the entrance to the church.

'I need to know where I am, and how I got here!' snapped Dorothy as she showed a fire unbeknown to most fourteen-year-old girls.

'Wheres you is...is here...' replied Two.

'Hows you gets here? Different for all Monkays,' chimed in Three, as it started to cough up the bones of a previously devoured meal.

'This place, is home. Neither there, neither here, but somewhere,' squawked One as it jumped onto the seat opposite Dorothy. 'Monkay come, Monkay go. But Monkay before not had fire on top.'

'Fire on top? You mean my hair?' said Dorothy as she placed a hand on the bright locks that rolled over her shoulder.

'Monkay before...no fire.' said Two.

'Monkay before was food,' followed up Three, as it regurgitated what looked like a small human bone. 'Monkay before, fell from sky too. Not land so well.'

'Maybe fire protect Monkay?' mused One.

'You ate them? Those that came before me?' asked Dorothy, as she stepped back towards the doorway. Her heart raced as the reality began to sink in. She had no idea where she was, whilst creatures that could not possibly exist spoke broken English to her. She was scared, she was alone and she needed her Dad. 'Fire...Yes, fire protects Monkay!' Dorothy fumbled as she pulled the band out of her hair and swished her hair around like a lions mane, instantly causing the flock of murderous vultures to panic and hop backwards. With that, Dorothy ran out into the open, shirking an opportunistic snap from one of the creatures as it's beak tore a hole in her dress. She saw a dark wood just a short distance away and instantly made for the safety that the trees would provide in such close formation. As if on cue, the heavens opened once more, and Dorothy felt her Converse slip with every footstep. The creatures instantly took to the sky and bore down on her position with ravenous intent.

'Monkay no escape us,' One cackled.

'All Monkay try though!' said Two.

'Make them taste good...' screeched Three as it swooped down, like a bird of prey that had set its sights upon a rabbit.

Dorothy stumbled into the treeline as brambles and thorns tore at her ankles. She hadn't the time to search for a path now though, and the direct approach would be the only one that kept her alive right now. Her lungs burning, she risked a look behind her as she pulled herself tight against a huge oak tree. To her amazement, the creatures were hopping about on outskirts of the wood, biting and snapping at each other as they bickered about whose fault it was that they had lost their quarry. 'Not so tough now, are you?' spat Dorothy as she fought back the tears, her anger overshadowing her youth. 'You big bags of feathers!'

'Monkay think she funny...' said One.

'Monkay no laugh long,' concluded Two.

'Oh, I'll laugh, alright!' called Dorothy, as she turned to look into the darkness of the wood, unaware that a thousand beady eyes were peering right back at her.

'Maybe Demon will laugh with you.' said One as it took flight.

'Maybe will throw us the Monkay bones,' said Three, as it joined its brethren in the air.

'Comes back tomorrows... Monkay won't last the darks for long,' howled Two, as the trio finally retreated back to church ruins.

Dorothy stepped further into the woods and eventually found the remains of a broken-down path. It was uneven and the broken stones were sharp, but it was still better than fighting through the thicket. The further she pushed on, the darker it became, and she realised quickly that the trio of murderous birds had not entered these woods for a reason.

-

Dorothy walked on for what seemed like hours. The only reason that she knew she was headed in any sort of direction was the fact that she hadn't encountered any turns or junctions. She was scared, and she desperately wanted her father to find her. Why had she been so angry at him? All he had ever done was love her and care for her. They had been the best of friends, and now she had hurt him. All he had wanted to do was protect her and her mother so that one day they might be able to build a relationship. Dorothy hated herself for pushing him away, and the fear that she might not see him again in order to make things right was progressively creeping over her with every step. The sun was almost completely obscured by the canopy of leaves above her, and it was becoming increasingly difficult to keep herself on the path without tripping over debris.

Who are you? said the voice, out of nowhere, it's sound resonating from all directions.

Dorothy spun on her heels and looked for the origin of the voice. The voice had sounded not unlike her mothers. Although the tone was a bastard mix of seductive and animalistic, like the monster under the bed that tried to coerce you to slip your leg out of the quilt.

I asked you who you were child, I won't ask again.

'My name is Dorothy...Dorothy Brooking,' she answered with a resilience that defied her tender years. 'Now, who are you and why are you hiding from me?'

Brooking? You are the child? My...you have grown haven't you? Actually, the more I look at you...Yes, I can see it, I see your mother in you.

'You know my mother?' asked Dorothy as she searched the darkness.

Once...a long time ago. We don't talk any more, said the voice almost disheartened by the admission.

'What? No...you're her, aren't you? My mother's mirror demon?' Dorothy tried to stand firm, but the pages of her mother's dairy kept flashing through her mind. She knew what this demon had done to her mother, she was under no illusions as to what it could do to her.

Is that what she called me? The mirror demon? She always did have a vivid imagination. How is your mother? Still alive?

Dorothy could not see the creature, but she was well aware that it was licking its lips as it spoke. 'I'm not scared of you. My mother beat you, and so will I.'

Your mother beat me? Did I not convince her to kill your precious Evan? Does your father feel like she beat me, when he's sitting alone at night crying?

'SHUT UP!' yelled Dorothy as she stepped forward, refusing to be scared by what was only a voice in her head.

NO

The creature placed a decaying hand upon her shoulder. Its tongue, black and forked, licked the side of Dorothy's neck as she found herself frozen by shock. You taste just like her, it whispered Now please, if you would... I need to work up an appetite

'What...what do you need me to do?' sputtered Dorothy.

Run, of course, child.
Always RUN!

4

A Mother's Torment
The Mirrorverse

Dorothy's heart felt like it was going to explode. She had never run so hard, or for so long, without seemingly taking a breath. She had found this place; cottage to some, stone shack to others, within a clearing in the wood. Even in such darkness it had been an easy spot; a gap in the canopy shone a glimpse of light on to the thatched roof, as if a dimming spotlight had been set to guide Dorothy straight through the front door. She slumped against the old wooden frame, a heavy iron bolt keeping her safe, at least for now. She could still feel the creature's cold touch upon her shoulder, it's acrid breath still tainting the air in her lungs. When she had first read her mother's diary, Dorothy had envisaged the demon in her own mind and, so far, she had been pretty spot on. Her mother's description had clearly been an accurate depiction. As Dorothy began to catch her breath, she pushed herself up and resolutely looked through the small latticed window. Dorothy fell back instantly to the floor and scrambled further into the cottage. It had been standing there, just outside the clearing, almost dubious of stepping in to the light of the setting sun. Dorothy searched desperately for something to use as weapon, while she was thought it was unlikely to find a shotgun sitting about, anything would be a boon right now. She pulled a heavy poker out of the fireplace and swung it about herself like a sword. Its tip pointed, and its weight was noteworthy. It would help, although just how much, she was unsure. Diary accounts of her mother physically fighting the mirror demon were rare, within Dorothy's memory at least. No part of this felt imagined to her though, as she searched for somewhere to hide. Her heart continued to pound in her chest and Dorothy feared that, regardless of where she hid, the demon would locate her from her heartbeat alone. She quickly moved about the stone building, realising that the tiny space had very little to offer in terms of security for her life. The place was filthy, spiders crawled the corners of each wall, mould and cobwebs adorned the peeling plaster, and the dank stench of death hung in the air like low-lying fog. A single bed sat in the corner, no sheet or pillow to make it a place of comfort, stained black and mouldy from neglect. The kitchen, complete with an ancient cast-iron Aga large enough to cook a pig whole, was littered with rotten meat and the mulch of composting vegetables. Maggots writhed upon the counter, as if disturbed by her presence in their space. A raven lay dead in an ornate birdcage that hung from the ceiling like a French oubliette, whilst the fireplace where she had found her weapon looked to be filled with ash and the bones of children who had failed to escape the demon's grasp. Dorothy threw up as she realised that what she thought to be an ashen log was actually a child's spine that lay upon the dead coals. Her throat burned and her eyes filled with tears as she realised that she was in real trouble here. She needed her Dad, and part of her was still hopeful that he would burst through the door and save the day. But he wasn't here, and she was alone. She ran over to the huge cooker and climbed inside the oven. It's grease-filled basin reeked of violence and murder, and she quickly felt relieved that it didn't seem to be a working oven any more. She closed the grated door behind her and clutched her iron poker as she peeked through the tiny vent in the door. She could feel something moving around her, among the grease and discarded meat. Dorothy wanted to fall to pieces, but she held firm. Her need to survive becoming more pressing than the scream that was all the harder to supress when the oven door burst open, the metal bolt magically dissolving as if had never existed.

I don't remember inviting you in to my home, growled the demon as it stood in the doorway.

Dorothy could see it now, a replica of her mother, yet it looked like a version of her mother that had been dug-up from the grave. Its hair was dirty and blackened, only hints of her fiery red crown still visible. Alice's crystal blue eyes had been replaced by the soulless blackened pools that only a creature from the very depths of hell could possess.

Where are you, child? You think you can hide from me, here, in my own world? I can smell you, your fear, you panic. You are not the woman your mother was.

Dorothy did not allow herself to breathe. The creature may have looked frail, it's limbs elongated and atrophied, but it reeked of supernatural power. Its teeth were razor sharp and its nails supplanted by long black talons.

*I have lived for a thousand lifetimes, child. I have devoured the hearts and minds of all those that I have blessed with my touch. You believe you are special? You think I haven't gorged on the hearts of other children just like you? I have seen worlds that exist outside of time. I have seen galaxies collapse as primitive beings like yourself bow down in front of masters greater than you can comprehend. I am the offspring of C'thiolkez. I was born into a darkness that you will never know, a place where the very concept of light does not exist. So, if you think you can hide from me, if you think I cannot see you hiding from me, **YOU ARE WRONG**. You are a pinprick* of light in a bottomless void, and I will drag your soul across the heavens so that you may be judged by those I deem worthy to say my name...'

'Get away from me!' screamed Dorothy as, all in an instant, the creature was at the oven door, talons ripping the thick metal plate from its hinges, as it bent down and smiled at Dorothy. Its smile widened as it hissed at her, its black forked tongue moving from side to side like a serpent in an attempt to seduce and hypnotise. Dorothy without thinking, lashed out with the iron poker and drove it through the demon's mouth.

The demon staggered backwards, gripping the poker with both clawed hands as it made a choking noise. It ripped out the iron rod and vomited both blood and bone onto the floor. You cannot truly hurt me, child. I told your mother the same thing. If you fight me, you might be able to delay me entering your head for a time, but that's it. I have survived the birth of civilisations-'

'Then that's what I'll do' said Dorothy 'You are not welcome in my head" She was shaking with fear as she climbed out of the oven to confront the demon.

But Dorothy, I'm not in your head. I was merely resting, contemplating, building my strength, you obstinate child. You came in to my world. The demon lurched forward and took Dorothy's head between its hands. For all her strength, Dorothy cried out in fear as she awaited the jaws of the creature to snap shut over her face.

You cannot fight me. But thank you, you will taste all the better for trying.

The creature's jaw opened wide enough to consume her head entirely and, at that moment, Dorothy knew she was going to die. To her surprise, though, as she awaited the razor sharp teeth to pierce her flesh, something else happened. The creature's body had been parted in twain as the woodsman's axe was brought down with extreme prejudice upon its head. In one motion its body fell quivering to the floor, black blood flowing out like an oil spill. Beyond the carnage, and still holding the axe, was her mother, beautiful and vibrant as every picture Dorothy had ever had of her, but with one difference. This Alice, this version of her, had no mouth. No opening at all, just another two inches of perfectly-toned ivory skin. 'MUM!' shouted Dorothy as she leapt in to her arms.

'Mum, where's...' Dorothy was cut short as Alice bought a finger to the place where her lips should have been, as she nodded at the demon and shook her head. She pulled Dorothy over to a dusty pile of children's clothes and began to search through the remains. She soon seemed to find what she was looking for, and with that, Alice pulled Dorothy out through the door, axe still firmly in hand. Dorothy looked down at the demon as she was hauled out of the cottage, and saw the one thing she had been dreading – the two halves of the beast, knitting themselves back together.

They moved quickly for an hour. Alice knew that she had not stopped the demon for long, and they needed to get out of the woods. Dorothy stayed quiet and followed her mother's lead until they reached the edge of the treeline, where they almost fell on to the sharp rocks of the canyon path. Rocks that stood at least twenty feet high surrounded them on each side, as a fast-running stream seemed to be the only way ahead. Dorothy collapsed by the edge and drank its clear water. She mused that just a few short days ago, you could not have paid her to drink from a natural stream, yet as she collapsed in to the fresh water, blood and grease washing off of her skin, she realised that nothing had ever tasted better.

'What happened to you, Mum?' asked Dorothy as she finished washing the blood of her mother's face.

Alice stared at Dorothy with sad eyes as she held up a finger to emulate the number one. Dorothy nodded in understanding as her mother motioned for her to undress. She pulled a white summer dress and a longline red hoodie out of her satchel.

'OK Mum, thank you' said Dorothy as she stripped off the rotten clothes and threw them to one side. The cold wind bit at her flesh as the sun finally dropped beneath the horizon. After slipping her socks and Converse back on, she turned to face her mother and saw that she was holding up two fingers now. 'OK, what's next?' Dorothy asked.

Alice put her hands together and motioned to sleep, before pointing to a small cave in the side of the rockface.

'OK, we sleep. I'm not about to argue with that.' said Dorothy, as she yawned and pulled the hoodie up around her ears. 'Then what?'

Alice pointed downstream and looked at Dorothy with un-resigned hope.

'What is it Mum? What aren't you saying?' said Dorothy realising, with a smile, the folly of her words. Alice looked about her and found a jagged stone loose about the stream bank. She started to draw something. Was it a dog? No...it looked more like a wolf. 'Wolves, that way?' asked Dorothy as her mother held her hand high. 'Big wolves?'

Alice gave her daughter a look which told her everything she needed to know; downstream was the only way out.

5

Finding Dorothy

Kansas, Missouri US

The local sheriff had found Dorothy unconscious in the remains of the derelict church. The building was a remnant of a time when the old Oaklake ranch had been much smaller, before that Tennessee family had come and bought up all the land. The sheriff didn't mind young Miss Palette, he just didn't agree so much with her sexual proclivities. Sheriff Brenan Wolfe wasn't a bigot by any means, he was just very old fashioned, as were a lot of people in this one-horse town. If Miss Palette wanted to court women, well that was her business, he just thought she could be a little more discreet about it. She had been living in England the past six years, with only occasional visits back to Kansas, so care of the property had fallen to her aging father who lived in the smaller estate down by the river. Ben Palette was a quiet old man who only left the safety of his home when the stock cars were in town for the speedway. He used to play a little football with Brenan when they were kids and, although he had never voiced it out loud, clearly shared the sheriff's misgivings on his only daughter's behaviour at times. He hadn't even know that this British family were staying until he had received the call from central, exclaiming that a worried father couldn't find his daughter after a small cluster of twisters had torn quickly across the state. Mr Brooking spoke of witnessing the most violent storm he had ever seen, and while Sheriff Wolfe knew that storms in Kansas were not to be over-exaggerated, ultimately this had been a drop in the ocean. Still, the young lady was out cold, and he hadn't wanted to move her from the recovery position until the EMT's had arrived, despite her very shallow breathing. There was no external damage, bar a few twigs in her hair, and certainly no blood seemed evident. Whilst this was certainly a positive, the sheriff had been doing this job long enough to know that there were many shades of grey between black and white; no indication of blood-loss did not necessarily mean there was no serious injury.

Worried about a potential head trauma, the ambulance crew had taken Dorothy to Stormont Vail hospital, in the city. Jacob had joined them on the journey and held on tightly to his daughter's hand the whole time. The senior EMT could not see any reason why Dorothy would still be unconscious, and with no signs of injury to her physical self it was hard to take an educated guess as to exactly what was wrong. He was hampered by a lack of equipment in the ambulance and would need a CAT scan to confirm any of the more outlandish theories that he had considered.

'You will need to wait outside, sir. I promise she is in good hands, but we can do our job better if we are focused on your daughter and not you,' said the nurse as she almost tackled a distraught Jacob into the waiting room the very second he tried to set foot into the ER.

This is all too familiar, thought Jacob as he once again found himself looking at the walls of a hospital waiting room. 'I need to know she's going to be OK...I have to know that I'm not going to lose her.'

'As soon as we know more, you will be the first person we communicate that information too. It doesn't look like there is any reason to panic just yet, her heart rate and breathing are well within the safe parameters.' the nurse used a reassuring tone to follow up her strong opening statement.

'You must understand, I nearly lost her mother in an emergency room many years ago, and then eight years later I lost my wife to a team of medical professionals who claimed that they could fix her. So don't tell me that all looks good. Don't tell me that there is no need to panic, just tell me that she is OK when you are able to do so, with no medium of doubt, For now, allow me the freedom to panic and worry until that time!' said Jacob forcefully, but without malice.

'Of course Mr Brooking. Please take a seat, and I'll send the doctor out the second we know more.' With that, the nurse disappeared through the plastic-screened door to leave Jacob to his thoughts.

Well, we have been here before old friend... said the calculated voice in the back of his mind, as he fell backwards into the chair, disappearing all at once into the void.

-

Jacob awoke gasping for air and clawing for purchase, except the arms of the chair were no longer there for him to hold. The waiting room had been transformed into the cold, clinical confines of an operating theatre. He sat bolt upright on the surgical bed and choked as if he had been underwater, whilst lights above him flickered on and off sporadically. He must have fainted, he thought, a nurse must have put him in here. How else could he have relocated without noticing? After rubbing his eyes and finding some composure, he swivelled round to the side of the bed and placed his feet gingerly upon the floor as he tested his balance from one foot to another. His head was swimming and his lungs burned still. Jacob drew deep breaths,, as if he had just come out of the womb. With a final blink, the lights above him failed, and the warm glow of the green emergency light flickered into life. The room and adjoining hallway now looked to him like the haunting corridors of a sea-life centre. Jacob made to move forward but stumbled and fell into the doorway, his legs not yet ready to take his full weight. As he fell into the corridor, instantly bracing himself against the wall, it became apparent to him that he had absolutely no idea which part of the hospital he had been placed into. With no signage to guide him, and seemingly no staff either, he was going to have to find a way back to reception on pure intuition. His only two perceivable options were left or right, yet both directions were bathed in darkness and, give or take the occasional glow of an exit sign, they looked identical. Why would the lights be off at all? Had they put him in some rarely used wing and forgotten that he was here? He didn't care for the reasons why, but not knowing how long he had been out for had left only one thought in his head; find reception and get to Dorothy. The choice was made for him as a noise, not dissimilar to a fog horn, roared down the corridor to his left. The noise almost brought him down to his knees as he felt pressure thundering down upon his ear drums. Jacob staggered to his right, moving away from the sound as quickly as his poorly functioning legs would take him. He removed his hands from the wall and covered his ears as the horn continued to assault his senses; blood seeped through his fingers as the deep bass of the horn's roar took its toll upon his flesh. Then, as if it sensed that he had made his choice of direction, the horn stopped and complete silence greeted him once more. That was of course, outside of the painful ringing that continued in his ears. Jacob felt sick, the noise had affected him right down to his stomach. What could possibly make such a sound within the confines of a hospital, and why would any such piece of equipment exist here at all? Jacob couldn't fathom the answers to such questions, and instead refocused his attempts to find the reception desk; all that mattered was Dorothy and her wellbeing. His legs seemed to find a rhythm as he picked up his pace a little. The disorientation he had awoken with was slowly leaving him with every step, yet, with every green-lit door he passed, no signage or sign of life greeted him, only darkness and silence. It all looked the same, it all looked...

Fear started to sink deep into Jacobs gut, he had experienced this feeling before; to be here but not *here*, to be in a dream, yet wide awake. The more identical doorways he passed, the more panicked he felt, for if this was here...here within his own subconscious, then It would be here, too. The lights blinked back and forth once more before finally coming back to life, and with that, Jacob again found himself surrounded by bustling nurses, and patients waiting to be helped by over-worked doctors. Jacob fell back against the wall as his senses were once more thrown full circle, his equilibrium tested beyond his capabilities to stand upright.

'Are you ok, Mr Brooking?' said the same stern-faced nurse who had forced him into the waiting room.

'Yes, I think so, at least...I'm not sure how I got here is all...' said Jacob as he took in his surroundings once more.

'I brought you here about an hour ago, do you not remember, Mr Brooking? Would you like me to get a doctor to see you? You have been through an awful lot today,'

'No, I'm fine. I just need to see my daughter, has anything changed? Can I see her?' asked Jacob as he suddenly remembered his focus once more.

'You can see her, but there is no change as such. Dr Ross will want to see you first, is that alright?' the nurse said, kindly.

'Yes, yes of course. Lead the way,' replied Jacob, as the ringing in his ears resumed again and a trickle of blood dripped from his ear.

-

Jacob sat listening to the consultant's theory on why his daughter wasn't responding but, ultimately, it was lost on him. The science just didn't seem to add up. If the senior medical staff were having to theorise, then how could he hope to understand? She was, by all accounts, in perfect health. Her breathing and heart rate were normal, whilst her bloods had come back clean, which ruled out a spider or rattler bite. She was, technically and medically, fine, yet she would not wake up. Of course, Jacob had seen this all before; Alice had dipped in and out of psychosis both during and after their relationship. Her eyes would glaze over as if she was in a daydream, and any sudden noise would shake her quickly back to reality. The doctor suggested that perhaps there was a hereditary bond between mother and daughter. Yet Dorothy was not snapping out of it at all. Due to her eyes reacting to light, they believed it to be some form of locked-in-syndrome, which put her under the category of coma, rather than a psychotic episode. Jacob only nodded occasionally as he let the consultant drive the conversation forward, until the lights once again started to flicker unto a spark-filled conclusion that left the room in total darkness as the bulb exploded above them. Jacob fell to the floor as he brought his arm up to protect his face from the shattered glass raining down upon him, his skin began to bleed from multiple, tiny, lacerations. He stood to assess the state of the room, and the darkness enveloped him again. Jacob realised that, once again, the green glow of the emergency lighting above the rooms exit was all he had to go by. He turned to check that the consultant wasn't injured in any way and found the man that he had been speaking with but a moment ago was now completely changed under the different light source. Where once there stood a man of no great stature, of only average height and weight, there was now a giant beast. He towered over Jacob, as trunk-like muscles tore the seams of the doctor's lab coat. Would that have been the biggest change in the consultant's image, Jacob warranted that he might have dealt with it all a little better, but where once there had been the balding head of a man, there were only giant tentacles now. Viscous and shaded like the colour of petroleum, all oily blues and garish greens, the two that protruded from his sleeves were long and intricate, as if formed to be used as hand, although much longer and wider than would be of any use for human equipment. The head of the creature, an appendage that gave the impression of some kind of oceanic fluke worm, opened up into an flower-like maw. Jacob fell in reverse, collapsing through the double doors as the haunting apparition pushed aside the heavy oak desk as though it were a polystyrene prop. It moved slowly toward him, not quite as though it was savouring the moment, more that it was just a simple puppet too slow to pick up on the commands of its master. Jacob shuffled backward towards the far side of the corridor, his legs kicking frantically as the tentacled monstrosity drew ever closer, its gigantic mass scraped the woodwork as it crouched under the doorframe to reach Jacob's feet. His heart pounding, and each breath that he took felt painfully short of what he needed to survive this situation, yet, as the creature came within touching distance...nothing happened. Jacob had seen things over the course of his life that would drive many men insane, oceanic leviathans that had ripped him from his own slumber, shadows that moved and spoke like puppets with no master in sight. Jacob knew that this couldn't be real...could it? The creature pulled Jacob to his feet as a father might pull up a naughty child, the mucus that covered its leathery skin gave off a sickening odour that had Jacob struggling to breathe without feeling as though he was about to empty his stomach. It was the stench that made this all too real for him, he could taste its scent. It rolled around the back of his throat, almost choking him with its foulness. The creature released Jacob as he found his footing, he could find no eyes within the creature, but its snub nose was quivering as if it was locating him through scent alone. With a groan, the giant creature raised what would have been the doctor's left arm, a tentacled finger outstretched as it pointed to a door at the end of the dark hallway. The mannerisms of the creature were not lost on Jacob. He could see all too well that this horrific thing had only one desire, and that was to kill Jacob where he stood, but something bigger and more powerful was guiding this creature's actions. Jacob didn't need any more direction. He pushed himself flush against the wall so as to head where he was clearly being directed. The door had looked to be over a hundred yards away when he first started, but within three steps he found himself already pushing through the swinging doors, unable to remember his approach towards them. His soul shattered at the sight of what lay in front of him.

'Evan, no...please don't do this to me, not her. Anyone but her...' cried Jacob as he ran over to his dead wife's side. She was lay, spread-eagled upon a cold steel surgical table. Her body had been cut open and pinned from womb to ribcage, yet she looked at Jacob with eyes full of life.

'Baby, is that you?' Evan reached out as much as her broken frame would allow and took Jacob's hand into her own.

'It's me, my love. I'm here, I have you,' whispered Jacob as he brushed a hair off her brow and kissed her forehead. 'I know this cannot be real...but I never thought I would see you again.'

'Baby...what have they done to me? Why can't I feel anything below my chest? I watched them put things inside of me, and now I can't feel anything anymore,' said Evan, unbridled fear in her voice.

'I'm not sure, my love. I don't know how you got here.' said Jacob with a stutter as he observed the steel pins that held her skin fast to the table that she lay upon.

'You do know how I got here,' said Evan, her tone switching instantly from fear to anger. 'You let this happen. You let Alice do this to me. You broke her, and she punished me!' Her voice was almost a screech as she pulled her hand away from him violently. 'YOU DID THIS!'

'Evan...no. No I could not have known this would happen. I did everything right, I told her about us. I divorced her, I married you, I did the right thing!' pleaded Jacob as he stepped back, unwilling to look inside the gaping black void where her innards should have been.

'You took her unborn child's life, then raised a daughter that she never knew she had, as if you were a single parent. All before falling in love once more with the very same woman you had broken her heart for in the first place,' Evan spoke the truth. Jacob could deny none of the accusations that she threw at him. 'You did everything right...by Jacob. Your narcissism has no end, and your justification for destroying lives has only ever been self-motivated-'

'I did it for you! It was all for you and Dorothy,' said Jacob, as tears began to choke him. 'It was only ever for you!'

'THEN WHY AM I HERE?' screamed Evan as blood exploded from her voided stomach, like a hot geyser erupting. The ceiling and walls were quickly covered in dark visceral fluid that, within seconds, had coated every inch of the room, including Jacob's voiceless self.

No words were coming to the fore as he watched Evan's back arch until it snapped violently, her head dropped to the side, and the screaming finally stopped. The last of the blood ran out of her like an overflowing sink. Jacob could not find the courage to look at her, yet somehow his body acted as if independent of free will, and he found himself staring back into his butchered wife. This time though, he saw no organs, no blood, nothing. Only darkness, as if there were a portal to another realm inside the empty cavity of his dead wife. Jacob could not stop his own movements; he was being controlled by unknown forces, compelled to explore the void that confronted him. His mind screamed for him to stop as his body slowly started to climb onto the blood-slicked operating table. Jacob could not have foreseen the things he had witnessed today, he never could have believed that he would once more fall so heavily into his own psychosis. All of that paled, though, as he unwillingly lunged forward into the vacuum that had been created in Evan's broken body, and his world fell once more into darkness.

6

Pack Mentality

The Mirrorverse

Dorothy had slept in her mother's arms the entirety of the night. If she hadn't already been sure that this wasn't Kansas, the deep snow that she had awoken to had confirmed it. Her breakfast may only have been an apple and some stream water, but surviving the night with her mother by her side made everything all the sweeter. They had been walking for what seemed like hours, yet Dorothy had not seen the sun's position move once since breakfast; not that it meant much in a place of talking vultures and immortal demon spawn. Dorothy mused that the sun probably behaved as haphazardly as everything else here. Alice set the pace, her bright red hair danced in the wind as the impromptu winter storm continued to batter them. Alice had argued, as best a woman with no mouth could, that Dorothy should take the lead, so that she could keep her eyes on her. Dorothy had rightly argued that, not only did she not know the way, but if something was to happen to Alice, it was not as if she could scream for help. So, it would be Dorothy who kept an eye out, whist her mother forged a way for them through the snow. The stream had begun to freeze over, and it's symphonic crackle became the soundtrack to Dorothy's journey. Alice turned on her heel and indicated that they would rest once they reached the ridge up ahead. Dorothy had quickly become accustomed to communicating with her mouthless mother. She still couldn't understand what had caused her lips to seal over; Alice had spoken in her diary of finding her voice, and how that had come only with courage. Dorothy watched her bound from rock to rock with the wood-axe still strapped to her back, and she could not imagine how this wonderfully strong woman could be considered anything but courageous. They reached the ridge, whereupon Alice instantly uncoupled her axe and dropped her satchel to the ground. Now was their chance to rest and rehydrate, and Dorothy gratefully accepted another apple as she dropped down on to the large boulder. That was when they heard the first howl.

They crept along the ridge line, keeping their silhouettes low and their scent against the wind. Alice couldn't put her finger on it, but she knew something was wrong. They stopped by the lip of the ridge and peered over a basin some hundred acres across, where the stream turned in to a lake and the source of the howling presented itself.

'Fuck!' said Dorothy, instantly drawing a slap from her mother and a glare that needed no words. 'Mum, they're not wolves - that big one was at least twelve foot tall!'

Alice looked on, trying to figure out what was missing from her equation. The largest wolf sat atop a large mound, overseeing the pack, whilst three more drank from the lake. Their fur was snowy white to perfectly blend in to the surrounding terrain, all except one, and both Alice and Dorothy noted that the beasts were all stained with blood, no doubt from the piles of massacred elk and deer whose bones littered the clearing. Panicked, Alice pulled Dorothy's face around to look at her.

'What is it, Mum?' she whispered, trying to keep her voice as low as possible. Alice held up four fingers and pointed at the wolves.

'Four wolves, I see that,' said Dorothy as she tried to understand. Alice then put one finger to her brow and then held up five fingers.

'But...you thought there were five of them-' said Dorothy under her breath as she staggered backward. The smallest of the wolves, still about ten feet tall, approached Alice from behind, it's blue eyes shining brightly against the snow-washed landscape.

'Alpha, I found them trying to flank our perimeter. I'm still not sure what they are, but they look like her...the Gorgon.' the wolf whispered the last two words as if to be heard mentioning that name would summon her forth.

'They are not like the Gorgon, Beta. But they are Hooman. The Alpha stood up to its full height and stretched, the hairs on its back all standing on end until it shook itself back to life. Its size was immense, and the beast bound down from its plateau and walked over to its new catch. 'Hoomans, meet my Betas. Betas, meet my daughter.'

The giant wolf circled Dorothy with a certain degree of caution. This Jacob-wolf had eyes of green so bright that an almost alien-like glow emanated from his stare. He bought his nose down to Dorothy's level, recognising her scent as his own, his snout almost as long as Dorothy was tall. He circled once more before stopping in front of them both.

'Dad? How could this be?' asked Dorothy as she bravely stepped forward, an act that caused the two flanking Betas to motion defensively. Jacob gave them both a look of assurance, albeit one that may have been steeped in more than a little threat. They recognised their Alpha's tone straight away and instantly dropped down to their bellies; they knew not to challenge his decisions.

'*She* is the reason that this can be. *She* is the reason I am trapped here,' Jacob snarled at Alice as the heavens thundered. The resonance within his voice caused Alice to drop to her knees in fear. Saliva dripped from the Jacob-wolf's mouth as if eager for his next meal.

'Don't you dare, Dad! That's Alice, that's my Mum! How would she be the reason that you are here?' said Dorothy with a growl not dissimilar to her fathers.

'Here? HERE?! Trapped in the body of a feral beast? Here, following my baser instincts to kill on sight? You don't understand "here", and because of that you will not understand the why,' the Jacob-wolf brought his eyes down to meet Dorothy's. 'Give me one reason to spare her life.'

'Dad, this isn't you. My father understood the concept of a journey. My father knew, with heart and reasonable thought, that the things my mum did were never to hurt him.'

'Reasonable thought!' growled Jacob 'She took that when she took Evan away from me. Now I am driven by instinct alone and, if you knew me, or know your father like you claim you do, well then, you would know that when I run on instinct - people get hurt. Delta, take her down.'

'Dad, what can I do? Tell me, please?' Dorothy stepped bravely forward and placed her hands on her father's nose. 'It's me, Dad. I know that you can feel our bond. Help me, what can I-' Dorothy hadn't even finished the question before the smallest wolf knocked Alice to the ground, pinning her to the surface with one giant paw.'

The Jacob-wolf closed its eyes and let out a sigh that caused the snow to steam around him.

'Delta, sit!' said the Jacob-wolf as Delta, without question, instantly obeyed to release Alice from her oppression. 'She's here you know...' said Jacob as he spun slowly around to sit, facing the same way he had started.

'Evan's here? Where? Why can I not bring her back to you?' asked Dorothy, as she searched for an angle that would enable her to save her mum's life.

'In the forbidden mansion, across the Murder Plains. Can you bring her back to me? Many have tried, my pack was once a hundred strong. She is not as you remember. The Gorgon has more in common with the demon in the woods than the Evan I knew and loved. Tell me, why do you think you have a better chance where so many have failed?' asked Jacob as he yawned.

'Because I know she has missed me as much as I've missed her,' said Dorothy as she stepped forward toward her father's giant paw, his fur soft between her fingers.

The Jacob-wolf looked deep in to Dorothy's heart, his eyes almost hypnotic. 'Fine, it would appear that the fates have brought us together for a reason. Delta will go with you.'

'But my lord, the Gorgon...she will end me...' yelped the smallest wolf.

Without blinking, another Beta leapt upon him, forcing him instantly to the ground, two massive paws pinning him down, as he had pinned Alice. 'You question the Alpha again, and I will end you myself, you pathetic whelp.' Dorothy realised, as she listened to the creatures fight, that all of the Betas were female and, clearly, the warriors of the pack.

'Beta, release him, he's no good to me torn to shreds. Delta, she needs a guide, so...guide her. Dorothy, the mute stays with me, do you understand?' said Jacob not looking for an answer.

'Yes, Dad, I understand' said Dorothy as she walked over to her mother. Dorothy helped her back to her feet and hugged her tightly. Alice looked at her daughter pleadingly, but she knew that her stubbornness would overthrow any argument. 'Goodbye, Mum' whispered Dorothy, as she turned to walk away.

'Dorothy, if you do not return by the rise of tomorrow's moon, I will take her as my own, you understand, don't you?'

'I'm going to bring her back, Dad, so your threats mean little to nothing.' said Dorothy as she once more place her hand upon his giant paw.

'Don't dally then my child, time is against you.' said the Jacob-wolf. 'And Delta...you come back all together, or not at all - do you hear me?'

'Yes, my lord. Of course.' replied Delta, fully aware that he would probably never return.

-

Delta had never let anyone ride him before, and in his meagre existence he had met very few Hoomans. It was not an issue; he may have been the smallest of the pack, but he was still the size of a shire horse, and having someone smaller than him now part of the pack was actually a refreshing change. The Hooman had chatted away politely, not asking him anything that he might have found intrusive. Mostly it had been about Alpha, but there was only so much that Delta knew about his origins. Alpha had united all the wolves of the Mirrorverse in to one pack, all the other alphas had fallen under his fangs. That was the limit of his knowledge on the origins of Alpha. Well that, and his lost love. Legend had it that before she was changed, the Gorgon and the Alpha were once in love. Delta had heard more than most as, being the smallest, the others would often pay him no mind as he sat in the background of every pack meeting. The Gorgon had been like the Alpha's conscience, she had taught the Alpha that he could forge his own path. Then, she was gone; taken by the mute. Now the Alpha was again slave to his feral nature, his baser instincts driving him to kill needlessly and dominate any mate of his choosing. That was the only version of Alpha that Delta had ever known, but this little Hooman was the only other one to seemingly halt the Alpha from doing what he was created to do.

7

Older & Wiser
Whitstable, Kent

A week passed, before Alice was ready to meet her parents again. Poppy had organised a luncheon at the Petalow's, with John and Angela eager to finally see their daughter as a free woman. John had struggled to understand the wait, but Alice had needed time to adjust to a world that had grown around her absence...at least that's what Poppy had told them. The truth would have sounded much more callous, and they didn't deserve to hear it. Poppy was applying what little make-up she wore whilst she watched Alice from the mirror. She hadn't even bothered to start getting ready, she just sat, as she always sat, surrounded by books. Her mind was made up, and nothing that Poppy said could convince Alice otherwise; she believed that a second universe, a much darker mirrored version, had bled into her own mind, and that the mental breakdown she had suffered was actually the result of a demon version of herself that had haunted her. Alice had spoken of these fears, long before the incident that left Evan dead but, back then, it was just something that she murmured about in her sleep. Now, it was an obsession - one that had taken over both of their lives. The books that were open upon the bed today all looked older than the two of them combined, and the bedroom had begun to smell like an old library, complete with the forlorn musk of unwashed shelves and dusty book sleeves. Her current theories on this "Mirrorverse" were far-fetched to say the least and Poppy had struggled not to be condescending in her appraisal of the situation. Unlike most Tennessee folk, and despite her strict conservative upbringing, Poppy had never believed in God, or even religion in general, so believing in this mystical second universe was never going to happen. Poppy's belief that life was finite, that once you were gone you were truly gone, was the reason that she enjoyed her life so much; each day precious, each day potentially your last. It was what had made the past six years so very difficult for her as she knew, without doubt, that Alice was the one for her, yet, she felt that each day she had been forced to wait was lost, with no promise of a tomorrow. There had been times when it had all become too much, her bags had been packed and the flight had been booked. Her skin missed the warm kiss of the Kansas sun, but something had always stopped her from getting in the taxi. It had been tough, knowing that Alice could have left the hospital so much sooner, and that her love voluntarily chose to be apart from her. Poppy knew that in reality, she was all that Alice had. Sure, her parents loved her, but they were retired now and it would be too much to ask them to run the shop. Jacob, understandably, could barely speak her name, and Poppy knew that he had been fighting his own demons since Evan had passed. Poppy now considered Jacob one of her closest friends; she had sat up many a night with both him and Dorothy as they tried to manage their new life with young Lachlan. She wept for the pain that she could see in his eyes, for she knew that Jacob, once the man of a hundred broken hearts, would likely never love again. Dorothy, on the other hand, wanted nothing more than to talk about her mother, as all young ladies do, and Poppy was happy to do so once Jacob had, rather uncomfortably, left the room. Alice had wanted to protect her daughter as much as possible over the course of her sentence and extended stay, so she had limited their contact to written letters and eventually Skype calls, once her stay had become voluntary. Dorothy was a fiery kid for sure, but the empathy she showed for her mother's plight was what had strengthened Poppy's own resolve when things had been tough. She wondered what Dorothy would make of this fantasy that Alice had created, her own love of Tolkien, Lovecraft and Arthur C. Clarke had worked to create a little girl with a hugely vivid imagination. Poppy wondered if it were best she resolve this avenue of exploration before the Brooking's returned from Kansas.

'Sugar, are you going to get ready or not? We have an hour to get to your parents and although they are only a short drive, I know it takes you longer to get ready than me, and I am ready to rock,' said Poppy as she turned to face Alice, who was still buried in the depths of some ancient chaos bible.

'I think I'll just go as I am, I don't really think my parents care what I look like.' said Alice without even looking up from the dirty yellow pages.

Poppy walked over to Alice and pushed the book away from her in order to get her full attention. 'No, they probably don't care, but I do. After six years of dressing in comfies, would it kill you to put a dress on, love?'

Alice looked up into Poppy's dark brown eyes and gave something close to a sigh of derision. 'OK, fine. I'll get dressed up, but when we get home I need to finish these passages.'

'Passages?' sighed Poppy as she ran her hand through piles of hand written notes that littered their bed. 'Alice, this has to stop. I didn't wait all these years for you to return home, just so that you could be lost in another fantasy.'

'You don't believe me, do you? That there was a driving force behind my actions? God, I knew it! When I thought you were listening, you were just laughing at me-' snapped Alice as she attempted to pull all her papers together into organised heaps.

'Does it look like I'm laughing at you? Or anything that's going on right now? Alice, I just want to help!' said Poppy as she tried, and failed, to take Alice by the hand.

'Well, you can help by going through all this with me. Help me find the answers that will complete this picture. Baby, I need you, don't you see?' Alice pleaded.

Poppy sat down on the bed, a move that panicked Alice into quickly moving her ordered mess of paperwork. 'When was the last time you heard a voice?' she asked as her eyes dropped to the ground.

'A couple of years, if I'm honest, but what does that matter in the context of my beliefs?' replied Alice, cautious of saying anything that might weaken her argument.

'It matters because, after years of therapy, years of refining your medication, and years of physical and mental well-being coaches, you still believe that this place exists. You were being treated for severe mental illness, and the treatments for that were extremely effective. Has it not occurred to you that, if you were right, then the voices wouldn't have stopped?'

Alice stood up and waved a fist full of notes in Poppy's face. 'No, what if the medication is blocking the signal? Or what if the Mirrorverse works in cycles related to the other planets or something? You can't tell me that you have all the answers, Poppy, because I know full well you bloody don't.'

'No, I don't have all the answers, honey, none of us do. But what we do have are a few simple facts that lead us towards one very obvious conclusion,' said Poppy as she stood to face Alice, afraid of the direction this conversation was taking. 'You cut your own throat Alice, you tried to kill Dorothy, and you took Evan's life.'

Alice almost collapsed from the shock of this straight-talking outburst from Poppy, and placed her hand on the bedside unit in an attempt to balance herself. 'It wasn't like that, it...'

'It wasn't your fault, Alice, and I am not saying it was. You were very ill and that's why you have gone through so much these past few years,' said Poppy as she braced Alice by the shoulders. 'You have to stop trying to find something to absolve you of the blame, that's not what you need. And it's not what Dorothy will need upon her return.'

'Then what do I need?' whimpered Alice as she fell into Poppy's waiting embrace. 'Tell me, help me.'

Poppy kissed Alice on the side of the head as she wrapped her arms tightly around her. Protecting her love was her only intention, as indeed it had been from the very start of the discussion. 'All you need, all you have ever needed, is to forgive yourself for what you did whilst you were unwell. No more, no less.'

-

John sat upon his old cast-iron bench and stretched himself over its rusty green back, feeling his spine crack not once, but twice, as he reached his arms above his head. He was feeling old, in mind, body and spirit. Yet here, at the end of his well-kept garden, he still found peace of mind. It had always been a source of mild amusement to him, considering what lay beneath, that this was the one spot that offered him clarity of thought. He watched Angela as she danced between the dahlias, she hadn't aged a day in the ten years since she had quit full-time work, and John loved her now more than ever. Some people faded when they retired, that was certainly how he felt, yet she had blossomed into something more wonderful than he ever could have hoped for. It was Angela, in her infinite wisdom, that had made him promise to remain calm in the face of Alice's impending arrival. She had thought of everything, including how easy it would be to overwhelm their little girl if they all jumped on her the second she walked through the door. He couldn't fathom what his Alice had been through. He may have spent a brief time in the cells at Colchester, after punching a gobshite Paratrooper back in the mid-seventies, but two weeks in isolation was hardly comparable to six years in a mental hospital. Granted, the last couple of years had been in open holding, but he still worried what it might have done to her mindset. Alice Petalow, his beautiful Alice, may well have been discharged from the hospital deemed no longer a danger to herself and others, but John knew that there was a big chance she would come out as a different person entirely.

'Hi, Dad,' smiled Alice, appearing as if from nowhere. His daydreaming was becoming an increasingly worrying issue as the years started to mount.

'Oh, Poppet, it's so good to have you home.' said John as he lifted himself up to meet her. John was still a big man, but he could see Alice weighing him up as he reached in to hold her.

'How are you Dad? You look well...a little slimmer, are you dieting?' asked Alice with an air of concern.

'No of course not my little love, you know how I feel about all that nonsense. Still the same three square meals a day that I've had since I met your mum, all those years ago,' laughed John as he held his daughter tightly. 'I'm just getting old, and it seems that Old Father Time speeds up the process with each year that passes. How are you feeling? Tell me, be honest.'

Alice joined her father as he sat back down upon the bench with a groan of aching muscles, John gave a quick wave to Poppy as she danced about the garden with his ever-youthful wife. I'm OK, Dad, really I am. It's just an adjustment really, having to cook my own dinner and such, but Poppy has helped immeasurably.'

'I have no doubt about that. She is, by a long shot, the best thing to ever happen to you.' said John with a wry smile.

'Apart from Dotty, you mean?' said Alice, knowing full well that he did.

'Obviously, apart from our little Dorothy. Have you spoke with her? She's eager to start this journey with you. She has become quite the young lady, and we are all very proud,' said John as he pushed his shoulder into Alice.

'I must confess, I haven't yet, but we have agreed to meet her at the airport. Poppy tells me that she is top of all her classes at school, as well as captain of the Lacrosse team, so it's nice that we have that in common.'

'Yes, but she plays defence, unlike you used to. She has a fiery side that is matched only by her rebellious nature...' smiled John.

'Well, that she must get from her father and own good self,' laughed Alice as she took her father's hand in her own. His grip still dwarfing her own. 'Dad, I need your help, and I need you to speak of things that I know you never have before, can you do that for me?'

'Well if I can help, then of course. But let's give this a little context before I commit,' said John with a little trepidation.

Alice took a deep breath before releasing his hand as she turned to face him. 'I know that you have killed. Being in those kind of situations was a part of your job for so long that it would be stupid of me to think otherwise-'

'But...' said John, fearing the worst part of this conversation was yet to come.

'But...have you ever killed someone, or hurt someone, that you were not ordered to?' asked Alice.

'You're struggling to deal with the guilt of Evan's death, and that is a completely normal thing, it shows you have a conscience,' replied John as he avoided a direct answer.

Alice looked back at her father with only love. She wanted to let him know that this was a safe place, because she knew that you did not get the Viking King to open up by squeezing him with pressure.

John looked down at the bench and swore he almost felt his own father glaring up at him. 'I did something once, that no man should ever have to do. I still, to this day, some forty-odd years later, cannot wash the blood stains that have endured from my skin,' John almost instinctively turned his hands over, as he had done a million times before. His giant paws bore the testimony of a man who had worked hard his whole life. Creases ran like dark trenches across every inch of his skin, tiny scars littered his arms from the very tips of his fingers unto the joint of his shoulder. 'I cannot tell you if what I did was right in the eyes of God. I can only tell you that I broke the law, despite the fact that every jury in the land might well have believed that my actions were justified.'

Alice waited, to make sure her father had finished before she asked another question. 'Have you forgiven yourself?'

'No, and I'm not sure I ever will. There was a line that I crossed. No-one made me cross it, no-one except me,' sighed John, as he looked back up to his daughter who was listening intently, eyes wide open, and her beautiful red air gently flowing in the summer breeze. 'But what I learned a long time ago, is not to let that guilt dictate the rest of my life in a negative way. I grew, I adapted, and I found a better version of myself on that journey.'

'I'm not sure I can do that, Dad. I'm trying so hard. God knows how I can ever look Jacob in the eye again...' said Alice as her heart began to sink once more.

'The only thing you can't do is bring Evan back. Everything else though, is within your power. You never meant to hurt anyone. Christ, I was there when you were born, and since that day you have struggled to even swear without blushing. You could never willingly hurt anyone, it's why you were so rubbish at defence when you played for Canterbury,' smiled John as he put his finger under her dropping chin. 'You never thought you would forgive Evan, or Jacob for that matter, but you did, and do you know what?'

Alice just looked at her father, as tears started to slowly fill her eyes.

'She would forgive you now, if she could, and Jacob already has. When you see him, at the airport, he will seem sad. He will seem like a husk of the man you once loved yourself, we notice it each time we speak with him. Yet he never talks of blaming you, only of how much he misses her,' said John as he pulled his daughter into a hug so overwhelming that she knew he was telling her the truth.

'I'm sorry I put you through all this, Dad,' cried Alice as she sobbed into his arms.

'Poppet, you have nothing to apologise for. I wouldn't change you for the world, neither would Mum, or that beautiful girlfriend of yours,' said John as he kissed her repeatedly upon the crown of her head. 'Now enough of this sad talk, this is a happy day. Now, go and tell your mother how she hasn't aged a day, unlike your old man.'

8

The Gorgon

The Mirrorverse

The mansion was huge; like Wayne Manor in those comics her dad used to read, and it stood out to Dorothy like a sore thumb in the rocky plateau. Her wolf, Delta, had become more subdued the closer they had got, and now they were within touching distance, he didn't want to take another step.

'What are you so afraid of, Delta? Can she really be so scary for a huge wolf like you?' asked Dorothy as she climbed down off the back of the giant beast, ruffling his mane as she spoke.

'See, young Hooman, look not at the walls, but the grounds that surround the great building,' said Delta as he gently pushed Dorothy with his nose. Dorothy poked her head out of a stony crater that had become their hiding place, and looked at the gardens surrounding the mansion.

'Those are just statues, right?' Dorothy asked as she gasped in horror.

'No, young Hooman, they are my kin, all sent to retrieve the Gorgon for our Alpha.'

Dorothy counted at least fifty wolves, each as big as the last, and all turned to stone in what looked like the middle of some epic battle. Some of them were reared up on two legs, giant paws ready to pin down their prey. Others had their front ends to the ground, teeth bared and haunches flexed, ready to drive them forward. Dorothy wondered if they had died where they stood, or if they had been positioned and presented to ward off potential visitors.

'Miss Hooman, I cannot go any further. I am sorry' said Delta as he lay upon the floor.

'I understand,' said Dorothy 'this isn't your fight, and I appreciate you bringing me this far. Will you wait for me?'

'Of course, I cannot return without you, my life would be forfeit to the Alpha,' said Delta as he began to chew on his own leg.

'Then, I promise that I will return with you.' smiled Dorothy as she once more ruffled his mane of black fur.

'Miss Hooman?' said Delta as he watched her turned to leave

'Yes, Delta?' replied Dorothy as she stepped out of the crater.

'Don't look her in the eye, promise me you won't!'

'I promise.' assured Dorothy as she scrambled over the top. Her confidence came from the knowledge of one thing; that, whatever she had become, Evan could not be any worse than the mirror demon.

-

Dorothy would never understand this place; The Mirrorverse, as her mother had named it in her diary. The sun had been high in the sky for fully twenty-four hours, yet the second she stepped over the threshold of the mansion, everything turned to darkness. Surprised to find the door unlocked, she peered down each corridor, one to each flank, a large hall opened up in front of her, ending in a massive double staircase that wound off both left and right. She quickly realised that this was true darkness, the occasional beam of moonlight breaking through the giant windows seemed only to cast more shadows, causing her to fumble on her way forward, and she took baby steps as she passed through the main hall. She hadn't the courage to call Evan's name just yet, preferring to scout the lay of the land before she announced herself. That was, until she was met with a sound that chilled her to her very soul. Dorothy had never heard a spider scuttle before, in fact she doubted if anyone ever really had. Yet, what she could hear was definitely a giant spider walking down the adjacent hall, and it was headed in her direction. As her heart began to race at the prospect of meeting a creature that she was petrified of in all its normal dimensions, she looked into the shadows for somewhere to hide. There was no shortage of darkness and it covered everything like a blanket, but Dorothy could not guarantee that whatever was approaching her could not see perfectly in the dark. She made for the huge double staircase in the centre of the hall, from the top of which she could observe undercover, whilst also having visibility of the ground floor from the balcony. Once again, she realised that she had been forced in to a situation where she was out of her depth. As she tripped over the top step, she quickly found a place to crouch that, in her mind, might make it more difficult to be picked out by sinister eyes. Dorothy peered through the gloom and watched as the broken moonlight picked at the silhouette of her approaching stepmother, but something was drastically wrong. The shadow upon the wall was of the arachnid whose sound had plagued her ears, it's bony aperture at least twelve feet high and barely fitting in to the mansion's giant hallway. It's movements robotic and jerky, each step out of sync with the last. Dorothy hated spiders, but the creature that the shadow portrayed was not what caught her off guard. As the entity rounded the corner and entered the foyer, it was apparent the shadow was not a true reflection of the subject that owned it, for it was Evan who was illuminated by the moonlight, and she looked more radiant and beautiful than ever. She walked elegantly into the room, whilst her spider shadow jerked aggressively behind her. Her golden hair draped down in curls around her waist, her perfect body dressed in an all-black bodysuit that made her appear almost naked within the darkness that surrounded them. She stopped, with her shadow pinned perfectly behind her, the silhouette of eight giant legs giving her a monstrous appearance at odds with her almost divine form.

'I recognise your scent, yet it feels like many lifetimes since it has graced me with its presence,' said Evan as she slowly started to ascend the staircase, ever closer to Dorothy's location. 'Is it really you, little one? It must have been a thousand years.'

'It's been six, and we have missed you in every single one,' replied Dorothy, unwilling to give her position away, yet unable to resist answering her.

'Time passes differently here my beautiful girl. I must confess, I have longed to see you grow up, to see the woman you would become.' Evan took each step as if she were savouring the time between them both. 'As glad as I am to have you here, Dorothy, you should leave while you still can. I am not the woman you remember, I am not like anything you have ever met, and I cannot promise that it will end well for you here.'

'You do not know who I have met and dealt with lately,' replied Dorothy with moxie. 'I'm not scared of you, Evan, no matter how many legs your shadow has.'

'You mean the Alice-thing the lurks in the woods? That horrid looking thing has never stepped foot inside my house. Ask yourself why, can you figure that out young lady?'

'I guess she's scared of you,' said Dorothy as she watched Evan's spider shadow continue to follow her up the stairs.

'Scared? I'm not sure that basic bitch knows what scared means, but she is at least smart enough to know that her powers are pale in comparison to mine. She is old, I'll give her that. Has she given you her famous "I've watched galaxies burn" speech?'

'She has,' replied Dorothy, as she backed in to the shadows, 'and I believed every single word.'

'Well while she was watching, it was I who was destroying. It was I who was burning, AND IT WAS I WHO GAVE LIGHT TO THE DARKNESS THAT VOMITED THAT ABOMINATION INTO THE UNIVERSE!' Evan boomed.

'So...you are evil like her? Merciless and hungry for the souls of the innocent?' asked Dorothy as she watched Evan and her shadow finally reach the top of the stairs. At this range Dorothy could see that, as beautiful as Evan was, her eyes were the same blood red as her long, sharp, fingernails.

'No, not like her, or that sea-beast that follows your father. They live only for evil, for petty hurt with delicious ends. I'm different. I have the ability to feel all of your human emotions, I can feel loss, and yes, I can feel love' said Evan as she slowly approached Dorothy's hiding spot. 'But do not be misled, mortal lives mean nothing to me when considered from the beginning of time; I could kill a billion souls just to prove the point that it changes nothing in the balance of the universe.'

Dorothy backed down the aisle, the shadows helping to hide her physical form. 'You know of the demon that follows my father?' she asked, falling in to an open bedroom.

'It is a primitive creature, not much older than your own pathetic race' said Evan as her spider-shadow entered the room before she did. 'It is one of the many children of Mobihtz, the Great Devourer. It is a simple creature that thrives on hate and fear. It rarely kills, and if does, it's often by accident.

'Well it made my dad sick' said Dorothy as she found her way in to the en-suite, knowing full well that Evan was right behind her now.

'Your father...' Evan paused briefly as she thought of her long-lost love. 'Your father should have been stronger.' said Evan as she drew closer.

'You made him stronger. He never recovered from losing you,' spoke Dorothy kindly.

'Does he still talk of me? Of us?' asked Evan as she put her hands on the door frame of the en-suite.

'Why do you think I'm here? Why do you think he sent an army of wolves to retrieve you? challenged Dorothy.

'To kill me, I think you mean!' snorted Evan with derision.

'You don't believe that do you? You were worshipped by my father, and you always will be,' Dorothy knew that she was trapped now, as she turned to the mirror that faced the entrance to the bathroom and awaited her fate.

Evan looked past Dorothy and saw her face in the mirror. 'You really have turned in to the most beautiful young lady haven't you? But I warned you against staying.'

'I thought you said you were not all evil, like the mirror demon that torments my mum or the kraken that weighs down so heavy on my father?' said Dorothy as she saw the reflection of Evan staring back at her. Her golden hair moved in the air as if by its own accord, her ruby eyes held the nightmares of the universe within, yet her beauty was such that even Dorothy, a thirteen-year old girl, felt compelled to drop to her knees in mortal worship.

'I am not like them,' repeated Evan, 'nor am I any better. You should have escaped whilst I presented the opportunity. Do you think I move so slowly for my other prey? I have given you a chance, rarely given and best not wasted.'

'Dad needs you. Mum needs you. For God's sake, Evan...I need you!' cried Dorothy as her heart began to pound and her eyes welled at the thought of her imminent demise. 'I will not leave this place without you.'

'Then you will die, my little love,' said Evan with sad certainty, her spider shadow now taking up the whole room, as it grew in both size and power.

'So be it!' shouted Dorothy as she closed her eyes and turned to wrap her arms around Evan. 'If I am to go, I am at least glad I got to see you one last time, Mumma Evan.' said Dorothy as the darkness came over her.

-

Dorothy walked out in to the mansion's garden, the summer sun baking down as she joined Evan upon a picnic blanket. Her spider shadow was gone, and only her pupils were still the colour of blood that previously her whole eye had been. Evan was pouring tea from an ornate china pot, whilst two faceless servants like mannequins, featureless and smooth, brought plates of miniature sandwiches and cream scones.

'I wondered when you would wake up little one, how's your head?' asked Evan as she took a delicate first sip of her tea.

'What happened? Am I dead?' asked Dorothy as she slowly sat upright, her head dizzy as if she had been spun about.

'Do you feel dead? I think not my child. Good Lord, you are beautiful. The light is certainly your ally,' said Evan as she pinched Dorothy's cheeks together.

'Why am I here? I was ready to die, what changed your mind from killing me?' Dorothy asked as she cautiously accepted a plate of cucumber sandwiches from Evan.

'Maybe the overwhelming thought that a being as ancient as myself could actually be wrong in matters of the heart,' said Evan as her attention was drawn to a noise in the bushes. 'Maybe Jacob wasn't trying to kill me with his little army, maybe I have wasted years out of stubbornness that could have been spent repairing my allegiance to the wolf. Years though, that seem such a short period of time when you are immortal, young Dorothy.'

Dorothy looked about her surroundings, the stone wolves only serving to make the vintage garden appear more gothic. 'All I want is for my family to be back together. I can't tell you how much we have all missed you. Honestly, I don't know what this place is, and frankly I don't care, all I know is that you are here, and my mum too...'

Evan halted Dorothy mid-sentence and rose up majestically. Her arachnid shadow instantly reappeared upon the ground and spread over the entirety of the lawn 'WHO ARE YOU?' she bellowed with a supernatural power that shook the very air. 'Come forward, and I may spare your life!'

Delta crawled out upon his belly from the safety of the hedgerow. The second he became fully exposed he rolled on to his side and relinquished to Evan. 'Be merciful, Gorgon, please be merciful. I am only here to guide the young Hooman, I meant no harm.'

Evan's blood-red eyes filled with black tears that quickly streamed down her face, like inky mascara.

'Lachlan, my son! I had no idea you were here!' exclaimed Evan as she fell to her knees, holding out her arms to Delta, who looked more than unsure.

'Lachlan? My brother? Why would you think that?' asked Dorothy. 'Delta is my guide, he's just another wolf. He doesn't know you beyond your reputation, he didn't recognise me when we met...' Dorothy was trying not to sound condescending to an all-powerful being.

'Do you not think I would know my own child? I am made up of stardust and worn souls; I am older than time, and I don't see like you see. That is my Lachlan, and he doesn't recognise me because he was but a baby when I was turned from his version of reality. His mirror-being formed from the loss of a parent, whether he realised it or not.'

Delta crept across the grass, scared to approach too quickly. The Gorgon was an enemy of legend to the pack, her reputation for destruction was unparalleled.

'Don't be scared. I'm not going to hurt you,' said Evan as she held out her hand to the giant wolf.

Delta sniffed at her before allowing Evan to run her hands through his mane. Her scent was familiar to him in a way he could not understand, but he felt safe within her grasp, and that had to mean something.

'I am sorry Miss Gorgon, but if there is something from your past that you see in me, I cannot. I do know you though, you smell as though you are from my pack.'

'That's because we are family, we all are,' said Evan as she took Dorothy's hand. 'You both have my power running through you. I see you as an essence, not as girl, or a wolf'

'I tell him stories about you, in my world. My Lachlan sits at the end of my bed and we talk about how you loved him right from the second you saw his face.' Dorothy began to cry as they all bundled against Delta's massive frame. 'He has a picture of us all by his bed, it's the only one with all four of us together.'

'This makes an old being very happy. Well...I guess we had better go see your father,' said Evan as she looked in to Dorothy's eyes, her shadow rescinding back to its normal shape and size.

'You both go, Delta will show you the way if you do not know it, but I have something else I need to do. And, Mumma Evan, I need your help to do it' said Dorothy with steely determination.

'I know what you seek my child. I see the events unfolding in front of you but, please, tell me what I already know, for I do miss the candour,' said Evan with an empty sadness.

'I need to find my mother's voice. I know you are powerful, but I am unsure of the gifts you possess, can you give it to her?' asked Dorothy.

'I cannot, because the only one stopping your mother's voice is your mother.' said Evan. 'Alice will find her voice as her story unfolds, a story that has already begun. To continue this journey you must travel to the Black Sea, where witches pray for an old master to return. There will be a trial, and it will come at a cost.' Evan reached over and took Dorothy's chin in her hand. 'My child, this is a journey you must take alone, for the story to unfold in your mothers favour. Are you sure this is your will?'

'Going alone seems to be something that I'm getting used to,' said Dorothy as she held Evan's face in return. 'You know, those red eyes don't suit you, but you are still the most beautiful woman I know.'

Evan smiled and kissed Dorothy on the cheek, her lips leaving a cold chill upon her skin as she pulled away, fluttering her eyes that had instantly transformed into the blue crystals that she was remembered for. She clicked her fingers at her faceless servants. 'Pack some of this food into a satchel for my girl, and find me a map to the Black Sea. Time is not on our side.'

9

Oyster Shells
Whitstable, Kent, UK

The waves lapped against the shore of Whitstable Bay as a man might pet his favourite dog. Reassuring strength mixed with a bonded understanding, they were beings that needed each other to be more than just water and rock. Jacob used to say that the sea without the shore was like riches kept inside a bank vault; entirely pointless. The shore needed the waves to crash upon it in order for it to evolve, to change. The very first day he had met Alice he had explained that, without the violence of the tide, it was likely that all the pebbles would be large colourless things that brought no value to the world. Today, Alice sat upon her quilted blanket, as she had done for many hours that day, and watched the waves stroke their mistress gently back and forth. The sun was slowly falling beneath the horizon and if it wasn't for the fire that Poppy had started before she disappeared, then Alice imagined that she would be starting to feel the chill that the end of the day always brought. Where Poppy had decided to go was anyone's guess. Apparently she had a surprise of epic proportions to bring to their beach party, if that's what two lovers found a campfire could be called. Alice watched the dying light reflect off of the oyster shells that littered the coastline. The town was famous for them, with most of the UK seeing them as a delicacy, whilst the good folk of Whitstable grew up snacking on them with an open bag of chips. Alice had never been a fan of them raw like most of the locals, but her father used to bring them home from work to steam on the barbeque with a little cucumber pickle, and she had loved them each and every time. For such a brute of a man, he held a delicate finesse that was lost on most people. He would religiously make Alice return the empty shells to the beach the next day, something to do with rebuilding oyster reefs for future generations, which she did, each and every time.

'I'm back! Don't panic people, the party can continue,' giggled Poppy as two handsome young teens carried a large crate to the spot where Alice was sitting. Both of them topless and shredded from a day's worth of bodyboarding, they lay the heavy wooden box down next to the fire and said their goodbyes to Poppy, who thanked them with a couple of beers from her tote bag.

'Damn,' said Poppy as she watched them walk back inland towards the car park. 'Almost makes me wish I was straight...'

'And twenty years younger you daft mare!' laughed Alice as she accepted the beer that Poppy opened for her, her bag was seemingly now just full of alcohol and marshmallows.

'You think Poppy gives a fuck about age gaps?' swaggered Poppy as she dropped down next to Alice, with very little grace.

'Well Poppy clearly doesn't give a fuck about anything of the sort, so thank the Lord she's as gay the day is long,' laughed Alice, gently mocking Poppy's third person referral. 'So, what's in the box?'

Poppy clinked her beer bottle with Alice's and looked smugly out to sea. 'What's in the box, you say?'

'Yes love, what's in the box?'

'This box?'

'Yes love, that box!'

'This box here?' Poppy teased, playfully.

'YES, the only bloody box on this pissing beach!' laughed Alice with hubris.

'Well why don't you open it and have a look? I got the fucker here, I've done my bit...' Poppy smiled.

It was at that moment that Alice noticed a measure of anxiety creep into Poppy's impenetrable and fun-loving demeanour. 'Baby, what's in the box?'

Kansas, Missouri, US

Jacob had awoken with his daughter's hand firmly in his grasp. Her hand, even as she became a young woman, was small and dainty compared to his own. The very moment that he realised his previous journey from the consultant's office to Dorothy's side had been fuelled by a psychosis of enormous magnitude, he knew that he had missed his medication. This was more than understandable given the situation, but the irony was not lost on him that this was the time he needed it most. It didn't take him long to find a nurse who could help him, understanding that his schizoaffective disorder was being adversely affected by the situation, she quickly found a doctor to help him get enough of a prescription to at least make it through the next couple of days. The teenage daughter of the ranch-hand that tended the land was kindly taking care of Lachlan in Jacob's absence. A simple girl of country charm and southern hospitality, she had done her best to keep him informed and demanded that under no circumstances was he to rush back. By virtue of the picture messages he had received during the time he was blacked out, he could only assume his boy was having the time of his life with young Miss Kitty, and his smile was the mirror of his mother's. Jacob made his way into the bathroom adjacent to Dorothy's bed and popped two of the lithium tablets into his mouth. He had been taking tablets for so long that he could swallow them dry with little to no effort, yet these now stuck in his throat as if trying to choke him. He took a handful of water from the tap and helped them on their way, before cupping his hands once more to wash his face. As he took in the reflection that stared back at him, more than aware of how tired he looked, he noticed how much his eyes had begun to fade. Where once were glistening emeralds that had been his most defining feature, they looked now a more pastel olive. Quite when the striking colour had started to fade, he could not have said, but he would have guessed it to be around the time he lost Evan. He still looked young for his age, but the journey he had taken was not easy to hide anymore. No amount of fake smiles would give him the visage required to trick anyone who might care to know how he really felt. He was tired, and when his reflection gave him an unnaturally toothy grin, a horror matched only by the shadowed tentacles that whipped about behind him, Jacob found a strength that he had become more than used to finding.

'You caught me off guard, I'll give you that, Ahab, but not again. You have no power here.'

His reflection just kept smiling back, its teeth pointed and razor sharp, its shadow a violent display of aggressive power.

'You can smile at me all you want,' said Jacob as he continued to wash his face. Unphased now by what he saw in front of him. 'For a moment, I forgot you were here, forgot the rules I have in place to stop you. But as I see you now, your wicked glare, your evil smile, I remember how little control you have over me.'

She's here with us now. Your child. Your Dorothy. She won't last the night.

The reflection spoke without moving its lips, the sound instead coming from the kraken-like shadow that danced in the background like an obsidian flame.

My daughter, who you will speak no more of, is not with you, nor has she ever has been. She is in the room opposite after taking a fall in the storm. You may think you have me, but you do not. I feel no fear, only annoyance that I briefly let you back in.

We will see who has her and who does not Jacob, and we shall see how much you fear us, once her soul is consumed. Your queen is not here to pull you from the brink once more.

Jacob patted his hands dry whilst looking his reflection square in the eye. 'You think Evan saved me? Oh no old friend, she did far more than that. That girl loved me; she showed me how to save myself, showed me my worth, reminded me every day what you were and how pathetic your powers were!'

You have…

'AND SHE WILL CONTINUE TO REMIND ME EACH AND EVERY DAY. Even though she is not by my side,' Jacob smiled back at the reflection with sadistic contempt. 'I'll see you around, Ahab.'

The creature watched Jacob from the mirror, as he left the bathroom with far too much confidence in his stride. A confidence that the creature did not believe he deserved.

I have little power here, of that you are correct. But if I catch her in my world, then you, boy, will never see her again.

Whitstable, Kent, UK

'How did you get hold of it?' asked Alice as she looked at her own Dorian Gray. The top of the crate now discarded, the image of her greatest and most terrible work looked straight back at her.

'I can't tell you it was easy, because it wasn't, but I feel that the potential reward will far outweigh any hardship I have incurred.' replied Poppy as she stood beside her stunned partner.

'So, my next question has to be why? I mean why would you think that I want such a thing? Am I proud of each and every stroke, yes of course, but this thing, it terrifies me for what it represents,' Alice could not draw her eyes from the girl in her painting, the whispers of the past already finding sanctuary in her mind.

'Listen, and please understand that it's not easy for me to be serious twice in one week,' said Poppy as she stepped between Alice and the painting, taking her hand in the process. 'I want to spend my life with you, the real you, who is fighting each morning to return to me in full. Now, I am trying to help you on that path and, of late, I have begun to see you flourish once more. But I know, as well as you do, that there are a few things that trigger you, pull you back, and I want to move you through these.'

'Things like this?' asked Alice with a nod to the canvas. 'My inability to forget?'

'No! You should never forget, my love. This is about looking at your scars and remembering how bad-ass you are, remembering that you are a survivor and that what tried to stop you, failed. You will never grow in any substantial way if you just forget your journey, so let's use that journey as a step up, and not a weight to bring you down,' said Poppy as she bent down to pick the canvas out of its crate.

'So I should paint over it?' Alice asked with a hint of whimsy.

'Fuck that, you're gonna burn this bitch!' laughed Poppy with absolute certainty. 'And then, I want you to marry me, yes this is a lame-ass proposal. Yes, it's all you're getting, and yes I'm still waiting for an answer, so I'm going to keep nervously talking until you make a positive gesture in response...'

Alice leaned in towards Poppy and kissed her squarely on the lips, pulling away with the painting in her grasp before turning to the fire that crackled beside them. 'Yes, I'll marry you! Tonight, tomorrow, in a castle or a barn, I don't care...' she lay her Dorian Gray on top of the burning driftwood and watched as it quickly devoured the canvas she had so gracefully laid upon it. 'We didn't pay for this did we? Please tell me I haven't just burnt a quarter-of-a-million pound painting.'

'You said yes, you are going to marry me, so the cost isn't relevant. It was not a quarter of a million, nor was it free, but was it worth it...'

'Yes, yes it was worth it,' agreed Alice. She kissed Poppy once more before they both collapsed back onto the beach in the kind of embrace that couples may only find once in their lifetimes.

The wine flowed and the embrace between lovers continued throughout the night. Poppy would never admit that the painting was a copy, the real work still hanging upon the walls of the Topeka gallery in Kansas. Whilst Alice would never tell anyone, especially her new fiancée, that she had heard the painting scream for the entirety of the time it was burning, like souls being tortured in the depths of hell.

The wailing was distant, yet it struck at her heart with a very familiar touch.

Kansas, Missouri, US

Jacob sat by his daughter's side and held her hand with the tenderness and care of a father unwilling to give up any fight to bring his little girl home. He held tight whilst he rested his brow upon a cushion that was pressed between his chair and her bed, and he continued to hold her hand whilst the nurses busied themselves around her with important tasks, and he held on while doctors poked and prodded at her soft skin, unable to solve the puzzle which was her condition. He knew that he was procrastinating though. He knew that there was something he was neglecting for, rightly or wrongly, he had done this job alone for so long, but now he needed to call home to let them all know what was happening. It was neither the call he wanted to make, nor the call Alice was yet strong enough to receive.

10

Finding Voice
The Mirrorverse

It had felt like days since Dorothy had left the wolf-pack, yet it was impossible to tell if her journey had been five minutes, or a thousand times that. Both the sun and the moon seemed to move around her in a circular ellipse that saw neither drop beneath the horizon, with one or the other always staring her squarely in the face and swapping places at a far more regular pace than the twelve hours she was used to. She had first spotted the black ocean when the last moon had joined her for the walk, and now near-darkness covered her approach to the location that Evan had marked upon her map. She had amazed Dorothy with her ability to heighten every emotional state within her young mind. Evan was easily the most beautiful woman that she had ever seen, yet her blood red eyes and arachnid shadow made her more frightening than any demon she had read about, or seen in the deep subconscious nightmares that used to plague her. Sure, the mirror demon that had hunted her through the forest was a more horrifying creature if you only used your eyes to see it, but Evan held a deeper power, as if the air around her trembled with power and the natural light was burned away by her own brilliance. The mirror demon, for all her teeth and talons, still felt like a physical entity that could be fought, even beaten, if the right circumstances were to fall in to play. The Gorgon, as she was known, felt more omnipotent, as if she could restitch the very reality in front of Dorothy's eyes with very little effort. As she had first entered the mansion, Dorothy had watched shadows dance to Evan's command. She had heard the Gorgon's voice as if it was coming from within her own mind, and she had seen the army of wolves that decorated the surrounding grounds, all turned to brittle stone with all but a glance. Yet, since arriving in this mirrored version of her own existence, Dorothy had never felt safer than when she had joined Evan for the brief picnic they had shared upon the lawn. Dorothy felt the ground underneath her feet slowly change as sharp gravel began to give way to the sinking texture of a sandy beach that was as dark as the ocean that lapped against it. The semi-circular outcrop of stone slabs that Evan had told her to find was positioned a few hundred yards ahead. The stones were at least five foot tall, each guarded by a cloaked figure that lit the area with burning torches. Dorothy did not feel safe, her bravery was being tested with every footstep, and breaking her mother's curse was her only driving force. She wished for Delta to be by her side, or even any of the ravenous Betas that had protected her father's pack with such gusto. The robed figures did not acknowledge her presence as she entered the redoubt that Dorothy wagered was a full circle, with half the outline submerged under the ocean's black surface. Whether or not this was down to her almost silent approach, or simply plain ignorance, Dorothy could not be sure but, as she listened to the murmured chanting of the four figures, one thing became clear. They were summoning something. Of course, it was near impossible for Dorothy to understand the words being spoken, as it sounded neither English nor even human in origin, and they spoke in unison whilst their vision was directed out to sea with focused intent.

'Excuse me, I'm here to see the guardians of the obsidian darkness, and I'm not sure if this is the right place. Can you help me find my way? For I am lost now, but for your guidance. My map would only bring me this far...' said

Dorothy as she help up the hand-drawn survey to the moonlight.

The figures continued to chant with only one purpose, the ocean was their colloquy, and no child would break that conversation.

'Rude!' grumbled Dorothy, as tiredness began to outweigh her need for politeness. 'I've been sent by the Gorgon, maybe you know her?'

All of a sudden, the chanting stopped and all eyes turned to Dorothy who now stood in the middle of them all. The light from their torches lit up her pale skin with every flicker.

'I assumed that would get your attention, now either tell me that you are the guardians I seek, or please point me in their direction, for I do not have time to spare.' said Dorothy with a well-earned confidence.

In unison, the figures dropped their torches to the ground. As the light now emanated from below, it instantly gave the figures a more haunting appearance, as they each pulled back the cowls that had previously cloaked their faces.

Dorothy recoiled at the faces that now confronted her, the taste of bile rose up within her throat and caused her mouth to water as she fought the desire to throw up in the middle of this clearly holy place. 'What are you?' she stuttered as she backed away, acutely aware that she had been very close to being surrounded.

The figures had clearly been human once, or at least from that heritage, but now something very different stared back at her. Black eyes far too large for the skulls that held were positioned over a nose-less maw filled with needle like teeth. 'Yomg ah worthy vulgtmor,' they chanted in unison. Their sickly olive-green skin quivered at the spray of the ocean, as Dorothy noticed slits upon their necks which could only be the sign of gills forming underneath the jawline. Or perhaps an attempt to self-mutilate themselves to at least look that way. 'Yomg ah worthy vulgtmor!' Once again, the words they muttered made no sense to Dorothy, as their voices became louder with each chant.

The tentacle burst violently from the ocean's surface with a thunderous roar that made Dorothy shrink back in terror. The creature that followed was of biblical proportions and as black as the voids of space. Seven more tentacles followed suit as it crashed forward without care of its guardians' safety. Dorothy saw that the creature, which resembled an octopus or squid of some kind, was not just black, but indeed so dark that it stood out as a silhouette against the midnight sky behind it.

Dorothy scampered backwards as the beast stretched out its limbs in an almost primal show of size and strength. The guardians were unmoved and continued to stare at Dorothy's fear stricken body, completely unnerved by their master's presence. Then, in almost trained unison, the guardians each stepped to the side, allowing their god to drag itself onto the land, which was no mean feat, considering its mass was undoubtably heavier without the aided buoyancy that the ocean freely gifted.

The beast slapped down one tentacle at a time as it drove itself towards Dorothy, each time sending an explosion of sand up into the air that showered down upon them all seconds later. Dorothy was frozen still, her instinct to survive much greater than the need to find her mother's missing voice, for, if she didn't survive this then the Alpha would tear her mother to shreds anyway.

None of this made any sense to Dorothy - Evan had sent her here and told of a trial that she had foreseen with her mirror-sight, a trial that would lead to her mother's freedom. She had not spoken of overcoming a Kraken-like creature that appeared as though it had been evicted from hell for being too extreme. This was an impossibility of a task, and Dorothy held no hope of completing it without her life being forfeit.

The creature raised itself up upon its largest limbs as it approached Dorothy, as a second pair reared up like a scorpion trying to intimidate its competition for a potential meal. Oily fluid dripped off its flesh as if it was continuously being secreted, while it's face stared at her from its centre with hundreds of jet-black eyes.

Dorothy felt her skin began to burn as the creatures breath escaped from its razor sharp beak, its necrotic power might kill her as easily as anything else if she did not move soon, yet she was struggling to move under the creature's terrifying gaze. That changed, though, as the creatures beak protruded forward and let out a blood-curdling shriek that cut Dorothy to the very heart. She watched as its mouth opened up to reveal another, smaller maw, filled with dagger-like teeth, and Dorothy ran. She ran while the beast screamed, she ran while the guardians chased, and she ran until her lungs stopped working and she fell into the darkness of unconsciousness once more.

-

Alpha brought a giant paw up to scratch at his head whilst an oversized mosquito played wistfully about his ear. He had been lay upon his sun plinth awaiting news of Dorothy and her quest to find the Gorgon, but the warmth of the midnight sun had begun to make him sleepy. His half-open eyes had barely managed to keep watch upon his Betas who, despite orders, continued to circle and growl at the mouthless one. Alice had sat quietly, legs crossed and eyes closed in silent contemplation. She had been no trouble to the pack, and would no doubt continue to be as such. Alpha hoped that his daughter would return with good news, because it would be a horrible shame to feed upon one he had once loved. He had been deprived of human flesh for far too long, and it's rich taste still danced on his tongue from memories long passed, as if taunting him with its decadence. As leader of the pack, he would be entitled to eat the whole of Alice's human form, but his Betas were loyal and had worked hard for the pack, so it paid to be magnanimous. He would enjoy her heart, her liver and other such organs, whilst his warriors would take the limbs. He would normally leave the bones for Delta, but as his life had been tied to the outcome of Dorothy's quest, her failure would mean that he, too, would have to give his life.

As if sensing their Alpha's train of thought, each Beta raised their nose to the sky in unison as they searched for a familiar scent, one that came first to the largest and most senior Beta, who let out a deep growl as its mane began to stand up on end.

'He's returned, my lord Alpha, and the whelp is not alone,' she barked as the other Betas fell into formation behind her.

'Dorothy?' asked Alpha as he rose and shook himself awake.

'No lord...it's her!'

-

'You requested me Jacob, and I am here. For centuries you have sent warriors, one after another, to take me down, to try to kill me. But sending our children, well...I could hardly ignore that could I?' said the Gorgon as she ruffled Delta's fur.

'Why do you presume I wanted you dead, my lady? I only wanted you here, with me.' said Alpha, as he jumped down from his raised plinth to see the woman he had once loved.

All the souls within the Mirrorverse were reflections of emotions. Alpha was a reflection of all the love and devotion that the human Jacob Brooking had felt for his family. His Betas were the plethora of women that, at his worst, he had fooled into following him. These souls were all immortal once born into existence, and within the non-linear time circuit that was the Mirrorverse, the Alpha Jacob had lived many lifetimes, contemplating the paradox that was his life. He loved the Gorgon Evan, for all that she was and all that she represented. He loved her look, her smell, her taste, like peaches holding too much juice for their tender skin. While this Jacob, the Alpha wolf, had never met or spoken to this Gorgon, he knew how he felt through the primal forces that were born unto him as a result of the real Jacob's own stirrings.

'You may not have sent them to kill me, Jacob, but you are naive to think that you are in control of such forces as a woman's desire. What did you think those thirsty bitches wanted for themselves?' the Gorgon smiled as she met Alpha's eye for the first time and continued towards where he now sat upon his rear haunches.

The Gorgon's comments had caused the Betas to begin circling in a pattern that could well have been tactical, or simply for the purposes of intimidation. Each of them bared their teeth as a low growl emitted from the largest wolf.

'Betas, all of you, back off. Now! Or, by our ever circling midnight sun, I swear I will kill you all myself,' snarled Alpha, expecting nothing less than obedience from his pack.

The pack though, continued to circle and make evident their hostile intentions towards the Gorgon; the only woman that their Alpha had ever truly loved. A Beta that had worked its way behind the Gorgon leapt like a coiled spring, covering many metres with an effortless bound. The beast's jaws opened wide, saliva dripping from glistening teeth, and paws extended with unnaturally sharp claws ready to tear at soft flesh, unprepared for such an assault.

Like all the wolves that had attacked the mansion before her, and even Dorothy, the Beta and her kin had no idea what they were facing. She was as old as the stars in the sky and the blanket of darkness that held them in place. If she so desired, although it would require considerable effort, she could restart the universe - her universe - from scratch. The Mirrorverse was her creation, and the very instant that the wolf found purchase on her body, it exploded into a flutter of butterflies. Thousands of them filled the air, in all the colours that the Alpha's eyes could recognise.

'ENOUGH!' yelled the Gorgon as her arachnid shadow rose up again behind her, even towering over Alpha and casting him into darkness.

The largest Beta yelped in submission and turned upon its heels as quickly as the beast had ever moved, throwing up grit and dirt, as it escaped towards the tree line that surrounded the rocky plane. The other Betas did not hesitate to follow suit and, before the Gorgon had receded her shadow, they were gone.

'See Lord Alpha, we are all simple creatures. We want what we want, and we act how we act,' she said as she reached Jacob's position, holding her hand up to pet his huge snout.

Alpha leaned into her touch and instantly felt a peace that he had never know upon this plane. 'Tell me, what must I do to make this right?'

'Well we can worry about what is right and wrong later, for time to us is as infinite as our love will ever be.

Right now we have much more pressing action that must be taken,' she said as she looked to her right.

'What is it? Tell me and I will make it so. What do we need?' said Alpha as he stood tall, ready for whatever action he would be asked to partake.

'What we need,' said the Gorgon as she pointed at Alice who had been sat upon her own rock, hugging her knees tightly as the drama had evolved around her. 'Is the voiceless one who took my human life.'

-

Dorothy awoke in darkness, inside an old building. The moonlight that shone through the open window did nothing for the aesthetics of what was clearly the remains of an ancient shrine of some kind. Dirt and cobwebs covered her clothes, and whilst the details of her journey here were a mystery, it was clear that, however it had occurred, it had been painfully hard. Every part of her body now felt bruised. Pulling herself up to the window, legs shaking beneath her as she struggled to put her full weight on them, it became apparent that the danger was not yet past. Two of the guardians were looking for her in the building opposite. Their movements were frantic and awkward, as if they were terrified to fail in their task. Despite the moonlight, the night seemed to keep Dorothy well hidden, and she was grateful for it. With no desire to be taken back to the Kraken's lair, she could hear the beast's high-pitched shrieking still carried on the wind.

The hand across her mouth caught her off guard and her screams were muffled by the oppressor's strength as he pulled her back into the rooms darkest corner.

'Shhhhhhh...I'm not here to hurt you. I wouldn't have bothered saving you if I wanted to give you up to them,' said the mysterious voice as it whispered into her ear uncomfortably.

The dark-haired man had taken Dorothy upstairs so that he could watch the prowling guardians from the first floor window with anonymity. They seemed to be vacating the area after a particularly loud screech from the sea-front told of their master's displeasure. The man had commented that if the guardians returned empty handed, it would likely be the case that one of their lives would be taken as tribute.

'Thank you for saving me. I just remember running until I didn't remember running any more, and then I was here,' said Dorothy as she sat on an old bed, watching her new companion scout the length of the pathway outside with curious eyes.

'You are welcome young Miss...?' The man paused, awaiting his new dependant to fill in the gap.

'Dorothy, or Dotty as my family call me.' She guessed that the man was roughly mid-thirties, one side of his body seemed much like her father's, well-built and full of lean muscle, but the other side far less so; his left arm was thin and decrepit, and there was a dark hue to the skin, as if it were infected.

'Well Miss Dotty, they seem to have left us alone, and we are all the better for it. They are not skilled warriors or even strong opponents, but they are relentless and greater in number,' said her saviour as he joined her to sit on the bed.

'There was only a handful of them at the beach, I assume that wasn't all of them?' Dorothy asked as she shuffled backwards to give the stranger some room.

'No, not at all. There is a town, once desolate, that lies not far from her, if you follow this road towards the never-sinking moon. It is filled with the creatures, neither man nor beast, but all loyal to the creature that lives within the reef.'

'You seem to know more than most in this darn place, have you been here long?' asked Dorothy, uneasy at their proximity to one another.

'Long? A year, maybe six. Maybe a thousand. Time...well it doesn't work as it should here.'

'So everyone keeps telling me,' smiled Dorothy as she tried to find some humour in her situation. 'So do you know why you are here? I spoke with the Gorgon and she claimed that everyone here is a reflection of some powerful emotional spike in the real universe.'

'You spoke with the Gorgon? The fallen angel that lives in the mansion at the crest of the Ruby Mountains? Well that tells me a little more about you, because she does not entertain guests lightly.'

'We have a complicated relationship, that is no less filled with love and compassion that bridges both of our worlds. Have you spoken to her yourself?' quizzed Dorothy, interested to know who this mysterious stranger was.

'Once, when I first arrived here, she laughed at me. Told me I was to die, and that my fate was sealed, yet, as I cowered before her magnificence, she said that my fate, although written, was in another woman's hands.'

'That sounds like her, at least she let you walk away. So, why do you think you're here?' said Dorothy as she realised that she had run out of bed to shuffle back upon.

'I don't honestly know. My real life, as you might call it, seems blurred beyond measure. I know that I was sick, that my body felt like it was being eaten away. That day-by-day the man that I was, became less than the man that I wanted to be.'

'That's a terrible way to live, and I'm sorry that you are as lost here as I am,' said Dorothy as he turned his face towards her. A smile crept across his face; a face of such non-descript features that Dorothy swore she would never be able to pick him out of a line-up.

'You don't need to be sorry, young Dorothy. I am here, and I have accepted that fate with open arms, because seeing you means that I am not alone here in this realm of madness.'

Dorothy began to feel increasingly uneasy of the man's gaze upon her, yet she was unsure what she could do without making it obvious that she was trying to escape. 'Tell me, do you remember your name at all?'

'My name? My name is Thomas, and you...you sweet child, look just like your mother.'

-

The Gorgon Evan, who had guided them here as quickly as she could, held out her hand out to stop Delta from following Alice into the building. What Alice was to find, she must face alone. Action and consequence was the nature of humanity, that was what the ancient demi-god had come here to find. They had made good time, the complexity of the journey nullified as they were led by the very creator of the world around them. Alpha sat on his haunches to her left, his size such that he could see straight into the upstairs window, and the sight that greeted him caused a growl of discontent to escape his jaws. Evan heard this and ran her fingers through his fur, it was a habit she never knew she had needed, but it was a habit that, in the short time since they had been introduced to one another, had sated both their lusts for violence to never before seen levels of calm.

'What our Dorothy needs, is just about to be delivered for her. Trust that I have seen this play out a thousand ways, and the only way that works my love, is to let Alice go it alone.' said Evan, her touch calming Alpha, whilst the much smaller Delta lost focus and began to chew upon his own tail.

-

Dorothy tried to lurch sideways as Thomas attempted to pin her tightly by both wrists, his facial structure changing each moment that passed. Dorothy knew who this was, she had read her mother's journal front to back and she was no fool. Could his morphing face be down to the fact that she had never seen this man, outside of words on a page? If that were true, then was this whole situation was based only on what she knew, was this whole world her own? It seemed irrelevant as the pain in her wrists shook her focus instantly back to the room, the fear of what her mother had endured was now a reality that she feared more than death.

'GET OFF OF ME, GET...OFF...OF-' screamed Dorothy as she turned her head away from his long, pointed, black tongue. It was turning her head that stopped her screaming as, looking through the darkness of the room, one thing was highlighted in the window frame beyond, two large, canine, emerald eyes.

The door to the room burst open, as if struck down by a much larger person than entered it. That was when Thomas saw his end, this was where he died.

Alice, who had not spoken for close to a thousand of the Mirrorverse's years, felt her sealed mouth tear open, as if she had been chewing on too much toffee. Her jaw cracked as it shifted into positions that had since become unnatural to it, and her throat burned as it accepted air into it for the first time in centuries. Dorothy somehow knew what was coming, she would call it instinct based upon the bond between mother and daughter. Evan would call it the power of foresight that she herself had passed down to her step-daughter. The second that Thomas turned to face Alice, releasing his captor at the same time, Dorothy pulled her hands to her ears and closed her eyes as Alice screamed. Not as a scared child, nor as a fearful mother, but as a Banshee, whose death-shriek tore through the very bones of the man assaulting her daughter.

Alpha turned away from the window, even with his primal instincts, he could not stomach what he now saw in front of him. Evan was unmoved, as if she was re-watching a horror movie, fully aware of where the jump scares were. Delta pawed at his ears, the painful wailing too much for his sensitive hearing.

Thomas felt his whole body contort into different poses, limbs and bones snapping violently with each jerk, like a puppet thrown into a hurricane. He had no control over the outcome of her assault, and Alice only stopped screaming when she saw his head snap violently in a full rotation, before falling limply against his shoulder.

'MUM!' Dorothy rushed to her mother's aid, catching her fall before she crashed into the frame of the bed.

'I'm OK, Dotty. I'm alright. I will never let a man like that hurt you, do you understand? Whatever I do in this life, that is what will keep me whole.' Alice spoke as though she had pulled a cactus through her vocal chords, and her joy at finding her voice seemed tempered by the pain it was causing her to speak.

'Don't speak if it's hurting you, Mum. You saved me, and we're together again. Nothing else matters,' said Dorothy as her eyes filled with tears of happiness. 'Are the others with you? I swear I saw my father's eyes through the window?'

Alice nodded and pointed to the stairway as she coughed and spluttered through the pain.

Dorothy raised her mother up and they leaned upon each other with all the love and support that, for so many years, had been the missing component in both of their lives, mirrored or otherwise.

11

Requiem

The Mirrorverse

The gate back to what Dorothy knew as the "real" world, was a mesmerising whirlpool of colour and, as they approached it, she couldn't help but feel as though they were about to walk through a giant rainbow bubble. She rode atop Delta's back, whilst her mother and Evan followed closely behind, riding the much larger wolf that her father had maintained the form of. Evan and her mother had never spoken as friends, but now they looked at each other with the mutual respect of two people who knew how much they each both endured. Alice sat upright, trying her best to balance herself against the bobbing of Jacob's giant back, whilst Evan, now in a completely human form, held onto her love as if frightened to lose him once more. Her fingernails, painted the same blood red that her eyes had previously shone, ran through Jacob's soft mane as she had once done with his human hair, and his tail wagged back and forth in joyful response. Dorothy had held her tongue for the course of the journey. She hadn't wanted to spoil the moment by saying anything that might remind her that none of this was real, she was just glad they were all together once more. Her heart overflowed with a joy that she could not measure in simple terms, and she kept her eyes on the glistening gate, unsure if she even wanted to go through it when they reached the plateau that it rested upon. Dorothy knew that she had to go, though. Her father had been through enough in losing Evan in the real world, and she knew that he would not survive another loss. So, she had resolved that she would go through the gate and return to Kansas. Her mother had warned of a guardian that protected the gate with absolute authority; a beast that would tower over even her father's wolf form. Yet, as they pulled around the last of the path's winding turns, nothing greeted them except for a huge pearlescent gate that sat upon an equally ornate plinth. Delta's quick feet skidded to a stop as the gravel beneath him sprayed up at the beast's abrupt change of pace, and that was where darkness struck them all.

Dorothy opened her eyes, and the sudden, painful exposure to the sunlight caused her to bring her hand up instantly to shade her vision. She had no idea for how long her eyes had been closed, only that her body felt as if it had been thrown to the ground, with her family suffering the same fate, by all accounts. Delta lay by her side, and Dorothy was more than grateful that the enormous beast had not landed on top of her. Beyond him, she saw her mother stumble to her feet, and her father shake his long white mane, as if stunned by some massive shockwave. Evan stood, unphased, by his side, her style and form untouched by whatever incident had brought them to this point. Dorothy watched her step confidently forward as her arachnid shadow imposed itself once more upon the ground, surrounding her like a giant black cape. It became apparent what had happened to them, as Dorothy followed the path with her eyes and she saw the guardian of the gate tear its giant hammer from the hole it had torn in the ground, the force of which had obviously been what had thrown them each skyward.

'Control yourself, beast. You know what I am - do not make me introduce myself formally, for my patience has limits, where as my eternal rage does not!' Evan's eyes filled with blood as she spoke, and soon Dorothy could not see her pupils for the mirrored scarlet that consumed them.

The beast in question was a gigantic, anthropomorphic polar bear, no less than fifty feet tall and half that wide. In its right paw, itself the size of a large car, it brandished a Warhammer almost as tall as the brute itself. Upon its back and chest were ornate pieces of golden armour that presented the bear like a Viking bear-king of god-like proportions. It was the most fearsome beast that Dorothy could ever have imagined. She had seen nothing to match it in terms of size and stature, not the Kraken, not even her wolf father. Yet as Evan approached it, the unimaginable happened. 'Apologies, my lady master. I did not see you here with this ramshackle party,' said the bear nervously as it dropped instantly to its knee, resting its weight upon the head of the hammer, its giant snout directing its eyes to the ground, unwilling to make eye contact with her.

'I do not desire your apology. I want you to behave yourself whilst I explain what is going to happen next.' said Evan as her arachnid shadow shivered and shrank back into her.

'But master, you made me swear to not let any single being through this gate other than you. It was the reason you created me, do I presume rightly that this is a test?' The beast's voice was a deep growl of resolute power, yet he still stared directly at Evan's feet, unable to find the fortitude to look his creator square in the eye.

'You are correct, that is why I created you. And you have done an admiral job at protecting what I have come to value, but this is no test,' said Evan as Jacob sat beside her. His size dwarfed her frame, yet it was her power that ruled this moment.

'An admiral job? With respect my lady, I have let no soul through this gate in the thousands of years it has stood,' the giant bear said, as it stood upright with military precision, his muscular shoulders back, and his gaze now fixed straight ahead as if searching for some far-off enemy.

'Yet, the Kraken beast has managed to attach itself to this wolf's human soul,' stated Evan as she ran her hand through the Alpha Jacob's soft fur. 'And that poor creature over there has had the mirror-witch taunting her for thirty years,' she continued as she pointed at Alice, who was sat quietly flexing her jaw, the muscles of which were still not used to being utilized.

The bear gave a growl of embarrassment as it tried to find an answer that excused his failure.

'I understand that those creatures, like many others here in this world I have created, do not possess souls. That the darkness and trickery that emanates from their very existence can be all but blinding to even the sharpest of minds,' said Evan kindly, as she stepped towards the magnificent creature. 'But let us not pretend that for all your dedication, loyalty and endeavour, you still have a tendency to hibernate in time with your Earth-mirror's wintertime. A kink that I have struggled to remedy,' smiled Evan as she looked up and caught his gaze for the first time. 'It's my own fault for making you a bear, I can own that mistake, and I know if you search your own soul, so will you, my guardian beast.'

'Pops!' shouted Dorothy, as all the pieces started to fall into place. 'I knew it, as soon as I saw you, I knew it.' Alice had appeared by her daughter's side and looked on in astonishment that her father could have been here with her the whole time.

'Pops?' repeated the bear as it looked down at the two flame-haired humans. 'I'm not sure I understand that word. If I am supposed to recognise you, then I am sorry, but I do not.'

'Do not be upset, he carries traits of his mirror, but I could not let him know too much of his real self. He would have become a liability if his love for those that resemble his real-world family were to manifest here,' said Evan as she walked over to Dorothy and placed a hand upon her shoulder.

'What are you?' asked Dorothy as she gently stroked Evan's cheek, her skin as flawless as it had been in life. 'I mean, really...'

'She is Darkness before light, and yet she illuminates,' barked the giant bear as if offended by the ignorance. 'She is both old and young, for time is just another dimension that falls at her feet. She is the architect of life and the destroyer of worlds. She is the beginning, the middle and the end. She is he, and he is It!' The bear dropped to its knee once more, the ground shaking at the sudden movement. 'May her benevolence guide our will.'

'So you're God?' whispered Dorothy, her soft voice barely audible.

'God is such a new word that is used to describe something that humans don't quite understand. It would also imply that I was but one, yet I am blessed, or cursed some might say, with three siblings.'

'If you are this mighty, why can't you just magic me home? Why could you not just save me from that Kraken thing, or my mother from the demon that haunted her?' asked Dorothy, with no malice in her tone.

'Because, sweet child, you are not puppets to me. I gave you souls so that you could make choices, so that I could learn from you the very nature of humanity,' answered Evan with assurance. 'Would you, or any of you, want me to control every action you make as a counter to every scenario I create? Where would it end, who would decide what was wrong and what was right, when only one vision understood the picture?'

'So I have to choose to leave this place? I have to walk through the gate?' said Dorothy as she looked up at the pearlescent frame.

'The power was always yours, as it was your mother's. You are stronger than can be measured and until you realise that, you will always ask me to click my fingers and send you to where you need to be. That, young Dorothy, is the key, because no one knows where you need to be...except you,' Evan smiled as she stepped behind Dorothy and ushered her forward towards the arch.

'Just remember this, small child with the fiery red hair,' said the bear as she walked slowly past him. 'Unless you are a creature born upon this side of the mirror, then this is a one-way journey. You can never return, even if you long to come back.'

Dorothy took the steps that led onto the giant plinth, each one requiring a certain amount of scrambling due to their immense size. As she reached the precipice and looked down upon her newly-reunited family, the bear's words started to weigh heavily upon her. She saw Evan, pressed against the Alpha-Jacob, the young Delta-Lachlan lay exhausted at their feet. She saw the mirrored version of her mother, alone, but confident and strong like never before, and she felt sadness that this is as complete as her family had ever felt. 'I guess this is goodbye, everyone,' she said as her eyes began to well.

'The choice is yours, my beautiful princess, it always has been. Just know you are loved, in this world, and the other,' said Alice as she stepped forward. 'I will see you on the other side, regardless.'

Dorothy turned and placed a hand upon the crystalline frame, like the inside of an oyster shell. The shimmering within its centre seemingly pulled at her like two magnets destined to never be separated. Something though, was stopping her from making the choice that had at first seemed so simple,. Her heart ached at what she knew was to be an impending loss, regardless of her decision. 'There's no place like home,' said Dorothy, as the irony weighed heavy upon her that she had no idea where "home" was.

Epilogue
Whitstable, Kent, UK

Poppy stood with her hand clasping Alice's, the ceremony was small and the congregation non-existent. It was just the two of them who stood in front of the registrar and their paid witness. They were both dressed in white flowing summer dresses, almost Pagan in design, and each had flowers protruding from French plaits. They had awoken together, prepared together, and they would leave as wives together, in the same perfect partnership. As the final words were spoken, and plain golden bands were exchanged, they kissed, they smiled, and they knew. They knew that no voices, no reflections and no worlds of fantasy would ever be strong enough to break the bond that they had fought for so long to find. They left the building, an old Edwardian bank now reformed for purpose, in a tight embrace, as the sound of the registry's speaker played a poorly honed version of an Elvis classic to see them out. The world felt right, and all its component parts were falling into place as they looked up to the blue skies that greeted them as a now married couple.

'I love you Sugar,' said Poppy with a smile that spread instantly to her wife.

'And I love you,' said Alice as she opened her car door. 'This won't be fun, but I guess we should go tell my parents.'

'They will be overjoyed, your parents only want you to be healthy and happy, you know this.' said Poppy as she climbed into the driver's seat.

'You're right, of course you are. I'm being silly, and once again it's you who grounds me,' smiled Alice as she pulled her phone from the car's glove box. 'Thank you for being my anchor to reality through the years that had thrown me in every direction but forward.'

'And thank you for being so crazy that the sex is the best I've ever had,' said Poppy with absolutely no regard for seriousness upon her wedding day. Her smile starting to make her cheeks ache as Alice playfully poked her in the ribs for the jibe about being crazy.

'Well, someone's been popular,' said Alice as she unlocked her phone.

'What do you mean? What bastard is trying to steal my woman?' smiled Poppy, with false bravado and a little giggle.

'Erm..,Jacob it seems. Then my parents, I have over fifty missed calls between them.'

HELLO AGAIN CHILD!

Said, in unison, every voice that Alice had ever heard.

The End

Born and raised on the Kent coast, PW Stephens is a fiction writer who takes real life horror straight out of the darkness and places it right here, in our own back yard. A mental health advocate, he has championed and fought his own battles and now brings you the much anticipated collective book in the Broken Pebbles series. PW Stephens resides in Cheshire with his American Akita, Beau.

Printed in Great Britain
by Amazon